Twenty Thousand Leagues under the Sea

JULES VERNE'S

Twenty Thousand Leagues under the Sea

The Definitive, Unabridged Edition
Based on the Original French Texts

Newly Translated and Annotated by
Walter James Miller
and Frederick Paul Walter

NAVAL INSTITUTE PRESS
Annapolis, Maryland

© 1993 by the UNITED STATES NAVAL INSTITUTE
Annapolis, Maryland

ISBN-13: 978-0-87021-678-7

LIBRARY OF CONGRESS CATALOGING-IN-PUBLICATION DATA

Verne, Jules, 1828–1905.
    [Vingt mille lieues sous les mers.   English]
    Jules Verne's Twenty thousand leagues under the sea : the definitive unabridged edition based on the original French texts / newly translated and annotated by Walter James Miller and Frederick Paul Walter.
        p.   cm.
    ISBN 1-55750-877-1
    ISBN 0-87021-678-3 (pbk.)
    1. Underwater exploration—Fiction.   2. Submarine boats—Fiction.
I. Miller, Walter James.   II. Walter, Frederick Paul.   III. Title.   IV. Title:
Twenty thousand leagues under the sea.
    PQ2469.V4E5   1993
    843′ .8—dc20   93-13835

First printing hardcover, 1993
Fourth printing paperback, 2003

Contents

Second Part

Contents

VI

INTRODUCTION

Jules Verne, Man of the Twenty-first Century

He's been world famous since the 1870s. Yet we have exciting reasons to believe that his greatest fame is yet to come. It makes good sense to call Jules Verne a hero of the twenty-first century.

For one thing, his many prophecies that reliably come true—one of his main claims to fame—will surely reach their crescendo in the 2000s. Even those of his myriad predictions that once seemed the most farfetched, the least likely to be realized, are now shaping up on the computer screen (itself one of his visions!) and destined for production in the foreseeable future.

Consider too that the twenty-first century will be the first time that readers of English will have complete and accurate translations of *all* of Verne's 65 books. Ironically, we will owe this windfall to a bizarre and tragicomic event of the 1960s. Some irresponsible critics and editors claimed they had discovered grave errors in Verne's science and mathematics, and serious omissions in his technical explanations. As proof they quoted from the standard English translations. They did not even bother to check those passages in Verne's original French! Had they done so, they would have found that Verne was guilty of none of these faults, which had appeared only in the English texts!

In this case at least, good came out of evil. Verne scholars (who themselves usually enjoy Verne in the original French) now cried out for new English editions that would restore the passages that readers of Verne had never known and correct the slapdash errors of the "standard" translations. Experts are even now hard at work on many Verne novels and short stories never before available in English. As a consequence of this reconstructive work on the English canon, Verne's reputation for accuracy in science and math is now greater than ever, and on this count too his prestige will reach a crescendo in the twenty-first century.

Happily, this new tidal wave of Verne scholarship, this new demand for more respectful English versions, is already raising Verne's literary (as well as scientific) reputation in nations that read him in English. The old "standard" translations of his most scientific novels granted us, on the average, only about 75 percent of the original story! Naturally, not only the scientific integrity but also the literary qualities were weakened beyond recognition. But critics and

A period portrait by Bertrand

teachers can now see, for the first time, that Verne creates magnificent settings, designs superb plots, and conceives complex characters of real flesh and blood who cope with deep philosophical questions and experience authentic dreams and fantasies. And so Verne is now a subject of serious literary study on the college and even graduate level. Many professors of literature or the humanities are now building their reputations on their lectures, books, and articles on Verne. Their students—who include the teachers, scholars, critics, and general readers of the twenty-first century—will constitute the largest readership Verne has ever enjoyed.

One major fruit of all these new studies is the book you now hold in your hands: the first English version of *Twenty Thousand Leagues under the Sea* to be totally free of the traditional ("standard") errors because it is based on a comparative study of the varying French texts and on new and original research into Verne's intentions, from his loftiest theoretical discussions down to his naming of the lowliest fish!

Prophecies and Praises

In World War II, the United States Navy honored two great men—and one of the sea's most talented *little* creatures!—when it christened a submarine the *Nautilus*. Then in 1955 the navy repeated the honors, transferring the name *Nautilus* to a nuclear submarine, the first vessel to sail across the North Pole by sailing *under* the ice cap.

The first great man honored here was the Father of Science Fiction, Jules Verne. He had given the name *Nautilus* to his fictitious-but-prophetic underwater-luxury-research-combat boat that travels more than twenty thousand leagues under the sea in the novel of that name. Verne's book, published in Paris in 1870, had predicted in great detail the maneuver of crossing the (South) Pole by sailing under it.

Now, Verne himself had named his underwater marvel after the one built by an earlier visionary, Robert Fulton, the second great man the navy was honoring. And surely both the American Fulton and the French Verne, when christening their ships, had in mind the spiral-shelled mollusk that can drop down to the ocean floor or rise to the surface by simply adjusting the amount of gas in its chambers.

The "chambered nautilus" belongs to a genus that has evolved over millions of years. Even adjusting our comparison to human scale, we can't begin to estimate how long it will take for all of Verne's prophecies to evolve into reality. They start with his correct prediction in *Five Weeks in a Balloon* (1863) that the main source of the Nile would be discovered in Lake Victoria. They continue through sixty-four more books, hundreds of prophecies in all, to *The Day of an American Journalist in 2889* (1889) and the end of our present round of civilization in "The Eternal Adam" (posthumous, 1910).

Consider just a few of the steady stream of forecasts in *Twenty Thousand Leagues under the Sea* alone. After Verne's *Nautilus* has for hours brazenly braved a fierce storm on the surface of the Atlantic, its captain, Captain

Nemo, finally submerges some 25 fathoms. And once down there, Professor Aronnax, the narrator, says "what tranquillity we found, what quiet, what peace all around us! Who could tell that a horrible hurricane was then raging on the surface of the sea?"

Then in 1898, just twenty-five years after this novel (or a miserly three-quarters of it!) first appeared in English, some 200 ships were driven onto the coasts of Florida by a "horrible hurricane." And Simon Lake, the inventor, and his crew, navigating the first submarine to operate successfully in the open sea, seemed trapped in that storm. But remembering Nemo's experience, Lake simply submerged to calm and safety. When he reached port he sent the news to Jules Verne, then 70 years old and still writing, that the prophecy he had made at the end of chapter 19, second part, of *Twenty Thousand Leagues* had proved true: in the most malicious tempest, a submarine need only drop down out of harm's way. In his autobiography Simon Lake would write: "Jules Verne was the director-general of my life," and Admiral Richard Byrd, on his way to the South Pole, would write that Verne was his main inspiration too.

In *Twenty Thousand Leagues,* Verne also correctly foresaw the modern technique of "driving" a submarine down by using inclined fins; he foresaw the development of scuba gear, of underwater workshops and towns. He provided his characters with a special underwater hunting gun that anticipates both our modern compressed-air weapons and our new electric "stun guns." (In *The Mysterious Island* Captain Nemo later uses this invention to dispatch some pirates to a "far, far better place.") And in *Twenty Thousand Leagues* Verne predicts our need to obtain new foods from marine plants and the ecological problems triggered by our wiping out the manatee, the dugong, and the whale.

Simon Lake's congratulatory message to Verne was the prototype of a myriad such confirmations to be addressed to the author and his descendants. Just one more major example: In 1969, Colonel Frank Borman, who commanded the first manned flight to the moon, wrote to Jean Jules-Verne, the novelist's grandson and biographer, expressing astonishment over the many similarities between the Apollo 8 space capsule and Verne's fictitious forerunner (in *From the Earth to the Moon,* 1865, and *All around the Moon,* 1870). "It cannot be a mere matter of coincidence," the astronaut wrote. Both capsules had the same weight (20,000 pounds) and height (12 feet). And "Our space vehicle was launched from Florida, like [Verne's] . . . and it splashed down in the Pacific a mere two and a half miles from the point mentioned in the novel."

No, fulfillment of Verne's prophecies has never been a mere coincidence. He had selected Florida for thoroughly scientific reasons and "splashdown" as the easiest form of returning to earth. He had correctly calculated the velocity needed to escape gravity: "I find that any projectile aimed at the moon with an initial velocity of 12,000 yards per second will arrive there out of scientific necessity." He correctly calculated a typical flight time for manned space craft to the moon and used it as his subtitle: *From the Earth to the Moon Direct in 97 Hours and 20 Minutes.* He foresaw both the need of preliminary experiments with animals to ascertain the effect of space travel on earth creatures, and the use of rockets as retrojets. This last was a self-fulfilling prophecy, since it inspired early space scientists like the Russian Konstantin Tsiolkovsky (1857–1935) and the German Hermann Oberth (1894–1989).

Verne in the 2000s — and Beyond

Which of Verne's predictions should we expect to come true in the twenty-first century and thereafter? Let's start with those in *Twenty Thousand Leagues* that we haven't yet caught up with.

Captain Nemo's *Nautilus* obviously and realistically serves as a supervessel for travel and exploration, for scientific research and observation, and for combat. So far, though, America and Russia have developed such superb craft solely for combat. We have experimented only with small submersibles for underwater research. Yet think of the tasks Captain Nemo left us, tasks best done in large submarines built for long-distance assignments. And built too with large windows making it easy to study the ocean depths from inside the boat, and with air locks making it easy for people in diving suits to step out on the ocean floor.

One task Nemo set for us is to find alternative ways to produce electricity. He himself considered, at one point, generating electricity from differences in seawater temperatures. And scientists now see this as a sure development of the twenty-first century. An "ocean power" plant can be built, e.g., any place where a cold current flows below warm tropical waters, say on the north coast of St. Croix in the Virgin Islands.

Nemo was already mapping the bottom of the sea in the mid-nineteenth century. We are told that even today only half of the ocean floor has been mapped; surely every square mile of it will be charted in the twenty-first century.

Captain Nemo was making the newcomer's inevitable transition from food-gathering to underwater farming. The giant oyster he was cultivating is just one small, simple symbol of the huge, complex marine agriculture our descendants will soon undertake.

Captain Nemo was also a pioneer in coal mining under the sea, a vast enterprise that our grandchildren probably will expand to include other minerals and metals. And the products of underwater farming and mining, and the work crews who accomplish them, will probably best be transported by large submarines.

Captain Nemo took Professor Aronnax and his other two "passengers on the *Nautilus*" on a world tour that was incredible in 1868 but surely feasible in 2068. Why can't tourists in 2068 gape at marvels on the ocean floor as easily as they now survey the Grand Canyon and Niagara Falls? Why, indeed, can't large classes in marine biology study their subject matter firsthand in new versions of Nemo's craft?

Which reminds us of the submarine villages that Nemo dreamed of. Both American and Russian experimental teams have lived for weeks, healthy and productive, in small underwater communities, but of course the full development of the concept lies in the future. We know that our descendants will have the option of living in metropolises under water, with shopping malls, schools, drive-in movies, sea-jeeps for commuters, shoppers, and students to get about, and garages and service stations for both jeeps and subs.

Finally, undersea living that now looks like an option could in the twenty-first century become a necessity if, for example, the loss of our ozone umbrella forces some of us to get in out of the sunlight.

Another rich source of prophecies is Verne's *2889*. In this short story Jules and his son Michel predicted moving pavements, solar heating (and storage of summer heat until winter), and weather control, all of them now in various stages of development, like Bernard Vonnegut's seeding of clouds with ice cubes to produce rainfall. Jules and Michel also foresaw telephoto opinion polls conducted to settle questions of peace or war, indeed even of innocence or guilt in criminal trials. And so, when in 1992 an American presidential candidate proposed an "electronic town hall" with referendums on political questions, and computerized voting after televised debates, Verne aficionados again saw this as a replay of *2889*.

As usually happens when such futuristic proposals are made, a journalist, in this case Margaret Slade of the *New York Times,* noted that they "evolve from nineteenth century social engineering concepts, like the utopian visions of H. G. Wells and Jules Verne."

And so it's not hard to imagine how reporters will keep us reminded, week by week, throughout the twenty-first century, that today's latest development was anticipated by Verne. Three-D holographic home movies? A replay of *Castle in the Carpathians* (1892). Turning the African deserts into lushly fertile farmlands? *The Barsac Mission* (posthumous, finished by Verne's son Michel, 1920).

But probably the most spectacular Verne prophecy now nearing realization is presented in *From the Earth to the Moon.* Verne's Baltimore Gun Clubbers *shoot* their space capsule into orbit with a giant gun *900 feet long.* Today, American space scientists, after relying for decades on rocket liftoff to heft their space ships into orbit, are developing a light-gas gun, maybe *two miles long,* that will be shooting first payloads and later people into outer space in the 2000s. And of course another *New York Times* reporter, Malcolm Browne, covering the early experiments in this project, describes it as "realizing Jules Verne's dream of firing a shell to the moon."

Indeed, Verne's dreams—including some of his nightmares—will pop up in the news with greater regularity as astronomers fine-tune their tools for spotting and tracking potential killer comets and asteroids. For example, in just a ten-week period, still another *Times* writer, William J. Broad, reports this series of developments:

"Big Comet May Strike Earth in August 2126—1 in 10 chance of devastating collision seen by astronomers." A week later he describes how "Scientists Ponder Saving Earth from a Comet," how experts are studying places in the inner solar system in which they could intercept Comet Swift-Tuttle with nuclear rockets. These experts are weapons scientists eager for a new job after the end of the Cold War. Their potential enemy is a six-mile-wide mass of ice and dirt that could blot out life on earth forever.

True, several weeks later Broad's headline is "Comet Alert Canceled, Thanks to New Data." But the new data do include a new date for the still possible direct hit: the year 3044. Meanwhile, it's clear that there are millions of asteroids whose orbits sometimes cross the earth's path. Broad's next story is about one of these, a four-mile-wide stony dumbbell photographed as it zips past us, at its closest just about ten times the distance from us to the moon! And Broad's last story in this perfect PR setup for Verne's space novels is headlined: "Study Finds Asteroid Leveled Siberian Area in 1908." Science has at last solved the mystery of what exploded over Siberia one summer night with a force of 1,000 Hiroshima-sized nuclear bombs, flattening forests more than half the size of New York City. And it was a stony asteroid just about 100 feet or so in diameter!

And these events are all, once again, replays of Jules Verne. For example, in his *Hector Servadac* (1877), the astronomer Palmyrin Rosette foresees a comet collision and takes pride in the infallibility of his science when "his" comet does indeed hit the earth right on schedule. And in *From the Earth to the Moon* (1865) it's the great weapons scientists of the American Civil War who, suddenly unemployed in 1865 and eager for a new job, tackle the task of shooting the moon. And in *All around the Moon* (1870), we learn that the capsule has not landed on the moon—just looped around it and headed for splashdown!— because its course has been altered by a near-hit from a passing stony asteroid.

But is there really any need, then, to give more examples of Verne prophecies about to come true in the next millennium? For obviously science reporters see it as their duty to report such new developments as part of Verne's unfolding plan for the future of humanity.[1]

Education of a Prophet

How do you become a prophet? In Jules Verne's case at least, that may not be the real question. For once you have invented *science fiction,* the *fiction* part of that occupation requires that you play imaginatively with the potential of the *science* part. So the real question may be, how did Verne come to invent sci-fi?

Born in 1828 in the seaport of Nantes, he was a Parisian in his mid-thirties before he discovered his true vocation. Maybe he was a late bloomer because it took a long time to integrate—and to see the new connections between—the literary and the scientific influences in his life. Maybe this was even harder

---

1. Our sampling here of the relevance of the *New York Times* coverage of science to Verne's prophecies is made from a ten-week period as follows: Margaret Slade's article, 4 October 1992; Malcolm Browne's, 29 October; and William J. Broad's, 27 October, 3 November, 29 December 1992, and 4 and 7 January 1993. It has been our experience that any similar period would yield comparable results.

because (as he himself saw) this meant integrating his feminine heritage and his masculine heritage, no easy task in a male chauvinist world.

He saw his mother as the very personification of creativity. Her imagination, he wrote, "was faster than a waterspout . . . very curious when I compare it with the way my own mind works." Although his father had decreed that Jules would become a lawyer, Jules wrote incessantly from his teens on, producing third-rate plays, articles, stories. Even when he did become a law student, he was taken under the wing of Alexandre Dumas, Sr., who produced Jules's first play. After many more mediocre productions and publications that yielded no hint of financial security, he still decided to leave the legal career for a literary one. But something was still needed to put verve and originality, *significance,* into his writing!

He saw his father as the first of his many scientific influences. Pierre Verne was extremely logical in all his doings, a fanatic about time, who was reputed to know the exact number of steps between his home and his office. Pierre's readings to his five children included Walter Scott, Fenimore Cooper, and the latest news about science. Jules's younger brother Paul started his life as a naval officer, and for Jules, Paul was a constant source of information and advice about marine matters. Also, the boys had a cousin, Henri Garcet, a mathematics professor whom Jules consulted when he was at work on any technical problem. Jules discussed the latest theories in astronomy, geology, and physiognomy with leading scientists he met at the home of Jacques Arago, famous world traveler. He argued the relative merits of lighter-than-air versus heavier-than-air aircraft at the Cercle de la Presse Scientifique, where he met the man who perhaps provided the spark: Gaspard Felix Tournachon, photographer and pioneer balloonist, better known to history as Nadar.

It seems like no surprise that Verne's work that really established the new genre of science fiction was *Five Weeks in a Balloon* (1863). He had found the right formula. He combined the kind of scientific invention and the area of exploration most in the news—in this case, aerial travel and Africa. *Five Weeks* established his audience and their expectations. He proved to be predicting developments they themselves would live to see in a matter of years. And so he had earned their confidence when he was extrapolating far into the future. The great integration had finally occurred. He was now able to assert his powerful maternal fancy against his powerful paternal logic to achieve the creative tension we now call sci-fi.

But if he was a late bloomer in matters professional, he was tragically even later in matters sexual. He failed five times to find happiness with a woman. He proposed marriage to three women before he was twenty-eight and was emphatically rejected each time. A fourth woman, a widow with children, accepted him when he was twenty-nine, but after they were married she proved indifferent to his needs as a writer, and his passion for her was quickly quenched. When, late in life, he finally found a true love, with a truly sympathetic woman, his lover died prematurely, plunging him into a despair he could ameliorate only through chronic workaholism.

We include his romantic failures because of their possible effect on his (and later sci-fi writers'?) work. He rarely gives a major role to a woman, and once indeed he begged his publisher not to keep asking for deep romantic passion in his writing. This might ironically have helped set the tone for the asexual science fiction that many of Verne's followers would also write: early sci-fi was regarded as a man's world, even an escape for men. Fortunately, all this has been changed by Ursula LeGuin, Doris Lessing, and other great women who have broadened and deepened the genre.

Evolution of Twenty Thousand Leagues

Verne's inspiration for *Twenty Thousand Leagues* must have been, like his invention of science fiction itself, a happy confluence of forces. There was first of all his passionate love for the sea. Brought up in the seaport of Nantes, Jules and Paul had learned how to manage small sailboats on the River Loire. Angry probably at facing a future in courts and law offices, jealous of Paul's freedom to join the navy, Jules actually ran away from home in his early teens and served a day on a seagoing sailing vessel before his father, consulting the time tables and taking a faster (steam) boat, caught up with him. As a bachelor and even as a new husband, Verne sailed to Britain and Scandinavia with the composer Aristide Hignard (for whom Verne wrote libretti), later with Paul to New York on the *Great Eastern.* On that voyage, typically, he interviewed both Cyrus Field, fresh from his final victory in laying the Atlantic Cable, and common seamen: Had they ever served on a ship attacked by a whale? Jules experienced on the *Great Eastern* what naval officer Paul described as the worst storm he had ever known at sea. And for most of his life as a writer, Verne also owned a yacht, each one in a series of three named after his (own) son Michel. He toured all the waters of Europe. All such experiences turn up in *Twenty Thousand Leagues.*

Verne's constant research into things marine extended even to underwater craft, and he knew well the history of some twenty-five experiments with submersibles that had all led to nothing. Add to this love of seascape and landfall another ingredient for *Twenty Thousand Leagues:* his political passion. He hated imperialism and sided with the oppressed everywhere. And then add one final ingredient: an 1865 letter to Verne from George Sand, Romantic novelist and feminist who was published, like Verne, by Pierre Hetzel, saying: "I hope you'll soon take us into the depths of the sea, making your characters travel in underwater equipment perfected by your science and your imagination."

These seem to be the forces that combined to spark the inspiration for *Twenty Thousand Leagues.* But the novel had a long and difficult birth. Verne got to work on it the summer of 1865, was interrupted by a nonfiction assignment from Hetzel in 1866, returned to his submarine epic in 1868, and finished it the following year. In a letter to your present translators, Dr. Arthur B. Evans, one of our leading Verne scholars, tells us that "Verne actually generated three different manuscripts of this text." His first draft was influenced by the 1863 Polish uprising against Tsarist Russia. Poland was quashed with a bestial savagery that appalled not just Verne but all Europe. As first conceived, the novel's protagonist, Captain Nemo, was a Polish aristocrat whose parents, wife, and children were brutally slaughtered by Russian troops. That was why, in Verne's original draft, Nemo went to sea to wage history's most unusual guerrilla warfare.

But in the late 1860s, France had to treat the tsar as an ally. Hetzel ruled out Verne's idea of Nemo as a Polish rebel. Both Dr. Evans and the author's grandson, Jean Jules-Verne, tell how Verne and Hetzel argued the matter throughout the development of the book. Verne finally left the identity of Nemo and of his great oppressor as something of a mystery, at least in *Twenty Thousand Leagues.* Readers who look carefully, however, can find slight clues to the new identities that Verne decided on for both Nemo and his persecutors. The nationalities of both Nemo and the enemy he fights are revealed in full in *The Mysterious Island.* But our annotations to the present translation will confirm the suspicions of those readers who sniff carefully enough.

The Literary Genius of Jules Verne

Properly translated, Jules Verne proves to be a master at plotting a story, planting suspense, inspiring us to like his people, creating internal as well as external conflict—in short, a writer adept at both action and characterization.

Verne tells his story through the eyes of Professor Aronnax who has just returned from research in *les mauvaises terres du Nébraska,* that is, the Nebraska Badlands. (This French phrase is rendered fatuously in the "standard" translation as "the disagreeable territory of Nebraska"!) The professor joins the staff of the USS *Abraham Lincoln,* a frigate under orders to seek out and destroy a mysterious whale-like monster that has been sighted by—and often collided with—ships in all the Seven Seas. Aronnax and his servant Conseil grow into a warm friendship with Ned Land, a Canadian on board as a master harpooner. When Ned sights and attacks the huge "whale," that monster cripples the warship and the trio, cast into the sea, are taken prisoner by the "monster's" captain, who calls himself Nemo ("nobody" in Latin).

Thus Verne launches his story with guaranteed built-in psychological conflict as well as physical conflict between people *and* between people and Nature. The professor, ironically, has a profound interest in *remaining* Nemo's prisoner. A scientist from the Paris Museum of Natural History, author of a treatise on *The Mysteries of the Great Submarine Depths,* he is now the first marine scientist in history able to study the ocean from deep *inside* the ocean! Furthermore, Verne steeps the professor in a serious psychological problem: he is unconsciously attracted to Captain Nemo as to a "perfect father." (As French psychoanalysts have made us realize, Jules Verne himself prospered and suffered, unconsciously, in such a relationship with his publisher, Pierre Hetzel.) But against these powerful internal needs to remain with Nemo, Aronnax must weigh the arguments for escaping from the submarine: Friend Ned is going mad in this imprisonment, and Captain Nemo, it becomes clear, is fighting a naval war of vengeance against some unknown power, a war that the trio can no longer abide. The professor must learn then, agonizing as it may be, that friendship is more valuable than the ultimate in scientific discovery.

But it is Captain Nemo who is Verne's greatest creation, indeed one of the stars of world literature, and a prototype of a major science fiction personality: the scientist run amuck, a Faustian man in a Baconian world. And Nemo also grows as a person, he too through internal conflict.

Naturalist, inventor, philosopher, musician, political idealist, and revolutionary—a man of great physical courage and noble desire to live by Reason—what a genius the world lost when this embittered man turned against society! And notice that it's not so easy for an author to create an authentic, convincing genius. How many such characters have we met in world literature?

Proud and disdainful as Nemo seems, he is actually deeply lonely and really grateful that chance has brought another marine scientist to his fugitive ship. Nemo endures the open hostility of Ned—suffers him to live—as the price he must pay for the professor's companionship and collaboration.

Nemo's tragedy is that he is caught in the contradiction between his love of absolute freedom and his passionate need for revenge. That is, he actually binds himself to his ugly enemy by his need for retaliation. But he yields to remorse, loses outer control, goes down in a moral maelstrom (Verne uses the real Maelstrom off Norway as a magnificent symbol!), and—as Verne will show in *The Mysterious Island*—experiences the classic death-and-rebirth in the whirlpool.

Properly translated, Verne clearly knows the separate artistic advantage of "developing" a character as opposed to using him or her as a type. With Conseil, for example, it is clear that Verne knew that some people *want* to be typed! They work hard to *become* a type! Conseil deliberately takes refuge in the stereotype of "the gentleman's gentleman" and is thus able actually to remain a permanent boy. And Nemo, too, to the limited degree that he is a type, deliberately strikes the pose of the Romantic exile, the misunderstood Byronic hero fighting for Greek independence. And as modern psychology makes clear, Nemo serves perfectly as the archetypal "perfect father" for the professor. Both Nemo and Conseil are further justified as types because they are seen as such through Aronnax's eyes, in both cases to serve his own psychological needs.

Verne, at least in our new, definitive text, proves to be talented, too, in characterizing group mood and group dynamics. We get to know much about the three companions through their long man-to-man bull sessions about pearls and whales and through a long scene in which, tormented and starving, they grate on each other's nerves.

Humor is one major element in Verne's style. Typical low-key joke: After the professor has swum all night and collapses on the deck of the *Nautilus,* he murmurs "Conseil?" The servant responds: "Has master rung for me?"

And wonderment is another of Verne's characteristics. As a Romanticist he is always astonished anew at the variety and plenitude in Nature. He can take a few facts, names, statistics, and whip up a pleasing paragraph of exclamations over "The Atlantic!" He is most content when he succeeds in catching the essence of each separate sight—like the unique qualities of a seal resting on land. He marvels at the shock of fresh perspective: what the bird hovering in the air looks like from under the water; how a fiery volcanic outpour looks when the absence of air precludes the chance of flame; why sea flowers "have no soul." In one succinct exclamation he can catch the very pathos of living: "How many of those oysters for which he risked his life would have no pearl in them!"

Verne's naive wonderment is stirred even by marine nomenclature. Giving us the names of ocean flora and fauna, he wants us to appreciate the insight of the people who have named them. Fishermen who dub certain sponges "elk horns, lion's paws, Neptune's gloves" Verne hails as "better poets than the scientists." Albatrosses, he thinks, are rightly known as "the vultures of the sea." Verne commends Baron Cuvier for comparing a certain mollusk shell to "an elegant skiff."

The newly translated novel also boasts Verne's own talent for metaphor, and it takes him even into the realm of what we now call depth psychology. Inside his helmet, the professor says, "my head rattled like an almond in its shell." Nemo exclaims that the ocean has a pulse, arteries, spasms. "And I side with the learned Maury . . . it has a circulation as real as the circulation of blood in animals." Verne describes Ned with exuberant phallic imagery: he's a "powerful telescope that could double as a cannon always loaded and ready to fire!" Verne reveals the professor's fear of sharks through slips of the tongue. He explores Aronnax's unconscious desire to retreat to the womb through four separate analogies: he yearns to meet Jonah's whale, he declares his contentment living like a snail in its shell, he is happy sleeping in a cave, and he dreams of himself as a mollusk with now the cave as his shell. And as Freud would point out, the professor's dream allows him to go on sleeping when he should be up on his feet.

Verne's true sense of dreams is what makes him a great Romantic genius for, as Freud also taught us, art is the dream of the artist. Verne's dreams are truly marvelous, giving us a chance to fight on the side of inoffensive right whales against vicious sperm whales, to travel through a natural sea-tunnel under the land, to *see* the Atlantic Cable sprawling on the seafloor, to visit the ruins of the lost continent of Atlantis! All aboard and full steam ahead!

Notes on the French Texts

Twenty Thousand Leagues first saw daylight as a magazine serial. It emerged in instalments between 20 March 1869 and 20 June 1870 in Hetzel's *Magasin d'éducation et de récréation*. Jean Jules-Verne reports his grandfather's anger over cuts inflicted on his text in its initial appearance. This disagreeable surprise on Verne's part suggests that Hetzel or his staff were wont to make textual changes without consulting the author. So, while we can note the differences between the various French texts of this novel, we cannot confidently say which, if any, were sanctioned by Verne himself. Lastly, the magazine serialization may have featured cuts, but it also contained occasional details missing from the hardcover first edition.

The novel's maiden book appearances occurred while the serialization was still under way: softcover editions (known as "in-18" by French bookmen) of the first part on 20 October 1869 and the second part on 13 June 1870, each issued to coincide with their respective completions in the *Magasin*. Presumably, the precise text of the serialization, including cuts and variants, was preserved in these cheap editions. Also presumably, the integral hardcover first edition would have appeared late in 1870, but it was evidently delayed a year by the Franco-Prussian War. (Verne, incidentally, served in that conflict as commander of the *Saint Michel* and its crew of 12. He patrolled the Bay of Somme while writing the first drafts of four novels!)

So the official first edition was issued by Hetzel in the fall of 1871—a big gorgeous volume in red and gold cloth (a format called by the French "grand in-8") and featuring two maps, plus more than a hundred black and white illustrations. *This is universally regarded as the essential, basic text.*

Still, we are aware of two other pertinent text sources: an obviously later Hetzel edition bound in mottled-green board covers that contains a few corrections of the 1871 text, and finally, a two-volume edition published in 1923 by Hachette, which has been excoriated by scholars for its cuts but which, like the *Magasin* texts, contains some detail missing from the 1871 first edition. Accordingly, while some have assumed its cuts were implemented by Hachette's staff, Dr. Evans suggests that this 1923 edition may simply have been set from the serialization (or possibly from the two-volume "in-18" paperback derived from that serialization).

Earlier English Versions

The novel's textual fortunes have been even more tangled in English. Published by the London firm of Sampson, Low, Marston & Co., the book's earliest English translation appeared in 1873. The translator was an Oxford cleric, the Reverend Louis Page Mercier, who hid his sins behind the byline "Mercier Lewis." As Walter James Miller, one of our present translators, fully documented in his 1965 and 1976 revisions of (and restorations to) this version, Mercier cut nearly a quarter of Verne's text and riddled the remainder with hundreds of translation errors. Whether these misrepresentations were politically motivated (British translations of Verne regularly tailored his ideas to conform to Victorian national propaganda) is open to discussion. But even the gentlest view is unfavorable: at best, the "standard" translation was simply a rush job to capitalize on the recent blockbusting success of Verne's *Around the World in Eighty Days.*

For nearly a century the Mercier remained the official English text. Reference books occasionally mention a second Victorian translation by the British boys' author Henry Frith, but to our knowledge this version wasn't marketed in the U.S. The text in Dent's "Everyman" series is credited to Frith, but it proves to be identical with the Mercier rendition. And not only has the Mercier endured on its own, but it seems to have influenced every subsequent version: a 1922 cutesyfied rewrite by Philip Schuyler Allen; Anthony Bonner's 1960 re-translation with many cuts restored but with some major Mercier blunders recycled; WJM's 1965 high school edition; Mendor Brunetti's 1969 redo, incorporating the reconstructive surgery of his predecessors; WJM's 1976 annotated edition; a 1989 juvenile edition by the illustrator Ron Miller, unfortunately sabotaged by careless typesetting; and even the imposing scholarship of Emanuel J. Mickel in his 1992 Indiana University edition. Undeniably we have come a long way, yet so insidious and pervasive were Mercier's errors, not one of the above versions succeeded in purging them all.

A From-the-Ground-up Translation

The edition you are now reading is, then, in several respects unprecedented and unique. Further, our collaboration proved to be an instance of pure serendipity.

Over the period 1989–1991, Frederick Paul Walter labored on behalf of a New York trade publisher to generate an entirely new, from-the-ground-up translation, the first such project to consider and scrutinize the differing French texts. En route FPW consulted with WJM and other Verne specialists and later copied WJM on the full first draft—at the precise moment, ironically, that WJM was himself retained by the Naval Institute Press to generate *his* entirely new translation. From that point on we proceeded as friendly rivals.

Then, abruptly, FPW's publisher canceled all plans. WJM suggested a pooling of resources: together we could produce a truly definitive *Twenty Thousand Leagues*.

Given the textual discrepancies, we don't always presume to know Verne's final intentions. But we are satisfied that we've taken every relevant source into account. The state of Texas is peculiarly rich in Verniana, and our translation derives from these three vintage sources: 1) the 1871 Hetzel edition ("grand in-8") at the University of Texas, Austin; 2) the undated later Hetzel edition in green board covers at Trinity University, San Antonio, an edition with slight revisions of the 1871 text; and 3) the 1923 two-volume Hachette edition at the University of Houston, which, per Dr. Evans, we treat as a stand-in for the serialization text. The current Livre de Poche paperback has served for day-to-day work: it reliably duplicates the 1871 text, although it recycles typos from a Swiss edition published by Rencontre, which indicates that it hails from that source rather than firsthand from a "grand in-8" copy.

In addition to this care over source materials, we've also attempted to set another precedent: the thorough new translation of Verne's marine biology. The novel's lengthy catalogs of fish and saltwater invertebrates have sorely taxed readers of previous English editions because these passages were often left in a quasi-French wording. Yet these notorious "laundry lists" *do* have clear English equivalents and we have done the necessary research to ferret them out.

In a similar vein, we have tried to clarify obscure geographical references by using contemporary U.S. spellings and terms, except where this would produce an obvious anachronism. Conversely, we have respected Verne's use of the metric system. Mercier and his followers have attempted to convert many of Verne's figures, leading not only to frequent errors but to grotesquely detailed citations where Verne clearly wanted an easy round number. Today such efforts are pointless: the metric system is firmly established in the U.S., and we have left Verne's figures as is.

Furthermore, we have taken an activist stand on textual errors in the original French. Once Mercier's many blunders are purged, we are still left with a handful of mostly minor typos in the Hetzel texts. By our estimate there are in this novel over 1,400 *numerical* references—dates, figures, latitude and longitude readings, depth and height citations, etc. In an era before computers and electronic calculators, such detail presented a stiff challenge to a compositor, and Hetzel's typesetters seem to have misset about two dozen items (not a despicable accuracy ratio—they're still batting better than 98 percent). However, in the interests of today's general reader, we thought it best to correct these slips in the text proper. But in the interests of scholars and students, we have carefully annotated each of these corrections, citing the original French in each case and including some discussion of the particular textual problem.

Finally, the present text displays the advantages that accrue when two independent scholars can harmoniously polish each other's work. Initially, FPW generated a rigorously faithful and literal text, adhering as tightly as possible to Verne's period French. For his part, WJM completed more than a third of his own new version before FPW's work became available to him. Thereafter, WJM drew heavily on FPW's text, massaging its period style for greater readability, color, and flow. Similarly, FPW retrieved most of the annotations from WJM's 1976 edition, adapting them for this new version and adding much recent scholarship. The result, we feel, is something approaching the best of all *possible* worlds.

About the Illustrations

The black and white engravings accompanying Verne's text initially appeared in the 1871 French first edition published by J. Hetzel et Cie. Two Parisian artists did the honors: Edouard Riou illustrated the first quarter of the book, Alphonse de Neuville finished the task, and one Hildibrand engraved the results. The present reproductions are from first-generation sources and are therefore exceptionally clear and clean.

That 1871 edition also featured two maps drafted under Verne's supervision and giving all the place names in French. These maps have been "translated" and redrawn for this edition by the Houston illustrator-cartoonist Jim Walter, brother of the present cotranslator.

Acknowledgments

Walter James Miller and Frederick Paul Walter hereby warmly acknowledge the generous help of several wonderful people, especially these Verne specialists for assistance with texts and variants and for their general encouragement: Dr. Olivier Dumas, president, Société Jules Verne, Paris; Dr. Arthur B. Evans, DePauw University; Steve Michaluk, United States Navy; Dr. Brian Taves, U.S. Library of Congress; and Sidney Kravitz of Dover, New Jersey; and these Houston colleagues, for help with editing and readability: Jacqueline Dodes, Marilyn Sacramento, Jim Walter, and Cheryl Young; and for their all-out practical help and faith in this project: Mary T. Hume of New York City and Mr. and Mrs. F. P. Walter of Indianapolis.

Walter James Miller
NEW YORK UNIVERSITY

Frederick Paul Walter
UNIVERSITY OF HOUSTON

Introduction

⬿

TERMS OF MEASUREMENT

CABLE LENGTH	In Verne's usage, 600 feet
CENTIGRADE	0° centigrade = freezing water
	37° centigrade = human body temperature
	100° centigrade = boiling water
FATHOM	6 feet
GRAM	Approx. 1/28 of an ounce
	• MILLIGRAM: Approx. 1/28,000 of an ounce
	• KILOGRAM (KILO): Approx. 2.2 pounds
HECTARE	Approx. 2.5 acres
KNOT	1 nautical mile, or 1.15 land statute miles, per hour
LEAGUE	In Verne's usage, 2.16 miles
LITER	Approx. 1 quart
METER	Approx. 1 yard, 3 inches
	• MILLIMETER: Approx. 1/25 of an inch
	• CENTIMETER: Approx. 2/5 of an inch
	• DECIMETER: Approx. 4 inches
	• KILOMETER: Approx. 6/10 of a mile
	• MYRIAMETER: Approx. 6.2 miles
TON, METRIC	Approx. 2,200 pounds

PUBLISHER'S NOTE

Both Verne experts and general readers are divided on the question of a proper English title for Jules Verne's novel. His title in the original French is *Vingt mille lieues sous les mers.* A literal translation would be *Twenty Thousand Leagues under the Seas.* This title would stress the fact that Verne's characters travel under *all* seven seas. It would also prevent anyone from thinking Verne meant twenty thousand leagues (43,200 miles) *downward,* an impossibility, of course, but a joke sometimes made in science fiction (as for example in Thomas Monteleone's Verne pastiche *The Secret Sea*).

On the other hand, readers who favor the usual English title—*Twenty Thousand Leagues under the Sea*—point out that in our language the phrase "the sea" can be an all-inclusive term for *all* the salt waters on our planet. When we hear that somebody "went to sea," we assume he or she is traveling all the seas.

Based on that understanding, then, the editors have decided to keep the usual title and rely on people's realizing that *under the Sea* means that Verne's characters travel under all of the salt waters of the earth.

First Part

90 105 120 135 150 165 180 165 150 135 120 105 90

ARCTIC OCEAN

New Siberian Islands

SIBERIA

ARCTIC CIRCLE

Bering Sea

Aleutian Islands

NORTH AMERICA

75 60 45 30 15 0 15 30 45 60 75

PEKING

SAN FRANCISCO

Crespo Island

Tropic of Cancer

CALCUTTA

Caroline Islands

Hawaiian Islands

MEXICO

PHILLIPINES

OCEANIA

PACIFIC OCEAN

BORNEO

Equator

INDIAN OCEAN

NEW GUINEA

Vanikoro

Marquesas Islands

Coral Sea

Fiji Islands

NEW CALEDONIA

Tonga Islands

Tuamotu Islands

Reao Island

AUSTRALIA

Tropic of Capricorn

SYDNEY

TASMANIA

NEW ZEALAND

ANTARCTIC CIRCLE

Sabrina Coast

Adélie Coast

ANTARCTIC OCEAN

Victoria Land

Mt. Erebus & Mt. Terror

90 105 120 135 150 165 180 165 150 135 120 105 90

CHART: First Part

Longitude Headings— PARIS MERIDIAN

cartography by Jim Walter after Jules Verne

ONE

A Moving Reef [1]

THE YEAR 1866 was marked by a bizarre situation, a phenomenon unexplained and inexplicable that probably no one has yet forgotten. Putting aside those rumors that upset people in the seaports and excited the public mind far inland, the significant fact is that seafaring men were especially agitated. Merchants, shipowners, ships' captains, skippers and masters from Europe and America, naval officers of all nations, and finally the various governments on those two continents, all became deeply concerned.

For some while, ships at sea had encountered "an enormous thing," a long spindle-shaped object, sometimes phosphorescent, infinitely bigger and faster than any whale.

Data relating to this apparition, entered in the logbooks of several ships, agreed in most respects as to the structure of the object or creature in question, its unprecedented speed, its amazing locomotive power, and the special vitality with which it seemed endowed. If it really was a whale or a related creature, it surpassed in size all large sea animals hitherto classified as "cetaceans." [2] Neither Cuvier nor Lacépède, [3] neither Duméril nor Quatrefages would have ad-

---

1. The very words "moving reef" were charged with excitement for Verne's original audience. Since 1861 the French had been reading news accounts of giant squid seen in the Atlantic. These reports revived earlier speculations (mainly by Scandinavian writers) about sea monsters huge enough to be mistaken for islands or reefs. Besides, for Verne himself the notion of a *moving reef* or *floating island* had profound subconscious significance. Large marine masses occur and recur throughout his novels, such as *A Floating City, The Fur Country, The Giant Raft,* and *Propeller Island,* which, in I 7, will lead us to a curious bit of psychohistory.

2. Today's scientists rank whales, dolphins, and porpoises as cetacea. In the nineteenth century, Verne was a little less strict, stretching the term to take in other fishlike mammals like seals and dugongs (see II 5 and II 14). Several types of oceangoing mammals will figure prominently in the subsequent narrative.

3. To give immediacy and verisimilitude to his fiction, Verne often uses the time-tested device of name-dropping with real-life personages. Cuvier and Lacépède were two of the great French pioneers in science's effort to set up systems of classification for natural phenomena. Bernard Germain Étienne de la Ville, Count of Lacépède (1756–1825), published his *History of Cetaceans* in 1804; his life's work was the study of fishes, and his classification system is cited more than once in the present novel. Baron Georges Leopold Cuvier (1769–1832) laid the broad

mitted that such a monster could exist unless they had seen it with their own eyes: the trained eyes of the scientist.

Striking an average of observations made at various times—rejecting those timid estimates that saw this object as only 200 feet long and ignoring those exaggerated opinions that it was a mile wide and three long—one could still conclude that this phenomenal creature greatly exceeded the dimensions of anything then known to ichthyologists—if indeed it existed at all.

But that it *did* exist was now an undeniable fact; and given that penchant for the marvelous that powers the human mind, one can understand the excitement produced all over the world by this supernatural apparition. As for classifying it as a fictitious event, that idea had to be discarded.

On July 20, 1866, the steamer *Governor Higginson,* of the Calcutta and Burnach Steam Navigation Company, had met this moving mass five miles off the east coast of Australia. At first Captain Baker thought he was in the presence of a hitherto undiscovered reef; he was all set to determine its exact position when two columns of water, projected by this inexplicable object, shot with a hissing sound 150 feet into the air. So, unless this reef suffered from the intermittent eruptions of a geyser, the *Governor Higginson* was facing, fair and square, some aquatic mammal, till then unknown, that could spout from its blowholes columns of water mixed with air and vapor.

Similar observations were made on July 23 of the same year, in Pacific waters, by the *Christopher Columbus* of the West India and Pacific Steam Navigation Company. This proved that this extraordinary cetacean could transport itself from one place to another with amazing speed, since, in an interval of just three days, the *Governor Higginson* and the *Christopher Columbus* had observed it at two points on the chart separated by more than 700 nautical leagues.4

Fifteen days later, and 2,000 leagues farther off, the *Helvetia* of the Compagnie Nationale and the *Shannon* of the Royal Mail Line, running on opposite tacks in that part of the Atlantic between the United States and Europe, respectively signaled each other that the monster had been raised in latitude 42° 15′ north, and longitude 60° 35′ west of the meridian of Greenwich. From this simultaneous observation, they were able to estimate the minimum length of

---

foundations for comparative anatomy and paleontology. The work of both men in the area of marine biology is still honored today, although many of their conclusions have, inevitably, been revised: both men were frequently forced to work from preserved specimens and published reports rather than from direct observation.

4. The league as a unit of distance has varied with time and place, becoming standardized only recently. In the nineteenth century seamen were apt to use the league as a rough unit of measure meaning somewhere between two and three miles. Repeatedly in this novel we can infer that Verne reckoned the nautical league as 2.16 nautical miles. Hence the *extraordinary cetacean* has traveled more than 1,500 miles in three days. And Verne's title, *Twenty Thousand Leagues . . .* could be read as *Forty-Three Thousand Two Hundred Miles. . . .*

Today a nautical league is three nautical miles or 5.556 kilometers. A nautical mile is about 6,080 feet. This is the length of one minute (1′) of arc of a great circle on the earth's surface.

the mammal at more than 350 English feet,[5] since the *Shannon* and the *Helvetia* were both 100 meters long, stem to stern, and still seemed shorter than the monster. Now the largest whales, those rorqual whales who frequent the waters of the Aleutian Islands, have never exceeded a length of 56 meters, if they attain that.

One after another, reports came in—fresh observations made by the transatlantic ship *Pereire,* news of a collision between the Inman Line's *Etna* and the monster, an official memorandum by the officers of the French frigate *Normandie,* dead-earnest reckonings by the staff of Commodore Fitz-James on board the *Lord Clyde*—all of this greatly influenced public opinion. In lighthearted countries, people joked about this phenomenon, but grave and practical countries, England, America, Germany, took the matter very seriously.

In every big city, the monster was in fashion. They sang of it in the cafes, ridiculed it in the newspapers, dramatized it on the stage. The scandal sheets found it a perfect occasion for all kinds of hoaxes. Newspapers that were short of copy resurrected all the imaginary and gigantic creatures, from the terrible white whale, "Moby Dick" of the hyperborean regions, to the immense kraken[6] whose tentacles could entwine a 500-ton ship and drag it down to the bottom of the sea. Even reports from ancient times were resurrected: the opinions of Aristotle and Pliny[7] who accepted the existence of such monsters, the Norwegian tales of Bishop Pontoppidan, the accounts of Paul Egede, and finally the reports of Captain Harrington[8] whose good faith is beyond suspicion when he claims to have seen, while aboard the *Castilian* in 1857, that enormous serpent which until then had frequented only the seas of the old *Constitutionalist.*[9]

5. About 106 meters. An English foot is only 30.4 centimeters. *Jules Verne*

6. Kraken was the Norwegian name given to a sea monster big enough to be mistaken for an island. With their multiple arms, the creatures were reputed to drag ships under. In Verne's time "kraken" was synonymous with the French "poulpe"—a monster with many limbs. Today's scientists would probably finger the giant squid (*Architeuthis dux*) as the likely culprit.

7. In his *Natural History,* Pliny (A.D. 23–79) described a 700-pound monster, with arms 30 feet long, that came out of the sea at night to steal food at Rocadillo, Spain. Probably Pliny was confusing accounts of two very real sea animals: the octopus, renowned for its ability to travel short distances on land, and the giant squid, which was often cast up on the Spanish coast in ancient times.

8. Again Verne salts his fiction with actual celebrities. These three men still figure prominently in the annals of sea-monster sightings. In his *Natural History of Norway* (1755) Erik Pontoppidan (1698–1764) described the kraken as "the largest and most surprising of all the animal creation." Once again it was probably a giant squid, and its likes were sighted by the Scandinavian cleric Hans Egede (1686–1758), whose experiences were written up and published by his son Povel (Paul) Egede (1708–1789). A famous nineteenth century sighting was reported by Britain's Captain George Henry Harrington, whose careful, uncolored observations garnered considerable attention.

9. A Parisian newspaper, known for its extreme political views, which had gone out of business. In referring to an "enormous serpent," Verne is punning on an alternate meaning of serpent: a traitor or snake-in-the-grass.

Then, in the learned societies and scientific journals a continuous controversy erupted between the believers and the nonbelievers. The "question of the monster" inflamed all minds. Journalists making a profession of science quarreled with journalists making a profession of wit, spilling seas of ink during this memorable campaign, some even spilling two or three drops of blood as they went from sea serpents to personal insults.

Lasting six months, war was waged back and forth. There were feature articles from the Geographic Institute of Brazil, the Royal Academy of Science in Berlin, the British Association, and the Smithsonian Institution in Washington; discussions in the *Indian Archipelago,* in *Cosmos,* published by Father Moigno, and in Petermann's *Mittheilungen;*[10] and scientific chronicles in the leading French and foreign newspapers—to all these the independent press retorted with inexhaustible zest. When the adversaries of the monster cited a saying of Linneaus that "Nature does not make jumps," witty writers for the independent press punned that "Nature does not make jackasses," and called on their contemporaries never to give the lie to Nature by admitting the existence of krakens, sea serpents, "Moby Dicks," and other lucubrations of drunken sailors. Finally, with an article published in a much-feared satirical journal, its most popular writer settled the matter: like Hippolytus spurning Phaedra, he dealt the monster a death-blow, dispatching it amid a universal chorus of laughter.[11] Wit had vanquished science.

During the early months of the year 1867, "the question" seemed to be buried, with no chance of being resurrected, when new facts were brought to the attention of the public. Now it was no longer just a problem for scientists, it was a real menace for the world at large. "The question" took on a new shape. The monster once again became an islet, a rock, a reef, but a reef that moved around, whose position was indeterminate and elusive!

On the night of March 5, 1867, the *Moravian,* of the Montreal Ocean Company, finding herself in latitude 27° 30′ and longitude 72° 15′, struck on her starboard quarter a rock not shown on any chart of those seas. Under the concerted efforts of wind and 400-horsepower engines, she was running at the rate of 13 knots. Had it not been for the superior strength of her hull, the *Moravian* would without doubt have been broken open by the shock and sunk with those 237 passengers she was bringing back from Canada.

The collision occurred just as day was breaking, about five o'clock in the morning. The officers on watch rushed to the stern. They scanned the sea with the most scrupulous attention. They saw nothing but a strong eddy about three cable lengths away,[12] as if those sheets of water had been violently agitated. The

---

10. German, meaning "Bulletin."

11. In Greek legend, Phaedra was the second wife of Theseus, who fathered Hippolytus by his earlier union. Phaedra lusts after her new stepson, but he repulses her advances. In revenge, she falsely accuses him before Theseus of being the initiator of the planned infidelity. Theseus curses his son, who later dies in a traffic accident.

12. A cable, or cable length, in nautical usage of the past was understood to be roughly equal to 100 fathoms or 600 feet. Officially, a cable is 608 feet in Great Britain, 720 feet in the United States.

exact bearings of the place were taken, and the *Moravian* continued on course, apparently without damage. Had it struck on a submerged rock, or on an enormous wreck? No one could tell. But when they examined its underside in the shipyard, they saw that part of its keel was broken.

This event, so grave in itself, might have been forgotten like so many others, if it had not, three weeks later, been reenacted under similar circumstances. But this time, thanks to the nationality of the victim of the collision, and thanks to the reputation of the company to which the vessel belonged, this event triggered a great outcry.

There is no one alive who has not heard of the celebrated English shipowner Cunard.[13] In 1840, this intelligent industrialist started a postal service between Liverpool and Halifax with three wooden paddle wheel steamers, each displacing 1,162 metric tons and driven by 400-horsepower engines. In 1848, the Cunard fleet was increased by four ships of 1,820 tons each with 650-horsepower engines, and two years later by two more vessels of even greater tonnage and power. In 1853, after Cunard's mail franchise had been renewed, they added to their fleet the *Arabia,* the *Persia,* the *China,* the *Scotia,* the *Java,* and the *Russia,* all ships of top speed and the biggest—except for the *Great Eastern*—that ever plowed the seas. By 1867, then, the company had twelve ships afloat, eight driven by paddle wheel and four by propeller.

If I give these very succinct details, it is to remind everyone of the importance of this shipping line, famous for its intelligent management. No oceangoing line has ever been better organized, no business enterprise ever rewarded with such success. In 26 years, the Cunard line had made 2,000 Atlantic crossings without so much as a voyage canceled, a delay recorded, a ship, a man, or even a letter lost. This must be the reason why—according to a recent survey of official records—passengers continue to prefer Cunard, in spite of powerful competition offered by France. So, as we might expect, it caused quite a stir when an accident befell one of Cunard's best steamers.[14]

---

13. For the climactic event of his opening chapter, Verne resorts to one of the heroes of nineteenth century industry. One historian explains Samuel Cunard's success by saying "he thought in services when other people thought in ships." Born in Halifax, Nova Scotia, in 1788, young Samuel became an agent for the East India Company. Stationed in Boston, he contracted to carry the British mail from New England to Bermuda.

He became an early advocate of conversion to steam in intercontinental shipping and by 1830 was working out detailed plans for a steamship line between Liverpool, Halifax, and Boston. Hence he was perfectly prepared when the Admiralty proposed to substitute steamships for sailing vessels in the transatlantic mail service. Cunard won the contract.

Part of his success surely was that he thought in terms of *classes* of ships, that is, fleets of sister ships that could offer identical services and, if need be, take each other's place. For his systematic improvement of transatlantic travel and communication, Cunard was made a baronet in 1859. Sir Samuel died in 1866, unaware that his line was shortly to run afoul of the "enormous thing."

14. In fact, at the very moment that the story is taking place, the *Scotia* holds the record for running from New York to Liverpool in 8 days, 22 hours.

The *Scotia* in dry dock

On April 13, 1867, the ocean being beautiful, the breeze favorable, the *Scotia* found herself in longitude 15° 12′ and latitude 45° 37′. She was running at 13.43 knots, propelled by her 1,000-horsepower engines. Her paddles treaded the water with perfect regularity. She was then drawing 6.7 meters of water, displacing 6,624 cubic meters.

At seventeen minutes past four in the afternoon, when the passengers were assembled for refreshments in the grand salon, a slight shock was felt on the hull, in that quarter a little aft of the port paddle.

The *Scotia* had not struck, she had *been* struck, and seemingly by something not blunt but sharp and penetrating. The collision had been so slight that no one would have been alarmed if some men working below had not rushed up on deck exclaiming: "We're sinking! We're sinking!"

At first, the passengers were frightened, but Captain Anderson hastened to reassure them. There could be no immediate danger: The *Scotia* was divided into seven compartments by watertight bulkheads, so she could brave any leak with impunity.

Captain Anderson then descended into the hold. He saw that the fifth compartment had been invaded by the ocean, and the rapidity of the invasion indicated that the leak was large. Fortunately, this compartment did not include the boilers, because the furnaces would at once have been extinguished.

Captain Anderson ordered the engines to be stopped and one of his seamen to dive down to assess the damage. Within moments they located a hole two meters wide in the ship's bottom. Such a leak could not be patched up, and the *Scotia* was obliged to resume her voyage with her paddles half-submerged. She was then 300 miles from Cape Clear, and after three days' delay, which built up much anxiety in Liverpool, she finally entered the Cunard basin.

After the *Scotia* was put in dry dock, Cunard engineers inspected her. They could scarcely believe their eyes. Two and a half meters below her waterline there was a regular gash, in the form of an isosceles triangle. This breach in the iron plates was so perfectly defined, it could not have been done more neatly by a punch. It required a perforating tool of no common stamp; and furthermore, after having been driven with prodigious strength to pierce an iron plate four centimeters thick, it had had to withdraw itself by a backward motion truly inexplicable.

This was the final fact needed to excite public passions anew. From then on, all marine casualties that could not be otherwise explained were attributed to the monster. This imaginary creature bore responsibility for all missing vessels, whose number, unfortunately, is considerable; for, of 3,000 ships whose losses are recorded every year by marine insurance bureaus,[15] the number of

15. Verne's French says *Bureau Veritas,* his country's equivalent of Lloyd's of London. Verne's statistics here came out of his personal experience. As a teen-ager he clerked at his father's law office, which was concerned largely with marine insurance. Young Verne had often to refer to data supplied by the Bureau and by its counterparts in other countries.

steam and sailing ships assumed to be totally lost, because of the absence of all news, amounts to no fewer than 200!

Now it was the "monster" that—justly or unjustly—was charged with their disappearance, and since, thanks to it, communication between the several continents had become more and more dangerous, the public demanded peremptorily that the seas be purged, at any price, of this formidable cetacean.

A Moving

Reef

✆

TWO

The Pros and Cons

WHILE THESE EVENTS were taking place, I came back from a scientific expedition into the Nebraska badlands[1] in the United States. The French government had assigned me to that work in my capacity as assistant professor at the Paris Museum of Natural History. After six months in Nebraska, I arrived in New York late in March laden with valuable collections. My return to France was scheduled for early May. While waiting, I kept busy classifying my mineralogical, botanical, and zoological specimens, and then that accident happened to the *Scotia*.

I was well up on the subject, which was the big news of the day—how could I have ignored it? I had read and reread every American and European newspaper without being any closer to the answer. This mystery fascinated me. Finding it impossible to form a solid opinion, I jumped from one extreme to the other. I did not doubt that something was there. Nonbelievers were invited to put their finger on the wound of the *Scotia*.

The debate was at its fiercest when I arrived in New York. The hypothesis of the floating islet, the moving reef, supported by minds not qualified to judge, was totally junked. And indeed, unless this reef had a machine in its guts, how could it change position with such prodigious speed? The idea of a floating hull or some huge wreck was junked for the same reason.

There remained only two possible solutions, creating two distinct groups of partisans: on one side, those who believed in a monster of incredible strength; on the other, those who swore by a submarine vessel of extreme motive power.

Now this second hypothesis, although entirely admissible, could not stand up against investigations in both the New World and the Old. It was not likely that a private individual could have such a marvel of mechanical engineering at

---

1. Deeply eroded to provide cross sections of several geological periods, the badlands are excellent grounds for fossil hunting. In the 1850s and 1860s, scientists and amateur collectors converged on the badlands, making discoveries that were to net them considerable reputations. It was natural enough for Verne, always on top of the latest scientific developments, to choose the badlands as the reason Aronnax would be in America. As we shall soon see, the professor has indeed returned with his share of Nebraska fossils.

his command. Where and when could he have built it? How could he have kept its construction a secret?

Only a government could possess such a destructive weapon. In these disastrous times, when man's ingenuity has multiplied the power of weaponry, it was possible that some government, without the knowledge of other nations, might be testing such a formidable machine. After the chassepot rifles came the torpedoes, after the torpedoes the submarine rams, and then—the reaction.[2] I hoped so, at least.

But this idea of a war machine faded as one country after another issued formal denials. Since public interest was at stake, and transoceanic communications were suffering, their veracity could not be doubted. And indeed, how could the building of such a submarine boat escape the public eye? For a private individual to keep such a secret under such circumstances would be very difficult, and certainly impossible for a nation whose every move is under constant surveillance by foreign spies.

And so, after inquiries were made in England, France, Russia, Prussia, Spain, Italy, America, even in Turkey, the hypothesis of a submarine *Monitor* was definitely rejected.[3]

And so the hypothesis of a monster had to be revived, in spite of the endless jokes heaped on it by the independent press, and in its wake, the human imagination indulged in the most absurd ichthyological reveries.

Upon my arrival in New York, several people did me the honor of consulting me on the question. In France I had published a two-volume work, in quarto, *The Mysteries of the Great Submarine Depths.* Well received in intellectual circles, this book had established me as a specialist in this rather obscure branch of natural history. My views were sought after. So long as I could deny the reality of the situation, I confined myself to an absolute "No comment." But soon driven into a corner, I was obliged to explain myself categorically. And in this vein, "the honorable Pierre Aronnax, professor at the Paris Museum," was called upon by the *New York Herald* to deliver an opinion for better or for worse.

I complied. I spoke for want of the power to hold my tongue. I discussed the question in all its forms, political and scientific, and here I give the conclusion from my carefully prepared article that was published in the April 30 edition:

"After examining these different hypotheses one by one, we find it necessary to admit, all other suppositions having been refuted, the existence of a marine animal of enormous power.

2. Named after its inventor, Antoine Chassepot, this rifle was a breech-loading weapon adopted by the French Army in 1866. As for the torpedoes, Verne is probably using the term in its older sense, to designate the underwater mines developed in the American Civil War. (When Admiral David Farragut said, "Damn the torpedoes! Full speed ahead!" he was looking at a minefield.)

3. Celebrated opponent of the *Merrimack,* the Union's *Monitor* was a Civil War ironclad with a low, flat deck; John Ericsson designed the vessel, whose remains were recovered off Cape Hatteras in 1974.

Professor Pierre Aronnax

"The deepest parts of the ocean are unknown to us. Soundings have not been able to reach them. What goes on in these remote abysses? What creatures live and could live twelve or fifteen miles beneath the surface of the water? What is the constitution of these beings? We can hardly imagine.

"However, the solution to this problem submitted to me can take the form of a dilemma. Either we know all the varieties of beings that inhabit our planet, or we do not know all of them.

"If we do not know them all, if Nature still keeps secrets in ichthyology, nothing is more admissible than to suppose the existence of fishes or cetaceans of new species or even new genera, with constitutions that can live in the strata inaccessible to our soundings, creatures that an accident of some sort, a fancy, a caprice if you will, brings back up to the surface for long periods.

"If, on the other hand, we do know all living species, we must look for the animal in question among those marine creatures already classified. In that case, I should be disposed to believe in the existence of a giant narwhale.

"The common narwhale, or sea unicorn, often attains a length of 60 feet. Increase its size five or even ten times, then give it strength proportionate to its size, lengthen its offensive weapon, and you have the animal we are looking for. It would have the proportions reported by the officers of the *Shannon,* the instrument needed to perforate the *Scotia,* and the power to pierce the hull of a steamship.

"The narwhale is armed with a type of ivory sword, or lance, as some naturalists call it. Essentially, it is a king-sized tooth with the hardness of steel. We find some of these teeth buried in the bodies of baleen whales, which the sea unicorn attacks always with success. Other of these teeth have been drawn out, with considerable difficulty, from the bottoms of ships that narwhales have pierced through and through, as a gimlet pierces a wine barrel. The museum of the Faculty of Medicine in Paris owns one of these tusks, 2.25 meters long, 48 centimeters wide at its base.

"So now! Imagine this tusk to be ten times stronger and the animal ten times more powerful, launch it at a speed of twenty miles per hour, multiply its mass by its speed, and you could create a collision capable of causing the catastrophe in question.

"Therefore, until we get more information, I shall assume the monster to be a sea unicorn of colossal dimensions, armed not with a mere lance but with a real spur, like the ironclad frigates or those called 'rams' of war, whose mass and motive power it also possesses. Thus we might explain this unexplainable phenomenon—unless there be something else, which, in spite of all one has surmised, seen, felt, or experienced, is still possible."

Those last words were cowardly; but I wanted to preserve my dignity as a professor and not expose myself to American ridicule—they laugh raucously when they do laugh. I reserved a way out for myself. In effect, though, I had admitted the existence of the "monster."

My article was hotly discussed, causing a great noise and gaining many partisans. And the solution it offered at least gave full play to the imagination.

The human mind delights in grand visions of supernatural beings. And the sea is precisely their best medium, the only medium that can produce and develop such giants, against which land animals, like the elephant and the rhinoceros, are mere midgets.

The liquid masses support the largest known species of mammals. Maybe the oceans also conceal mollusks of unimaginable dimensions, crustaceans too fearful to contemplate, like lobsters 100 meters long or crabs weighing 200 metric tons. Why not? After all, in remote, prehistoric, geological epochs, the land produced quadrupeds, apes, reptiles, birds of enormous sizes. The Creator cast them in a colossal mould which time has gradually reduced. Now why shouldn't the seas, in their unknown depths, have preserved some of these specimens of gigantic life from the prehistoric ages? For the seas never change, while the shores undergo continuous mutation. Maybe the bosom of the ocean conceals the last varieties of those titans, for whom years are centuries, centuries millennia.

But I have been getting carried away. Enough of these fantasies that time has now transformed into terrible realities for me. To repeat: opinion had crystallized as to the nature of this phenomenon, the public now accepted the existence of a prodigious creature distinct from the sea serpents of myth and fable.

While some persisted in seeing this as a purely scientific problem, more practical people, especially in England and America, felt strongly that the oceans must be purged of this fearsome monster, to guarantee the safety of transoceanic enterprise.

The industrial and commercial papers treated the question mainly from this point of view. *The Shipping and Mercantile Gazette, Lloyd's List,* the *Packetboat,* and the *Maritime and Colonial Review,* all papers devoted to insurance companies (which threatened to raise their premium rates), were unanimous on this point.

Public opinion thus pronounced, the United States was the first in the field. In New York they made preparations for an expedition destined to pursue this narwhale. A fast frigate, the *Abraham Lincoln,* was put into commission as soon as possible. The naval arsenals were unlocked for Commander Farragut,[4] who hastened to arm his ship.

But, as it always happens, the moment it was decided to pursue the monster, the monster did not appear. For two months no one heard a thing about it. No ship met with it. It seemed as if the sea unicorn knew all about these plots being woven around it. It had been so much talked of, even through the Atlantic Cable, that jokesters claimed this sly fellow had stopped a cablegram on its way and was making the most of it.

The frigate was supplied for a long voyage, and equipped with formidable

The Pros and Cons

15

---

4. Verne selects many names for their echo value. Here he names the frigate after the martyred president and her commander after the great Civil War naval hero, Admiral David Glasgow Farragut. The admiral did a diplomatic tour of France and England in 1867 and was accordingly well known in Europe.

fishing gear, but no one could tell it where to go. Impatience grew until suddenly, on June 2,[5] it was learned that the *Tampico*,[6] a steamship of the San Francisco Line sailing between California and Shanghai, had sighted the animal three weeks before in the North Pacific.

This news caused intense excitement. Commander Farragut was given less than twenty-four hours to prepare for departure. His ship was restocked with food, his coal bunkers overflowed. Not a single man was absent from his post. All that was left to be done was to fire and stoke the furnaces, heat the boilers, and weigh anchor. Half a day's delay would have been unforgivable. But he asked for nothing better than to get going.

I received a letter just three hours before the *Abraham Lincoln* left its Brooklyn pier;[7] it read as follows:

Pierre Aronnax
Professor at the Paris Museum
Fifth Avenue Hotel[8]
New York

Sir,

If you would like to join the expedition on the *Abraham Lincoln,* the government of the Union would take great pleasure in having you represent France in this enterprise. Commander Farragut has a cabin at your disposal.

Very cordially yours,
J. B. Hobson
SECRETARY OF THE NAVY[9]

5. The Hetzel and Hachette editions both give July 2, contributing to some muddled dating in I 2 and 4, while furnishing the first of several apparent typographical or editorial errors that dot the original French texts. The current Livre de Poche paperback gives July 3, but this is no improvement because the overall chronology makes it clear that the action described must have occurred in May or June. Some twentieth-century French editions correct this detail to read June 2, and we have followed their lead.

6. The steamship is so named in the Hachette edition; but in Hetzel, the vessel unaccountably remains anonymous. The deletion of this detail was probably a typesetter's accident; hence we have followed Hachette.

7. A pier is a type of wharf expressly set aside for each craft. *Jules Verne*

8. The original establishment was second only to the Astor in world renown, and on April 9, 1867, its guest register included the names Jules and Paul Verne. The author and his brother had made a transatlantic voyage on the *Great Eastern,* and Jules's autobiographical delight in his writing is manifest in the passages devoted to New York: in the next chapter his detailed memories of the hotel will add to the credibility of his story.

9. In 1867 this U.S. cabinet post was actually held by Gideon Welles.

THREE

Whatever Pleases Master

T HREE SECONDS *BEFORE* receiving J. B. Hobson's letter, I no more thought of chasing the unicorn than of attempting the Northwest Passage.[1] Three seconds *after* reading this letter from the honorable Secretary of the Navy, I felt that my true vocation, my main goal in life, was to pursue this monster and rid the seas of it.

But I had just returned from a painful trip, exhausted, and I desperately needed a rest. I had wanted nothing more than to see my country again, my modest quarters near the Botanical Gardens, my precious collections of rare specimens. But now nothing could hold me back. Now I forgot all that, fatigue, friends, collections, and without reflecting further, I accepted the American government's invitation.

"Besides," I told myself, "all roads lead back to Europe, and the unicorn may be thoughtful enough to lead me back toward the coast of France. That worthy animal may even allow itself to be caught in European waters (for my special benefit), and I'll try to bring back no less than half a meter of its ivory lance to the Museum of Natural History."

In the meantime, though, I would have to hunt this narwhale in the North Pacific. That meant going to France via the Antipodes.

"Conseil," I called out impatiently.

Conseil was my manservant. A faithful Flemish lad who had accompanied me on all my trips. I liked him and he liked me. He was phlegmatic in temperament, punctual on principle, zealous from habit, rarely disturbed or even surprised, adroit with his hands, apt at any service required of him. Despite his name, he never gave "counsel," even when not asked for it.

---

1. In 1867 no one had yet found the Northwest Passage, although European mariners had long sought a quick route from the Atlantic to the Pacific across the top of the world through the Arctic Archipelago of Canada and Alaska. Those who failed included such big names as Henry Hudson and Captain Cook. One of Verne's earliest tales, "A Winter Amid the Ice," published in 1855, was inspired by the heroism of early Arctic explorers. But Verne was to die only months before the first successful east-to-west negotiation of these frozen waterways: by the great Norwegian explorer Roald Amundsen in 1906.

Rubbing shoulders with learned men in our little world at the Botanical Gardens, Conseil had come to know a thing or two. In Conseil I had a well-versed specialist in biological classification. With acrobatic agility he could run up and down the ladder of branches, groups, classes, subclasses, orders, families, genera, subgenera, species, and varieties. But his knowledge stopped there. To classify in the abstract was his whole life, but he was helpless on the practical side. I do not think he could tell the difference, in real life, between a sperm whale and a baleen whale. But still, what a fine, decent chap!

For ten years, Conseil had followed wherever science led. Never once did he complain of the length or the hardships of a journey. Never did he object to packing his trunk for whatever place it might be, China or the Congo. He went here and everywhere without question. He enjoyed good health, which defied all ailments; solid muscles; and no nerves! Not even an appearance of nerves—mentally speaking, of course.

This boy was thirty years of age, and his age to that of his master was as fifteen is to twenty. Please forgive me for using this roundabout way of admitting I was forty.

But Conseil had one fault. He was formal to the nth degree. He never spoke to me except in the third person, and to the point of aggravation.[2]

"Conseil!" I repeated, while preparing feverishly to embark.

I felt sure of this devoted lad. Ordinarily, I never asked him if it was convenient for him to follow me on my trips. But this time, the expedition could be indefinitely prolonged, the enterprise could be dangerous in pursuit of an animal that could sink a frigate as easily as a walnut shell. Here was good reason to stop and think, even for the world's most impassive man. What would he say?

"Conseil!" I cried a third time.

Conseil presented himself.

"Has master called me?"

"Yes, my boy. Get me ready, get yourself ready. We leave in two hours."

"Whatever pleases master," he answered quietly.

2. Verne plants this observation here for two reasons: (1) to prepare us for Conseil's behavior on his first entrance; (2) to prepare us for a scene late in the book when Conseil's grammar—and his character—will undergo a sudden, tragicomic change. Since Conseil's keeping himself at third-person distance is "aggravating" to the professor, this helps characterize the phlegmatic Conseil as more interested in formality, and the sensitive Aronnax as lonely for a human relationship.

Verne considered this mode of address a major clue to Conseil's characterization, using one of the servant's catchphrases as the chapter title to underscore the point. However, the standard Mercier translation badly mishandled Conseil's dialogue, and until recently this crucial speech mannerism has been pretty much lost to American readers.

As for Conseil's *name,* among French critics it is commonly supposed to commemorate one of Verne's real-life friendships: with Jacques-François Conseil, the inventor of a steam-powered submarine that he tested in the Seine during the 1860s.

Presumably, "Conseil" is the manservant's *surname.* Verne neglects to give the lad a Christian name, and he is called simply "Conseil" or "Mr. Conseil," much as the British operate with their valets (e.g., Jeeves, Bunter, and other fictional men-in-waiting).

"There's not a second to spare. Pack everything into my trunk—my traveling kit, suits, shirts, socks—don't bother to count—just as many as you can squeeze in, and hurry."

"And master's collections?" he wondered.

"We'll worry about them later."

"What! The *Archaeotherium,* the *Hyracotherium,* the oreodonts, the *Cheiropotamus,* and master's other skeletons?"[3]

"The hotel will keep them for us."

"And master's live babirusa?"

"They'll feed it while we're gone. Anyhow, I'll have our menagerie sent on to France."

"So then, *we* are not going back to Paris?" Conseil asked.

"Yes, we are, of course," I said evasively, "but by a detour."

"Whatever detour pleases master."

"Oh, it's nothing really, a route not quite so direct, that's all. We sail on the *Abraham Lincoln.*"

"Whatever master thinks proper."

"You see, my friend, it's the monster, the famous narwhale. We're going to rid the seas of it! The author of a two-volume treatise, in quarto, on *The Mysteries of the Great Submarine Depths* can't excuse himself from going with Commander Farragut. A glorious mission, but dangerous. We can't predict where we'll be going. These animals can be capricious. But let's go anyhow. Our commander is a determined man."

"Whatever master does, I'll do," Conseil responded.

"But think it over. I don't want to hide anything from you. Not everybody comes back from this kind of a trip!"

"Whatever pleases master."

In fifteen minutes our bags were packed. Conseil had done everything in a jiffy. I knew nothing was missing, for that lad could classify shirts and suits as neatly as birds and mammals.

The hotel elevator took us down to the grand vestibule on the mezzanine. I went down a short stair to the ground floor. I settled my bill at that vast desk, which as usual was besieged by a large crowd. I gave instructions for sending my cartons of stuffed animals and dried plants to Paris. I opened a credit account for the babirusa and, Conseil at my heels, I jumped into a carriage.

Available at a fare of twenty francs, the carriage went down Broadway to Union Square, followed Fourth Avenue to its junction with the Bowery, turned into Katrin Street and stopped at Pier 34. From there the Katrin Ferry took us, men, horses and carriage, to Brooklyn, that great annex of New York, situated on the left bank of the East River. In a few minutes we arrived at the pier where the *Abraham Lincoln* was belching clouds of black smoke from her two funnels.

3. These are fossil skeletons, prehistoric relatives of the wart hog, horse, deer, and raccoon.

Our baggage was immediately carried to the deck of the frigate. I hastened on board. I asked for Commander Farragut. One of the sailors conducted me to the afterdeck, where I met a good-looking officer. He held out his hand to me.

"Professor Pierre Aronnax?" he asked.

"Himself," I replied. "Commander Farragut?"

"In person. Good to have you aboard, professor. Your cabin is ready."

I bowed, and leaving the commander to his last-minute preparations, I was conducted to the cabin they had reserved for me.

The *Abraham Lincoln* had been perfectly chosen and fitted out for its new assignment. It was a very fast frigate, with superheating apparatus allowing it to build up to as much as seven atmospheres of steam pressure. Under these conditions the *Abraham Lincoln* could attain a mean speed of 18.3 miles per hour, a considerable speed, but not enough to cope with our giant cetacean.

The way the frigate was fitted out inside corresponded favorably with its nautical qualities. I was quite pleased with my cabin, located in the stern and opening into the officers' mess.

"We'll be quite comfortable here," I told Conseil.

"With all due respect to master, as comfortable as a hermit crab inside the shell of a whelk."

I left Conseil to the proper stowing of our luggage, and I went back up on deck to watch the preparations for weighing anchor.

Just then, Commander Farragut was giving the order to cast off the last moorings holding the *Abraham Lincoln* to its Brooklyn pier. That meant that if I had been delayed a quarter of an hour, or even less, the frigate would have left without me, and I would have missed out on this extraordinary, supernatural, and unimaginable expedition, a true account of which might well meet with incredulity.

But Commander Farragut did not want to lose a day nor an hour in setting out for those waters where the animal had been sighted. He called for his engineer.

"Do we have pressure up?" he asked of him.

"Oh yes, sir!" the engineer responded.

"*Go ahead,*" cried the commander.

By means of a compressed-air apparatus, his order was relayed to the engine room where the mechanics activated the start-up wheel. Steam whistled into the half-open valves. The long horizontal pistons groaned and pushed the tie-rods of the drive shaft. The blades of our propeller beat the water faster and faster, and the *Abraham Lincoln* moved out majestically amid an escort of a hundred ferryboats and tenders, all jammed with well-wishers.[4]

The wharves of Brooklyn, and every part of New York bordering the East River, were also crowded with spectators. Three cheers burst from 500,000 throats. Thousands of handkerchiefs were waving above the crowds, saluting

---

4. A tender is a small steamboat assisting the large liners. *Jules Verne*

The *Abraham Lincoln* sets out

the *Abraham Lincoln* until she reached the waters of the Hudson River, at the tip of that elongated island forming New York City.

Then the frigate followed the New Jersey coast on the right bank of that beautiful river, a bank covered with mansions, and passed the forts, which saluted us with their biggest guns. The *Abraham Lincoln* responded by lowering and hoisting the American colors three times. Its 39 stars shone resplendent from the gaff of the mizzenmast.[5] Reducing speed to take the narrow channel, marked by buoys, that curves into that inner bay formed by Sandy Hook, she coasted the long sandy beach where thousands of spectators gave us a rousing final cheer.

The escort of boats and tenders still followed the frigate, not leaving her till we came abreast of the lightship whose two signal lights mark the entrance to New York harbor.[6]

Three o'clock sounded. The pilot descended into his dinghy and returned to the little schooner that was waiting for him to leeward. The furnaces were stoked up, the propeller beat the waves faster now, the frigate skirted the low, yellow coast of Long Island. At eight in the evening, after we lost sight of the lights on Fire Island, off to the northwest, we ran full steam ahead into the dark waters of the Atlantic.

5. There were only 37 stars on the American flag in 1867, and there would not be 39 until 1889. This error appears to be Verne's own: in chapter 7 of *All Around the Moon,* published the same year as the present novel (1870), he makes the identical mistake.

6. The last of these famous lightships can now be seen in the South Street Seaport Museum in Manhattan.

FOUR

Ned Land

COMMANDER FARRAGUT WAS a distinguished mariner, deserving of
the ship he commanded. He and his frigate were one. He was the very soul
of the *Abraham Lincoln*. And on the Cetacean Question, there were no
doubts in his mind: he would not allow the existence of the sea unicorn to
be debated aboard his vessel. He believed in it as certain pious women believed in
the Leviathan[1]—on faith, not through reason. The monster did exist, and Commander Farragut would purge the seas of it, he had sworn so. The man was a sort
of Knight of Rhodes, a Sir Dieudonné of Gozo, on his way to meet the dragon
wasting the island. Either Commander Farragut would slay the narwhale or the
narwhale would slay Commander Farragut. No other possibility!

The officers on board shared their leader's views. They were endlessly
chatting, discussing, arguing, calculating the chances of an encounter, studying
intently the vast expanse of the ocean. Several of them voluntarily stood watch
in the crosstrees of the topgallant sail—officers who would have cursed such an
assignment under any other circumstances. The common sailors also were too
impatient to stay on deck; so long as the sun was in the sky, they were up in the
rigging. And the prow of the *Abraham Lincoln* had not yet even reached the
suspected waters of the Pacific.

In short, the ship's company wanted nothing more than to meet the unicorn, harpoon it, hoist it on board, and carve it up. They surveyed the waves
with scrupulous attention. Incidentally, Commander Farragut had mentioned
a certain sum of $2,000, set aside for that person—cabin boy or able bodied
seaman, mate or officer—who first sighted the narwhale. I leave it to the imagination how men used their eyes on board the *Abraham Lincoln*.

As for me, I did not lag behind the others; I yielded to no one my role in
these daily observations. The frigate would have had a hundred good reasons
for calling itself the *Argus*.[2] Only one person on board, Conseil, seemed indifferent and out of keeping with the general enthusiasm.

1. A colossal sea monster described in the Book of Job and by modern commentators, assumed to be a whale of some kind.

2. Since 19th century Europeans received classical educations, Verne could count on his

As I said earlier, Commander Farragut had carefully equipped his ship with every apparatus for catching a gigantic cetacean. No whaling vessel had ever been better armed. We possessed every known device, from the harpoon hurled by hand to the blunderbuss firing barbed arrows, to the duck gun with explosive bullets. On the forecastle was mounted the latest model breech-loading cannon, thick of barrel, narrow in the bore, a model that would figure at the 1867 Universal Exposition. With the greatest of ease, this American-made gun could hurl a conical projectile weighing four kilograms to a mean distance of sixteen kilometers.

And so, the *Abraham Lincoln* lacked no means of destruction. But it had still more. It had Ned Land, the King of Harpooners.

Ned Land was a Canadian with an extraordinary manual ability who knew no equal in his dangerous occupation: He surpassed all harpooners in dexterity, poise, boldness, and cunning. It would have to be a truly wily baleen whale or an exceptionally shrewd sperm whale to escape Ned's harpoon.

He was about forty. More than six English feet in height, strongly built, he was grave, taciturn, sometimes violent, very ill-tempered when frustrated. His appearance demanded attention, especially the power of his gaze, which accentuated his facial expression.

I feel Commander Farragut had acted wisely in engaging this man. Because of his eye and his arm, he alone was worth as much as the rest of the crew. I can do no better than to compare him with a powerful telescope that could double as a cannon always loaded and ready to shoot.[3]

Whoever calls himself Canadian calls himself French. As uncommunicative as Ned Land was, I must admit he took a liking to me. My nationality attracted him, no doubt. It was a chance for him to speak, and for me to hear, that old language of Rabelais still heard in some Canadian provinces. The harpooner's family originated in Quebec, and they were already a tribe of bold fishermen back in the days when that town still belonged to France.

Gradually, Ned became a bit more talkative, and I loved to hear of his exploits in the polar seas. He spoke of fishing and of combat with whales in a naturally poetic manner. His stories took the form of an epic: I seemed to be hearing a Canadian Homer reciting his *Iliad* of the Arctic.

I am writing of this bold companion now as one speaks of an old acquaintance. Because we have become close friends, united in that deep comradeship born of dangers shared. Ah, my gallant Ned, I ask nothing more than to live another hundred years, the longer to remember my time with you.

---

readers knowing that the Argus was, in Greek myth, a monster with one hundred eyes, only a few of which were ever closed at any given time (to get some sleep) while the remainder kept watch. Following the brute's demise, Hera placed its hundred eyes in the tail of the peacock.

3. Freudians will delight in Aronnax's unabashed use of phallic symbolism. Although Freud's achievements were decades in the future, Verne's usage is consistent and true: later in the novel, it will be Land who suffers most from having no "targets" for his "cannon," while Aronnax will express, in symbolic terms, his sweet satisfaction with narcissism.

Now then, where did Ned stand on the Cetacean Question? To tell the truth, he did not believe that such an animal existed; he alone on board did not share the general conviction. He even avoided the subject, which I felt one day it was my duty to press upon him.

On the magnificent evening of June 25,[4] three weeks after our departure, the frigate found itself parallel with Cabo Blanco, 30 miles to leeward of the coast of Patagonia. We had crossed the Tropic of Capricorn, and the Strait of Magellan opened less than 700 miles to the south. Within eight days, the *Abraham Lincoln* would plow the waters of the Pacific.

Seated on the afterdeck, Ned Land and I were chatting about one thing and another, gazing out at that mysterious sea whose depths to this day remain impenetrable by human vision. I naturally led our conversation to the giant narwhale, and I commented on the expedition's chances of success or failure. Seeing that Ned let me talk on without saying much himself, I pressed him more closely.

"Ned," I asked, "is it possible you doubt the existence of this cetacean we're hunting? Do you have any particular reasons for being so skeptical?"

The harpooner gazed stonily at me, slapped his wide forehead with his hand in a gesture habitual to him, closed his eyes as if to collect his thoughts, and said at last:

"Maybe I do, Professor Aronnax."

"But Ned, *you?* A professional whaler, you who are familiar with the great marine mammals, you whose imagination might easily accept this hypothesis of an enormous cetacean, you ought to be the last one to doubt it under these circumstances."

"That's just what deceives you, professor. The common man still believes in super-comets crossing outer space, in prehistoric monsters thriving in the interior of the earth, but neither astronomers nor geologists believe such myths.[5] Whalers don't either. I've hunted many a cetacean. I've harpooned a great many, I've slain many, but however powerful and well armed they were, neither their tails nor their tusks could have pierced the iron plates of a steamship."

"But Ned, we've heard of ships that had been pierced through and through by narwhale teeth."

---

4. Continuing the dating confusion launched in I 2, both the Hetzel and Hachette editions give July 30. Some later French editions amend this to June 30, but it doesn't work: I 5 finds the frigate 400 miles farther south on that date. The context makes it clear that this particular "magnificent evening" had to be on or about June 25, and we have adjusted the text to reflect as much.

5. Scientific skepticism notwithstanding, Verne had great fun with "super-comets" in a later novel, *Hector Servadac,* while an earlier book, *Journey to the Center of the Earth,* featured "prehistoric monsters thriving in the interior of the earth." It is a cliché in sci-fi criticism to call Verne factual and H. G. Wells fanciful; but both of the aforementioned books are brilliant stunts in which Verne juggles facts to kerflummox the reader into accepting fancies more typical of Wells.

Ned Land

"Maybe wooden ships," the Canadian said. "But I myself have never seen it done. Until I have proof, I shall doubt that baleen whales, sperm whales, or sea unicorns can produce the effect you describe."

"Listen here, Ned—"

"No, professor, no, anything you want, except that. A giant squid, perhaps?"

"Even less likely, Ned. The squid is only a mollusk, and even that name indicates the relative softness of its flesh.[6] Even if a squid were 500 feet long—and remember, it is not a vertebrate—it would be incapable of damaging ships like the *Scotia* or the *Abraham Lincoln*. We must reject fables about the prowess of krakens or other monsters of that species."

"So, Mr. Naturalist," Ned said in a bantering tone, "you persist in accepting the existence of an enormous cetacean?"

"Yes, Ned, I persist with a conviction based on the logic of the facts. I believe in the existence of a mammal with a powerful constitution, belonging to the branch Vertebrata, like baleen whales, sperm whales, or dolphins, and equipped with a horn-covered tusk of great penetrating power."

"Hmm," the harpooner responded, shaking his head with the air of a man who would not let himself be convinced.

"Mark my word, my worthy Canadian," I resumed. "If such a mammal exists, if it inhabits the depths of the sea, if it frequents those strata lying miles beneath the surface, it must necessarily have a constitution so solid it defies comparison."

"And why such a powerful constitution?" Ned asked.

"Because it requires incalculable strength just to exist in those strata and resist their pressure."[7]

"Really?" He winked at me.

"Really, and I can prove it with just a few figures."

"Oh figures! Figures can lie!"

"In business, Ned, but not in mathematics. Listen to me. Let's remember that the pressure of one atmosphere is represented by a column of water 32 feet high. Actually, the column would not be so high because we're talking of salt water, which is denser than fresh water. Anyhow, when you dive beneath the waves, Ned, for every 32 feet of water above you, your body is supporting one more atmosphere, that is to say, one more kilogram per each square centimeter on the surface of your body. So it follows that at 320 feet down, that pressure equals ten atmospheres, at 3,200 feet 100 atmospheres, at 32,000 feet—about two-and-a-half vertical leagues down—1,000 atmospheres. That means that if

6. Aronnax is reminding Ned that the word mollusk derives from New Latin *mollusca,* the soft ones, and from classic Latin *mollis,* soft. English readers may recall our verb *mollify,* to soften.

7. Aronnax is hampered here by the prevailing beliefs of his era. Today, we know that many life forms have adapted to the ocean's deepest strata: living tissue is largely composed of water, which is practically incompressible.

you could attain that depth in the ocean, each square centimeter on the surface of your body would be supporting 1,000 kilograms of pressure. Now Ned, my gallant lad, do you know how many square centimeters there are on the surface of your body?"

"I haven't the slightest idea, professor."

"About 17,000."

"So many?"

"And since the atmosphere's pressure actually weighs a bit more than one kilogram per square centimeter, your 17,000 square centimeters are supporting 17,568 kilograms at this very moment."

"Without my noticing it?"

"Without your noticing it. And if you're not crushed by so much pressure, it's because the air penetrates the interior of your body with equal pressure. With perfect equilibrium between inside pressure and outside pressure, they neutralize each other, so you can bear it without discomfort. But in the water, it's different."

"Yes, I can see that," Ned responded, becoming more interested. "Because the water surrounds me but doesn't penetrate me."

"Exactly, Ned. So at 32 feet below the surface, you'd undergo a pressure of 17,568 kilograms; at 320 feet, or ten times greater pressure, it's 175,680 kilograms; at 3,200 feet, or 100 times greater pressure, it's 1,756,800 kilograms; and finally, at 32,000 feet, or 1,000 times greater pressure, it would be 17,568,000 kilograms. You'd be squashed as flat as if they had pulled you from between the plates of a hydraulic press."

"The devil!" Ned exclaimed.

"So my worthy harpooner, if vertebrates several hundred meters long— and proportionate in bulk—can exist at such depths, their surface area must be millions of square centimeters, and they must support billions of kilograms. Figure it out then, what their bone structure must be like, and the power of their constitution, to resist such pressures."

"They'd have to be made of sheet iron eight inches thick, like ironclad frigates."

"Right, Ned. Then think of what damage such a mass could inflict if it were hurled with the speed of an express train against the hull of a ship."

"Yes, right, maybe," the Canadian responded, shaken by these figures but not yet willing to give in.

"So have I convinced you, Ned?"

"You've convinced me of one thing, Mr. Naturalist. If such animals do exist at the bottom of the sea, they must be as strong as you say they are."

"But if they don't exist, my obstinate harpooner, how do you explain what happened to the *Scotia*?"

"It's just maybe—"

"Yes, go on—"

"Maybe because it's not true." Without knowing it, the Canadian had reproduced a celebrated remark by the astronomer Arago.[8]

But this answer merely proved how stubborn Ned could be, and nothing else. I didn't press him any further that day. The damage to the *Scotia* was undeniable. The hole in her side was real enough so that it had to be patched. What better proof of the existence of a hole can you have? That puncture was the effect of a cause. Rocks beneath the surface had not been the cause, nor had submarine engines. So the hole had to be the work of an animal armed with a perforating tool.

So, for all the reasons so far deduced, I believed that this animal belonged to the branch Vertebrata, class Mammalia, group Pisciforma and, finally, order Cetacea. As for the family in which it would be classified—baleen whale, sperm whale, dolphin—and the genus of which it formed a part, and the species with which it was properly aligned, these were questions that would require more work. To answer them, we would have to dissect the monster; to dissect it, catch it; to catch it, harpoon it, which was Ned's business; to harpoon it, sight it, which was the crew's business; and to sight it, meet it, which was a chancy business.

8. This remark was well known to Verne's audience, if only because his earlier novel *From the Earth to the Moon* had cited it in a detailed anecdote. Domenique-François Arago (1786–1856), famous French astronomer and physicist, became embroiled in a discussion of "lunacy," which in those days was taken to mean mental illnesses caused by phases and eclipses of the moon. The discussion had reached the point where someone was attributing dizzy spells, sleepwalking, and attacks of malaria to "the influence of the moon."

"How come? Why?" Arago was asked.

"Maybe," he answered, "because it's not true."

FIVE

At Random

DAY AFTER DAY, the voyage of the *Abraham Lincoln* proved uneventful. The monotony was broken by just one memorable incident, one that demonstrated Ned Land's remarkable talent and showed how much we could depend on him.

On June 30, off the Falkland Islands, we communicated with some American whalers and we learned that they had no new information about the narwhale. But one of them, the captain of the *Monroe,* knowing that Ned Land had signed on board the *Abraham Lincoln,* asked for his help in chasing a baleen whale they had sighted. Commander Farragut welcomed a chance to see Ned at work and authorized him to go aboard the *Monroe.* And Ned's luck was such that instead of one whale he harpooned two, striking one to the heart, and catching the other after just a few minutes' chase.

I decided that if the monster ever had to reckon with Ned's harpoon, I would not bet on the monster.

The frigate skirted the eastern coast of South America with great speed. On July 3 we were at the opening into the Strait of Magellan, parallel with Cabo de las Virgenes. But Commander Farragut was unwilling to try such a tortuous passage and maneuvered instead to double Cape Horn.

The crew agreed with him unanimously. After all, was it likely that they would find the monster in such a narrow strait? A good number of sailors thought the monster could never get through that passage: "He's much too big for that!"

Toward three o'clock in the afternoon of July 6, the *Abraham Lincoln* rounded that solitary island, passing it fifteen miles to the south, that desolate cape at the very end of the American continent, on which Dutch sailors had imposed the name of their native town, Hoorn. Our course was then changed to the northwest, and the next day, the propeller of our frigate finally churned the waters of the Pacific.

"Keep your eyes peeled! Keep your eyes open!" the sailors exhorted each other.

And they opened them inordinately wide. Eyes and spyglasses—a bit dazzled, true, by the prospect of $2,000—had not a moment's rest. Day and night we scanned the sea, and men with a faculty for seeing in the dark had a 50 percent better chance of winning the prize.

Even I, for whom silver has little charm, was constantly on the alert. Eating quick meals and taking only short naps, indifferent to sun or rain, I no longer left the deck. Now I was leaning on the forecastle rail, now propped on the stern rail, my hungry eyes devouring the cotton-colored wake that whitened the ocean as far as eye could reach. And how often I shared the feelings of officers and crew when some capricious whale lifted its black back above the waves! In a moment, the deck of the frigate would be crowded. The hatches would vomit forth a torrent of sailors and officers. With chest heaving and an anxious look in his eye, each man would watch the cetacean's progress. I stared enough to wear out my retina, enough to go blind, while Conseil, impassive as always, would calmly repeat:

"If master would not open his eyes so wide, master would see more."

But oh frustration! The *Abraham Lincoln* would alter its course and make for the creature, which turned out to be an innocent baleen whale or a common sperm whale, that would soon vanish amid a chorus of curses.

But the weather held good. We were conducting our search under the most favorable circumstances. It was supposed to be the bad season in the southernmost regions, because July there corresponds to our January in Europe, but the sea was beautiful and easily visible over a vast perimeter.

Ned Land continued to affect the greatest skepticism.[1] When he was off-duty, he even pretended that he never looked at the water, unless somebody else had sighted a whale. His prodigious vision might have made a great difference. But that stubborn Canadian spent eight hours out of every twelve reading or sleeping in his cabin. A hundred times I chided him for his indifference.

"Bah" was his answer, "nothing's there, professor, and even if there were some animal out there, what chance would we have of sighting it? Aren't we just wandering about at random? People say they've seen this elusive creature again in the Pacific high seas, and I'm willing to believe it, but that was two months ago. Judging by the temperament of your narwhale, he does not enjoy hanging out in the same place. On the contrary, he has a great facility for getting around. Now professor, you know even better than I that Nature doesn't violate good sense. She would not give a naturally slow animal the faculty of rapid movement unless there was some need for it. And so, if your beast exists, it's far away from here by now."

I did not know how to answer that. Obviously we *were* just stabbing in the dark. But how else could we go about it? Granted, that way our chances were

---

1. Ned is a man of action, but he cannot get excited by a seemingly false mission. In this brief exchange, Verne prefigures Land's growing depression later in the novel, the result of his repeated frustration in every area of manly endeavor. Simultaneously, Verne begins to detail Aronnax's weaknesses: he sees Ned as willfully *affecting* indifference, sulking because he is "ill-tempered when frustrated." A Freudian might accuse the professor of *projecting*: ironically, it is he himself who is tenacious in his views.

limited, to say the least. But the crew never doubted we would be successful. Not a sailor on board would have bet against our sighting the narwhale, and soon.

On July 20, we cut the Tropic of Capricorn at longitude 105°, and on July 27 we crossed the equator on the 110th meridian. These bearings taken, the frigate took a decidedly western course and committed itself to central Pacific waters. Commander Farragut felt, and with good reason, that it was better to stay in deep waters, keeping clear of continents and islands, which the beast itself seemed to avoid—because, as the boatswain thought, "Coastal waters are too shallow for him!" The frigate accordingly kept well out when passing the Tuamotu, Marquesas, and Hawaiian Islands, cut the Tropic of Cancer at longitude 132°, and made for the China Seas.

Now we were in the arena where the monster's antics had last been reported and, truly, we no longer lived normal lives. Hearts beat wildly, preparing for incurable aneurisms. The entire ship's company was undergoing a nervous excitement that I can hardly describe. They did not eat, they did not sleep. Twenty times a day a mistake in perception, or the optical illusion of a sailor perched in the crosstrees, would get us all into a deep sweat, and this anguish, repeated over and over, kept us in a state of irritability so violent that a reaction was bound to set in.

And it didn't take long. For three months, during which each day seemed like a century, the *Abraham Lincoln* plowed Pacific waters, chasing whales, veering suddenly off course, swerving from one tack to another, stopping suddenly, putting on steam and reversing its engines in quick succession, at the risk of wrecking her machinery, and leaving no Japanese or American waters unexplored. And with no results. We saw nothing except an immense, deserted sea. Nothing that resembled a gigantic narwhale, or a submerged island, or a floating wreck, or a moving reef, nothing at all supernatural.

And so the reaction did set in. Discouragement took hold and opened the door to disbelief. A new sentiment grew on board, three-tenths shame, seven-tenths fury. For the men felt embarrassed at having been fooled by a myth, and then that infuriated them. The mountains of arguments piled up over a year collapsed suddenly, and each man wanted now only to catch up on his eating and sleeping, to make up for the time he had sacrificed.

With human fickleness, the crew's morale went from one extreme to the other.

The most enthusiastic supporters of the project now became its fiercest enemies. This reaction mounted upward from the bowels of the ship, from the quarters of the coal trimmers to the officers' mess, and indeed, without Commander Farragut's special obstinacy, the frigate would have put back to that cape in the south.

But this useless search could not go on much longer. The *Abraham Lincoln* had done nothing to deserve reproach and everything to succeed. Never had a crew in the American Navy shown more zeal or more patience; this failure was not their fault; there was nothing to do but go home.

Exploring every point

These arguments were presented to the commander. He held fast. His men did not conceal their discontent, and their duties suffered because of it. I will not say there was mutiny, but after a reasonable period of obstinacy, Commander Farragut, like Christopher Columbus before him, asked for just three days more. If in those three days they had not sighted the monster, the man at the helm would give three turns of the wheel, and the *Abraham Lincoln* would make for the Atlantic.

This agreement was reached on November 2. It had the immediate effect of rallying the crew, who watched the ocean with new attention. Each sailor wanted one last look with which to sum up his experience. Spyglasses were worked feverishly. It was a supreme challenge issued to the giant narwhale, and he could not fail to answer this summons.

Two days passed. The *Abraham Lincoln* cruised at half-steam. We tried a thousand schemes to attract the animal or rouse it from its lethargy. We trailed enormous sides of bacon in our wake, to the great satisfaction, I must say, of some sharks. While the *Abraham Lincoln* heaved to, its longboats radiated in every direction, leaving not a point of the sea unexplored. But the evening of November 4 arrived with the mystery still unresolved. Next day, at noon on November 5, the delay would expire, and the commander, faithful to his promise, would have to turn to the southeast and finally abandon the North Pacific.

The frigate found itself in latitude 31° 15′ north and longitude 136° 42′ east. The coast of Japan was still less than 200 miles to our leeward. Night was coming on. Eight o'clock was struck. Huge clouds covered the face of the moon, then in its first quarter. The sea undulated peacefully under the stempost of the frigate.

At that moment I was in the bow, leaning over the starboard rail. Conseil, standing next to me, stared straight ahead. Perched in the ratlines, the crew studied the horizon, which contracted and darkened little by little. Officers were scouring the growing dark with their night glasses. Sometimes the ocean sparkled with the rays of the moon, which darted between the fringes of two clouds. Then all traces of light were gone.

Looking at Conseil, I imagined he was feeling, for a change, a bit of the general excitement. Perhaps for the first time his nerves were vibrating with curiosity.

"Come, Conseil, this is your last chance to pocket that $2,000."

"May I be permitted to say that I never reckoned on getting that prize, and the Union government could have offered $100,000 and been none the poorer."

"I think you're right, Conseil. It was a foolish, rash thing to get involved in. How much time I've lost, how many stupid frenzies we've been through! Six months ago we could have been back in France—"

"In master's little apartment," he added, "in master's museum! I would by now have classified all of master's fossils. And master's babirusa would have been installed in its cage at the zoo in the Botanical Gardens, attracting all the curious Parisians."

"Yes, you're right, Conseil, and I guess we'll be laughed at for our troubles too."

"I think," Conseil said quietly, "they will make fun of master. And, need it be said—?"

"It needs be said, Conseil."

"Well, master will be getting his just deserts."

"How true!"

"When one has the honor of being a great savant, one doesn't expose oneself to—"

Conseil didn't have time to complete the compliment. Amid a general silence, a voice had just rung out. It was Ned Land's voice:

"Ahoy! The thing itself! Abeam to leeward!"

At Random

35

SIX

At Full Steam

T THIS CRY, the whole ship's crew hurried toward the harpooner—commander, officers, mates, seamen, cabin boys, even engineers leaving their engines, stokers their furnaces. Commander Farragut gave the order to stop, and the frigate just coasted.

By now, the darkness was profound, and no matter how good Ned's eyes were, I still wondered how he could see and what he could see. My heart was pounding as if to burst.

But Ned was not mistaken. By now we could all make out the thing he was pointing at. Two cable lengths off the frigate's starboard quarter, the ocean seemed to be illuminated from below. This was no mere phosphorescent phenomenon, I was sure of that. Immersed some fathoms[1] below the surface, the monster was throwing off that intense but inexplicable light that several captains had mentioned in their reports. This magnificent radiance had to be the work of some great illuminating power. Now the edge of its luminescence swept out over the sea in an immense and elongated oval; its center burned with unbearable intensity which diminished by degrees outward.

"That's only a mass of phosphorescent organisms," one of the officers said.

"No sir," I answered emphatically. "Not even angel wing clams, not even salps[2] have ever produced a light that powerful. No, that brightness is essentially *electric* in nature. Besides, look! Look! It's moving back and forth! It's coming toward us!"

A chorus of cries rose from the frigate.

"Quiet!" Commander Farragut shouted. "Helm hard to leeward! Reverse engines!"

Sailors rushed to the helm, engineers back to their machinery. Under reverse steam, the *Abraham Lincoln* beat to port, describing a semicircle.

"Right your helm! Engines forward!" the commander cried. "Engines forward!"

---

1. Officially, a fathom is a distance of six feet. Traditionally, it is the distance between a man's fingertips when his arms are outstretched. A seaman finds this to be the maximum convenient length for gathering up the sounding line used to "fathom the depths."

2. Tiny, larvalike semivertebrates that cluster by the thousands on the ocean's surface.

As these orders were carried out, the frigate moved speedily away from that core of luminescence.

No, excuse me. It *tried* to move away, but that supernatural creature came at us with a speed double our own.

We gasped for breath. Amazement more than fear left us speechless and motionless. The animal overtook us and played with us! It circled the frigate, then making 14 knots, and enveloped us in its electric rings which were like luminous dust. Then it moved away two or three miles, leaving a phosphorescent track comparable to those masses of steam that express trains leave behind. Then suddenly, from the dark horizon where it had regained its momentum, the monster came rushing at the *Abraham Lincoln* with alarming speed, stopping abruptly about 20 feet from our hull and extinguishing its light—not by plunging under the waters, since its glow did not diminish gradually but all at once, as if its source had simply been switched off. Then it appeared again on the other side of the frigate, either by circling it or by going under it. At any moment a collision could have occurred that would have been fatal—to us.

And I was astonished at the maneuvers of the frigate. It was fleeing, not fighting. Assigned to pursue, it was *being* pursued, and I expressed my amazement to the commander. His usually impassive look had changed to one of bewilderment.

"Professor Aronnax," he said, "I don't know what kind of terrible creature I'm up against! I'm unwilling to risk my frigate in this darkness. Furthermore, how do you attack the unknown, or defend yourself from it? Let's wait for daylight, and then the monster and my frigate will switch roles."

"You have no doubts, commander, about the nature of the monster?"

"No, sir—evidently it's a giant narwhale, but an electric narwhale too."

"Maybe," I said, "we can't approach it any more than we could an electric eel or electric ray."

"Doubtless," the commander responded, "and if it has their power to electrocute, it's certainly the most terrifying animal ever conceived by our Creator. That's why, professor, I have to be careful."

No one thought of sleeping, and the ship's company stayed on their feet all night long. Unable to compete with the monster's velocity, the *Abraham Lincoln* slowed down, sailing at half speed. The narwhale seemed to be mimicking the frigate, just riding the waves, standing by in the arena of the conflict.

Toward midnight, though, it just disappeared or, to use a better expression, it "went out," like a huge glowworm. Had it fled us after all? We were obliged to fear so, not hope so. But at 12:53 in the morning, we were almost deafened by a hissing sound, as though a waterspout were being expelled with great violence.

By then, Commander Farragut, Ned Land, and I were all on the afterdeck, peering through the darkness.

"Ned Land," the commander asked, "you've often heard whales roar?"

"Often, sir, but never a whale the very sight of which earned me $2,000."

"Oh, of course, Mr. Land, you've won the prize. But now tell me, isn't that the noise cetaceans make as they spout water out of their blowholes?"

"The same kind of noise, sir, although this is incomparably louder. But there's no mistaking it. That is certainly a cetacean out there. With your permission, sir," the harpooner added, "we will speak a few words with him at daybreak."

"If he's in a mood to listen to you, Mr. Land," I responded skeptically.

"Just let me get within four harpoon lengths of him," the Canadian retorted, "and he'll have to listen to me."

"But for that," the commander went on, "I'd have to put a whaleboat at your disposal."

"Certainly, sir."

"That would be risking the lives of my men."

"And mine too," the harpooner simply added.

Toward 2 a.m. the great core of luminescence reappeared, no less intense, five miles to windward. In spite of the distance, and the noise of sea and wind, we could hear the loud strokes of the beast's tail, even its panting breath. It seemed that the moment when the gigantic narwhale came to the surface to take a breath, air was sucked into its lungs like steam sucked into the vast cylinders of a 2,000-horsepower engine.

"Hmm," I wondered. "A whale with the strength of a cavalry regiment, now that's some whale!"

All night we stayed on the alert, prepared for action. The fishing gear was laid out along the railings. Our first mate loaded the blunderbusses, which can throw harpoons as far as a mile, and the long duck guns, which fire explosive bullets and can inflict fatal wounds on even the most powerful creatures. Ned Land just sharpened his harpoon, a terrifying weapon in his hands.

Day began to break at six o'clock, and then the narwhale's electric light went out. By seven a thick fog obscured our view, and the best spyglasses couldn't pierce it. Everybody was disappointed, even angry.

I climbed to the crosstrees of the mizzen sail; some officers were already perched on the mastheads. By eight o'clock the fog rolled heavily over the waves, and its huge whorls were rising little by little. The horizon grew wider, clearer all at once. Suddenly, just as on the preceding day, we heard Ned Land's voice:

"There's the thing itself, astern to port!" he cried out.

Every eye looked where he was pointing.

There, a mile and a half away, a long black body emerged a meter above the surface. Its tail quivered violently, creating a considerable eddy. Never had a fish's tail beat the sea with such power. An immense white track described the animal's course, a long curve. As we approached the cetacean, I studied it carefully, objectively. The captains of the *Shannon* and the *Helvetia* had exaggerated its dimensions. I estimated its length as only 250 feet. As for its girth, that was difficult to judge, but all in all, the animal appeared to be well proportioned in all three dimensions.

While I was watching this phenomenal creature, two jets of water and vapor were ejected from its blowholes and rose to a height of 40 meters, and so I ascertained its method of breathing. Hence I was able to conclude definitely that it belonged to the branch Vertebrata, class Mammalia, subclass Monodelphia, group Pisciforma, order Cetacea, family . . . but here I was stumped. The order of cetaceans comprises three families: baleen whales, sperm whales, dolphins, and it's in this last group that narwhales are classified. Each family is divided into several genera, each genus into species, each species into varieties. So I had not yet established variety, species, genus, and family. But I did not doubt that with the aid of Providence and Commander Farragut, I would be able to complete my classification.

Impatiently the crew awaited orders from their chief. After watching the animal intently, the commander called the engineer, who came running.

"Sir," the commander asked, "you've got pressure up?"

"Yes sir!"

"Fine. Stoke your furnaces and put on full steam."

Three cheers greeted this command. The moment for battle had arrived. Just moments later, the frigate's two funnels vomited forth torrents of black smoke, and its deck quaked from the trembling of its boilers.

Driven by her powerful propeller, the *Abraham Lincoln* made straight for the monster. Seemingly indifferent, the beast let us come to within half a cable length. Then, disdaining to dive, it retreated with a burst of speed, and seemed content to maintain its distance.

For three-quarters of an hour we chased the monster without gaining two fathoms on it. It was clear that at this rate we should never catch up with it.

In a rage, the commander twisted the thick growth of hair that bristled under his chin.

"Ned Land!" he called out, and the Canadian reported at once.

"Mr. Land, do you still think I should put out my longboats?"

"No, sir," Ned answered. "That beast won't be taken against its will."

"In your opinion, what should we do then?"

"Build up more steam, sir, if you can, and, with your permission, I'll post myself on the bobstays under the bowsprit. If we get within harpoon range, I'll harpoon him."

"Permission granted, Ned," Commander Farragut said. "Engineer! Keep the pressure climbing!"

Ned Land went to his post. The furnaces were forced to greater heat, the propeller was doing forty-three revolutions per minute, and steam shot from the valves. We heaved the log and calculated that the *Abraham Lincoln* was making 18.5 miles per hour.[3]

3. The "log" is really a wedge-shaped *chip of wood* that is weighted with lead and attached to a line reeled out from a ship's stern. When a seaman "heaves the log," the chip settles vertically in one spot on the surface of the sea while the vessel moves away from it, unreeling the line. This line is *knotted* at intervals of 47.25 feet. The number of knots payed out in 28 seconds

But that accursed animal was also swimming at the rate of 18.5 miles. We kept up this pace for an hour without gaining a fathom! This was humiliating for one of the fastest men-of-war in the United States Navy. The crew was working up an anger. They cursed the beast, who disdained to answer. The commander no longer simply twisted his goatee—he was chewing on it. He called the engineer once more.

"You've reached your top pressure?"

"Yes, sir."

"And what is it?"

"Six and a half atmospheres."

"Get it up to ten atmospheres."

A typical Yankee command, if I ever heard one, the way it's done during those paddlewheeler races on the Mississippi, "to leave the competition behind."[4]

"Conseil," I said to my gallant servant now beside me, "are you aware that we will probably blow ourselves up?"

"Whatever pleases master," he said. And I admit, I *was* pleased to be taking this chance.

The valves were charged. More coal was flung into the furnaces, which were ventilated with torrents of air. The *Abraham Lincoln* built up speed. Its masts trembled down to their blocks, and clouds of smoke could hardly crowd out of the narrow funnels.

We heaved the log again.

"Well, helmsman?" the commander asked.

"19.3 miles, sir."

"Clap on more steam."

The engineer complied. The pressure gauge reached ten atmospheres. But the cetacean was getting up steam, too, no doubt, for without a bit of strain, it also made 19.3!

What a chase! No, I cannot describe those emotions that shook my very being. Ned Land was ready at his post, brandishing his harpoon. Once or twice the animal allowed us to get closer.

---

shows the ship's speed, which is reported, logically enough, in "knots." Timing is done with a sandglass and is based on this equation:

$$\frac{47.25 \text{ feet}}{6,080 \text{ feet}} = \frac{28 \text{ seconds}}{3,600 \text{ seconds}}$$

In other words, a knot is the same part of a "nautical mile" (6,080 feet) as 28 seconds is of an hour (3,600 seconds).

4. Riverboat captains were notorious for recklessly racing each other. They would doctor the safety valves on their boilers to double the steam pressure and, running out of coal in mid-race, even resorted to stoking their furnaces with items of furniture on board. Boiler explosions were common, and for Verne they symbolized the excesses of technology, especially American technology. In his first novel, *Five Weeks in a Balloon,* one character predicts that "the end of the earth will come when some enormous boiler, charged to three billion atmospheres of pressure, explodes and blows up the world!"

To which another character adds: "And I bet the Yankees will have a hand in it."

"We're catching up with it!" the Canadian cried. "We're getting closer!" But just as he was poised to strike, the cetacean stole away very easily with a speed that I estimated at no less than 30 miles per hour. And even during our bursts of top speed, the monster ridiculed the frigate by making a full circle around us! Cries of fury broke from the crew.

By noon, we were no further ahead than we had been at eight a.m. The commander decided on more direct measures.

"Bah!" he expostulated. "So that beast is faster than my frigate! All right, we'll see if it can outrun our conical shells! Mate, man the gun in the bow!"

They loaded our forecastle cannon and took aim. The cannoneer fired but his shell passed over the cetacean, then half a mile away.

"Somebody with better aim!" the commander cried. "Five hundred dollars to whoever can pierce that animal's hide."

An old gunner with a grey beard—I can see him yet—a man with steady eye and cool expression, stepped up to the gun, made some adjustments, and aimed for a long time. A mighty boom was followed by cheers from the crew.

For the shell did reach its target, but it glanced off the animal's rounded back and splashed into the sea two miles away.

"Oh blast it!" the old cannoneer shouted in a rage. "That beast must be armored with six-inch plates."

"Curse it!" the commander cried.

He resumed the chase and leaning toward me he vowed:

"I shall pursue that beast until my frigate explodes."

"Yes," I said, "and you're right to risk it."

We could still hope that the monster would get tired and not be as insensitive to fatigue as a steam engine. But no such luck. Hour after hour slipped by without its showing any sign of exhaustion.

It must be noted, however, that the *Abraham Lincoln* itself was struggling with indefatigable tenacity. I figure that it covered a distance of not less than 500 kilometers on that ill-fated day of November 6. But night fell and enclosed the surging ocean in its shadows.

Now I felt that our expedition had ended, that we would never see that fantastic creature again. I was deceiving myself. At 10:50 that evening, the electric brilliance reappeared three miles to windward, just as pure and as intense as the night before.

The narwhale seemed motionless, though. Was it sleeping, tired from its workday, just riding with the waves? Whatever, here was a chance that Commander Farragut could not miss.

He gave his orders. The *Abraham Lincoln* kept at half steam, advancing cautiously so as not to awaken its adversary. It is not unusual in mid ocean to find whales so sound asleep they are easily taken. Ned Land had harpooned more than one that way. Now he went to take his post on the bobstays under the bowsprit.

The frigate approached quietly, stopping two cable lengths from the animal and then coasting. No one dared breathe. A deep silence reigned on deck.

We were not 100 feet from the burning core of light, whose brilliance dazzled us. Leaning on the forecastle railing, I could see Ned Land below me, one hand grasping the martingale, the other brandishing his harpoon.

When he was hardly 20 feet from that motionless animal, his arm suddenly straightened, and the harpoon shot out. I heard the weapon strike sonorously, as if it had hit something with a hard outer surface.

The electric light was instantly extinguished and two enormous waterspouts cascaded over the deck of the frigate, flooding us from stem to stern, knocking men down, breaking spare masts and yardarms from their lashings.

There was a hideous collision, and without having a chance to catch hold of something, I was flung over the rail and hurled into the sea.

SEVEN

An Unknown Species of Whale

EVEN THOUGH I was shocked by this unexpected descent, I still have very definite impressions of my experience. First I was dragged about 20 feet under. I am a good swimmer and, while I'm not as good as authors like Byron or Edgar Allan Poe, who were master divers,[1] I didn't lose my head on the way down. With two vigorous kicks of the heel I regained the surface.

My first thought was of the frigate. Had the crew seen me go overboard? Would the *Abraham Lincoln* turn around? Was Commander Farragut putting a longboat into the water? Could I hope to be rescued?

The darkness was profound, but I could glimpse a black mass disappearing into the east, its running lights fading away. It was the frigate. And I felt lost.

"Help! Help!" I shouted, desperately swimming after the *Abraham Lincoln.* My clothes hampered me. The water seemed to glue them to my skin, paralyzing me. I was going down, I was suffocating.

"Help!"

That was my final cry. My mouth filling with water, I struggled against being pulled into the depths. Suddenly my clothes were clutched by firm hands, and I felt myself being pulled up to the surface. And yes, I heard these words uttered close to my ear:

"If master would oblige me by leaning on my shoulder, master would be able to swim so much more easily."

With one hand I reached out for the arm of my loyal Conseil.

"You!" I said. "You!"

"Myself," Conseil answered, "awaiting master's instructions."

"So that collision threw you overboard along with me?"

"Not exactly, but being master's servant, I followed him."

---

1. Byron was indeed a heroic swimmer, crossing the Hellespont (the Dardanelles) in 1810, like Leander going to his nightly tryst with Hero. Why Verne thought of Poe as a master diver is less clear: perhaps he was daydreaming of the American poet's great sea stories "A Descent into the Maelstrom" and *The Narrative of Arthur Gordon Pym,* both of which surely influenced Verne in his handling of the present novel's conclusion.

The worthy lad thought that only natural.

"And the frigate?" I gasped.

"The frigate?" Conseil rolled over onto his back. "I think master had better not rely on the frigate."

"Why?"

"When I jumped overboard, I heard someone at the helm saying that the propeller and rudder were broken."

"Broken?"

"Yes, by the monster's tusk. That's all the damage the *Abraham Lincoln* suffered. But for us that's everything—she can't answer her helm."

"Then we are finished."

"Maybe," Conseil said calmly. "But we can last for several hours yet, and a lot can happen in that time."

His coolness gave me new strength. I tried to swim more vigorously, but my clothes weighed me down like a cloak of lead, and I had trouble keeping my head above water. But Conseil was on top of the situation.

"Master should allow me to make an incision for him," he said. And slipping an open knife under my clothes, he slit them from top to bottom. He pulled them off me while I swam for us both. Then I disencumbered him of his clothes, and we swam more easily, side by side.

However, our situation hadn't improved very much. Even if they now missed us aboard ship, the frigate could not return to leeward for us, being helpless without a rudder. We could only count on the longboats.

Conseil calmly figured that out and then laid his plans accordingly. He had an astonishing temperament, behaving in the sea as if he were at home. Since our only chance now lay in our being picked up by the *Abraham Lincoln*'s longboats, we had to do everything possible to stay alive until they could find us. We had to divide the work so that we wouldn't both be exhausted at the same time. This was our plan: One of us would lie on his back, with arms crossed, legs outstretched, while the other would swim and tow or push his partner. Relieving each other every ten minutes or so, we could stay afloat for hours, perhaps even until daylight.

A slight chance! But hope is so firmly rooted in the human heart! And there were two of us. And I must admit, if I tried deliberately to destroy all my illusions, tried to will despair, I certainly could not do it.

The cetacean had rammed our frigate about eleven o'clock in the evening. I therefore figured we should have to swim, at most, eight hours until sunrise. A strenuous task, but feasible, thanks to our relaying. The sea was lovely and hardly tired us. Once in a while I would try to see through the thick gloom that was broken only by the phosphorescence our movements created. I watched the luminous ripples splashing over my hand, their glistening surface spotted with silvery rings. It seemed as if we were swimming in a bath of quicksilver.

Toward one a.m., I fell prey to intense fatigue. My limbs stiffened in the grip of strong cramps. Conseil had to keep me afloat. Our survival now devolved on him alone. I heard the poor boy gasping, his breathing became shallow and quick. I did not think he could last much longer.

"Leave me, leave me!" I ordered him.

"Abandon master? Never," he replied. "I would rather drown first."

At that moment, the moon emerged from the edge of a large cloud that the wind was driving east. The sea glittered under its rays. This kindly light reinvigorated us. Able to hold up my head again, I scoured the horizon. I located the frigate! She was about five miles off, a dark mass, barely perceptible. But no longboats—not a one in sight.

I tried to shout. True, that seemed pointless at such a distance. And my swollen lips could produce no sounds. But Conseil could still speak a bit, and I heard him shouting at intervals:

"Help! Help!"

We stopped swimming for a few seconds to listen. It could have been a ringing in my ear—that organ was crowded with impeded blood—but I thought I heard an answer.

"Did you hear something?" I murmured.

"Yes, yes!" And Conseil shouted another desperate appeal.

This time there could be no mistake. A human voice had responded! Was it the voice of some poor wretch abandoned at sea, some other victim of the collision we had suffered? Or maybe it was a sailor in one of the longboats, hailing us from the dark?

We both made a supreme effort, Conseil hefting himself up on my shoulder as I tried my utmost to stay afloat, and he rose half out of the water, then slipped back exhausted.

"Did you see anything?"

"I saw," he murmured, "I saw—but we must not talk—save our strength."

What had he seen? I don't know why, but the thought of the monster occurred to me for the first time. But that voice? Gone are the days when Jonahs took refuge in the bellies of whales!

But Conseil was pushing me again. At times, he raised his head, looked ahead of us, and shouted a question, and it was answered by a voice that sounded nearer each time. But now I could hardly hear. My strength vanished, my fingers stiffened, my hand no longer functioned, my mouth opened convulsively, and I swallowed brine, its coldness numbing me. I raised my head once more and collapsed.

At that moment, something hard knocked against me. I clung to it. I felt that someone was lifting me, pulling me back up to the surface, that my chest caved in, that I was fainting.

I revived soon, because someone was rubbing me so vigorously I felt furrows in my flesh. I half opened my eyes.

"Conseil?" I murmured.

"Has master rung for me?"

In the last brightness of a moon settling on the horizon, I saw a face, not Conseil's but one I recognized instantly.

A floating islet

"Ned!" I gasped.

"In person, professor, and still after his prize!"

"You were thrown into the sea by the collision?"

"Yes, professor, but I was luckier than you. I was able to set foot on this floating islet."[2]

"Islet?"

"Well, to be more specific, on our giant narwhale."

"Explain yourself, please, Ned."

"I soon realized why my harpoon hadn't pierced its hide, why it was blunted."

"Why, Ned?"

"Because this beast, professor, is made of boiler-plate steel!"

At this point in my story I must pull myself together, remember precisely how I felt, and make doubly sure of everything I write.

The Canadian's last words stirred up a revolution in my brain. I quickly lifted myself up to the summit of this half-submerged being or object that had become our refuge. I kicked it. Obviously it was a hard, impenetrable substance, not the soft matter that covers the bodies of our great marine mammals. Still, this hard substance could be a bony carapace, like those that covered some prehistoric animals. And I might almost have let it go at that, classifying this monster among the amphibious reptiles, like turtles or alligators.

But no! That blackish back on which I was sitting was glossy and smooth, with nothing like overlapping scales. When I kicked it, it gave off a metallic sonority. Incredible as this sounds, it seemed to be made of bolted plates.

There could be no question now. This animal, this monster, this natural phenomenon that had intrigued the world of science, overthrown and confused the imaginations of seamen in both hemispheres, was, I had to admit it now, an even more amazing phenomenon, a phenomenon made by man!

To come upon the most fabled, most mythical being could not have shocked me so much. It is quite simple to believe that prodigious things come from the Creator. But suddenly to find that the impossible had been shaped by human beings: that staggers the mind.

An Unknown

Species of

Whale

47

2. From Aronnax and Land we have now heard enough about a *moving reef* and a *floating islet* to discuss the relation of this notion to Verne's own psychohistory.

As a child Verne lived on the Île Feydeau, an island in the Loire River off Nantes. In March the swollen Loire smashed against the island's quays, sometimes flooding the streets. *Jules was afraid that the island would be torn from its underpinnings and float out to sea.* Hence, much of the speculation in this novel has been a reenactment of Jules's boyhood fantasy: recall the ongoing confusion over whether this *moving mass* is a ship, a gigantic animal, or a runaway rock.

Verne's nightmare is most thoroughly explored in his novel *The Fur Country* (1873). The Hudson Bay Fur Company has established an outpost at the very edge of the Arctic Ocean. Unknown to its builders, this post rests upon an ancient shelf of ice now covered over with vegetation and soil deposits. Abruptly, an earthquake separates this shelf of ice from the mainland, and the fort becomes a *floating islet.*

But there was no room for doubt. We were stretched out on the back of some sort of submarine boat, which was shaped, so far as I could judge, like an immense steel fish.[3] Ned was absolutely certain of this, and Conseil and I could only line up behind him.

"Then," I asked, "does this apparatus include some motive power inside it, and a crew to operate it?"

"Apparently," the harpooner answered. "But in the three hours I've inhabited this floating islet, it has shown no signs of life."

"You mean this boat hasn't moved?"

"No, professor, it just rides the waves, but it doesn't move of its own accord."

"But we know, beyond any doubt, that it is capable of great speed. Now it needs machinery to develop that speed, and an engineer to direct the machinery, so I conclude that we are saved."

"Humph," Ned replied in his most skeptical tone.

At that moment, as if to prove my point, a bubbling began at one end of this strange thing, which was apparently driven by a propeller, and we started to move. We barely had time to hang on to its topside, which rose about 80 centimeters out of the water, and fortunately it was moving slowly.

"So long as it navigates horizontally," Ned muttered, "I won't mind it too much. But if it takes a mind to dive, I wouldn't give $2.00 for my hide."

The Canadian might have quoted a much lower price. It became necessary now to communicate with the beings, whatever they were, inside this machine. I searched all over the outside for an opening, a panel, a hatch, a manhole. But the iron plates were joined tight and solid with rows and rows of iron rivets.

Then the moon disappeared and left us in deep darkness. We were obliged to wait for daylight before we could find some means of getting inside this submarine craft.

Thus our fate depended entirely on the whims of the mysterious helmsmen who maneuvered this boat, for if they submerged, we were doomed. But unless that happened, I didn't doubt the possibility of making contact with them. As a matter of fact, if they did not manufacture their own air, they would be forced to spend time on the surface in order to replenish their supply

---

3. In Verne's day this was an exciting prospect: some twenty-five known experiments with submersible boats had attained only the most modest results—none had proved capable of a long-distance voyage in the open sea. In 1620 the Dutchman Cornelius van Drebbel successfully maneuvered a submarine device in the river Thames. In 1720 the Englishman John Day built a similar contraption in which he stayed thirty feet under for twelve hours, then perished when he attempted to repeat the feat. In 1776 the American David Bushnell launched his *Turtle* into New York harbor, a one-man vessel that became the first functional submarine and introduced guerrilla warfare to naval operations. In 1800 the American Robert Fulton built a larger variant, the two-man *Nautilus*. Finally, during the American Civil War, the Confederate Army built three operating submersibles and carried out the first successful attack on a surface vessel. But, again, at the time of our story no submarine craft existed that could be trusted out of sight of shore.

of oxygen. So there had to be some opening, some duct or channel between the inside and the outside.[4]

As for hoping to be saved by Commander Farragut, we had to forget all about that. We had been swept to the west, and I estimated our moderate speed to be about 12 miles per hour. The propeller was beating the water with mathematical regularity, sometimes protruding above the surface and throwing phosphorescent spray to great heights.

At about 4 a.m., the craft increased its speed. We found it more difficult to hang on, and the waves battered us at close range. Fortunately, Ned by chance felt a large mooring ring fastened to the upper part of that iron back, and we all held on for dear life.

At last, that long night faded away. My memories of it are vague in some respects. I can recall just one important detail. When sea and wind were calm, I fancied I heard some indistinct music, a kind of fugitive harmony, distant chords. What was the mystery behind this submarine navigation, for which the whole world was seeking an explanation? What kind of beings inhabited this strange boat? What mechanical agent enabled it to move with such prodigious speed?

Day came at last. Morning mists encompassed us, but they vanished soon. I was about to resume my examination of the hull, which formed on top a kind of raised platform, when I realized we were sinking bit by bit.

"Oh damnation!" Ned Land screamed, kicking the sonorous iron. "Open up there, you antisocial navigators!"

But it was difficult to make oneself heard above the beating of the propeller. Fortunately, the submerging maneuver stopped. From within the boat, there came noises of iron fastenings pushed violently aside. One of those iron plates was raised, a man appeared, uttered a strange cry, and at once disappeared.

Moments later, eight strapping fellows, with faces masked, came out quietly and dragged us down into their formidable machine.

---

4. Aronnax seems to be grappling with the uneasy thought that the submarine can seal itself into a self-sufficient container for indefinite periods. If so, this constitutes one of Verne's thousands of successful predictions, because modern nuclear subs can indeed stay under indefinitely.

EIGHT

Mobilis in Mobile

THIS BRUTAL ABDUCTION was accomplished with the speed of lightning. My companions and I had no time to collect ourselves. I did not know how they felt as we were being dragged down into that floating prison, but as for me, I was shivering all over. With whom were we dealing? No doubt with some new species of pirates, exploiting the seas after their own fashion.

As soon as the narrow hatch was closed again over me, I was enveloped in profound darkness. My eyes, still drenched with the outside light, could make out nothing. I could tell that my naked feet were touching the rungs of an iron ladder. Firmly gripped by those men, Ned Land and Conseil were following me. At the foot of the ladder, a door opened and then closed behind us with a loud clang.

We seemed to be alone. Where? I could not say, couldn't even imagine. Everything was black, such a thick blackness that after several minutes I still couldn't pick up even the faint glimmers you can always find on the darkest nights.

Meanwhile, furious at these goings on, Ned was giving free rein to his indignation.

"Damnation!" he cried. "These people could teach the savages of New Caledonia[1] a thing or two about hospitality. And I wouldn't be a bit surprised if they *do* turn out to be cannibals! But I'm warning them, they won't eat me without having to fight me first!"

"Calm yourself, friend Ned, please be calm," Conseil answered serenely. "Don't cry before you're hurt. We're not in the roaster yet."

"In a roaster, no, but in an oven, yes. It's dark enough for one. Fortunately, I still have my Bowie knife and I can use that even in the dark.[2] The first of these bandits who dares lay a hand on me. . . ."

---

1. Verne says simply "Caledonians," which earlier English translators render as "the Scotch." It's true that Caledonia is a poetic synonym for Scotland, but the context of Ned's gibes about cannibals suggests that *New* Caledonia is indicated. The Melanesian natives of this French territorial island did indeed practice cannibalism: in 1850 French surveyors were slain and eaten by the islanders, a calamity surely well known to Verne and his readers.

2. A Bowie knife is a wide-bladed dagger that Americans are forever carrying around. *Jules Verne*

Two strangers

"Ned, take it easy," I told the harpooner. "Don't compromise us with pointless violence. How can you be sure they're not listening to us? It's better to try to find out where we are."

Groping my way, I took five steps and reached an iron wall; I could feel the plates bolted together. Turning around, I knocked against a wooden table and found stools set by it. The floor of our prison was covered with a thick hemp-like matting that muffled the sound of our footsteps. I could find no evidence of a door or window in the naked walls. Conseil, having gone around the opposite way, bumped into me and together we stepped to the middle of the cabin which, I now calculated, was about twenty feet by ten. As for its height, not even Ned, with his great stature, could reach the ceiling.

Half an hour passed with no change in our situation, when suddenly we went from extreme darkness to harsh light. Our prison just brightened abruptly, filled with a luminosity so strong that I could not bear it at first. In its whiteness and intensity I recognized the electric light that had played around the submarine boat with such magnificent phosphorescence. After shutting my eyes involuntarily, I opened them and saw that this illumination came from a frosted half globe curving out of the ceiling.

"Finally we can see!" cried Ned, knife in hand, poised for action.

"Yes," I risked a witty antithesis, "but we are still in the dark about our situation."

"Master must be patient," said my imperturbable Conseil.

The sudden lighting enabled me to examine the cabin more thoroughly. It was furnished with only a table and five stools. I could not locate the door, which was probably sealed hermetically. We could hear nothing. Everything seemed dead in the interior of this craft. Was it moving, floating on the surface of the sea, or diving? I couldn't tell. However, that luminous globe had not been turned on without good reason. I hoped that some crewmen would soon appear. For if you want to consign people to oblivion, you do not light up their dungeon.

And I was not wrong. We heard an unlocking noise, the door opened, and two men entered.

The first was short, strongly muscled, broad shouldered, with robust limbs, sturdy head, an abundance of black hair and a thick mustache, and a gaze sharp and penetrating. His whole personality was stamped with that southern vivacity we usually associate with the people of Provence. Diderot has maintained, with some justification, that a man's behavior is metaphoric, and this short man was certainly the living proof.[3] One could sense that his everyday speech sparkled with prosopopeia, metonymy, and hyphallage.[4] But I

---

3. Denis Diderot (1713–1784) was a renowned French poet, playwright, philosopher, and critic.

4. Aronnax shows an occasional interest in classical rhetoric, the source of these three terms. *Prosopopeia* is the figure of speech in which something nonhuman is given human attributes; e.g., this bit of personification by Verne's great contemporary Victor Hugo: "The insolent sea

could never verify this, because in my presence at least he always spoke a language I could not understand or even identify.

The second stranger merits a more detailed description. A disciple of Gratiolet or Engel would have been able to read his features like an open book.[5] With no hesitation, I could tell his dominant characteristics: self-confidence, because his head was set like a nobleman's well above the line of his shoulders, and his black eyes looked around with cool assurance; calmness, because his skin, rather pale than ruddy, showed coolness of blood; energy, because of the rapid contractions of his brows; and finally, courage, because his deep breathing indicated an expansive nature of great vitality.

I would add that this was a proud man, that his firm, calm gaze reflected thinking of a lofty nature, and that the harmony of his facial expression and bodily movements indicated—if the physiognomists are right—a man of great candor.

I felt "involuntarily" reassured by his presence. I thought it boded well for our interview.

But whether this person was 35 or 50 years of age, I could not tell. He was tall, with a broad forehead, straight nose, mouth clearly defined, beautiful teeth, fine tapered hands, that were eminently "psychic," to use a word from chirognomy[6] meaning that they were worthy of serving a lofty, passionate soul. This was certainly the most admirable specimen of manhood I had ever seen. One outstanding feature was his eyes, set rather far apart, which—I verified this later—could take in nearly a quarter of the horizon at once. This faculty gave him a range of vision far greater than even Ned Land's. When this stranger fixed his gaze on an object, his eyebrows met, his heavy eyelids closed around his pupils so as to contract the field of his vision, and he *looked!* And what a look—as if he could magnify objects far away, as if he saw through to your soul, as if he could penetrate strata of water opaque to our eyes, could read the very depths of the sea.

These two strangers wore caps made of sea-otter fur and boots of sealskin, and garments made of some special material that fitted loosely and allowed the limbs great freedom of movement.

The taller of the two, apparently the chief on board, examined us with great care without uttering a word. Then he turned to his companion and talked to him in a tongue I could not recognize. It was a sonorous, harmonious, flexible language with vowels that underwent a varied accentuation.

---

was in a good humor." *Metonymy* uses a concrete object to symbolize something; thus, *the crown* can stand for the reigning monarch, or *the bottle* for alcohol. *Hyphallage* is the interchange in syntax between two terms; thus, Spenser mentions "Sansfroy's dead dowry," meaning "dead Sansfroy's dowry."

5. Louis-Pierre Gratiolet (1815–1865), French physician, and Josef Engel (1816–1874), Austrian anatomist, were physiognomists or "experts" in judging character from facial features.

6. Reading a person's character in his hands. Like physiognomy, this typology is in discredit today, but Verne used these two *vogues* to good artistic ends in this chapter: having Aronnax try out these fashionable theories makes the character descriptions more dynamic. Verne continually experiments with such contrapuntal techniques for advancing the action.

The other replied with a shake of the head and two or three words I could not understand. Then he seemed to question me with a long stare.

I replied in simple French that I was not conversant in his language, but he seemed not to understand, and the situation grew embarrassing.

"Still, if master were to tell our story," Conseil said, "maybe these gentlemen could make out the key words."

I started over, recounting our adventures, sounding every syllable very clearly, omitting not a single detail. I announced our names and titles. I formally presented Professor Aronnax, his servant Conseil, and Mr. Ned Land, harpooner. The tall man with the soft, calm eyes listened to me patiently, even politely, and paid unusual attention, but nothing in his face showed that he understood my story. When I concluded he said nothing at all.

Another possibility was to speak English. Perhaps they would know that nearly universal language. I knew it, as I knew German, well enough to read fluently but not well enough to speak correctly. But we just *had* to make ourselves understood.

"Come," I told the harpooner, "it's your turn. Speak your best Anglo-Saxon and try to do better than I have."

Ned needed no persuading, and recommenced our story, most of which I could follow. His basic message was the same, but his manner was different. True to his nature, he spoke with great animation. He complained vigorously about being imprisoned in violation of his civil rights, demanded to know the legal basis for his detention, mentioned a writ of *habeas corpus,* threatened to take to court anyone holding him without due cause, ranted, gesticulated, shouted, and at last, by a very expressive sign, showed that we were dying of hunger.

That was absolutely true, but we had nearly forgotten it.

To his consternation, the harpooner seemed no more successful than I had been. Our visitors did not bat an eye. Apparently they understood neither the language of Arago nor that of Faraday.7

Really embarrassed now, thinking we had exhausted our philological resources, I no longer knew what tactic to pursue when Conseil said:

"If master will permit, I'll tell our story in German."

"What! You speak German?" I exclaimed.

"Like most Flemings, with all due respect to master."

"On the contrary, we are respectful of you, go ahead, my boy."

And Conseil, in his calm voice, rendered our third account of our adventures. But in spite of the narrator's elegant turns of phrase and excellent accent, German failed too.

7. Aronnax is again indulging in uneasy speculation. To preside over such a technological marvel as this underwater boat, the captain had to be familiar with the principles of physics. At that time, the two chief authorities on the subject were French (Arago) and English (Faraday); and if the ship's commander understood neither of these tongues, then Aronnax is worrying that the captain's technology comes from some body of knowledge unknown to international science.

Nonplussed, straining to recall my earliest lessons in Latin, I started to tell our story in that tongue. Cicero would have shut his ears and sent me back to the kitchen, but I did get through our tale. And with the same results, our fourth failure. The two strangers exchanged a few words in their incomprehensible language and withdrew, without so much as a reassuring nod in our direction, as might have been expected in any country on earth. The door was bolted again.

"This is infamous!" Ned Land exploded for the twentieth time. "We speak to those rogues in French, English, German, and Latin, and neither of them has the decency to answer!"

"Calm yourself," I told the impetuous Ned. "Anger will get us no place."

"But professor," continued our irate companion, "do you realize we could starve to death in this iron cage?"

"Bah," Conseil said philosophically. "We can hold out for some time yet."

"Friends, we mustn't despair," I said. "We have been in worse situations than this. So do me the favor of waiting a bit before you form an opinion of the commander and his crew."

"My opinion is formed already," Ned Land retorted. "They are villains."

"Yes? And from what country, Ned?"

"From the Land of Villainy!"

"My gallant Ned, that country is not clearly marked on the maps of the world, and I admit that it's hard to figure out the nationality of these two strangers. Neither English, German, nor French, that's all we can say right now. But I'm inclined to think the commander and his first mate were born in the low latitudes. There must be southern blood in their veins. But I cannot decide from their looks whether they are Spaniards, Turks, Arabs, or Indians. As for their language, it's beyond my comprehension."

"Now we see the disadvantage of not knowing many languages," Conseil added, "or is it the disadvantage of not having one universal language?"[8]

"What good would that do?" said Ned. "Don't you see, these people have invented their own private language with which to torment gallant folk who are asking for a little dinner! Why, in every country, what does it mean when you move your jaws up and down, click your teeth, smack your lips? Whether you are in Quebec or the Tuamotu Islands, in Paris or the Antipodes, doesn't it mean: 'I'm hungry, please feed me?'"

"Oh," Conseil said, "some people are just unintelligent by nature—"

And as he said that, the door opened. A steward came in.[9] He brought us some clothes, jackets and sailor's trousers, made of a fabric I didn't recognize. I hastened to change into them, and my companions did likewise. Meanwhile,

8. Verne was a great believer in the need for an artificial international language. In the 1890s, shortly after Esperanto was invented, Verne served as chairman of the Esperantist group of his region.

9. A steward is a waiter on board a steamer. *Jules Verne*

our silent steward—dumb, perhaps deaf as well—had set the table with three place settings.

"Something's brewing," Conseil murmured, "and it bodes well."

"Bah," said the rancorous harpooner, "what do you suppose they eat? Turtle livers, loin of shark, dogfish steaks?"

"Let's find out," said Conseil.

The steward placed platters with silver dish-covers on the table and we took our places. Doubtless we were dealing with civilized people, and except for that flood of electric light, I could imagine I was in the dining room of the Hotel Adelphi in Liverpool, or the Grand Hotel in Paris. But there was no bread nor wine. The water was fresh and clear, but it was still water and so did not suit Ned's taste. Among the dishes we were served I recognized several fish beautifully prepared, but I could not identify certain otherwise excellent platters, not even the kingdom, animal or vegetable, to which they belonged. The dinner service was elegant and in perfect taste. Each utensil, spoon, fork, knife, plate, bore a letter encircled by a motto, of which this is an exact facsimile:

"Mobile within the mobile element!" That Latin motto was certainly appropriate for this submarine craft, so long as the preposition "in" was translated as "within" and not "upon." The letter *N* was no doubt the initial of that enigmatic person in command at the bottom of the ocean.[10]

Ned and Conseil were not meditating on such matters. They were devouring the food, and now so was I. I felt reassured about our fate, since it seemed clear that our hosts would not let us starve. But all earthly things must end, even the hunger of people who have not eaten for fifteen hours. Our appetites appeased, we were overcome with drowsiness. A natural reaction to having spent an interminable night contending with death.

"Ye gods, but I'll sleep soundly," drowsed Conseil.

10. This hybrid Latin phrase caused some concern to the original French compositors. The Hachette edition gives it as *Mobilis in Mobili* in the table of contents, the chapter part title, the page heads, and the chapter body, then in a later reference (II 6) corrects it to *Mobilis in Mobile.* The 1871 Hetzel edition corrects everything to the latter except the I 8 body appearance (a logo), and a later Hetzel edition corrects that appearance as well. It would seem that *mobile* is right, but in III 16 of this novel's sequel, *The Mysterious Island* (1875), Hetzel reverts to the former spelling.

So which is it? We reason it out this way: (1) In Verne's usage, *mobile* would function as a singular noun whereas *mobili* would be its plural; (2) Verne himself translates the term as *l'element mobile;* (3) Since his French gives the singular (*l'element*) rather than the plural (*les elements*), we accordingly give the Latin singular throughout.

As for the motto's significance, helpful English variations might include *flexible within flux, changing with change,* or, as Allen Klots, Jr., has suggested, *free in a free world.*

"And me—I'm sleeping already," said Ned.

My companions stretched out on the carpet, deep in slumber. But for me, too many thoughts crowded my head, too many insoluble questions pressed on me, too many fancies kept my eyes half open. Where were we? What strange power was propelling us? I felt—or I believe I felt—the machine sinking toward the lowest depths of the sea. Dreadful fantasies besieged me. I saw in this mysterious refuge a world of unknown creatures, to which this submarine boat seemed related, living, moving, formidable like them. Then I grew calmer, my imagination dissolved into vague unconsciousness, and I fell into a miserable slumber.

Mobilis in

Mobile

☙

NINE

The Wrath of Ned Land

I HAD NO WAY of knowing exactly how long we had slept, but I felt completely rested, so I figured we had slumbered for many, many hours. I awoke first. My companions were still stretched out, like inert masses, in their corners.

I had scarcely risen from my somewhat hard bed when I felt my brain clear, my mind grow alert. So I began an intensive reexamination of our cell. Nothing had changed inside. The prison was still a prison, the prisoners still prisoners. But, taking advantage of our slumber, the steward had cleared the table. So there was nothing to indicate that our situation would change, and I worried now whether we were destined to live forever in this cage.

This prospect was all the more painful to me because, even though my mind was clear of the obsessions of the night before, I now felt a strange weight on my chest. I was breathing with difficulty. The air was heavy and insufficient for my lungs. Although our cell was large, it was clear we had consumed a great portion of the oxygen it had contained. Basically, each person consumes, every hour, the oxygen contained in 100 liters of air, and then this air, charged with a nearly equal amount of carbon dioxide, becomes unbreathable.

It was now urgent to renew the air in our cell, and probably in the entire submarine boat. This raised a question in my mind. How did the commander of this seagoing dwelling accomplish this? By chemical means, perhaps, releasing the oxygen contained in potassium chlorate by heating it, and absorbing the carbon dioxide with potassium hydroxide? This would force him to make regular visits to shore to get the chemicals required. Or did he simply store air in high-pressure tanks and dispense it according to the needs of his crew? Maybe. Or, using a more convenient, more economical, and therefore more likely method, did he just rise to the surface and take breath there, like a cetacean, and so renew his air supply every 24 hours? No matter what his method was, it seemed to me urgent to use it now.

As a matter of fact, I was already breathing faster, in an effort to get more of whatever oxygen remained,[1] when suddenly I was refreshed by a current of

---

1. The professor is getting so little oxygen that he's not thinking straight. It would be better for him to take slow, shallow breaths—as magicians and fakirs have repeatedly demonstrated. For instance, in 1926 Houdini was locked in a coffin, then plunged into a swimming pool, where he remained for ninety minutes by keeping still and using shallow breathing.

pure air, perfumed with a salty aroma. It was an invigorating sea breeze, charged with iodine. I opened my mouth wide, and my lungs glutted themselves. At the same time I felt a swaying, a rolling, slight but definitely perceptible. This craft, this iron-plated monster, had apparently risen to the surface to breathe, after the fashion of whales. And so the ship's method of ventilation was established. But, when I had absorbed a chestful of pure air, I wondered where the conduit was that conveyed this beneficial stuff to us. It didn't take long to find it. Above the door there was an air vent through which masses of fresh air poured into our cabin.

I was making these observations when Ned and Conseil awoke almost simultaneously, probably under the influence of this abrupt freshening of the air. They rubbed their eyes, stretched their arms, then sprang to their feet.

"Has master slept well?" Conseil asked with his perennial politeness.

"Very well, my gallant lad. And you, Ned?"

"Profoundly, professor. But do I deceive myself, or am I breathing a sea breeze?"

A seaman couldn't be wrong about that, and I told the Canadian what had happened during his slumbering.

"Good!" he answered. "That explains those roarings we heard when our so-called narwhale neared the *Abraham Lincoln*."

"Right, Ned, it was taking breath."

"But professor, I have no idea what time it is, except that maybe it's dinnertime."

"Dinnertime, my valiant harpooner? I'd say at least breakfast time, because we've certainly begun another day."

"Then," Conseil asked, "we slept 24 hours?"

"That's my estimate."

"I won't challenge that," Ned joined in, "but dinner or breakfast, that steward will be mighty welcome whether he brings the former or the latter."

"The former *and* the latter," said Conseil.

"Fine," Ned concluded. "We deserve two meals, and speaking for myself, I'll do justice to them both."

"But," I cautioned, "we must be patient. It's clear these strangers don't intend to let us starve to death. Otherwise that last meal they fed us wouldn't make any sense."

"But suppose they're just fattening us up."

"Ned, cut that out!" I admonished. "There's no reason to think we've fallen in with cannibals."

"One occasion doesn't establish a custom," he said in all seriousness. "Suppose these people have had to go for a long time without fresh meat. In that case, three healthy specimens like the professor, his servant, and me—"

"Banish such thoughts, Mr. Land," I told the harpooner. "Don't let such ideas make you angry at our hosts. That might just aggravate the situation."

"In any case," he said, "I'm as hungry as the devil, and dinner or breakfast, not one paltry meal has arrived."

"Mr. Land," I replied, "we must conform to the regulations on board, and I imagine our stomachs are running ahead of the chef's dinner bell."

"Well then," Conseil observed calmly, "we'll have to adjust to the chef's schedule."

"That's so like you, friend Conseil," the impatient Canadian retorted. "You never lose your temper, you're always calm. You'd be willing to say thanks for a meal they never served you, and you'd die of hunger before you'd complain."

"What good would complaining do?" Conseil asked.

"Complaining doesn't have to *do* good, it *feels* good. And if these pirates—out of respect for the professor I call them pirates, since he forbids us to call them cannibals—if these pirates think they can suffocate me in this cage without hearing my favorite curse words, they are mistaken. Now professor, speak frankly. Do you think they plan to keep us locked up in this iron box for long?"

"Truthfully, friend Land, I know only what you know, no more, no less."

"But what do you *think*?"

"I think that mere chance has put us in possession of some important secret. And if this submarine crew wants to keep their secret *secret,* and if that is more important to them than the lives of three strangers, then I think that our very existence has been compromised. If such is not the case, then this monster that has swallowed us will take us back to the world of civilized people."

"Unless they impress us into their crew," Conseil suggested, "and force us to serve—"

"Until," Ned took over, "a frigate that is faster or more maneuverable than the *Abraham Lincoln* captures these pirates and hangs the whole crew—us included—from the tip of a mainmast yardarm."

"Good thinking, Mr. Land," I said. "But so far we're not faced with anything like that. There's no point talking about what we would do in that case. I repeat, we must be guided by developments, and do nothing until we see what is to be done."

"On the contrary, professor." The harpooner could not imagine retreating. "We've got to do something."

"Oh? Like what, Ned?"

"Escape!"

"To escape from a prison on land is hard enough. To escape from a prison underwater seems to me quite impossible."

"So, friend Ned," Conseil demanded, "how can you meet master's argument? I cannot believe that an American is at the end of his rope!"

Visibly embarrassed, the harpooner said nothing. To escape the trap into which we had fallen seemed out of the question. But a Canadian is half-French, as Ned Land demonstrated in the response he finally gave.

"So, professor, you can't imagine what men do when they can't break out of their prison?"

"No I cannot, my friend."

"It's quite simple. They arrange things so they can afford to stay."

"Of course!" Conseil said. "I would rather stay inside this boat than above or below it in the water."

"But only after we jettison our jailers, turn-keys, and guards."

"What, Ned! You're seriously thinking of taking command of this ship?"

"Very seriously."

"That's impossible."

"Why do you say that? If a good chance presents itself, why shouldn't we take advantage of it? Suppose there are only some twenty men in the crew, how can they hold back two Frenchmen and a Canadian!"

It seemed wiser at that moment to accept his plan than to discuss it. So I was content to say: "Let's be guided by such circumstances when they develop. But until something does develop, contain yourself. Our only chance is to invent some stratagem, and flying into a rage won't help us do that. So promise me you'll accept this situation without going into a tantrum over it."

"You have my promise," he said, but he didn't sound sincere. "Not a word of anger, no brutal gestures, even when they don't feed us on time."

"Word of honor, Ned."

Our conversation petered out. Each of us withdrew into his own thoughts. In spite of the harpooner's self-assurance, I entertained no illusions. I saw no chance at all of carrying out Ned's wild plans. Navigation of this boat required a large crew, and so if it came to an all-out fight, we would be hopelessly outnumbered. Besides, you must be able to get at your enemy to fight him, and we were immobilized. I couldn't see any way to escape from that hermetically sealed iron box. And if the strange commander of that submarine had some secret that he must maintain at all costs—and that seemed likely to me—then he would have to limit our actions on board. Would he get rid of us in some direct, violent way, or would he leave us stranded on some remote coast? Too many unknowns. Each of these hypotheses seemed plausible, and only one thing was certain: You had to be a harpooner to hope for freedom through use of force.

Now I could see that Ned was thinking things over too, and getting madder by the minute. I could hear those favorite curse words growling in his gullet, and I saw him making menacing gestures. He prowled around like a wild beast in a cage, hitting the walls with his feet and his fists. Time was slipping by, we were fearfully hungry, and the steward made no appearance. It was too long to leave us like this, castaways, if they really had good intentions toward us. Ned Land, tormented by the cravings of hunger, was boiling with wrath, and despite his promise, I dreaded an explosion when he found himself in the presence of one of the crew.

For two hours more, Ned Land's rage increased; he shouted, he cried, but in vain. Those iron walls were deaf. There were no sounds in the interior of that submarine boat, which seemed dead. I knew it hadn't moved, for I would have felt its hull trembling under the influence of its propeller. No longer a part of the world, it had doubtless sunk into the watery abyss. The silence was horrifying.

Abandoned, isolated, I had no idea how long this could go on. Hopes I had entertained when the captain interviewed us were fading away. His gentle gaze, the generosity implied in his physiognomy, his noble bearing, all that vanished from my mind. I was forming a new impression of this enigmatic person. He was pitiless, cruel, outside humanity, an implacable foe of humankind, against whom he could well have sworn an oath of everlasting hatred.

Could he really intend to let us starve, one by one, shut up in this cramped prison, exposed to those awful temptations induced by extreme hunger? I was becoming obsessed with this grim possibility. I felt an insensate dread overtaking me. Conseil remained calm while Ned Land roared.

Just then, I heard a noise outside. Footsteps resounded on the metal flags. The locks were turned, the door opened, the steward entered.

Before I could rush forward to stop him, the Canadian had thrown the steward down, and was holding him by the throat. The steward was choking in the grip of Ned's powerful hands.

Conseil was already trying to loosen the harpooner's hands from his half-suffocated victim, and I was going to join in the rescue, when suddenly I was nailed to the spot by hearing these words pronounced in French:

"Calm down, Mr. Land. And you, professor, will you kindly listen to me?"

TEN

~~~~

The Man of the Waters

IT WAS THE commander speaking.

At his words, Ned stood up quickly. The commander motioned the steward toward the door. Nearly strangled, the man staggered out. Such was the power of the commander that the steward betrayed none of the resentment he surely must have felt toward Ned. Conseil, in spite of himself, seemed interested. I was stupefied. We waited in silence for the outcome of this scene.

Leaning against the table with his arms folded,[1] the commander looked us over carefully. Did he hesitate to speak again? Was he regretting those words he had just spoken in French? One might have thought so.

After several moments of silence, which none of us dreamed of breaking, "Gentlemen," he said in a calm, penetrating voice, "I speak French, English, German, even Latin equally well. I could have answered you during our first interview, but I wanted to learn something about you first, and then to reflect on what I had learned.

"Since your four separate accounts agreed completely on all the main points, I was convinced you had identified yourselves truthfully. I now know that chance has brought to my vessel Pierre Aronnax, professor of natural history at the Paris Museum, on a scientific mission abroad; Conseil, his manservant; and Ned Land, Canadian harpooner on duty aboard the *Abraham Lincoln,* a frigate in the United States Navy."

I bowed in agreement. Since he had not addressed a question to me, I felt no obligation to respond. This man expressed himself with perfect ease, with not a trace of accent. His sentences were well phrased, his words well chosen, his fluency in French remarkable. Yet I did not feel that he was a Frenchman. He went on:

---

1. This may have been Verne's own characteristic posture. Riou's 1869 portrait of Aronnax (reproduced here in I 2) used Verne himself as its studio model and shows the subject staring alertly into the distance, arms folded. And a photograph of the young Verne by his friend Nadar (not reproduced here but viewable in many sources) shows the same pose. Apparently Verne saw this as the natural posture of the independent man—*aloof physically but involved mentally.* (Of course, both the professor and Nemo were created out of two contrasting sides of Verne's own nature.)

"Surely you have thought, professor, that I have waited a long while to pay you this second visit. But, once I realized who you were, I wanted to consider very, very carefully how to treat you. I hesitated. Most annoying circumstances have brought you into the life of someone who has broken all ties with humanity. You have invaded my life."

"Unintentionally!" I protested.

"Unintentionally?" He raised his voice a little. "Was it unintentionally that the *Abraham Lincoln* chased me all over the ocean? Was it unintentionally that you accepted the invitation to board that frigate? Was it unintentionally that your conical shells bounced off my hull? Was it unintentionally that Mr. Land hit me with his harpoon?"

I detected a barely restrained irritation in his words. But there was a very natural reply to make to these charges, and I made it.

"Sir, you are apparently unaware of the discussions you have provoked all over Europe and America. You are unaware that reports from vessels that have collided with your submarine craft have excited public feeling on two continents. I'll spare you for the moment the innumerable hypotheses by which people have attempted to explain this phenomenon to which you alone possess the secret. But you must know that in pursuing you all over the Pacific high seas, we on the *Abraham Lincoln* thought we were chasing some powerful monster that had to be destroyed at any cost."

Half a smile curled his lips. Then, in a calmer tone, he replied:

"Professor, do you dare affirm that your frigate would not have pursued and cannonaded a submarine boat as readily as a monster?"

That embarrassed me. I knew that Commander Farragut would have shown no such hesitation. He would have seen it as his duty to destroy a contrivance of this kind just as well as a giant narwhale.

"Therefore, professor, you see that I have the right to treat you as enemies?"

I said nothing, for a good reason. What good would it do to debate such a proposition when force could shatter the best arguments?

"I have hesitated," he resumed, "because nothing obliges me to show you the least hospitality. I could decide to part company with you, because I would have no interest in seeing you again. I could station you on the deck of this boat, where you have taken refuge, I could submerge and forget that you had ever intruded in my life. Wouldn't that be my right?"

"The right of a savage," I couldn't help blurting out, "but not the right of a civilized man."

"Professor," he shot back, "I'm not what you call a civilized man.[2] I am

---

2. In this crucial speech, Verne introduces a major motif of the novel and indeed of his entire body of work. The captain by his phrase "what you call" challenges the standard definition of civilization, questioning whether our world *is* civilized. As in Thoreau's *Civil Disobedience* (1849), the captain stakes out the position of the Higher Conscience, the Great Refusal, foreshadowing the worldwide "dropout" movement that has continued from the 1960s to the present day.

finished with society, for reasons I alone can appreciate. I don't obey its laws, and I suggest you never again refer to them in my presence."

That was plain speaking. Disdainful anger kindled in this stranger's eyes, and I had a glimpse of a terrible past in his life. Not only had he put himself outside the pale of humanity's laws, but also he had made himself independent, free in the ultimate sense of the word, quite beyond all law! Who could pursue him to the depths of the sea when he defied all attacks on the surface? What vessel could withstand the shock of a collision with his submarine monitor? What armor, no matter how thick, could stand the blows of his ram? What man could call him to account for his actions? God, if he believed in Him, his conscience if he had one, were the sole judges to whom he would answer.

These reflections crossed my mind while the stranger stood silent, wrapped up in his own ideas. I regarded him with mingled fear and attention, as maybe Oedipus regarded the Sphinx.[3] After a while the commander spoke again:

"So I have wondered, could my own interests be reconciled with that pity that every human being has a claim to? So, you will remain on board my boat, since fate has placed you here. You'll be free here, and in exchange for this liberty you must accept just one condition. Your word of honor that you will submit to it will suffice."

"What is it, sir? I suppose this condition is one an honorable man can accept?"

"Certainly. Just this. Certain unforeseeable developments might force me to confine you to your cabins for some hours or even days. Since I prefer never to use violence, I expect from you, more than ever, your passive obedience under such circumstances. In acting this way, I shield you from any responsibility, I absolve you completely, for I make it impossible for you to see what ought not be seen. You accept?"

So, things did happen on board that, to say the least, were unique and egregious, that ought not to be witnessed by people still under the influence of society's laws. Among the surprises in store for us, this might not be the least.

"We accept," I said. "But I ask your permission to pose one question. Just one."

"Speak, professor."

"You said we'd be free on board."

"Entirely."

"But what do you mean by such liberty?"

3. A provocative simile, as we can see by comparing Oedipus's situation with Aronnax's. In a state of uncertainty about himself and his antecedents, Oedipus confronts the Sphinx, a monster who promised death to anyone not answering her riddle. As for Aronnax, he must, like Oedipus, *fear death* in a crucial interview; and, again like the mythical hero, the professor seems to be engaged in an underlying identity crisis. Aronnax is, both literally and symbolically, lost at sea: earlier, in I 7, he talked of Jonahs taking "refuge in the bellies of whales," which Jungians would regard as an archetypal descent into the self, a retreat into the womb in order to be reborn. Now the professor is *in* the whale's belly . . . or, to extend the present metaphor, at the crossroads with Oedipus.

"The liberty to come and go, to observe everything happening, except under those rare circumstances, in short, the liberty that my crew and I enjoy."

Clearly we did not understand each other.

"Pardon me, sir, but that is the liberty that every prisoner has, the freedom to pace his cell. That would not be enough for us."

"Nevertheless, it must suffice."

"What, we must give up homeland, friends, family?"

"Yes, professor, but renouncing that unendurable worldly yoke that men call liberty is not so painful as you think."

"By thunder!" cried Ned Land. "Never will I give my word of honor not to escape."

"Mr. Land," the commander replied coldly, "I didn't ask for *your* word of honor."

"Sir," I was getting angry in spite of myself, "you are taking advantage of us. This is cruelty."

"No, it is clemency. You are my prisoners of war. I keep you alive although I could, by a simple command, plunge you back into the sea. You assaulted me! And you have stumbled on a secret that no one must penetrate—the secret of my very existence. Do you think I can send you back to that world that must know nothing about my present life? Never! In detaining you, it's not you I protect. It's me."

No arguments could prevail in such a situation.

"You give us then," I asked, "just the choice between life and death?"

"Just that."

"My friends," I said to Ned and Conseil, "faced with such a choice, we can have only one answer. But we have not sworn any loyalty to the master of this ship."

"None," he said, and then in a gentler tone: "Allow me to finish. I know of you, Professor Aronnax. You, if not your companions, will not find life aboard this boat so unbearable. You will find among my favorite books a copy of your two-volume treatise on the depths of the sea. I have read and reread it. You have pursued your studies as far as *terrestrial* science can go. But you don't know all because you have not seen it all. So let me tell you, professor, you won't regret the time spent on board my ship. You are going to tour the land of marvels. Astonishment, amazement will become your everyday state of mind. You won't get bored with the spectacles I will provide for you. I'm going on another tour of the submarine world—for all I know, my last tour—and I'm going to review everything I've ever studied at the bottom of the seas, and you can be my fellow student. Starting today, you'll enter a new element, and you will see what nobody has ever seen—since my crew and I no longer count—and thanks to me, you will discover the ultimate secrets of our planet."

I can't deny that these words had an overpowering effect on me. He had touched my weak spot. For a moment I forgot that contemplation of these sublime phenomena was not worth the loss of my liberty. And I counted on the future to resolve this grave situation. So I contented myself with saying:

"Sir, even though you have broken with humanity, I cannot believe you still reject all human sentiment. We are castaways, charitably taken aboard by you, and we can't forget that. And I must admit that, if my interest in science could cancel out my love of liberty, this promised voyage would offer me tremendous compensations."

I expected him to extend his hand, so we could shake as a sign of our agreement. He did nothing of the kind. I regretted that.

"One last question," I said as he seemed ready to leave.

"Yes, professor?"

"By what name or title are we to call you?"

"Sir," the commander replied, "to you I am nothing but Captain Nemo.[4] You and your companions are nothing to me but passengers on the *Nautilus.*"[5]

Captain Nemo called and a steward appeared. The commander gave him his orders in that strange language I could not even identify. Then he turned toward the Canadian and Conseil:

"A repast awaits you in your cabin," he told them. "Be so good as to follow this man."

"I won't refuse *that* offer!" the harpooner declared. And so Ned and Conseil left the cell where they had been confined for more than 30 hours.

"And now, professor, *our* lunch is ready. Permit me to lead the way."

"At your service, captain."

Following him, I passed through the door and found myself in a passageway, lighted by electricity, otherwise similar to a gangway on a more conventional vessel. After we walked ten meters or so, a second door opened before me. I then entered a dining room decorated and furnished in austere good taste. Tall oaken sideboards, inlaid with ebony, stood at the two ends of the room, their shelves sparkling with china, porcelain, and cut glass of incalculable value. Silver plate shone in the light shed by fixtures set in the ceiling, where fine painted designs tempered the glare.

A table richly spread stood in the center of the hall. Captain Nemo pointed to my place.

"You must be famished," he said. "Sit down and enjoy a good meal."

4. In Latin, nemo means *no one, nobody.* As "Captain No one," the man is reflecting by his very name his withdrawal from society: he is the romantic outcast, the "nameless one." Of course this is ironic, because he is *far from a nobody,* as we shall soon discover. In addition, his choice of incognito ties him to Odysseus of classic legend: "nemo" is what that famous wanderer called himself when he encountered the Cyclops.

5. The captain has been equally artistic in naming his submarine. He has commemorated Robert Fulton's early submersible (see note 3 for I 7), which, in its turn, had honored one of the ocean's most intriguing inhabitants: the nautilus is a spiral-shelled mollusk whose genus has survived for over 350,000,000 years. It sinks or rises in the sea by adjusting the amount of gas in its chambers. The U.S. Navy evenhandedly honored Verne, Fulton, and mollusk by giving the name *Nautilus* both to a WWII submarine and to the celebrated atomic sub that cruised under the North Pole in 1958.

Lunch beneath the sea

Our luncheon included several familiar seafood dishes and others completely new to me. They were good, but with a peculiar taste that I would soon become accustomed to. They seemed rich in phosphorus, and I assumed they too came from the sea.

Captain Nemo was watching me. I asked him no questions, but he read my thoughts.

"Most of these dishes must be absolutely new to you," he said, "but eat them without anxiety. They are healthful and nourishing. I long ago renounced foods of the land, and I am none the worse for it. My crew eat the same food, and they are all healthy and vigorous."

"You mean *all* these foods come from the sea?" It was hard to accept.

"Yes, professor, the sea supplies all my wants. Sometimes, when I cast my nets in tow, I drag them in ready to snap. Sometimes I hunt on the ocean floor, which seems inaccessible to man, and stalk the game that dwells in my submarine forests. My flocks, like those of Neptune's old shepherd,[6] graze without fear on the immense prairies of the ocean. I own vast properties, forever sown by the hand of the Creator and harvested by me."

I gaped at Captain Nemo with amazement, and I responded:

"I can understand that your nets furnish you with excellent fish for your table. I understand less how you can hunt aquatic game in your submarine forests. But I can't understand at all how a slice of meat, no matter how small, can be included in your bill of fare."

"Oh no, professor," Captain Nemo replied. "I never eat the flesh of land animals."

"Then what is this?" I pointed to a dish on which some slices of filleted meat were left.

"That, which you take to be meat, professor, is fillet of sea turtle. And that, which you might take to be stewed pork, is dolphin liver. My cook is clever in preserving these ocean products. Try all of these dishes, I beg of you. Here is some preserved sea cucumber that any Malaysian would declare to be unrivaled in the whole world, here's cream from milk supplied us by the udders of cetaceans, and sugar by the huge fucus plants of the North Sea, and finally, let me offer you some jam made from sea anemone, equal to that of the most savory fruits."

I sampled and tasted, more out of curiosity than as a connoisseur, while Captain Nemo charmed me with his amazing stories.

"But this ocean, Professor Aronnax, this prodigious, inexhaustible provider, does more than nourish me. She clothes me as well. That cloth covering you was woven from those masses of filaments that anchor certain seashells. It has been dyed with the purple the ancients used, purple from the murex snail, and shaded with violet that I extract from a marine slug, the Mediterranean sea hare. The perfumes you'll find on the washstand in your cabin we produce by

6. This would be Proteus, an allusion Verne will repeat in II 6 and II 14. Proteus was often represented as herding flocks of seal or dolphin.

distilling various sea plants. Your mattress we made from the softest eelgrass. Your quill pen is made from whalebone, your ink is a juice secreted by cuttlefish or squid. I get everything from the sea, just as, some day, the sea will claim me."

"Captain, you are enamored of the sea!"

"Yes I am. The sea is everything. It covers seven-tenths of the planet. Its breath is pure and healthful. It's an immense wilderness where a man never feels lonely, because he feels life astir on every side. The sea fosters a wondrous, supernatural existence. It's all movement and love, 'the living infinite' as one of your poets called it. Basically, as you know, professor, Nature manifests herself in the sea through all three of her kingdoms: mineral, vegetable, and animal. The animal kingdom is well represented by the four groups of zoophytes, the three classes of articulates, by the five classes of mollusks, and three vertebrate classes: mammals, reptiles, and myriad legions of fish, an infinite order of animals comprising more than 13,000 species, only one-tenth of which also belong to fresh water.

"The sea is the vast reservoir of Nature. Our globe began with the sea, and maybe it will end with it. Here is supreme tranquillity! The sea does not belong to despots! Up there on the surface, men can still exercise their iniquitous claims, fight each other, tear one another to pieces, and transport their terrestrial horrors. But thirty feet below the surface, their reign ceases, their influence is quenched, their power vanishes. Ah professor, why not live—*live* in the bosom of the seas! Here alone will you find true independence! Here I recognize no master! Here I'm free!"

In the midst of this enthusiasm, Captain Nemo suddenly became silent. Had he been carried beyond the bounds of his usual reserve? Did he feel he had said too much? For several minutes he paced back and forth, upset. Then he grew calm, regained his cool expression, and turned toward me:

"Now, professor, if you would like to inspect the *Nautilus,* I am at your service."

ELEVEN

The Nautilus

APTAIN NEMO STOOD UP. I followed him. At the rear of the dining room a double door opened and I entered another room of about the same size.

It was a library. Tall pieces of furniture, made of black rosewood inlaid with copper, contained in their deep shelves a vast number of books uniformly bound. These bookcases followed the contours of the room, leading at the lower end to long couches upholstered in maroon leather and curved to provide maximum comfort. There were light, movable reading stands on which one could rest a book and which could be pulled over or pushed away as one required. In the center of the room stood an immense table covered with pamphlets and newspapers way out-of-date. Electric light, originating in four frosted globes half-set in the ceiling, flooded the whole harmonious ensemble. I gaped with genuine admiration at this room, so ingeniously fitted out, and I could hardly believe my eyes.

"This library," I said to my host, who had thrown himself onto one of the couches, "would do honor to more than one Continental palace, and I truly marvel when I think you can take it with you to the bottom of the ocean!"

"Where could you find greater silence or solitude, professor? Did you have such perfect tranquillity in your office at the museum?"

"No, sir, I must confess my study is a very poor one compared to yours. Why, you have here some six or seven thousand books—"

"Twelve thousand, Professor Aronnax. They are my only ties with the shore. I gave up the world the day my *Nautilus* plunged beneath the waters for the first time. That day I bought my last books, my last pamphlets, my last newspapers. Since then I wish to believe humanity no longer thinks or writes.[1] These books, professor, are at your disposal; make free use of them."

---

1. Here, and in his later remark that "The masters belong to all time," Nemo voices a desire for total regression to a Garden of Eden—a timelessness, stasis, immortality, in which all history is simultaneous. This wish to escape time is a denial of his basic suffering. But, as we shall see, he is the prisoner of a traumatic experience that simply will not let him get outside history.

Thanking the captain, I went up to the shelves. Works of science, ethics, literature, in many languages, were in abundance; but I did not see a single book on economics, apparently a subject strictly proscribed on board. And, strange to say, these books were not grouped according to the languages they were written in, and the resultant mixture suggested that the captain could read fluently whatever books came to hand, regardless of language.

Among these books I found masterpieces both ancient and modern, everything worthwhile in history, poetry, fiction, science, from Homer to Victor Hugo, from Xenophon to Michelet, from Rabelais to Madame Sand.[2] But science predominated in that library: books on mechanics, ballistics, hydrography, meteorology, geography, geology, etc., held a place no less important than works on natural history. It was clear these were the captain's main studies. I found all of Humboldt, all of Arago, the works of Foucault, of Henri Sainte-Claire Deville, of Chasles, Milne-Edwards, Quatrefages, Tyndall, Faraday, Berthelot, the Abbe Secchi, Petermann, Commander Maury,[3] Agassiz, and others, plus the transactions of the Academy of Sciences, bulletins of geographical societies, and—in a position of prominence—those two volumes that probably had earned me this relatively charitable welcome from Captain Nemo.

Among the works of Joseph Bertrand, his book *The Founders of Astronomy* gave me a major clue. Since I knew it had appeared in 1865, I now assumed that the *Nautilus* had not been launched before that. So, Captain Nemo had been at sea for no more than three years. Maybe more recent works would enable me to pinpoint the time more precisely. But I could check on that later. Right now I wanted to continue our inspection of the marvels of the *Nautilus*.

"Sir," I turned to the captain, "thank you for putting this library at my disposal. It contains great treasures of science, and I shall take advantage of them."

"This room is not just a library," he said, "it's also a smoking room."

2. George Sand (pseudonym of Aurore Dupin, 1804–1876) was a French romantic novelist. A pioneering force in the women's liberation movement and an early advocate of sexual freedom, she was regarded as one of the literary greats in Verne's Paris. But her connections to this author and this novel run still deeper: first, both she and Verne were under contract to the same publisher, J. Hetzel; second, in an 1865 letter to Verne praising his first two novels (*Five Weeks in a Balloon* and *Journey to the Center of the Earth*), Sand made the following plea for a new book from Verne's pen: "I hope you'll soon take us into the depths of the sea, making your characters travel in diving equipment perfected by your science and your imagination." Accordingly, say French scholars, she provided the inspiration for the present book.

3. Virginia-born Matthew Maury (1806–1873) was appointed officer in charge of the U.S. Navy's depot of charts and instruments. In this capacity he generated wind and current charts that were used worldwide, supervised the development of new depth-sounding machinery, then prepared the first depth map of the North Atlantic. In 1855 Maury published a seagoing classic that made him a household word, *The Physical Geography of the Sea and Its Meteorology*, a cornerstone work in every 19th century captain's shipboard library. In the course of their 20,000-league association, Nemo and Aronnax will often engage in a pet intellectual pastime of that period: discussing Maury's theories and accomplishments. Some of his conclusions have been rebutted since, but his methods and data were invaluable assists to world shipping.

"A smoking room?" I cried. "Then one may smoke on board?"

"Of course."

"Then, sir, I'm led to believe you've maintained relations with Havana."

"Not at all," he answered quickly. "Try this cigar, professor. It does not come from Havana, but you will like it, if you're a connoisseur."

I accepted a cigar whose shape resembled a Cuban cigar, but this one was made of golden leaves. I lighted it at a little brazier on an elegant bronze stand, and I drew the first whiffs with the delight of the smoker who hasn't had a puff in days.

"Excellent," I concluded, "but it's not from the tobacco plant."

"Right," he agreed, "this tobacco comes from neither Havana nor the East. It is a kind of seaweed rich in nicotine with which the ocean supplies us, but sparingly. Now, do you think you will miss your Havanas?"

"Captain, from this day on I shall scorn them."

"Good then, smoke these at your pleasure. And do not worry about their origin. They may not bear an official excise-tax stamp, but they are none the worse for that, I imagine.

"On the contrary."

Captain Nemo now opened a door facing the one by which we had entered the library and I passed into an immense salon, splendidly lighted. It was a large quadrilateral with the corners canted, ten meters long, six wide, five high. A luminous ceiling, decorated with light arabesques, shed a gentle light clear as day over all the marvels assembled in this—museum! Yes, it was a museum, really, in which a lavish and intelligent hand had gathered all the treasures of nature and of art with the artistic confusion that distinguishes a painter's studio.

Some thirty pictures by the masters, uniformly framed and separated by glittering panoplies of arms, decorated the walls, which were hung with tapestries of severe, classic design. There I gazed at canvases of enormous value, most of which I had at one time or another admired in private collections or at public exhibitions in Europe. The several schools of the old masters were represented by a Madonna by Raphael, a Virgin by Leonardo da Vinci, a nymph by Correggio, a woman by Titian, an Adoration by Veronese, an Assumption by Murillo, a portrait by Holbein, a monk by Velazquez, a martyr by Ribera, a town fair by Rubens, two Flemish landscapes by Teniers, three little genre paintings by Gerard Dow, Metsu, and Paul Potter, two canvases by Gericault and Prud'hon, and some seascapes by Backhuysen and Vernet. Modern art was represented by works signed Delacroix, Ingres, Decamps, Troyon, Meissonier, Daubigny, etc., and on pedestals in the corners of this magnificent museum stood some admirable statues in marble or bronze modeled on some of the loveliest works of antiquity. As the captain had predicted, amazement began to take hold of me.

"Professor," this strange man was saying, "you must excuse the unceremonious way in which I receive you, and the disorder of this salon."

"Sir," I replied, "without seeking to know who you are, I am certain I know what you are—an artist."

"Only an enthusiast, professor, an aficionado. I used to love to collect beautiful works created by human hands. I sought them out greedily, ferreted them out indefatigably, and I've been able to bring together a few objects of great value. These are my last souvenirs of those shores that are dead for me. In my eyes, the modern artists are already as old as the ancients, two or three thousand years old. I confuse them in my mind. The masters belong to all time."

"And these composers?" I pointed to sheet music of Weber, Rossini, Mozart, Beethoven, Haydn, Meyerbeer, Herold, Wagner, Auber, Gounod, Massé,[4] and others scattered over a large organ standing against one wall of the salon.

"These musicians are the contemporaries of Orpheus, because in the memory of the dead, all chronological differences are blurred, and I am dead, professor, as dead as any of your friends sleeping six feet under."

He fell silent and seemed lost in reverie. I contemplated him with strong feelings, silently analyzing his strange expression. Leaning on an elbow against a costly mosaic table, he no longer saw me, he had forgotten me. I did not disturb his meditations, but continued to study the curiosities in this extraordinary room.

Next to the works of art, natural rarities predominated. These comprised mainly plants, shells, and other marine products that the captain must have collected himself. In the middle of the salon, a jet of water, lighted by electricity, tumbled back into a large bowl made from a single giant clam. This shell had come from the largest of the acephalous mollusks. Its rim was delicately scalloped and measured about six meters in circumference. Hence it was larger than those beautiful giant clams given to Francois I by the Venetian Republic and made into two huge holy-water basins for the Church of Saint-Sulpice in Paris.

Around this fountain, in elegant glass cases framed in copper, I found the most precious specimens of the sea ever presented to the eye of a naturalist, and all classified and labeled! My professorial joy may easily be imagined.

The cases containing the zoophytes displayed some very curious specimens from the two groups, the polyps and the echinoderms. In the first group there were organ-pipe coral, some gorgonian coral arranged like a fan, soft sponges of Syria, isis coral from the Molucca Islands, sea-pen coral, an admirable genus *Virgularia* from Norwegian waters, some various genus *Umbellularia,* some alcyonarian coral, a whole series of those madreporic polyps that my mentor Milne-Edwards[5] has so wisely classified into divisions, and among which I

4. Victor Massé (1822–1884), composer at the Paris Opera and a personal friend of Verne's, is a musician whose output is all but unknown outside France. Hachette includes his name in the midst of some very fast company (Mozart, Beethoven, Wagner), which may account for his absence from the list reprinted in Hetzel.

5. Henri Milne-Edwards (1800–1885) was one of science's first field researchers in marine biology: when not busy as a classroom lecturer or as senior staff member at the Paris Museum, Milne-Edwards donned the diving equipment of his day and studied aquatic conditions first-

saw some wonderful genus *Flabellina,* and some genus *Oculina* from Réunion Island, plus a "Neptune's Chariot" from the Caribbean, superb varieties of corals, and, in short, every species of those curious polyparies of which entire islands are formed, islands that could someday become continents. And there was a complete collection of echinoderms, those marine animals remarkable for being enveloped in spines: starfish, feather stars, sea lilies, free-swimming crinoids, brittle stars, sea urchins, sea cucumbers, etc.

Now, a nervous conchologist would have fainted before the other, more numerous glass cases in which the mollusks were classified. There I found a collection of inestimable value that time does not allow me to do justice to. Among these displays I will cite for the record: an elegant royal hammer shell from the Indian Ocean, whose evenly spaced white spots stood out vividly on a red and brown ground; an imperial spiny oyster, brightly colored, bristling with thorns, a specimen rarely seen in European museums: I estimated its worth at 20,000 francs; a common hammer shell from the waters of Queensland, difficult to obtain; exotic cockles from Senegal with fragile white bivalve shells that a strong breath could shatter like a soap bubble; several varieties of watering-pot shell from Java, a kind of calcareous tube edged with leafy folds and highly prized by collectors; a whole series of top shell snails, some a greenish yellow fished up in American waters, others a reddish brown, natives of Queensland waters, the former from the Gulf of Mexico and remarkable for their overlapping shells, the latter some sun carrier shells found in southern seas; and the rarest of all, the magnificent spurred star shell from New Zealand.

Also there were some admirable peppery furrow shells; precious specimens of cytherean clams and venus clams; the trellis wentletrap snail from Tranquebar waters; a marbled turban snail with its resplendent pearly gleam; the green parrot shell from the China Seas; the rare cone snail from the genus *Coenodullus;* all the varieties of the polished cowries used as money in India and Africa; a "glory of the seas," the most precious East Indies shell; and finally, common periwinkles, delphinula snails, turret snails, violet snails, some European cowries, volute snails, olive shells, miter shells, helmet shells, murex snails, whelks, harp shells, some spiky periwinkles, triton snails, horn shells, spindle shells, conch shells, spider conches, limpets, glass snails, some sea butterflies, every kind of delicate, fragile shell to which science has given such charming names.

In separate cases there were spread out strings of pearls of the greatest beauty, reflecting the electric light in little sparks of fire; some pink pearls torn from marine fan shells of the Red Sea; green pearls from the iridescent abalone; yellow, blue, and black pearls, the curious output of various mollusks in every ocean, and of certain mussels in streams of the North; lastly, samples of incalculable worth that were oozed by the rarest of shellfish. Some were larger than

hand. His books are in Nemo's library, as Aronnax has noted, and the professor will refer more than once to Milne-Edwards's classification of undersea invertebrates as the novel proceeds.

a pigeon egg and worth more than the pearl the explorer Tavernier[6] sold to the Shah of Persia for 3,000,000 francs, more even than the one owned by the Imam of Muscat, which I had believed to be unrivaled anywhere in the world.

So it was simply impossible to estimate the value of this collection. Captain Nemo must have spent millions collecting these specimens. I was wondering what financial resources he could have drawn on to satisfy his fancy for collecting when I was interrupted:

"You are examining my shells, professor? Surely they must be interesting to a naturalist. But for me they have a far greater charm. I have collected them all with my own hands, and there is not a sea on the globe that I have not ransacked for them."

"Captain, I can understand your delight in browsing amid these riches: you are one of those who collect their own treasures. No European museum possesses such a collection of marine exhibits. Still, if I exhaust my admiration on them, I'll save none for the ship that carries them. I do not want to pry into your secrets. But I confess that the *Nautilus,* the motive power it encloses, the contrivances that you use to control it, the powerful agent that propels it, all these matters excite my curiosity to fever pitch. For example, I see on the walls of this salon some instruments entirely unfamiliar to me. May I presume to ask—?"

"Professor," he replied, "I have told you, you have complete liberty aboard my ship. No part of the *Nautilus* is off-limits to you. You may inspect it in detail. And it would please me to serve as your guide."

"I don't know how to thank you, captain, and I won't abuse the privilege. But would you mind telling me something about these instruments, what they are for, how you use them?"

"There are identical instruments in my own room, professor, where I shall be pleased to explain their use to you. But first come and see the cabin I have set aside for you. See how you will be accommodated aboard the *Nautilus.*"

I followed Captain Nemo. Through one of the doorways that pierced the canted corners of the salon he led me again into the corridors, toward the bow. There I found not just a cabin but an elegant room with a bed, a washstand, and other furniture.

I could only thank the commander.

"Your room adjoins mine," he said as he opened another door, "and mine opens into the salon we just left."

I went into his room. It had a severe, almost monastic air. A small iron bedstead, a worktable, a washstand, and very subdued lighting. No luxuries. Just the barest necessities.

He pointed to a bench:

"Please be seated," he said.

I sat, and he began to talk.

6. Jean-Baptiste Tavernier (1605–1689) was a famed travel author of the day: he made six long journeys to the Orient, hobnobbing with the greatest princes of the East, pioneering European trade with India, and publishing three separate books about his journeys.

TWELVE

Everything by Electricity [1]

P ROFESSOR," HE SAID, pointing to the instruments on the walls of his cabin, "these are all the apparatus I need to navigate the *Nautilus*. Here, as in the salon, I have them always in sight, telling me my position and my exact direction in the midst of the seas. I'm sure you recognize some of these like the thermometer, which gives me the temperature inside the boat; the barometer, which tells the weight of the outside air and so helps me anticipate changes in the weather; the humidistat, which indicates the degree of dryness in the atmosphere; the storm glass, whose contents, if they decompose, foretell the approach of tempests; the compass, which directs my course; the sextant, with which I can shoot the altitude of the sun and so determine my latitude; chronometers, with which I reckon my longitude; and telescopes for day or night, with which I can survey the horizon when I go to the surface."

"So far," I responded, "I recognize all the usual navigating equipment. But these other devices—no doubt these are designed for the special needs of the submarine *Nautilus*? This dial with the moving needle—isn't this a pressure gauge?"

"Actually, yes. But in showing me the water pressure on our hull, it also shows me how deep down we are."

"And these seem to be a new kind of sounding line."

"They're thermometric sounding lines. They report temperatures in the different strata of the sea."

"And these other instruments—I can't imagine what they do."

"At this point, professor, I must give you some theoretical background. So, bear with me." He paused. "There is a powerful agent, obedient, rapid, facile, which can be put to any use and reigns supreme on board my ship. It does

---

1. When this novel appeared in 1870, electricity was only a curiosity at carnivals and World's Fairs. The first practical dynamos had been demonstrated at the Paris Exhibition of 1867, but two decades would pass before electric lighting enjoyed widespread use. Further, Verne's readers were fascinated to discover that Captain Nemo had gone beyond mere lighting and employed electricity for propulsion, heating, cooking, ventilation—-even security.

everything. It illuminates our ship, it warms us, it is the soul of our mechanical apparatus. This agent is—electricity."

"Electricity!" I cried in surprise.

"Yes, sir."

"But captain, you are capable of such fantastic speed! That doesn't suggest electric power. Until now, electricity has been able to produce only small amounts of power—"

"Professor," the captain responded, "my electricity is not the usual electricity. With your permission, that's all I'll say at the moment."

"All right, captain, I won't press you. Suffice it to say, I'm astonished at the results you get. But there is one question, if you don't mind. The electric cells you use to produce this marvelous power must be depleted so quickly. For example, how can you replenish your supply of zinc, since you have forsworn all contact with the land?"

"That question I shall answer," the captain said. "First, consider that in the ocean floor there are not only veins of zinc, but also veins of iron, silver, and gold, all of which I could easily mine. But I do not want to use the same metals that landsmen use. I want to get my electricity from the sea itself."

"The sea itself?"

"Of course, professor. Such means are not lacking to me. I could, for example, establish a circuit between wires set at different depths and get electricity by means of the reaction to different temperatures 'sensed' by those wires. But I prefer a more practical method."

"And what method is that?"

"You know what seawater is composed of. In 1,000 grams you find 96.5 percent of water, and about 2.66 percent of sodium chloride. Then, in smaller quantities, magnesium chloride, potassium chloride, magnesium bromide, sulfate of magnesia, calcium sulfate, calcium carbonate. So you know then that sodium chloride is there in good proportions. And it's that sodium that I extract from seawater, that sodium that composes my electric cells."

"Sodium . . . ."

"Yes, professor. Mixed with mercury, sodium forms an amalgam that takes the place of zinc in Bunsen batteries. The mercury is never consumed, only the sodium is used up, and the sea resupplies me with that. Moreover, I can tell you, sodium batteries are more powerful. Their electric motive force is twice that of zinc batteries."[2]

2. The standard English translation of this novel (the Rev. Louis Mercier's rendition, published in London in 1873) omitted nearly a quarter of the book, including this immediate passage on the *Nautilus*'s batteries; in addition, Mercier's text commits, literally, hundreds of detail errors in rendering Verne's French into English. Accordingly, modern commentators who work only from Mercier have been inappropriately hard on Verne's science. For example, Theodore L. Thomas in a December 1961 *Galaxy* article, "The Watery Wonders of Captain Nemo," excoriated this novel's technical integrity: "The purported science in it is not semi-science or even pseudo-science. It is non-science." Thomas then adduced various gross content errors to support his condemnation; but

"Captain, I can see how sodium meets your needs. And there is plenty of it in the ocean. But you have to produce it, to extract it. How? You could use your batteries to extract it, but, if I'm not mistaken, your apparatus would use up more sodium than you would be producing."

"And so of course I don't use batteries, at least not for the extraction process. I use heat from coal in the earth."

"In the *earth*?" I lingered on that word.

"Let us call it *sea* coal," he responded.

"You mean you mine veins of coal in the floor of the ocean?"

"Some day you'll see how we do it, professor. I ask you to be patient. You'll have enough time for patience. Just remember one thing: I owe all to the ocean. It produces electricity, and electricity gives the *Nautilus* heat, light, movement, and in a word, life."

"But not the air you breathe?"

"Oh, I could manufacture the air I need if I had to, but why should I go to that trouble, since I can surface at will? But if electricity doesn't manufacture my air, at least it works the powerful pumps that store the air under pressure in special tanks. That enables me, if need be, to stay under as long as I have to."

"Captain," I summed it up, "I'm lost in admiration. You are the first to discover what other men must also find out one day: the genuine motive power of electricity."

"I doubt they'll find it out," he said coolly. "In any event, now you at least understand this first use that *I* have made of this precious power. It gives us an even and continuous light that the sun does not. Now, look at this clock. It's electric and runs with a regularity that defies the best chronometers. I have divided it into 24 hours, like the Italian timepieces, because for me there is neither a.m. nor p.m., day nor night, sun nor moon, but only this artificial light that I take with me to the bottom of the sea. See, just now it's ten o'clock in the morning."

"Exactly."

"Here's still another application of electricity: this dial hanging before our eyes indicates the speed of the *Nautilus*. An electric cable connects it to a patent log,[3] and this needle shows our actual progress . . . at this moment, as you can see, we're traveling at a moderate speed of fifteen miles an hour."

---

had he checked Verne's French, he would have discovered that *every one of the cited shortcomings existed only in the English text;* Verne was the innocent victim of slovenly translation.

Hence, Thomas charged that Verne had failed to describe "the storage batteries used aboard the *Nautilus*. There are none," he said flatly. But the French *does* provide a responsible description of these batteries, and it is properly included in our complete translation. To conclude, Verne commentaries that rely solely on the old Victorian translations, without cross-checking the French, are themselves unreliable almost by definition.

Although discredited, Thomas's other criticisms still have some academic currency, and these notes will continue to rebut his assessments as the appropriate occasions arise.

3. A propeller-like device trailed in a ship's wake to measure speed and miles made good.

"Marvelous! I agree, captain, you're right to exploit this source of energy. It's sure to take the place of wind, water, and steam."

"And that's not all, Professor Aronnax," Captain Nemo said as he stood up. "If you'd like to come with me, we can inspect the after part of the *Nautilus*."

So then, I already knew the whole forward part of this submarine boat. I reviewed its subdivisions in my mind going from amidships to the ram on its prow: the dining hall, five meters long, separated from the library by a watertight bulkhead; the library, also five meters long; the grand salon, ten meters long, separated from the captain's cabin by a second watertight bulkhead; the captain's room, five meters; mine, two-and-a-half meters; and lastly, air tanks, extending about seven-and-a-half meters to the stempost. All together, a length of thirty-five meters. The watertight bulkheads were pierced by doors that were shut hermetically with india-rubber seals. This guaranteed the safety of the *Nautilus* in case of a leak in any one section.

I was following Captain Nemo through corridors arranged for easy transit, and we arrived amidships. There I found myself at the base of a deep shaft between two watertight bulkheads. An iron ladder, clamped to a bulkhead, led upward. I asked the captain what the ladder was used for.

"It takes us to our dinghy," he answered.

"What! You have a dinghy?" I exclaimed.

"Of course. An excellent longboat, light and insubmersible, perfect for fishing and sightseeing."

"But when you want to embark in your dinghy, don't you have to take the *Nautilus* to the surface first?"

"Not at all. The dinghy is attached to the topside of the *Nautilus*'s hull. It's set in a cavity made expressly to receive it. It's decked over, completely watertight, held in place with strong bolts. This ladder takes me up to a hatch in the hull of the *Nautilus* that corresponds to a similar hatch in the side of the dinghy. Through that double opening I can enter the dinghy. The crew close up the hatch in the *Nautilus,* I close up the one in the longboat, simply by screwing it into place. I undo the bolts holding the dinghy to the *Nautilus,* and the dinghy shoots to the surface. Then I open the paneling of the deck, kept closed until now, step my mast and hoist my sail—or I set my oars—and I'm off!"

"But how do you get back on board?"

"I don't come back, professor. The *Nautilus* comes after me."

"How do they know when to come?"

"An electric cable connects us. I telegraph my orders to the ship. That's it."

"Indeed." I was intoxicated with all these marvels. "Nothing could be simpler, I guess."

After we passed the well of the staircase that led to the platform, I looked into a cabin two meters long in which Conseil and Ned Land, seemingly enchanted with their food, were devouring it with gusto. Then a door led into the galley, three meters long, located between two large storage lockers.

There electricity, more powerful and obedient than gas, did most of the cooking. Platinum griddles, connected to electric wires, gave off an even heat on the top of the stoves. Electricity also operated a distilling apparatus which, through evaporation, provided excellent drinking water. An adjoining bathroom, comfortably arranged, supplied hot and cold running water.

Next came the crew's quarters, five meters long.[4] But the door was closed, and I couldn't study the accommodations, which might have told me how many men it took to run the *Nautilus*.

Separating the crew's quarters from the engine room was a fourth watertight bulkhead. A door opened and I found myself in the compartment where Captain Nemo—obviously a first-class engineer—had set up his locomotive apparatus.

Evenly lighted, this engine room was at least twenty meters long. It was divided, by function, into two sections: the first enclosed the equipment for generating electricity, the second the mechanism for transmitting this power to the propeller.

I was surprised to sniff a strange odor, absolutely *sui generis,*[5] which pervaded this compartment. Captain Nemo noticed my concern.

"That," he reassured me, "is a gas produced by our use of sodium. It's only a slight inconvenience. Anyhow, we surface every morning to ventilate the ship in the open air."

Meanwhile, I was examining the *Nautilus*'s machinery with impatient curiosity.

"You see," the captain said, "I use Bunsen cells instead of Ruhmkorff cells, which aren't powerful enough.[6] You use fewer Bunsen cells but they're large and strong. Experience shows that they're better. The electricity I generate here is conducted aft. There large electromagnets actuate a special system of levers and gears that in turn transmit the power to the propeller shaft. The propeller has a diameter of six meters, a pitch of seven and a half meters, and can make 120 revolutions per second."

"And that gives you?"

4. Conseil and Ned share a cabin two meters long, and the crewmen a five-meter berthroom. Compare Nemo's quarters, which include a five-meter bedroom, a five-meter private dining room, and the ten-meter salon. Nemo is one of those 19th century liberals who believe in freedom but not necessarily in equality. Aronnax likewise believes in freedom within hierarchy, as is shown by his unquestioning acceptance of the segregation of Ned and Conseil. Verne's output consistently displays these bourgeois values: in *The Mysterious Island* Captain Harding's Negro manservant, Neb, and the captain's dog, Top, are both considered admirable for their total willingness to die for their master. We recall, of course, Conseil's voluntary plunge into the sea, following Aronnax's involuntary one.

5. Latin: "in a class by itself."

6. Robert Wilhelm Bunsen (1811–1899) was professor of chemistry at Heidelberg and inventor of the then-unrivaled Bunsen cell. Heinrich Daniel Ruhmkorff (1803–1877) was a German instrument maker who relocated to Paris, where he attained fame as the inventor of the Ruhmkorff induction coil. Nemo's comparison soon suggests to Aronnax that maybe the captain has developed a new, higher-voltage coil.

The engine room

"A speed of fifty miles an hour."

There was still a mystery here, but I didn't insist on exploring it. How could electricity produce such power?[7] What source of energy was he really tapping? Was it in the exorbitant voltage developed by a new kind of induction coil? Had he worked out a new transmission system, a secret system of levers that could step up the power infinitely?[8] This was hard to understand.

"Captain, I have witnessed the results, and I'm not pressing you to explain them. I've seen the *Nautilus* maneuvering around the *Abraham Lincoln,* and so I have firsthand evidence of its swiftness. But it isn't enough just to move, we must also see where we're going. We must be able to steer to the right, left, up, down. How do you descend to the great depths, where you must resist hundreds of atmospheres of pressure? How do you manage to climb up to the surface again? Finally, how do you keep your ship at whatever level suits you? Am I being indiscreet, posing all these questions?"

He hesitated. "I guess not. After all, you will never leave the *Nautilus*. So come into the salon. That's actually our workroom, and that's where you'll learn everything you want to know about the *Nautilus*."

7. Aronnax is doubtless recalling early experiments in electric propulsion—-which all seemed to lead nowhere. In 1834 Thomas Davenport of Vermont successfully powered a small railroad car on electricity, and in 1838 Aberdeen's Robert Davidson did likewise with a five-ton locomotive. But these developments attracted little commercial interest: they relied on storage batteries that were prohibitively expensive.

8. And sure enough, there is now talk of such a discovery, in which a new set of levers produces great power. Did its inventor meet up with Captain Nemo? *Jules Verne*

THIRTEEN

Some Figures

A MOMENT LATER we were relaxing on a divan in the salon, smoking cigars. The captain placed before me a drawing that gave the floor plan, cross section, and side view of the *Nautilus.* He began his explanation with these words:

"Here, Professor Aronnax, are the several dimensions of the boat that is now transporting you. It's a very long cylinder with conical ends. In shape it very much resembles your cigar, a shape already used in London in several vessels of the same sort. From end to end, the cylinder is exactly 70 meters long, and its beam, at its widest point, is eight meters. And so it isn't altogether constructed on the ten-to-one ratio like your fast ships, but its lines are sufficiently long, and the curves sufficiently gradual, so that the displaced water is easily moved aside and acts as no obstacle.

"Those two dimensions give you, via a simple calculation, the surface area and the volume of the *Nautilus.* The area comprises 1,011.45 square meters, its volume 1,507.2 cubic meters, which is to say that when entirely submerged, it displaces 1,500 cubic meters of water, or weighs 1,500 metric tons.[1]

"When I designed a ship intended for submarine navigation, I wanted it, when floating, to lie nine-tenths below the surface, to stand only one-tenth out of the water. Therefore, under those conditions, it ought to displace only nine-tenths of its volume, or 1,356.48 cubic meters, meaning that it must weigh that same number of metric tons. And so in building the boat I had to be careful not to exceed that weight while following those dimensions.

"Now, the *Nautilus* has two hulls, one interior, one exterior, and they are joined by iron T-bars, which gives the boat terrific rigidity. Because of this cellular arrangement, it has the resistance of a solid block. The plating can't

---

1. In Verne's day, an era without computers and electronic calculators, it was more difficult for a publisher to herd large quantities of numerals accurately into print. And *some figures,* in this chapter of that name, seem to have been misset by the original French compositors. We have rectified these seeming errors, but the changes should be noted: a) "1,507.2 cubic meters" was originally given as 1,500.2; b) soon after, our "displace 1,507.2 metric tons" restores the .2; c) in the full paragraph just above item (b), our "961.52 metric tons" corrects the French 961.62.

yield; it's self-adhering and not dependent on its rivets; and the homogeneity of its construction, due to the perfect union of the materials involved, permits it to defy the most violent of seas.

"These two hulls are manufactured from steel plates whose relative density is 7.8 times that of water.[2] The inner hull has a thickness of no less than five centimeters and weighs 394.96 metric tons. The second envelope, the outer hull, includes a keel 50 centimeters high and 25 wide, which by itself weighs 62 metric tons; add to this the engine, the ballast, the accessories and accommodations, the bulkheads and interior braces, and we have 961.52 metric tons, which, added to 394.96, gives us the desired total of 1,356.48 metric tons. Right?"

"Right," I replied.

"So," the captain continued, "when the *Nautilus* is afloat, she does stand one-tenth out of water. And if I design some ballast tanks equal in capacity to that one tenth, tanks able to hold 150.72 metric tons, and if I fill them with water, the boat would now displace 1,507.2 metric tons—or weigh that much— and would be completely immersed.

"And that's how it works, professor. Those ballast tanks are conveniently located in the lower parts of the *Nautilus*. I open the stopcocks, the tanks fill up, and the ship sinks until it is just flush with the surface."

"I see, captain. But now I come to a serious problem. That you can sink flush with the surface, that I can understand. But lower down, plunging deeper, doesn't your submarine encounter a pressure, and therefore an upward thrust, of one atmosphere for every thirty feet of water,[3] or just about a kilogram per each square centimeter?"

"Right so far, professor."

"Therefore, unless you fill the *Nautilus* completely with water, I don't see how you can force it down to such depths."

"Professor," he responded, "you mustn't confuse statics with dynamics, or you'll be liable to serious error. We spend very little labor in reaching the bottom, for all bodies tend to sink. Now follow my reasoning carefully."

"I'm listening, captain."

"When I wanted to find out the increase in weight required to submerge the *Nautilus,* I had only to calculate the reduction in volume that seawater experiences at greater and greater depths."

"That's clear," I said.

"Now if water is not absolutely incompressible, it at least compresses very little. According to recent studies, this reduction is only .0000436 per atmosphere, or per every thirty feet of depth. For example, to dive 1,000 meters

2. An elementary fact known even to schoolchildren. But Mercier's 1873 English translation blunders ludicrously, saying that the iron's "density is from .7 to .8 that of water." Accordingly, T. L. Thomas's 1961 *Galaxy* article blames Verne for this inanity, but his Victorian translator is the guilty party.

3. Earlier, in I 4, Aronnax used 32 feet for his column; here he rounds the figure out. The English figure of 15 pounds per square inch is another convenient round figure commonly used in general discussion.

down, I must reckon the reduction in volume under a pressure equivalent to that from a 1,000-meter column of water, that is, under a pressure of 100 atmospheres. In this case, the reduction would be .00436. And so, I would have to increase our weight from 1,507.2 metric tons to 1,513.77. An increase of only 6.57 tons."

"That's all?"

"That's all, and it's easy to verify. Now I have supplementary ballast tanks that can ship 100 metric tons of water. You see, I can sink to quite a depth! If I want to rise and lie flush with the surface, I need only pump the supplementary water out, and if I want the *Nautilus* to float one-tenth above the surface, I empty all the ballast tanks all the way."

This line of reasoning, fortified with figures, gave me not much room for argument.

"I accept your calculations, captain—after all, your daily experience confirms them entirely—but I still sense one real difficulty."

"And what is that?"

"When you're at a depth of 1,000 meters, the walls of the *Nautilus* withstand a pressure of 100 atmospheres. If then, at this moment, you want to empty the supplementary ballast tanks to lighten your ship and so rise to the surface, your pumps must overcome that pressure of 100 atmospheres, which is about 100 kilograms per square centimeter. That would require a power—"

"That only my electricity can give me," he said hastily. "I must repeat, professor, the motive power of my engines is almost infinite. My pumps have prodigious power, as you must have noticed when their streams of water burst like a torrent over the *Abraham Lincoln*. Anyhow, I use my supplementary tanks only to reach a depth of 1,500 to 2,000 meters, and that with a view to saving my engines. When I have a mind to visit the ocean depths two or three vertical leagues below the surface, I use slower but equally sure means."

"What are they?"

"That leads me to telling you how the *Nautilus* is maneuvered."

"I'm impatient to hear it."

"To steer this boat to starboard or to port—that is, to turn on a horizontal plane—I use an ordinary wide-bladed rudder attached to the rear of the sternpost and operated by a wheel-and-tackle. But I can also make the *Nautilus* descend or ascend, on a vertical plane, by slanting its two fins. These are attached to the sides at the center of flotation. They can move in any direction and they're worked from inside by means of powerful levers. If the fins are kept parallel with the boat, it moves horizontally. If they are slanted, the *Nautilus* follows the angle of the slant and, under the thrust of the propeller, either descends on a diagonal as steep as I decide, or ascends diagonally. And if I want to rise very rapidly to the surface, I disengage the propeller, and the pressure of the water causes the *Nautilus* to rise vertically, like a balloon filled with hydrogen going up in the air."

"Bravo!" I cried. "But how can your helmsman follow the course you've given him when he's under the waters?"

The *Nautilus*

"The helmsman is stationed in a glass-windowed pilothouse that protrudes above the hull; biconvex lenses are set in the walls."

"Can glass resist such pressures?"

"Perfectly. Crystal can be shattered by a sharp blow, but it nevertheless can resist tremendous water pressure. During experiments with fishing by electric light in the North Sea in 1864, glass plates less than only seven millimeters thick were found capable of resisting a pressure of 16 atmospheres, and they let through strong rays whose warmth was distributed unevenly. Now I use glass windows measuring no less than 21 centimeters at their center—thirty times thicker!"

"I understand. But in order for the helmsman to see, some light must pierce the darkness, so I wonder how, in the midst of the black depths—"

"Behind his pilothouse I have placed a powerful electric reflector. Its rays light up the sea for half a mile ahead."

"Ah! bravo, three bravos, captain. That accounts for the phosphorescence from this so-called narwhale that so puzzled us scientists. But while we're on the subject, may I ask if the *Nautilus*'s collision with the *Scotia,* which caused such a stir, was an accident?"

"Quite accidental, professor. I was navigating two meters beneath the surface when the collision occurred. And I could see it had no serious effect."

"No. But how about your collision with the *Abraham Lincoln?*"

"I'm sorry for what happened to one of the best ships in the gallant American navy. But they attacked me and I had to defend myself. I contented myself, however, with simply putting the frigate out of action. She won't have any trouble getting repaired at the nearest port."

"Ah, commander," I cried out with new conviction, "your *Nautilus* is truly a marvelous ship!"

"Yes, professor," he responded with deep feeling, "I love it as though it were my own flesh and blood. In a conventional ship, facing the dangers of the open sea, you feel hazards everywhere. And sometimes, on the surface, your chief sensation is that there's an abyss beneath you, as the Dutchman Jansen so aptly phrased it. But in the depths, aboard the *Nautilus,* your heart never fails you. No structural weaknesses to worry about, since the double hull has the rigidity of iron. No rigging to wear out in the rolling and pitching of the sea. No sails for the winds to carry away. No boilers to be torn apart by steam. No fear of fire since this ship is built of steel not wood. No running low on coal since electricity is our mechanical agent. No chance collision to worry about, since we're all alone down here in the depths of the sea. No tempests to face, because a few meters below the surface, we can find absolute tranquillity. There you are, sir, the ship *par excellence.* And if it's true that the engineer has more confidence in the craft than the builder has, and the builder more than the captain himself has, then you can understand the total abandon with which I trust my *Nautilus!* For I am its captain, its builder, and its engineer all in one!"

Captain Nemo spoke with captivating eloquence. The fire in his eyes and the passion in his gestures transfigured him. Yes, he loved his ship as a father loves his child!

But one question, perhaps indiscreet, naturally leapt to mind, and I could not resist the temptation to ask it:

"So you're an engineer by profession?"

"Oh yes, I studied in London, Paris, and New York, back in the days when I still frequented dry land."

"But how were you able to build this wonderful ship in total secrecy?"

"Each section, professor, came to me from a different point on the globe and was sent to a cover address. The keel was forged by Creusot, in France; the propeller shaft by Pen and Company in London; the sheet iron plates for the hull by Laird in Liverpool; the propeller itself by Scott in Glasgow. The tanks were manufactured by Cail and Company in Paris; the engine by Krupp in Prussia; the ram by the Motala shops in Sweden; the precision instruments by Hart Brothers in New York, and so on. Each of these firms got my specifications under a different name."

"But," I persisted, "once these sections were manufactured you had to have some place to assemble them . . . ."

"Professor, I set up my workshops on a desert isle in the middle of the ocean. There my workmen—that is to say my gallant comrades whom I have trained and educated—and I myself put together the *Nautilus*. When our work was finished, we burned all evidence of our stay on the isle. I would have blown it up if that had been possible."

"From all this, am I allowed to believe that such a boat costs a fortune?"

"Professor Aronnax, an iron ship costs about 1,125 francs per metric ton. The *Nautilus* displaces 1,500 metric tons. It cost, therefore, 1,687,000 francs, or 2,000,000 francs with all its furnishings, or 4,000,000 or 5,000,000 francs with the art works and other collections it contains."

"Then just one more question, captain."

"Ask it, professor."

"You must be fabulously wealthy."

"Infinitely wealthy, professor, and I could—without missing it—pay off the twelve-billion-franc national debt of France."[4]

I gaped at this bizarre person as he spoke these words. Was he playing on my credulity? The future would let me know.

---

4. Hachette gives twelve billion here, Hetzel ten billion. We flipped a coin and followed Hachette. In any event, this "punch line" had great impact on Verne's readers, because France was considerably hobbled by financial burdens incurred under Emperor Louis Napoleon and by huge indemnities owed Germany after the 1870–71 war.

FOURTEEN

The Black Current

THAT PART OF the earth covered by the seas is calculated at 3,832,558 square myriameters or 147,323,530 square miles—in other words, more than 38,000,000,000 hectares[1] or 94 billion acres. This liquid mass comprises 2,250,000,000 cubic miles, which could form a sphere with a diameter of sixty leagues, which would weigh three quintillion metric tons. To appreciate that figure, we should remember that a quintillion is to a billion what a billion is to one, or in other words, there are as many billions in a quintillion as there are ones in a billion! And this mass—this 3,000,000,000,000,000,000 tons of fluid—almost equals all the water discharged by all the world's rivers in the past 40,000 years!

During bygone geological epochs, the period of fire gave way to the period of water. At first, ocean prevailed everywhere.[2] But by degrees, during the Silurian period, the tops of mountains began to appear, islands emerged, disappeared in partial floods, rose again, joined to form continents, till at length the earth became geographically arranged as we know it now. The solid had wrested from the liquid 37,657,000 square miles, that is, 12,916,000,000 hectares or more than 32 billion acres.

The shape of the continents makes it convenient to divide the waters into five major areas: the frozen Arctic Ocean, the frozen Antarctic Ocean, the Indian Ocean, the Atlantic Ocean, and the Pacific Ocean.

The Pacific extends north to south between the two polar circles, and east to west between the Americas and Asia, over 145 degrees of longitude. It is the most tranquil of the oceans;[3] its currents are broad and slow, its tides middling,

---

1. The Hetzel edition's compositors seem to have misset this as *trente-huit millions d'hectares;* it should read *milliards d'hectares.* (*Note:* The Hachette edition omits the citation altogether.)

2. Aronnax here espouses the theory of German geologist A. G. Werner (1750–1817), who maintained that originally there was a universal ocean that held in solution the mineral matter for nearly all rocks. Werner's followers were known as Neptunists. Geologists in the opposing school were known as Vulcanists or Plutonists because they recognized the role of subterranean heat in forming the earth's crust.

3. It was because of its serene, tranquil nature that the Pacific was so named; *pacific* means peaceful.

its rain plentiful. And this was the first ocean that I was destined to explore under these strange auspices.

"Professor," Captain Nemo said, "if you would like to come along, we can take our bearings and fix the starting point of our voyage. It's fifteen minutes before noon. Time to surface."

He pressed an electric bell three times. The pumps began to expel water from the ballast tanks. The needle of the pressure gauge indicated, through the decreasing pressures, the rising of the *Nautilus*. Then it stopped.

"We're at the surface," he said.

I walked to the central companionway, which led up to the platform, climbed the iron steps, passed through the open hatches, and found myself topside.

The platform emerged only 80 centimeters or so, less than three feet, out of water. The bow and stern of the *Nautilus* formed that spindle shape that properly caused it to be compared to a long cigar. I noticed that its iron plates, slightly overlapping each other, resembled the scales covering the bodies of large terrestrial reptiles. This proved to me how natural it was that, in spite of all the intense scrutiny through telescopes, this boat had been viewed as a marine animal.

Near the middle of the platform the dinghy was half buried in the hull, forming a slight bulge. Fore and aft rose two cupolas, of medium height, partly enclosed in thick biconvex glass: one was for the steersman, the other held the brilliant electric beacon that lighted his way.

The sea was splendid, the sky pure. Our long aquatic vehicle could scarcely feel the broad undulations of the Pacific. A mild eastern breeze rippled the waters. The horizon was free of mist, ideally visible for our purposes.

There was nothing in sight. Not a reef, not an isle. No more *Abraham Lincoln*. A vast desert.

Sextant in hand, Captain Nemo was set to take the altitude of the sun, which would give him our latitude. He waited for a few moments until its disk touched the horizon. As he shot the sun he moved not a muscle. The sextant could not have been more stabilized in a hand of marble.

"Twelve noon, professor," he said. "If you're ready. . . ."

I cast one last look over the sea, slightly yellowish as it neared the coast of Japan,[4] and we descended to the salon.

There the captain determined our position, using a chronometer to calculate his longitude and checking that against his previous observations of hour angles.

"Professor, we are in longitude 137° 15′ west. . . ."

"Of which meridian?" I asked too eagerly, hoping his answer would give me a clue to his nationality.

---

4. The *Nautilus* is east of the Yellow Sea, which is named for its sediment-laden waters, the muddy discharge of the great rivers of China.

Noon observations

"Sir, I have chronometers set to the meridians of Paris, Greenwich, and Washington. But to honor you, I am using Paris."

I bowed. I had learned nothing. He went on:

"We're in longitude 137° 15′ west of the Paris meridian,[5] and in latitude 30° 7′ north, which is to say, about 300 miles off the Japanese coast. So, it's at noon on November 8 that we begin our exploration of the submarine world."

"May God preserve us," I said.

"And now, professor, I leave you to your studies. I've set our course east northeast at a depth of 50 meters. Here are some large-scale maps on which you can follow our course. The salon is at your disposal, and with your consent I will withdraw."

Captain Nemo bowed and I remained alone with my thoughts, all focused on the commander of the *Nautilus*.

Would I ever be able to discover the nationality of this strange person who boasted that he had none? What had provoked his hatred for humanity, a hatred that maybe was in search of some awful vengeance? Was he one of those neglected savants, one of those "frustrated geniuses," as Conseil had put it, a modern Galileo, or one of those scientists like the American Maury, whose career had been shattered by a political upheaval?[6] I couldn't say yet. As for me, chance had placed me aboard his ship, my fate was in his hands, he had received me hospitably but coldly. He had never shaken hands with me when I extended mine, and he had never extended his.

For an entire hour I was sunk in these reflections, hoping to pierce this mystery that had so intrigued me. Then my gaze fell on the vast map spread out on the table, and I put my finger on the very spot where our just determined latitude and longitude crossed.

Like the land, the sea has its rivers.[7] These are unique currents known by their temperature and their color; the most remarkable of these is called the

5. Except where he expressly refers to the meridian of Greenwich, Verne's longitude citations appear to use the Paris meridian throughout. In this clever little passage, Verne not only gives his readers their rightful chance to follow the voyagers on the map, but he permits Nemo and Aronnax to indulge in some nice psychological fencing, as the latter gropes for clues to Nemo's nationality.

6. Maury had never suffered the kind of overt persecution experienced by Galileo Galilei (1564–1642), who was forced by the religious authorities to retract his teachings that the sun (not the earth) was the center of our universe; Galileo spent his last years under house arrest. As for Maury, Aronnax sees the Civil War as blighting the American's career, but that might be a simplification. Maury resigned his position at the U.S. Navy's depot of charts and instruments in order to serve the Confederacy, for whom he invented an electric torpedo (harbor mine) that was to wreak havoc on Union warships. But whether working for the North or the South, Maury suffered the petty miseries that bureaucracies provide for the genius, and he earned neither wealth nor notable advancement. But the last five years of his life were relatively satisfying: he settled down as professor of meteorology at the Virginia Military Institute–and simultaneously saw his textbooks widely adopted in American schools.

7. Here Aronnax echoes a famous sentence in Maury's *Physical Geography of the Sea*. A superb phrasemaker, Maury opens his chapter on the Gulf Stream thus: "There is a river in the ocean . . ."

The Black

Current

ॐ

93

Gulf Stream. Science has mapped out the paths of five principal currents: one in the North Atlantic, another in the South Atlantic, a third in the North Pacific, a fourth in the South Pacific, and the fifth in the southern Indian Ocean. Probably at one time there was a sixth current in the northern Indian Ocean, when the Caspian and Aral seas were joined with the great Asian lakes to form one single uniform expanse of water.

Now where my finger rested on the map one of these oceangoing rivers was rolling by, the Kuroshio, as the Japanese call it, the Black Current.[8] It starts in the Bay of Bengal where it is heated by the perpendicular rays of the tropical sun, crosses the Strait of Malacca, flows along the Asian coasts, curves into the North Pacific up to the Aleutian Islands, carrying along with it the trunks of camphor trees and other indigenous products, and cutting a clear path through the sea with the pure indigo of its warm waters. This was the current the *Nautilus* would cross. I followed it with my eyes on the map, I saw it lose itself in the vast Pacific, and I felt I was being swept along with it—when Ned Land and Conseil appeared at the door of the salon.

My gallant companions seemed petrified at the sight of the wonders on display.

"Where are we?" cried the Canadian. "Where? In the Quebec Museum?"

"With master's permission," Conseil ventured, "in the Sommerard Palace."[9]

"My friends"—I motioned them to come in—"you're not in Canada, not in France, but on board the *Nautilus,* 50 meters below the surface."

"If master says so, it must be so," Conseil replied, "but frankly, this room is enough to astonish even a Fleming like me."

"Be astonished, Conseil, and feast your eyes. For a classifier of your caliber, there's plenty here to keep you busy for a long time."

There was no need to urge him on. Leaning over the glass cases, he was already murmuring, in the language of naturalists, "Class Gastropoda, family Buccinoidea, genus cowry, species *Cypraea madagascariensis,*" and so on.

Meanwhile Ned, who couldn't care less about conchology, queried me about my conversation with Captain Nemo. Had I found out who he was, where he came from, where he was going, toward what depths he was taking us? In short, a thousand questions I had no time to answer.

I told him all I knew, which meant all I didn't know, and asked him whether he had seen or heard anything himself.

"Nothing seen, nothing heard," the Canadian reported. "Not even a sign of the crew. You don't imagine that they are run by electricity too, do you?"

8. The Kuroshio Current is also known today as the Japan Current. It (allegedly) warms southeastern Japan just as the Gulf Stream (allegedly) warms Britain. We shall come back to that "alleged" warming in II 19.

9. Alexandre du Sommerard (1779–1842) was a French archaeologist specializing in the ancient monuments of France and Italy. His collections were exhibited at the Sommerard Palace and the Hôtel de Cluny in Paris.

"Electric sailors?"[10]

"Ye gods, I'm ready to think so. But professor," asked Ned, still obsessed with certain ideas, "can you tell me how many men there are on board? Ten, twenty, fifty, a hundred?"

"I have no way of knowing, Mr. Land. But believe me, for the time being it's better to give up any idea of seizing control of the *Nautilus,* or even of escaping. This craft is a masterpiece of modern technology, and I'd be sorry not to have seen it. Many people would accept the circumstances forced on us, just to be able to see such wonders. So let's be calm and try to appreciate what we see."

"See!" cried the harpooner. "But we can't see anything, we'll never see a thing from this iron prison. We're traveling and navigating blindly—"

Ned Land had no sooner uttered this latest plaint than the room was plunged into total darkness. The lights in the ceiling had gone out so suddenly that my eyes ached, just as if we had had the opposite experience of going from deep darkness to brilliant light.

We remained quiet, not moving, not knowing what surprise was in store for us, pleasant or unpleasant. I could hear a sliding noise, as though the side walls were moving.

"It's the end of the end," said Ned Land.

"Order Hydromedusa," Conseil was murmuring.

Suddenly, through two oblong openings, light broke into each side of the salon. The liquid medium outside was vividly lit up by the electric beacon atop the *Nautilus.* Two glass panels separated us from the sea. At first I trembled at the thought that those fragile partitions could break, but copper frames held them in place with seemingly infinite strength.

The sea world was distinctly visible for a mile all around the *Nautilus.* What a sight! What pen could describe it? Who could paint the effects of light penetrating these transparent layers of water and growing dimmer as it reached the upper and lower strata?

The clarity of seawater is often remarked upon. It is more diaphanous than spring water. The mineral and organic substances it holds in suspension actually increase its transparency. In certain parts of the ocean, for example in the West Indies, a sandy bottom 145 meters down can be seen from the surface with amazing clarity, and the sun's rays can reach down as far as 300 meters. But here the *Nautilus* was originating its own light in the very depths of the sea. It was no longer luminous water, it was liquid light.

If we accept the hypothesis of Ehrenberg[11] that the submarine depths are illuminated by phosphorescent organisms, then we must conclude that Nature has reserved one of her most prodigious spectacles for inhabitants of the seas.

10. Ned's notion that Nemo's crew seem to be run by electricity is an excellent commentary on the sailors' robotlike impassivity.

11. The German biologist Christian Gottfried Ehrenberg (1795–1876) was internationally honored for his work on microorganisms.

And I was able to judge it myself by the thousand ways the light played before my eyes. On each side I had a window opening over these unknown abysses. The darkness of the salon showed to advantage the brightness outside, and we could look out as if this clear glass were the window of an immense aquarium.

The *Nautilus* seemed to be standing still because there was nothing nearby to serve as a point of reference.[12] But every once in a while, the water, parted by the ship's ram, would swirl by in swift eddies and we could see we were moving at great speed.

Astonished, we leaned against the window and none of us broke that silence of stupefaction until Conseil said:

"You wanted to see something, friend Ned—and now there's something to see!"

"Curious!" muttered the Canadian. "Curious!" Forgetting his anger and his plans to escape, he seemed to yield to some irresistible attraction. "A man would come farther than this to admire such a sight."

"Ah!" I cried out. "Now I understand this man's mode of living. He's found a separate world for himself, and it reserves its most astonishing wonders for him alone."

"But the fish!" the Canadian remarked. "I don't see any fish!"

"What do you care," Conseil teased. "You couldn't identify them anyhow."

"Me? I'm a fisherman!" Ned Land protested.

And so began a strange argument between the two friends, since they were both familiar with fish but in entirely different ways.

All the world knows that fish constitute the fourth and last class of the vertebrate branch. They are properly defined as "vertebrates with a double circulatory system and cold blood, breathing through gills and destined to live only in water." There are two distinct series: bony fish, whose spinal column is made of bony vertebrae, and cartilaginous fish, whose spine is made of cartilaginous vertebrae.

Now Ned was probably aware of this gross distinction, but Conseil could carry the classification down to the finest detail. And since Ned was now his friend, Conseil could not appear to be less informed than Ned. And so he said:

"Ned, you're a killer of fish, a professional. You've caught great numbers of these fascinating creatures. But I bet you don't know how to classify them."

"I sure can," the harpooner responded in all seriousness. "There are two classes: fish we eat and fish we don't eat."

"That's how a glutton classifies fish. But could you tell me the essential differences between bony fish and cartilaginous fish?"

"Maybe, Conseil."

"And the subdivisions of those two main classes?"

"Well now, you see—"

---

12. Here Verne seems to have a fine (pre-Einstein) appreciation of relativity.

"Well now, listen and concentrate! Bony fish are subdivided into six orders. First, the acanthopterygians. Their upper jaw is fully formed and free-moving, their gills are shaped like a comb. This order includes fifteen families, that is to say, three-quarters of all known fish. Type: the common-perch."

"Pretty good eating," Ned pronounced.

"Second," Conseil went on, "are the abdominals. Their pelvic fins hang under the abdomen, behind the pectorals, but are not attached to the shoulder bone. This order is divided into five families, including most of the freshwater fish. Types: carp and pike."

"Pee-yew!" Ned said scornfully. "Freshwater types!"

"Third," Conseil continued, "the subbrachians. Their pelvic fins are beneath the pectorals and attached to the shoulder bone. There are four families in this order. Types: plaice, dab, turbot, brill, sole, etc."

"Superb! Superb!" cried the harpooner, still classifying fish according to their culinary value.

"Fourth," Conseil persisted unabashed, "the apods. They have elongated bodies and no pelvic fins. They're covered with thick—often sticky—skin. There's only one family in this order. Types: the common eel and the electric eel."

"Mediocre," Ned grumbled, "mediocre."

"Fifth, the lophobranchians. Their jaws are fully formed and free-moving; their gills consist of little tufts arranged in pairs along their branchial arches. Again, only one family. Types: sea horses and dragonfish."

"Awful, just plain awful."

"Sixth and last," Conseil said, "the plectognaths. Their maxillary bone is attached to the side of the intermaxillary that forms the jaw, and their post-temporal bone is united with the skull, making the jaw immovable. They have no true pelvic fins. Two families. Types: puffers and moonfish."

"They're an insult to the pot they're cooked in."

"Have you understood so far?" Conseil asked in his most didactic manner.

"Not at all, friend Conseil. But go right on, it sounds impressive."

And the imperturbable Conseil did go right on. "There are only three orders of cartilaginous fish."

"Good news."

"First, the cyclostomes. Their jaws are welded into a flexible ring. Their gills consist of a large number of holes. This order consists of only one family. Type: the lamprey."

"You must learn to like them."

"Second, the selacians. Their gills are like the cyclostomes, but they have free-moving lower jaws. This order is the most important in its class and comprises two families. Types: the ray and the shark."

"What!" cried Ned Land. "Rays and man-eating sharks in the same order! Well, friend *Conseil,* on behalf of the rays, I don't *counsel* you to put them in the same tank!"

"Third," Conseil responded, "the sturionians. Their gills have the usual single opening with a gill-cover. There are four genera in this order. Type: the sturgeon."

"Ah, friend Conseil, you saved the best for last. It is the last, I hope?"

"Yes, my gallant Ned. But when you have mastered what I have already recited, you still know very little. For these families are subdivided into genera, subgenera, species, varieties—"

"It's good you know all that, Conseil," Ned exclaimed, leaning against the glass panel. "Because here come some of your varieties!"

"Fish!" Conseil was amazed. "Like in the aquarium."

"No," I stepped in. "An aquarium is like a cage, and those fish are as free as birds in the air."

"What are you waiting for, Conseil?" Ned said. "Tell us their names!"

"Me?" Conseil replied. "I can't. That's the professor's job."

And that was the situation. Conseil was a fanatic classifier but not a working naturalist, and I don't think he could have distinguished a tuna from a bonito. And Ned was the opposite: he could identify each fish but could not classify them scientifically.

"A triggerfish," I remarked.

"A Chinese triggerfish," Ned added.

"Genus *Balistes,* family Scleroderma, order Plectognatha," Conseil murmured.

No doubt about it, Ned and Conseil together could make one distinguished naturalist.

The Canadian was not mistaken. Frolicking around the *Nautilus* was a school of triggerfish, with flat bodies, grainy hides, armed with stings on their dorsal fins, their four rows of sharp quills quivering on both sides of their tails. Their skin was admirable: grey on top, white on the bottom, with touches of gold scintillating in the somber waters. And among the triggerfish some rays were undulating like sheets in the wind. I was delighted by a Chinese ray, yellow on top, pink underneath, with three stings behind his eye. This is a rare species whose actual existence was still in doubt in Lacépède's day, since he had never seen one except in an album of Japanese drawings.

For two hours, an entire aquatic army escorted the *Nautilus.* As they leaped and frolicked, vying with each other in beauty, brightness, and speed, I could distinguish some green wrasse; some bewhiskered mullet, marked with a double line of black; some round-tailed gobies from the genus *Eleotris,* white with violet spots on the back; some Japanese specimens of the genus *Scomber,* a beautiful mackerel of those seas with a blue body and silvery head; some brilliant azure goldfish, whose name alone describes them; varieties of porgy or gilthead: some banded with variegated fins of blue and yellow; others with horizontal heraldic bars, with a black strip around the caudal area; others boasting color zones and elegantly corseted with six waistbands; some trumpetfish with fluty beaks, genuine seafaring woodcocks, specimens of which attain a meter in length; some Japanese salamanders; some moray eels from the

An aquatic army

genus *Echidna,* serpents six feet long, with small but keen eyes and a big mouth bristling with teeth; and many other species.

Our admiration was rekindled every moment. Exclamations followed exclamations. Ned named the fish, Conseil classified them, and I was in ecstasies over the vivacity of their movements and the beauty of their forms. Never had it been given to me to surprise these creatures, alive and at liberty, in their natural element. I cannot mention all the varieties that streaked past my dazzled eyes, all the collections of China and Japan. More numerous than the birds of the air, they raced up to us, no doubt attracted by the brilliance of our electric beacon.

Suddenly there was daylight in the salon, the sheet-iron panels slid shut, and the enchanting vision vanished. But for a long time I dreamt on until my eyes fell on the instruments hanging on the partition. The compass still showed our course as east-northeast,[13] the pressure gauge indicated a pressure of five atmospheres, equivalent to a depth of 50 meters, and the electric log showed our speed to be 15 miles an hour. I expected Captain Nemo but he didn't appear. The clock marked the hour of five.

Ned Land and Conseil returned to their cabin and I retired to mine. There I found my dinner awaiting me. It consisted of turtle soup made from the daintiest hawksbill; a red mullet with white, slightly flaky flesh; its liver, prepared separately, was delicious; and some fillets from the imperial angelfish, whose taste I found superior to salmon.

I spent the evening reading, writing, meditating. As weariness overpowered me I stretched out on my eelgrass bed and slept profoundly, while the *Nautilus* glided through the rapid waters of the Black Current.

13. The French gives "north-northeast," a minor verbal discrepancy that mildly conflicts with Verne's map and with comments in the respective first parts of this chapter and the chapter immediately following. Most likely this was an editorial/authorial oversight, and we have regularized the citation to match the others.

FIFTEEN

A Letter of Invitation

THE NEXT DAY, November 9, I got up only after a long sleep of twelve hours. Conseil came, as was his custom, to hear "how master passed the night" and to offer his services. He had left his friend the Canadian sleeping like someone who would spend his entire life sleeping.

I let the gallant lad chatter on as he pleased, without giving much thought to answering him. I was preoccupied with the absence of Captain Nemo the evening before, and I hoped to see him today.

Quickly I got into my clothes, which were all woven from byssus. Several times Conseil had asked for details about this fabric. I told him it was made from the glossy, silken filaments with which the fan mussel—a type of mollusk quite common along Mediterranean shores—attaches itself to the rocks. In olden days, people wove these silken filaments into a soft, warm cloth from which they made beautiful gloves and stockings. And so the crew of the *Nautilus* could clothe themselves at little cost. For they had ready access to byssus and did not have to depend on sheep, silkworms, or cotton plants, all terrestrial products.

As soon as I was dressed I went into the grand salon, only to find it deserted.

For a while I studied the conchological treasures displayed in the glass cases. Then I went through the vast albums of rare marine plants which, although they had been pressed and dried out, still retained their admirable colors. Among these precious hydrophytes, I especially studied various seaweeds: some *Cladostephus verticillatus,* some peacock's tails, some caulerpa shaped like fig leaves, some graniferous beauty bushes, some delicate scarlet-tinted rosetangle, some fan-shaped sea colander, and some mermaid's cups, which look like the tops of squat mushrooms and which for a long time were classified as zoophytes—in short, a perfect series of algae.

The whole day passed without my being honored by a visit from Captain Nemo. The panels never opened. I thought maybe they did not want us to tire of these wonders.

Our course was still east-northeast, our speed 12 miles an hour, our depth varying between 50 and 60 meters.

Next day, November 10, the same isolation, the same solitude. I saw none of the ship's personnel. Ned and Conseil, who spent the better part of the day with me, were also astonished by the captain's inexplicable absence. Was that extraordinary person ill? Had he changed his mind about us?

But after all, as Conseil pointed out, we enjoyed the freedom of the ship and were served good food in abundance. Our host was keeping his part of the bargain. We could not complain, and moreover the very uniqueness of our situation promised such wonderful compensations for us that we had no right to reproach him.

On that day, I started my diary of our adventures, which has made it easy to recount them with detailed accuracy. And there was one peculiar thing about this diary: it was written on paper made from eelgrass.[1]

Early on the morning of November 11, fresh air spread through the ship, telling me we had surfaced to renew our oxygen supply. I walked to the central companionway and mounted to the platform.

It was six o'clock. The weather was cloudy, the sea grey but calm. Scarcely a billow. I hoped to see Captain Nemo—would he come up? I saw no one but the steersman in his glass-windowed cupola. Seated on the ledge provided by the hull of the dinghy, I inhaled the salty breeze with great delight.

Gradually the mist was dissipated by the sun's rays as it rose from behind the eastern horizon. Under its gaze, the sea flamed like a trail of gunpowder. The clouds, scattered on high, were tinted with beautiful, vivid colors, and numerous "ladyfingers" warned of daylong winds.[2] But what was wind to the *Nautilus*, which no tempest could intimidate!

I was admiring this joyous sunrise, so gay and so lifegiving, when I heard steps mounting to the platform. I was prepared to salute Captain Nemo, but it was his first mate, whom I had already seen on the captain's first visit. He advanced over the platform without seeming to see me. With a powerful telescope he scrutinized the horizon in every direction. When his examination was over, he walked to the hatch and pronounced these words (I have remembered them because every morning, under the same conditions, they were repeated):

"Nautron respoc lorni virch."

What this phrase meant I could not say.[3]

1. A marine plant with long, narrow leaves that is found in abundance along the North Atlantic coast. Also called grass wrack.

2. "Ladyfingers" are small, thin, white clouds with serrated edges. *Jules Verne*

3. But Aronnax will make an excellent (and probably accurate) guess at the start of I 18. Meanwhile he is still too bedazzled by the many new circumstances to analyze this phrase right off. But he has the necessary tools: a knowledge of English, German, and Latin, plus his native French, and an interest in etymology. When the phrase's meaning finally "occurs" to him three chapters from now, Aronnax may have sensed that meaning in the following manner.

Nautron respoc lorni virch, he hears. *Nautron* should readily suggest the French *nautique* and its English cognate, *nautical*, which promptly suggests the *sea* or *ships*. *Respoc* is tougher going, but the classical prefix *re-*, meaning *back* or *again*, might suggest to Aronnax that this language is in the Indo-European family, and he might then recall *spoko-*, an ancient form of the root *spec-*, to observe, found in French words like *spectateur* or the English *inspect*. Finally, *lorni* echoes English words like *lorn*, bereft of, or *forlorn*, deserted, and German words like *verloren*, lost.

These words pronounced, the first mate returned below. I thought the *Nautilus* was about to dive, so I regained the hatch and returned through the gangways to my cabin.

In this way five days slipped by with no change in our situation. Each morning I mounted to the platform, heard the same man pronounce the same phrase, but never saw Captain Nemo.

I had made up my mind that I would never see him again when, on November 16, returning to my cabin with Ned and Conseil, I found on my table a note addressed to me.

I opened it impatiently. It was written in script that was clear and neat but a bit "gothic," its characters suggesting the German style. It was couched in these terms:

Professor Aronnax
On board the *Nautilus*

November 16, 1867

Captain Nemo invites Professor Aronnax to a hunting party tomorrow morning in his Crespo Island forests. He hopes nothing prevents the professor from accepting, and he looks forward with pleasure to the professor's companions joining him.

The commander of the *Nautilus,*
Captain Nemo

"A hunting party!" Ned exclaimed.

"In his forests on Crespo Island," Conseil added.

"Does that mean he sometimes goes ashore?" Ned Land surmised.

"That's what it seems to mean," I said as I reread the letter.

"Well then, we must accept," said the Canadian. "And once on dry land, we'll figure out what to do next. Anyhow, I won't be sorry to eat some fresh venison."

Without trying to reconcile the contradiction between Captain Nemo's professed aversion to continents and islands and this invitation to hunt in *his* forest, I contented myself with saying:

"Let's first see where this Crespo Island is."

Consulting the map, I found in latitude 32° 40′ north and longitude 167° 50′ west a small island: It had been visited in 1801 by Captain Crespo and it was marked on old Spanish maps as Rocca de la Plata, "Silver Rock." So we were then about 1,800 miles from our point of departure, and the *Nautilus,* changing course somewhat, was bringing us back toward the southeast.

So, when he puts it all together, Aronnax will sense that the phrase means something like *The vista is devoid of ships,* or *There is nothing in sight.*

I pointed out to my companions this little stray rock in the middle of the North Pacific.

"If Captain Nemo does occasionally go on dry land," I said, "at least he chooses desert islands!"

Ned Land shook his head without answering, and he and Conseil left me. After my supper, served by the mute and impassive steward, I went to bed, not without some anxiety.

On awakening on the morning of November 17, I could feel that the *Nautilus* lay perfectly still. I dressed hurriedly and entered the grand salon.

Captain Nemo was there waiting for me. He rose, bowed, and asked if it was convenient for me to go with him. Since he made no reference at all to his eight-day absence, I said nothing about it either, saying simply that my companions and I were ready to accompany him.

"But captain, may I indulge in one question?"

"Indulge yourself, professor, and if I'm able to answer, I'll answer."

"Well, captain, how is it that after severing all ties with the land, you can still own forests on Crespo Island?"

"Professor," he replied, "the forests I possess depend on the sun for neither light nor heat. Neither lions nor tigers nor panthers nor any other quadrupeds frequent my forests. They're known only to me, they grow only for me. In short, they are not terrestrial forests, they are submarine forests."

"Submarine forests!" I exclaimed.

"Yes, professor."

"And you propose to take me there."

"Exactly."

"On foot?"

"And without getting your feet wet."

"While hunting?"

"While hunting."

"Gun in hand?"

"Gun in hand."

I stared at the commander of the *Nautilus* in a way that must have seemed quite unflattering.

"Surely," I thought, "he's mentally ill. He's had a bad attack that's lasted eight days and he's not over it yet. Pity! I liked him better eccentric than insane."

My apprehension must have shown clearly on my face, but Captain Nemo remained content with inviting me to follow him, and I did, prepared for almost anything.

We entered the dining room, where we found breakfast served.

"Professor Aronnax," he said, "pray share my breakfast without ceremony. We'll chat as we eat. For though I promised you a walk in my forest, I didn't say we'd find a restaurant there. So eat breakfast like a man who probably will eat dinner very late today."

I did honor to the breakfast. It consisted of various fish and slices of sea cucumbers, those superb zoophytes, all spiced with very tasty seaweeds, like *Porphyra laciniata* and *Laurencia primafetida*. Our drink consisted of clear water to which, following the captain's example, I added some drops of a fermented liquor extracted by the Kamchatka process from the seaweed known as *Rhodymenia palmata*. At first Captain Nemo ate without speaking a word, but at last he said:

"Professor, when I invited you to hunt with me in my Crespo forests, you thought I was contradicting myself. When I made it clear that they are *submarine* forests, you thought I was out of my mind. Professor, never pass judgment so lightly on any man."

"But captain, please believe me—"

"Be kind enough to listen, and then decide whether you have any reason to accuse me of contradiction or madness."

"I'm listening."

"You know as well as I do, professor, that a human being can live under water if he carries a sufficient supply of breathable air. When a man works under water, he wears a waterproof suit and a metal helmet and receives air from above by means of force pumps and flow regulators."

"That's the standard diving suit," I agreed.

"Right, but under those conditions the workman isn't free to go very far. He's attached to the pump that sends him air through an india-rubber hose, but it's like a chain that binds him to one small area, and if we were thus bound to the *Nautilus,* we couldn't go far either."

"And how do you get free?"

"We use the Rouquayrol-Denayrouze apparatus, invented by two of your compatriots, but which I have perfected for our special use, permitting you to venture into these new physiological conditions without suffering any organic disorders.4 It consists of a tank made of thick iron in which I store air under a

4. Benoit Rouquayrol, mining engineer, and Auguste Denayrouze, naval officer, were able to design their diving equipment only after scientists understood the problem of equalizing the pressure. As a diver descends, the water pressure on his chest increases and he can't expand his chest if his lungs are filled with air at normal pressure. The solution was to fill the diver's lungs with compressed air that equals the pressure of the surrounding water. Rouquayrol and Denayrouze equipped their tank with a "demand valve" (or "bellows mechanism," in Nemo's phrase) that automatically supplies air at the proper pressure for the particular depth reached by the diver.

One of Nemo's improvements is that he is able to charge his tank with air so highly compressed that the diver need not return to the surface for several hours. Another modification Nemo has made is that he exchanges the Rouquayrol-Denayrouze "mask" for "a copper sphere," a version of the closed helmet developed by Auguste Siebe around 1840. Siebe's contrivance came equipped with check valves that made it unnecessary for the diver to use his tongue to control incoming and outgoing air. A careful scrutiny of the French makes it apparent that Nemo used exactly this contrivance, but a particularly insidious translating error by the Victorian Louis Mercier not only misled modern commentators but temporarily bamboozled your present translators as well. See the very next note, as well as note 1 in I 17.

pressure of 50 atmospheres. This tank is strapped on your back like a soldier's pack. The upper part of the tank is a compartment from which the air, regulated by a bellows mechanism, can be released only at the proper pressure. In the Rouquayrol apparatus that has been in use,[5] two india-rubber hoses go from that upper compartment to a mask that covers the man's nose and mouth; one hose is for breathing in fresh air, the other for exhaling stale air; the tongue closes off one or the other according to the man's needs. But for myself, since I have to move around under considerable pressure on the sea floor, the mask would not suffice. I have to protect my head inside a copper sphere, such as divers use, and so I fix those two hoses, for inhaling and exhaling, into that sphere."

"Splendid, captain. But what do you do about the fact that your air supply is used up quickly? Once it drops down to 15 percent oxygen, it's no longer good for breathing."

"That's right, but as I've said, Professor Aronnax, the *Nautilus*'s pumps enable me to store air under considerable pressure; I can put enough breathable air in the tanks of my diving apparatus to last nine or ten hours."

"Then I can have no further objections," I said. "But I am curious about one thing. How can you light your way at the bottom of the sea?"

"With the Ruhmkorff apparatus, professor. While the breathing equipment is carried on the back, the Ruhmkorff is attached to the belt. It's composed of a Bunsen battery that I activate not with potassium dichromate but with sodium. An induction coil collects the electricity that is produced and conducts it to a special lantern. In this lantern, there is a glass tube in the form of a spiral that contains only a residue of carbon dioxide. When the apparatus is turned on, this gas becomes luminous and gives off a continuous whitish light. Thus equipped, I can breathe and can see perfectly well."

"Captain Nemo, you meet all my objections with such convincing answers that I hardly dare have any more doubts. But if I'm forced to believe in your Rouquayrol and Ruhmkorff devices, I still have some reservations about the gun I'm going to carry."

"Well, it's not a gun that uses powder," the captain responded.

"Then it's an air gun?"

"Of course. How could I manufacture gunpowder on board, without either saltpeter, sulfur, or charcoal?"

"Even so," I said, "to fire under water, in a medium 855 times denser than air, you'd have to overcome terrific resistance."

5. Verne's French reads *Dans l'appareil Rouquayrol, tel qu'il est employé.* Unfortunately, Louis Mercier's 1873 standard translation renders this innocuous phrase as "In the Rouquayrol apparatus such as *we* use." This is a subtle but far-reaching error that leads the reader to believe that Nemo's diving helmet required tongue control of the air flow. This misperception will create a thundering discrepancy in I 17, once again exposing the innocent Verne to modern critical sneers—and causing a momentary loss of faith even in the devoted bosoms of your present translators. To be concluded.

A waterproof suit

"That would be no problem. There are certain guns—modeled after Fulton's and perfected by the Englishmen Philippe, Coles, and Burley, by the Frenchman Furcy, and by the Italian Landi—that have a device for closing out the water, thus making it possible to fire under such conditions. But I repeat to you, having no gunpowder, I use instead compressed air, which the *Nautilus*'s pumps supply in great abundance."

"But the air in an air gun must be used up fast."

"Yes, but don't I carry my Rouquayrol tank, which can recharge my gun as needed? All I had to do was add an *ad hoc* spigot.[6] But you'll see for yourself, professor, on these underwater hunting trips we don't use much air or many bullets."

"But it seems to me that in this semi-darkness, surrounded by liquid so much denser than air, shots wouldn't carry far and wouldn't do much damage."

"On the contrary, professor, with this gun every shot proves fatal, and as soon as an animal is hit, or even just touched, it drops as if hit by lightning."

"How come?"

"Because this gun doesn't shoot ordinary bullets, it shoots little glass capsules invented by the Austrian chemist Leinebroch. And I have a large supply.[7] These glass capsules are sheathed in steel and weighted with lead. They are veritable little Leyden jars charged with high-voltage electricity. At the slightest impact they discharge, and the animal, no matter how large or strong, falls dead. Furthermore, these capsules are no bigger than number 4 shot, and the chamber of any ordinary gun could hold ten of them."

"There's nothing left for me to say except"—I got up from the table—"that I'll shoulder my gun and where you go, I shall go."

Captain Nemo led me toward the stern. Passing Ned and Conseil's cabin, I summoned them and they immediately followed us.

We came to a cell near the engine room, where we were to put on our underwater walking suits.

6. Latin: ad hoc, here, means "tailor-made."

7. A supply that lasts the captain well into this book's sequel, *The Mysterious Island*. There we learn how those Leinebroch bullets affect a hostile human target. When pirates threaten the benign castaways on the island, Nemo discreetly intervenes. The ruffians' corpses are found stretched out near a stream: "The bodies bore no obvious trace of any wound. Only after carefully examining them did Pencroft find—on the forehead of one, the chest of another, the shoulder of a third—a little red spot, a sort of scarcely visible bruise, the cause of which it was impossible to imagine."

SIXTEEN

A Walk on the Ocean Plains

THIS CELL WAS, properly speaking, both the arsenal and the wardrobe of the *Nautilus*. A dozen deep-sea diving outfits were hanging on the walls, awaiting the hikers.

As soon as he saw them, Ned Land showed his abhorrence for the idea of getting into one of them.

"But my gallant Ned," I pointed out, "the forests of Crespo Island are *submarine* forests."

"Fine!" Disappointment spread over his face as his dreams of fresh meat faded away. "And you, Professor Aronnax, are you going to insert yourself into these clothes?"

"I have no alternative, Mr. Land."

"Well, you're free to do what you want, professor," the harpooner replied, shrugging his shoulders, "but as for me, unless I'm forced to, I'll never climb inside one of those."

"No one will force you, Mr. Land," the captain said.

"And Conseil's going to risk it?"

"Where master goes, I go," Conseil answered.

At a signal from the captain, two of the crew helped us to dress in these heavy, waterproof garments, made of seamless india rubber and designed expressly to withstand considerable pressure. I thought of mine as a suit of armor but flexible as well as resistant. It consisted of jacket and pants. The pants terminated in thick boots, with heavy lead soles. The fabric of the jacket was stretched over copper mail that protected the chest from the crushing pressure and allowed the lungs to function freely; the sleeves terminated in supple gloves that made it easy to work with the hands.

I could appreciate the vast difference between this perfected diving apparatus and the cork breastplates, leather jumpers, seagoing tunics, barrel helmets, etc., invented and so highly praised in the eighteenth century.

Captain Nemo, one of his companions—who looked like Hercules and must have been prodigiously strong—and Conseil and I were soon dressed to the neck in these diving garments. The only thing remaining was to encase our heads in their metallic spheres. But first I asked the captain's permission to examine the guns the crew had ready for us.

One of them handed me a seemingly ordinary gun, but the butt end, made of boiler plate steel and hollow inside, was rather large. This served as a tank for the compressed air that a trigger-operated valve could release into the metal chamber. In a groove where the butt was thickest, a clip held twenty electric bullets which, by means of a spring, could be moved automatically one-by-one into the barrel of the gun. As soon as one shot had been fired, another one was ready to go off.

"Captain Nemo," I said, "this gun is perfectly easy to use. I just hope I have a chance to try it out. But how do we get out there?"

"At this moment, professor, the *Nautilus* is resting on the bottom in ten meters of water. We're all set to leave."

"But how?"

"You'll see."

Captain Nemo thrust his head into his metal sphere, Conseil and I followed suit, not without first hearing the Canadian throw us a sarcastic "Good hunting!" The jacket terminated in a collar of threaded copper, into which the metallic sphere was screwed. Three holes, covered with thick glass, allowed me to look in any direction simply by turning my head inside the copper sphere. I could feel the Rouquayrol apparatus being strapped on my back, and as soon as it was in position I could breathe with great ease.

With the Ruhmkorff lamp fastened on my belt, my gun in hand, I was all set to leave. But I must admit that, while imprisoned in this heavy apparatus and nailed to the floor by my lead-soled boots, I couldn't take a step.

But the crew knew how to handle that problem, and I felt myself being propelled into another room contiguous to the wardrobe. My companions followed, pushed and pulled like myself. I heard a door with watertight seals close and we were enveloped in deep darkness.

In a few minutes, I could hear a sharp hissing and felt coldness mounting from my knees to my chest. Obviously someone inside the ship had opened a stopcock and allowed seawater to overrun us and soon fill that cell. A second door, placed in the side of the *Nautilus,* opened and a dusky light fell over us. A second later we were treading the bottom of the sea.

And now, how can I recapture the impressions made on me by that stroll under water? Words are impotent to recount such wonders! When the painter is incapable of reproducing with his brush the precise qualities of the liquid element, how can the writer hope to achieve it with his pen?

Captain Nemo walked ahead of us, and his Herculean companion strode a few steps behind us. Conseil and I walked side by side, as if a conversation might still be possible through our metallic helmets! Already I no longer felt the weight of my suit, of my lead-soled boots, of my air tank, or of my helmet, inside which my head rattled like an almond in its shell. All these objects, once immersed in water, lost a portion of their weight equal to the weight of the water they displaced, and I was profiting now by this law of physics discovered by Archimedes. I was no longer an inert mass, I had, relatively speaking, great freedom of movement.

I was astonished to see the power of the sun, which illuminated the soil thirty feet below the surface of the ocean. Solar rays easily pierced that aqueous mass and dissipated its dark coloration. I could easily distinguish objects 100 meters away. Beyond that, the bottom was shaded by fine gradations of ultramarine, and still farther away it turned blue and faded into vague obscurity.[1] Truly this water surrounding me was another air, denser than the terrestrial atmosphere but almost as transparent. Above me I could see the calm surface of the ocean.

We were walking on sand fine and smooth, not wrinkled like sand along a beach that retains the impressions made by waves. This dazzling carpet, really a reflector, threw back the rays of the sun with wonderful intensity, which accounted for the great vibrations of light that penetrated every molecule of water. Will you believe me when I say that at a depth of thirty feet, I could see as if I was in broad daylight?

For a quarter of an hour, I trod this blazing sand, strewn with an almost impalpable dust of seashells. The hull of the *Nautilus,* resembling a long reef, disappeared by degrees, but when night fell amid the waters, the ship's beacon light would surely guide us on our return trip, since its rays pierced darkness with perfect distinctness. This phenomenon is difficult to understand for anyone who has seen searchlight rays only on land. There the dust suspended in the air gives these rays the appearance of a luminous mist; but on the water, as well as under the water, shafts of electric light are transmitted with incomparable purity.[2]

We continued to stroll, and the vast sandy plain seemed endless. My hands seemed to be parting liquid curtains that closed in again behind me, and my footprints were erased abruptly under the pressure of the water.

Some objects looming in the distance soon became visible. I recognized a foreground of magnificent rocks, carpeted with splendid specimens of zoophytes, and I was struck by the unique effect produced by the medium we were in.

It was then ten in the morning. The sun's rays struck the surface at an oblique angle, and decomposing by refraction as though passing through a prism, they shaded the edges of the flowers, rocks, buds, seashells, and polyps

1. One of the sea's mysteries is how its colors are determined. Formerly scientists thought those colors resulted from the light scattered by minute particles suspended in the water. But today they also acknowledge the relative absorption of solar-energy spectrums by the water molecules themselves. The light we see consists of rays that range from the longer wavelengths of red through orange, yellow, and green, to the shorter wavelengths of blue, indigo, and violet. Water absorbs the longer wavelengths more rapidly, so James B. Rucker of the U.S. Naval Oceanographic Office reports that red colors are reduced to 2 percent of their surface visibility only 15 feet down, while deep blues are the last to be extinguished.

So Aronnax correctly reports that "the bottom was shaded by fine gradations of ultramarine, and still farther away it turned blue"; the longer, redder waves have been absorbed first.

2. This entire passage indicates that Aronnax is walking in an exceptionally clear part of the ocean. By comparison, 99 percent of the light is extinguished 26 feet down at Woods Hole, Massachusetts, and in some inshore areas 50 percent of the light is lost just 6 feet down.

On the ocean floor

with all seven colors of the solar spectrum. It was marvelous, a mixture of florid hues, a feast for the eyes, a living kaleidoscope of red, orange, yellow, green, blue, indigo, violet—the whole palette of a madcap colorist! If only I had been able to communicate to Conseil the lively sensations mounting to my brain, to compete with him in expressions of wonder! If only I had known—like Captain Nemo and his Hercules—how to exchange thoughts by a system of signals! So, lacking such outlets, I talked to myself—I declaimed inside the copper sphere that boxed my head, wasting more of my air supply than was wise.

In the midst of that splendid spectacle, Conseil had also stopped. Evidently that fine lad, in the presence of so many specimens of zoophytes and mollusks, was busy classifying, always classifying. Polyps and echinoderms covered the floor of the sea. There were various kinds of isis coral; some cornularian coral that live apart; some tufts of virgin genus *Oculina,* formerly called "white coral"; bristling fungus coral shaped like mushrooms; sea anemones holding onto the rocks with their muscular disks—all forming what seemed a flowerbed embellished by jellyfish from the genus *Porpita,* sporting collars of azure tentacles; starfish studding the sand, including some veinlike feather stars of the genus *Asterophyton,* like delicate lace embroidered by water nymphs, their festoons moving slightly with the eddies created by our passing.

I hated to be squashing underfoot the brilliant specimens of mollusks strewn over the seafloor by the thousands: concentric comb shells; hammer shells; coquina, which can actually leap about; top shell snails; red helmet shells; angel-wing conchs; sea hares;[3] and many other products of the inexhaustible sea. But we had to keep going, and as we walked, we could see scudding above us schools of Portuguese men-of-war with their ultramarine tentacles trailing along behind them; medusas, whose milk-white or delicate pink umbrellas were edged with blue, all shading us from the sun's rays; and jellyfish of the species *Pelagia panopyra,* which, if it had been dark, would have lighted our path with their phosphorescence.

All these wonders I enjoyed in the space of a quarter of a mile, hardly pausing, for Captain Nemo was always beckoning us on. Soon the nature of the seafloor changed. Leaving the sand, we walked into slimy mud, what Americans call "ooze," composed of siliceous and calcareous shells. Then we crossed a prairie of algae, open-sea plants the waters had not yet uprooted, growing in wild profusion. This soft, thick lawn could rival the most velvety carpet woven by humanity. But while verdure sprawled at our feet, it did not abandon us overhead. A light network of marine plants, of that inexhaustible algae family of which more than 2,000 species are known, crisscrossed the surface of the water. I saw long ribbons of fucus floating above, some globular, others tubular; some *Laurencia,* some *Cladostephus* with most delicate foliage;

---

3. Both the Hetzel and Hachette editions give "les aphysies," which we take to be a misspelling of "les aplysies"—the genus *Aplysia,* which houses a wide selection of that marine slug nicknamed the sea hare.

and some *Rhodymenia palmata* that looked like the fan shapes of cactus. I noticed that the green plants lived nearer the surface, while the red ones occupied a medium depth, leaving to the black or brown hydrophytes the task of forming gardens and flower beds in the deeper parts of the ocean.[4]

These algae are truly a prodigy of creation, one of the marvels of world flora. This family produces both the smallest and the largest plants on earth. For, just as one can count 40,000 of these almost imperceptible buds in a five-square-millimeter space, so one can gather fucus plants more than 500 meters long!

We had been away from the *Nautilus* for about an hour and a half. It was almost noon. I could tell the time because the sun's rays were no longer refracted since now they entered the water perpendicularly. The magical colors were disappearing by degrees, emerald and sapphire were fading away from our world. We walked with a regular step that rang on the ground with amazing intensity. The slightest noise was transmitted with a speed to which the ear is unaccustomed on land. Indeed, water is a better conductor of sound than air, and carries it four times as fast.

Now the seafloor sloped downward. The light took on a uniform shade. We reached a depth of 100 meters, undergoing a pressure of 10 atmospheres. My diving apparatus was so well designed that I felt no effects of this pressure. True, at the start I had had a little trouble moving my fingers, but by now even that minor stiffness had disappeared. I would have expected to be exhausted after walking in such a harness for two hours, but I still felt no sign of fatigue. On the contrary, aided by the buoyancy of the water, I could move with surprising ease.

Even at this 300-foot depth, I could still make out the sun's rays, though feebly. Their brilliance had diminished to a reddish twilight, halfway between day and night. But we could still make our way without resorting to the Ruhmkorff apparatus.

Then Captain Nemo paused. He waited until I caught up with him. He pointed to some dark masses looming in the shadows just a short distance ahead.

"It must be the forests of Crespo Island," I thought, and I wasn't mistaken.

---

4. But these color differences that Aronnax cites may have been the effect of light absorption. Plants of the same surface color could, at changing depths, appear to be different colors.

SEVENTEEN

A Submarine Forest

AT LAST WE HAD reached the edge of this forest, doubtless one of the most beautiful of Captain Nemo's vast domains. He looked upon it as his own, he felt he had the same right to it that the first people had in the early days of the world. And indeed, who was there who could challenge his claim to this underwater property? What other, bolder pioneer would come, ax in hand, to chop down these dark copses?

This was a forest of large tree-like plants; and the moment we entered its vast arcades, I was struck by the unique arrangement of their branches, a pattern I had never seen before. None of the weeds carpeting the seafloor, none of the branches of the shrubbery, crept or inclined or extended horizontally. They all stretched straight up! Every filament, every ribbon, no matter how thin, was standing as straight as a ramrod. Fucus and creepers grew in stiff perpendicular lines controlled by the density of the medium that produced them. They seemed incapable of movement, but when I parted them with my hand, they immediately returned to their original positions. This was truly the regime of verticality.

I soon grew accustomed to this bizarre situation and to the relative darkness that enveloped us. The seafloor was now littered with sharp stones that were difficult to avoid. Here the submarine flora seemed pretty comprehensive, richer than it would have been in the Arctic or tropical zones, where such products are not so numerous. But at first I confused the two kingdoms, involuntarily seeing zoophytes as hydrophytes, animals as plants. I think anybody would have made the same mistake. The fauna and flora are so closely allied in the submarine world.

I noticed that all these specimens of the vegetable kingdom had only the flimsiest foundation in the earth. Without roots and seemingly indifferent as to which solid objects they adhere to—sand, shells, husks, pebbles—they ask of the ground not nourishment but simply a point of support. These plants are self-propagated, and the principle of their existence resides in the water that sustains and nourishes them. Most of them shoot forth not leaves but blades of capricious shapes, in a narrow range of colors, pink, crimson, green, olive, tan, brown. There I saw—but of course not dried out like our specimens aboard the

Nautilus—some peacock's tails spread out like fans to catch a breeze; some scarlet rosetangle; sea tangle, stretching out their young and edible shoots; some thread-like, wavy kelp of the genus *Nereocystis* attaining a tallness of fifteen meters; some bouquets of mermaid's cups, with stems that grow thicker at the top; and many other open-sea plants—all without flowers!

"It's a curious anomaly in this bizarre element," as one witty naturalist has quipped. "The animal kingdom flowers, and the vegetable kingdom doesn't!"

Among these various shrubs, as big as trees of the temperate zone, there were crowded together in their damp shadows real bushes of moving flowers, hedges of zoophytes in which there blossomed some stony coral striped with twisting furrows; some yellow sea anemone of the genus *Caryophylia*, with their diaphanous tentacles; some anemone with grassy tufts of the genus *Zoantharia*, and—to complete the illusion—fish flies flitted from branch to branch like a flock of hummingbirds. Meanwhile some yellow fish of the genus *Lepiso-canthus*, with bristling jaws and pointed scales, some flying gurnards, and some pinecone fish rose underfoot like a flock of snipe.

At about one o'clock, Captain Nemo signaled us to halt. I was pleased to obey, and we stretched out under an arbor of winged kelp, whose long thin tendrils stood up like arrows.

In this short but delicious rest, there was nothing lacking but the charm of conversation. But it was impossible to talk, impossible to respond. I could only place my great copper headpiece next to Conseil's headpiece. I saw his eyes glistening with delight, and to show his pleasure, he bobbed his head around inside his helmet in the most comical way imaginable.

After walking for four hours, I was amazed to realize that I wasn't really hungry. What kept my stomach in such a good mood I was unable to say. But, maybe in exchange, I felt an irresistible need to sleep, a feeling that I understand comes over all divers. My eyes closed behind the thick glass windows and I fell into a deep slumber,[1] which until then I had been able to fight off only by

---

1. At last, we reach the payoff of notes 4 and 5 in I 15. In his December 1961 *Galaxy* article, T. L. Thomas cited this underwater nap as a choice example of Verne's alleged slovenly science: "Things have been happening so fast and furiously," says Thomas, "that both Verne and the reader alike forget that Verne's SCUBA gear demands that the tongue alternately pop into and out of the two breathing tubes, a good trick when one is asleep." Alas, Thomas has been misled by yet another translating error in the Victorian text perpetrated by Louis Mercier. As we indicated in our notes for I 15, Verne merely observes that the tongue device was in general use; he does *not* say that Nemo used it—that assertion was Mercier's alone. Clearly, Nemo's equipment utilized a Siebe helmet with standard check valves, a device that had been around for a quarter century at the time of the novel's publication. The captain's innovation was, as he stated, the combining of this helmet with the portable air tank developed by Rouquayrol and Denayrouze. The verdict: while modern diving coaches might consider such an underwater siesta imprudent, the feat was far from impossible.

As for Mr. Thomas, this is one instance, perhaps, where we are moved to greater tolerance: your present translators jumped to the same wrong conclusion. In his 1976 annotated edition of the Mercier text (with notes, corrections, and cuts opened), WJM concluded that this episode seemed to be "one of Verne's worst bloopers," and FPW had privately agreed. The truth didn't

walking. Captain Nemo and his herculean companion had actually set an example, falling into a nap before I did.

How long I dozed I had no way of knowing, but when I awoke it seemed as if the sun were sinking toward the horizon. Captain Nemo had already gotten up, and I was lazily stretching my limbs when an unexpected apparition brought me promptly to my feet.

Just a few paces away, a monster sea spider, a meter tall, was eyeing me malignantly, poised to leap at me. My diving apparatus was thick enough to protect me from the monster's bite, but I could not help shuddering with horror. Conseil and the sailor from the *Nautilus* were getting up too. Captain Nemo pointed to the hideous crustacean, and the sailor brought it down with a swing of his rifle butt. I saw the creature's horrible legs writhing in its death throes.

This encounter reminded me that other, even more fearful animals haunt these dark depths, and that my diving suit wouldn't protect me against all of them. I hadn't thought of this earlier, but now I was determined to be more alert. Indeed, I had assumed this halt would be the turning point in our walk, but I was wrong. Instead of turning back, Captain Nemo continued his bold excursion.

The seafloor sloped downward now at a greater angle, taking us deeper and deeper. It must have been almost three o'clock when we entered a narrow valley between high, vertical walls, a gorge 150 meters deep. Thanks to the perfection of our diving equipment, we had thus gone 90 meters below the limit that Nature had heretofore set on submarine walks by human beings.[2]

I say 150 meters, but of course I had with me no instrument by which to measure the depth. But I knew that the sun's rays, even in the clearest water, could reach no deeper. And at precisely that moment the darkness became profound. I could see nothing ten paces ahead. I began to grope my way when suddenly I saw a brilliant white light. Captain Nemo had turned on his Ruhmkorff lamp. His companion did likewise, and Conseil and I followed their example. By turning a switch, I connected the induction coil and the glass spiral, and the sea, lighted up by four such lamps, was illuminated for a radius of 25 meters.

Captain Nemo plunged farther into the forest's dark depths, and the shrubbery began to thin out. I noticed that vegetable life was disappearing faster than animal life. Open-sea plants were already abandoning the soil, which was be-

out until our correspondence in the summer of 1990. FPW finally copped to Mercier's subtle mistranslation, exposed it, and concluded: "Since Nemo doesn't say he uses the tongue system, and since it's *never mentioned again* in the book, it's clear to me that Verne never thought of it as part of Nemo's apparatus. Hence I don't think our man can fairly be accused of discrepancy."

2. Actually, at 150 meters (450-plus feet), they are considerably below the limits now recommended for amateur divers using modern scuba equipment. The U.S. Divers Corporation's basic rule number 12 is: "Although record dives have been made to 300 feet, amateur divers should not exceed 130 feet."

coming more and more arid, but the area was still swarming with animals—zoophytes, articulates, mollusks, and fish.

As we were walking, I thought the light from our Ruhmkorff apparatus would automatically attract some of the inhabitants of these somber depths. But if they did approach us, they kept far enough away that we couldn't shoot them. Several times I saw Captain Nemo halt, put his gun to his shoulder, look through his sights, then lower his gun and resume his hike.

And at last, about four o'clock, this marvelous excursion came to an end. A wall of superb rocks, an imposing mass, rose before us: a heap of gigantic stone blocks, an enormous granite cliffside opening into grottoes but offering no surfaces up which we could climb. This was the underpinning of Crespo Island, this was—land!

Captain Nemo stopped abruptly. With a gesture he terminated our trip. However much I wanted to try to scale that wall, I was obliged to stop too. Here ended the captain's domains, and he would not go beyond them. Beyond was a portion of the earth that he would never again tread underfoot.

We began our return trip. Captain Nemo resumed his place as the leader, directing our course without hesitation. I realized we were not taking the same route back. This new way, much steeper and almost painful, led us upward rapidly toward the surface. Nevertheless, this rise to the upper strata was not so sudden as to cause overly fast decompression, which would have led to severe organic disorders, to those internal injuries so fatal to divers.[3] Soon the light reappeared and grew stronger, and since the sun was low on the horizon, the refraction once again edged every object with a rainbow-like border.

At a depth of ten meters, we were walking amid swarms of small fish of every species, more numerous than the birds of the air, and also more agile. But no aquatic game worthy of a shot presented itself.

---

3. These *severe organic disorders,* known in Verne's day as "caisson disease," are now called "the bends." This condition is caused by formation of minute nitrogen bubbles in the joints, muscles, and nerve control centers. The result can be crippling or even fatal.

At depths approaching 300 feet, enough nitrogen could dissolve into a diver's blood to disrupt his brain and nervous system, leading to physical and mental disorientation. Below 400 feet, even a veteran diver in "hard hat" gear may experience difficulty in concentrating on even the simplest tasks. Then, as the diver surfaces, excess nitrogen in his system can cause still greater problems: if his ascent is overhasty, "the bends" result, bringing pain to the joints and even fatally blocking the blood flow to heart, lungs, or brain.

How credible, then, is this stroll on the seafloor? First, we have to accept as a given the ability of Nemo's tanks to supply air for ten hours. At the start, the men are walking at a safe depth of 30 feet; over the next several hours they descend gradually to a depth of 150 meters by three o'clock. Now maybe Nemo and his Herculean sailor could have developed the necessary ruggedness for such a depth, but surely Aronnax and Conseil would have been very hard-pressed. But at least their return journey seems more realistic: *much steeper and almost painful*—no doubt in the knees and ankles. Still, their ascent is much too fast for safety, and probably Verne would have written this episode differently after 1875, when Paul Bert won a 20,000-franc prize from the French Academy of Sciences for his research into proper rates of ascent.

Then suddenly I saw the captain shoulder his gun and follow a moving object into the shrubbery. He fired, I actually heard a slight hissing, and an animal, struck by lightning, dropped some paces away.

It was a magnificent sea otter of the genus *Enhydra,* the only quadruped that lives exclusively in the ocean. It was one-and-a-half meters long, sure to be worth a high price. Its coat, chestnut brown above and silver underneath, would have made one of those beautiful furs so much in demand in the Russian and Chinese markets. The fineness and luster of its pelt guaranteed it a value of at least 2,000 francs. I greatly admired this curious mammal, with its rounded head and short ears, round eyes, white whiskers like a cat's, its feet webbed and clawed, its tufted tail. Hunted and trapped by fishermen, this precious carnivore has become very rare. It has taken refuge mainly in the northernmost parts of the Pacific, where it might soon become extinct.[4]

Our herculean crewman picked up the animal and tossed it on his shoulder, and we continued our journey homeward. For an hour, a plain of sand stretched before us. Sometimes our trail rose to within two meters of the surface of the ocean. Then I could see our images clearly reflected on the surface, but upside down: above us there walked an identical group, mimicking our motions and gestures, like us in every detail, except that they walked with heads down and feet in the air.

Another unusual effect. Thick clouds formed above us and vanished quickly. But when I thought it over, I realized that what appeared to be clouds were due to the varying height of the water in the midst of a ground swell, and when I studied the phenomenon further, I could see the foam breaking on the crests and spreading "white caps" over the water. I could even see the shadows of huge birds overhead as they swiftly skimmed the surface.

Then I witnessed one of the finest shots ever to thrill a hunter. A large bird of great wingspread hovered over us, clearly visible. When it was just a few meters above the surface, Captain Nemo's companion shouldered his gun, aimed, fired. The creature fell, struck by lightning, and the force of its fall brought it within reach of our adroit hunter.[5] It was a superb albatross, a magnificent specimen of these open-sea birds.

This incident hardly interrupted our march. For two hours, we hiked now over sandy plains, then over seaweed prairies that were difficult to cross. To be honest, I was near exhaustion when I suddenly saw a glimmer of light a half mile ahead. It was the beacon of the *Nautilus.* We should have been on board in twenty minutes when I could breathe easy again: for I was worried now that

4. Indeed, by 1900 it was believed that the sea otter *had* become extinct. But a few individuals still survived, and through efforts by conservationists, the species was placed under strict protection and is now making a comeback in Pacific Northwest waters.

5. Whose shot really was remarkable—because he occupied one medium (water) and his target another (air). In taking aim he had to compensate for the light rays bending as they pass from the one to the other.

my oxygen supply seemed very low. But I wasn't reckoning on an accidental meeting that delayed our return.

I was lagging some twenty steps behind him when suddenly I saw Captain Nemo rushing back toward me. With his powerful hands he sent me sprawling on the ground while his crewman did the same to Conseil. I did not know what to make of this brusque assault, but I was reassured to see the captain lying motionless beside me.

I was stretched out on the seafloor underneath a thicket of algae when, raising my head a bit, I saw some enormous shapes hurtling by, leaving a phosphorescent trail behind them.

My blood froze! We were being threatened by powerful sharks, a pair of blue sharks, terrible man-eaters with huge tails and a dull, glassy stare, who secrete a phosphorescent substance through holes around their snouts. They are like gigantic fireflies that can crush a man in their iron jaws! I don't know whether Conseil was taking the trouble to classify them, but as for me, I looked at their silver bellies, their huge maws bristling with teeth, from a viewpoint less than scientific—more as a potential victim than as a professor of natural history.

Fortunately, these voracious animals see poorly. They passed by without noticing us, barely touching us with their brown fins. We had miraculously escaped a danger greater than meeting a tiger deep in the jungle.

Half an hour later, guided by the ship's beacon, we reached the *Nautilus*. The outer door was already open, and Captain Nemo closed it after we reentered the first cell. Then he pressed a button. I heard pumps at work, I felt the water sinking around me, and soon that cell was completely dry. The inside door was opened and we entered the wardrobe.

I shed my diving apparatus—it was not an easy job—and worn out from lack of food and rest, I returned to my cabin, in spite of everything marveling over this extraordinary excursion on the bottom of the sea.

EIGHTEEN

Four Thousand Leagues under the Pacific

NEXT DAY, NOVEMBER 18, I felt fully recovered from my fatigue of the night before, and I mounted to the platform just as the first mate was pronouncing his usual daily phrase. It occurred to me that his routine expression either referred to the weather conditions or meant something like "There is nothing in sight."

And truly, the ocean was deserted. Not a sail on the horizon. The heights of Crespo Island had disappeared during the night. The sea was absorbing all the colors of the spectrum except blue, reflecting it in all directions, leaving the water itself a magnificent indigo. The sea looked like watered silk printed with a broad, wavy pattern.

While I was admiring this splendid spectacle, Captain Nemo appeared. He did not seem to notice me as he began a series of astronomical observations. Then he leaned an elbow on the beacon housing and gazed out over the sea.

Meanwhile, a score of the *Nautilus*'s crew—all vigorous and well built—had also mounted to the platform. They had come up to take in the nets that had been trailing in our wake during the night. These seamen obviously hailed from many different countries, but I surmised they were all European in origin. I thought I could recognize some Irishmen, some Frenchmen, a few Slavs, and a native of Greece or Crete. They spoke very little, and when they did utter a word or two it was in that bizarre language whose origin I could not even guess.[1] And so I gave up any idea of questioning them.

They hauled the nets on board. These were large dragnets like those used for trawling on the Normandy coast. They were like huge pockets held half open by a floating pole and a chain laced through the lower meshes. These pockets dragged along the seafloor and collected everything in their path. That

---

1. Verne is building up suspense about this. Perhaps we're dealing with an actual if obscure tongue—how can Aronnax and the average reader be certain this phrase is *not* from Old Persian? Or modern Assamese? Or, like J. R. R. Tolkien, was Verne tinkering with developing a language of his own? In either case, this strange dialect could have been Nemo's answer to the communication problems posed by the international makeup of his crew. Unfortunately, the text will fail to clarify the mystery—so, to paraphrase Aronnax himself, "these are questions that require more work."

morning they brought up many curious specimens from those waters so rich in marine life. I saw anglerfish, whose comical movements qualify them for the stage; black commerson anglers equipped with antennas; undulating triggerfish with red stripes encircling their bodies; some bloated puffers whose venom is extremely subtle; some olive-colored lampreys; snipefish with their silvery scales; cutlass fish, which can give you as strong a shock as the electric eel and the electric ray; scaly featherbacks with brown transverse stripes; a green variety of cod; and several varieties of goby, etc. Finally, I saw several larger types: a one-meter jack with a prominent head; several lovely bonitos, genus *Scomber,* decked out in blue and silver; and three magnificent tuna whose great speed had not saved them from our dragnets.

I reckoned that cast of the nets brought in more than 1,000 pounds of fish. It was a fine catch but no surprise. These nets were always left trailing for several hours and captured in their meshes an infinite variety of undersea life. We never lacked excellent food on board the *Nautilus,* for its speed and the attraction of its beacon light guaranteed us a continual supply.

These various products of the ocean were lowered through the hatch and taken to the food lockers, some to be eaten fresh, the rest to be preserved.

With the fishing finished and our air supply renewed, I thought we were set to dive and resume our submarine excursion, and was preparing to return to my cabin when, without any preamble, Captain Nemo turned toward me and said:

"Professor, look at that sea! Who can say it isn't actually alive! It expresses its anger and its tenderness! Yesterday it went to sleep as we did, and now like us it is awakening after a peaceful night."

No good morning, no good day! It was as if this strange personality were simply resuming a conversation he had begun earlier.

"Yes, watch it," he said, "as it awakens under the caresses of the sun. It's going to renew its diurnal existence. It's fascinating to study its functions as an organism. It has a pulse, arteries, sudden movements, and I side with the learned Maury who discovered that it has a circulation as real as the circulation of blood in animals."

I sensed that Captain Nemo expected no responses from me, and it seemed pointless to say "Oh yes," "How right you are!" or "Precisely." He was talking to himself, with long pauses between sentences. He was meditating aloud.

"Yes, the ocean does indeed have an actual circulation, and to set it going, the Creator of all things has only to increase its temperature or its salinity or its population of microscopic animals. Changes of temperature cause changes in density, thus creating currents and countercurrents.[2] Evaporation, which is

---

2. The causes of ocean currents have been debated for centuries. Benjamin Franklin (the first to chart the Gulf Stream) blamed the frictional drag of winds over the surface. By contrast, Maury theorized that deep ocean currents circulate upward to replace surface waters, driven by the difference in density between equatorial and polar waters, the former moving "downhill" toward the poles. Twentieth-century studies show that both views are reflected in the total

nonexistent in the upper Arctic areas but very active in the equatorial zones, brings about a perpetual interchange of polar and tropical waters. Furthermore, I have discovered currents that go from the surface to the bottom, and from the seafloor back to the surface, vertical currents that constitute the true respiration of the sea. I have seen a molecule of ocean water, heated at the surface, drop into the depths, attain its maximum density at two degrees below zero centigrade, then cool off, become lighter, and rise again. At the Poles, professor, you will see the consequences of this phenomenon, you will realize why, through this law of prescient Nature, water can freeze only at the surface."[3]

When he finished that sentence I was thinking: "The Pole! Does this audacious character intend to take us even there?"

He fell silent, surveying that element that was to him a subject of deep and endless study, and then resumed:

"As you know, professor, salts are so abundant in the sea that if you extracted every dissolved grain, you could form a mass equal to 4,500,000 cubic leagues. Spread out all over the earth, that mass would form a layer more than ten meters high. And don't think the presence of these salts is a mere whim of Nature. Not so. They render the oceanic waters less evaporable, so winds cannot pick up too much vapor which, when condensing, would submerge the temperate zones! These salts play a major role in stabilizing the general ecology of the globe."

He paused again, straightened up, took several steps along the platform, and came back to me:

"And as for those billions of microscopic animals, those infusoria, millions of them in a drop of water, 800,000 needed to add up to one milligram of weight—their role is no less important. They absorb marine salts, they assimilate the solid elements in water, they make corals and madreporic polyps, they

---

explanation. The Norwegian physicist Vilhelm Bjerknes (1862—1951) demonstrated that varying water densities *do* generate fluid motion.

Likewise, the Swedish oceanographer Vagn Walfrid Ekman (1874—1954) revealed that wind-drag *does* cause currents, their direction being affected by the earth's rotation—a force called the Coriolis effect. Thus, a wind abetted by Coriolis force will drive the surface waters at a 45° angle to the wind direction, inducing successively deeper currents moving at successively sharper angles; 200 to 500 feet down, the current will actually flow in a direction exactly opposite to the wind—in short, a countercurrent.

3. "This law of prescient Nature" is crucial to the existence of life. Nemo casually notes that as water will "cool off" it will "become lighter." Generally, cooling substances contract and grow *heavier,* and water does so up to a certain point ($-2°$ centigrade in the case of salt water) where it unorthodoxly begins to expand again and lighten. Hence, when Nemo's "*molecule of ocean water*" freezes, it will "rise again" and float as ice—which the sun can proceed to melt, starting the cycle all over. Without this circular process, if ice formed in the oceans from the bottom up, the seas would soon freeze solid. Even more likely, the oceans would not have been able to develop at all. Either way, there wouldn't be any life on earth, because life began in the water. "This phenomenon," as Nemo terms it, is due to the peculiar molecular structure of water.

are the true creators of limestone continents! And so, that drop of water, lighter when deprived of its mineral nutrients, ascends to the surface again, absorbs the salts left by evaporation, becomes heavier, descends to bring the tiny animals new materials to absorb. And so we have a double current, ascending and descending, constant movement, perpetual life! Marine life is more intense than land life, more exuberant, more infinite, spread out all over the ocean that some people have said is the element of death for humanity, but an element of life for myriads of animals—and for me!"

When Captain Nemo spoke like this, he seemed transfigured and aroused extraordinary emotions in me.

"There," he added, "out there is true existence. And I can imagine the founding of nautical cities, clusters of submarine households which, like the *Nautilus,* would ascend to the surface to renew their air supply, free towns, independent towns such as we've never known. But then, probably some despot . . . ."

He finished with a violent gesture. Then, as if to dispel some tragic thought, he addressed me directly:

"Professor Aronnax, do you know how deep the ocean is?"

"Well, I know at least what the main soundings have taught us."

"Could you cite them for me, so I can check them against my own?"

"Here are a few," I said, "that spring to mind. If I'm not mistaken, a mean depth of 8,200 meters was found in the North Atlantic, and 2,500 meters in the Mediterranean. The most remarkable soundings have been taken in the South Atlantic, near the 35th parallel, and they gave 12,000 meters, 14,091 meters, 15,149 meters. To sum it up, it's estimated that if the bottom of the sea were leveled, its mean depth would be about seven kilometers."[4]

"Well, professor," he responded, "we shall show you better than that, I hope. As for the mean depth of this part of the Pacific, let me tell you, it's only 4,000 meters."

And with that, Captain Nemo headed toward the hatch and disappeared down the ladder. I followed and again I repaired to the grand salon. Almost at once the propeller started up and the log gave our speed as 20 miles per hour.

In the days that followed, indeed for weeks, Captain Nemo made few appearances. The first mate regularly marked our position on the chart, so I could always plot our course precisely.

But Conseil and Ned did spend many hours with me. Conseil had told Ned about all the marvels of our underwater walk, and the Canadian was sorry he had not gone along with us. I reassured him though that he would probably have another chance to visit the forests of Oceania.

---

4. Aronnax's "most remarkable soundings"—exceeding 15,000 meters—were based on faulty sounding procedures. After Maury instituted more accurate practices, such figures were no longer reported. Today's record soundings (e.g., the Challenger Deep near Guam) scarcely exceed 12,000 meters, and modern oceanographers give the average depth of the world's oceans at about half of Aronnax's figure (roughly 2 miles, or 3½ kilometers).

Nearly every day, for several hours, the panels of the salon would open and we never tired of peering into the mysteries of the submarine world.

The general direction of the *Nautilus* was southeast, and we cruised at depths between 100 and 150 meters. One day though, and I don't know by what caprice of the captain's, we descended diagonally, by means of the slanting fins, to a depth of 2,000 meters. The thermometer gave a temperature of 4.25° centigrade, a temperature that seemed common to all latitudes at that depth.

At three a.m. on November 26, the *Nautilus* crossed the Tropic of Cancer at longitude 172°. On November 27, we passed in sight of the Hawaiian Islands, where the famous Captain Cook met his death on February 14, 1779.[5] We had then navigated 4,860 leagues from our point of departure. When I mounted to the platform that morning, I could see, two miles to leeward, Hawaii, the largest of the seven islands in that archipelago. I could clearly see the cultivated fields along the shore, the various mountain chains running parallel to the coast, and the volcanoes, dominated by Mauna Kea, which rises to 5,000 meters above sea level. Among other specimens from those parts that our nets brought up, I saw some peacock-tailed flabellarian coral—polyps pressed into pleasant shapes and peculiar to those waters.

The *Nautilus* continued on its southeasterly course. We cut the equator at longitude 142° on December 1 and on December 4, after a speedy but uneventful crossing, we sighted the Marquesas Islands. From three miles away, I saw, in latitude 8° 57′ south and longitude 139° 32′ west, Martin Point on Nuku Hiva, largest of this island group that flies the French flag. I could see only its wooded mountains on the horizon, because Captain Nemo didn't like getting close to land. Here our nets brought in beautiful specimens of fish. I saw dolphinfish, with azure fins and golden tails, whose flesh is unrivaled the world over; wrasse of the genus *Hologymnosus,* almost destitute of scales but rich in taste; some knifejaws with bony beaks; and some yellowish albacore, as good to eat as bonito—all worthy of being classified as fish for the table.

After leaving these charming islands that belong to France, the *Nautilus* traveled about 2,000 miles from December 4 to 11. This navigation was noteworthy for our meeting with an immense school of squid, curious mollusks who are closely related to the cuttlefish. French fishermen call them "cuckoldfish"; they belong to the class Cephalopoda, family Dibranchiata, which also includes the cuttlefish and argonauts. These creatures were carefully studied by naturalists in ancient times, and they supplied numerous metaphors for orators in the Greek marketplace,[6] as well as excellent dinners for the rich, if we can believe Athenaeus, a Greek physician who lived before Galen.

5. James Cook (1728–1779) led the first genuine scientific expeditions. When Cook's *Endeavor* sailed from England in 1768, it was the first ship staffed with scientists and equipped for modern navigation. In three separate voyages, Cook left to science its first complete survey of the Pacific, from the Bering Strait to the Antarctic, before perishing in a skirmish with Hawaiian islanders. Both Aronnax and Nemo will speak reverently of him on several occasions.

6. Another of Aronnax's tongue-in-cheek remarks. Given the phallic shape of the "cuckoldfish," the metaphors were probably ribald ones.

It was during the night of December 9–10 that we encountered this army of mollusks, which are distinctly nocturnal. We could have counted them by the millions. They were migrating from temperate regions to warmer climes, following in the wake of herrings and sardines. We watched them through our thick glass panels, swimming backward with great speed, propelling themselves by means of their locomotor tubes, chasing fish and other mollusks, eating the smaller ones, eaten by the larger ones, tossing about in indescribable confusion the ten feet Nature has placed on their heads like a crest of pneumatic serpents. In spite of its speed, it took the *Nautilus* several hours to pass through this swarm of animals, and our nets brought in great quantities of them, among which I recognized all nine species that d'Orbigny has classified as native to the Pacific.[7]

During this trip, the sea showed us its greatest marvels. It varied them continuously. It changed the scenery for our pleasure, and we were called upon not simply to witness the works of the Creator in the liquid element, but also to penetrate the most fearsome mysteries of the ocean.

On December 11 I was busy reading in the grand salon. Ned Land and Conseil were gazing out at the luminous waters through the panels, which were half open. The *Nautilus* stood motionless, its ballast tanks full, holding at a depth of 1,000 meters, in a relatively uninhabited section of the ocean where only larger fish would make occasional appearances.

I was deep in a charming book by Jean Macé, *The Servants of the Stomach,*[8] savoring its ingenious lessons, when Conseil interrupted.

"Would master please come over here a moment?" he was saying in a strange tone of voice.

"What is it, Conseil?"

"Something master should see."

I got up and went over to the window—and stared.

In the full electric illumination, an enormous black mass, quite motionless, hung suspended in the water. I watched it carefully, trying to identify this gigantic cetacean. But a sudden thought struck me.

"A ship!" I cried.

"Yes," the Canadian responded, "a disabled ship that has sunk straight down."

Ned Land was right. We were in the presence of a vessel whose severed shrouds still hung from their clasps. Its hull still looked in good condition; it couldn't have sunk more than a few hours before. The stumps of three masts, cut off about two feet above the deck, suggested that when the ship was already

7. Like Aronnax himself, Alcide d'Orbigny (1802–1857) had been a traveling naturalist for the Paris Museum. He is credited with laying the foundations of cephalopod systematics, a subject upon which he published a landmark monograph.

8. Along with Verne, Jean Macé was a codirector of J. Hetzel's young people's review, *Magasin d'education et de récréation.* A man of republican sympathies, Macé also founded the League of Education.

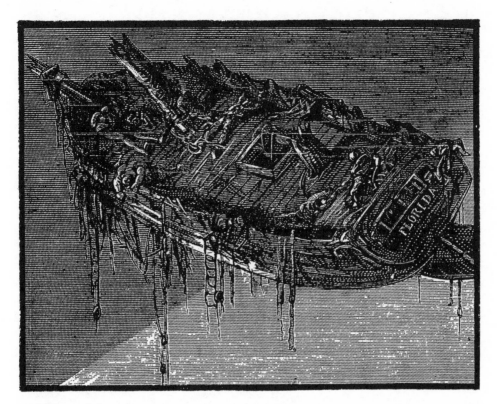

A shipwreck in progress

taking on water, the captain tried to save it by sacrificing his masts. But it must have heeled sideways and filled up completely—it still listed to port. A sorry spectacle, this carcass lost beneath the waves. But sadder still was the sight on deck, where some people, who had been lashed to the ship with ropes to prevent their being washed overboard, had drowned. I could count four men, one still standing at the helm—then a woman halfway out of a skylight on the afterdeck, and holding a child in her arms. The woman was young. By the brilliant light of the *Nautilus*'s beacon I could make out her features, not yet decomposing. In a supreme effort, she had held her child high overhead and the poor little creature's arms were still tight around its mother's neck. The positions of the four sailors were frightful, twisted from convulsive movements, probably from making a final effort to burst the ropes binding them to the ship. And the helmsman, alone, calmer, his face clear and serious, his gray hair plastered to his brow, his hands clutching the wheel, seemed still to be steering his wrecked three-master through the ocean depths.

O what a scene! We were dumbfounded, with hearts beating fast, at the very idea of catching a shipwreck in progress, photographing, so to speak, its last moments with our minds. And already I could see huge sharks advancing, eyes on fire, attracted by human flesh.

Meanwhile the *Nautilus* was making a slow turn around the ship, and for an instant I could read the board on its stern:

The Florida
Sunderland, England

*Four
Thousand
Leagues
under the
Pacific*

128

NINETEEN

Vanikoro

THIS TERRIBLE SIGHT was the first of a series of marine disasters that the *Nautilus* was to encounter on its voyage. Whenever we ran through frequented seas, we would often see wrecked hulls rotting away in mid-water, and guns, cannonballs, anchors, chains, and a thousand other iron objects rusting away on the bottom.

Forever swept along by the *Nautilus,* in which we lived in virtual isolation, we sighted on December 11 the Tuamotu archipelago, which Bougainville had named "the dangerous group";[1] it extends from Ducie Island to Lazareff Island over 500 leagues from the east-southeast to the west-northwest, between latitudes 13° 30′ and 23° 50′ south, and longitudes 125° 30′ and 151° 30′ west. This archipelago covers an area of 370 square leagues, and it is formed of some 60 groups of islands, including the Gambier group, which is a French protectorate. These islands are coral formations. A slow but steady upheaval, due to the work of polyps, will someday connect these islands to each other. Then this new, combined island will be welded to its neighbor archipelagos, and a fifth continent will extend from New Zealand and New Caledonia as far as the Marquesas Islands.

When I suggested this possibility to Captain Nemo, he responded coldly:

"This planet doesn't need new continents, it needs new men."

Our course chanced to lead the *Nautilus* directly toward the island of Clermont-Tonnerre,[2] one of the most curious in this group, which was discovered in 1822 by Captain Bell of the *Minerva.* And so I was able to study the madreporic system that has created the islands in this ocean.

Madreporic polyps—which one must be careful not to confuse with precious coral—cover their tissue with a limestone crust; their variations in structure have led my illustrious mentor, Professor Milne-Edwards, to classify them into five sections. The tiny microscopic animals that secrete this polypary live

---

1. Another famous explorer whose exploits were well known to Verne's readers was the Frenchman Louis de Bougainville (1729–1811), whose so-called "dangerous group" is also nick-named the "Low" Archipelago.

2. On today's maps called Reao Island.

by the billions in the depths of their cells. Their limestone deposits build up into rocks, reefs, islets, islands. Sometimes they form a circular ring to create a lagoon or a little interior lake, a ring with gaps through which the lagoon communicates with the sea. Other times they form barrier reefs like those off the coasts of New Caledonia and some of the Tuamotu islands. In still other places, like Réunion Island and Mauritius, they build fringing reefs, high, straight walls from which the ocean drops off to great depths.

While cruising along just a few cable lengths off the shores of the island of Clermont-Tonnerre, I gazed in admiration at this gigantic structure built by these microscopic workers. These walls were especially the work of those madreporic polyps known as fire coral, finger coral, star coral, and stony coral. These polyps develop specifically in the agitated water near the surface, and so they build their foundations from above, substructures that slowly sink along with the rubble of secretions that support them. At least, that's the theory of Mr. Charles Darwin, who thus explains the formation of atolls[3]—and his theory, in my opinion, is superior to the rival theory that says these madrepores build on the peaks of mountains or volcanoes that are submerged just a few feet below sea level.[4]

I was able to study these strange walls close up. Our sounding lines indicated that they dropped perpendicularly for more than 300 meters, and our light made the brilliant limestone sparkle all the way down.

Conseil asked me how long it had taken for these colossal walls to develop. I astonished him by saying that scientists reckoned the rate of growth at about an eighth of an inch per biennium.[5]

3. Although Darwin published his theory of atolls in 1842 as part of his book *The Structure and Distribution of Coral Reefs,* that theory could not be proved until 1952. Coral reefs, Darwin argued, develop around the edges of a volcano standing above the waves. As the volcano subsides gradually into the sea, "various minute and tender animals" keep building the reef's surface upward, always continuing their building at their normal depth, the top 150 to 180 feet of tropical water, for coral can only grow in depths illuminated by strong light. Eventually, the volcano's central peak disappears, leaving nothing but a circular reef enclosing a lagoon—an atoll. About a century later, this theory was verified by U.S. scientists who took borings over 4,000 feet down the coral of Eniwetok Atoll: they hit volcanic rock, then discovered that the limestone directly resting on it contained the remains of shallow-water organisms!

4. The trouble with this hypothesis, Darwin said, is that it "implies the existence of submarine chains of mountains of almost the same height, extending over areas of many thousand square miles."

5. The French gives *per century,* an editorial or authorial blunder that makes hash of the accompanying arithmetic. The coral wall under discussion has a depth of "more than 300 meters," or about 1,000 feet. Yet if it grew at the rate of an eighth of an inch per century, its attainment of that depth would take *9,600,000* years, rather than Aronnax's 192,000 years. But Darwin's treatise, which Verne has been paraphrasing, suggests that the growth rate would be nearer an eighth of an inch *every two years.* (Today's scientists believe coral growth to be even more rapid—check a modern edition of the *Britannica.*) Now then, if *biennium* is substituted for *century,* the result not only squares with Darwin but it instantly straightens out the arithmetic: the figures are now right on the button.

Whose error was this? It's hard to imagine Verne letting such a howler slip by on a proofing

"So, to build these walls," he said, "it must have taken—?"

"One hundred and ninety-two thousand years, my gallant lad. And that means we have to see those 'days of Creation' mentioned in the Bible as really longer periods of time.[6] Furthermore, the formation of coal—that is, the mineralization of forests swallowed by floods—and the cooling off of basaltic rocks[7] also required a much longer time. So I'll say that those 'days' mentioned in the Bible must represent epochs, and not literally the hours between sunrise and sunrise. Because, according to the Bible itself, the sun doesn't date from the first day of Creation."

When the *Nautilus* returned to the surface, I could see the entire island of Clermont-Tonnerre with its low, wooded growth. Indeed, I could visualize its history. Its madreporic rocks had evidently been fertilized by waterspouts and storms. One day, a seed, carried by some hurricane from nearby land, fell on these limestone beds, mixing with the decomposing particles of marine plants and fish to form a vegetable humus. A coconut, floating in on the waves, arrived on the new shore and germinated. The tree that grew prevented water from evaporating and so a stream was born. Vegetation gradually flourished. Some tiny animals—worms, insects—came ashore on tree trunks that winds had wrenched from nearby islands. Turtles came and laid their eggs. Birds built their nests in the young trees. Thus animal life developed. Attracted by the green vegetation and the fertile soil, human beings settled. That was how these islands came to be, the great work of microscopic animals.

Toward evening, Clermont-Tonnerre faded into the distance and the *Nautilus* noticeably changed course. After touching the Tropic of Capricorn at longitude 135°, it sailed west-northwest, making its way through the intertropical zone. Although the summer sun was very strong, we did not suffer from the heat because, thirty or forty meters below the surface, the temperature never rose above 10° to 12° centigrade.

On December 15, we passed to the west of the bewitching Society Islands and gracious Tahiti, queen of the Pacific. In the morning, I spotted Tahiti's lofty peaks a few miles to leeward. Its waters supplied us with excellent fish for menus on board; mackerel, some bonito, some albacore, and several varieties of that sea serpent called the moray eel.

By then the *Nautilus* had traveled 8,100 miles. We logged 9,720 miles as we passed between the Tonga archipelago, where the crews of the *Argo,* the *Port-au-Prince,* and the *Duke of Portland* had all perished, and the archipelago of the Navigators, where Captain de Langle, the friend of La Pérouse, was slain.

---

check. So did he nod off? Or was he, perhaps, not sent a proof at all? We leave the puzzle to future researchers.

6. Aronnax, like many scientists since, reconciles Darwin's theory of evolution with Genesis by concluding that the six "days" of Creation are simply metaphors for six major epochs of geological time.

7. This detail appears in Hachette but was (accidentally?) dropped from Hetzel. For completeness' sake we've followed the former.

Then we sighted the Fiji Islands, where the natives had massacred the sailors of the *Union* as well as Captain Bureau, of Nantes, commander of the *Aimable Josephine.*

Extended over 100 leagues north to south, and over 90 leagues east to west, this archipelago is contained between latitude 2° and 6° south and between longitude 174° and 179° west. It is composed of islands, isles, and reefs, including the islands of Viti Levu, Vanua Levu, and Kadavu.

Tasman discovered this island group in 1643, the same year that Torricelli invented the barometer and that Louis XIV ascended the throne. I leave it to the reader to decide which of these three deeds was more beneficial to humanity. Then came Cook in 1774,[8] d'Entrecasteaux in 1793, and finally Dumont d'Urville in 1827, who untangled the entire chaotic geography of this archipelago. The *Nautilus* headed for Wailea Bay, scene of the terrible adventures of Captain Dillon, who was the first to throw light on the mystery of the shipwreck of La Pérouse.[9]

We repeatedly dragged our nets across the bay, gathering in a huge number of superb oysters. As Seneca had advised, we opened them right at the table, and stuffed ourselves. These mollusks belonged to the species known as *Ostrea lamellosa,* quite common in Corsican waters. The Wailea oyster beds must have been extensive. If they had not been controlled by various natural checks, these shellfish would have jam-packed the bay, since as many as 2,000,000 eggs have been counted in one single oyster.

If Ned suffered no gastric disturbances at our oyster fest, it was only because oysters are the only food that never causes indigestion. Indeed, one would have to consume sixteen dozen of these headless mollusks in order to gain the 315 grams of nitrogen one needs daily.

On December 25 the *Nautilus* was navigating among the New Hebrides, which were discovered by Queiros in 1606, explored by Bougainville in 1768, and given their present name by Cook in 1773. This group is mainly composed of nine large islands stretching out over 120 leagues from north-northwest to south-southeast, situated between latitude 2° and 15° south, and between longitude 164° and 168°. We passed close to Aurou Island, which, at the moment of our noon observations, looked like a mass of green woods dominated by a very tall mountain peak.

That day was Noël, and Ned Land seemed sad that there was no celebration on board of Christmas, which Protestants observe so fervently with a great family feast.

I had not seen Captain Nemo for a week, when, on the morning of December 27, he entered the grand salon, acting as always as if he had left me only five minutes ago. I was busy tracing our course on the map when he came up to me,

8. The French gives 1714, an obvious typo that persists in every text we've seen. Cook visited the Fiji Islands during his second voyage (1772–1775).

9. The disappearance of an entire expedition under France's Commander La Pérouse was one of the great maritime riddles.

put his finger on a position on the chart, and pronounced just one word:

"Vanikoro."

That word was magic. That was the name of those islets where La Pérouse's ships had foundered. I leaped to my feet.

"Is the *Nautilus* heading for Vanikoro?" I asked.

"Yes, professor," the captain replied.

"And I'll be able to visit those celebrated islands where the *Boussole* and the *Astrolabe* went aground?"

"If you'd like to, professor."

"When will we reach Vanikoro?"

"We're there, professor."

Followed by the captain, I mounted to the platform and greedily scanned the horizon.

In the northeast I discovered two volcanic islands of unequal size, surrounded by a coral reef whose circumference, I knew well, measured forty miles. We were close to the island properly called Vanikoro, which Dumont d'Urville had tagged Isle de la Recherche, "Island of the Search." We lay directly before the little harbor of Vanou, situated in latitude 16° 4′ south, longitude 164° 32′ east. The island seemed covered with verdure from the beach to the heights inland, crowned by Mt. Kapogo, 476 fathoms high.

Clearing the outer belt of rocks via a narrow strait, the *Nautilus* found itself inside the breakers where the sea was 30 to 40 fathoms deep. Under the green shade of some tropical evergreens, I spied a few natives. They seemed greatly surprised at our approach. To them this long black object, advancing flush with the water, must have seemed like some giant whale that they should view with distrust.

Just then Captain Nemo asked what I knew about La Pérouse's shipwreck.

"Only what everybody knows, captain."

"Then can you tell me just what it is that everybody knows?" he asked sarcastically.

"Oh of course."

I gave him a succinct summary of all that the last labors of Dumont d'Urville had made known to us:

In 1785, King Louis XVI commissioned La Pérouse and his second in command, Captain de Langle, to circumnavigate the globe. They embarked in two sloops of war, the *Boussole* and the *Astrolabe,* and were never seen again.

In 1791, the French government, justifiably anxious over the fate of the two sloops of war, outfitted two large supply ships, the *Recherche* and the *Espérance,* which left Brest on September 28 under the command of Bruni d'Entrecasteaux. Two months later the government learned, from a certain Bowen, commanding the *Albemarle,* that debris of shipwrecked vessels had been seen on the New Georgia coast. But d'Entrecasteaux, unaware of Bowen's information, which seemed dubious anyhow, headed for the Admiralty Islands, which a certain Captain Hunter had reported as the scene of La Pérouse's shipwreck.

D'Entrecasteaux searched in vain. The *Espérance* and the *Recherche* passed right by Vanikoro without stopping there. And the voyage was a disaster. It cost the lives of d'Entrecasteaux, two of his officers, and several of his sailors.

It was an old hand at sailing the Pacific, Captain Dillon, who was the first to find unmistakable evidence of the wrecks. On May 15, 1824, his ship, the *St. Patrick,* was passing near Tikopia Island, one of the New Hebrides. A native boatman pulled alongside in a dugout canoe and sold Dillon a silver sword hilt bearing the imprint of characters engraved with a burin.[10] This native said that when he had visited Vanikoro six years before, he had seen two Europeans from ships that had run aground many years earlier on the reefs of the island.

Dillon surmised that the ships were La Pérouse's, whose disappearance had startled the whole world. He tried to get to Vanikoro where, according to the native boatman, he would find much debris from the shipwreck, but wind and currents prevented him.

Dillon returned to Calcutta where he was able to interest the Asiatic Society and the East India Company in his discovery. They put a vessel, which was named after the *Recherche,* at his disposal and, accompanied by a French official, he embarked on January 23, 1827.

The new *Recherche,* after putting in at several Pacific ports, dropped anchor off Vanikoro on July 7, 1827, in that same harbor of Vanou where our *Nautilus* was now floating.

There Dillon collected numerous remains of the wrecked ships, iron utensils, anchors, grommets from pulley blocks, a few swivel guns, an 18-pound cannonball, fragments of astronomical instruments, a piece of stern rail, a bronze bell inscribed "Made by Bazin," the foundry mark of the Brest arsenal around 1785. There could no longer be any doubt.

Dillon stayed on at Vanikoro until October, until he was certain he had gleaned all available evidence. Then he left Vanikoro, headed for New Zealand, dropped anchor at Calcutta on April 7, 1828, and returned to France where he was warmly received by the grateful King Charles X.

Meanwhile, Dumont d'Urville, unacquainted with Dillon's discoveries, was searching for La Pérouse's wrecks elsewhere. For a whaler had reported that some medals and a Cross of St. Louis had been found in the hands of natives of the Louisiade Islands and New Caledonia.

And so Dumont d'Urville had put to sea in a vessel named after the *Astrolabe,* and two months after Dillon had left Vanikoro, he put into Hobart. There he read about Dillon's labors, and also about a certain James Hobbs, first mate on the *Union* out of Calcutta, who had gone ashore on an island, situated in latitude 8° 18′ south and longitude 156° 30′ east, and had seen some natives using iron bars and wearing red cloth.

Dumont d'Urville was puzzled, wondering whether he could give cred-

---

10. A pointed, steel cutting tool used by sculptors and metalworkers.

ence to these stories that he had read in newspapers not known for their accuracy. But he decided to follow Dillon's trail.

On February 10, 1828, the new *Astrolabe* hove before Tikopia Island where d'Urville took on, as a guide and interpreter, a deserter who had settled there. He sighted Vanikoro on the 12th, skirted its reefs until the 14th, and not until the 20th did he anchor inside its barrier, in Vanou harbor.

Three days later, several ship's officers walked around the island and collected some trifles. Adopting a system of denial and evasion, the natives refused to take them to the scene of the disaster. This equivocal conduct led d'Urville's men to suspect that the natives had mistreated the castaways; at least the natives seemed fearful that d'Urville had come to avenge La Pérouse and his unfortunate crews.

Finally, on February 26, appeased with gifts, assured there would be no reprisals, the natives led the first mate, Mr. Jacquinot, to the scene of the wreck.

There, in three or four fathoms of water, between the Paeu and Vanou reefs, lay some anchors, cannons, iron and lead ballast, all caked with limestone deposits. A launch and a whaleboat from the new *Astrolabe* were brought to the scene, and—after long exhausting labor—their crews managed to raise an anchor weighing 1,800 pounds, a cast-iron eight-pounder cannon, a piece of lead ballast, and two copper swivel guns.

Questioning the natives, d'Urville learned that after La Pérouse lost his two ships on the reefs, he built a smaller boat, only to lose that one too. Where? No one could say.

Under a copse of mangroves, the commander of the new *Astrolabe* erected a memorial to the famous navigator and his men. This was a simple four-sided pyramid, set on a coral base, with no ironwork to tempt the natives' avarice.

Now Dumont d'Urville was set to leave, but fever rampant in those unsanitary islands had undermined the health of his crews and, sick himself, he was unable to cast off until March 17.

Meanwhile, the French government was worried that Dumont d'Urville did not know about Dillon's discoveries, and they sent to Vanikoro a sloop of war, the *Bayonnaise,* which had been stationed on the American west coast. Under the command of Legoarant de Tromelin, the *Bayonnaise* anchored off Vanikoro a few months after the new *Astrolabe* had departed. De Tromelin found nothing new except that he could report that the natives had respected the memorial honoring La Pérouse.

Such were the events that I had summarized for Captain Nemo.

"So," he responded, "no one knows where that third ship, the one the castaways built on Vanikoro Island, sailed to, or where it sank?"

"No, nobody knows."

Captain Nemo said nothing but signaled me to follow him to the salon. The *Nautilus* dropped some meters below the surface. He opened the panels.

I rushed to the window and beneath encrustations of coral—fungus coral, siphonula coral, alcyon coral, sea anemone from the genus *Caryophylia*—and

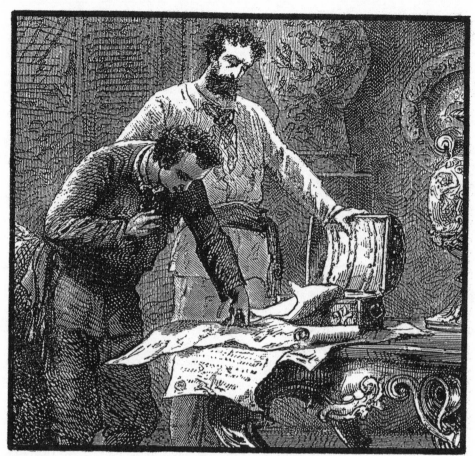

Military orders

through myriads of lovely fish—greenfish, damselfish, sweepers,[11] snappers, squirrelfish—I could see objects that the dredges had been unable to bring up: iron stirrups, anchors, cannon, shot, capstan fittings, a stempost, all objects from the sunken ships, now carpeted in moving flowers.

While I gaped at this pitiful wreckage, Captain Nemo said gravely:

"Commander La Pérouse set out on December 7, 1785, with his ships the *Boussole* and the *Astrolabe.* He anchored first at Botany Bay, visited the Tonga Island group and New Caledonia, headed for the Santa Cruz archipelago, and then put in at Nomuka in the Hapai Islands. Finally his ships approached the unknown reefs of Vanikoro. The *Boussole* was in the lead and ran afoul of breakers on the southern coast. The *Astrolabe* came to the rescue and likewise ran aground. The first ship was destroyed almost immediately. The second, stranded to leeward, held together for several days. The natives welcomed the castaways warmly enough. The crews stationed themselves on the island and built a small craft from the remains of the two larger ones. Several sailors stayed voluntarily in Vanikoro. The others, weak and sick, sailed with La Pérouse. He headed for the Solomon Islands and there all hands perished on the west coast of the main island in that group, between Cape Deception and Cape Satisfaction!"

"And how do you know all this?" I cried out.

"Here's what I found at the very scene of their final disaster."

Captain Nemo showed me a tin box, stamped with the French coat-of-arms and all corroded by salt water. He opened it. I saw a sheaf of papers, yellowed but still legible.

They were the actual military orders given by the French Minister of the Navy to Commander La Pérouse, annotated along the margins in the handwriting of Louis XVI!

"Ah, what a beautiful death for a sailor," the captain was saying. "A tomb of coral is a peaceful tomb. Heaven grant me that my companions and I rest in no other!"

---

11. Both the Hachette and Hetzel editions give *pomphérides,* which we take to be a typo for pimphérides—the genus *Pimpherida,* fish nicknamed sweepers or catalufa.

TWENTY

The Torres Strait[1]

URING THE NIGHT of December 27–28, the *Nautilus* left the waterways of Vanikoro with great speed. Our course was southwesterly, and in three days we had covered the 750 leagues that separate La Pérouse's islands from the southeastern tip of New Guinea.

Bright and early on January 1, 1868, Conseil joined me on the platform.

"Will master," the gallant lad said, "permit me to wish him a Happy New Year?"

"What, Conseil—you're acting just as if I were still in my study at the Botanical Gardens in Paris! I accept your good wishes and I thank you for them. Only, I'd like to know what you mean by a 'happy year' in our present situation. Do you mean a year that will end our imprisonment, or a year in which we make the best of it as this strange voyage continues—?"

"Good lord," Conseil responded, "I really don't know *how* to respond to master's question. Certainly we've been seeing some great marvels, and for the last two months we've had no time for boredom. The latest marvel is always the most marvelous, and if this progression continues, I can't imagine how it will end. In my opinion, we'll never again have such an experience."

"Never again, Conseil."

"Besides, Mr. Nemo really lives up to his Latin name.[2] He couldn't bother us less if he didn't exist at all."

"That's right, my boy."

"And so, with all due respect to master, I think a happy new year would be the one that allows us to see everything but get it over with!"

"Everything? That would be a very long year. But what does Ned Land think?"

---

1. To nineteenth century Europeans, Verne's chapter title created suspense with a mere place name: by itself, this strait connoted the impenetrable mysteries of the South Pacific. Discovered by Spain's Luis Vaez de Torres in 1606, the strait's barrier reefs repelled most vessels, and Holland's Abel Tansman even denied their existence in 1644. But in 1770 Captain Cook confirmed the presence of these treacherous waters. So, for Verne's early readers, this chapter title promised dangerous adventure in exotic territory.

2. As we discussed in note 4 for I 10, Nemo's Byronic incognito means "no one" or "nobody."

"Ned Land thinks exactly the opposite of what I think. He has a practical mind with a demanding stomach. He is tired of looking at fish and eating nothing but fish. The lack of wine, bread, and meat is an affront to the dignity of an Anglo-Saxon. He is accustomed to beefsteak, brandy, and gin—in moderation, of course."

"As for me, Conseil, that isn't what bothers me. I've adjusted very well to the diet on board."

"And so have I. I am as happy to stay on board as Mr. Land is eager to escape. If this new year is bad for me, it will be good for him, and vice versa. No matter what happens, one of us will always be satisfied. But as for master, I hope that all his wishes come true."

"Thank you, my boy. Only we must postpone the question of New Year's gifts, and let a handshake suffice until later. That's all I have on me right now!"

"Master was never so generous," Conseil said, as he bowed and then went about his business.

By January 2, we had traveled 11,340 miles, or 5,250 leagues,[3] since our point of departure in the Japan Sea. Before the ram of the *Nautilus* there stretched the dangerous waters of the Coral Sea, off the northeast coast of Australia. We cruised along a few miles off that fearsome shoal where Captain Cook's ships almost went down on June 10, 1770. The craft Cook was aboard charged into some coral rock, and if it did not founder it was because a piece of the coral broke off in the collision and plugged the very hole it had made in the hull![4]

I had hoped to visit this reef, 360 leagues long, against which the seas, always rough, break with great violence and thunderous noise. But the *Nautilus*'s slanting fins dragged us down to a great depth and I could see nothing of those tall coral walls. I had to content myself with studying the various specimens of fish brought up by our nets. Among others I saw some long-finned albacore, a species in the genus *Scomber,* as large as tuna, with bluish flanks and vertical stripes that disappear when it dies. These fish followed us in schools and furnished our table with very dainty flesh. We also caught great numbers of yellow-green giltheads half a decimeter long and tasting like dorado, and some flying gurnards, veritable submarine swallows that on dark nights alternately streak air and water with their phosphorescent gleams. Among mollusks and zoophytes I found in our dragnet various species of alcyonarian coral, some sea urchins, hammer shells, spurred star shells, wentletrap snails, horn shells, and glass snails. Local plant life was represented by beautiful floating algae, sea tangle, kelp from the genus *Macrocystis,* impregnated with the gum that trans-

3. Here we can see that Verne is reckoning a league as 2.16 miles.

4. On that memorable night of June 10, 1770, Captain Cook dumped six cannons overboard in a successful effort to lighten his ship. Those cannons were finally recovered on January 10, 1969, by a salvage expedition from the Philadelphia Academy of Natural Sciences under Virgil Kauffman. At least ten diving expeditions of record had searched for them before Kauffman's crew arrived.

udes through their pores, from which I selected an admirable *Nemastoma gel-iniaroidea* to be placed among the curiosities of Nature in the museum.

Two days after crossing the Coral Sea, on January 4 we sighted the coasts of Papua. On that occasion Captain Nemo informed me of his intention to get into the Indian Ocean through the Torres Strait. That was all he said. But it pleased Ned. For this route would take us, once again, closer to European waters.

The Torres Strait is regarded as dangerous not only for its bristling reefs but also for the hostile inhabitants who live along the coasts. It separates Queensland from the huge island of Papua, also known as New Guinea.

Papua is 400 leagues long and 130 leagues wide, with a surface area of 40,000 square leagues. It is located between latitude 0° 19′ and 10° 2′ south, and between longitude 128° 23′ and 146° 15′. At midday, as the first mate was shooting the sun, I spied the summits of the Arfak Mountains. They rise in terraces that terminate in sharp peaks.

This land was discovered in 1511 by the Portuguese Francisco Serrano. It was visited successively by Don Jorge de Meneses in 1526; by Juan de Grijalva in 1527; by the Spanish general Alvaro de Saavedra in 1528; by Inigo Ortiz in 1545; by the Dutchman Schouten in 1616; by Nicolas Sruick in 1753; by Tasman, Dampier, Fumel, Carteret, Edwards, Bougainville, Cook, McClure, Thomas Forrest, and by d'Entrecasteaux in 1792; by Duperrey in 1823; and by Dumont d'Urville in 1827. De Rienzi has declared this to be "the very heartland" of the blacks who inhabit the Malay Archipelago, and I had no suspicion that chance would bring me face to face with those fearsome Andaman aborigines.

In short, the *Nautilus* was entering the world's most dangerous strait, one that even the boldest navigators hesitated to clear, the strait that Luis Vaez de Torres braved on his return to Melanesia from the South Seas, the strait in which Dumont d'Urville ran aground in 1840 and nearly went down with all hands. And even the *Nautilus,* superior to every danger in the sea, was about to become intimate with these dreaded reefs.

The Torres Strait is about 34 leagues wide but obstructed by a countless number of islands, islets, reefs, and rocks that make it nearly impossible to sail through. And so Captain Nemo took every necessary precaution in crossing it. Floating flush with the water, the *Nautilus* moved ahead at a moderate speed. Its propeller churned the waves slowly like the tail of a giant whale.

Taking advantage of this situation, my two companions and I took seats on the usually deserted platform. Before us rose the pilothouse in which, I was pretty sure, Captain Nemo himself was at the helm. On my lap I had those excellent charts of the Torres Strait prepared by the hydrographic engineer Vincendon Dumoulin and Ensign Coupvent-Desbois, now an admiral, who were on Dumont d'Urville's staff during his last circumnavigation of the globe. Along with those made by Captain King, these are the best charts for unraveling the snarl of this narrow passage, and I consulted them attentively.

The sea was boiling furiously around the *Nautilus*. Traveling from southeast to northwest at a speed of two-and-a-half miles an hour, the current broke over the coral heads that stood out here and there.

"That's a very rough sea," Ned Land said.

"Detestable indeed," I acknowledged, "and hardly suitable for a boat like the *Nautilus*."

"That damned captain," the Canadian continued, "must really be sure of his course, because I can see clusters of coral that would only have to graze his hull to knock it into a thousand pieces."

Indeed, the situation was downright dangerous, but the *Nautilus* seemed to slip through these terrible reefs as if by magic. The captain didn't follow the exact course of the second *Astrolabe* and the *Zelee*, since that proved disastrous for Dumont d'Urville. Rather he ran more to the north along the Murray Islands, then came back toward the southwest and toward Cumberland Passage. I expected he would charge right into that opening, but he climbed to the northwest, through a great number of almost unknown islands and isles, and headed for Tound Island and the Bad Channel.

Now I was wondering whether Captain Nemo, rash almost to the point of madness, planned to urge his craft into the strait where Dumont d'Urville's two sloops of war had gone aground, when once again he changed his course and headed due west toward Gueboroar Island.

By now it was three o'clock in the afternoon. The current was easing, it was almost full tide. The *Nautilus* was nearing the island, which I can still recall vividly because of its remarkable border of screw pines. We hugged the coast less than two miles out.

Suddenly I was knocked down. The *Nautilus* had struck a reef. It remained motionless, listing slightly to port.

When I regained my feet, I could see Captain Nemo and his first mate out on the platform, examining the ship's position, talking in their incomprehensible dialect.

This was our situation. Gueboroar Island rose two miles to starboard, its coast curving north to west like a huge arm. Toward the south and the east, we could already see the tops of several coral formations, uncovered by the ebbing tide. We had run aground at high tide, in one of those seas whose tides are middling, a sorry circumstance for refloating the *Nautilus*. But the ship itself had suffered no damage, so solidly joined was its hull. True, it could neither founder nor crack open, but it was in serious danger of being forever attached to these reefs, and that would be the end of Captain Nemo's submarine.

I was mulling this over when the captain came up to me looking as calm and cool as always, neither alarmed nor unhappy, in perfect self-control.

"An accident?" I ventured.

"No, an incident," he replied.

"But an incident that could force you once again to live on land!"

Captain Nemo gave me a strange look and shook his head in denial. It was his way of reaffirming his intention never to set foot on land again. After a pause he spoke:

"No, professor, the *Nautilus* is not yet consigned to perdition. It will still take you on a tour of all the marvels of the marine world. Our journey has just begun, and I have no desire to deprive myself so soon of the honor of your company."

"Nevertheless, captain," I went on, ignoring his ironic turn of phrase, "the *Nautilus* ran aground at high tide. In the Pacific the tides are not very strong, and if you can't unballast the *Nautilus*—and that seems impossible—I can't imagine how it can be refloated."

"You're right, professor, tides are not strong in this ocean. But in the Torres Strait there is still a meter-and-a-half difference between high and low tides. This is January 4. In five days we'll have a full moon. Now I'll be amazed if that helpful satellite doesn't raise these waters again and render me a service for which I shall be forever grateful."

So saying, Captain Nemo, followed by his first mate, descended into the interior of the *Nautilus*. The ship was immobilized, just as still as if those coral polyps had already walled it in with their indestructible cement.

"Well, sir?" Ned Land had come up to me as soon as the captain had gone below.

"Well, Ned, we're calmly waiting for the tide of January 9 when the moon will be good enough to lift us back into the sea."

"Just like that?"

"Exactly like that."

"You mean our captain isn't even going to put down his anchors, connect the chains to his engines, and try to pull himself off the reef?"

"No," Conseil joined in. "Why go to all that trouble if the tide will get us off?"

The Canadian gaped at Conseil, then shrugged. It was the seaman in him talking now.

"Professor, believe me when I say this hunk of iron will never sail again, on the water or under the water. It's only fit to be sold for its weight. And so I think our time has come to give Captain Nemo the slip."

"Friend Ned," I replied, "I don't think this stout *Nautilus* is in such trouble as you say. Anyhow, in four days we'll know how much faith we can put in these Pacific tides. Thinking of escape would be reasonable if we were near the coasts of England or Provence, but in the waterways of Papua it's unreasonable. And there's always time for such extreme measures if the *Nautilus* can't right itself—which I would regard as a very grave event."

"But can't we at least get the lay of the land?" he implored. "Over there is an island. On that island I see some trees. Under those trees there must be some animals, *land* animals with cutlets and chops and legs of roast beef, into which I wouldn't mind sinking my teeth."

"Now here I think friend Ned has something," Conseil spoke up. "This time I agree with him. Couldn't master get his friend the captain to take us ashore, if only to see if we still have the knack of walking on dry land?"

"Oh I can ask him," I said, "but I'm sure he'll refuse."

"Let master give it a try," Conseil urged, "and then we'll know where we stand with the captain."

To my great surprise, the captain gave us the permission I asked for, and with grace and alacrity, not even exacting my promise to return to the ship. But escaping across New Guinea would be very perilous and I would never advise Ned to try it. Better to be a prisoner aboard the *Nautilus* than to fall into the hands of the Papuan natives.

The dinghy was put at our disposal for the next morning. I hardly needed to ask whether Captain Nemo would go along. I imagined that none of the crew would be assigned to us, but that Ned Land would be expected to handle the boat. Besides, the island was only two miles away, and it would be child's play for the Canadian to steer that nimble dinghy between those reefs so fatal for larger vessels.

On the morning of January 5 the dinghy, its deck panels opened, was wrenched from its socket and launched into the sea. Only two men were needed for that task. The oars were in the boat and we had only to take our seats.

At eight a.m., armed with guns and axes, we rowed clear of the *Nautilus*. The sea was calm and a mild breeze came off the shore. Conseil and I rowed vigorously while Ned steered us through the narrow passages between the rocks. The dinghy handled well and glided along smoothly.

Ned could hardly contain his joy. He was like a prisoner breaking out of jail with no thought of how he had to return.

"Meat!" he kept saying. "We're going to eat meat! And what meat—real game! A real mess call, by thunder! Now I don't say fish isn't good for you, but you mustn't overdo it. It'll be nice for a change to eat fresh venison, grilled over live coals!"

"Glutton!" Conseil complained. "You're making my mouth water."

"It remains to be seen," I cautioned, "whether those forests do contain game, and whether that game isn't big enough to hunt the hunter himself."

"All right, professor," replied the Canadian, whose teeth seemed to be as honed as the blade of an ax. "But if there are no other four-legged animals on that island, I'll eat tiger—sirloin of tiger."

"Ned is making me nervous," said Conseil.

"Whatever it is," Ned went on, "any animal having four legs without feathers, or two legs with feathers, will be welcomed with a bullet."

"Oh my," I sighed. "Here we go again with the unpredictable Mr. Land."

"Don't worry about me, professor, and keep rowing. Give me just twenty-five minutes and I'll serve you my kind of tasty dish."

At 8:30, after we had successfully cleared the ring of coral that surrounds Gueboroar Island, we ran gently aground on a sandy beach.

TWENTY-ONE

A Few Days on Land

I WAS TREMENDOUSLY excited to be touching dry land once again! Ned sort of tested the soil with his foot—he looked as if he were about to take possession of it. Yet it had been only two months since we had become, in Captain Nemo's words, "passengers on the *Nautilus*," but in reality, in our language, his prisoners.

In just a few minutes we were a rifle shot away from the surf. The soil was almost entirely madreporic, but some dried-out stream beds were strewn with bits of granite, showing that this island was of primordial origin. Its entire horizon was hidden behind a curtain of beautiful forest. Huge trees, some of them 200 feet tall, were linked to each other by garlands of tropical vines, natural hammocks rocking in a mild breeze. There were mimosas, banyans, beefwood, teakwood, hibiscus, some screw pines, and palm trees, all mingled in wild profusion. Beneath the shade of their green canopies, at the feet of their gigantic trunks, grew orchids, leguminous plants, and ferns.

But without pausing to enjoy all these splendid specimens of Papuan plant life, the Canadian preferred the functional to the decorative. He went straight for a coconut palm, knocked down some coconuts, broke them open, and we drank their milk and ate their meat with a pleasure that was a protest against the usual fare on the *Nautilus*.

"Excellent!" Ned said.

"Exquisite!" Conseil added.

"I don't imagine your Nemo would object to our taking some coconuts aboard?" Ned wondered.

"I don't think so," I replied. "But he wouldn't eat any himself."

"So much the worse for him," Conseil said.

"So much the better for us," Ned replied. "We'll have them all for ourselves."

"But just one word, Mr. Land," I told the harpooner as he began to ravage another coconut tree. "Coconuts are fine, but before we fill the dinghy with them, we should find out if this island can provide us with other foods just as useful. It would be good, for example, to have some fresh vegetables on board the *Nautilus*."

"Master is right," Conseil said. "I suggest we reserve three places in the dinghy—one for fruit, another for vegetables, the third for venison—of which I haven't yet seen the slightest sign."

"Conseil, don't give up yet," the Canadian urged him.

"So let's continue our search," I suggested, "but keep a sharp lookout. This island seems uninhabited, but maybe we'll still run into some people who are less fussy than we are about what they eat."

"Ho, ho!" said Ned, moving his jaws in a very significant way.

"Horrors, Ned!" Conseil cried out.

"Yes," the Canadian continued his mock threats, "I'm beginning to appreciate the charms of cannibalism!"

"Ned, what are you thinking of?" Conseil said, "You, a cannibal? I won't feel secure any more, sharing a cabin with you. I don't want to wake up some morning to find myself half devoured!"

"Conseil, my friend, I like you a lot but not enough to eat you unless I really have to."

"I can't count on that," Conseil concluded, "so let's get back to hunting. We've got to shoot some game to placate this man-eater. Otherwise some morning master won't find enough pieces of his manservant to serve him."

During this bantering we had penetrated the darkest part of the forest, and for two hours we explored it in every direction. In our search for edible vegetation we had the good luck to come upon one of the most useful products of the tropics. I mean the breadfruit tree, which flourishes on Gueboroar Island. I saw mainly the seedless variety that in Malaysia is called "Rima."

This tree is distinguished by its straight trunk forty feet high. Its top is gracefully rounded and composed of large multilobed leaves. This makes it easy for the naturalist to identify it as the artocarpus that has been so happily transplanted to the Mascarene Islands. Its big globe-shaped fruit, about a decimeter wide, with hexagonal wrinkles on the outer rind, hang down from its heavy foliage. This useful plant has been a godsend in areas that lack wheat, for without demanding any special attention, it provides fruit eight months out of the year.[1]

Ned Land was on good terms with this plant. He had eaten it on many of his voyages, and he knew how to prepare its edible fruit. The very sight of it delighted him, and he could no longer contain himself.

---

1. The *Artocarpus altilis* tree has played a dramatic role in world exploration. After Captain Cook saw the breadfruit tree in the Pacific Islands, he recommended transplanting it to the New World to feed the Negro slaves. The task fell to Captain William Bligh aboard HMS *Bounty*. But as readers of sea lore know by heart, part of his crew mutinied on April 28, 1789. Bligh and eighteen others were set adrift in an open boat, miraculously made it to safety, and Bligh was able to make a return voyage in 1792, this time successfully transplanting the breadfruit to the West Indies. Unfortunately, the Negroes continued to prefer bananas.

Still, *Artocarpus* has flourished from Brazil to Mexico. As Verne makes clear, it is not "fruit" in the usual sense—it must be cooked and then garnished with butter, salt, or gravy, because it is tasteless by itself.

"Professor," he announced, "I'll die if I can't taste a little breadfruit pasta!"

"Go ahead and taste some, Ned. We're here to conduct experiments—so let's experiment."

"It won't take long," he promised.

Armed with a magnifying glass, he started a fire of deadwood that was soon crackling joyously. Meanwhile Conseil and I picked the best fruit of the artocarpus that we could find. Some were not yet ripe: their thick skins covered their white and slightly fibrous pulps. But others, in great numbers, were yellowish and gelatinous, just waiting to be picked.

These fruits contained no pits. Conseil took a dozen or so to Ned Land who cut them into thick slices and placed them over a fire of live coals.

"You'll see, sir," he kept repeating, "just how good this bread is. You'll see for yourself."

"Especially when you haven't had any for a long time," Conseil sympathized.

"It's much more than bread," the Canadian added. "It's more like a dainty pastry. Haven't you ever had any, professor?"

"No, Ned."

"Well then, get ready for something special. If you don't come back for seconds, I'm no longer the King of Harpooners."

In a few minutes, the parts of the fruit exposed to the fire were well toasted. The inside had turned into a kind of white pasta, a sort of soft bread-center with a flavor somewhat like artichoke.

I had to admit it, this bread was excellent, and I ate it with gusto.

"But it's too bad," I realized, "breadfruit can't be kept fresh. So there's no point in taking any back to the ship."

"By thunder, professor," he said incredulously. "You're talking like a naturalist. But I'm going to act like a baker. Conseil, harvest some of this fruit and we'll pick it up on our way back."

"But how will you preserve and prepare it?" I persisted.

"From the pulp I can ferment a batter that will stay fresh indefinitely. When I get a yen for some, I'll cook it in the galley. It'll have a slightly tart taste, but you'll like it."

"So you think this breadfruit is a meal in itself?"

"Not quite—you have to eat it with real fruit, or at least with vegetables."

"Well then, let's get those too."

When we had completed our harvest of breadfruit, we set out to find the rest of this "terrestrial" meal. And not in vain. By noontime we had picked a great supply of bananas. These delicious products of the Torrid Zone ripen throughout the year. Malaysians call them "pisang" and eat them raw. We also gathered some enormous jackfruit, which has a very strong taste, some savory mangoes, and pineapples of an incredible size. This took a long time but we had no reason to regret it.

I noticed that Conseil was keeping an eye on Ned. The harpooner led the way through the forest, gathering with a sure hand still more fruit which might well have completed his foraging.

"Isn't this enough, Ned?" Conseil finally asked.

"Humph!" the Canadian looked sullen.

"What, you're still not satisfied?"

"All this plant life doesn't make a meal. This is just the end of the meal, the dessert. What about the soup? What about a roast?"

"Indeed," I broke in, "Ned did promise us some cutlets. But that seems doubtful now."

"Sir," Ned said stoutly, "this hunt can't end when it hasn't even begun. Patience! We'll surely find some animal with feathers or fur, if not around here, then in some other area."

"And if not today, then tomorrow," Conseil added, "because we shouldn't go too far. I think we ought to get back to the dinghy."

"What, already?" Ned cried.

"We should get back before nightfall," I said.

"What time is it then?" the Canadian asked.

"Two o'clock at least," replied Conseil.

"Ye gods," Ned sighed, "how time flies on solid ground."

"Let's go," Conseil urged.

Heading back through the forest, we completed our harvest by gathering some palm cabbages from the tops of their trees, some small beans that I recognized as the "abrou" of the Malaysians, and some excellent yams.

We were overloaded when we arrived at the dinghy, but Ned wanted even more. And fortune favored him. When we were all set to push off, he spied several trees, from 25 to 30 feet tall, belonging to the palm species. As precious as the breadfruit, these trees are justly considered among the most useful products of Malaysia.

Called sago palms, they grow wild. Like mulberry trees, they reproduce via both shoots and seeds.

Ned Land knew exactly what to do with these trees.[2] Wielding his ax with great vigor, he soon stretched out on the ground two or three sago palms. I could tell they were fully grown by the white dust on their branches. More as a naturalist than as a hungry man, I watched him at work. He was stripping bands of bark off each trunk. This bark was about an inch thick and covered networks of long fibers that were inextricably knotted and puttied with a kind

2. The Canadian, indeed, is the ultimate do-it-yourselfer, Verne's glorification of man's ingenuity in the face of nature. He now emerges as a man who does more than merely crave meat and liquor. He exults in his ability to combine brainwork with brawn, is happiest in situations that challenge the total unified man. He is amused when Aronnax talks only *like a naturalist* (and his scorn of scientists for their bookish impracticality runs slyly through the novel) while he, Ned, can serve as harpooner, baker, cook, quartermaster, woodsman, and you-name-it. Verne and his readers had great admiration for this kind of person. Ned is a zesty version of Daniel Defoe's Robinson Crusoe and the heroes of Johann David Wyss's *The Swiss Family Robinson*. Verne tells the Crusoe story over and over again, not only in chapters like "A Few Days on Land" but in whole novels like *The Mysterious Island* or *The Island of the Robinsons*.

of glutinous flour. This flour is the starch-like sago, an edible substance that is a principal food for Melanesians.

Ned was content for the moment to chop the trunks into short logs, as if he were making firewood. Later he would extract the flour by sifting it through cloth to separate it from the fibrous ligaments, let it dry out in the sun, and then put it into molds to harden.

Finally, at five p.m., our treasures loaded aboard the dinghy, we quit the shore of the island and half an hour later we pulled alongside the *Nautilus*. No one appeared to greet us. The enormous sheet-iron cylinder seemed deserted. Our provisions stowed away, I descended to my room. There I found my supper ready. I ate and afterward fell sound asleep.

The next day, January 6, there was no change on board. Not a sound inside, not a sign of life. The dinghy lay alongside the hull, exactly as we had moored it. We decided to go back to Gueboroar Island. Ned Land thought we might have more luck hunting than the day before if we tried another part of the forest.

We set out at sunrise. Riding on a tidal current that was going our way, we reached the island in a matter of minutes.

We disembarked and, thinking it best to follow the Canadian's instincts, we let him lead the way. His long legs soon threatened to leave us behind. He headed west along the coast, forded some riverbeds, and then reached a high plain bordered by splendid forests. We saw several kingfishers along the streams, but they stayed away from us. Their caution indicated to me that these birds knew what to expect from two-legged creatures like us, and I decided that either the island was inhabited or at least sometimes visited by human beings.

Crossing a rather lush prairie, we came to the edge of a small forest enlivened by the singing and the flitting about of a great number of birds.

"Nothing here but birds," said Conseil.

"But some of them are edible," the harpooner replied.

"Wrong, Ned. I see only ordinary parrots."

"Friend Conseil," Ned said gravely, "a parrot is like a pheasant if you have nothing else to eat."

"And what's more," I joined in, "if these birds are cooked right, they're worth knife and fork."

Indeed, beneath the dense foliage of that wood, a whole world of parrots were fluttering from branch to branch, needing only the proper upbringing to speak like human beings. As it was, they were cackling in concert with parakeets of every color, with solemn cockatoos seeming to meditate on deep philosophical questions. Glowing red lories passed by like bunting borne on the breeze, in the midst of kalao parrots noisy on the wing, papuan lories painted in fine shadings of blue, and a whole variety of winged creatures, charming but not especially edible.

There was one bird missing from that collection, one native to these shores that never flies beyond the Arrou Islands and Papuan Islands. But fortune would smile on me and I would see it before long.

Passing through a fairly dense copse, we again found a plain covered with thickets. There I saw some magnificent birds taking flight, their long feathers so arranged they had to head into the wind. I gazed in awe at their undulant flight, the graceful curves they described in space, their shimmering colors. I had no difficulty identifying them.

"Birds of paradise!" I cried out.

"Order Passeriforma, division Clystomora," Conseil responded.

"Partridge family?" asked Ned.

"I don't think so, Mr. Land. But I'm counting on your skill to get us one of these charming products of the tropics!"

"I'll try, professor, but I'm better with a harpoon than a gun."

Malaysians, who carry on a brisk trade in these birds with the Chinese, use various methods for catching them, none of which we could employ. Sometimes they arrange snares in the summits of the high trees the bird of paradise prefers to inhabit, and sometimes they use a strong glue that paralyzes its movements. They will even go so far as to poison the springs where these fowl go to drink. But all we could do was fire at them in flight, which left us little chance of getting one. And so we wasted a good part of our ammunition.

By eleven a.m. we had reached the foothills of the mountains which form the center of the island and still we had bagged nothing. Hunger drove us on. The hunters had relied on what they could kill and they had miscalculated. But then Conseil, luckily and to his own surprise, brought down two birds and assured us at least of breakfast. We briskly plucked the white pigeon and the ringdove he had bagged, hung them from a spit, and roasted them over a blazing fire of deadwood. While these interesting animals were cooking, Ned prepared some breadfruit. Then we ate the birds down to the bone and declared them excellent. Nutmeg, on which these birds gorge themselves, sweetens their flesh and makes it delicious.

"It's as if chickens were nourished on truffles," Conseil decided.

"And now, Ned," I asked, "what next?"

"Four-legged game, Professor Aronnax. These pigeons are just appetizers, trifles. I won't be content until I've bagged an animal with cutlets."

"And I won't be content, Ned, until I've caught a bird of paradise."

"So let's resume our hunt," Conseil advised, "but head back toward the sea. We've reached the foothills of these mountains, and I think it would be better to return to the forest."

Good advice and we took it. After hiking for an hour we reached a veritable forest of sago palms. Some harmless snakes glided away beneath our feet. Birds of paradise fled as we approached and I despaired of catching one. Then Conseil, who was in the lead, suddenly bent down, uttered a cry of triumph, and ran back to me holding a magnificent specimen.

"Bravo, Conseil!"

"Master is too generous with his praise."

"No, my boy. What you did is nothing less than a stroke of genius. Catching one of these birds alive, and with your bare hands!"

Conseil makes a capture

"But if master will examine the bird closely, he will see that I've done nothing of great merit."

"And why not, Conseil?"

"Because this specimen is as drunk as a lord."

"Drunk?"

"Yes, master, drunk from all the nutmeg it was eating under that nutmeg tree where I caught it. See, my friend Ned, the terrible effects of intemperance."

"Damnation!" the Canadian exclaimed. "It isn't right to accuse me of drunkenness, given all the gin I haven't had these past two months."

I was examining this curious bird. Conseil was right. Drunk from nutmeg, our bird of paradise was helpless, unable to fly, barely able to walk. But that didn't bother me—I just let him sleep it off.

This bird belonged to the loveliest of the eight species found in Papua and the neighboring islands. It was the "great emerald" bird of paradise, one of the rarest kinds. It was about three decimeters long. Its head was relatively small, and its tiny eyes were located near the opening of its beak. It boasted a wonderful range of colors, with a yellow beak, brown feet and claws, hazel wings with purple tips, pale yellow head and scruff-of-the neck, emerald throat, maroon belly and chest. Two strands of a horn substance covered with down arose over its tail, lengthened by long, light feathers of admirable delicacy, and they completed the costume of this marvelous bird that the natives have given the poetic name "bird of the sun."

I wished that I could take this superb bird of paradise back to Paris and present it to the zoo at the Botanical Gardens, which does not possess one single live specimen.

"You mean they're rare?" Ned spoke as the hunter who does not rate game according to aesthetic standards.

"Very rare, friend Ned, and hard to capture alive. But even dead they command a good price on the market. And so the islanders often make fake ones, just as people make fake pearls or diamonds."

"What," exclaimed Conseil, "they make fake birds of paradise? Does master know how they do it?"

"Oh yes. During the easterly monsoon season, the birds of paradise lose these magnificent tail feathers, which naturalists call 'below-the-wing' feathers. The counterfeiter will gather these feathers, kill a parakeet, attach these bird of paradise feathers to the parakeet, sew up the wounds, paint the suture, varnish the bird, and send the end product of their unique industry to museums and collectors in Europe."

"All right," Ned said, "if they don't get the right bird, at least they get the right feathers, and if it isn't sold as food, I don't see what difference it makes."

If my desires had been fulfilled by the capture of a bird of paradise, those of our Canadian had not yet been met. Fortunately, though, near two p.m. Ned Land bagged a magnificent wild boar, of the species the natives call "bari-outang." This animal favored us just when we most needed quadruped meat, and he was warmly received. Ned Land proved himself gloriously with his shot. Hit by an electric bullet, the pig just dropped dead on the spot.

The Canadian skinned it and cleaned it, and removed a half dozen cutlets destined to serve as the grilled meat course of our evening meal. Then we resumed our hunt, with Ned and Conseil set once again to perform great feats.

Beating the bushes, my two friends flushed out a herd of kangaroos who fled bounding along on their elastic legs. But they couldn't flee so fast that our electric bullets couldn't catch up with them.

"Ah, professor," exclaimed Ned Land, whose hunting mania had gone to his head, "what superb meat, especially when it's cooked in a stew! What supplies for the *Nautilus!* Two—three—no, five on the ground! And to think all this meat is ours, and those fools on board won't have a bite of it!"

I think that if Ned, in his excess of joy, had not gloated so much he might have massacred the entire herd. But he was content with a mere dozen of these fascinating marsupials, which form the first order of aplacental mammals, as Conseil of course reminded us.

They were small, a species of those "rabbit kangaroos" that live in hollowed-out trees and can move at great speed. But although middling in stature, they furnish a flesh most esteemed.

Needless to say, we were satisfied with the results of our hunt. Ned was overjoyed and suggested coming back to this enchanted island the very next day, to depopulate it of all its edible quadrupeds, but he was reckoning without events.

By six p.m. we were back on the beach, near our dinghy aground in its usual place. The *Nautilus,* two miles off shore, looked like a long reef.

With no further delay, Ned Land got down to the important business of dinner. He was a master at this kind of cooking. Grilling over the coals, the "bari-outang's" cutlets soon filled the air with a delicious aroma.

But here I am gushing like Ned Land, in ecstasy over the grilling of fresh pork! May I be forgiven now, as I forgave the Canadian then, and for the same reasons.

In short, the dinner was unsurpassed. Two ringdoves rounded out our extraordinary menu. Sago pasta, some breadfruit, some mangoes, half a dozen pineapples, liquor fermented from coconuts—all this left us in a state of ecstasy. I even noticed that my companions weren't expressing themselves with their usual good sense.

"What if we don't go back to the *Nautilus* tonight?" Conseil was saying.

"Suppose we never go back?" Ned added.

And just then a stone, falling at our feet, cut short the harpooner's proposition.

TWENTY-TWO

Captain Nemo's Lightning

WITHOUT GETTING UP, we stared into the forest. My hand halted halfway to my mouth, but Ned's went all the way to his.

"A stor e," Conseil coolly reasoned, "doesn't drop from the sky, unless it's a meteorite."

A second stone, well polished, knocked the savory leg of a ringdove out of Conseil's hand, supporting his argument.

We all three reached for our rifles, ready to respond to any attack.

"Could it be apes?" Ned asked.

"Close to it," Conseil replied. "They're savages."[1]

"Get into the dinghy," I said, heading toward the water.

It was necessary to retreat because some 20 natives, armed with slings and bows and arrows, appeared hardly a hundred paces away, emerging from a copse that hid the horizon on our right.

Our dinghy was beached about ten fathoms to our left.

---

1. This dialogue sums up Verne's contradictory feelings about such minorities. Conseil says in effect that *these savages are close to the apes.* But in the next scene, Nemo will have the best answer to that kind of racism: *"Where aren't there savages? Are they any worse than other men, the local natives you call savages?"*

Verne's ambivalence about these questions is perceptively treated in Jean Chesneaux's *The Political and Social Ideas of Jules Verne* (1971). At one extreme, Chesneaux says, Verne's writings "naively reflect the racist, ethnocentric prejudices that provided easy rationalization for colonial expansion and the pillage of colonial lands." At the other extreme, Chesneaux finds Verne's novels "redolent of 18th-century elitist views about the superiority of a 'state of nature' " with its "noble savage."

Verne's contradictions begin in his very first novel *Five Weeks in a Balloon* (1863), where blacks are described as being "as naturally imitative as monkeys." In later books, Verne's scorn for African and Pacific natives seems often directed at their ruling classes. In *Propeller Island* (1895), for example, he describes the Polynesian notion of *taboo* as "laws invented by the strong for use against the weak . . ." Conversely, in *César Cascabel*, Verne applauded the Eskimos for "the most perfect equality that prevails among them."

No doubt the main reason for Verne's inconsistency was his "progressiveness," which in his day meant the technological exploitation of Nature for human good. When primitive cultures welcomed the white man's technology and commerce, Verne approved; when they did not, he probably saw them as willfully obstructing progress.

The natives advanced slowly but with definitely hostile gestures. Stones and arrows rained all around us.

In spite of the obvious danger, Ned was unwilling to leave his game behind. He carried a pig on one side and kangaroos on the other, still managing to depart with great rapidity.

In a few minutes we were at water's edge, instantaneously loading provisions and weapons into the dinghy, pushing it to sea and positioning its two oars. We had not rowed two cable lengths when the natives, now a hundred strong, howling and gesticulating, entered the water to their waists. I was hoping that the sight of them might bring some of the *Nautilus*'s men out on deck. But no. Lying well out, that big machine still seemed deserted.

About 20 minutes later, we boarded her. The hatches were open. We moored the dinghy and descended into the interior. I hastened into the salon, which was filled with resonant chords. Captain Nemo was bent over his organ keyboard, deep in a musical trance.

"Captain!" I shouted.

He had not heard.

"Captain!" I repeated, touching his hand.

He was startled and, turning toward me, said:

"So it's you, professor. Have you had a good hunt? Have you botanized to your heart's content?"

"Yes, captain, but unfortunately we've brought back a troop of bipeds whose very presence is alarming."

"What bipeds?"

"Savages."

"Savages indeed," he grew more ironic. "Are you surprised, professor, at setting foot on land, any land, and finding savages there? Where aren't there savages? Are they any worse than men elsewhere, the local natives you call savages?"

"But captain—"

"All I can say, professor, is that I have encountered savages everywhere."

"In that case, captain, if you don't wish to entertain them aboard the *Nautilus,* you'd better take some defensive measures."

"Relax, Professor Aronnax, there's nothing to be so upset about."

"But there are so many of them!"

"How many?"

"At least a hundred."

"Professor," he started to finger the keys again, "when all the natives of Papua are assembled on this coast, the *Nautilus* will still have nothing to worry about."

His fingers raced over his keyboard and I noticed that he was playing only the black keys, giving his melodies a Scottish character. Soon he ignored me and was plunged into a reverie I no longer sought to disturb.

I returned to the platform. Night had fallen, rather suddenly, as it always does in those low latitudes, and without twilight. I could see Gueboroar Island indistinctly, but there were numerous fires on the beach suggesting that the natives had no intention of leaving in the immediate future.

For several hours, I was alone, now musing on the natives—no longer fearing them, having been reassured by the calm captain—now forgetting them entirely to admire the splendors of the tropical night. My thoughts took wing to France, in the wake of those zodiacal stars that would shine over my homeland in just a few hours. The moon shone resplendent amid the constellations at the zenith.

Then I remembered that the day after tomorrow, this faithful, helpful satellite would return to this same place, raise the tide, and wrench the *Nautilus* off this coral reef. By midnight, seeing that all was peaceful over the dark waves as well as under the trees on the coast, I repaired to my cabin and relaxed into a calm sleep.

The night slipped by without mishap. The captain must have assumed that the natives were frightened by the mere sight of this monster aground in the bay, for he kept the hatches open and they would have had no trouble getting inside.

At six a.m. on January 8, I mounted to the platform. The morning fog was lifting. I could soon see the island through the mists, first the beaches and then the mountain peaks.

The natives were still there, many more than the day before, maybe as many as 500 or 600. Taking advantage of the low tide, some of them had advanced over the coral heads and were less than two cable lengths away. I could distinguish them easily as true Papuans, athletic in stature, men of fine stock, with broad and high forehead, large, well-formed nose, and white teeth. Their hair was woolly and red-tinted, contrasting with black and glistening bodies that resembled the Nubians'. Strings of beads, probably made from bone, dangled from their pierced and distended earlobes. Generally, these Papuans were naked. Now I could distinguish some women among them, dressed from hip to knee in grass skirts held up by waistbands made from vegetation. Men who seemed to be chieftains wore necklaces made of crescent-shaped objects or beads of red and white glass. Nearly all of them were armed with bows and arrows and shields, and many carried, in nets hanging from the shoulder, those polished stones that they could launch from their slings with such dexterity.

One of the chieftains came nearer to the *Nautilus* to examine it closely. He must have been a high-ranking "mado" because he was dressed in banana leaves with scalloped edges and painted in glowing colors.

I could easily have dropped him with a bullet, he was well within range. But I thought it best to see if they were really going to attack us. Between Europeans and savages, it's proper for Europeans to strike back but not to attack first.[2]

2. A good example of the sanctimonious attitudes so prevalent in Verne's day. For a European like Aronnax to say that he will be noble and *only strike back, not attack first* is hypocritical. As the natives see it, the very presence of Europeans on the natives' land is already an

During the low tide, they lurked nearby but did not become troublesome or even noisy. Often I heard them repeating the word "assai." From the gestures that accompanied this word, I assumed they were inviting me to go ashore with them. I felt I should decline the invitation.

And so the dinghy did not leave shipside that day. This annoyed Ned who could not complete his provisions. Instead that adroit Canadian spent his time preparing the meat and flour he had already brought back from Gueboroar Island. Meanwhile, about 11 a.m., when the coral heads began to disappear under the rising tide, the Papuans returned to the shore. But I could see that their numbers were increasing on the beach. Were the newcomers from neighboring islands, or from the Papuan mainland? I couldn't see a single native dugout canoe.

With nothing better to do, I thought of dredging these beautiful, clear waters in which I could see a profusion of shells, zoophytes, and open-sea plants. After all, it was the last day we were to spend in these waters if, on the next day, the *Nautilus* would float free again as Captain Nemo had promised.

Therefore I enlisted the help of Conseil, who brought me a small, light dragnet similar to those used in oyster fishing.

"How about those natives?" Conseil asked. "With all due respect to master, they don't seem very menacing to me."

"They're still cannibals, my boy."

"A person can be a cannibal and still be honorable, just as one can be a glutton and still be honest. One does not exclude the other."

"All right, Conseil! I agree with you that there are honest cannibals and that they devour their prisoners with a sense of decency. Still, I do not want to be devoured, even honorably, so I will stay on my guard, especially since the captain seems to be taking no precautions. And so, to work!"

For two hours, we fished energetically without finding anything really rare. Our dragnet was filled with Midas abalone, harp shells, obelisk snails, and especially the finest hammer shells I had ever seen. We also brought up a few sea cucumbers, some pearl oysters, and a dozen small turtles that we set aside for the ship's pantry.

But when I least expected it, I put my hands on a marvel, what you could call a natural deformity, something genuinely rare. Conseil had just made a cast of the net and it came up laden with a variety of fairly ordinary shells, when suddenly I plunged my arms hastily into the net, withdrew a certain shelled creature, and uttered a conchological cry, that is to say, the most piercing cry the human throat can produce.

"Oh, what's wrong?" Conseil asked in surprise. "Has master been bitten?"

"No, my boy, but I would willingly have given up a finger for this discovery!"

---

aggression. The colonialist/imperialist view is that as soon as the native tries to repel the invader, it is the native who has commenced hostilities. The white man will be the innocent victim justified in protecting himself—in a land he has invaded.

"What discovery?"

"This shell." I held up my trophy.

"But that's just an olive shell of the 'tent olive' species, genus *Oliva,* order Pectinibranchia, class Gastropoda, branch Mollus—"

"Yes, of course, Conseil. But instead of coiling from right to left, notice, this olive shell rolls from left to right!"

"Is it possible?" he cried.

"Yes, my boy, it's a left-handed shell!"

"A left-handed shell," he repeated excitedly.

"Just look at this spiral."

"Ah, believe me, master," Conseil said, taking the precious shell in trembling hands, "never have I experienced such a thrill!"

Indeed, it was something to get excited about. As naturalists will tell you, "dextrality" is a law of Nature. In their rotational and orbital movements, stars and their satellites go from right to left. Human beings use their right hands more than their left, and so their instruments and apparatus, like staircases, locks, watch springs, etc., are designed to operate from right to left. And Nature has usually followed this rule in coiling her shells. They are right-handed with only rare exceptions, and when by chance a shell's spiral is left-handed, collectors are ready to pay its weight in gold for it.

Conseil and I were deeply immersed in studying our trophy, and I was solemnly promising myself that I would enrich the Paris Museum with it, when a stone shot from the sling of a native shattered the precious object in Conseil's hands.

I cried out in despair. Conseil seized his rifle and aimed at a native who was raising his sling just ten meters away from us. I tried to stop Conseil, but he had already pulled the trigger and shattered a bracelet of amulets dangling from the native's arm.

"Conseil," I cried out, "Conseil!"

"What? Didn't master see that that cannibal attacked first?"

"But a shell isn't worth a human life," I insisted.

"Oh that rascal," he said. "I would rather he had shattered my shoulder than that shell!"

Conseil was serious but I couldn't agree. Meanwhile, the situation had worsened and we hadn't noticed it. Some twenty dugout canoes now surrounded the *Nautilus*. Scooped out of tree trunks, these dugouts were long, narrow, and designed for speed; each canoe maintained its balance with two bamboo poles floated out over the water. They were maneuvered by skillful paddlers, half-naked, and I watched their advance with some uneasiness.

It seemed evident that these Papuans had already had some dealings with Europeans and knew their ships. But this long iron cylinder stretched out in their bay, with no masts, no funnels, what could they make of it? Nothing good, apparently, because at first they kept at a respectful distance. But they seemed to be gaining confidence bit by bit, maybe because they had ascertained that this boat was immobilized, and they sought to become more familiar with it. Now then, such familiarity was exactly what we had to prevent. Our guns were noiseless, and could produce only a moderate effect on natives who reputedly respect mainly noisy mechanisms. The lightning bolt without claps of thunder would scare people less, although the danger lies in the flash, not the noise.

Now the dugouts drew closer to the *Nautilus* and sent a cloud of arrows over us.

"The devil," cursed Conseil, "it's hailing and maybe the hailstones are poisoned."

"We've got to alert Captain Nemo," I said as I went down the hatch.

In the salon I found no one. I dared to knock on the door of the captain's room.

I heard the word "Enter." I did and I found the captain immersed in calculations studded with X and other algebraic signs.[3]

"Am I disturbing you?" I asked out of politeness.

"Yes, professor," the captain replied, "but I assume you have serious reasons for doing so?"

"Quite serious. We're surrounded by natives in dugout canoes and in a few minutes we'll be attacked by hundreds of savages."

"So," the captain was calm, "they've arrived in their canoes?"

"Yes, sir."

"Well, sir, closing the hatches should suffice."

"Right, and I came to tell you—"

"Nothing could be simpler." Captain Nemo pressed an electric button and transmitted an order to the crew's quarters.

"There, sir, it's all done," he remarked in a few moments. "The dinghy is in place and the hatches are closed. I don't imagine that you're worried these gentlemen will stave in walls that shells from your frigate couldn't pierce?"

"No, captain, but there's still a real danger—"

"What's that, sir?"

3. Aronnax's wry comment was, in Louis Mercier's standard translation, twisted into the following mistranslated gibberish: "algebraical calculations of X and other quantities."

You can imagine how Verne's American detractors sneered at *that*! "Nobody with even a smattering of mathematics would put it that way," T. L. Thomas wrote in his *Galaxy* article. "People don't sit around calculating 'X and other quantities' as an end in itself. Such a remark could only be made by a man with no mathematical background whatsoever." But, of course, it wasn't Verne who made that remark, it was his inept Victorian translator.

Again, the remark is cast in Aronnax's characteristically underhanded humor. Here is his simultaneous grasp of the situation's gravity along with its irony and absurdity. The *Nautilus* is under attack by primitive warriors packing concrete spears and arrows, while the submarine's sophisticated captain is immersed in the serene abstractions of higher mathematics.

Actually, Verne was compulsive about the accuracy and finesse of his calculations. In *From the Earth to the Moon,* the mathematical passages were so gracefully expounded that the rumor spread that Sir John Herschel himself had collaborated with Verne.

"Tomorrow at this time we must open the hatches again to renew the air on board."

"Absolutely true, professor, since our craft breathes the way cetaceans do."

"Now then, if these Papuans are occupying our platform at that moment, I don't see how you can stop them from coming inside."

"You suppose they'll board us?"

"I'm sure they will."

"Well, professor, let them come aboard. I see no reason to stop them. They're just poor creatures, these Papuans, and I don't want my visit to Gueboroar Island to cost the life of a single one of these unfortunate people."

I turned to go, but Captain Nemo stopped me and signaled for me to sit down next to him. He asked about our excursions on shore, and about our luck in hunting, but he couldn't understand the Canadian's passion for meat. Our conversation ran to various subjects, and without being more communicative, Captain Nemo proved more amiable.

Our talk drifted to the *Nautilus*'s situation, aground in exactly that strait where Dumont d'Urville was nearly lost.

"He was one of your great seamen," the captain told me, "one of your most intelligent navigators. He was the Captain Cook of the French people. A man of wisdom but unlucky! Having braved the ice banks of the South Pole, the coral of Oceania, the cannibals of the Pacific, only to die miserably in a railroad accident! If that energetic man had the power to think in those final seconds of his life, imagine what his last thoughts must have been."

Captain Nemo seemed quite moved, and his emotions gave me a better opinion of him.

Then, chart in hand, we reviewed the achievements of the French navigator: his circumnavigations of the globe; his two attempts at the South Pole, which led to his discovery of the Adelaide Coast and the Louis Philippe Peninsula; finally, his hydrographic surveys of the main islands of Oceania.

"What your d'Urville did on the surface of the seas," Captain Nemo pointed out, "I have done under them, but more easily, more thoroughly, than he could. Tossed about by hurricanes, the *Zelee* and the new *Astrolabe* couldn't function like the *Nautilus,* my quiet work room, always steady and reliable amid the waters."

"Still, captain, there is one point of resemblance between Dumont d'Urville's sloops of war and the *Nautilus.*"

"Yes?"

"Like them, the *Nautilus* has run aground."

"Professor, the *Nautilus* is not aground," the captain replied coldly. "I designed the *Nautilus* to rest on the ocean floor. I won't be repeating the painful labor, those maneuvers forced on d'Urville to refloat his ships. The *Zelee* and the second *Astrolabe* almost perished, but my *Nautilus* is in no danger. Tomorrow, on the appointed day, at the appointed hour, she will rise with the tide and resume her navigation of the seas."

"Captain, I don't doubt—"

"Tomorrow," he added, rising, "tomorrow at 2:40 p.m. the *Nautilus* will float and exit the Torres Strait unharmed."

Having curtly pronounced these words, the captain bowed slightly. Thus I was dismissed and went back to my own cabin.

There I found Conseil, eager to know the results of my interview with the captain.

"My boy," I explained, "when I appeared to be worried that the *Nautilus* is seriously threatened by the Papuans, he treated the idea with sarcasm. So I have just one thing to say: Have confidence in him and go to sleep in peace."

"Master has no need of my services?"

"No, my friend. And what's Ned Land up to?"

"If master doesn't mind my saying so," Conseil said, "our friend Ned is making a kangaroo pie that will surely be a marvel!"

Left to myself, I went to bed but slept poorly. I could hear those savages stamping on the platform and uttering deafening cries. And so the night passed without rousing the crew from their customary inertia. They were no more distracted by the presence of these man-eaters than soldiers in an armored fortress would be disturbed by ants running over their armament.

I got up at six a.m. The hatches had not been opened. The air in the interior had not been renewed. But our air tanks were kept full, ready for any emergency: they could always discharge as many cubic meters of fresh oxygen as might be needed to improve our atmosphere.

I worked in my cabin until midday without seeing Captain Nemo. No one on board seemed to be preparing for our departure. After a while I made my way to the salon. The clock said 2:30. In ten minutes the tide would reach its maximum elevation, and if Captain Nemo hadn't made a rash promise, the *Nautilus* should instantly float clear of the coral. If not, many months might pass before we had another such chance.

Now I could feel some vibrations of the hull. I could hear the plating grind against the limestone of the coral reef.

At 2:35 Captain Nemo entered the salon.

"We're about to leave," he said.

"Ah!" I exclaimed.

"I have given the order to open the hatches."

"But the Papuans—"

"The Papuans?" The captain shrugged his shoulders.

"Won't they enter the ship?"

"How could they do that?"

"By coming down the hatches you've opened."

"Professor," the captain calmly replied, "the *Nautilus* can't be entered that way even when its hatches are open."

I stared at him.

"You still don't understand?" the captain asked.

"No, sir!"

"Well, then, come along and watch."

A shocking reception

We headed toward the central companionway. There Ned Land and Conseil, greatly intrigued, watched as some crewmen were opening the hatches. A great clamor, cries of rage, assailed our ears.

The hatches were opened outward. Twenty hostile faces appeared. But the first native to put his hand on the companionway railing was flung backward by some invisible power and fled crying out in fear and dancing wildly.

Ten of his companions succeeded him, all meeting the same fate.

Conseil was overjoyed. But Ned, answering to his violent instincts, sprang up the staircase. And as soon as he grasped the railing, he was in his turn overthrown.

"Damnation!" he cried. "I've been hit by lightning!"

His words explained everything. That was no simple rail that just led up to the platform. It was also a metal cable charged with the ship's electricity. Whoever touched it received a powerful shock, a shock that could have been fatal if Captain Nemo had turned the current all the way up. It could be said in truth that he had set up between himself and his enemies an electric barrier that no one could clear with impunity.

Crazed with terror, the unhinged Papuans were in full retreat. As for us, half laughing, we massaged and consoled the unfortunate Canadian, who was swearing like one possessed.

Then, lifted by the final sweep of the tide, the *Nautilus* rose from its coral bed at exactly that fortieth minute specified by the captain.[4] The propeller churned the waves with lazy majesty. Our speed increased gradually, and navigating on the surface of the ocean, we left the dangerous narrows of the Torres Strait—safe and sound.

4. Such perfect timing is reminiscent of Verne's father Pierre, with his telescope trained on the town clock, and his knowledge of the precise number of steps he had to take from house to office.

TWENTY-THREE

Aegri Somnia[1]

THE NEXT DAY, January 10, the *Nautilus* resumed its midwater cruising but at a great speed that I guessed to be at least 35 miles per hour. Its propeller was turning so fast I could neither follow nor count its revolutions.

Until now I had been greatly impressed by that marvelous electric power because it provided the *Nautilus* with motion, heat, and light. But to those wonders I had now to add the fact that electricity also protected the ship from outside attack, transforming it into a sacred ark no profane hand could touch without being struck by lightning. My admiration was boundless not only for the ship but for the engineer who had created it.

We were heading directly west and on January 11 we doubled Cape Wessel, in longitude 135° and latitude 10° north, the western tip of the Gulf of Carpentaria.[2] Reefs were still numerous but more widely scattered and were precisely marked on the chart. The *Nautilus* had no trouble avoiding the Money breakers on our port side and the Victoria reefs to starboard, located at longitude 130° on the tenth parallel, which we followed rigorously.

On January 13, arriving in the Timor Sea, Captain Nemo sighted Timor Island at longitude 122°. This island has a surface area of 1,625 square leagues. It is governed by rajahs who call themselves "the sons of crocodiles," in other words, descendants with the loftiest origins that humans can claim. The rajahs' scaly ancestors swarm in all the rivers and are especially venerated. They are sheltered, nourished, flattered, pampered, and offered a ritual diet of young maidens. Woe to the stranger who raises a finger against these sacred lizards.[3]

But the *Nautilus* wanted nothing to do with these horrible animals. Timor Island was visible just for a moment at noon, when the first mate determined

---

1. Latin: "troubled dreams."

2. Verne's French mistakenly gives the eastern tip.

3. A good example of Verne's scorn for primitive beliefs and the rulers who profit by these beliefs. Aronnax emphasizes the cruelty to women in such societies. In Verne's time, of course, should any European question any European takeover of such places, the objection would be silenced with arguments about the white man's duty to save "young maidens" and beautiful women from crocodiles and slavery.

our position. I also caught only a glimpse of little Roti Island, part of the same archipelago, whose women have a well-established reputation for beauty in the Malaysian marketplace.

After our position was established, the captain altered our course toward the southwest. Our ram pointed to the Indian Ocean. Where would Captain Nemo's caprices take us next? Would he mount toward the coasts of Asia? Would he prefer the beaches of Europe? These were choices not likely in a man who avoided populated areas. So, would he descend southward? Would he double the Cape of Good Hope, then Cape Horn, and push on to the South Pole? Would he return finally to the Pacific where his *Nautilus* could sail freely and independently? Only time would tell.

We cruised along the Cartier, Hibernia, Seringapatam, and Scott reefs, the solid element's last assertions against the liquid element, and we were beyond all sight of land by January 14. The *Nautilus* slowed down, swimming underwater some times, on the surface other times, here too, it seemed, at the caprice of the captain.

During this phase of our voyage, Captain Nemo conducted interesting research into ocean temperatures at different depths. Under ordinary conditions, such readings are obtained with rather complicated equipment and the results are dubious, whether obtained with thermometric sounding gear, whose glass often shatters under the water pressure, or with devices that make use of the varying resistance of metals to electric currents. Results so obtained cannot be verified with any accuracy. But to ascertain the sea's temperatures, all Captain Nemo had to do was descend into its depths in person and read his thermometer at regular intervals, and he would immediately have the reliable data he sought.

And so, sometimes by filling his ballast tanks, sometimes by driving us down with his side fins set at an angle, the captain reached depths of 3,000, 4,000, 5,000, 7,000, 9,000, 10,000 meters. One conclusion he came to is that the sea maintains, at a depth of 1,000 meters, a permanent temperature of 4.5° centigrade in every latitude.

I followed these observations with great interest. Captain Nemo threw himself into all such work with a passion. I could not help wondering *why*? Was it for the benefit of humanity at large? That seemed unlikely, since some day or other, his labors would perish with him beneath some unknown sea. Unless he intended to pass on his results to me. But that would mean he planned to release us some day, and so far there was no sign of that.

Be that as it may, he also shared with me the data he had obtained on the relative densities of water in the principal seas. From this communication I learned something of personal benefit that had nothing to do with science.

It happened during the morning of January 15. We were walking on the platform. The captain asked me if I knew how salt water differs in density from sea to sea. I replied that I did not because we had not yet conducted rigorous enough scientific observations of these phenomena.

"But I have conducted such observations," he told me, "and I can vouch for their reliability."

"Fine," I answered, "but the *Nautilus* exists in a world apart. The discoveries its scientists make are not shared with that larger world."[4]

He was silent for a few moments. "You are right, professor, the *Nautilus* is a separate world. It is as foreign to the earth as are the other planets. We'll never know what scientists on Saturn and Jupiter have discovered. But since chance has brought you and me together, I can share my data with you."

"I'm all ears, captain."

"As you know, professor, salt water is denser than fresh water, but not uniformly so. Now if I represent the density of fresh water as 1.000, then I can tell you I find a density of 1.028 in Atlantic waters, 1.026 in Pacific waters, 1.030 in the Mediterranean, and—"

Aha! I thought, so he *does* venture into the Mediterranean!

"—1.018 in the Ionian Sea, and 1.029 in Adriatic waters."

Decidedly, then, the *Nautilus* did not avoid the frequented seas of Europe, and I inferred it would take us—maybe soon—toward our own civilization. This would be such great news to share with Ned Land!

For several days more, we made observations of many kinds, on the salinity of seawater at various depths, its electric properties, coloration, transparency. All through this work, Captain Nemo's ingenuity was equaled only by his graciousness toward me. Then he disappeared for some days and I worked all alone once more.

On January 16 the *Nautilus* seemed to fall asleep just a few meters below the surface. Its electrical apparatus was not functioning and its motionless propeller let it drift at the mercy of the currents. I assumed that the crew was busy repairing something inside the boat that was damaged or worn down by the constant strain on the *Nautilus*'s engine.

My companions and I then witnessed a strange spectacle. The panels were open in the salon, and since the *Nautilus*'s beacon had been turned off, a vague darkness reigned amid the waters. Above us the sky was stormy, covered with thick clouds, and so it barely lighted the upper layers of the sea.

I was observing the state of the ocean under these conditions. The largest fish appeared before me as nothing more than ill-defined shadows. Then the

---

4. Verne is here preoccupied with *Faustian man versus Baconian man*. These two opposing attitudes have long tugged at science. Faust was medieval in the sense that his discoveries weren't shared, they were his selfish secrets, his source of power and leverage. Conversely, Francis Bacon (1561–1626) promulgated the modern doctrine: if scientists publish and share their results, they will mutually benefit each other and humanity will advance that much faster.

Hence we see that Aronnax implicitly is accusing Nemo of being a Dr. Faustus when he could be a famous Baconian. But, in actuality, the struggle between these two influences still continues in our 20th century world. On the one hand we have the various professional societies and national academies that work to foster openness and sharing. But since World War II, this pooling of knowledge has declined: all too often, graduate-level dissertations in the sciences are stamped TOP SECRET; corporations try to hide their promising innovations from the competition, and the military organizations of nations worldwide are automatically secretive about their technological advances.

Nautilus seemed suddenly transported into broad daylight. At first I thought our beacon had been turned on again and was throwing its electric radiance into that mass of liquid. I was wrong, and after a moment's closer observation I understood my mistake.

The *Nautilus* had drifted into some phosphorescent strata, which in that darkness seemed positively dazzling. This effect was produced by myriads of tiny luminous animals whose brightness increased as they glided over the metal hull of our boat. And in the midst of those luminous sheets of water I saw flashes of brighter light, like those that appear inside a blazing furnace from streams of molten lead or from large masses of metal brought to a white heat—flashes of such intensity that by contrast certain areas of the light became shadows in a fiery setting from which all shadows should seemingly have been banished. No, this was not the even light thrown by our beacon. This light throbbed with unprecedented life and vigor! Yes, this truly was living light!

Speaking objectively, of course, this was an aggregation of innumerable open-sea infusoria and of noctiluca an eighth of an inch wide, genuine globules of translucent jelly supplied with a threadlike tentacle—as many as 25,000 have been counted in 30 cubic centimeters of water. And their illumination was doubled by those glimmerings peculiar to medusas, starfish, common jellyfish, angel wing clams, and other phosphorescent zoophytes impregnated with the grease from organic matter decomposed by the sea and perhaps with mucus secreted by fish.

For several hours the *Nautilus* drifted in those brilliant waters, and our wonderment increased when we saw huge marine animals frolicking in them like the fire-dwelling salamanders of mythology. In the midst of that nonburning fire, I saw some swift, elegant porpoises, those tireless clowns of the sea, and some sailfish three meters long, those wise harbingers of hurricanes, whose formidable broadswords sometimes knocked against our salon window. And we saw smaller creatures: miscellaneous triggerfish, some leather jacks, some unicornfish, and a hundred others who swam by as dark streaks in the luminous water.

We were enchanted by this dazzling spectacle! Had some atmospheric condition enhanced the intensity of this phenomenon? Had a storm been unleashed on the surface of the sea? But even at that depth of just a few meters the *Nautilus* could not feel its fury. The ship swayed peacefully down in the tranquil water.

And so we lived, always charmed by some new marvel. Conseil observed and classified his zoophytes, articulates, mollusks, fish. Days passed swiftly and I no longer counted them. Ned tried, as usual, to vary the diet on board. Like real snails we were at home in our shell, and I declare it is easy to become a full-fledged snail.

This way of life seemed simple and natural, and we no longer envisaged a different mode of existence on land, and then something happened to remind us of the strangeness of our situation.

On January 18 the *Nautilus* lay in longitude 105° and latitude 15° south.[5] The weather was threatening, the sea rough and rolling. There was a strong east wind. Our barometer, which had been falling for several days, now foretold a struggle of the elements.

I had mounted to the platform just when the first mate was taking his measurements of hour angles.[6] Out of habit I waited for him to pronounce his usual phrase. That day, however, he uttered a different sentence, but one no less incomprehensible. Almost immediately Captain Nemo appeared, lifted his telescope, and began to watch something on the horizon.

For some minutes the captain stood motionless, transfixed by what he saw. Then he lowered his telescope and exchanged ten or so words with his first mate. The mate seemed to be the victim of some emotion he tried in vain to control. But Captain Nemo contained himself, remaining cool. He seemed to be raising certain objections, which the first mate seemed to be answering with strong reassurances. That's what I inferred from the differences in their tones and gestures. I myself had stared assiduously in the direction they were pointing to but couldn't see a thing. Sky and sea met along the horizon in a perfectly clear, unbroken line.

Captain Nemo was pacing from one end of the platform to the other without looking at me, maybe without even seeing me. His step was firm but not so regular as usual. At times he would stop, cross his arms over his chest, and stare at the sea. What could he be looking for in that grand expanse? At that time the *Nautilus* lay hundreds of miles from the nearest land.

Then the first mate would take up his telescope again, peer obstinately at the horizon, pace up and down, stamp his foot, obviously much more nervous than his superior.

But this mystery would soon be cleared up, for Captain Nemo had given the order to increase our speed and the propeller was beating faster now.

At that moment the first mate pointed out something new to the captain, who stopped pacing up and down and directed his telescope toward the place indicated. He studied it for a long time. Greatly intrigued, I went down to the salon and brought back an excellent long-range telescope I habitually used. Leaning my elbow on the beacon housing, which jutted out on the forward section of the platform, I got set to scan that entire stretch of sky and sea.

But no sooner had I put my eye to the eyepiece than the instrument was wrenched from my hands.

I turned around. Captain Nêmo was standing before me but I could scarcely recognize him. His features were transfigured. Flashing sullenly, his eyes withdrew under his frowning brow. His teeth were half bared. His body tense, his fists clenched, his head bowed between his shoulders, he betrayed a

5. The *Nautilus* is now out in the Indian Ocean, roughly 800 miles from the west coast of Australia, 500 miles south of Java.

6. The first mate measures the angle of the sun's altitude and then consults hourly tables and his chronometer to determine his position.

Captain Nemo transfixed

violent hatred breathing from every pore. He did not move. My telescope had dropped from his hand and rolled at his feet.

Had I unwittingly provoked this show of anger? Did this incomprehensible person think I had unveiled some secret forbidden to the passengers of the *Nautilus*?

No! I was not the object of his fury: he wasn't even looking at me. His gaze was focused on that invisible spot on the horizon.

At last Captain Nemo regained his usual self-control. His features, so profoundly distorted, resumed their customary calm. He spoke a few words to his first mate in their strange tongue and then he turned to me.

"Professor Aronnax," he said in a tone of command, "I expect you now to honor one of the promises you made to me."

"Which one, captain?"

"That whenever I so decide, you and your companions will be confined below until I deem it advisable to set you free again."

"You're in command," I said gaping at him. "But may I ask just one question?"

"No, sir."

After such an answer, argument was out of the question. I could only obey, since any resistance would be impossible.

I went below to the cabin occupied by Ned Land and Conseil and told them of the captain's decision. I leave it to the reader to imagine how the Canadian greeted this news. And there was no time for explanations. Four crewmen came to the door and escorted us to that cell in which we had spent our first night aboard the *Nautilus*.

Ned Land tried to lodge a complaint but the door was shut in his face.

"Could master tell us what this means?" Conseil asked.

I told them what had happened. They were as astonished as I was but no wiser. I fell into a deep speculation, and Captain Nemo's strange facial seizure haunted me. But I couldn't link two ideas in logical order, and I had drifted into the most absurd hypotheses when I was yanked out of my reverie by these words from Ned Land:

"Hey look! Lunch is served!"

Indeed the table had been set. Apparently Captain Nemo had ordered our lunch at the same time he had called for an increase in the *Nautilus*'s speed.

"Will master permit me to make a suggestion?" Conseil asked.

"Yes, my boy."

"Well, then, it would be best if master ate lunch because we have no idea how we'll be treated later."

"And you're right, Conseil."

"Unfortunately," Ned Land said, "they've given us the usual food."

"Friend Ned," Conseil replied, "what would you say if they had given us no food at all?"

That stopped the harpooner in his tracks.

Troubled dreams

We sat down at the table and ate in silence. I couldn't eat much. Conseil "forced himself" to eat because it was "prudent" and Ned Land didn't miss a bite. Our lunch finished, each of us propped himself up in a corner.

Just then the lights went out, leaving us in total darkness. Ned Land fell asleep almost at once, and to my surprise, Conseil followed suit. I was wondering what could have produced their sudden need for sleep, when I felt myself sinking into a stupor. I tried to keep my eyes open but they closed of their own accord. I fell prey to acute hallucinations. Some strong sedative had been laced into the food we had just eaten! So, imprisoning us was not enough to conceal Captain Nemo's activities from us—putting us to sleep was necessary too!

I could hear the hatches closing. The gentle rocking of the sea ceased. Did this mean we had left the surface? Was the *Nautilus* sinking into the motionless strata, into calmer water?

Now I tried to fight off my drowsiness, but it was getting harder and harder to stay awake. My breathing grew weaker, I could feel a mortal chill creeping over my almost paralyzed limbs. Now my eyelids fell shut like lead weights that I could not raise again. A morbid sleep, haunted by hallucinations, took hold of me. The visions vanished, leaving me in complete oblivion.

TWENTY-FOUR

◊

The Realm of Coral

THE NEXT DAY I awoke with a perfectly clear head. I was further surprised to find myself in my own cabin. Probably my companions had also been carried to their own room while still unconscious. Probably they were just as ignorant of what had gone on during the night as I was. We could only hope that future events might unravel this mystery.

I considered leaving my cabin. Was I free now or still a prisoner? Quite free, free to open my door, to walk down the corridor, and mount the central companionway. Hatches that had been closed the day before were open now. I arrived on the platform.

Ned Land and Conseil were there waiting for me. I questioned them. They knew nothing. Lost in a heavy sleep that had left them with no memories of the night, they were quite astonished to find themselves back in their cabin.

As for the *Nautilus,* it seemed to be as calm and mysterious as always. It cruised on the surface of the sea at a moderate speed. Nothing seemed changed on board.

Ned Land scanned the ocean with his sharp eyes. It was deserted. The Canadian raised nothing new on the horizon, no sail, no shore. A noisy breeze blew from the west, and disheveled by the wind, long waves were making the submarine roll very noticeably.

After renewing its air supply, the *Nautilus* submerged only to a mean depth of fifteen meters, apparently so it could surface again quickly. And, contrary to custom, it did surface several times during that day of January 19. Each time the first mate mounted to the platform and once again his usual sentence rang through the ship's interior.

As for Captain Nemo, he did not appear. Of the other people aboard, I saw only my impassive steward, who served me with his usual mute efficiency.

Toward two p.m. I was in the salon busy sorting my notes, when the door opened and the captain entered. I bowed. He responded with an almost imperceptible bow, without speaking. I resumed my work, hoping he might give me some explanation of the night's events. He gave me none. I gazed at him. His face looked tired; his eyes were red from lack of sleep; his features revealed profound sadness and chagrin. He walked to and fro, sat down and got up again, picked up a book at random, put it aside almost at once, consulted his instruments but didn't take his usual notes, plainly unable to rest easy for a minute.

Finally he came over to me and said:

"Are you a physician, Professor Aronnax?"

That particular question was so unexpected that I just gaped at him for a moment.

"Are you a physician?" he repeated. "Several of your colleagues in science took their degrees in medicine—Gratiolet, Moquin-Tandon, and others."[1]

"Oh yes," I said, "I am a doctor, I was on call at the hospitals. I practiced for several years before I joined the museum."

"Good, sir."

That information obviously pleased him. But not knowing what he was after, I waited for more questions, ready to respond as circumstances required.

"Professor Aronnax," the captain said, "would you please treat one of my men?"

"Someone is sick on board?"

"Yes."

"All right. I'm ready to help."

"Come then."

I confess my heart was pounding, I'm not sure why, but I sensed a distinct connection between the illness of a crewman and yesterday's events, and that mystery interested me at least as much as the sick man.

Captain Nemo conducted me to the stern of the *Nautilus,* into a cabin near the crew's quarters.

On a bed lay a man about 40 years old, with a strongly molded face, the very model of the Anglo-Saxon.

I bent over him. He was not only ill, he was badly wounded. Swathed in blood-soaked linen, his head rested on a folded pillow. I undid the bandages, while he gaped with great staring eyes and let me work on him without complaint.

It was a horrible wound. His cranium had been smashed open by a blunt instrument, leaving his naked brain exposed, and the cerebral matter had suffered deep abrasions. Blood clots had formed in this dissolving mass, taking on the purple color of wine dregs. He had incurred both contusion and concussion of the brain. The injured man's breathing was labored, and muscle spasms quivered in his face. Cerebral inflammation was complete, bringing on a paralysis of sensation and movement.

1. The anxiety in Nemo's inquiry stems from the fact that in Aronnax's day, a naturalist might or might not have had medical training. Medical studies could well serve as a route to a career in natural history, zoology, paleontology, comparative anatomy, etc. But Aronnax could have entered natural history directly by studying under specialists like Milne-Edwards and d'Orbigny.

I felt his pulse. It was intermittent. The body's extremities were already growing cold, and I could see that death was approaching without my being able to do anything to stop it. I dressed the wound of this doomed man, readjusted the bandages around his head, and turned to Captain Nemo.

"How did he get this wound?" I asked.

"What does it matter?" the captain replied evasively. "The *Nautilus* suffered a collision that shattered one of the engine levers, and it struck this man. My first mate was standing next to him. This man flung himself forward to intercept the blow. A brother sacrifices himself for his brother, a friend for his friend, what could be simpler? That's the law for all of us on board the *Nautilus*.[2] But what do you think are his chances?"

I hesitated to say.

"You may speak freely," the captain explained, "because this man doesn't understand French."

I looked once more at the patient and then said:

"This man will be dead within two hours."

"Nothing can save him?"

"Nothing."

Captain Nemo clenched his fists, a few tears slid from his eyes, which I had thought incapable of weeping.

For a few moments I watched the dying crewman, whose life was waning bit by bit. He grew paler under the electric light that bathed his deathbed. I looked at his intelligent face, furrowed with premature wrinkles that misfortune, maybe misery, had long ago carved. I was hoping to learn the secret of his life in whatever last words might escape his lips.

"You may go now, Professor Aronnax," the captain told me.

I left the captain in the doomed man's cabin and sought out my own room again, much moved by that terrible scene. All that day I was haunted by gruesome forebodings. I slept poorly that night, and my dreams were interrupted by

2. The guts of this paragraph (from "My first mate" through "on board the *Nautilus*") appear in Hachette but have been *deleted* from Hetzel—and from most reprints and translations based on the latter.

Because these egalitarian sentiments seem significant and their deletion puzzling, we enlisted the investigative aid of Dr. Arthur B. Evans of DePauw University and Dr. Olivier Dumas, President of the *Société Jules Verne* in Paris. They graciously complied and discovered that the passage first appears intact in the novel's magazine serialization in Hetzel's *Magasin d'éducation et de récréation* (where it ran from March 20, 1869, through June 20, 1870). Why Hetzel made the deletion in the first hardcover edition is still undetermined (political squeamishness? or just a compositor's oversight?), but Dr. Evans speculates that the Hachette text may have been set from the *Magasin* rather than from the first hardcover. In any event, the various detail distinctions between these French texts are a fruitful field for future scholarship, and it seems that even the French are only now becoming aware of work to be done in this area.

One thing is certain: the intact passage contrasts strongly with earlier scenes in which Nemo's crewmen are seen as robotlike. The wounded man seems more human: he has voluntarily suffered to save another from suffering, and we learn that such altruism is "*the law*" on board. Even so, our best information is that the crewmen are grim, depressed, melancholy men.

distant sighing sounds, like a funeral dirge. Was it a hymn for the dead, murmured in that language I could never fathom?

The next morning I mounted to the platform. Captain Nemo was already there and as soon as he saw me he came over.

"Professor," he asked, "would it be convenient for you to make a submarine excursion today?"

"With my companions?" I asked.

"If they're agreeable."

"We're at your service, captain."

"Then kindly get into your diving suits."

As for the dead or dying man, there was no mention of him. I rejoined Ned Land and Conseil and told them of Captain Nemo's invitation. Conseil was eager to accept and this time the Canadian seemed anxious to come with us.

It was eight a.m. In half an hour we were all dressed for this new venture and equipped with our apparatus for breathing and for lighting our path. The double door was opened and, accompanied by Captain Nemo and a dozen of the crew, we set foot on the solid seafloor where the *Nautilus* rested ten meters down.

A gentle slope led to a rough bottom at a depth of fifteen fathoms. This seabottom was entirely different from the one I had walked on during my first excursion under the waters of the Pacific. Here I saw no fine-grained sand, no submarine prairies, no open-sea forest. At once I recognized the marvelous region through which we were guided by Captain Nemo. It was the realm of coral.

In the zoophyte branch and in the class Alcyonaria, the order Gorgonaria contains three groups: sea fans, isidian polyps, and coral polyps. It is in this last group that precious coral belongs, a curious substance that has been classified, at different times, as belonging to the mineral, the vegetable, and the animal kingdom! Medicine to the ancients, jewelry to the moderns, it was not permanently placed in the animal kingdom until 1694, by Peysonnel of Marseille.

A coral is a unit of tiny animals assembled over a polypary that is brittle and stony in nature. These polyps have a unique generating mechanism that reproduces them via the budding process, and they have an individual life while taking part in a community life. Hence they constitute a kind of natural socialism. I was familiar with the latest research on this bizarre zoophyte which, as some naturalists have aptly noted, turns to stone while assuming the shape of a tree. Nothing could have pleased me more than visiting one of these petrified forests Nature has planted on the floor of the sea.

We turned on our Ruhmkorff lamps and followed a coral shoal that was in the process of formation and that will some day shut off this portion of the Indian Ocean. Our route was bordered by inextricable thickets formed from tangled shrubs covered with little star-shaped, white-streaked flowers. But unlike plants that grow on land, these arborizations become affixed to rocks on the seafloor by heading downward.

Our lamps created a thousand charming effects as they played about amid these brightly colored boughs. I fancied I was seeing those cylindrical, membrane-filled tubes trembling beneath the undulations of the waters. I was tempted to gather their fresh petals, ornamented with delicate tentacles, some newly in bloom, others scarcely opened, while nimble fish with fluttering fins brushed past them like flocks of birds. But if I tried to touch the moving flowers of these sensitive, lively creatures, an alarm would immediately spread throughout the colony. The white petals withdrew into their red sheaths, the flowers vanished before my eyes, the thicket changed into a block of stony nipples.

Chance had brought me into the presence of the most precious specimens of this zoophyte. This coral was just as valuable as those fished up from the Mediterranean off the Barbary Coast or off the French and Italian coasts. Its vivid hues justify those poetic names—*blood flower* and *blood foam*—that the industry confers on its best specimens. Coral sells for as much as 500 francs per kilogram, and here there was enough of it to make a host of coral fishermen wealthy. Often merging with other polyparies, this precious material then forms compact, inseparable units called "macciota," and I noted some admirable pink samples of this type of coral.

But soon the thickets grew closer together and the treelike forms grew taller. Veritable petrified copses and long alcoves from some fantastic school of architecture appeared before us. Captain Nemo entered a dark gallery that sloped gently down to a depth of 100 meters. The light from our glass lamps sometimes created magical effects when it was reflected off the wrinkled roughness of those natural arches and those formations hanging down like chandeliers; our lamps flecked them with fiery dots.

Amid this precious coral shrubbery I observed other polyps no less curious: some melita coral; some rainbow coral with jointed branches; then, a few tufts of genus *Corallina,* some green, others red, genuine algae that become encrusted with calcareous salts and which, after long arguments, naturalists have finally placed in the vegetable kingdom. But as one intellectual has put it, "This might be the actual point where life arises obscurely from its sleep of stone without as yet detaching itself from its crude point of departure."

Finally, after a two-hour walk we had reached a depth of about 300 meters, which is to say, the lowermost depth at which coral begins to form. But now it was no longer a matter of an isolated thicket or a low clump of trees. Rather, there was an immense forest, with great mineral vegetation, enormous petrified trees joined by garlands of elegant hydras from the genus *Plumularia,* those tropical creepers of the sea, all adorned in shadings and reflections. We passed freely under their lofty boughs, extending into the shadows of the waves, while at our feet organ-pipe coral, stony coral, star coral, fungus coral, and sea anemone from the genus *Caryophylia* formed a carpet of flowers strewn with dazzling gems.

What an indescribable spectacle! Oh if only we had been able to communicate our feelings! Why did we have to be imprisoned behind our masks of metal and glass! Why prevented from talking with each other! Why couldn't we share the life of the fish that inhabit this liquid element, or better yet, the life of those amphibians who, for hours on end, can live at sea or on shore, as their whim determines![3]

Meanwhile, Captain Nemo had halted. When my companions and I stopped and turned around, I saw the crewmen forming a semicircle about their commander. Taking a closer look, I could see that four crewmen were carrying on their shoulders an object that was oblong in shape.

We were in the center of a vast clearing surrounded by the lofty foliage of the submarine forest. Over that area our lamps created a kind of twilight that extended the shadows on the seafloor out of all proportion. Beyond the boundaries of our clearing the darkness deepened again, relieved only by those little sparkles given off by the sharp crests of the coral.

Ned Land and Conseil stood next to me. As we watched I had the feeling we were about to witness a strange scene. Glancing over the seafloor, I could see that it was raised at certain points by mounds that were encrusted with limestone deposits and arranged with a symmetry that betrayed the hand of man.

In the middle of the clearing, on a pedestal of rocks roughly stacked, there stood a cross of coral with extended arms that one might have thought were made of petrified blood.

At a sign from Captain Nemo, one of the crew came forward and, a few feet from the cross, detached a pickaxe from his belt and began digging a hole.

At last I put it all together![4] That clearing was a cemetery, that hole a grave, that oblong object the body of the man who was dying during the night! Captain Nemo and his people had come to inter their companion in this communal resting place, at the bottom of this inaccessible ocean!

No, never had my feelings been excited to such a pitch! Never had such staggering impressions invaded my psyche. I did not want to see what my eyes could not help seeing.

The grave was taking shape slowly. Fish fled in all directions as their retreat was invaded. I heard the pick resound on the limestone floor, its iron point now and then giving off sparks when it hit some stray flint on the seabottom. The hole grew longer, wider, then deep enough to receive the body.

Now the pallbearers carried it to the graveside. It was wrapped in white fabric made from filaments of the fan mussel. They lowered the body into its watery grave. Captain Nemo, arms crossed on his chest, and all the friends of him who had loved them, knelt in an attitude of prayer. . . . My two companions and I bowed reverently.

3. Verne almost seems here to be suggesting that Aronnax is experiencing "rapture of the deep," that he has reached the euphoric—even hallucinatory—stage of nitrogen overload discussed in a note for I 17.

4. You may be heaving a sigh of relief that Aronnax has finally put it all together. But here we have to connive at a *literary convention*. If an author tells his story via a narrator, then it's best that the narrator have slowish mental reflexes. This builds suspense and allows *you the reader* to make connections all by yourself—and to listen as the professor asks all those questions that get *you* the answers. Would Sherlock Holmes ever get a chance to explain the case if Dr. Watson weren't a bit slow?

A coral grave

Crewmen then covered over the grave with the rubble that had been dug out of the seafloor, forming a small mound.

When this had been done, Captain Nemo and his men stood up, walked closer to the grave, sank again on bended knee, and all stretched out their hands in a gesture of final farewell.

The funeral procession resumed the path to the *Nautilus,* passing beneath the arches of the forest, through the copses, along the coral thickets, climbing steadily higher.

At last we could make out the ship's lights. Their luminous track guided us to the *Nautilus.* By one p.m. we had returned.

As soon as I had changed my clothes, I mounted to the platform and, prey to my terribly obsessive thoughts, I sat near the beacon.

Captain Nemo rejoined me and I stood up and said:

"So, as I feared, that man died during the night?"

"Yes, Professor Aronnax," he responded.

"And now he rests next to his companions in that coral cemetery."

"Yes, forgotten by the world but not by us. We dig the graves, and we entrust to the polyps the task of sealing away our dead for eternity."

With a brusque gesture the captain hid his face in his clenched fists in a vain effort to repress a sob. Then he added:

"Yes, our peaceful cemetery lies hundreds of feet beneath the surface of the sea."

"At least, captain, your dead can sleep quietly there, out of the reach of sharks."

"Yes, sir," Captain Nemo replied solemnly, "of sharks and . . . men."

Second Part

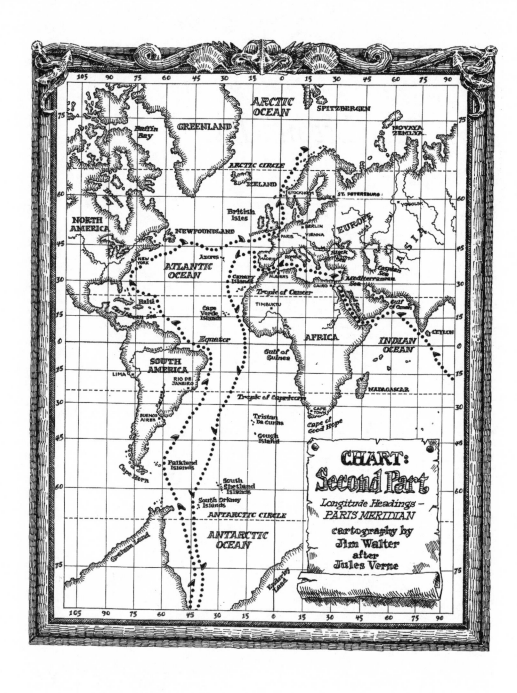

CHART: Second Part

Longitude Headings –
PARIS MERIDIAN

cartography by
Jim Walter
after
Jules Verne

ONE

The Indian Ocean

WE BEGIN NOW the second part of our voyage under the seas. The first ended in that moving scene in the coral cemetery, which left such a deep impression on my mind. For not only would Captain Nemo spend his entire life in the bosom of this immense sea, but he had already prepared his tomb in its most impenetrable abyss. There, the last sleep of the *Nautilus*'s men, friends bound together in death as in life, would be forever secure from sea monsters.

"And from men, too," the captain had added.

Always that same fierce, implacable defiance of society!

As for me, I could no longer consider the hypothesis that so satisfied Conseil. That worthy lad persisted in seeing the *Nautilus*'s commander simply as one of those unappreciated scientists who repay humanity's indifference with contempt. For Conseil, the captain was still a neglected genius who, weary of earth's deceptions, had been driven to take refuge in this inaccessible medium where he was free to follow his instincts. But to my mind, this theory explained only one side of Captain Nemo.

Indeed, the mystery of that night when we had been restrained by confinement and involuntary sleep, after the captain had taken the precaution of violently wrenching from me a telescope poised to scour the sea, and of that next night when that man died from an unexplained collision suffered by the *Nautilus*—all this led me down a different trail. No, Captain Nemo was not content simply with avoiding humanity. His formidable submarine served not only his instincts for freedom but also, perhaps, his needs for some terrible revenge.

Still, as I write these words nothing is completely clear to me, I still glimpse only glimmers in the dark, and I must limit my pen to taking dictation from events.

Nothing really tied us to Captain Nemo. He thought we could not easily escape from the *Nautilus*. But we were not constrained by any agreement, we had not given our word of honor to stay on board. We were simply captives, prisoners masquerading as "guests" for the sake of everyday courtesy. Surely Ned Land, for one, had never give up hope of regaining his freedom. Certainly he would seize the first chance to escape. And no doubt so would I. But I would not get away without some regrets at making off with those secrets of the *Nautilus* that Captain Nemo had so generously shared with us. Another dilemma— were we to hate or to admire that man? Was he a martyr or an executioner? And to be candid, I did not want to leave him forever until we had completed this tour of the submarine world, the first part of which had been so magnificent. I wanted to see the entire sequence of those marvels hidden beneath the oceans. I wanted to see what no one had yet observed, even if I had to pay for this curiosity with my life. What had I observed so far? Nothing, relatively speaking, since we had so far traveled only 6,000 leagues under the Pacific.

Still, I was well aware that the *Nautilus* was approaching inhabited shores, and if some chance for salvation presented itself, it would be cruel to sacrifice my companions to my passion for the unknown. I would have to go with them, maybe even lead them. But would such an opportunity ever arise? As a man deprived by force of his free will, I craved such an opportunity; but as a scientist lusting for knowledge, I dreaded it.[1]

That day, January 21, 1868, the first mate was ready at noon to take the sun's altitude. I mounted to the platform, lit a cigar, and watched him at his work. It seemed clear to me that this man did not know French, because I made several remarks in a loud voice that were bound to provoke from him some involuntary sign of recognition had he understood them. But he remained mute and impassive.

While he was peering through his sextant, one of the *Nautilus*'s sailors— that powerful man who had gone with us to Crespo Island on our first submarine walk—came to clean the glass panes around the beacon. I examined the components of that apparatus. It contained biconvex lenses which, as in lighthouses, increased its strength a hundredfold and sent its rays out in the desired direction. That electric apparatus was so constructed as to yield its maximum illuminating power. Its light was produced in a vacuum, ensuring both its steadiness and its intensity. The vacuum also reduced the wear on the graphite points between which ran the electric arc. This was an important economy for Captain Nemo who could not easily replace them. Under these conditions, they scarcely suffered any attrition at all.

---

1. Here is a perfect instance of Verne's talent for anticipating the social and psychological problems arising out of a scientific endeavor. Aronnax is torn between his humanitarian and scientific needs: he has ideal conditions for making unprecedented progress in his field, but he must work under dubious auspices.

Kurt Vonnegut discussed this all-too-modern conflict in a 1969 speech to the American Physical Society. He defined virtuous physicists as those who "don't . . . work on the development of new weapons. . . . They don't work for corporations that pollute water or atmosphere or raid the public treasury." He added that some "physicists . . . are so virtuous that they don't go into physics at all."

Through Aronnax's conflicts, Verne foreshadowed one of the greatest psychological problems faced in our time by physicists, oceanographers, meteorologists, chemists, geologists, and even cetologists.

When the *Nautilus* was ready to dive again, I went back down to the salon. The hatches were shut and our course set due west.

We were plowing the Indian Ocean, a vast liquid plain with an area of 550,000,000 hectares whose waters are so transparent it makes one dizzy to lean over their surface and look down. Here we generally cruised at a depth somewhere between 100 and 200 meters. We went on this way for several days. For anyone but myself, with my passion for the sea, those hours would probably have seemed long and monotonous. But my daily stroll on the platform where I was invigorated by the bracing ocean air, the spectacle in those rich waters beyond the salon windows, my enjoyment of the books in the library, my work on my memoirs, all this took all my time, leaving me with not a moment of weariness or boredom.

We all managed to stay in perfect health. Ship's fare agreed with us marvelously, and for my part, I could easily have done without those variations in diet that Ned Land had so ingeniously worked to serve us, all in a spirit of protest. And because of that constant temperature maintained on board, we were less liable to catch colds. Besides, we had a good supply of that madreporic coral, of the genus *Dendrophylia,* known in Provence as "sea fennel," and a poultice dissolved from the flesh of its polyps would have made us an excellent cough medicine.

For several days we saw a great number of aquatic birds with webbed feet, known as gulls or sea mews. The crew shot some with great skill, and when they were cooked our chef's special way, they furnished us with a very agreeable dish of sea game. Among the great riders of the wind, resting on the waves from their tiring flights from faraway shores, I saw some magnificent albatross, birds of the Longipennes (long-winged) family, whose discordant cries sound like the braying of an ass. The Totipalmes (fully webbed) family was represented by some swift frigate birds, nimbly catching fish swimming near the surface, and by numerous tropic birds of the genus *Phaeton,* among others the red-tailed tropic bird, as large as a pigeon, its white plumage shaded pink, which contrasts sharply with its dark wings.

The *Nautilus*'s nets brought up several kinds of sea turtle from the hawksbill genus with dome-shaped backs and very valuable shells. These reptiles can dive easily and stay under a long time simply by closing the fleshy valves at the external orifices of their nasal passages. Some of these hawksbills were still sleeping inside their carapaces after we captured them; that is how they manage to sleep and still protect themselves from other marine animals. Their meat was nothing memorable, but their eggs made an excellent dish.

As for fish, they always provoked our admiration when, gazing through the open panels, we could spy on the secrets of their aquatic life. I noted several species I had never before been able to observe.

I will cite mainly some trunkfish peculiar to the Red Sea, the sea of the East Indies, and that part of the ocean washing the coasts of equatorial America. These fish, like turtles, armadillos, sea urchins, and crustaceans, are protected by armorplate that is neither chalky nor stony but true bone. Their armor is sometimes shaped like a solid triangle, sometimes like a solid quadrangle. Among the triangular I noted some half a decimeter long, brown of tail and yellow of fin; their flesh is wholesome and delicious, and I recommend that they be acclimatized to fresh water, a change that many saltwater fish can undergo with ease. Among the quadrangular, I would cite some topped with four large protuberances along their back; some trunkfish with white spots on their underside that make good house pets like certain birds; some boxfish armed with stings formed by extensions of their bony crusts, who are nicknamed "sea pigs" because of the way they can grunt; finally, some trunkfish called dromedaries because of their large, conical humps, whose flesh is tough and leathery.

From the daily notes kept by Mr. Conseil, I also retrieve certain fish from the genus *Tetradon* peculiar to those waters: some southern puffers with red backs and white chests that can be identified by their three longitudinal rows of filaments; and some jugfish, seven inches long and decked out in the most vivid colors. And then some specimens of other genera: some blowfish resembling a dark brown egg, with white bands and no tail; some globefish, genuine porcupines of the sea, supplied with stings and able to inflate themselves until they form a pincushion bristling with darts; sea horses common to all the oceans; some flying dragonfish with long muzzles and highly distended pectoral fins shaped like wings, which enable them, if not to fly, at least to spring into the air; some spatula-shaped paddlefish with tails covered with many scaly rings; snipefish with long jaws, excellent fish 25 centimeters long, glittering with pleasant colors; some livid dragonets with wrinkled heads; myriads of jumping blennies, with black stripes and long pectoral fins, gliding over the surface of the sea with prodigious speed; delicious sailfish that can hoist their fins and use them like sails to catch a favorable current; splendid nursery fish over which Nature has showered yellow, azure, silver, and gold; some yellow mackerel with wings made of filaments; bullheads forever mud-spattered and able to make hissing sounds; sea robins whose livers are believed to be poisonous; some ladyfish that can flutter their movable eyelids; finally, some archerfish with long tubular snouts, genuine flycatchers of the sea, armed with a rifle unforeseen by either Remington or Chassepot: it can kill insects by shooting them with a simple drop of water.

In the eighty-ninth genus of fish as classified by Lacépède, and belonging to his second subclass of bony fish, characterized by gill covers and a bronchial membrane, I noticed some scorpionfish whose heads are armed with stings and who have only one dorsal fin; these creatures may or may not be covered with small scales, depending on their subgenus. The second subgenus gave us some specimens of *Didactylus* three to four decimeters long, streaked with yellow, with fantastically shaped heads. The first subgenus furnished several specimens of that bizarre fish aptly nicknamed "toadfish." Its large head is sometimes gouged with deep cavities, sometimes swollen with protuberances. Bristling with stings and strewn with nodules, it sports hideous and irregular horns; its body and tail are adorned with calluses; its stings can inflict serious injuries. It is repulsive and horrifying.

From January 21 to 23, the *Nautilus* traveled at the rate of 250 leagues every twenty-four hours, or 540 miles at the rate of 22 miles per hour. If we were able to identify all these different varieties of fish, it was because they were attracted by our electric glow and tried to follow alongside: outdistanced by our speed, most of them fell behind, but some of them managed to keep pace with the *Nautilus* for a while.

On the morning of January 24, in latitude 12° 5' south and longitude 94° 33', we sighted the Keeling Islands,[2] upheavings of madreporic coral planted with magnificent coconut trees. They had been visited by Mr. Darwin and Captain Fitzroy.[3] The *Nautilus* cruised along a short distance off the shores of these deserted islands. Our dragnets brought up numerous specimens of polyps and echinoderms plus some curious shells from the branch Mollusca. Some precious exhibits from the delphinula snail species were added to Captain Nemo's treasures, and I contributed some pointed star coral, a kind of parasitic polypary often found attached to seashells.

Soon the Keeling Islands disappeared beneath the horizon, and our course was set to the northwest toward the tip of the Indian peninsula.

"Civilized countries!" Ned exclaimed to me that day. "They'll be better than those Papuan islands where we met more savages than deer! On that Indian shore, professor, there are roads and railways, English, French, and Hindu villages. We wouldn't walk five miles without meeting a fellow countryman. Hey now, hasn't the time come for our sudden departure from Captain Nemo?"

"Oh no, Ned," I said very emphatically. "Let's ride it out, as you seafaring people say. The *Nautilus* is heading toward inhabited places. It's returning toward Europe, so let it take us there. Once we arrive in home waters, then we can decide what is best. Besides, I don't imagine Captain Nemo will let us hunt on the coasts of Malabar or Coromandel as he did in the forests of New Guinea."

"But sir, why can't we do it without his consent?"

I didn't answer the Canadian. I didn't want an argument. Deep down, I wanted to take full advantage of the fact that fate had put me on board the *Nautilus*.

On leaving the Keeling Islands, our pace generally slackened. Our course seemed more capricious and often took us to great depths. Several times the

---

2. Some twenty-seven coral islets also known as the Cocos Islands, about 1,400 miles southeast of Sri Lanka (Ceylon). Discovered in 1609 by Captain William Keeling of the East India Company, they are now administered by Australia.

3. The fame of evolutionary theorist Charles Darwin (1809–1882) overshadows that of his colleague Robert Fitzroy (1805–1865), also a man of accomplishment. In command of HMS *Beagle,* Fitzroy took Darwin on a world tour of Cape Verde, the South American coasts, Tahiti, New Zealand, Australia, and numerous other places that Darwin described in his *The Voyage of the Beagle* (1839). Fitzroy concurrently published a two-volume narrative of his voyages and, after retiring, the *Weather Book,* which expressed some surprisingly advanced meteorological views.

captain used our side fins; internal levers could set them at oblique angles to our waterline. Thus we went as deep as two or three kilometers down but without ever verifying the extreme depths of this sea near India, which soundings of 13,000 meters have been unable to reach. As for the temperature of the lower strata, our thermometer always and invariably indicated 4° centigrade. But I did notice that the upper strata of shallow seas were always colder than the upper strata of the open seas.

On January 25, the ocean being absolutely deserted, the *Nautilus* spent the day on the surface, churning the waves with its powerful propeller, making the water leap to great heights. Who, under such circumstances, would not have seen it as a giant cetacean? I spent three-quarters of the day out on the platform. I gazed at the sea. Nothing on the horizon, except toward four p.m. a long steamer to the west, running on our opposite tack. Its masting was visible to us for a moment but it could not sight the *Nautilus* because we lay too low in the water. I imagine that steamboat belonged to the Peninsular & Oriental line, providing service from the island of Ceylon to Sydney, calling, too, at King George Sound and Melbourne.

At five p.m., just before that brief twilight that links day to night in the tropics, Conseil and I marveled at a most curious spectacle.

It was a charming animal that—the ancients said—it was good luck to meet. Aristotle, Athenaeus, Pliny, and Oppian studied its habits and described it with all the poetic resources of Greece and Rome. They called it "nautilus" and "pompilius." But modern science has not endorsed those names. This mollusk is now known as the argonaut.

Anyone asking Conseil would soon learn from that gallant lad that the branch Mollusca is divided into five classes; that the first class features the Cephalopoda whose members are sometimes naked, sometimes covered with a shell; that this class comprises two families, the Dibranchiata and the Tetrabranchiata, which are distinguished by the number of their gills; that the family Dibranchiata includes three genera, the argonaut, the squid, and the cuttlefish; and that the family Tetrabranchiata contains only one genus, the nautilus.

After hearing Conseil's catalog, it would be unforgivable for the listener to confuse the argonaut, which is *acetabuliferous* (that is, a bearer of suction tubes), with the nautilus, which is *tentaculiferous* (a bearer of tentacles).

Now, it was a school of argonauts then traveling on the surface of the sea. We could count several hundred of them. They belonged to that species of argonaut covered with protuberances and unique to the seas near India.

Those graceful mollusks were swimming backward by sucking water into their locomotive tubes and then expelling it. Of their eight tentacles, six were long and thin and floated on the water, while the other two, rounded and shaped like palms, were held up to the wind like flimsy sails. I could see perfectly their undulating, spiral-shaped shells, which Cuvier aptly compared to an elegant skiff. And this shell is a genuine boat indeed, for it transports the animal that creates it without the animal's adhering to it.

The argonauts

"The argonaut," I explained to Conseil, "is free to leave its shell, but it never does."[4]

"Like Captain Nemo, then," Conseil said sagely. "He should have named his ship the *Argonaut*."

For about an hour the *Nautilus* cruised amid this school of mollusks. Then, I do not know what fear suddenly seized them. As if at a command signal, every sail was abruptly lowered; the tentacles were withdrawn, the bodies contracted, the shells turned over by changing their center of gravity, and the entire flotilla disappeared beneath the waves. It was instantaneous. No squadron of ships ever maneuvered with greater unanimity.

Night also fell abruptly, and scarcely swelling in the breeze, the waves died down peacefully all around the *Nautilus*.

Next day, on January 26, we crossed the equator at the 82nd meridian and reentered the Northern Hemisphere.

That day a formidable school of sharks decided to escort us. These terrible animals teem in those waters and make them extremely dangerous. Some of them were Phillips sharks, with a brown back, a whitish belly, and eleven rows of teeth; others were bigeye sharks whose necks are marked by a great black spot encircled in white and so resembling an eye; and there were some Isabella sharks whose rounded snouts were covered with dark speckles. Often these powerful animals would rush against the salon window with a violence that made me nervous. In no time at all Ned Land could no longer contain himself. He wanted to ascend to the surface and harpoon those monsters, especially certain smooth hound sharks whose maws were paved with teeth arranged like a mosaic, and some huge tiger sharks five meters long that seemed most intent on provoking him. But soon the *Nautilus* stepped up its speed and outdistanced the fastest of those man-eaters.

On January 27, at the mouth of the vast Bay of Bengal, we repeatedly came across a gruesome spectacle: human corpses floating on the surface of the water. They were the dead from villages in India, carried by the Ganges out to the high seas, carcasses that the vultures, the country's only morticians, had not yet devoured. But now there were plenty of sharks to help the vultures with their funereal chores.

Toward seven p.m. the *Nautilus,* half submerged, cruised in a sea of milk. Yes, as far as the eye could see, the ocean seemed lactified. Was it an effect of the moon's rays? No, for the new moon was scarcely two days old and was still lost below the horizon in the sun's rays. Although the sky was lit up by the stars, it seemed pitch-black by contrast with the whiteness of the water.

Conseil couldn't believe his eyes and asked me what caused this strange phenomenon. Happily I was able to give him an answer.

---

4. Biologists have changed their minds about the argonaut since Verne's day. We now know that she doesn't spread two tentacles like sails but uses these expanded arms to clasp her shell. We say "she" because only the female argonaut is known to inhabit the *elegant skiff*—she uses it as an egg case. Finally, she not only is free to come and go, but she does so.

"That is called a milk sea," I said, "a vast expanse of white waves often seen along the coasts of Amboina and in these waterways."

"But could master tell me what produces such an effect?" Conseil asked. "I can't believe that the water has actually changed to milk!"

"No, my boy. This whiteness that so astonishes you is caused by the presence of myriads of tiny creatures called infusoria, a kind of small luminous worm that is colorless and gelatinous in appearance, as thick as a hair, whose length is not more than one-fifth of a millimeter. Many of these tiny beings will stick together over an area of several leagues."

"Several leagues!" Conseil cried.

"Yes, my boy, and don't try to compute the number of infusoria out there. You won't be able because, if I'm not mistaken, some navigators have cruised through milk seas for more than 40 miles."

I can't be sure he took my advice, for he seemed to be deep in thought, maybe trying to calculate how many one-fifths of a millimeter are contained in 40 square miles. I myself continued to observe this phenomenon. For several hours the *Nautilus*'s ram sliced through those whitish waves. I watched its noiseless gliding over that soapy water as it drifted in those foaming eddies sometimes seen between currents entering and leaving a bay.

Toward midnight the sea suddenly resumed its usual color, but behind us, all the way to the horizon, the sky reflected the whiteness of those waters and for a good while seemed impregnated with the vague glimmering of an aurora borealis.

TWO

A New Proposition from Captain Nemo

A T NOON ON January 28, when the *Nautilus* surfaced in latitude 9° 4′ north, it lay in sight of land about eight miles to the west. The first thing I noticed was a group of mountains rising in very whimsical shapes to a height of about 2,000 feet. When our midday observations were completed, I went back down to the salon and when our bearings were reported on the chart, I realized we were off the island of Ceylon, that pearl dangling from the lower lobe of India's peninsula.

I went searching in the library for a book about this island, which is one of the most fertile in the world. Sure enough, I came upon a book by H. C. Sirr, Esq., *Ceylon and the Singhalese.* Settling down in the salon, I first noted the bearings of Ceylon, on which the ancients bestowed so many different names.[1] It is situated between latitudes 5° 55′ and 9° 49′ north, and between longitudes 79° 42′ and 82° 4′ east of the meridian of Greenwich. It is 275 miles long; its maximum width is 150 miles; its circumference, 900 miles; its surface area, 24,448 square miles: in other words, slightly smaller than the area of Ireland.

At that moment Captain Nemo and his first mate appeared. The captain glanced at the chart and, turning toward me, he said:

"The island of Ceylon is celebrated for its pearl fisheries. Would you like to visit one of them, professor?"

"I certainly would, captain!"

"Fine. It's easy enough. We'll see the fisheries, but we won't see any fishermen. The annual harvest hasn't begun. No matter. I'll give orders to bear toward the Gulf of Mannar. We'll get there during the night."

The captain said a few words to his first mate who left us immediately. Soon the *Nautilus* submerged and the pressure gauge indicated that we were traveling at a depth of 30 feet.

---

1. In ancient times Ceylon was known as *Taprobane.* The island has also been called *Sri Lanka* or *Sinhala,* as well as *Tamil Ilam* or *Ilanka,* after its two principal language groups, the Singhalese and the Ceylon Tamil. Ceylon's name was officially changed to *Sri Lanka* in 1948, and it remains the home of one of Verne's notable successors in science fiction, Arthur C. Clarke.

I searched the chart for the Gulf of Mannar. There it was, along the 9th parallel, off Ceylon's northwest coast. It is bounded on the north by the elongated little island of Mannar. In order to reach it we had to travel up the entire western shore of Ceylon.

"Professor," Captain Nemo told me, "they fish for pearls in the Bay of Bengal, the seas of the East Indies, the seas of China and Japan, and in those seas south of the United States, the Gulf of Panama, and the Gulf of California. But it's off Ceylon that such fishing brings in the greatest rewards. No doubt we're getting there a bit too early, since the fishermen won't gather in the Gulf of Mannar until March. For about a month, then, some 300 boats will engage in that lucrative harvest of these treasures of the sea. Each boat will be manned by ten oarsmen and ten fishermen. The fishermen divide into two groups, and they take turns diving. They descend to a depth of about 12 meters by holding a heavy stone between their feet, the stone attached by a rope to their boat."

"You mean," I asked, "that such primitive methods are still all that they use?"

"That's all," Captain Nemo replied, "though these fisheries belong to the most industrialized people in the world, the English. They got them via the Treaty of Amiens in 1802."

"But it seems to me that diving suits, like yours, would be very useful in such operations."

"Yes, since these poor fishermen cannot stay down very long. On his trip to Ceylon the Englishman Percival made much of a Kaffir[2] who stayed down five minutes without coming up for air. I find that hard to believe. I know that some divers can last up to 57 seconds, and highly skillful ones to 87 seconds.[3] But such men are rare, and when these unfortunates do come back up on board, the water pouring out of their noses and ears is tinted with blood. I believe the actual average time down for pearl fishermen is 30 seconds, during which they hastily stuff their small nets with all the pearl oysters they can tear free. And these fishermen don't live to advanced age: their vision weakens, they develop ulcers on their eyes and sores on their bodies, and some of them are even stricken with apoplexy while they're under the water."[4]

"A grim occupation," I agreed, "and one that only serves to gratify the whims of fashion. But tell me, captain, do you know how many oysters a boat can gather in a workday?"

2. Originally the Mohammedans gave this name to a South African Bantu people who were *Kafir,* that is, infidels or non-Muslims. European colonists picked up the word as a term of contempt to distinguish "colored" people from "whites."

3. Nemo seems to be underestimating the stamina of the pearl divers. Captain Edward L. Beach, Naval War College expert on underwater activities, says that a five-minute dive "appears to be a reasonable maximum." The divers "hyperventilate": they take many deep diaphragmatic breaths before each dive.

4. Male pearl divers of the South Pacific do suffer effects similar to those that Verne describes. But it is not apoplexy that kills them. It's the bends.

"Maybe 40,000 to 50,000. They say that in 1814, when the English government went fishing on its own behalf, its divers brought up 76,000,000 oysters in twenty days of work."

"But are these fishermen well paid, at least?" I asked.

"Hardly, professor. In Panama they get a dollar a week. In most places they get one penny for each oyster that contains a pearl. And how many they bring up contain nothing!"

"One penny to these poor people who make their employers rich! That is— odious!"[5]

"On that note, professor, you and your companions will visit the oysterbank of Mannar, and if by chance some eager fisherman will already be there, well, we can watch him at work."

"That suits me, captain."

"By the way, Professor Aronnax, you're not afraid of sharks, are you?"

"Of sharks!" I cried out. That seemed to me to be a rather unnecessary question.

"Well?" the captain resumed.

"I admit, captain, I'm not yet on intimate terms with that genus of fish."

"We've grown accustomed to them, the rest of us," Captain Nemo replied. "And in time you will be too. Besides, we'll be armed, and on our way we might be able to do a little shark hunting. It's fascinating work. So, professor, I'll see you bright and early tomorrow."

That said in a carefree manner, Captain Nemo left the salon.

If you're invited to hunt bears in the Swiss mountains, you might say: "Very good, we're going to hunt bear tomorrow!" If you're invited to hunt lions on the Atlas plains or tigers in the India jungles, you might say: "Hey, we've got a chance to bag a lion (or a tiger) tomorrow!" But if you're invited to hunt sharks in their native element, you might want to think it over before giving your answer.

As for myself, I passed a hand over my forehead and found it wet with cold beads of sweat.

"Let's think this over," I cautioned myself, "and let's take our time. Hunting otters in underwater forests, as we did in the forests of Crespo Island, is one thing. But to roam the floor of the sea where you're almost sure to meet some man-eaters, that's something else! I'm aware that in certain countries, especially the Andaman Islands, some Negroes don't hesitate to attack sharks, a dagger in one hand and a noose in the other, but I'm also aware that many men who confront these formidable animals don't come back alive. Besides, I'm not a Negro, and even if I *were* a Negro, I don't think a little hesitation on my part in such a situation would be considered out of place."

5. Aronnax's horror at this ruthless exploitation is another example of Verne's conflict over colonialism. Generally his sympathies lie with "the most industrialized people," who stand for progress in Verne's scale of values. But as a humanitarian, Verne cannot ignore the victimization of colonial peoples by their *"employers."*

There I was, daydreaming of sharks, envisioning those huge jaws bristling with multiple rows of teeth that can cut a man in half. I could already feel a definite pain around my pelvic girdle. Then too I was offended by the offhand manner in which the captain had extended that deplorable invitation. As if it were a matter of going into the woods and trapping some harmless fox!

"Oh well," I thought, "Conseil will never want to go, and that could be my excuse for not accompanying the captain." As for Ned Land, I admit I couldn't be so sure of *his* wisdom. Danger, however great, held a perpetual fascination for his combative nature.

I resumed my study of Sirr's book, but I realized I was turning the pages mechanically. Between the lines I saw jaws opening wide!

At that moment Conseil and the Canadian came in, quite composed, even happy. Little did they know!

"Ye gods, professor," Ned Land began. "Your Captain Nemo, the devil take him, has just made us a very pleasant proposition."

"Oh," I said. "So you know—"

"With all due respect to master," Conseil replied, "the commander of the *Nautilus* has invited us, along with master, to visit the magnificent fisheries of Ceylon. He asked us very cordially and acted like a true gentleman."

"He didn't say anything else?"

"Nothing else, professor," the Canadian answered, "except that he had already discussed this little outing with you."

"He had indeed," I said. "And he gave you no details about—"

"None at all, Mr. Naturalist. But you will come with us, won't you?"

"Me? Oh surely, yes, of course. I can see that you are looking forward to this, Mr. Land."

"Yes, it could be very interesting."

"And maybe dangerous?" I said in an insinuating tone of voice.

"Dangerous?" Ned Land replied. "A little trip to an oysterbank?"

Captain Nemo had obviously decided not to plant the idea of sharks in *their* minds. For my part, I looked at them a bit anxiously, as if they were already missing a limb or two. Shouldn't I warn them? Yes, no doubt, but I scarcely knew how to go about it.

"Would master please," Conseil asked, "give us some background on pearl fishing?"

"On the fishing itself?" I asked. "Or on the sidelights?"

"On the fishing," the Canadian answered. "The more we know in advance, the more we'll get out of it."

"Well then, sit down, friends, and I'll teach you everything I myself have just been taught by the Englishman H. C. Sirr!"

Ned and Conseil sat down on a divan and right off the Canadian asked:

"When you get down to it, professor, just what is a pearl?"

"My gallant Ned," I began, "for the poet a pearl is a tear from the sea; for some Orientals, it's a drop of solidified dew; for the ladies it's a jewel they can wear on their fingers, necks, and ears, a jewel oblong in shape, glossy in luster,

A New Proposition from Captain Nemo

☙

195

and nacreous in substance;[6] for the chemist it's a mixture of calcium phosphate and calcium carbonate with a little gelatin protein; and finally, for the naturalist it's an abnormal secretion from the nacre-producing organ housed in certain bivalves."

"Branch Mollusca," Conseil murmured, "class Acephala, order Testacea."

"Precisely, my learned Conseil. Now then, among those Testacea capable of producing pearls we find the rainbow abalone, turbo snails, giant clams, and saltwater scallops—in short, all those that secrete nacre, that is to say, the blue, azure, violet, or white substance, that mother-of-pearl, that lines the insides of their valves."

"How about mussels?" the Canadian prompted.

"Yes, also the mussels found in certain rivers in Scotland, Wales, Ireland, Saxony, Bohemia, and France."

"Good," he replied. "We'll pay closer attention to them from now on!"

"But," I continued, "for secreting pearls, the mollusk *par excellence* is the pearl oyster, *Meleagrina margaritifera,* that precious shellfish. A pearl itself is simply a nacreous concretion that assumes a globular shape. Either it sticks to the oyster's shell or becomes embedded in its flesh. On the valves a pearl is adherent, in the flesh it lies loose. But it always has as its nucleus a small hard object, like a sterile egg or grain of sand, around which the nacreous material is deposited, in thin, concentric layers, over a period of years."[7]

"Do they ever find more than one pearl in the same oyster?" Conseil wondered.

"Yes, my boy. Some shellfish are veritable jewel boxes. There was one oyster I heard about—and I find this hard to believe—that was supposed to contain no fewer than 150 sharks."

"A hundred and fifty sharks!" Ned cried.

"Did I say sharks?" I said quickly. "I meant 150 pearls. Sharks wouldn't make sense."

"Of course not," Conseil said. "But now would master tell us how they extract the pearls from the oysters."

"There are several ways. Sometime if the pearls are stuck very fast to the valves, fishermen pull them off with pliers. But most often the shellfish are spread out on mats made from the esparto grass you find on the beaches. They die when they're exposed to the open air, and after ten days they have rotted sufficiently. Then they are immersed in big tanks of salt water, opened, and washed.

"At this point the sorters begin their twofold task. First they remove the plates of nacre, that is, the layers of mother-of-pearl, distinguished in the busi-

6. Nacre is the shell-like matter from which pearls form.

7. Scientists in decades immediately following this novel's publication tended to believe that the main cause of pearl formation was the dead body of a minute parasite. But today's scientists generally support Aronnax's claims: the nacreous material is gradually deposited around some irritating object that becomes trapped in the oyster's tissue.

ness as true silver, or bastard white, or bastard black. These are shipped out in cases weighing 125 to 150 kilograms. Then the sorters remove the oyster's meaty tissue, they boil it and finally strain it, to extract even the smallest pearls."

"Does the price of a pearl depend on its size?" Conseil asked.

"It depends not only on its size," I explained, "but also on its shape; on its 'water,' that is, its color; and on its *orient*—that is, that dappled, shimmering glow that makes it so charming to the eye. The finest pearls are called virgin pearls, or paragons. They grow in isolation in the mollusk's flesh. They're white, often opaque, but sometimes of an opalescent transparency, and most often spherical or pear-shaped. The spherical ones are made into bracelets; the pear-shaped ones into earrings and, since they're the most precious, they are priced individually. The other pearls that stick to the shell are more irregular in shape and they are priced by weight. Finally, classed lowest on the scale, are the smallest pearls, called seed pearls. They are priced by the measuring cup and they're used mainly in the embroidery on church vestments."

"But it must be a long and difficult job, to separate all those pearls according to their sizes," the Canadian said.

"No, my friend, they use a series of eleven sieves, or strainers, punctured with a varying number of holes. Pearls too large to pass through a strainer with 20 to 80 holes are first class. Pearls that don't slip through sieves pierced with 100 to 800 holes are second class. And finally, pearls for which they have to use strainers with 900 to 1,000 holes are the seed pearls."

"Ingenious," Conseil said, "to reduce dividing and classifying pearls into a mechanical operation. And does master know how much money they make from harvesting these oysterbanks?"

"According to Sirr's book," I replied, "the Ceylon fisheries are farmed annually for 3,000,000 man-eaters."

"Francs," Conseil corrected me.

"Of course, francs, 3,000,000 francs," I went on. "But I don't think these fisheries are yielding that much today. Likewise, the Central American fisheries yielded 4,000,000 francs a year in the time of King Charles V, and now they bring in maybe two-thirds that amount. The total proceeds from the entire pearl-fishing industry must now be about 9,000,000 francs."

"But," Conseil asked, "weren't some famous pearls quoted at very high prices?"

"Yes, my boy. They say Julius Caesar offered Servilia[8] a pearl worth 120,000 francs in our currency."[9]

"I've even heard stories," the Canadian said, "about a lady in ancient times who drank pearls in vinegar."

---

8. She was the daughter of Quintus Servilius Caepio. She married Marcus Innius Brutus, and their son, Marcus Junius Brutus, was one of the assassins of Caesar in March of 44 B.C.

9. Suetonius in his *Lives of the Twelve Caesars* says that this pearl was valued at six million sesterces, roughly $150,000.

"Cleopatra," Conseil retorted.[10]

"Must have tasted awful," Ned Land added.

"Detestable, friend Ned," Conseil responded. "But a little glass of vinegar worth 1,500,000 francs is not to be despised."

"Too bad I didn't marry that lady," the Canadian said, throwing up his arms with an air of defeat.

"Ned Land married to Cleopatra?" Conseil cried.

"I was all set to tie the knot, Conseil," Ned explained in all seriousness, "and it wasn't my fault that it fell through. I even bought a pearl necklace for Kate Tender, my fiancée, but she married someone else. Those pearls, you can trust me on this, professor, they were so large they wouldn't have passed through that strainer with 20 holes. And I got that necklace for just $1.50."

"My gallant Ned," I laughed, "those must have been artificial pearls, hollow glass beads coated inside with a substance called *essence d'Orient*."

"Wow, that Essence of Orient must be very expensive stuff," the Canadian wondered.

"No. It comes from the scales of the bleak, a European carp. It's nothing more than a silver substance that collects in the water and is preserved in ammonia. It's almost worthless."

"Maybe that's why Kate Tender married somebody else," Ned said philosophically.

"But, returning to pearls of great value," I said, "I don't think any monarch ever owned one more valuable than Captain Nemo's."

"Master means that one?" Conseil was pointing to the magnificent pearl in one of the glass cases.

"Exactly. And I'm not far off when I estimate its value at 2,000,000—uh—"

"Francs!" Conseil said quickly.

"Yes," I said, "2,000,000 francs, and all it cost our captain was the work of picking it up."

"And who knows!" cried Ned. "During our stroll tomorrow, maybe we'll find one just like it!"

"Bah!" Conseil exclaimed.

"And why not?"

"What good would a pearl worth millions do us on board the *Nautilus*?"

"On board, no," Ned Land said. "But . . . someplace else?"

"Oh, someplace else," Conseil shook his head.

"Actually," I said, "Mr. Land is right. If we could take a pearl worth millions back to Europe—or to America—it would make our story more credible, and it would also command a higher price."

"I would think so," the Canadian said.

10. She and other aristocrats possibly "*drank pearls in vinegar*" because powdered pearl was believed to be an antidote for poison. In the Orient, a dissolved pearl was part of the love potion. In Renaissance Italy, powdered pearl was thought to be a cure for epilepsy and hysteria.

"But," asked Conseil, who forever returned to the didactic side of things, "is this pearl fishing dangerous?"

"No," I replied hastily, "especially if one takes the proper precautions."

"What risks could you run in a job like that?" Ned said. "Swallowing a few gulps of salt water?"

"Thou sayest, Ned. Incidentally," I asked, trying to affect Captain Nemo's casual tone, "are you afraid of sharks, gallant Ned?"

"Me?" the Canadian responded. "A harpooner by profession? It's my job to make light of them."

"But it's not a question," I pointed out, "of fishing for them with a swivel hook, hoisting them onto the deck of a ship, chopping off the tail with a blow of the ax, opening the belly, wrenching out the heart and tossing it into the sea."

"Then it's a question of—?"

"Exactly."

"In the water?"

"In the water."

"Ye gods, give me a sharp harpoon! You know, professor, those sharks are badly designed! They have to roll their bellies over in order to snap you up,[11] and in the meantime—"

Ned Land had a way of pronouncing "snap" that sent chills down the spine.

"Well, how about you, Conseil? What do you feel about sharks?"

"Me? I'll be candid with master."

Thank God, I thought.

"If master is willing to face these sharks, I don't see why his faithful man-servant shouldn't be willing to face them too."

11. An old belief now discredited. Sharks are quite able to attack in an upright position.

THREE

A Pearl Worth Ten Million

WHEN NIGHT FELL, I retired but slept poorly: Sharks played a major role in my dreams! And I found it both just and unjust that the French word for shark, *requin,* should be so close, etymologically speaking, to the word *requiem.*[1]

The next day I was awakened at 4 a.m. by the steward whom Captain Nemo had placed expressly at my service. I rose hurriedly, dressed, and went into the salon.

Captain Nemo was waiting for me.

"Professor Aronnax," he said, "are you ready to start?"

"I'm ready."

"Please follow me."

"What of my companions, captain?"

"They've been alerted. They're waiting for us."

"Aren't we going to get into our diving suits?" I asked.

"Not yet. I don't want the *Nautilus* to get too close to the coast, so we're fairly far out from the Mannar oysterbank. But I've had the dinghy made ready. It will take us to the exact spot where we'll disembark and that'll save us a long trek. Our diving suits are in the dinghy, so we'll get into them just before we start our underwater journey."

Captain Nemo led me to the central companionway whose steps led onto the platform. Ned and Conseil were there, delighted at the idea of the "pleasure jaunt" now under way. Oars in position, five of the *Nautilus*'s crew were already aboard the dinghy, which was moored alongside.

The night was still dark. Layers of cloud cloaked the skies and left only a few stars visible. My eyes flew toward the land, but I could see only a blurred line running along three-quarters of the horizon from southwest to northwest. Sailing up the west coast of Ceylon during the night, the *Nautilus* now lay west

---

1. In English, too, the words are close. The *requin,* a voracious shark, is grimly known as the *requiem shark. Requiem* is the first word in the mass for the dead, which begins: *Requiem aeterna dona eis, Domine* (Grant them eternal rest, O Lord). In other words, Aronnax has lost a night's rest over fears that the requin will bring him eternal rest.

of the bay, or rather of the gulf formed by the mainland and Mannar Island. Under those somber waters lay the oysterbank, an inexhaustible field of pearls stretching for over twenty miles.

Captain Nemo, Conseil, Ned, and I found seats in the stern of the dinghy. The coxswain took the tiller, his four crewmen leaned into their oars, the painter was cast off, and we pulled clear.

We headed south. The oarsmen took their time. I watched their strokes catch the water powerfully, and they waited ten seconds between strokes, according to the system used in most navies. While their oars were in the air and the dinghy coasted, drops of water would flick off and strike the dark bases of the waves, spattering like splashes of molten lead. Coming from well out, a gentle swell made the dinghy roll slightly, and a few cresting billows lapped at our bow.

We were quiet. What was Captain Nemo thinking about? Perhaps that the shore we were approaching was too close for his comfort, contrary to the Canadian's thoughts, probably that the shore was too far away. As for Conseil, he had come along out of simple curiosity.

Toward 5:30 a.m., the first glimmers of dawn defined the upper lines of that coast with greater distinctness. Fairly flat to the east, it rose a little toward the south. Five miles still lay between us, and the beach was still indistinct owing to the mists on the water. Between us and the shore, the sea was deserted. Not a boat, not a diver. Profound silence prevailed in this meeting place of pearl fishermen. Just as Captain Nemo had predicted, we were arriving in these waters a month too early.

At 6 a.m. the day broke suddenly, with that rapidity characteristic of the tropics, which know neither real dawn nor real dusk. The sun's rays pierced the curtain of clouds piled up on the eastern horizon and that radiant orb rose rapidly.

Now I could clearly see the shore, with a few trees scattered here and there.

The dinghy was advancing toward Mannar Island, which curved to the south. Captain Nemo rose from his thwart and studied the sea.

When he gave the signal, the anchor was lowered but its chain scarcely ran out because the bottom lay no more than a meter down; this was one of the shallowest spots near that oysterbank. The dinghy swung around at once under the ebb tide's outbound thrust.

"We're there, Professor Aronnax," Captain Nemo announced. "You see how well enclosed this bay is? Right here, in just a month from now, numerous fishing boats will gather, and these are the waters their divers will ransack so boldly. This bay is well situated for their kind of fishing. It's protected from strong winds, the sea is never very turbulent here, all of which is highly favorable for divers.

"Now let's get into our underwater suits, and set out on our stroll."

Looking at those suspicious waters I said nothing, and with the help of the crewmen, I put on my heavy aquatic garb. Captain Nemo and my two companions were also getting dressed. None of the *Nautilus*'s crew would accompany us on this new excursion.

Soon we were enveloped up to the neck in india-rubber clothing, and our air tanks were strapped to our backs. But I couldn't see any of our Ruhmkorff lamps. Before inserting my head in its copper helmet, I asked the captain about this.

"Our lamps would be useless," he told me. "We won't be going very deep, and the sun's rays will suffice to illuminate our activities. Besides, it's not wise to take an electric lantern under these waves. Its glow might have the unhappy effect of attracting the more dangerous inhabitants of these waters."

As Captain Nemo pronounced those words, I turned toward Conseil and Ned Land. But their heads were already encased in their metal headgear and they could neither hear nor respond.

I had one last question for Captain Nemo.

"What about our weapons?" I asked. "Our firearms?"

"Firearms? What for? Don't your mountaineers attack bears dagger in hand? And isn't steel surer than lead? Here's a sturdy blade. Put it in your belt and let's get going."

I gazed at my companions. They were armed like us, but Ned Land was also brandishing an enormous harpoon he had stowed in the dinghy before we left the *Nautilus.*

Following the captain's example, I let myself be crowned with my heavy copper sphere, and our air tanks immediately went to work.

Then the crewmen helped us overboard one after the other until we were all standing on a sandy bottom in about a meter and a half of water. Captain Nemo waved us on. We followed him down a gentle slope until we disappeared under the waves.

Once I was in the water, my obsessive fears vanished. I became serenely calm, much to my surprise. The ease with which I could move gave me new confidence, I suppose, and the strangeness of the spectacle took hold of my imagination. The sun's rays were already lighting up the water and I could see even the smallest objects very clearly. After walking for ten minutes, we reached a depth of five meters and the terrain flattened out.

Like a covey of snipe over a marsh, schools of curious fish rose underfoot, members of the genus *Monopterus* that have no fin but their tail. I identified the Javanese eel, a veritable serpent eight decimeters long, with a livid belly: without the golden stripes on its sides it could easily be mistaken for a conger eel. From the genus *Stromateus,* the butterfish, whose oval bodies are highly compressed, I saw some adorned in brilliant colors and sporting a dorsal fin like a sickle: when dried and marinated they make an excellent dish known as "karawade"; also, some sea poachers, fish of the genus *Aspidophoroides,* their bodies covered with scaly armor in eight longitudinal sections.

The sun lit up the waters more and more as it rose higher and higher. The seafloor changed little by little. The fine-grained sand gave way now to a veritable pavement of smooth stones covered by a carpet of mollusks and zoophytes. Among the specimens in those two branches, I noticed some windowpane oysters with thin valves of unequal size, a kind of ostracod peculiar to the Red Sea and the Indian Ocean; some orange-colored lucina with circular shells; awl-shaped auger shells; some of those Persian murex snails of the kind that supplied Captain Nemo with an admirable dye; spiky periwinkles fifteen centimeters long, rising in the water like hands ready to seize us. There were also some horn-covered turban snails bristling with spines; some lamp shells; some duck clams, edible mollusks that stock the Hindu marketplaces; some subtly luminous jellyfish of the species *Pelagia panopyra;* and finally, some superb *Oculina flabelliforma,* magnificent sea fans that form one of the most remarkable tree-like growths in that ocean.

In the midst of that moving vegetation, and under those arbors of water plants, there raced legions of clumsy articulates, in particular some fanged frog crabs whose carapace is shaped like a slightly rounded triangle; some robber crabs unique to those waterways; and horrible parthenopian crabs repulsive to the eye.

Another hideous animal that I met several times was the enormous crab that Mr. Darwin saw. Nature has given this creature the instinct and necessary strength to feed on coconuts! It clambers up trees on the beach and sends the coconuts tumbling down. They split when they hit the ground and the crab forces them open with its powerful claws. There, under those well-illuminated waves, that crab raced with unparalleled agility, while by contrast, green turtles from the species frequenting the Malabar coast moved slowly among the crumbling rocks.

Toward seven a.m. we finally surveyed the area where pearl oysters reproduce by the millions. These precious mollusks were attached to the rocks by their brown byssus, a mass of filaments that prevents them from moving about. In this respect oysters are inferior to mussels, which enjoy some slight freedom of movement.

The shellfish *Meleagrina,* that womb for pearls, has valves nearly equal in size, making a rounded shell with heavy partitions and a gnarled exterior. Some of these were furrowed with flaky green bands that radiated down from the top. These were the young oysters. Others, which had black and rough surfaces and measured up to 15 centimeters in width, were ten years old or older.

Captain Nemo pointed to those prodigious piles of shellfish, and I could understand that these mines were genuinely inexhaustible, since Nature's creative powers are greater than man's destructive instincts. And true to those instincts, Ned Land started stuffing the finest specimens into a net at his side.

But we could not stop. We had to follow the captain who was heading down trails seemingly known only to him. The seafloor then rose discernibly, and sometimes when I raised my arms, my hands protruded above the surface. Then the floor of the oysterbank would capriciously sink again, and we walked around high, pointed rocks that rose like pyramids. In their somber crevices, huge crustaceans would rear up on their long legs, like engines of war, and stare out at us. Underfoot there crept some millipedes, some bloodworms, some aricia worms, and some annelid worms whose antennas and tubular tentacles were preposterously long.

Now there opened in our path a vast cave hollowed out in a picturesque pile of rocks whose glossy heights were covered with submarine flora. At first it seemed to me to be profoundly dark inside this cave. The sun's rays seemed to grow weaker the farther inside we looked. Their vague transparency became no more than drowned light.

Captain Nemo was leading the way and as we followed him, my eyes did grow accustomed to that relative gloom. I could make out natural pillars that supported a whimsically contoured vaulting, pillars based on a granite foundation like the weighty columns of Tuscan architecture. Why had our mysterious guide taken us to the bottom of this submarine crypt? I would soon know.

After negotiating a fairly steep slope we trod the floor of a kind of circular pit. There Captain Nemo halted and pointed toward an object I had not yet noticed.

It was an oyster of extraordinary dimensions, a titanic giant clam, a font that could have held a lake of holy water, a basin more than two meters wide, hence, needless to say, larger than the one that already enhanced the *Nautilus's* salon.

I walked over to this phenomenal mollusk. It was attached by its byssus, its mass of filaments, to a granite table and there it grew in isolation amid the calm waters of this cave. I estimated the weight of that giant clam at 300 kilograms. Such an oyster would contain about fifteen kilos of meat: only a Gargantuan stomach could consume a couple dozen of these.

Clearly, Captain Nemo had been well aware of the existence of this bivalve. This was not the first time he had paid it a visit. Initially I thought his sole reason for taking us into this cave was to show us a natural curiosity. But I was wrong. Captain Nemo had a vested interest in checking on the current condition of that giant clam.

The mollusk's twin valves were partly open. The captain approached and inserted his dagger vertically between them to prevent their closing again. Then with his hands he raised the fringed membranes that formed the animal's mantle.

There, between the leaflike folds, I saw a loose pearl the size of a coconut.[2] Its globular shape, its perfect clarity, and wonderful *orient* made it a jewel of inestimable value. Carried away by curiosity, I stretched out my hand to take it, weigh it, feel it! But the captain stopped me, indicating he did not want me to touch it, removed his dagger in one swift motion, and let those two valves close abruptly.

I could see Captain Nemo's plan. In leaving this pearl hidden in the giant clam's mantle, he was allowing it to grow slowly. With each passing year the mollusk's secretions added new concentric layers. And only he was acquainted with this cave where this admirable "fruit" was ripening. He was cultivating it, so to speak, so that someday he could add it to his museum of precious rarities.

2. By contrast, the largest pearl on record is the Hope pearl, which has a maximum circumference of 4½ inches and weighs about 3 ounces.

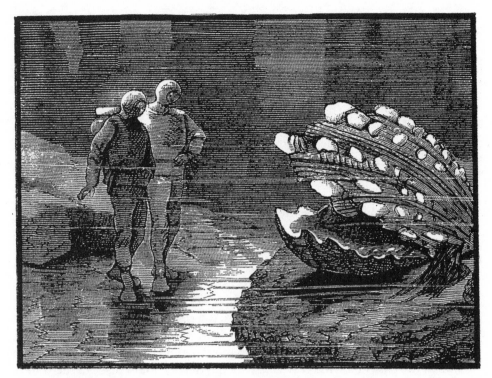

An extraordinary oyster

He might even have done what some Chinese and East Indians do: predetermine the growth of his pearl by inserting a piece of glass or metal beneath the mollusk's mantle so that little by little it became covered with nacreous material.3 In any case, comparing that pearl to others I had known about and to those shimmering in the captain's collection, I estimated its value at no less than 10,000,000 francs. It was a superb natural curiosity rather than a piece of jewelry—I knew of no woman's ear that could handle it.

Our visit to that opulent giant clam was over—Captain Nemo was leaving the cave and we climbed back up to the oysterbank in the midst of clear waters not yet disturbed by divers at work.

We each wandered on his own, true loiterers stopping or straying as our separate fancies dictated. For my part, I was no longer obsessed by those dangers my imagination had so ridiculously enlarged upon. The shallows were rising closer to the surface and soon, as I walked in just a meter of water, my head and chest were above the level of the ocean. Conseil rejoined me, and putting his huge copper capsule next to mine, he gave me a friendly greeting with his eyes. But this lofty plateau measured only a few fathoms, and then we reentered Our Element. I think I now have the right to call it that.

Ten minutes later Captain Nemo suddenly stopped. I thought that meant we were about to start back. But no. He motioned for us to crouch down next to him at the base of a wide crevice. He pointed to a certain place in the waters and I gazed intently in that direction.

Five meters away a shadow appeared and dropped to the seafloor. The disquieting thought of a shark shot through my mind but I was wrong, once again that was not the problem.

It was a man, a live man, a black Indian fisherman, a poor devil who doubtless had come to glean what he could before harvest time. I could see the bottom of his little boat, moored some feet over his head. He would dive and go back up in rapid succession. To help him dive rapidly, he gripped between his feet a stone, shaped like a sugar loaf and connected to the boat by a rope. This was all the equipment he had. Arriving on the seafloor at a depth of about five meters, he hurriedly fell on his knees and stuffed a sack with shellfish plucked at random. Then he would swim back up, empty his sack into his boat, haul up his stone, and begin the process—which took him about 30 seconds—all over again.

That diver didn't see us. We were hidden in the shadow cast by a rock. And anyhow, how could that poor Indian ever imagine that human beings, creatures like himself, were there near him under the water, watching his every movement, every detail of his work?

3. The first Chinese credited with breeding his own pearl was Ye-jin-yang of Hoochow in the thirteenth century. He placed not pieces of glass, as Aronnax says, but pellets of mud or bits of bone, wood, or brass under the flesh of river mussels. Some Chinese, by using molded lead or tin, even grew pearls in the shape of seated Buddhas.

He repeated his cycle many times, gathering no more than ten shellfish each time, because he had to wrench them from the banks where each clung with its tenacious byssus. And how many of those oysters for which he risked his life would have no pearl in them!

I watched him closely. His movements were regular and systematic, and for half an hour he seemed to work in no danger. I was becoming quite familiar with this interesting process when suddenly, at a moment when he was kneeling on the seafloor, I saw him make a gesture of fright; he stood up and braced himself for the leap upward.

Now I could understand his terror. A gigantic shadow loomed above that unfortunate diver—a huge shark, angling toward him, eyes on fire, jaws open wide.

I was mute with horror, unable to move.

With one powerful movement of its fins the voracious animal shot toward the Indian, who leaped aside and avoided the shark's bite but not the thrashing of its tail, which struck him across his chest and stretched him out flat on the seafloor.

This scene had lasted for just a few seconds. The shark returned, rolled over onto its back, and made ready to chop the Indian in two. Then I could feel Captain Nemo, who was next to me, jump up, and knife in hand, he strode right toward the monster, ready for close combat.

Just when it was set to snap up that wretched fisherman, the man-eater spied its new adversary, repositioned itself on its belly, and streaked toward him.

To this day I can still see Captain Nemo's stance. Bracing himself, he waited for that formidable man-eater with admirable poise, and when the beast rushed at him, the captain leaped aside with prodigious speed, avoiding a collision and sinking his knife into its belly. But that didn't end it. A terrible battle was joined.

The shark seemed to roar, so to speak. Its blood was pouring into the sea, dyeing the water red, and through that murk I could see nothing.

Nothing until the water cleared enough for me to spot the brave captain hanging on to one of the beast's fins, in close combat with it, belaboring the shark's belly with dagger blows yet unable to deliver the decisive thrust, that is, a direct hit to the heart. In its struggles the man-eater churned the water so violently it almost knocked me down.

I wanted to help the captain, but I was paralyzed with horror.

I gaped wildeyed as the struggle took a new turn. The captain was overthrown by the massive monster and fell to the seafloor. Now the shark's jaws opened wide like a pair of industrial shears. That would have been the end of Captain Nemo if Ned Land, quick as thought, harpoon in hand, hadn't rushed forward and hurled it into the monstrous fish.

The waves were bloody. The water quivered from the movements of the man-eater, which thrashed about with indescribable fury. Ned Land had not missed his target. This was the monster's death rattle. Though stabbed to the heart, it still struggled dreadfully, and its convulsions knocked Conseil down.

Meanwhile Ned Land was pulling the captain out of danger. The captain immediately went over to the Indian, cut the rope binding him to his stone, lifted the fellow in his arms and, with one strong kick of the heel, mounted to the surface.

Saved by a miracle, we all three of us followed him up to the fisherman's boat.

Captain Nemo's first concern was to revive that unlucky man. I wasn't sure he would succeed. I hoped so—after all, the poor devil had not been under very long. But that blow from the shark's tail could have been fatal.

Fortunately, after vigorous massaging by Conseil and the captain, the almost drowned man regained consciousness slowly and finally opened his eyes. What must have been his surprise, maybe even his terror, to find four huge copper craniums bending over him!

But most of all, what must he have thought when Captain Nemo pulled a bag of pearls from a pocket in his diving suit and placed it in the fisherman's hands? This magnificent benefaction from the Man of the Waters to the poor Indian from Ceylon was accepted with trembling hands. His bewildered eyes showed that he could not imagine to what superhuman creatures he owed both his life and his fortune.

At the captain's signal we descended again to the oysterbank and, retracing our steps, walked for half an hour until we reached the anchor connecting the seafloor with the *Nautilus*'s dinghy.

Helped by the five crewmen, we got back into the boat and were relieved of our heavy copper carapaces.

Captain Nemo's first words were spoken to the Canadian.

"Thank you, Mr. Land," he said.

"One good turn deserves another, captain," Ned answered. "I owed it to you."

A vague smile passed over the captain's face and that was all.

"To the *Nautilus*," he ordered.

The dinghy flew over the waves. A few minutes later we encountered the shark again: floating and dead. By the black markings on the tips of its fins I identified it as the terrible *Squalus melanopterus* of the Indian seas, a variety of that species properly termed shark. It was more than 25 feet long, and its enormous mouth occupied a third of its body. From the six rows of teeth forming an isosceles triangle in its upper jaw, I could tell that it was an adult.

Conseil gazed at it with a purely scientific fascination, and I'm sure he located it, not without good reason, in the class of cartilaginous fish, order Chondropterygia with fixed gills, family Selacia, genus *Squalus*.

While I myself was contemplating that inert mass, suddenly a dozen of those voracious *melanoptera* appeared around the dinghy and, ignoring us entirely, threw themselves on the carcass and fought among themselves for every bite of it.

By 8:30 we were back on board the *Nautilus*.

There I fell into a reverie over our experiences at the Mannar oysterbank. Two impressions were inevitable, one bearing on the captain's unparalleled courage, the other on his devotion to a human being, a member of that race from which he had fled beneath the sea. Whatever he might say, this strange man had not yet succeeded in wholly stifling his heart.

When I voiced these reflections to him, he answered me in a slightly emotional tone:

"That Indian, professor, lives in the land of the oppressed and I am to this day, and will be until my last breath, a native of that same land!"[4]

---

4. Maintaining suspense over Nemo's nationality, Verne is deftly ambiguous with this curtain line. By "*land*" is Nemo speaking *figuratively* of an imaginary land of the oppressed to which all victims of oppression belong? If so, then he has not yet revealed his own nationality. Or is he speaking *literally* of India as *the* land of the oppressed and hence of himself as an Indian? If yes, then his oppressor, the target of his hatred, is Great Britain. Or does he intend both meanings? The grand ambiguity suits Nemo's romantic character and adds to the suspense.

Verne does not fully reveal Nemo's origin and life story until the end of *The Mysterious Island*. Since at this point we're to remain mystified, we shall not discuss that revelation till much later.

FOUR

The Red Sea

URING THE DAY of January 29 the island of Ceylon disappeared under the horizon, and at a speed of 20 miles per hour the *Nautilus* glided into those labyrinthine channels that separate the Maldive and Laccadive Islands.[1] We likewise hugged Kiltan Island, which is of madreporic origin, discovered by Vasco da Gama in 1499 and one of nineteen principal islands in the Laccadive archipelago, situated between latitudes 10° and 14° 30′ north, and between longitudes 50° 72′ and 69° east.

We had by then traveled 16,220 miles, or 7,500 leagues[2] since our point of departure in the seas of Japan.

When we surfaced the next day, on January 30, there was no longer any land in sight. The ship set its course to the north-northwest and we headed toward the Gulf of Oman, which lies between Arabia and the Indian peninsula, and through which one enters the Persian Gulf.

This was obviously a dead end, there was no possible way out. So the question was, where was Captain Nemo taking us? I had no idea. But that did not satisfy the Canadian, who queried me that day about our destination.

"We're going, Mr. Land, wherever the captain's fancy takes us."

"His fancy," the Canadian responded, "can't take us very far. The Persian Gulf has no exit, and if we enter it, we'll soon have to come back out the way we went in."

"Well then, we'll come back out, Mr. Land, and if after that the *Nautilus* wants to visit the Red Sea, the Strait of Bab el Mandeb is always there to let us through."

"I needn't tell you, sir," Ned Land persisted, "that the Red Sea is just as landlocked as the Persian Gulf. The Isthmus of Suez hasn't yet been cut through,[3] and even if it had been, a boat as secretive as ours couldn't take any

---

1. The nature of Nemo's navigation problems here will be explained by the islanders' original name for these coral isles: *laksha diva,* or "100,000 isles." This name applied to both the Maldives and the Laccadives.

2. Here again we see Verne's own conversion ratio. He has been reckoning a league as 2.16 miles.

3. The Suez Canal was still under construction, and thanks to France's Ferdinand de Lesseps, it would open just twenty months after the present action.

chances in a canal intersected with locks. So we won't get back to Europe by means of the Red Sea either."

"But I didn't say we were heading for Europe."

"Where do you think we're going then?"

"My guess is that after visiting these curious waterways of Arabia and Egypt, the *Nautilus* will go back to the Indian Ocean, navigate either through the Mozambique Channel or off the Mascarene Islands, and so head to the Cape of Good Hope."

"And once we're at the Cape of Good Hope?" the Canadian asked with characteristic tenacity.

"Well then, we'll enter that Atlantic Ocean which we still haven't visited. But friend Ned, what's wrong? You're getting tired of this voyage under the seas? You're sated with this continually varying spectacle of submarine wonders? For my part, I'll be extremely vexed to see the end of a voyage like this, which so few people could have the chance to make."

"But Professor Aronnax," replied the Canadian, "do you realize that soon it'll be three months that we've been prisoners on the *Nautilus?*"

"No, Ned, I don't realize that, I don't want to realize it, I don't count the days and the hours."

"But when will it all end?"

"The end will come in its own time. Besides, there's nothing we can do about it, and there's no point in talking about it. My gallant Ned, if you come to tell me, 'I see a chance to escape,' I'll discuss it with you. But that isn't the case right now, and to tell you the truth, I don't think Captain Nemo ever does venture into European seas."[4]

This short dialogue made it clear that in my mania for the *Nautilus,* I had begun to identify with its commander.

As for Ned Land, he ended our talk in fine speechifying style: "That's all well and good. But to my mind, a man is not really alive unless he's free."

For four days, until February 3, the *Nautilus* toured the Gulf of Oman at various speeds and depths. It seemed to cruise at random, as if hesitating over which course to take, but we never crossed the Tropic of Cancer.

When leaving that gulf we had a quick look at Muscat, the most important town in the country of Oman. I admired its unusual appearance, the whiteness of its houses and forts standing out in sharp contrast to the blackness of the rocks surrounding it. I saw the round domes of its mosques, the elegant spires of its minarets, and its fresh, green terraces. But it was just a fleeting vision, for the *Nautilus* soon dived beneath the dark waves.

Then it cruised along at a distance of six miles from the Arabic coasts of Mahra and Hadhramaut with their wavy lines of mountains broken by a few

4. Aronnax seems to be telling an outright lie here. In I 23, he learned that Nemo *"does venture into the Mediterranean,"* news the professor expected Ned Land to welcome. Instead, Aronnax now conceals that news. This shift in loyalty and honesty is what's on the naturalist's conscience as he writes his very next sentence.

ancient ruins. On February 5 we finally put into the Gulf of Aden, a perfect funnel inserted into the neck of Bab el Mandeb, bottling the waters of the Indian Ocean inside the Red Sea.

On February 6 the *Nautilus* cruised in sight of the city of Aden, perched on a promontory joined to the mainland by a narrow isthmus, a sort of inaccessible Gibraltar that the English refortified after taking it in 1839. I glimpsed the octagonal minarets of that town, which, as the Arab historian Idrisi tells us, used to be one of the richest, busiest commercial centers along that coast.[5]

I was sure that when Captain Nemo reached this point, he would back out again, but I was wrong, and to my great surprise, he did nothing of the sort.

The next day, February 7, we entered the Strait of Bab el Mandeb, whose name in Arabic means "The Gate of Tears." Twenty miles wide, it is only 52 kilometers long, and it took the *Nautilus*—traveling at top speed—barely an hour to clear it. But I couldn't see a thing, not even Perim Island where the British government built fortifications to strengthen Aden's position. There were many English and French steamers of the lines going from Suez to Bombay, Calcutta, Melbourne, Réunion Island, and Mauritius, all plowing that narrow passage, too many for the *Nautilus* to dare show itself. So it prudently cruised in midwater.

Finally, at noon, we were plowing the waves of the Red Sea.

The Red Sea, so famous in Biblical traditions, is rarely replenished by rain and never by any important rivers. Moreover, it is continually drained by a high rate of evaporation, and its water level is dropping by a meter and a half every year! A singular gulf which, if landlocked like a lake, would probably have dried up entirely. It is inferior in that sense to the neighboring Caspian and Dead seas, whose levels remain constant: their evaporation precisely equals the amount of water that enters them.

The Red Sea is 2,600 kilometers long with a mean width of 240. In the days of the Egyptian Ptolemies and the Roman emperors, it was a great commercial artery for the world; when the Suez Canal is completed, the region will win back much of its lost prestige, a prestige that the Suez railroads have already partly regained.

I would not even attempt to understand the whim that made Captain Nemo take us into this gulf. But I approved wholeheartedly of the *Nautilus*'s entering it. It traveled at a moderate pace, sometimes on the surface, sometimes underwater to avoid some ship, and so I could observe this curious sea both inside and topside.

5. Abu 'Abdullah Mohammed Ibn Mohammed Ash-Sharif al-Idrisi (1100–c. 1166), Arab geographer, was hailed to the court of Roger II, Norman king of Sicily, who commissioned Idrisi to do an illustrated treatise on "the whole of the known world." Idrisi worked on his *Book of Roger* for fifteen years. He consulted Arabic experts, ancient authorities like Ptolemy and Orosius, the court records of Roger's dominions, and travelers' accounts of the day. Hence his description of twelfth-century Sicily has great historical value, and his map of the Mediterranean and Near East is superior to any European map of that period. His comments on the Red Sea would be well known to such a nautical scholar as Nemo.

On February 8, in the early daylight hours, Mocha appeared before us: a town now in ruins, whose walls would collapse at the mere sound of a cannon, but which shelters here and there some green date trees. At one time it was a city of some importance, boasting six marketplaces and twenty-six mosques, and its walls, defended by fourteen forts, formed a girdle three kilometers in circumference.

Then the *Nautilus* approached the African beaches, where the sea is considerably deeper. There, through the open panels and in a midwater of crystalline clarity, our ship enabled us to study admirable thickets of dazzling coral and huge chunks of rocks clothed in a splendid green fur of algae and fucus plants. What an indescribable spectacle, what a variety of beautiful scenery where those reefs and volcanic islands level off next to the Libyan coast! But soon the *Nautilus* hugged the eastern shore where those treelike forms appeared in all their glory. This was off the coast of Tihama, where those masses of zoophytes not only flourished *below* sea level but also formed picturesque networks that unfolded themselves as high as ten fathoms *above* it; the latter were more whimsical in shape but less colorful than the former, whose hues were kept vivid by the vitality of the waters.

How many charming hours I spent this way at the salon windows! How many new specimens of submarine flora and fauna I was able to admire beneath the rays of our electric beacon! I saw mushroom-shaped fungus coral; some slate-colored sea anemone, among others the species *Thalassianthus aster;* some organ-pipe coral arranged like flutes and just waiting for a puff from the god Pan; some seashells peculiar to this sea that lie inside hollows in the madreporic formations and whose bases are twisted into squat spirals; and finally, a thousand specimens of a polypary I had not observed until then: the common sponge.

The first division in the polyp group, the class Spongiaria has been created by scientists precisely for this curious product whose usefulness is incontestable. The sponge is by no means a plant, although some naturalists still insist it is, but an animal of the lowest order, a polypary inferior to those associated with coral. To me its animal nature is no longer in question; I cannot accept even the view of those ancient savants who saw it as halfway between plant and animal. I will concede that naturalists are not all of one mind on the structure of the sponge. For some it is a polypary, for others, including Professor Milne-Edwards, it is a solitary individual.

The class Spongiaria comprises about 300 species found in many seas and even in certain rivers, these last called freshwater sponges. But their favorite waters are the Red Sea and the Mediterranean near the Greek isles and off the Syrian coast. Those waters witness the reproduction and growth of the soft, delicate bath sponges that can command prices up to 150 francs apiece: the yellow sponge from Syria, the horn sponge from Barbary, etc. But since I had no hope of studying these zoophytes in the seaports of the Levant—from which we were separated by the insuperable Isthmus of Suez—I had to be content to observe them in the Red Sea.

Along the shore

So I asked Conseil to join me while the *Nautilus,* at a mean depth of eight or nine meters, slowly skimmed the beautiful rocks near the east coast.

There sponges were growing in every shape—globular, stalklike, leaflike, fingerlike. They certainly justified, with some exactitude, the nicknames given them by fishermen, who are better poets than the scientists: basket sponges, chalice sponges, distaff sponges, elkhorn sponges, lion's paws, peacocktails, and Neptune's gloves.[6] A gelatinous, semifluid substance coated the fibrous tissue of those sponges, and from that tissue there escaped a steady trickle of water that carried sustenance to each cell and was then expelled by a contracting movement. That gelatinous substance disappears when the polyp dies, giving off ammonia as it rots. What remains finally are just those horny or gelatinous fibers that we call the household sponge, which takes on a russet color and is put to various uses, depending on its elasticity, permeability, or resistance to saturation.

Conseil and I saw these polyparies stuck to rocks, to mollusk shells, even to the stalks of water plants. They decorated the smallest crevices, some sprawling, others standing or hanging like outgrowths of coral. I told Conseil that these sponges are fished up in two ways, either by dredging or by diving. And diving is preferable because picking them by hand does not damage the polypary's tissue, and so guarantees better prices.

Other zoophytes germinating near those sponges consisted mainly of a very elegant species of jellyfish; mollusks were represented by some varieties of squid that, according to Professor d'Orbigny, are unique to the Red Sea, and reptiles by virgata turtles of the genus *Chelonia,* which supplied our table with a dainty but healthful dish.

As for fish, they were plentiful and often remarkable. Those that the *Nautilus*'s nets hauled in most frequently were: rays, including some spotted rays, oval in shape, brick red in color, their bodies strewn with erratic blue speckles and identifiable by their jagged double stingers; some silver-backed skates; some common stingrays with stippled tails; some butterfly rays, two meters long, flapping like huge overcoats in the midst of the waters; some guitarfish, absolutely toothless, a kind of cartilaginous fish closer in shape to the shark; trunkfish called dromedaries, eighteen inches long with humps that end in a backward-curving sting; some serpents, genuine moray eels boasting a silver tail, a bluish back, and brown pectorals trimmed with gray piping; a species of butterfish known as the fiatola, striped with narrow streaks of gold and decked in the three colors of the French flag; some Montague blennies four decimeters long; some superb jacks decorated with seven transverse black stripes, boasting blue and yellow fins plus gold and silver scales; some snooks; some standard mullet with yellow heads; parrot fish,

6. Here Aronnax the romanticist seems happily at odds with Aronnax the scientist as he relishes the lyrical and imaginative names that fishermen give to the sea's inhabitants. As a romanticist, Aronnax feels that a man close to nature will intuitively express that unity in metaphoric descriptions. Hence his claim that fishermen "are better poets than the scientists."

Fish of the Red Sea

wrasse, triggerfish, gobies, etc.; and a thousand other fish I had already observed in other waters.

On February 9 the *Nautilus* cruised in the widest part of the Red Sea, which measures 190 miles straight across from Suakin on the west coast to Qunfidha on the east coast.

At noon that day, after our position had been fixed, Captain Nemo came out on the platform, where I happened to be. I vowed not to let him go below again without at least sounding him out on his future plans. As soon as he saw me, he came over, graciously offered me a cigar, and said:

"Well now, professor, how do you like this Red Sea? Have you seen enough of its hidden wonders, its fish and zoophytes, its flowerbeds of sponges, its forests of coral? Have you had a look at the towns spread out on its shores?"

"Yes, Captain Nemo," I answered, "and the *Nautilus* is marvelously suited to such a survey. Ah, it is such an—*intelligent* boat!"

"Yes sir, intelligent, bold, and invulnerable! It has nothing to fear from the terrible storms of the Red Sea, or from its currents or reefs."

"Indeed," I said, "this sea is supposed to be one of the worst, and in ancient times, if I'm not mistaken, it was reputed to be detestable."

"Quite detestable, Professor Aronnax. The Greek and Latin historians can find nothing to say in its favor, and Strabo says it's very rough when the Etesian winds are blowing[7] and during the rainy season. The Arab Idrisi, who speaks of it as the Gulf of Colzoum, says that ships perished in great numbers on its sandbanks, and no one dared to navigate it at night. This, he claims, is a sea subject to fearful hurricanes, strewn with inhospitable islands, 'with nothing good to offer' either below or on the surface. And you find pretty much the same views in Arrian, Agatharchides, and Artemidorus."

"It's easy to see," I added, "that those historians didn't sail on the *Nautilus*."

"Indeed," he responded with a smile, "but as far as that's concerned, the moderns haven't progressed much beyond the ancients. It took many a century to find the mechanical power of steam. Who knows whether we'll see a second *Nautilus* within the next century? Progress is slow, Professor Aronnax."

"That's true," I said. "Your ship is a century ahead of its time, maybe several centuries. How unfortunate that such a secret must die with its inventor!"

He had no response to that. After some moments of silence:

"We were discussing," he said, "the views of ancient historians on the dangers of navigating the Red Sea."

---

7. Strabo's *Geography* (completed about 7 B.C.) is the only ancient treatise on its subject to survive. He gives us broad outlines of the conditions in many countries and, as Nemo remarks, tells us the effect on the Red Sea of the *Etesian winds*. They come from the north down across the Mediterranean. Strabo calls them Etesian ("annual," from Greek *etos*, "year") since they return every summer.

"Yes," I resumed, "but weren't their fears a bit exaggerated?"

"Yes and no, Professor Aronnax," answered Captain Nemo, who seemed to have learned "his Red Sea" backward and forward. "What is no longer dangerous for a modern ship—well rigged, solidly constructed, in control of its direction thanks to obedient steam—presented all kinds of perils to the vessels of the ancients. Picture to yourself those early navigators setting forth in sailboats made of planks lashed together with palm-tree ropes, caulked with powdered resin, and coated with dogfish grease.[8] They didn't even have instruments for taking their bearings, they navigated by guesswork amid currents they hardly knew. Under those conditions, shipwrecks were inevitable and numerous. But nowadays steamers providing service between Suez and the South Seas have nothing to fear from the fury of this gulf, in spite of the contrary winds of its monsoons. Their captains and passengers no longer make sacrifices to placate the gods before they embark, nor do they dress in wreaths and gold headbands to thank their gods at the nearest temple after they disembark."

"Admitted," I said, "and steam seems to have killed all gratitude in the hearts of sailors. But since you seem to have made a special study of this sea, captain, can you tell me how it got its name?"

"There are many explanations, Professor Aronnax. Would you like to hear the view of one fourteenth-century chronicler?"

"Gladly."

"This fanciful writer claims the sea got its name after the crossing of the Israelites,[9] when the Pharaoh died in those waves that closed in again at Moses' command:

To mark that miraculous sequel
the sea turned a red without equal.
So there was nothing else to do
except to name it for its hue."

"Very poetic, Captain Nemo," I responded, "but not a very satisfactory explanation. I'm interested in *your* opinion on this matter."

"Here it is, Professor Aronnax. The name 'Red Sea' must be seen as a translation of the Hebrew word 'Edrom,' and if the ancients gave it that name, it was because of the peculiar color of its waters."

"Until now, though, I've seen only clear water without any peculiar color."

"Right, but as we advance toward the far end of this gulf, you'll note its unique appearance. I recall seeing the bay of El Tur completely red, like a lake of blood."

8. Maybe the Red Sea's first navigators sailed in reed boats, with the "clinker" construction that Nemo describes coming later.

9. Modern biblical scholars say the Israelites crossed the Sea of Reeds (a site near the Suez Canal) rather than the Red Sea. The Hebrew text, according to the Jewish Publication Society of America, gives the name of the crossing area as *Yam Suf,* sea of reeds, or bullrushes. The area was then marshland, but today it is covered with sand.

"And you attribute this color to the presence of microscopic algae?"

"Yes. It's a purplish, mucilaginous substance produced by those tiny buds called trichodesmia, 40,000 of which are needed to occupy the space of one square millimeter. Perhaps you'll see them when we reach El Tur."[10]

"So, Captain Nemo, this is not the first time you've run the *Nautilus* through the Red Sea?"

"No, sir."

"Well then, since you already mentioned the crossing by the Israelites and the catastrophe that befell the Egyptians, I'd like to know whether you've found any evidence under the waters of that great historic event?"

"I haven't, and there's a good reason why I haven't."

"Which is?"

"Because that area where Moses crossed with all his people is now so clogged with sand that camels can hardly even bathe their legs there. You will understand that my *Nautilus* wouldn't find enough water to operate in."

"And where is that area?" I asked.

"It's a little above Suez in a sound that once formed a deep estuary when the Red Sea stretched as far as the Bitter Lakes. Now whether or not their crossing was a miracle, the Israelites nonetheless did cross there to reach the Promised Land, and the Pharaoh's army did perish precisely in that area. And so I believe that digging in those sands would uncover a great quantity of weapons and instruments of Egyptian origin."

"Obviously," I agreed. "And for archaeology's sake, I hope those excavations are begun sooner or later, once new towns spring up on that isthmus after the Suez Canal is completed. But speaking of the canal, it won't be of much use to a ship like the *Nautilus!*"

"True, but very useful to the rest of the world," Captain Nemo said. "The ancients fully understood the value to commerce of linking the Red Sea to the Mediterranean. But they never dreamed of digging a direct canal and they chose the Nile as their link. In all likelihood, a canal connecting the Nile to the Red Sea was begun, if we can trust tradition, under Egypt's King Sesostris. What's certain is that in 615 B.C. King Necho II started work on a canal that was fed by Nile water and crossed the Egyptian plains opposite Arabia. It took four days to travel this canal and it was so wide that two triremes could pass through it side by side.[11] Its construction was continued by Darius the Great, the son of Hystaspes, and probably completed by King Ptolemy II. Strabo saw it used for shipping, but because it sloped down somewhat from its point of departure near Bubastis to the Red Sea, it was navigable for only a few months of the year. This canal served commerce until the century of Rome's Antonine

10. Nemo may be describing what is now called "the red tide." Parts of the Red Sea are rich in phytoplankton, minute floating plants. In a "plankton bloom," there may be forty million such cells in a quart of salt water. Because these plants contain red pigments, they can discolor the surface over wide areas.

11. A trireme is a galley having three tiers of oarsmen.

emperors. Then it was abandoned and filled in with sand, but reinstated by order of Arabia's Caliph Omar I. It was filled in for good in 761 or 762 A.D. by Caliph Al-Mansur in an effort to prevent supplies from reaching Mohammed ibn Abdullah, who had rebelled against him. During his Egyptian campaign, your General Napoleon Bonaparte discovered traces of that old canal in the Suez desert, and—surprised by the tide—he almost perished a few hours before rejoining his troops at Hadjaroth, where Moses had pitched camp 3,300 years before."

"Well, captain, what the ancients didn't dare undertake, Mr. de Lesseps has. His joining of these two seas will shorten the route from Cádiz to India by 9,000 kilometers, and before long he will have changed Africa into an immense island."

"You have a right, professor, to be proud of your compatriot. Such a man brings more honor to a nation than the greatest generals! Like so many others, he began with difficulties and rebuffs, but he triumphed because he has the willpower of a genius. And it's sad to think that this work, which ought to have been an international work, which would suffice to make any nation famous, will succeed only through the efforts of one man. So, all honor to Mr. de Lesseps!"[12]

"Yes, all honor to that great man," I agreed, completely surprised by the emphatic way in which Captain Nemo had spoken of genius and rebuffs.

"Unfortunately," he went on, " I can't take you through that Suez Canal, but you'll still see the long jetties of Port Said the day after tomorrow when we'll arrive in the Mediterranean."

"In the Mediterranean!" I exclaimed.

"Yes, professor. Does that surprise you?"

"What surprises me is the notion that we'll be there the day after tomorrow."

"Really?"

"Yes, captain, although since I've been aboard your ship, I should be accustomed to letting nothing surprise me!"

"But just what is it that startles you?"

"The speed at which you'll have to travel, to go around Africa and double the Cape of Good Hope, to be in the Mediterranean the day after tomorrow!"

"Who told you we'd go around Africa, professor? And what's this about doubling the Cape of Good Hope?"

12. As Nemo and Aronnax are talking, Ferdinand de Lesseps (1805–1894) is nearing the end of his herculean labors on the Suez Canal, which will officially open on November 17, 1869. Returning home in triumph, de Lesseps, a great admirer of Verne, will nominate "the great romancer" for the Legion of Honor.

And so Verne will experience painful conflict when de Lesseps is convicted of fraud in the Panama Canal scandal of 1893. As Kenneth Allott, Verne's English biographer, summed it up, "Lesseps . . . suffered because the magnitude of his ideas drove him into underestimating expense and then into dishonesty to hide his difficulties."

"Because unless the *Nautilus* sails on dry land and crosses over the isthmus—"

"Or under it, Professor Aronnax."

"Under it?"

"Certainly," Captain Nemo replied quietly. "Nature long ago made under that tongue of land what man today is making on its surface."

"What! There is a passage?"

"Yes, a subterranean passage that I have named the Arabian Tunnel. It starts below Suez and leads to the Bay of Pelusium."

"But isn't that isthmus composed entirely of quicksand?"

"Only part way down. At a depth of 50 meters one meets a layer of solid rock."

"Did you discover this passage by chance?" I asked, more and more surprised.

"By chance plus logic, and by logic even more than by chance."

"I'm listening, captain, but my ears are resisting what they hear!"

"Oh well, sir, the old saying is an eternal truth: *Aures habent et non audient.*[13] Not only does this tunnel exist, but I have used it several times. Without it, I would not have ventured today into such a dead end as the Red Sea."

"Would it be presumptuous to ask just how you discovered this tunnel?"

"Sir, there can be no secrets between people who will never separate."

I ignored this innuendo, waiting instead for his explanation.

"Professor, the simple reasoning of the naturalist led me to discover this passage, and I alone know of its existence. I had observed that the Red Sea and the Mediterranean both contain a distinct number of identical species of fish: eels, butterfish, greenfish, bass, jewelfish, and flying fish. Sure of this fact, I wondered if there weren't some link between the two seas. If there were, its underground current must of necessity flow from the Red Sea to the Mediterranean, simply because of the latter's lower level. So I hauled up a large number of fish around Suez. I slipped brass rings around their tails and threw them back into the sea. Some months later, off the coast of Syria, I recaptured several specimens of my fish embellished with their telltale rings. So I had proved that some passage existed between the two seas. I looked for it with my *Nautilus,* I discovered it, I ventured inside it; and very soon now, professor, you too will have traveled through my Arabian Tunnel!"

13. Latin: "They have ears and hear not."

The Arabian Tunnel [1]

LATER THAT DAY, I reported to Conseil and Ned Land that part of my talk with Captain Nemo that I knew would interest them most. When I explained that within two days we would be in Mediterranean waters, Conseil clapped his hands but the Canadian shrugged his shoulders.

"An underwater tunnel," he cried out, "a tunnel connecting two seas! Whoever heard of such a thing!"

"Friend Ned, whoever heard of the *Nautilus?*" Conseil pointed out. "Nobody, but it exists all the same! You shouldn't be so willing to shrug something off just because you never heard of it."

"We'll soon see," Ned answered with a shake of his head. "After all, I'd like nothing better than believing in your captain's little passageway, and I hope to God it can really take us into Mediterranean waters."

That same evening the *Nautilus* surfaced at latitude 21° 30′ north and drew near the Arabian coast. I spied Jidda, an important financial center for Egypt, Syria, Turkey, and India. I could clearly make out the shape of its buildings, the ships made fast along its wharves, and those larger vessels whose draft of water obliged them to anchor at the port's offshore mooring. Fairly low on the horizon, the sun struck full force on the houses of the town, accenting their whiteness. Outside the town, some wood or reed huts showed us where the bedouins lived.

Soon Jidda disappeared into the evening shadows, and the *Nautilus* dived beneath the surface of the slightly phosphorescent waters.

---

1. In 1863 Verne spent time with Charles Sainte-Claire Deville, a geographer. Deville had explored the interiors of numerous volcanoes and discussed with Verne the possibility that their craters are connected by underground tunnels. Verne subsequently developed a fictional obsession with tunnels and, according to Kenneth Allott, wanted to "return to the womb." But few womb-returners ever produce novels like *A Journey to the Center of the Earth* (1864) or notions like Nemo's Arabian Tunnel.

Today it is known that natural underground passages are almost as common as Verne had imagined. Recent research on "continental drift" indicates that the Red Sea marks the boundary of two of the continental plates. This greatly increases the chances of there being undersea passages in that area, and it makes Verne's Arabian Tunnel all the more prophetic.

The next day, February 10, several ships appeared, running on our opposite tack. The *Nautilus* resumed its submarine navigation. But at noon, when our bearings were taken, the sea was deserted and the ship rose again to her waterline.

Accompanied by Ned and Conseil, I found a seat on the platform. The coast to the east looked like a blurred mass in the damp fog.

Leaning against the side of the dinghy, we were chatting of one thing or another, when Ned Land extended his hand toward a point in the water and said to me:

"Do you see anything right there, professor?"

"No, Ned," I answered, "but you know my eyes aren't as good as yours."

"Take a good look," he insisted. "There, off the starboard bow, almost level with the beacon! Don't you see a mass that seems to be moving about?"

"Yes," I said after watching carefully, "I can see something long and black moving on the surface."

"Another *Nautilus?*" Conseil suggested.

"No," the Canadian said, "but unless I'm terribly mistaken, that's a marine animal."

"Are there whales in the Red Sea?" Conseil asked.

"Yes, my boy," I told him, "they're sighted in these waters now and then."

"That's not a whale," Ned said, keeping his eyes on the object they had discovered. "Whales and I know each other. I couldn't mistake their little ways."

"So let's wait and see," Conseil said. "The *Nautilus* is heading for that quarter. We'll soon find out what it is."

Indeed, that black object was soon only a mile away. It looked like a huge reef set down in mid-ocean. What was it? I still couldn't figure it out.

"Oh, it's moving off! It's diving," Ned cried. "Damnation! What can that animal be? It doesn't have the forked tail of a baleen whale or a sperm whale, and its fins look like sawed-off limbs."

"But in that case, . . ." I ventured.

"Good Lord," the Canadian was saying, "it's rolled over on its back, and it's lifting its breasts into the air!"

"It's a siren," Conseil cried, "a genuine mermaid, with all due respect to master."

That word "siren" put me on the right track. I realized that this animal belonged to the order Sirenia: marine animals that legends have turned into mermaids, half women, half fish.[2]

"No," I told Conseil, "that's not a mermaid, but a strange creature nevertheless. Only a few specimens remain in the Red Sea. That's a dugong."

"Order Sirenia, group Pisciforma, subclass Monodelphia, class Mammalia, branch Vertebrata," Conseil said.

2. When the dugong floats half upright, with a suckling baby under one flipper, she indeed looks "half woman," especially when the observer is not too close. It helps, of course, if the observer is a prurient sailor who has been too long between ports.

And when Conseil has spoken, there's nothing more to say.

Meanwhile Ned Land watched intently, his eyes burning with desire at the mere sight of that cetacean. His hands seemed set to hurl a harpoon. You might have thought he was waiting for the right moment to leap into the sea and attack the creature in its own element.

"Oh sir," he told me in a voice trembling with emotion, "I've never fought anything like . . . that!"

All his being focused on the word *that*.

Just then Captain Nemo appeared on the platform. He spied the dugong. He could sense how the Canadian felt and spoke to him directly:

"If you held a harpoon right now, Mr. Land, would it be burning your hand?"

"Oh yes, sir!"

"And it would not displease you to resume for one day your trade as a fisherman, and to add that cetacean to the list of those you have already caught?"

"It wouldn't displease me one bit!"

"Well then, go ahead and try."

"Thank you, sir!" Ned's eyes were aflame.

"Only," the captain added, "I advise you for your own sake to aim carefully at that animal."

"Is the dugong dangerous when attacked?" I asked, in spite of the Canadian's shrug of his shoulders.

"Yes," replied the captain, "sometimes that animal may turn on its assailants and capsize their boat. But for Mr. Land that's not a serious worry. His eye is sharp, his arm is certain. I am only urging that he aim carefully because the dugong is justly regarded as great game, and I know Mr. Land does not dislike a choice morsel."

"You mean to say," the Canadian exclaimed, "that in addition to being a good fight that beast is also good food?"

"Yes, Mr. Land. Its flesh is real meat, held in high regard, and throughout Malaysia it is reserved for the tables of monarchs. And so this excellent animal is hunted so relentlessly that—like its relative the manatee—it is close to extinction."[3]

"In that case, captain," Conseil said in all seriousness, "this particular dugong could be the last of its race, so wouldn't it be better to spare it, for the sake of science?"

"Maybe," the Canadian cut in, "it would be better to harpoon it, for the sake of cuisine!"

"Then go ahead, Mr. Land," the captain decided.

As mute and impassive as always, seven crewmen mounted to the platform. One was carrying a harpoon and line of the type used by whalers. Its

3. Today the dugong is classed as an endangered species, while its close relative, Steller's sea cow, became extinct in the eighteenth century.

deck paneling removed, the dinghy was wrenched from its socket and let down into the sea. Six oarsmen took their places on the thwarts, and the coxswain took the tiller. Ned, Conseil, and I found seats in the stern.

"You're not joining us, captain?" I asked.

"No, sir, but I wish you happy hunting."

The dinghy was pushed off, and driven along by its six oarsmen, it moved swiftly toward the dugong, now floating about two miles from the *Nautilus*.

When we got within a few cable lengths of the cetacean, the dinghy slowed down, and the oars dipped quietly into those tranquil waters. Harpoon in hand, Ned Land went to take his stand in the bow. Harpoons used for striking whales are usually attached to a very long line that is payed out rapidly when the wounded beast drags it with him. But this line was no longer than ten fathoms or so, and it was attached to a small barrel which, while floating, would mark the beast's movements beneath the waters.

Standing up, I could closely observe the Canadian's quarry. That dugong—which is also known by the name halicore—greatly resembled the manatee. Its oblong body ended in a long caudal fin and its side fins in veritable fingers. It differs from the manatee in that its upper jaw is armed with two long, pointed teeth, tusks sticking out on each side.[4]

This dugong that Ned Land was getting ready to attack was enormous, easily exceeding seven meters in length.[5] It wasn't moving and seemed to be sleeping on the surface, which should have made it easier to capture.

The dinghy approached cautiously to within three fathoms of the animal. The oars were held suspended above the oarlocks. I was crouching. Ned Land leaned slightly back, brandishing his harpoon with expert hands.

Suddenly I heard a hissing sound and the dugong disappeared. Ned had flung the harpoon with great force but it seemed to have struck only water.

"Damnation!" he cried in a fury. "I missed it!"

"No," I said, "you wounded it. See the blood over there? But your harpoon didn't stick in its body."

"My harpoon! Get my harpoon!"

The sailors started rowing again and the coxswain steered us toward the floating barrel. We fished up the harpoon and started off in pursuit of the animal.

From time to time it would rise to breathe at the surface. Obviously its wound had not weakened it because it moved with great speed. The six oarsmen pulled vigorously and the dinghy flew on its trail. Several times we got within a few fathoms of it, and the Canadian hovered ready to strike, but the dugong disappeared in an abrupt dive, and it proved impossible to catch up with it again.

4. But only the male has such tusks. So Ned could not have seen "its breasts." In Verne's day naturalists had not yet observed dugongs closely enough to supply the new profession of science fiction with all the science fact it needed.

5. This is truly enormous. Recent sightings of dugongs report their length as three yards on the average, with four yards considered exceptional.

Imagine the anger boiling over in our impatient Ned Land! He hurled the most furious swearwords in the English language at the hapless beast. For my part, I was simply disappointed to see the dugong outwit us repeatedly.

We pursued it without pause for an hour. I had begun to think it would be almost impossible to capture it, when this animal got the unfortunate idea of retaliating, which it would regret. It turned toward us, jockeying for position.

This maneuver did not escape the Canadian.

"Watch out!" he warned.

The coxswain spoke some words in his bizarre language, no doubt alerting his men to keep on their guard.

The dugong halted within 20 feet of us, brusquely sniffing the air with its vast nostrils, pierced not at the end of its muzzle but on its topside. Gathering momentum, it rushed at us.

The dinghy could not avoid the collision. Half overturned, it shipped a few tons of water that we had to bail out. But thanks to our expert coxswain, we took the blow on the bias rather than broadside, and so did not capsize. Clinging to the stempost, Ned Land was harpooning the gigantic animal again and again. Then it sank its teeth into our gunwale and lifted the dinghy out of the water as a lion would lift a deer. We were flung one on top of the other, and I have no idea how the battle might have ended if the relentless Canadian had not finally hit it in the heart.

I heard its teeth scraping on the iron hull, and the dugong disappeared dragging our harpoon with it. But the barrel soon popped up on the surface, and a few minutes later the corpse appeared and rolled over on its back. Our dinghy reached it, took it in tow, and headed for the *Nautilus*.

We had to use very powerful tackle to hoist that dugong up onto the platform. It weighed 5,000 kilograms. The Canadian watched every detail of the work as the crew cut it up. That night my steward served me some slices of that flesh, perfectly prepared by our chef. I found it excellent, even better than veal if not beef.

Next morning, February 11, the *Nautilus*'s pantry was enriched by more dainty game. A covey of terns alighted on the platform. They were of a species called *Sterna nilotica,* peculiar to Egypt. The beak is black; the head gray and stippled; the eyes surrounded by white dots; the back, wings, and tail grayish; the belly and throat white, the feet red. We also captured a few dozen Nile duck, another excellent dish; these birds are white on their necks and at the top of their heads, with black spots all over.

The *Nautilus* had reduced its speed, advancing at a saunter, so to speak. And I noticed that the Red Sea's water was getting less salty the nearer we got to Suez.

Toward five p.m. we raised Cape Ras Mohammed to the north. This cape forms the tip of Arabia Petraea, the land between the Gulf of Suez and the Gulf of Aqaba.

The *Nautilus* then entered the Strait of Jubal, which opens into the Gulf of Suez. I could see clearly a lofty mountain dominating Ras Mohammed be-

The dugong attacks

tween the two gulfs. It was Mount Horeb, that biblical Mount Sinai on whose summit Moses met God face to face, that summit the mind's eye always pictures as crowned with lightning.

Around six p.m., sometimes afloat and sometimes submerged, the *Nautilus* passed well out from El Tur, situated at the far end of a bay whose waters seemed tinted with red, as Captain Nemo had predicted. Then night fell amidst a heavy silence occasionally broken by the cry of a pelican or a nocturnal bird, by the roar of surf crashing against rocks, or by the faraway drone of a steamer as its paddle wheels churned the gulf's waves.

From eight to nine p.m. the *Nautilus* cruised just a few meters beneath the surface. According to my reckoning, we had to be quite close to Suez. Through the windows of the salon, I saw rocky bottoms brilliantly illuminated by our electric light. It seemed to me that the strait was getting narrower and narrower.

At 9:15 we surfaced and I mounted to the platform. Impatient to get through Captain Nemo's tunnel, I could not hold still and so came up for a breath of fresh night air.

Soon I spied a pale signal light glimmering a mile away, half discolored by the mist.

"A floating lighthouse," someone said next to me.

I turned and discovered the captain.

"The floating signal light of Suez," he continued. "It won't be long now before we reach the mouth of the tunnel."

"It can't be very easy to enter it."

"No, sir, and that's why I stay in the pilothouse and direct the entire operation myself. So, if you would like to go below, Professor Aronnax, the *Nautilus* is about to submerge, and we won't surface again until we've passed through my Arabian Tunnel."

I followed the captain below. The hatch was closed, the ballast tanks were taking in water, and our submarine dropped down about ten meters.

As I headed toward my cabin, the captain stopped me.

"Professor, would you like to join me in the wheelhouse?"

"Yes, but I didn't know how to ask," I confessed.

"Come along then. This way you'll be able to see all there is to see about this combination submarine—and subterranean—navigating."

Captain Nemo led me toward the central companionway. Halfway up he opened a door, walked through the upper gangway, and entered the wheelhouse which, as the reader already knows, rises at the end of the platform.

It was a cabin about six feet square, closely resembling those occupied by the helmsmen of steamboats plying the Mississippi and Hudson rivers.[6] In the

6. This is the second time Aronnax invokes such a comparison with the American riverboat. And once again the analogy is most apt. The *Nautilus*'s pilothouse does resemble the riverboat's (described by Mark Twain as "all glass . . . perched on the top of the deck"). And both the river pilot and Nemo face some nasty navigating: the former had to take his craft out on a shallow river beset with snags, driftwood, and shoals; the latter must steer through a subway tunnel that spills one sea into another!

The captain takes the helm

center stood an upright wheel geared to rudder cables running to the *Nautilus*'s stern. Four deadlights, windows of biconvex glass, were set one in each wall, enabling the man at the helm to see in every direction.

The cabin was dark, but my eyes soon grew accustomed to the darkness and I saw the pilot, a powerfully built man whose hands rested on the pegs of the wheel. Outside, the sea was brilliantly illuminated by the beacon behind us at the other end of the platform.

"Now," Captain Nemo said, "let's find our tunnel."

Electric wires linked the pilothouse with the engine room, and from the cabin the captain could signal simultaneously the direction and the speed he desired. He pressed a metal button and at once the propeller slowed down considerably.

I gazed in silence at the lofty, sheer wall we were skirting at that moment, the solid rock base of the sandy mountains on that coast. For an hour we followed it, keeping it just a few meters away. Captain Nemo never took his eyes off the two concentric circles of the compass hanging in the cabin. At a mere gesture from him, the helmsman would instantly alter the *Nautilus*'s course.

Standing by the port deadlight, I could see magnificent coral substructures, zoophytes, algae, and, in crevices in the rock, crustaceans waving their huge claws.

At 10:15 Captain Nemo himself took the helm. Dark and deep, a wide gallery opened up ahead of us. The *Nautilus* boldly entered it. I heard strange rumblings on either side of us. It was the waters of the Red Sea, rushing down the slope of the tunnel toward the Mediterranean! Although the captain reversed the engines to lessen the force of the current, the *Nautilus* shot forward like an arrow.

Along the narrow walls of the passageway I could now make out nothing but brilliant streaks, straight lines, fiery furrows, all scrawled hastily by our speeding electric light. With my hand pressed on my chest, I tried to slow down the flutterings of my heart.

At 10:35 Captain Nemo left the wheel and turned to me:

"The Mediterranean," he announced.

Swept along by that torrent, the *Nautilus* had just crossed the Isthmus of Suez in less than twenty minutes.

SIX

The Isles of Greece

AT SUNRISE THE next day, February 12, the *Nautilus* rose to the surface and I rushed up onto the platform. I could see the vague silhouette of Pelusium three miles to the south. An underground torrent had carried us from one sea to another. We had traveled downstream on that current, of course; it must have been impossible to go back upstream through that tunnel.

Toward 7 a.m. Ned and Conseil joined me. Those inseparable companions had slept so soundly they were totally unaware of the feat the *Nautilus* had accomplished.

"Well, Mr. Naturalist," the Canadian asked in a mildly scoffing tone, "what about that Mediterranean?"

"We're floating on it, friend Ned."

"What!" Conseil put in. "Last night . . .?"

"Yes, last night, in just a few minutes, we cleared that insuperable isthmus."

"I don't believe it," the Canadian insisted.

"Then you're wrong, Mr. Land," I continued. "That low coast curving south is the coast of Egypt."

"Tell it to the marines," the stubborn harpooner said. "I'm not that gullible."

"But if master says it's so," Conseil told him, "then it's so."

"Furthermore, Ned, the captain did me the honor of letting me stand at his side in the pilothouse while he himself steered the *Nautilus* through his narrow tunnel."

"You heard that, Ned?" said Conseil.

"And Ned," I added, "with your sharp eyes you ought to be able to make out the jetties of Port Said stretching out into the sea."

The Canadian peered in that direction.

"Yes, you're right, professor, and your captain is a superman. Yes, we are in the Mediterranean. Good, then! Let's talk a bit about our own private concerns, in such a quiet, casual way that nobody catches on."

I could see exactly what he was driving at. In any event, I thought it best to let him get it off his chest. We all three went to find seats near the beacon, where we were less exposed to the spray from the waves.

"We're listening, Ned," I said. "What's it all about?"

"What I have to say is very simple," the Canadian replied. "We're near Europe, and before Captain Nemo's whims drag us down to the polar seas or back to Oceania, I say, let's leave the *Nautilus*."

I confess, such talks with the Canadian always upset me. I did not want to deprive my companions of their freedom, yet I did not want to leave Captain Nemo. Thanks to him and his submarine apparatus, I was day by day nearer the completion of my undersea research, and I was rewriting my book on the great submarine depths in the midst of the very place I was describing.[1] How would I ever again find such opportunities to observe the wonders of the ocean? No way! And so I could not entertain this idea of leaving the *Nautilus* before my researches had been completed.

"Friend Ned," I said, "tell me frankly. Are you bored on this ship? Do you regret that destiny has cast you into Captain Nemo's domain?"

The Canadian hesitated. Then crossing his arms he said:

"Frankly, I don't regret having taken this trip under the sea. I'll be glad to have done it, but in order to have done it, it's got to end! That's how I see it."

"It will end, Ned."

"Where and when?"

"Where—I don't know. When—I couldn't say. I can only suppose it will end when the seas have nothing more to teach us. Everything that begins in this world must of necessity come to an end."

"I think as master thinks," Conseil said. "It's possible that after researching all the seas, Captain Nemo will end our captivity too."

"End our captivity?" the Canadian cried. "You mean end our lives!"

"Let's not exaggerate, Mr. Land," I resumed. "I don't think we have anything to fear from the captain, but neither do I agree with Conseil. We now know the secrets of the *Nautilus,* and I can't imagine that its commander, just to set us free, would let us reveal those secrets to the world."

"In that case, what *do* you expect?" the Canadian demanded.

"That we'll get our chance, if not now, then maybe six months from now."

"Ye gods!" Ned exploded. "And tell me where, if you please, we shall be six months from now, Mr. Naturalist?"

"Perhaps here, perhaps in China. You know the *Nautilus* moves fast. It crosses oceans as swallows cross the sky or express trains cross continents. It doesn't even avoid seas that are heavily traveled. Who can guess whether it will coast France, England, or America, where we would have as good a chance to escape as we have here."

---

1. Verne's elegant control of his plot is typified by his timing at this point. The *Nautilus*'s arrival in the Mediterranean offers Ned his best chance for escape. And, inevitably, Aronnax sees that his book must be rewritten. Each man now has maximum motivation for resisting the other.

Of course Verne himself has known all along that the ongoing underwater discoveries would render Aronnax's book obsolete. But the author saved the news of the professor's rewrite till this crucial moment. That's shrewd storytelling.

"Professor Aronnax," the Canadian said, "your arguments are rotten to the core! You talk about some future day: 'We'll be here! We'll be there!' Me, I'm talking about *now*. We *are* here, and we must take advantage of it!"

I was hard pressed by Ned Land's good sense, and I felt I was losing ground. I couldn't find one sound argument to use next.

"Sir," Ned resumed, "let's assume an impossibility: suppose Captain Nemo offered you your freedom this very day. Would you accept it?"

"I don't know."

"And if he adds that this offer he's making you now won't ever be made again, then would you accept?"

I didn't say anything.

"And what does my friend Conseil have to say?" Ned Land asked.

"Your friend Conseil," that gallant lad calmly replied, "has nothing to say for himself. He's a completely disinterested person in this whole matter. Like his master, like his friend Ned, Conseil is a bachelor. Conseil has no wife, no parents, no children waiting for him back home. He serves master, he thinks like master, he speaks like master, and to his great regret he can't be counted on to make a majority. Only two persons are involved here: master on one side, Ned Land on the other. That settled, Conseil is here to listen and to keep score."[2]

I couldn't help smiling at Conseil's total self-annihilation. And Ned must have been relieved to discover he did not have to contend with Conseil too.

"So, professor," Ned summed it up, "since Conseil does not exist, let's settle this matter just between the two of us. You know where I stand. What's your decision?"

It was clear the matter had to be settled. I could not procrastinate much longer.

"Friend Ned," I said, "this is what I think. Your reasoning is correct, and my arguments can't stand up to yours. We must not rely on Captain Nemo's good will. Common sense would prevent him from setting us free. Conversely, common sense should make us take advantage of the first chance we get to leave the *Nautilus*."

"Great, Professor Aronnax, wisely said!"

"But one proviso," I said, "just one. The opportunity must be viable! Our first attempt to escape must be realizable, because if it aborts we won't get another chance, and Captain Nemo will not forgive us!"

"That's also wisely said," the Canadian acknowledged. "But your proviso holds for any attempt at escape, whether it's made in two years or two days. So the problem is this: If a favorable chance arises, we must seize it."

"Agreed. But now, Ned, tell me, what do *you* mean by a favorable chance?"

2. Verne displays more virtuosity in characterization than he's usually given credit for. Conseil has now turned his third-person habit on himself for some objective self-analysis. He also makes it clear that he and his employer are content in their celibacy. Ned, by contrast, is obviously frustrated.

"One that takes the *Nautilus* within a short distance of some European coast on a cloudy night."

"And you'd try to get away by swimming?"

"Yes, if the ship's on the surface and near enough to a coast. No, if the ship is submerged and we're too far out."

"And in that event?"

"In that event I'd try to get hold of the dinghy. I know how it works. We'd get inside it, undo the bolts, and mount to the surface without even the helmsman—up there in the bow—seeing us take off."

"Good, Ned, be alert for such a chance, but don't forget—one failure finishes us."

"I won't forget, sir."

"And now, would you like to hear what I think about your plans?"

"Gladly, Professor Aronnax."

"Well, I think—and I'm not saying 'I hope'—that such a favorable chance will never arise."

"Why not?"

"Because Captain Nemo can't possibly believe that we've given up all hope of gaining our freedom, and he'll keep on his guard, above all in seas within sight of the coasts of Europe."

"I share master's opinion," Conseil said.

"Well, we'll see," Ned Land replied, shaking his head in a very determined way.

"And so, Ned Land," I summed up my feelings, "let's leave it at that. There's no need for more talk. The day you're ready, tell us and we'll follow you. I leave it entirely up to you."

That's how we ended our talk, which was to have such dire consequences later on. I must say that events worked out at first as I had predicted, to the Canadian's great despair. Was Captain Nemo wary of what we might try in those frequented waters, or did he simply want to stay out of sight of the many ships of every nation plowing the Mediterranean? I don't know, but most of the time we cruised beneath the surface and far away from any shore. Either the *Nautilus* would come up just enough to let the pilothouse emerge,[3] or it would dive to great depths. Even so, between the Greek isles and Asia Minor, we could not *find* the bottom even at 2,000 meters down!

---

3. Like most early submarine designers, Nemo had no use for a periscope. Simon Lake didn't add one to his designs until 1893, and John Philip Holland didn't use one at all on his 1900 model.

The periscope was distrusted because early models had proved almost worthless. To be of any value, a periscope must be long enough to allow the submarine to run well below the surface. But the long tubes absorbed light and left the image practically in the dark. The vessel's pitch and roll caused further problems. Only in the twentieth century were effective periscopes conceived: they used prisms, which absorbed less light and were mounted to automatically compensate for the boat's pitching. But that's fifty years ahead of our story.

Accordingly, I learned that we were near Karpathos Island, one of the Sporades group, only when Captain Nemo pointed to a spot on the map and quoted this verse from Virgil:

Est in Carpathio Neptuni gurgite vates
Caeruleus Proteus . . .[4]

It was indeed that legendary abode of Proteus, the old shepherd of Neptune's flocks: an island between Rhodes and Crete that the Greeks now call Karpathos and the Italians Scarpanto. But I could see only its granite foundations through the window of the salon.[5]

Next day, February 14, I intended to spend a few hours studying the fish of that island group, but for whatever reason, the panels remained hermetically sealed. On checking the *Nautilus*'s course, I realized we were heading for the ancient island of Crete, also called Candia. I remembered that months before, when I had shipped aboard the *Abraham Lincoln,* this entire island was rebelling against its despotic overlords, the Ottoman Empire of Turkey. Recently, of course, I was totally ignorant of what had happened to that revolution, and Captain Nemo, also cut off from communication with the land, was hardly the person to keep me informed.

Hence I made no mention of that rebellion even when I found myself alone with him in the salon that night. Anyhow, he was silent and seemed to me preoccupied. Then too—and this was quite unlike him—he ordered that the panels be opened and he paced back and forth between them, peering attentively into the surrounding waters. What was going on? I couldn't figure it out, and I turned to studying the fish that passed before us.

Among others I noted that sand goby cited by Aristotle and commonly known by the name sea loach, which is found particularly in the salty waters near the Nile Delta. Swimming near them were some semiphosphorescent red porgy, a variety of gilthead that the Egyptians ranked among their sacred animals; they were honored in religious ceremonies when their arrival in the Nile announced the fertile flood season. I also noted some wrasse known as the tapiro, three decimeters long, bony fish with transparent scales and livid coloration mixed with red spots; they eat large quantities of marine plants and that gives them an exquisite flavor. Accordingly these tapiro were in great demand

---

4. Latin: "There, in King Neptune's abyss by Karpathos, his spokesman is azure-hued Proteus . . ."—Virgil, *Georgics,* Bk. 4.

5. Of all the literary references to Karpathos, why does Nemo pick one involving *Proteus?* The answer, again, underlines Verne's elegant narrative control.

Virgil retells the story of how Proteus, the Old Man of the Sea, can change his shape endlessly—from him we get the adjective *protean,* meaning capable of *infinite variation.* Now Nemo knows that many seemingly stable conditions can undergo sudden, radical transformation. We are soon to hear of the map changing before our eyes, of a cold sea turned boiling hot, of empires toppling in a day. And remember that one interpretation of Nemo's motto *Mobilis in Mobile* is "Changing with Change." This chapter and the next will furnish detailed illustrations.

among the epicures of ancient Rome: their entrails were dressed with peacock brains, flamingo tongues, and testes of moray to compose that divine platter that delighted the emperor Vitellius.

Another inhabitant of those seas brought back still more memories of what I had learned about classical times. This was the remora, which travels attached to the bellies of sharks.[6] As the ancients tell it, these little fish can cling to the bottom of a ship and halt it in its course, and by holding back Mark Antony's vessel during the Battle of Actium, one of them actually helped Augustus win the day! The destiny of nations can hang by a thread![7] I also observed some admirable snappers of the order Lutianida, sacred fish for the Greeks, who claimed they had the power to drive off sea monsters. Their Greek name *anthias* means "flower," and they justify it by the play of their colors and by those fleeting reflections that turn their dorsal fins into watered silk; their shadings are confined to a gamut of reds from the pallor of pink to the glow of ruby. I couldn't take my eyes off these marine marvels when suddenly they took in an unexpected apparition.

A man appeared in the midst of the water, a diver carrying a small leather bag at his belt. It was not a body lost in the sea. It was a living man, swimming vigorously, now disappearing to catch his breath at the surface, then instantly diving again.

I turned to Captain Nemo and said excitedly:

"A man drowning—a castaway!" I cried. "We must save him, at any price!"

Without answering, the captain went to lean against the window.

The man drew closer, looking at us with his face pressed against the glass.

To my astonishment, Captain Nemo gave him a signal. The diver answered with a wave of his hand, at once mounted to the surface, and did not reappear.

"Don't be alarmed," the captain reassured me. "That's Nicolas from Cape Matapan, nicknamed 'Il Pesce'.[8] He's well known throughout the Cyclades

---

6. The remora's dorsal fin has evolved into a veritable suction cup. It can attach itself to turtles, rays, sunfish, and especially sharks. One reason the latter are preferred is that sharks are sloppy eaters, gouging ragged chunks of meat from their prey while letting lots of scraps drift free. The remora detaches and feasts away.

He earns the free ride and meal by cleaning crustaceans off the shark's skin. But he retains his independence: should the host shark get caught by fishermen, the guest remora discreetly departs.

Verne will make productive use of the remora's American cousin in II 17.

7. Verne knew that his nineteenth-century readers recalled how the one-day Battle of Actium changed the course of history. On September 2, 31 B.C., the combined fleets of Antony and Cleopatra seemed about to win the day. But some mysterious, still-unexplained chain reaction took place: Cleopatra's sixty ships fled, Antony apparently deserted his men, and the rebels surrendered to Octavian—who became Augustus Caesar, one of history's most powerful and influential rulers. As Virgil and Nemo both knew, reality is protean. Verne will now provide further demonstrations on both the political and geological levels.

8. Italian: "The Fish."

The Cretan diver

Islands. An audacious diver! Water is his true element, he lives in it more than on the land, constantly going from one island to another, even to Crete."

"And you know him, captain?"

"Why not, Professor Aronnax?"

With this, Captain Nemo went over to a cabinet near the port panel. Next to the cabinet was a chest banded with hoops of steel; on its lid was a copper plaque bearing the *Nautilus*'s monogram with its motto *Mobilis in Mobile*.

Ignoring me entirely, the captain opened the cabinet, which turned out to be a kind of safe containing a great number of ingots.

And they were gold ingots! Where had it come from, this supply of precious metal worth such enormous sums! Where had the captain gathered this gold? What was he going to do with it?

I didn't say a word. I just gaped. He took the ingots out one by one and arranged them methodically in the chest, which was soon filled to the top. I estimated that it now held more than 1,000 kilograms of gold, that is to say, nearly 5,000,000 francs!

Fastening the chest securely, the captain wrote an address on the lid in characters that must have been modern Greek.

Then he pressed a button that sent signals to the crew's quarters. Four men appeared, and, not without some difficulty, pushed the chest out of the salon. Then I heard them hoisting it up the iron companionway by means of pulleys.

Then Captain Nemo turned to me.

"You were saying, professor?"

"I wasn't saying a thing, captain."

"Then, with your permission, sir, I will bid you good evening."

And with that, Captain Nemo left the salon.

I went to my own cabin, puzzled, as one might imagine. I couldn't get to sleep. I was trying to figure out the connection between the diver and the chest of gold. Soon I felt we were rolling and pitching and realized we had surfaced.

I heard the sound of footsteps on the platform. I realized the dinghy was being detached and put to sea. Once it banged against the *Nautilus*'s side, then all was quiet.

Two hours later, similar sounds, similar comings and goings. Hoisted back on board, the dinghy was set down in its socket, and the *Nautilus* plunged back beneath the waves.

So, those millions had been delivered to their address. Where on this continent? Who was Captain Nemo's addressee?

Next day I told Conseil and the Canadian what had happened, things that had raised my curiosity to fever pitch. My companions were no less surprised than I.

"But where does he get all that gold?" Ned Land asked.

I had no answer to that question. After breakfast I went to the salon and got down to work. I was writing up my notes until 5 p.m. At that moment—I thought at first it was due to some personal indisposition—I felt intensely hot and had to take off my byssus coat. A strange reaction because we were not in the low latitudes and, in any event, once the *Nautilus* was submerged, it should not be subject to any rise in temperature. I checked the pressure gauge. It showed a depth of 60 feet, a depth beyond the reach of atmospheric heat.

I went on writing but soon it got so hot I couldn't stand it any longer.

"Could there be a fire on board?" I wondered.

I was on my way out when Captain Nemo appeared, consulted the thermometer, and turned toward me and remarked:

"Forty-two degrees centigrade."

"I've noted as much, captain," I responded, "and if it gets even a little bit hotter, we won't be able to stand it."

"Professor, it can't get any hotter unless we want it to."

"You mean you can control this heat?"

"No, but I can back away from the fireplace producing it."

"It's outside then?"

"Of course. We're cruising through a current of boiling water."

"Is that really possible?"

"Look."

The panels opened and I could see a completely white sea around the *Nautilus*. Steaming sulfurous fumes bubbled up through the waves, which were boiling like water on a stove. I placed my hand against one of the windows, but it was so hot I removed it at once.

"Where are we?" I asked.

"Near Santorin Island,[9] professor, and exactly in the channel that separates the volcanic isles of Nea Kameni and Palea Kameni. I wanted you to experience an underwater volcanic eruption firsthand."

"I thought the formation of these new islands was about completed."

"Nothing is ever completed in these volcanic waterways," Captain Nemo replied, "and the earth is constantly being reworked by subterranean fires. According to the Latin historians Pliny and Cassiodorus, in the year 19 of our era a new island, the divine Thera, had already appeared in the very place where these islets were formed more recently. Later, Thera sank under the waves, only to reappear and sink again in 69 A.D. From then to our own day these plutonic labors seemed suspended. But on February 3, 1866, a new islet, named George Island, emerged amid sulfurous vapors near Nea Kameni and was welded to it on February 6. Seven days later, February 13, the island of Aphroessa appeared, leaving a ten-meter channel between itself and Nea Kameni. I was in these seas then and I was able to watch the phenomenon develop phase-by-phase. Circular in shape, Aphroessa measured 300 feet in diameter

---

9. Taking its name from Saint Irene, this island is also known as Thira or Thera and has figured prominently in recent geological and archaeological research. Teams from the U.S. and Sweden determined that Santorin was the site of a gargantuan volcanic eruption about 3,500 years ago, a genuine catastrophe accompanied by 100-foot tidal waves. Finding unmistakable traces of a city inside the hardened volcanic ash, archaeologists have even speculated that this cataclysm may have been the inspiration for Plato's narrative of Atlantis. But we're getting ahead of ourselves—and Verne's story.

and was 30 feet high. It was composed of black, vitreous lava mixed with fragments of feldspar. On March 10 a smaller islet, called Reka, showed itself next to Nea Kameni, and since then, these three islands have fused into one single, selfsame island."

"What about this channel we're in currently?"

"Right here," he responded by pointing to a spot on his chart of the isles of Greece. "Notice that I've drawn in the new islets in their place."

"Do you think this channel will also fill up some day?"

"Probably, professor. Since 1866 eight little lava islets have surged up in front of the port of St. Nicholas on Palea Kameni. So it's clear that Nea and Palea will join in days to come. In the mid-Pacific we have tiny infusoria making continents, but here we have volcanoes making islands. Look, sir! Look at the work going on out there beneath the waves."

I went back to the window. The *Nautilus* was no longer moving, the heat had become absolutely unbearable. The presence of iron salts was turning the sea from white to red. Although the salon was sealed hermetically, it was filling now with the stink of sulfur, and outside I could see scarlet flames brighter than our electric light.

I was swimming in sweat, I was stifling. I was about to be cooked. Yes, I really felt I was about to be roasted alive!

"We can't survive much longer in this boiling water," I told the captain.

"No, that wouldn't be very wise," agreed Nemo the Impassive.

He gave an order. The *Nautilus* tacked about and withdrew from that furnace it could no longer brave with impunity. Fifteen minutes later we were breathing fresh air on the surface.

The thought hit me then that if Ned had chosen those waters for our escape, we would never have gotten through that fiery sea alive.

Next day, February 16, we left that basin which, between Rhodes and Alexandria, reaches depths of 3,000 meters, and passing well out from Cerigo Island after doubling Cape Matapan, the *Nautilus* left the isles of Greece behind.

Through the Mediterranean in 48 Hours

THE MEDITERRANEAN, THE blue sea *par excellence:* to Hebrews "the great sea"; to the Greeks simply "the sea"; to the Romans, *mare nostrum.*[1] Bordered by orange trees, aloes, cactus, and sea pines; perfumed with the scent of myrtle; framed by rugged mountains; saturated with pure, transparent air but incessantly troubled by volcanic action, this sea is a true battlefield where Neptune and Pluto still struggle for world domination.[2] Here on these beaches and waters, as Michelet says, humanity gains new strength in one of the most invigorating climates of our globe.[3]

But beautiful as it was, I could get only a quick look at that basin whose surface area comprises 2,000,000 square kilometers. Even Captain Nemo's personal observations were denied me, because that enigmatic personage did not appear once during our rapid crossing. I estimate that the *Nautilus* traveled

---

1. Latin: "our sea."

2. Throughout this chapter there are images of protean change. Here, Aronnax means that the sea has to contend with underground eruptions. Aronnax has been long concerned about this dispute: in I 14 he noted the victory of solid over liquid matter. Meanwhile, Verne indulges his flair for double meanings: just as the gods Neptune and Pluto struggled for domination of the physical world, so the Neptunists and Plutonists (or Vulcanists) were still disputing their theories in the scientific world.

3. Jules Michelet (1798–1874), the great romantic historian, saw man himself as Protean: man makes his own history in a continuous struggle against fate. He saw the emergence of the French republic as a human victory over racial and geographic determinism, and his book *The People* (1846) accurately predicted the Revolution of 1848. When he refused to swear allegiance to Emperor Louis Napoleon, he was blacklisted. Hence, Verne's very mention of Michelet while Napoleon is still in power is itself a political act.

In addition, Michelet's *The Sea* (1861) is reputed to have directly influenced much of the marine content of the present novel. "Jules Verne," writes Christian Chelebourg, "borrowed from Michelet a large number of imaginative situations: the milk sea, the Black Current, the waters of the Pole, the microscopic organisms, the madreporic master builders, the 'blood flower' coral, the submarine forests. . . . the fight between baleen whales and sperm whales is also found in Michelet, and with descriptions close to those coming from Jules Verne. Finally, a chapter devoted by the historian to crustaceans contains the seeds of the episode about the monsters seen by Aronnax and Nemo on the way to Atlantis: in this book Verne found the warlike imagery with which he depicts these animals, plus the idea of making them gigantic."

some 600 leagues under the waves of that sea, and that the trip was accomplished in just 24 hours times two. Quitting the waterways of Greece on the morning of February 16, we cleared the Strait of Gibraltar by sunrise on February 18.

It was clear to me that Captain Nemo did not enjoy the Mediterranean, locked in as it was by those countries he was fleeing. Its waves and winds apparently brought back too many memories, if not too many regrets. There he no longer had the freedom and independence that the larger seas had allowed him, and his *Nautilus* felt cramped between the nearby shores of Africa and Europe.

And so we were speeding at twenty-five miles (that is, twelve four-kilometer leagues) per hour. Needless to say, Ned Land was greatly vexed that he had to give up his plans to escape to Europe. Swept along at the rate of twelve to thirteen meters per second, he could not hope to make use of the dinghy. Leaving the *Nautilus* under those conditions would have been like jumping from a railroad train racing at that speed, a rash move if ever there was one. Moreover, the *Nautilus* surfaced only at night to renew its air supply, and, giving up its noon observations, traveled only by compass and log.[4]

Inside the Mediterranean, then, I could spy no more of its fast-passing scenery than a traveler might see from an express train; in other words, I could view only the distant horizons because the foregrounds flashed by like lightning. However, Conseil and I were able to observe some of those species of Mediterranean fish that could match the speed of the *Nautilus* long enough for us to identify them. We stayed on watch at the salon windows, and our notes enable me to reconstruct, in a few words, the ichthyology of that sea.

Among the varied species inhabiting it, some I really observed, others I merely glimpsed, and the rest I missed entirely because of the *Nautilus*'s speed. So permit me to sort them out according to this fanciful mode of classification. It will at least convey the rapidity of our observations.

In the midst of the water brilliantly illuminated by our electric light, there snaked past some of those meter-long lampreys common to nearly every sea. There was a type of ray, five feet wide, from the genus *Oxyrhynchus* that boasted a white belly, with a spotted ash-gray back, and unfolded like a vast shawl carried off by the currents. Other rays passed so fast I could not tell whether they deserved the name of "eagle ray," given them by the ancient Greeks, or the names "rat ray," "bat ray," or "toad ray," given them by modern fishermen. Twelve-foot long dogfish called topes, especially feared by divers, vied with each other in speed. Resembling great bluish shadows, some thresher sharks went by, eight feet long and gifted with an acute sense of smell. Some dorados of the genus *Sparus,* some of them up to thirteen decimeters long, appeared in

4. This is the traditional "dead reckoning" method of navigation. Nemo is simply steering by compass, calculating the distance covered each day, then finding his position on the map. In the confined Mediterranean this method is feasible, but on the high seas deviations caused by winds and currents would make use of the sextant and chronometer imperative.

silver and azure dress, encircled with ribbons, that contrasts with the somber color of their fins; these fish, whose eyes are set in brows of gold, were once sacred to the goddess Venus; they are a valuable species, equally at home in fresh or salt water, living in rivers, lakes, and oceans, in every clime, tolerating any temperature; they are a rarity too in this: their line dates back to early geologic epochs of our earth's prehistory, yet preserves all its beauty from those Edenic times. Some magnificent sturgeons, nine to ten meters long, creatures of great speed, knocked their powerful tails against our window panes, showing off their bluish backs with small brown spots; encountered in every sea, they resemble sharks but lack their strength; in the spring they are fond of going up large rivers, struggling against the currents of the Volga, Danube, Po, Rhine, Loire, and Oder; they live on herring, mackerel, salmon, codfish; although they belong to the class of cartilaginous fish, they rate as a delicacy;[5] they are eaten fresh, dried, marinated, or salted, and in ancient Rome they were taken in triumph to the table of the epicure Lucullus.[6]

But whenever the *Nautilus* cruised near the surface, those denizens of the Mediterranean I could observe best belonged to the sixty-third genus of bony fish. These were tuna from the genus *Scomber,* blue-black on top, with silver breastplates, their dorsal stripes giving off a golden gleam. They are said to follow ships in search of shade from the hot tropical sun, and they did just that with the *Nautilus,* as they had done with the ships of La Pérouse. For hours on end they would race with our submarine. I never wearied of admiring these creatures so perfectly built for racing, with their small heads, bodies sleek and spindle-shaped, in some cases more than three meters long, their pectoral fins endowed with great strength and their caudal fins forked. Like certain birds whose speed they emulate, these tuna swam in triangle formation, which prompted the ancients to say they knew both geometry and military strategy. Still, they can't escape the Provençal fishermen, who esteem them as highly as did the ancient inhabitants of the Propontis[7] and of Italy; and these precious but heedless creatures go leaping blindly by the thousands into the nets of the Marseillaise.

Just for the record, I will cite those Mediterranean fish that Conseil and I merely glimpsed. There were some whitish eels of the species *Gymnotus fasciatus,* sweeping by like vague mists; some conger eels, serpents three to four meters long, tricked out in green, blue, and yellow; hakes three feet long, whose liver makes a dainty morsel; some wormfish drifting like thin seaweed; some sea robins, which poets call lyrefish and seamen call pipers, whose muzzle is

5. Aronnax is reminding us that back in I 14 while Ned and Conseil bantered over the classification of fish, Ned had declared the sturgeon his personal favorite. Perhaps he was fond of caviar.

6. Lucius Licinius Lucullus (c. 114—57 B.C.) was born poor, earned great wealth in the military, and retired in luxury. He is said to have introduced the cherry to Italy. His biography is in Plutarch's *Lives.*

7. Propontis was the ancient name for the Sea of Marmora in northwestern Turkey. It feeds into both the Black Sea and the Aegean.

embellished with two serrated triangular plates shaped like Homer's lyre; swallowfish, which swim as fast as swallows fly; some redheaded groupers, their dorsal fins adorned with filaments; shad, covered with spots of black, gray, brown, blue, yellow, and green, a fish actually responsive to the silvery sounds of little bells; some splendid turbot, like seagoing pheasant, diamond-shaped bodies with yellowish fins stippled in brown and their topside usually marbled in brown and yellow; finally, schools of marvelous red mullet, genuine seagoing birds of paradise, for which the ancients paid up to 10,000 sesterces apiece, and which they put to death at the table so they could watch with merciless eyes as it changed from the cinnabar red of the living to the pallid white of the dead.

As for other fish common to both the Atlantic and the Mediterranean, I was unable to observe miralets, triggerfish, puffers, seahorses, jewelfish, trumpetfish, blennies, gray mullet, wrasse, smelt, flying fish, anchovies, sea bream, porgies, garfish, or the chief representatives of the order Pleuronecta, such as sole, flounder, plaice, dab, and brill, simply because of the dizzying speed with which the *Nautilus* dashed through those rich waters.

As for sea mammals, I thought I saw, near the mouth of the Adriatic Sea, two or three sperm whales,[8] equipped with that single dorsal fin denoting the genus *Physeter;* some pilot whales, genus *Globicephalus,* unique to the Mediterranean, the forepart of the head striped with little bright lines; and a dozen seals, white bellied and black coated, known as monk seals and truly looking just like three-meter Dominicans.

As for Conseil, he thought he had spotted a turtle six feet wide with three ridges running down its back. I regretted missing that reptile, because from Conseil's description I believe I recognized the leatherback turtle, a pretty rare species. The only turtles I myself saw were a few loggerheads with elongated shells.

As for zoophytes, for a few moments I was able to admire a beautiful orange hydra from the genus *Galeolaria,* which clung briefly to the port window; it consisted of a long lean filament spreading out into innumerable branches and ending in the most delicate lace ever spun by the rivals of Arachne herself.[9] Unfortunately, I could not capture that splendid specimen, and I doubtless would have seen no other Mediterranean zoophytes if the *Nautilus* hadn't slowed down considerably on the evening of February 16. This is what happened.

We were passing between Sicily and the Tunisian coast. In that cramped space between Cape Bon and the Strait of Messina, the sea bottom rises almost

8. The originals of Moby Dick, sperm whales are the only giant-size cetaceans with teeth. They have been so heavily hunted in the past 200 years that they are now an endangered species.

9. In Greek myth, Arachne was a Lydian princess who was such a superb weaver that she challenged the goddess Athene to a weaving contest. Arachne's textile was flawless, plus its design depicted some of the gods' more notorious amours. Furious, Athene tore the fabric and subsequently changed Arachne into a spider. *Arakhne* is Greek for spider, and in today's science spiders are known as "arachnids."

Mediterranean life

abruptly. It forms a genuine ridge that comes up to about seventeen meters from the surface, while the depth before and after is 170 meters. And so the *Nautilus* had to maneuver carefully so as not to strike against that underwater barrier.

I showed Conseil the position of that long reef on our Mediterranean chart.

"But with all due respect to master," Conseil undertook to observe, "it's like a real isthmus linking Europe to Africa."

"Correct, my boy," I agreed, "it cuts across the entire Strait of Sicily. Smith's soundings prove that these two continents were indeed once linked between Cape Boeo and Cape Farina.[10]

"I can easily believe that," Conseil said.

"And what's more," I resumed, "there's a barrier like this between Gibraltar and Ceuta, and during prehistoric times it closed off the Mediterranean completely."

"Heavens!" Conseil thought aloud. "Suppose someday some volcanic upheaval raises these two barriers again above the surface!"

"That's not likely, Conseil."

"What I mean—if master will allow me to finish—is that if this ever did happen, it would prove annoying to Mr. de Lesseps, who has taken so much trouble to cut through his isthmus."

"Yes it would but it won't happen. The violence of these subterranean forces is constantly diminishing. Volcanoes were numerous in the world's early days, but they're becoming extinct one by one. The heat inside the earth is weakening, the temperature in the lower strata of our planet is declining appreciably each century, all this to our detriment, because that heat is life."

"But there's the sun—"

"The sun isn't enough, Conseil. Can it restore heat to a corpse?"

"Not that I'm aware."

"Well then, my friend, the earth itself will someday be such a cold body. Like the moon that long ago lost its vital heat, our planet will become uninhabitable and uninhabited."

"In how many centuries?" he asked.

"In some hundreds of thousands of years, my boy."[11]

"Well then," Conseil concluded, "we have plenty of time to complete our voyage—unless Ned Land messes things up!"

Thus reassured, Conseil went back to studying the shallow bottom that the *Nautilus* was skimming at moderate speed.

On the rocky, volcanic seafloor there bloomed quite a collection of moving flora: sponges; sea cucumbers; jellyfish called the sea gooseberry, with reddish

---

10. Aronnax's remarks foreshadow today's theories of continental drift. It is now believed that the Mediterranean originated when the African plate swung away from the European plate. Belts of volcanoes around the world tend to fall along the meeting places of the great plates.

11. Here Aronnax is projecting much too quick an end for the planet earth. The most modest of today's theories speak at least in terms of millions.

tendrils, emitting a faint phosphorescence; some genus *Beroe,* commonly called melon jellyfish, bathing in a gleaming rainbow of colors; some ambulatory, indeed free-swimming crinoids a meter wide, reddening the water; treelike basket stars of great loveliness; some sea fans of the genus *Pavonacea* with long stems; great numbers of edible sea urchins of various species; and some green sea anemone, with grayish trunk and a brown disk, almost lost in their olive-colored tentacles.

Conseil was busy identifying mollusks and articulates. While his catalog might make for dull reading, I ought not to do him the injustice of ignoring his observations.[12]

From the branch Mollusca he cites numerous comb-shaped scallops; hooflike spiny oysters stacked pell-mell on top of each other; some triangular coquina; some trident-shaped glass snails with yellow fins and transparent shells; some orange snails from the genus *Pleurobranchus,* like eggs with green dots; some genus *Aplysia,* also called sea hares; and sea hares from the genus *Dolabella;* some plumpish paper bubble shells; umbrella shells found only in the Mediterranean; abalone that provide a good mother-of-pearl; pilgrim scallops; saddle shells that folk in the French province of Languedoc are said to prefer to oysters; some of those cockleshells so dear to the Marseillaise; some oversize Venus shells, plump and white, among the clams abounding off North America and eaten in such quantities in New York; variously colored comb shells with gill covers; date mussels, hiding in their holes, whose peppery taste I enjoy; furrowed heart cockles, whose shells have riblike protrusions at their arched summits; triton shells, covered with scarlet bumps; carinaria snails turned up at each end, resembling flimsy gondolas; crowned ferola snails; atlanta snails with spiral shells; gray nudibranches of the genus *Tethys,* speckled white and covered with fringed mantles; some nudibranches from the suborder Eolidea that look like little slugs; sea butterflies creeping along on their backs; seashells from the genus *Auricula,* including the oval shaped *Auricula myosotis;* some tannish wentletrap snails; common periwinkles; violet snails; cineraria snails; rock borers; ear shells; cabochon snails; pandora shells; and others.

As for the articulates, in his notes Conseil has properly divided them into six classes, three of which belong to the marine world: the Crustacea, Cirripedia, and Annelida.

Crustaceans are subdivided into nine orders, the first of which comprises the decapods, or animals whose head and thorax are usually united, whose cheek-and-mouth apparatus is made up of several pairs of jaws and whose thorax has four, five, or six pairs of walking legs.

Conseil followed the method of our mentor, Professor Milne-Edwards, and divided the decapods into three sections: Brachyura, Macrura, Anomura.

---

12. Verne probably expected some readers to skip such passages, so he often devises clever *detour signs* like this one.

Although these names sound barbarous, they are correct and precise.[13] Among the Brachyura, Conseil cites amanthia crabs, with fronts armed with two great diverging tips, that inachus scorpion which—I can't imagine why—the Greeks used as a symbol of wisdom; spider crabs, including some of the massena and spinimane varieties that usually live at great depths but had, apparently, gone astray over these shallows; xanthid crabs; pilumna crabs; rhomboid crabs; granular box crabs, easy to digest, as Conseil noted; toothless masked crabs; ebalia crabs; cymopolia crabs; woolly-handed crabs; and others.

The Macrura are subdivided into five families: hardshells, burrowers, crayfish, prawns, and ghost crabs. Among these Conseil cites some common spiny lobsters, the female of which furnishes flesh very good to eat; some slipper lobsters, or common shrimp; some waterside gebia shrimp; and many other edible species. But he says nothing of the crayfish subdivision, which includes the lobster proper, because spiny lobsters are the only kind found in the Mediterranean. Finally, among the Anomura he saw some common drocina crabs that take shelter in the rear of whatever abandoned seashells they can squat in; homola crabs with spiny fronts; hermit crabs; hairy porcelain crabs; and others.

And there Conseil stopped. He didn't have enough time to complete the class Crustacea via a study of its stomatopods, amphipods, homopods, isopods, trilobites, branchiopods, ostracods, and entomostraceans. And in order to complete his study of the sea's articulates, he would have had to cite the class Cirripedia, including water fleas and carp lice, and the class Annelida, which he would have been careful to divide into tubifex worms and dorsibranchian worms. But having passed the shallows of the Strait of Sicily, the *Nautilus* resumed its usual deep-water speed. No more studies of mollusks, zoophytes, articulates. Just a few large fish seen passing like shadows.

During the night of February 16–17 we entered the second basin of the Mediterranean, the greatest depth of which we found at 3,000 meters. The captain got us to the deepest strata by driving the ship down, full-throttle, with his slanting fins.

We saw no more natural marvels but instead terrible, moving spectacles. We were then crossing that portion of the Mediterranean so fecund with tragedies. From the coast of Algiers to the beaches of Provence, how many ships have wrecked, how many vessels disappeared! Compared to the vast liquid plains of the Pacific, the Mediterranean is only a lake, but it is a capricious lake, with temperamental waves, now kindly caressing the frail one-master floating between the twofold ultramarine of sky and water, later waxing ill-tempered and turbulent, lashing with its winds, smashing the strongest vessels with the powerful wallop of its waves.

13. That is, *brachyura* means short-tailed ones with greatly reduced abdomens; *macrura* means long-tailed ones with well-developed abdomens; *anomura* means irregular or unusual tails with short, flexed abdomens.

And so, in our rapid cruise through those deep strata, how many vessels I saw lying prone on the seafloor, some already caked with coral, others only covered with a layer of rust, plus anchors, cannon, shells, iron fittings, propeller blades, parts of engines, broken cylinders, staved in boilers; and higher up in midwater, hulls floating, some upright, others upside down.

Some of these wrecked ships had been rammed in collisions, others had struck granite reefs. I saw some that had sunk straight down, their masting still upright, their rigging stiffened by the water. They had the air of being at anchor by an immense, open, offshore mooring, waiting for the order to cast off. When the *Nautilus* passed between them, bathing them in floods of electricity, they seemed about to salute us with a dip of their colors and to signal us their serial numbers! But no, nothing but silence and death in that field of disasters.

The number of gruesome wrecks increased the nearer the *Nautilus* drew to the Strait of Gibraltar. By then the coasts of Africa and Europe were coming closer together and collisions occur more frequently as ships converge there. I saw numerous iron undersides, the eerie wrecks of steamers, some lying flat, some standing up on end like huge animals. One of these boats made a terrible first impression: sides gashed open, funnel bent, paddlewheels gone from their frame, the rudder parted from the sternpost but still held on by an iron chain, its rear nameplate eaten away by marine salts! How many lives had been snuffed out in that wreck? How many victims had been swept under the waves? Had even one sailor survived to tell the tale of that catastrophe, or has the sea kept it secret? I don't know why, but it occurred to me that this boat buried beneath the waves could be the *Atlas,* missing with all hands some twenty years before, and never heard from again! What a gruesome tale those Mediterranean depths could tell, that vast boneyard where so many treasures have been lost, so many victims have met their end!

But with total indifference the *Nautilus* moved at full speed among those ruins. On February 18, toward 3 a.m., we arrived at the entrance to the Strait of Gibraltar.

There are two currents here: an upper current long since known, which brings Atlantic Ocean water into the Mediterranean basin; and a lower countercurrent now known to exist through scientific reasoning. Essentially, the Mediterranean constantly receives that current from the Atlantic as well as waters from the rivers falling into it. Since local evaporation is not enough to reestablish equilibrium, the sum of the waters in this sea should raise its level every year. But this is not the case, the water level in fact remains the same; so we are obliged to accept the existence of a lower current which—via the Strait of Gibraltar—pours the Mediterranean surplus into the Atlantic basin.

A fact indeed! The *Nautilus* profited by the "theoretical" existence of that countercurrent. It advanced swiftly through that narrow passage. For an in-

The Temple of Hercules

stant I got a glimpse of the wonderful ruins of the Temple of Hercules buried, as Pliny and Avienus have mentioned, along with that low island on which it stood.[14] A few minutes later we were floating on the surface of the Atlantic.

14. Both writers were probably required reading for Aronnax in his student days. Pliny the Elder published a *Natural History* that still survives. He himself perished while studying the eruption of Vesuvius.

Rufius Festus Avienus left us, in the fourth century, Latin translations of two Greek poems on geographical subjects.

EIGHT

The Bay of Vigo[1]

THE ATLANTIC! THAT vast sheet of water with a surface area of 25,000,000 square miles, a length of 9,000 miles, and a mean width of 2,700. An important sea virtually unknown to the ancients, except maybe to the Carthaginians, those Dutchmen of antiquity who, in their commercial exploring, did sail the west coasts of Europe and Africa! An ocean, whose parallel winding shores form an immense perimeter that is fed by the world's greatest rivers: the St. Lawrence, the Mississippi, the Amazon, the Plata, the Orinoco, the Niger, the Senegal, the Elbe, the Loire, and the Rhine, which bring it waters from the most civilized and the most undeveloped areas of the globe. A magnificent plain of waves, plowed incessantly by ships of every land, shaded by every flag in the world, terminating in those two terrible headlands feared by every mariner, Cape Horn and the Cape of Tempests.[2]

The *Nautilus* broke those waters with the tip of its ram after sailing almost 10,000 leagues in three and a half months, a distance greater than a great circle of the earth. But where were we going? What did the future have in store for us?

Emerging from the Strait of Gibraltar, the *Nautilus* headed for the open sea. It could surface now, and we could once again enjoy our walks on the platform.

I went up there at once with Ned Land and Conseil. We could vaguely make out Cape St. Vincent, twelve miles away, the southwestern tip of the Hispanic peninsula. A fairly strong wind was blowing from the south, the sea was swelling and surging, the *Nautilus* rolling and rocking violently. It was almost impossible to stand up on the platform, which was buffeted by that enormously heavy sea. After inhaling a few deep breaths of sea air, we went back down.

1. Again Verne uses a place name that promises suspense and exotic complications. To European readers, the Bay of Vigo was a colorful port that had been a center of romance and heroism. A spacious fjord, the Bay of Vigo extends inland some twenty miles, furnishing a normally peaceful harbor.

But there were a few tensions in its history. In 1585 and again in 1589, Sir Francis Drake's English fleet attacked the town of Vigo. And in 1702, this bay was the scene of yet another incident . . . as described in this chapter.

2. Better known as the Cape of Good Hope.

I took to my room again. Conseil returned to his cabin, but the Canadian, looking rather preoccupied, followed me. Our swift crossing of the Mediterranean had not allowed him to carry out his plans, and I could read his disappointment in his face.

As soon as I had closed my door, he sat down and gazed silently at me.

"Friend Ned," I said, "I know how you feel, but you mustn't blame yourself. Given the way the *Nautilus* navigated, it would have been madness to think of escaping."

Ned Land did not respond. I could tell by his pursed lips and frowning brow that he was in the grip of an *idée fixe*.

"Look," I resumed, "we needn't despair so soon. We're sailing up the Portuguese coast. France and England aren't far off, we'll easily find refuge up there. Oh, I grant you, if the *Nautilus* had left the Strait of Gibraltar and headed for that cape in the south, if it were sweeping us toward those regions where there are no continents, then I would share your anxiety. But now we know that Captain Nemo doesn't avoid civilized areas, and so I think in a few days it'll be safe to take action."

Ned Land stared still more intently at me. Finally he unpursed his lips:

"Tonight. We'll do it tonight."

I straightened suddenly. I confess I was less than ready for this. I wanted to reply but words failed me.

"We agreed to wait for the right circumstances," Ned Land resumed. "Now we have a good chance. Tonight we'll be only a few miles off the Spanish coast. The nights now are cloudy. The wind's blowing toward the shore. You promised me, Professor Aronnax, and I'm counting on you."

Since I still said nothing, the Canadian got up and came over to me:

"Tonight at nine," he said. "I have alerted Conseil. At that time Captain Nemo will be shut up in his room, probably in bed. Neither the mechanics nor the crew will be able to see us. Conseil and I will make for the central companionway. And you, Professor Aronnax, you'll stay in the library, just two paces away, and wait for my signal. The oars, the mast, the sail are already in the dinghy. I've even managed to stow some provisions in it. I've also gotten hold of a monkey wrench to undo the bolts that attach the dinghy to the hull of the *Nautilus*. So, everything is ready. I'll see you tonight."

"But the sea is rough," I said.

"Granted," he acknowledged, "but that's the risk we've got to take. Freedom is worth the price. Besides, the dinghy is built solid, and sailing a few miles with the wind behind us is no big deal. You know, if we stayed on board, we might be 100 leagues out to sea by tomorrow. But if things go according to plan, by 10 or 11 p.m. tonight we'll be landing on some spot of *terra firma*—or we could be dead. We're in God's hands! Tonight, then!"

With that, he left me—dumbfounded. I had imagined that if it ever came to this, I would have time to think it over, *talk* it over. My stubborn friend had given me no such chance. But after all, what could I have said? Ned Land was right a hundred times over. The circumstances were nearly ideal and he was taking advantage of them. For purely selfish reasons, could I go back on my promise and be responsible for jeopardizing the future of my friends? Ned was right, by tomorrow Captain Nemo could sweep us far away from any shore.

At that moment, a tolerably loud hissing told me that the ballast tanks were filling up. The *Nautilus* was sinking down into the Atlantic.

I stayed in my cabin, wanting to avoid the captain, to hide from him the feelings that were sweeping over me and could betray me. It was a sad day for me, torn between the desire to regain my freedom and my regret at leaving this marvelous *Nautilus,* leaving my submarine research unfinished! How could I give up "my Atlantic," as I had begun to think of it, without wresting from its depths its profoundest secrets, as I had done with the Indian Ocean and the Pacific! It was like leaving a novel half read, or being interrupted at the most exciting point of a dream! What miserable hours I spent, now thinking of us as safe on shore, then finding myself hoping that some unforeseen circumstances would frustrate Ned Land's plans.

Twice I visited the salon to consult the compass. I wanted to see if the *Nautilus*'s course was taking us closer to the coast or farther out to sea. Oh no! The *Nautilus* stayed in Portuguese waters. Heading north, it was cruising the beaches.

So I had to resign myself to the situation and get ready to escape. But I didn't have much luggage. My notes—that was *all*.

As for Captain Nemo, I wondered what he would think of our escaping, what distress or maybe what harm it would cause him, and what he would do in case our breakout failed or was discovered. Certainly I had no right to complain. On the contrary, never was hospitality more wholehearted than his on board the *Nautilus*. Yet in leaving him I could not be accused of ingratitude. No solemn promises bound us to him. He counted on the force of circumstances, not on promises, to keep us on board. And so his openly stated plan of keeping us prisoners forever certainly justified our every effort to escape.

I had not seen the captain since our visit to Santorin Island. Would chance bring us face-to-face again before I left? I desired it and I dreaded it. I listened for footsteps in his cabin, next to mine. Silence. His cabin was undoubtedly empty.

I began to wonder if that enigmatic man was even on board. My ideas about him had changed a bit since that night when the dinghy had left the *Nautilus* on some mysterious mission. I had come to think now that regardless of what he claimed, he still maintained some relations with the shore. Did he himself never leave the *Nautilus*? I could recall sometimes not seeing him for weeks at a time. What was he doing then? Was he sulking in antisocial seclusion, or was he on some secret mission, the nature of which I could not imagine?

Thousands of such questions crowded my mind. In our strange situation the scope for conjecture was unlimited. I felt an unbearable uneasiness. That day of waiting seemed endless. The hours struck too slowly to keep pace with my impatience.

As usual, dinner was served in my cabin. I was too preoccupied to eat very much. I got up from the table at seven o'clock. One hundred and twenty minutes—I was counting them!—still separated me from that moment I was to join Ned Land. I was getting more and more nervous. My pulse was pounding. I could not stay put. I walked up and down, hoping to calm myself with physical activity. The thought of dying in this reckless venture was the least of my worries. What did upset me, though, was the thought that our plans might be discovered before we could get away, that we would be hauled before Captain Nemo, who would be furious, or worse yet, saddened by our desertion.

I wanted to spend some time—one last time—in the salon. I went through the corridor and arrived at the museum where I had passed so many pleasant, productive hours. I gazed at all those riches, all those treasures, like a man about to be exiled for life, to leave and never come back. For so many days now these marvels of Nature, these masterworks of art, had been central to my life, and I would never see them again. I wanted to stare one last time through the windows out into the Atlantic, but the panels were hermetically sealed, and a curtain of steel separated me from this ocean I had not yet explored.

Wandering through the salon, I came to the door, set into one of the canted corners, that led into the captain's cabin. To my great surprise it was open. I stepped back involuntarily. I was afraid Captain Nemo would see me if he were in there. But I heard no sounds and looked in. The room was deserted. I pushed the door all the way open and stepped inside. Still that same, stark, monastic look.

But then I saw something I had not noticed during my earlier visit—some etchings hanging on the wall. They were portraits of great men of history who had devoted their lives zealously to a great human ideal: Thaddeus Kosciusko, the hero whose dying words had been *Finis Poloniae;*[3] Markos Botzaris, for modern Greece the reincarnation of the Spartan King Leonidas; Daniel O'Connell, defender of Ireland; George Washington, the founder of the American Union; Daniele Manin, the Italian patriot; Abraham Lincoln, felled by the bullet of a proponent of slavery; and finally, that martyr for the redemption of the black race, John Brown—hanging from his gallows just as Victor Hugo has so terrifyingly depicted him.

What was the bond that Captain Nemo felt with those heroic souls? Would these portraits help me unravel the mystery of his life?[4] Was he, like these heroes, himself a fighter for oppressed people, a liberator of enslaved races? Had he taken an active part in some recent political or social upheaval? Had he

3. Latin: loosely, "Save Poland's borders!"

4. Indeed, these portraits are crucial to our understanding of Nemo's character and of the rationale behind his strange behavior. Nemo's gallery of personal heroes includes men who have not hesitated to take up arms against established government when that government has proved to be evil. And, rebels or not, what all these heroes had in common was their devotion to the ideals of human freedom and civil rights.

And let's not forget that the *Nautilus*'s library seems to have a ban on books about economics. Does Nemo feel that this subject is the *root* of governmental evil?

served heroically in that terrible civil war in America, a war lamentable yet forever glorious? . . .

The clock suddenly struck eight. The first blow of the hammer on the bell wrenched me out of my musings. I shuddered as if some invisible eye had plunged into my most secret thoughts, and I rushed out of the room.[5]

My eye fell on the compass. We were still on a northerly course. The log indicated a moderate speed, the pressure gauge a depth of about sixty feet. Circumstances still favored the Canadian's plan.

I went back to my cabin and dressed warmly: fishing boots, otter cap, byssus coat lined with sealskin. I was ready. I was waiting. Only the propeller's vibrations broke the deep silence on board. I listened carefully. Would I hear sudden shouts telling me that Ned Land had been caught preparing to escape? A deadly disquiet stole through me. I tried in vain to be cool and calm.

A few minutes before nine I put my ear to the captain's door. Not a sound. I left my room and went back to the salon. It was dimly lit and deserted.

I opened the door to the library. The same dim lighting, the same solitude. I went over to man my post near the door that led to the central companionway. I was waiting for Ned Land's signal.

At that moment the propeller's vibrations slowed down noticeably—then it stopped altogether. Why had the *Nautilus* stopped? Whether this would help or hinder Ned's plans I had no way of knowing.

Now the silence was broken only by the pounding of my heart.

Suddenly I felt a slight jolt. I realized the *Nautilus* had come to rest on the ocean floor. My anxiety deepened. Still no signal from Ned. How I wanted to be with him to urge him to postpone our attempt! I sensed we were no longer navigating under normal conditions.

Suddenly the door to the salon opened and Captain Nemo appeared. He saw me, and without further preamble he said, in a genial tone:

"Ah, professor, I've been looking for you. How well do you know your Spanish history?"

---

5. Aronnax's behavior here reveals much about his psychology and even more about Verne's psychohistory.

Aronnax worries that Nemo will be hurt by the professor's *desertion*. He worries whether he can be *accused of ingratitude*. He fears he will *be hauled before Captain Nemo, who would be furious*. He feels as if he's being watched by an *invisible eye*. His feelings culminate in a dread of being *exiled for life*. Unmistakably, he is the dependent son fearful of angering the Omnipotent Parent.

According to Marcel Moré, a major theme in Verne's work is *the search for the perfect father*. Verne's own search, Moré says, ended when he signed on with publisher Pierre Hetzel. Hetzel took charge of the author's professional and personal life, whereat Verne flourished. In this scene Aronnax feels as Verne would if he were forced to consider deserting Hetzel.

Aronnax's attack of conscience also replays a crisis in Verne's life with his *real* father. The eleven-year-old Jules ran away to be a cabin boy on a ship bound for the West Indies. But as the vessel made its last stop in France, he was *caught* by his father, who was *furious* about the boy's *desertion*. He had to promise his parents that he would conduct all future journeys only in his imagination.

Even if one knew his *own* country's history backward and forward, in my disturbed, bewildered state he could not have recalled one single date!

"Well?" he repeated. "Did you hear my question? How well do you know Spanish history?"

"Not at all well."

"The most learned among us," the captain said, "still have a lot to learn. Take a seat and I'll tell you about a strange chapter in Spain's history."

The captain stretched out on a divan as I mechanically sat down near him but, as much as I could, in the shadows.[6]

"Professor, now listen carefully. This bit of history will interest you because it will answer at least one question you've never been able to resolve."

"I'm listening, captain," I said, wondering what this was all about, whether it had anything to do with our attempted escape.

"Professor, with your permission, we'll go back to 1702. You're surely aware that in those days your King Louis XIV thought an imperial gesture could subdue the Pyrenees, and he had imposed his grandson, the Duke of Anjou, on the Spaniards. Reigning more or less badly under the name of King Philip V, this prince had a rough time in foreign affairs.

"In fact, the year before, the royal houses of Holland, Austria, and England had signed a treaty of alliance at The Hague. Their goal was to wrench the Spanish crown from Philip V and to place it on the head of an archduke whom they prematurely dubbed King Charles III.

"Spain had to face this coalition with practically no army or navy. But it was not short of money, provided that its galleons, laden with gold and silver from America, could enter its ports. Now then, late in 1702 Spain expected a rich convoy, which France was escorting with a fleet of twenty-three ships, commanded by Admiral de Chateau-Renault, because, you see, the coalition's navies were roving the Atlantic.

"This convoy was supposed to put into Cádiz, but when the admiral heard that an English fleet was cruising thereabouts, he decided to head for a French port.

"But the Spanish commanders in the convoy wouldn't hear of it. They insisted on being escorted to a Spanish port, if not to Cádiz, then to the Bay of Vigo, on the northwest coast of Spain and not blockaded.

"Admiral de Chateau-Renault was so weak as to give in to these demands and the galleons put into the Bay of Vigo.

"Unfortunately, this bay forms an open offshore mooring that's impossible to defend. So it was necessary to work fast and unload those galleons before the

6. Does Nemo notice that Aronnax is all dressed up for the outside cold? Even though Aronnax sits carefully *in the shadows,* Nemo could hardly miss that heavy byssus overcoat and otter cap the professor is wearing. Is it possible that some crewman spied Ned and Conseil in outdoor garb, and that Nemo has surmised the escape plan? In any event, Nemo's present undertaking, whether coincidental or not, is sure to thwart Ned's scheme. And it suits Nemo's role as the mysterious, ironic, all-knowing genius that he would be content to frustrate Aronnax without ever letting on that he knew the truth.

coalition fleet arrived. There was time enough for this unloading, but a miserable question of trade rivalry suddenly changed everything.

"Are you following this chain of events?" Captain Nemo asked.

"Perfectly." I still couldn't figure out why I was getting this history lesson.

"Then I'll go on. This is what developed. The merchants of Cádiz had a charter that gave them the right to receive all goods from the West Indies. To unload the ingots from those galleons at the Bay of Vigo was to violate their rights. So they lodged a complaint in Madrid; they obtained an order from the weak King Philip V—the convoy would stay at Vigo, without unloading, until the enemy fleets went away!

"Now then, while that order was in the works, English ships arrived in the Bay of Vigo on October 22, 1702. Although he was outnumbered, Admiral de Chateau-Renault fought courageously. But when he saw that the convoy's riches would fall into enemy hands, he burned and scuttled the galleons, which went to the bottom with their immense treasures."[7]

Captain Nemo paused. I still couldn't see why he thought this should be of interest to me.

"So?" I said.

"So, Professor Aronnax," Captain Nemo resumed, "we're now in the Bay of Vigo. It's up to you now to get to the bottom of that mystery."

He rose and bade me follow him. I had had time to collect myself and I obeyed. The salon was dark but the sea sparkled through the transparent windows. I looked out.

Within a half-mile radius of the *Nautilus*, the waters were bathed now in electric light. The sandy bottom was clear and bright. Crewmen in their diving suits were busy, in the midst of the black wrecks of ships, clearing away half-rotted barrels and disemboweled trunks. From those kegs and coffers spilled ingots of gold and silver; the sand was strewn with jewels and pieces of eight. Laden with this precious booty, the men would take it to the *Nautilus,* then go back to fish for more silver and gold.

I understood now. This was the site of that battle on October 22, 1702. This was the very place where galleons carrying treasure to the Spanish government had gone to the bottom. This was where Captain Nemo came when he needed millions with which to ballast his *Nautilus*. It was for him, for him alone, that America had yielded up its precious metals. He was the direct, sole heir of this treasure snatched from the Incas and those Indians conquered by Hernando Cortez!

"Did you ever imagine, professor," he asked, smiling, "that the sea contained such riches?"

7. But the admiral did not succeed in sinking *all* the treasure. The combined British and Dutch fleet succeeded in capturing about a million pounds in silver—only a *fraction* of the total treasure!

⸝ Louis XIV did not hold Chateau-Renault responsible for this great loss. In 1703 he made the admiral a marshal of France and in 1704, governor of Brittany.

The scuttling

"I know it's estimated that there are 2,000,000 metric tons of silver held in suspension in seawater."

"Surely, but if you set about extracting *that* silver, your expenses would outweigh your profits. Here, conversely, I've only to pick up what other men have lost, not only in this Bay of Vigo, but at a thousand other sites of shipwrecks that I've marked on my underwater charts. Now you can understand why I am a billionaire."

"I do understand, captain. But let me tell you that by harvesting this Bay of Vigo, you are forestalling the efforts of a rival company."

"What company?"

"A company chartered by the Spanish government to search for these sunken galleons. Its investors have been lured by the promise of enormous gains, because these scuttled riches are estimated to be worth 500,000,000 francs."

"There used to be 500 million here," the captain responded, "but not now."

"Indeed. Then a timely warning to those stockholders would be a charitable act. Yet who knows if the warning would be well taken. Usually what gamblers regret most is not the loss of their money so much as the loss of their insane expectations. But in the end I feel less sorry for them than for those thousands of poor people who would have benefited from such wealth if it had been fairly distributed—but now it will be forever useless to them."

No sooner had I voiced this regret than I felt it must have wounded Captain Nemo.

"Useless!" he replied animatedly. "What makes you, professor, think these riches go to waste when I'm the one gathering them? Do you think I toil to collect these treasures for selfish reasons? Who told you I don't put them to good use? Do you think I'm unaware of the suffering peoples and oppressed races on this planet, the poor to be comforted, the victims to be avenged? Can't you . . . understand? . . ."

Captain Nemo stopped there, perhaps regretting he had said so much. But yes, I did understand. Whatever had driven him to seek independence beneath the waves, he remained a human being before all else. His heart still beat for suffering humanity, and his immense charity went out to downtrodden races as well as to individuals.

And I also understood where those millions had been sent by Captain Nemo, when the *Nautilus* navigated the waters where Crete was in rebellion against the Ottoman Empire!

NINE

A Lost Continent

THE NEXT MORNING, February 19, as I had expected, the Canadian came to my cabin. He looked terribly dejected.

"Well, sir?" he asked.

"Well, Ned, the fates were against us last night."

"You said it! That damned captain just had to call a halt at the exact time we were all set to escape from his boat."

"Yes, Ned, he had business with his bankers."

"His bankers!"

"Or rather his bank vaults. I mean the ocean, where his riches are safer than in any national treasury."

I told the Canadian everything that had happened the night before, with the secret hope of making him give up the idea of deserting the captain. But my story had no such effect; instead he deeply regretted that he himself had not been able to stroll over the battlefield of Vigo.

"Besides," he added, "it's not over yet. My first harpoon missed, that's all. We'll succeed the next time, tonight, if we have—"

"Which way are we sailing now?"

"I have no idea," Ned admitted.

"Well, we'll find out at noon."

The Canadian rejoined Conseil. As soon as I was dressed I went to the salon. The compass was not reassuring. The *Nautilus* was heading south-southwest. We were turning our backs on Europe.

I was impatient to see our position marked on the chart. Toward 11:30 a.m. I heard the ballast tanks emptying and we rose to the surface. I sprang to the platform. Ned Land had got there ahead of me.

No more shore in sight. Nothing but the vastness of the sea. On the horizon, though, were several sails, probably ships going all the way to Cape São Roque to find favorable winds for doubling the Cape of Good Hope. The sky was overcast. I could sense a squall on the way.

Furious, Ned tried to see something beyond the mists. He still hoped that behind all that fog he would see those shores he so desperately desired.

At noon the sun made a momentary appearance. The first mate took advantage of this rift in the clouds to take his bearings. Then, with the sea getting rougher, we went below and the hatch was closed.

When I consulted the chart an hour later, I found that our position was marked at longitude 16° 17′ and latitude 33° 22′, just about 150 leagues from the nearest land. It was pointless to think of escaping. The reader can well imagine the intensity of the Canadian's rage when I told him this bad news.

For myself, I confess I was not really sorry. I actually felt as if a great burden had been lifted from my shoulders, and I was able to return to my work with a new calmness.

Toward 11 p.m. I received a most unexpected visit from Captain Nemo. He inquired most graciously whether I felt fatigued from my late vigil the night before. I said no.

"Then, Professor Aronnax, I'd like to suggest a very curious excursion."

"I'm all ears."

"So far you've visited the ocean depths only by day, when the sun is out. How would you like to see them on a dark night?"

"Oh what a good idea!"

"I warn you, though, this will be a very exhausting hike. We'll walk long hours and climb a mountain. And the roads aren't kept in good repair."

"Everything you say, captain, just increases my curiosity. I'm all set to go."

"Then come, professor, let's go get into our diving suits."

In the dressing room I saw that neither my companions nor any crewmen were to go with us this time. Captain Nemo had not even suggested that I call Ned or Conseil.

It took us just a few minutes to get into our suits. Then the tanks, abundantly charged with air, were set on our backs. But the electric lamps had not been prepared, and I remarked on this to the captain.

"They would be useless to us," he replied.

I was sure I had not heard him correctly, but I couldn't pursue the matter because the captain's head was already hidden in his helmet. I finished harnessing myself, I felt an alpenstock being placed in my hand, and a few minutes later, after the usual procedures, we set foot on the bottom of the Atlantic, 300 meters down.

It was nearly midnight. The waters were profoundly dark, but Captain Nemo pointed to a red spot in the distance, a broad gleam shimmering about two miles from the *Nautilus*. What that fire could be, what was feeding it, how it could sustain itself in this liquid environment, I could not imagine. Anyhow, it lit our way, vaguely it is true, but I soon became accustomed to that peculiar gloom and could see now why the Ruhmkorff apparatus had been left behind.

Captain Nemo and I walked side by side toward that conspicuous glow. The level seafloor had begun to rise, almost imperceptibly. We took long strides and made good use of our alpenstocks. Still, our progress was slow, for we kept sinking in a slimy mud mixed with seaweed and littered with flat stones.

As we advanced I heard a pitter-patter above my head. Sometimes this sound would increase in intensity, becoming a continuous crackle. Then I understood—it was a violent rainfall rattling on the surface of the waves. Instinctively I worried that I was going to get drenched! Drenched by water in the midst of water! I had to grin at that absurd notion. But to tell the truth, wearing a heavy diving suit, one no longer has the sensation of being in the water, one simply feels in the midst of an atmosphere denser than the air we walk in on land. Nothing more.

After half an hour, we were treading on a rocky bottom. Jellyfish, microscopic crustaceans, and sea pen coral faintly illuminated it with their phosphorescent glimmering. I saw piles of stones covered by millions of zoophytes and jumbled algae. My feet often slipped on that viscous seaweed carpet—without my alpenstock I would have fallen more than once. Whenever I turned around, I could still see the *Nautilus*'s whitish beacon light, but it had begun to grow paler in the distance.

I began to realize that those piles of stone were laid out on the ocean floor with a distinct but inexplicable regularity. I noticed, too, huge furrows trailing off into the distant darkness, so long I could not even estimate how long. There were many other details I found hard to explain. I had the sensation that my heavy lead soles were crushing bones that made a dry crackling sound. What was this vast, strange plain we were crossing? I wanted to ask the captain, but unfortunately I did not know that sign language he and his companions used on these underwater excursions.

Meanwhile, that reddish light guiding us had expanded, it now ignited the horizon. The existence of fire underwater aroused my curiosity to fever pitch. Was it some electrical discharge? Was I walking toward some natural phenomenon still unknown to scientists on land? Even this notion hit me: was this conflagration produced by human beings? Had human hands fanned that flame? In those deep strata was I about to visit friends of Captain Nemo who led lives as strange as his own? Would I find a whole colony of exiles down here, people weary of a miserable existence on land, who had sought and found independence in the extreme depths of the sea? All these absurd, inadmissible notions pursued me, and overexcited by the sequence of marvels passing before my eyes, I would not have been surprised to run into one of those underwater cities Captain Nemo dreamed about![1]

Our route brightened more and more. That red glow had turned into a white glare, radiating from the summit of a mountain about 800 feet high. But now I realized that that glare was simply a reflection produced by the water

1. Nemo's "dream" is one of Verne's predictions that has come true only in fairly recent times. In 1969–70 teams of 4 to 5 scientist/aquanauts lived from 1 to 2 months at a depth of 50 feet near the island of St. John in the Virgin Islands, working, cooking, and sleeping in submersible dwellings under a minimum pressure of one and a half atmospheres. This was the first successful instance of living under such sustained pressures.

itself. The furnace that was the real source of this inexplicable light was on the opposite side of the mountain.

Captain Nemo advanced without hesitation amid those stone mazes furrowing the floor of the area. He knew this somber route. Doubtless he had often made this trip, and there seemed to be no danger he would lose his way. I followed him with unshakable confidence. He seemed like some genie of the sea, and as he walked ahead of me, I admired his tall build, which stood out in black against the lights on the horizon.

It was one a.m. when we reached the first slopes of the mountain. But to climb it we had to venture up difficult trails through a vast forest.

Yes, a forest of dead trees! Trees with no leaves, no sap, turned to stone by the action of the waters, with here and there a gigantic pine towering over all the others. It was like a still-erect coalfield, its roots clutching broken soil, its boughs outlined against the ceiling of the waters like thin black paper cutouts. Picture a forest clinging to the sides of one of the Harz Mountains, but a forest all underwater. The trails were cluttered with algae and fucus plants, among them swarming hosts of crustaceans. I plunged on, climbing rocks, stepping over fallen tree trunks, snapping those marine vines that swayed from tree to tree, startling the fish flying from branch to branch. In my enthusiasm I no longer felt weary. I followed a guide who never tired.

What a sight! How can I describe it! How can I portray those woods and rocks in their liquid setting, their undersides somber and sullen, their upper parts tinted red in that light whose intensity was doubled when it was reflected by that water! We scaled rocks that crumbled behind us, breaking up in enormous chunks with the dull rumble of an avalanche. To our right and left were hollowed-out gloomy caves where the gaze lost its way. Vast glades would open out, seemingly cleared by the hand of man, and I sometimes wondered whether some residents of these underwater regions would suddenly appear before me.

But Captain Nemo kept on climbing. It wouldn't do to fall behind, so I followed him boldly. My alpenstock was a great help. One false step would have been dangerous on those narrow paths gouged out of the sides of those chasms, and I walked with a firm step and not the slightest feeling of dizziness. Sometimes I leaped a crevasse whose depth would have made me hesitate had it been in a glacier on dry land; sometimes I ventured out on a wobbling tree trunk fallen across a chasm, without looking down, having eyes only for the savage scenery. Monumental rocks, leaning on strangely shaped bases, seemed to defy the laws of equilibrium. From between their stony knees, trees sprang like jets under heavy pressure, supporting other trees that supported them in turn. Natural towers with wide, steeply carved battlements, leaned over at angles that the laws of gravity would not tolerate on dry land.

And I too could tell the difference created by the density of seawater, for in spite of my heavy diving suit, copper headpiece, and lead soles, I could climb slopes of incredible steepness with the agility of a chamois or a Pyrenees mountain goat.

I know this account of my underwater hike must sound scarcely believable. I must set down experiences apparently impossible yet real and undeniable. These were not daydreams. These were things I saw and felt!

Two hours after leaving the *Nautilus* we had cleared the timberline, and 100 feet above us rose the mountain peak that stood silhouetted against the brilliant light coming from its opposite slope. Some petrified shrubs ran in sprawling, zigzag lines. Fish rose in schools at our feet like birds surprised in tall grass. The rocky mass was gouged with impenetrable crevices, deep grottoes, unfathomable holes at the bottom of which I could hear formidable creatures moving. My blood would curdle when I saw an enormous antenna move across my path, or heard some frightful claw snap shut in the shadow of some hollow. Thousands of luminous spots glittered in the gloom. They were the eyes of gigantic crustaceans crouching in their lairs; of giant lobsters drawing themselves up like spear carriers and moving their claws with a scrap-iron clanking; of titanic crabs aiming their bodies like cannon on their carriages; of hideous squid intertwining their tentacles like a moving thicket of snakes.

What was this extravagant world that even I as a naturalist did not know? To what order do these articulates belong, these jointed invertebrates who use rocks as a second shell? Where had Nature found the secret of their vegetating existence, and for how many centuries had they lived like this in the deepest strata of the sea?

But I could not pause to wonder. Captain Nemo, well acquainted with these terrible creatures, no longer minded them. We reached a kind of first plateau where still other surprises were in store for me. I could make out picturesque ruins clearly the work not of the Creator but of humanity! Here were vast stacks of stones among which I discerned the vague shapes of palaces and temples, now arrayed in hosts of blossoming zoophytes, and over it all, not ivy but a mantle of seaweed and fucus plants.

But what portion of the globe could this be, this country swallowed by some cataclysm? Who had arranged these rocks and stones like the dolmens of prehistoric days? Where was I, where had Captain Nemo's fancies taken me?

I wanted to ask him. Since I couldn't, I stopped him and seized his arm. But he shook his head, pointed to the highest point on the mountain, seeming to say:

"Come on! Follow me! Farther up!"

With one last burst of energy, I followed him and in a few minutes I had reached that peak that rose ten meters above the rest of the mountain.

I looked back down the side we had just scaled. On that side the mountain rose only 700 to 800 feet above the plain; but turning, I could see that on the other side, it rose twice that height over a much lower part of the Atlantic. My eyes roved over a vast area lit by violent flashes. This mountain was in fact a volcano. Fifty feet below this peak, amid a shower of stones and cinders, a wide crater vomited up torrents of lava that were dispersed in a fiery cascade into the masses of water. So situated, that volcano was an immense torch lighting those lower plains to the farthest reaches of the horizon.

Notice that I said this underwater crater was throwing up lava, but I didn't mention *flames*. For flames need oxygen from the air and would be unable to spread under water. But a lava flow—having in itself the principle of its incandescence—can attain a white heat, fight victoriously against the surrounding water, and turn it into steam on contact. Fast currents swept away all that diffuse gas, and torrents of lava slid to the foot of the mountain like those of a Mt. Vesuvius over the city limits of another Torre del Greco.

Indeed, there beneath my eyes was a town destroyed, ruined, overwhelmed, its roofs caved in, its temples fallen down, its arches dislocated, its columns stretched out on the seafloor. In those ruins I could still sense the solid proportions of a Tuscan-like architecture. Farther off I could see remnants of a gigantic aqueduct, over these the encrusted heights of an acropolis along with the fluid forms of a Parthenon, elsewhere the remains of a wharf, as if some ancient port had long ago sheltered merchant ships and triremes on the shore of a vanished sea; still farther off, long lines of crumbling walls, wide and empty streets, a whole buried Pompeii that Captain Nemo was resurrecting before my eyes!

Where was I? *Where?* I had to know at any price, I wanted to speak, to wrench off that copper sphere that imprisoned my head.

But Captain Nemo came over and, with a gesture, bade me watch him while he picked up a piece of chalky stone, walked toward a black basaltic rock, and scrawled just one word:

ATLANTIS

A bolt of light flashed through my mind. Atlantis, that ancient land of Meropis cited by the historian Theopompus; the Atlantis of Plato: the continent whose objective existence has been denied by such thinkers as Origen, Porphyry, Iamblichus, d'Anville, Malte-Brun, and Humboldt, who wrote it off as legend; that land whose reality has nevertheless been accepted by other thinkers like Posidonius, Pliny, Ammianus Marcellinus, Tertullian, Engel, Scherer, Tournefort, Buffon, and d'Avezac.[2] I was looking at that land, its own unimpeachable witness of its existence and its catastrophic end! This was that now submerged region that had once existed outside Europe, Asia, and Libya, beyond the Pillars of Hercules,[3] home of those powerful Atlantians against whom the early Greeks had waged their first wars!

2. Verne lists a mere platoon of the many battalions of authors who have written about Atlantis. We'll pluck out only Buffon for special attention, because he was one of the best-known naturalists in the civilized world. George Louis Leclerc, Count de Buffon (1707–1788), was author of a thirty-six-volume reference work, *Natural History.* His fame was so universal that Charles Dickens could pun on his name (Buffon = buffoon) in *The Old Curiosity Shop.*

3. Two high points of rock at the eastern end of the Strait of Gibraltar. They were regarded by many in the ancient world as the outer limit of feasible navigation. Legend has it that Hercules erected them: the one on the European side is today known as the Rock of Gibraltar; the other, on the African headland, is Mount Acho.

The writer who recorded the lofty deeds of those heroic times was Plato himself. His dialogues *Timaeus* and *Critias* were written, so to speak, under the inspiration of Solon, poet and legislator.

One day Solon was talking with some wise old men in Saïs, the Egyptian capital, a town already 8,000 years old, as indicated by its annals engraved on the sacred walls of its temples. One of those elders told the story of another town yet another thousand years older. That town, the original Athens, ninety centuries old, had been invaded and partly destroyed by the Atlantians.[4] These Atlantians, he said, inhabited a continent greater than Africa and Asia combined, an area extending from latitude 12° to latitude 40° north. Their dominion stretched even to Egypt. They had tried to conquer Greece too, but they were forced to retreat before the indomitable resistance of the Hellenes. Centuries later they were overwhelmed by a terrible cataclysm—floods and earthquakes. One night and one day sufficed to obliterate Atlantis, whose highest peaks still stand above the sea: Madeira, the Azores, the Canaries, the Cape Verde islands.

Such were the historical memories that this single word inscribed on stone sent rushing through my mind. Brought here by the strangest of destinies, I was now standing on one of the mountains of that lost continent! My hands were touching ruins many thousands of years old, contemporary with prehistoric, geologic epochs.[5] I was walking in the very place where the contemporaries of earliest humanity had walked. Under my lead soles I was crushing the bones of animals from the age of fable, animals that had once sought the shade under these trees now turned to stone!

Oh, why is there never enough time! I would have liked to descend the steep slopes of that mountain, travel across the entire huge continent that had doubtless linked Africa to America, and visit its great prehistoric cities.[6] Maybe I was now looking at the warlike town of Makhimos or the pious village of Eusebes, whose gigantic citizens lived for centuries and had the strength to stack these stone blocks that still resisted the action of the sea. Maybe some day some new volcanic phenomenon will lift these sunken ruins back to the surface of the waves! Many submarine volcanoes have been sighted in this part of the Atlantic, and many ships have felt extraordinary vibrations while sailing over these turbulent depths. Some have heard muted noises that announce some

---

4. Verne is paraphrasing Plato here, but somehow the French compositors seemed to have muddled the Greek's chronology. In place of Plato's 8,000 years, both the Hetzel and Hachette editions give *800* years; in place of Plato's ninety centuries, the French texts give *nine hundred* centuries! These "wrong numbers" not only contradict Plato, they contradict themselves. We have rectified them for this edition.

5. In 1975 University of Miami scientists reported finding evidence that torrents flowing down the Mississippi from a melting ice sheet some 11,600 years ago raised worldwide sea levels enough to explain many ancient stories of a great flood—including the destruction of Atlantis by flooding.

6. In Verne's posthumous tale *The Eternal Adam,* archeologists of a future culture do find the ruins of Atlantis.

contest of the elements far below, others have collected volcanic ash shot above the waves. As far as the equator this entire seafloor is still worked over by plutonic forces. Who knows whether, in some remote future, the summits of these fire-belching underwater mountains, augmented by volcanic ash and successive layers of lava, will rise again above the surface of the Atlantic!

While I was musing like this and trying to fix in my mind every detail of that magnificent landscape, Captain Nemo was leaning his elbows on a moss-covered monument, motionless as if himself petrified in mute ecstasy. Was he dreaming of those lost generations, seeking here the secret of human destiny? Was this the place where this strange person came to renew himself, bathing in historical memories, reliving that bygone life, he who had resigned from our modern life? I would have given anything to know his thoughts, to share them, understand them.

We stayed there an entire hour, contemplating the vast plains in the glow of that lava, which occasionally took on a surprising intensity. Inner bubblings sent quick shivers running over the crust of the mountain. Noises from the deep, carried very clearly by the water, reverberated with majestic amplitude.

For a moment the moon appeared and cast its pale rays through the waters down onto the lost continent. It was just a passing glimmer, but the effect was indescribable. The captain stood up, took one final look out over those vast plains, then motioned for me to follow him.

It didn't take us long to get down the mountain. Once past the petrified forest I could see the *Nautilus*'s beacon light beaming like a star. The captain walked straight toward it, and we were back on board just as the first rays of dawn were whitening the surface of the ocean.

TEN

The Submarine Coalfields

THE NEXT DAY, February 20, I was very late in getting up. I was so exhausted from the adventure of the night before that I actually slept until 11 a.m. But I dressed quickly. I wanted to check on our course. The instruments told me that the *Nautilus* was still racing south, at twenty miles per hour, and a depth of 100 meters.

When Conseil came in, I told him about our excursion and, since the panels were open, he was able to get a glimpse of the submerged continent.

Indeed, the *Nautilus* was skimming just about ten meters over the soil of the plains of Atlantis. The ship scudded along like a balloon borne by the wind over prairies on land. But it would be more accurate to say that sitting in that salon, we were more like passengers in a coach on an express train. The foregrounds passing by outside were rocks carved into fantastic shapes, forests of trees that had crossed over from the vegetable kingdom to the mineral kingdom, their motionless silhouettes sprawling beneath the waves. There were also solid masses of stone buried beneath carpets of axidia and sea anemone, bristling with tall, vertical marine plants; then blocks of lava whose strange shapes bore witness to the violence of volcanic action.

While that bizarre scenery gleamed under our electric light, I told Conseil the story of the Atlantians, and how they had inspired the old French scientist Jean Bailly to write so many charming—albeit fictitious—pages.[1] I told him about the wars of those heroic people. I discussed the question of Atlantis with the new fervor of someone who could no longer have the slightest doubt. But I realized that Conseil was distracted, and his indifference to my discourse on ancient history was soon explained.

Schools of fish were swimming by, and when fish passed by, Conseil would vanish into the depths of classification and depart the real world. In that case I could only follow him back into ichthyology.[2]

---

1. Jean Sylvain Bailly believed the Atlantians actually lived at the North Pole, as Dr. Clawbonny relates in Verne's *Adventures of Captain Hatteras* (1866). Bailly was a French astronomer whose scientific writings were interrupted by the French Revolution. He went to the guillotine in 1793.

2. Conseil appears to be making progress. Early on, he could only classify fish, not identify

These Atlantic fish, however, differed little from those we had observed earlier. There were some gigantic rays, five meters long, with muscles so powerful they could leap out of the water; sharks of several species, among others a fifteen-foot glaucous shark with sharp, triangular teeth, so transparent as to seem almost invisible in the water; some brown lantern sharks; prism-shaped humantin sharks armored with protuberant hides; sturgeon like their cousins we had seen in the Mediterranean; and some trumpet-snouted pipefish a foot and a half long, yellow brown with small gray fins and no teeth or tongue, unreeling like slim, supple serpents.

Among bony fish, Conseil identified some blackish marlin three meters long, their upper jaw fitted with a piercing sword; some sprightly colored weevers, known in Aristotle's time as sea dragons, with dorsal stingers that make them quite dangerous to pick up; dolphinfish with brown backs striped with blue and edged in gold; some fine dorados; moonlike opahs that resembled bluish dishes but which, when lighted by the sun's rays, turn into silver spots; finally, swordfish from the genus *Xiphias,* eight meters long, swimming in schools, sporting yellowish sickle-shaped fins and six-foot broadswords, bold animals who eat plants rather than other fish, and, like well-trained husbands, obey the slightest signals from their females.[3]

But while observing these various specimens of marine fauna, I kept one eye on the long plains of Atlantis. Strange lumpy shapes in the terrain would sometimes force the *Nautilus* to slow down and slip like a graceful cetacean into narrow gaps in those hills. If this labyrinth became impossible, our submarine would simply rise above it like a balloon, and having crossed the obstacles, would resume its speedy course just a few meters above the seafloor. This charming, admirable way of navigating kept reminding me of maneuvering in a balloon, except that the *Nautilus* was much more under the control of its helmsman.[4]

That terrain began to change little by little toward four p.m. Generally composed of thick slime mixed with petrified branches, it grew more stony, and seemed strewn with conglomerates, or "pudding stones," and a basaltic gravel called "tuff," along with bits of lava and sulfurous obsidian. I expected these long plains to change into a mountainous area; and indeed, when the *Nautilus*

---

them. Apparently on this journey he has at last learned the faces that go with the names.

3. Is Verne slyly ridiculing the institution of marriage? It wouldn't be the only time in his works. Among Verne scholars the conventional wisdom is that the author was unhappy in his marriage and sought solace in a long-running affair with some "unique siren." A hint of this situation is supposedly to be found in his *A Castle in the Carpathians* (1892), a story about the strange effects of a deceased opera singer on two men who loved her.

4. Verne's comparison of the *Nautilus*'s cruising with a balloon trip is perfect and instructive. Both vehicles are *buoyed* by their respective mediums. Verne, of course, had a lifelong interest in ballooning, dating from his youthful friendship with the flamboyant aeronaut Nadar. Balloon feats figure not only in his maiden novel *Five Weeks in a Balloon* but in later yarns like *The Mysterious Island* (1875) or *Robur the Conqueror* (1886).

was making certain turns, I saw that the southerly horizon was blocked by a high wall that seemed to close off every exit. Obviously its summit rose above the surface. It had to be a continent or at least an island, either one of the Canaries or one of the Cape Verde Islands. Now our location had not been marked on the chart—maybe on purpose—and so I was ignorant of our real position. In any case, that wall seemed to mark the end of Atlantis, of which we had in reality toured only a small part.

Nightfall did not interrupt my observations. Conseil had returned to his cabin and I was alone. The *Nautilus* slowed down, hovering over those muddled masses on the seafloor, sometimes grazing them as though seeking a place to settle down, sometimes mounting capriciously to the surface. Then I glimpsed a few bright constellations, especially five or six of those zodiacal stars on the tail end of Orion.

I would have stayed longer at my window admiring those beauties of sea and sky but the panels closed. The *Nautilus* had just arrived at the face of that high perpendicular wall. I had no idea what specific maneuvers the ship was attempting. I took to my cabin. The *Nautilus* wasn't moving. I fell asleep with the firm intention of getting up in just a few hours.

But it was eight a.m. when I returned to the salon. I checked the pressure gauge. It told me that the *Nautilus* was afloat on the surface, and I could hear footsteps on the platform. Yet there was no rolling of the ship to indicate that surface waves were hitting its hull.

I went up the companionway as far as the hatch. It was open. But instead of the broad daylight I expected, I found myself surrounded by total darkness. Where were we? Had I made some mistake? Was it still night? No, not one star was shining, and besides, night is never so totally dark.

I couldn't figure it out, but then a voice said:

"Is that you, professor?"

"Ah, Captain Nemo! Where are we?"

"Underground, professor."

"Underground! And the *Nautilus* is still floating?"

"It always floats."

"But I don't understand!"

"Wait a few moments, we're about to turn on the beacon. If you want some light shed on the situation, you'll be satisfied."

I set foot on the platform, waiting. The darkness was so profound I couldn't see even Captain Nemo. But gazing at the zenith exactly up above my head, I thought I caught an indecisive glimmer, a kind of twilight filtering through a round hole. Then the beacon blazed forth and its vividness dispelled that vague glimmer.

For a moment my eyes were dazzled, but soon I could open them and look around. The *Nautilus* was stationary. It was floating next to an embankment shaped like a wharf. The water it was floating on was a lake contained inside a ring of walls about two miles in diameter, hence about six miles in circumference. As the pressure gauge had indicated, the level of the water was necessarily the same as that outside, because there had to be a passage between this lake and that ocean. Slanting inward over their foundations, those high walls converged to form a vault, an immense overturned funnel about 500 or 600 meters high. At its peak there was the round hole, through which I had detected that vague glimmer—it was sunlight.

I wanted, of course, to examine the interior of this enormous cavern, to ask myself if it was the work of Nature or of humankind, but first I went over to Captain Nemo and asked:

"Where are we?"

"In the very heart of an extinct volcano," he explained, "a volcano invaded by the ocean after some upheaval in the earth. While you were sleeping, professor, the *Nautilus* entered this lagoon through a natural channel ten meters below the surface of the ocean. This is my home port, safe, convenient, secret, sheltered from any wind! Show me, if you can, a single harbor that is so protected from the fury of hurricanes."

"Indeed," I agreed, "you're safe here, Captain Nemo. Who could reach you in the heart of a volcano? But isn't that an opening up there at the top?"

"That's the crater. It was once filled with lava, steam, flames, but now it brings us this bracing air we're breathing."

"But which volcanic mountain *is* this?" I asked.

"It's one of those numerous islets with which this sea is strewn. For ships a simple reef, for us a huge cavern. I discovered it by chance, and chance served me well."

"But couldn't someone come in through that crater up there?"

"No more than I could go out through it. You can climb the inside base of this mountain up to about 100 feet. But after that the inner walls lean too far in, they overhang, you couldn't scale them."

"It's clear, captain, Nature is on your side, any place, any time. You're safe on this lake, and no one else could come here. But what's your reason for being here? The *Nautilus* doesn't need a harbor."

"No, professor, but it needs electricity for power, batteries to produce the electricity, sodium for the batteries, coal to make the sodium, and coalfields from which to extract the coal. Right at this spot the sea covers entire forests that were buried during the geologic epochs, millions of years ago; now they are mineralized, changed into carbon fuel—inexhaustible mines in my control."

"So then, captain, here your sailors become miners?"

"Precisely. These mines extend out under the waves like the coalfields at Newcastle. My men get into their diving suits, take pick and shovel, *go into the water* to extract the coal—making me independent of mines on dry land. When I burn this coal to manufacture sodium, the smoke rising from this mountain's crater make it look as if the volcano is still active."

"And may I watch your companions doing this?"

"No, not this time, professor—I'm eager to resume our tour of the submarine world. This time I'll simply draw sodium from my reserve stocks. We'll stay here just long enough to load it on board, a simple day's work, then we'll be off again. And so, Professor Aronnax, if you'd like to explore this cavern, or walk around the lagoon, seize the day!"

I thanked the captain and went to get my two friends, who had not yet left their cabin. Without telling them where we were, I invited them to follow me.

They mounted to the platform. Surprised by nothing, Conseil acted as if it were perfectly natural to go to sleep under the waves and wake up under a mountain. But Ned Land had just one idea in his head: was it possible to escape from this cavern?

After breakfast, about ten o'clock, we stepped down onto the wharf.

"Well, here we are, back on land," quipped Conseil.

"I'd hardly call this land," muttered the Canadian. "And anyhow, we're not on it but under it."

We were walking along a sandy beach that stretched, at its widest place, 500 feet from the water back to the base of the mountain walls. Via that beach one could easily circle the lake. Near the walls, where the sand became broken soil, there were picturesque piles of volcanic blocks and huge pumice stones. All these crumbling masses were covered with an enamel polished by volcanic fires, and they glistened from our electric light. As we walked along the shore, our footsteps stirred the mica dust up into clouds of sparks.

As we moved away from the sand flats by the water, the ground rose noticeably, and we reached some long, sinuous ramps, steep paths that allowed us to climb little by little. But we had to tread carefully on those loose conglomerate stones, and our feet skidded on glassy trachyte, made from feldspar and quartz crystals.

Every detail of that enormous cavern—as I pointed out to my companions—proved its volcanic origin.

"Can you imagine what this funnel must have been like," I asked them, "when it was full of boiling lava rising to the crater up there, like molten iron up the insides of a furnace?"

"I can well imagine it," Conseil responded. "But will master tell me why this great smelter suspended its operations and was replaced by a calm lake?"

"Probably, Conseil, because some upheaval opened up an underwater channel, that channel that serves as a passageway for the *Nautilus*. The waters of the Atlantic rushed into the volcanic interior of the mountain. There was a terrible struggle between the elements of fire and water, a contest ending in King Neptune's favor. But many centuries have passed since then, and now this submerged volcano has changed into a peaceful grotto."

"All right," Ned Land replied, "I can accept that explanation, but for our sake it's too bad that the channel the professor mentions didn't open up *above* sea level."

"But friend Ned," Conseil replied, "if the channel hadn't opened up under the sea, the *Nautilus* couldn't have gotten in!"

"And I'll add this, Mr. Land," I said. "The waters wouldn't have rushed under the mountain, and the volcano would still be a volcano. So your regrets are irrelevant."

We continued to climb. The ramps became steeper and narrower. Sometimes there were deep ditches we had to jump across, or masses of overhanging rock we had to get around. We slid on our knees, we crept on our bellies. But helped by Conseil's dexterity and the Canadian's strength, we overcame every obstacle.

When we had climbed about thirty meters up, the terrain changed without becoming any easier. Leaving conglomerate stones and trachyte behind us, we confronted black basalt: here, eaten away and honeycombed; elsewhere, shaped like prisms arranged like a series of columns that supported that immense vaulting, a magnificent sample of natural architecture. Later, among the basalt rocks there snaked some long, hardened lava flows, inlaid with veins of bituminous coal, and sometimes covered with carpets of sulfur. The daylight falling through the crater was stronger now, shedding a vague glimmer over this volcanic waste forever buried in the heart of this extinguished mountain.

However, at an elevation of about 250 feet our climb was halted by insurmountable obstacles. That interior vaulting leaned out so far it became a massive overhang. And our climb became a horizontal, circular stroll. At this level the vegetable kingdom began to struggle against the mineral kingdom. Some shrubs and an occasional tree were growing out of crevices in the wall. I identified some spurges with their caustic, purgative sap leaking from the bark. There were heliotropes unable to justify their name as sunworshipers, here where the sun never reached them; their clusters of flowers drooped sadly, their colors and scents were faded. Here and there some chrysanthemums sprouted timidly at the feet of aloes with long, sad, sickly leaves. But between the lava flows I spied some little violets with their subtle perfume, and I confess I inhaled it hungrily. The soul of a flower is its scent, and splendid as they may look, sea flowers have no soul.

We had reached a clump of robust dragon trees, prying the rocks apart with their muscular roots, when Ned Land cried:

"Oh professor, a hive!"

"A hive!" I said with a gesture of disbelief.

"Yes, a hive," the Canadian repeated, "with bees buzzing around it!"

Getting closer I was forced to believe what I saw. Around a hole in the trunk of a dragon tree there swarmed thousands of those ingenious insects so common to the Canary Islands, where their produce is highly esteemed.

Of course, the Canadian wanted to stock up on honey, and it would have been ungracious to deny him. He mixed some sulfur with dry leaves, lit them with a spark from his tinderbox, and began to smoke out the bees. Little by little the buzzing died down, and Ned broke open the hive, which gave him several pounds of sweet honey. He filled his knapsack with it.

"I'll mix this honey with breadfruit batter," he told us, "and then I'll offer you a delectable cake!

"But of course," Conseil put in, "that would be gingerbread!"

"I'm all for gingerbread," I said, "but for now let's resume our walk. It's an interesting place."

At certain turns in the trail we could see the entire lagoon. The ship's beacon completely lighted up that peaceful body of water which knew neither ripples nor waves. The *Nautilus* lay perfectly still. On its platform and its embankment-wharf, the crew was milling about, black shadows outlined clearly in that luminous space.

We now reached the high point on that wall of rock supporting the vault. Now I could see that bees were not the only representatives of the animal kingdom inside this volcano. Birds of prey soared and whirled in the shadows, or started up from nests on the tips of rocks. There were a few sparrow hawks with white bellies, and some screeching kestrels. Some fine plump bustards decamped over those slopes as fast as their stilt-like legs would carry them. The reader can well imagine how the Canadian's appetite was whetted by the sight of such savory game, how he cursed the fact that he had no gun with him. He made stones do the work of bullets, and after several fruitless efforts, he finally wounded a splendid bustard. It is no exaggeration to say he risked his life twenty times in order to lay hold of that bird, but he fared so well that the animal joined the honeycombs in his sack.

We were forced now to head back down toward the beach because that ridge had become impossible. Above us the yawning crater looked like the wide mouth of a well. From where we stood I could see the sky pretty clearly, with clouds racing by, disheveled by the west wind, with tatters of mist grazing the mountain summit. That was proof positive that the clouds held at a middling altitude, because the volcano did not rise more than 1,800 feet above sea level.[5]

Half an hour after the Canadian's latest triumph, we were back on the beach. There I found the local flora represented by a wide carpet of samphire, a small umbrella-like plant that preserves quite well, also known as glasswort, saxifrage, and sea fennel. Conseil gathered a few bunches. And the local fauna included thousands of crustaceans of every kind: lobsters, hermit crabs, prawns, mysid shrimp, daddy longlegs, rock crabs, and prodigious numbers of seashells, including cowries, murex snails, and limpets.

While studying the flora and fauna, we spotted the mouth of a magnificent cave. Its floor was composed of fine-grained sand, and we happily stretched out on it! Fire had polished the enamel of its interior walls, which were sprinkled with mica-rich dust. Ned Land got up to tap the walls, trying to find out how thick they were! I could not repress a smile. Our conversation inevitably turned to his everlasting plans to escape, and I felt I could give him this hope, without too great a risk of being wrong: Captain Nemo had only come south to stock up on sodium. I thought he'd now hug the coasts of Europe and America, which should give Ned more opportunities to plan our escape, with greater luck this time.

5. The French gives *800* feet, evidently a typo since Aronnax previously estimated the volcano's height at "about 500 or 600 meters." We've corrected the later reference to jibe with the earlier.

After we had rested in that charming grotto for an hour or so, our conversation, lively at the start, languished. Drowsiness overcame us. Since I could see no reason to resist the call of sleep, I fell into a heavy doze. I dreamed—one does not determine his own dreams!—that my existence had shrunk to the vegetating life of a simple mollusk. It seemed to me that this grotto was the double valve of my shell . . .[6]

But all at once I was awakened by Conseil's voice:

"Master must get up!"

"What is it?" I asked, up on my elbows.

"We're being swamped!"

I stood up. The sea was storming into our retreat, and since we were not mollusks, we had to get out.

In a few minutes we were safe, on higher ground above the cave.

"What happened?" Conseil inquired. "Some new phenomenon?"

"Not at all, my friends," I replied. "It's the tide, just the tide, which took us by surprise as it did Sir Walter Scott's hero.[7] The ocean outside is rising, and by the natural law of equilibrium, the level of the lake inside is rising too. We got off easy, just with a little bath. Let's go back to the *Nautilus* and get into some dry clothes."

Three-quarters of an hour later, we completed our circular walk and were back on board. The sailors finished loading the sodium and we could have left right away.

But Captain Nemo gave no orders for casting off. Did he want to go through his submarine passageway under the secrecy of night? Maybe.

Whatever the reason, the *Nautilus* waited until the next day to leave its home port. Then we were navigating a few meters beneath the surface of the Atlantic, away from any land.

6. Despite his disclaimer, Aronnax has now had his ultimate Freudian dream. He has talked of Jonahs taking refuge in whales' bellies. He has described the sheltered life on the *Nautilus* as resembling that of a snail in its shell. And now, inside a cave, he makes a full return to the womb: he is an oyster inside its double-valved shell. He is nearing the identity crisis from which he will emerge reborn.

7. Verne's father read Scott aloud to his sons, and the French author retained an admiration for his Scottish predecessor throughout his life. Our guess is that Verne's present reference is to Scott's *The Antiquary,* which features a violent storm tide off the southeast coast of Scotland.

ELEVEN

The Sargasso Sea[1]

T HE *NAUTILUS* HADN'T changed its course. For the time being then, we had to put aside any hope of returning to European waters. Captain Nemo kept his ram pointed south. I didn't dare think about where he was taking us.

That day the *Nautilus* crossed a singular part of the Atlantic Ocean. Everyone has heard of that great current of warm water known as the Gulf Stream. After emerging from channels off Florida, it heads toward Spitzbergen. But near latitude 44° north, this current divides into two branches: the first heads for the coasts of Ireland and Norway; the second flexes southward parallel with the Azores, touches the beaches of Africa and swings back, in an elongated oval, to the Caribbean.[2]

Now this second branch forms a ring—more accurately, a collar!—of warm water around an area of colder water called the Sargasso Sea, an area always calm and motionless. It's like a lake in the middle of the Atlantic, and the waters of the Gulf Stream take no less than three years to circle around it.

The Sargasso Sea, properly speaking, covers every submerged part of Atlantis. Some authors have maintained that the numerous weeds strewn over the surface were wrenched from the prairies of that ancient continent. But it's more likely that those grasses, algae, and fucus plants were carried off from the beaches of Europe and America, then swept into the Sargasso Sea by the Gulf Stream. There lies one of the reasons that Christopher Columbus felt confirmed in his belief that a New World existed. When this bold explorer's ships arrived in the Sargasso Sea, they had great trouble navigating through all that

---

1. Again Verne uses a well-known place name as an attention-getter. The Sargasso Sea is the most famous of the Atlantic's mystery regions. Only in recent years has some of its mystery dissipated, but—as we shall see—the legends linger on.

2. Twentieth century research indicates that the Gulf Stream really meanders. No reliable maps of its current can be established. For example, in early June 1950 the principal current made a big loop to the south between longitude 60° and 65° west. But later that same June, the Gulf Stream took a shortcut, eliminating the loop, which broke off as an eddy.

plant life, which to their great dismay slowed them down to a halt. They wasted three long weeks crossing this sector.3

Such was the region the *Nautilus* was visiting at the moment: a genuine prairie, a closely woven carpet of algae, gulfweed, and bladder wrack so dense and compact that a ship's stempost could not cut through it without difficulty. And so, not wanting to get his propeller tangled up in this mass of plants, Captain Nemo kept his ship a few meters below the surface.4

The name Sargasso comes from the Spanish word "sargazo," which means gulfweed (here, the swimming gulfweed, or berry carrier), the chief material forming this immense bed.5 The American scientist Matthew Maury, in his classic *The Physical Geography of the Sea,* tells us why these water plants gather in that peaceful Atlantic basin.

His explanation seems identical to a condition known the world over. He points out that "if bits of cork or chaff, or any floating substance, be put into a basin, and a circular motion be given to the water, all the light substances will be found crowding together near the center of the pool, where there is the least motion. Just such a basin is the Atlantic Ocean to the Gulf Stream, and the Sargasso Sea is the center of the whirl."6

I share Maury's view, and I was able to study this phenomenon in its very midst, where ships rarely penetrate. Above us, huddled among those brown weeds, all sorts of strange objects were floating: tree trunks uprooted from the Andes or the Rocky Mountains, and sent floating here via the Amazon or the Mississippi;7 many pieces of wreckage, remnants of keels and ship-bottoms, bulwarks staved in and so weighted down with seashells and barnacles they could no longer rise to the surface. And someday Maury's other notion will be realized, that by collecting like this over the centuries, these materials will be turned to coal by the action of the seawater, forming vast inexhaustible coal-fields, precious reserves prepared by prescient Nature for that day when humanity will have used up the coal mines on land.

---

3. Columbus's men panicked in the Sargasso because they believed that these weeds signified that they were close to land and in danger of cracking up on an unknown coast. But their soundings failed to find bottom.

4. Even today legend has it that large vessels become hopelessly entangled in these weeds. But modern ships often go right through the Sargasso. The Reader's Digest book *Secrets of the Seas* declares that the weeds occur in patches "no larger than a doormat." Hence the Sargasso Sea's sinister reputation is greatly exaggerated.

5. Actually, it was the Portuguese who named this kelp: they noted the resemblance between the air-bladder floats of the weed and a small grape called *sarga* in Portugal.

6. Writing in French, Verne naturally quoted from the *French translation* of Maury's English—a rather free and unrigorous translation as it turns out (instead of Maury's basin, the anonymous translator substitutes a *vase*). Rather than retranslating the French back into English, we have simply quoted Maury directly.

7. It is unlikely that Rocky Mountain trees could float such a distance, because the tributaries of the Upper Missouri are too small to carry trees except in floods. Besides, trees that grow in the Rockies are not identifiable as such: the same trees grow elsewhere along the Mississippi.

Amid that impossibly intricate fabric of weeds and fucus plants, I noted some charming pink, star-shaped alcyon coral; some sea anemone, trailing the long tresses of their tentacles after them; some red, green, and blue jellyfish, especially those huge rhizostome jellyfish described by Cuvier, with their blue umbrellas bordered with violet festoons.

We spent the whole day of February 22 in the Sargasso Sea where fish, which love marine plants and crustaceans, find plenty to eat.[8] The next day the ocean resumed its standard appearance.

For nineteen days, then, February 23 to March 12, the *Nautilus* sailed the middle of the Atlantic, hurrying along at a constant speed of 100 leagues every 24 hours. Captain Nemo obviously was eager to advance his underwater research program, and I felt certain he would double Cape Horn and return to the Pacific South Seas.

So Ned Land had good reason to worry. In those wide seas, without islands, it was not feasible to jump ship. Nor did we have any way to oppose Captain Nemo's whims. There was nothing to do but give in. Still, what we could not attain through force or trickery, I liked to think we might achieve through persuasion. Once this voyage was over, wasn't it possible that Captain Nemo might set us free in return for our solemn oath never to reveal his existence? Our solemn word of honor, which we would have kept religiously. But this delicate question would have to be negotiated with the captain. Would he even listen to our appeal for freedom? At the very beginning he had declared, very explicitly, that the secret of his life required that we be kept prisoners permanently. Wouldn't he see my four-month silence as tacit acceptance of this situation? Would my raising the question again arouse suspicions that might jeopardize our plans, if some favorable circumstances made us consider escape again? I mulled over all these questions, weighed them, tried them out on Conseil, but he was no less perplexed than I. In short, I am not easily discouraged, but I realized that my chances of ever seeing my fellow men again were shrinking day by day, especially on a day when Captain Nemo was recklessly racing toward the South Atlantic!

During those nineteen days nothing happened worth mentioning. I saw little of the captain. He was working. In the library I would find books he had left open, especially books on natural history. He had leafed through my work on the great submarine depths, and the margins were full of his notes, which sometimes contradicted my systems and theories.[9] But the captain seemed content with this way of refining my work, which he rarely discussed with me in person. Sometimes I would hear melancholy sounds reverberating from the

8. Among the diners, surprisingly, are *freshwater eels* from both European and American rivers. Scientists now know that such eels migrate to the Atlantic in the winter, then spawn in the Sargasso Sea. The larvae take three years to drift back to their predestined habitats in the Old and New Worlds.

9. Including the professor's classification systems. For instance, Aronnax might classify a certain crab in the *Brachyura*. Nemo might disagree and place it in the *Anomura*.

organ, which he played expressively but only at night, amid the most secretive darkness, while the *Nautilus* slumbered in the wilderness of the sea.

During this segment of our voyage we navigated on the surface for entire days. The sea seemed deserted. We spotted only a few sailing vessels laden for the East Indies via the Cape of Good Hope. One day we were actually pursued by longboats from a whaling ship—no doubt they saw us as some enormous baleen whale of fantastic value. But Captain Nemo decided not to waste the time and effort of those gallant men, so he ended the hunt by plunging below the waves. Ned Land observed this incident with great concentration. I'm sure he regretted that those harpooners could not pierce our iron whale and mortally wound it.

The fish that Conseil and I identified during this period differed little from those we had already studied in other latitudes. Chief among them were specimens of that terrible cartilaginous genus that is divided into three subgenera comprising no fewer than thirty-two species: striped sharks five meters long, the head squat and wider than the body, the caudal fin curved, with seven large black parallel stripes running down the back; and some perlon sharks, ash gray, with seven gill openings and a single dorsal fin placed fairly near the middle of the body.

We also saw some large dogfish, a voracious species of fish if there ever was one. Fishermen's stories are always taken with a grain of salt, but I'll repeat a few for what they're worth. In the body of one dogfish they found a buffalo head and an entire calf; in another, two tuna and a sailor in uniform; in still another, a soldier with his saber; and in one last example, a horse and its rider! To tell the truth, these stories sound less than divinely inspired. But since no dogfish ever allowed itself to be caught in the *Nautilus*'s nets, I can't vouch for their voracity.

Schools of elegant, playful dolphin accompanied us for entire days. They came in groups of five or six, hunting in packs like wolves over the countryside. Moreover, they are just as voracious as dogfish, if I am to believe a certain Copenhagen professor who claims he removed from one dolphin thirteen porpoises and fifteen seals. True, it was a killer whale, of the largest known species, who can grow up to twenty-four feet long. The family Delphinia numbers ten genera, and the dolphins I saw were akin to the genus *Delphinorhynchus,* remarkable for a narrow muzzle four times as long as their cranium. Three meters long, their bodies were black on top, pinkish white with scattered spots underneath.

In those seas I also noted some strange specimens of croakers, fish from the order Acanthopterygia, family Scienidea. Some authors—better poets than naturalists—claim that these fish sing melodiously, and when they sing together they are unequaled by choirs of human voices. I can't say, much to my regret, for these croakers did not serenade us as we passed.[10]

---

10. Also nicknamed "drums," these fish do produce an audible throbbing sound in the water. But few modern listeners would be moved to assert that the creatures "sing melodiously."

Finally, Conseil classified a great number of flying fish. Nothing could be more curious than the precise timing with which dolphins hunt these fish. No matter how far they flew, however evasive their trajectory (even up and over the *Nautilus*), the hapless flying fish always found a dolphin to welcome it with open mouth. These were either flying gurnards or kitelike sea robins; they have luminous mouths, and at night they would trace fiery streaks through the air before plunging into those somber waters like shooting stars. That was what our journey was like until March 13. On that day the *Nautilus* was used in some depth-sounding experiments that proved of great scientific interest to me.

By then we had covered nearly 13,000 leagues from our starting point in the Pacific high seas. As marked on the chart, our position was latitude 45° 37′ south, longitude 37° 53′ west. These were the same waters in which Captain Denham, aboard the *Herald,* payed out 14,000 meters of sounding line without finding bottom. And it was there too that Lieutenant Parker, of the American frigate *Congress,* could not touch the submarine soil with soundings of 15,149 meters.[11]

Captain Nemo decided to take his *Nautilus* down to the ultimate depths to check these different soundings. I was all set to take notes on the results of the experiment. The panels were opened, and the necessary preparations begun to reach those prodigious depths.

It was considered obviously out of the question to achieve such a dive simply by filling the ballast tanks. Maybe they would not sufficiently increase the ship's specific gravity. Moreover, in order to come back up, it would be necessary to expel that water, and our pumps might not have been powerful enough to overcome the outside pressure.

Captain Nemo decided to make for the ocean floor by diving on an appropriate diagonal: he set his side fins at a 45° angle to the *Nautilus*'s waterline. Then he brought the propeller up to its top speed, its fourfold blade churning the waves with indescribable violence.

Under this powerful thrust the *Nautilus*'s hull quivered like a resonating chord as the ship sank steadily into the waters. Posted in the salon, the captain and I watched the pressure gauge as its needle moved rapidly across the dial. Soon we had dropped below the zone in which most fish can live. If some of those creatures can live only at or near the surface of seas or rivers, a still smaller

11. The French compositors apparently produced a mild bobble here, giving 15,140. We have corrected the citation to match its first appearance in I 18.

In any event, this measurement could not have been literally accurate, because it's nearly equivalent to 50,000 feet. When such reports reached Maury, he feared something was wrong and overhauled the whole theory and practice of sounding. He suspected that at great depths the line would continue to pay out even after the plummet touched bottom, the line's own weight continuing to tug fresh lengths. Maury therefore ordered that the line be marked every 100 fathoms so that the speed of payout could be observed. When that speed suddenly diminished—even if the line still payed out—the fathom marker at which the diminution had been noted was to be recorded as the bottom depth.

number can thrive at significant depths. Among the latter I saw the cow shark, a species of dogfish with six respiratory slits; the telescope fish with its enormous eyes; the armored gurnard with gray thoracic fins, black pectoral fins, and pale red slabs of bone as its breastplate; and finally, the grenadier, whom I saw at a depth of 1,200 meters—in other words, tolerating a pressure of 120 atmospheres.

I asked Captain Nemo if he had seen any fish at lower depths.

"Fish? Rarely," he replied. "But given the present state of marine science, what can we presume to say, what do we really know of such depths?"

"Well, let's see, captain. We know that as we descend into the lowest strata, vegetable life disappears sooner than animal life. We know that where we still encounter moving creatures, we will not find marine plants. We know that oysters and pilgrim scallops live in 2,000 meters of water, and that Admiral McClintock, England's hero of the polar seas, brought up a live sea star from a depth of 2,500 meters. We know that the crew of the Royal Navy's *Bulldog* fished up a starfish from 2,620 fathoms, that is, from more than a league down! Would you still say, captain, that we really know very little?"

"No, professor," he replied, "I wouldn't be that impolite. But still, I'd like to know how you can account for the fact that animals can live at such depths?"

"I explain it on two grounds," I answered. "First of all, there are vertical currents, caused by differences in the salinity and the density of seawater. They create enough movement to sustain the rudimentary lifestyle of, say, sea lilies and starfish."

"Exactly," the captain said.

"Secondly, we know that oxygen is the basis of life, that the amount of oxygen dissolved in salt water actually increases with depth (instead of decreasing), or, in other words, the greater the depth, the more oxygen goes into solution."

"So! We know that, do we?" Captain Nemo seemed somewhat surprised. "And we have good reason to know it—because it's true. Let me merely add that when fish are caught near the surface, their air bladders contain more nitrogen than oxygen, and conversely, when they're pulled up from the extreme depths, their bladders contain more oxygen than nitrogen. And that bears out your observation. But let's get back to our experiment."

I glanced at the pressure gauge. It showed we were at a depth of 6,000 meters. We had been 'driving down' for an hour, and we were still sliding down on our slanting fins. The waters were deserted and wonderfully transparent, with a diaphaneity no painter could ever reproduce. An hour later we were 13,000 meters down—about three and a quarter vertical leagues below the surface—and there was still no sign of the bottom.

However, at 14,000 meters I saw blackish peaks surging up into view. Those summits, of course, could have topped mountains as high or even higher than the Himalayas or Mt. Blanc, and we still had no way of calculating the depth of the valleys between them.

In spite of the powerful pressures it was sustaining, the *Nautilus* drove down deeper yet. I could feel its iron plates trembling at the bolts; metal bars arched, bulkheads groaned; the salon windows seemed to bulge inward under the pressure. And that entire sturdy apparatus would no doubt have caved in if, as its captain had told me, it had not been built to resist like a solid block.

While grazing those rocky slopes lost beneath the sea, I spied again some seashells, tube worms, lively annelid worms from the genus *Spirorbis,* and some specimens of starfish.

But soon these last representatives of animal life vanished, and three vertical leagues down the *Nautilus* passed the limits of submarine life just as a balloon rises into heights where no one can breathe.[12] We had reached a depth of 16,000 meters—four vertical leagues!—and at that point the *Nautilus*'s hull was tolerating a pressure of 1,600 atmospheres, that is, 1,600 kilograms per each square centimeter on its surface![13]

"What a situation to be in!" I exclaimed. "Sailing such depths where humanity has never been! Look, captain, look at those magnificent rocks, those grottoes with no life in them, these final global repositories where no life is *possible!* What extraordinary scenery, and why are we reduced to preserving it only as a memory!"

"Would you like," Captain Nemo asked, "to take back more than just the memory?"

"What can you mean?"

"I mean that nothing would be easier than taking a photograph of this spectacle."

Before I had time to express the surprise this new proposition gave me, the captain had ordered a camera to be set up in the salon. Beyond the wide-open panels, that liquid mass was absolutely clear. Our artificial illumination allowed no shadows, no blurs. Not even the sun could have served our operation so well. With the thrust of its propeller checked by the inclined fins, the *Nautilus* stood still. The camera was aimed at that spectacle on the ocean floor, and in a few seconds we had a perfect negative.

And here I present a print of the positive. In it one can view the primeval rocks that have never seen the light of day, that nether granite that forms the solid foundation of our planet, those deep caverns gouged out of the stone mass, and everything distinctly outlined as if recorded by the brush of certain Flemish masters. Farther off, the wondrously undulating line of a mountainous horizon, the background of that seascape. And the general effect of those glossy rocks is indescribable—black, polished, without moss or any other growth to

12. On January 21, 1960, Jacques Picard and Lieutenant Donald Walsh made their historic dive in the *Trieste.* They descended 35,600 feet into the Challenger Deep. On the bottom they saw a shrimp, about an inch in diameter, and a sole about a foot long.

13. The normal conversion of 1,600 atmospheres would be 23,520 pounds per square inch of surface. This would make the *Nautilus* almost six times as strong as the *Trieste,* which was built to withstand 4,000 pounds per square inch.

A deep-sea photograph

mar their surface, cut into bizarre shapes, all firmly based on a carpet of sand sparkling beneath our electric light.

Then, having taken his picture, Captain Nemo told me:

"Let's surface, professor. We mustn't push our luck too far, we shouldn't expose the *Nautilus* too long to such pressures."

"Up we go, then!" I responded.

"Hold on tight!"

Before I had time to realize why he had so advised me, I was flung to the carpet.

At a signal from the captain, the fins had been set vertically and the propeller disengaged. The *Nautilus* rose with terrific speed, like a balloon shooting into the sky. Vibrating sonorously, it knifed up through those waters. We could see nothing at all. In four minutes we traveled those four leagues between the bottom and the surface. After emerging out into the air like a flying fish, the *Nautilus* fell back into the water, making it leap up like a fountain to a prodigious height.

TWELVE

Sperm Whales and Baleen Whales

URING THE NIGHT of March 13–14 the *Nautilus* resumed its southerly course. I had thought that once it was parallel to Cape Horn, it would sail west of the cape, return to the Pacific, and complete its tour of the world. It did nothing of the sort; instead it continued moving toward the southernmost regions. Where were we headed then? To the pole? That was insanity. I was beginning to think that the captain's recklessness more than justified Ned Land's worst fears.

For some time now the Canadian had not said anything to me about escaping. He had become less sociable, more subdued. I could see how his long imprisonment was weighing on him, how anger was building up in him. Whenever he met the captain, his eyes would gleam with sullen resentment, and I was always afraid that his innate tendencies to violence would lead him to do something rash.

On that day, March 14, he and Conseil happened to find me in my room. I asked them what they had in mind.

"We want to ask you a simple question, sir," the Canadian said.

"Go ahead, Ned."

"How many men, would you say, are on board the *Nautilus*?"

"I can't really say, my friend."

"It seems to me," he went on, "that it doesn't take a very large crew to run a ship like this."

"Certainly," I responded, "under present conditions, you wouldn't need more than ten men to operate it."

"Well then," the Canadian asked, "why should there be more than that?"

"Why?" I repeated.

I stared fixedly at him: his intentions were so easy to read.

"Because, Ned, if I'm to believe my own presentiments, if I really understand this man, his *Nautilus* isn't just a ship. It's a refuge for people like its commander, people who have severed all ties with life on land."

"All right," Conseil broke in, "but to put it succinctly, the *Nautilus* can carry only a certain number of persons. Could master estimate the largest possible number?"

"How, Conseil?"

"By scientific calculation. Master knows the ship's dimensions and hence the amount of air it contains. Master knows too how much air each person needs, and comparing these data with the fact that the *Nautilus* must surface every 24 hours . . ."

Conseil left his sentence hanging but I could see clearly what he was trying to get at.

"I follow you," I said, "but even though such calculations are easy, the results would prove to be approximate at best, because conditions vary, and . . ."

"Never mind, go ahead," Ned urged.

"Well, here it is," I responded. "Each person needs, every hour, the oxygen contained in 100 liters of air. So, in 24 hours, we each need the oxygen in 2,400 liters. The problem then is simply to calculate how many times 2,400 liters the *Nautilus* can hold."

"Precisely," Conseil murmured.

"The *Nautilus*'s capacity is 1,500 metric tons, and since a ton contains 1,000 liters, the *Nautilus* contains 1,500,000 liters of air. Now, dividing that by 2,400 . . ."

I resorted to pencil and paper.

". . . we get 625. In other words, there is enough air in the *Nautilus* for 625 people for 24 hours."

"Six hundred and twenty-five people!" Ned exclaimed.

"But rest assured," I added, "counting passengers, sailors, and officers, we don't make up one-tenth of that figure."

"Still too many for three men," Conseil murmured.[1]

"And therefore, my poor Ned, I can only recommend patience."

"And," Conseil went on, "even more than patience. Resignation."

Conseil had hit on the exact word.

"Even so," he added, "Captain Nemo can't go south forever! He'll have to stop someplace—maybe the Ice Bank will stop him—and he'll come back to more civilized regions. Then it will be time to take up Ned's plans again."

The Canadian shook his head, rubbed his forehead, said nothing, and left the room.

---

1. Nemo's crewmen are so subdued and retiring, that after living in the same boat with them for four months, Ned still doesn't know their actual number. The professor is no help. He once saw *some twenty* of them on deck in I 18, but was that the whole crew or just one watch? We don't know whether Nemo posts watches at all, but he does seem to use a different detail of men for differing projects: one gun carrier on the Crespo hunt, a crew of five for the dinghy on one occasion and seven on another, eight men to drag in the prisoners, a dozen to assist at the underwater funeral. Twenty or thereabouts will remain to the end the top figure. But we can't be sure there aren't more.

Nemo's men are so restrained and emotionless that they almost seem in a state of chronic depression. The only signs we've had of any team spirit or positive attitude were (1) the self-sacrifice of one man to save another from a falling lever; (2) the crew's work at running funds ashore to aid the Cretan revolution. Theirs may be a life of grim altruism.

"With master's permission, I would like to point out one thing," Conseil said. "Our poor Ned dwells on all the things he can't have. He's haunted by his past life. He's obsessed with anything that is denied us. His memories oppress him, he's on the verge of tears. We must try to understand him. There's nothing here for him to do. He isn't a scientist like master, he doesn't get excited by the marvels of the sea. He would risk anything just to be able to walk into a tavern in his own country!"

Certainly the monotony on board must have seemed intolerable to the Canadian, accustomed as he was to a life of freedom and action. Rarely did anything happen that could satisfy him. But that day something occurred that at least reminded him of his happy times as a harpooner.

Toward eleven a.m., while on the surface, the *Nautilus* fell in with a herd of baleen whales. I was not surprised, because I knew that these creatures were hunted down so relentlessly that they were taking refuge in the higher latitudes.

Whales have played a major role in the history of navigation and geographic exploration. Dragging in their wake first the Basques, then Asturian Spaniards, Englishmen, and Dutchmen, they are the animals who emboldened these people against the dangers of the sea, who actually led them from one end of the earth to the other. Baleen whales like to frequent the Arctic and the Antarctic waters. Old legends even claim that these cetaceans have led fishermen to within a mere seven leagues of the North Pole! Although that feat is fictitious, it is also prophetic, for it is highly likely that by chasing whales into the polar seas, humanity will finally reach one of those unexplored points: the North or the South Pole.

We were sitting on the platform in the midst of a tranquil sea. March—the equivalent of October in those latitudes—was giving us some fine autumnal weather. It was the Canadian—and on this question he could not be mistaken—who raised a baleen whale on the eastern horizon. And by looking carefully I could see it too, its blackish back rising and falling above the waves, about five miles from the *Nautilus*.

"Wow!" Ned Land cried out. "If only I were on board a whaler now—what fun this would be! That's a big animal! Look how powerful it is, to send up such jets of air and vapor! Damnation! Why do I have to be chained to this hunk of iron!"

"Poor Ned," I remarked. "You never give up hope."

"How could a whaler ever forget his trade, professor? There's never a dull moment when you're hunting a whale!"

"You've never fished these seas, Ned?"

"Never, professor. Only the northern waters, and just as much in the Bering Strait as in the Davis Strait."

"Then the southern right whale is new to you. Until now it's the bowhead whale you've hunted. That species won't risk going past the warm waters of the equator."

"Professor, what is this you're trying to put over on me?" the Canadian asked in a skeptical tone of voice.

"Just the facts, Ned."

"Just nonsense! Only two and a half years ago—in 1865—I, the man to whom you're telling that nonsense, I myself walked the carcass of a whale near Greenland, and in its flank we found another harpoon stamped with the mark of a Bering Sea whaler. Now I ask you, after it was wounded *west* of America, how could that beast be killed *east* of America, unless it had crossed the equator and doubled the Cape of Good Hope or Cape Horn?"

"I'm inclined to agree with our friend Ned," Conseil said. "And I want to hear what master will say to *that*."

"Master will say, my friends, that baleen whales are localized, according to species, and they never leave their native sea. So if one of those animals went from the Bering Strait to the Davis Strait, it's because there's a passageway from one sea to the other, either along the Canadian coast or along the Siberian coast."

"You expect us to fall for that?" the Canadian asked with a wink.

"If master says it . . ." Conseil put in.

"What you mean," the Canadian resumed, "is that if I've never fished these waters, then I don't know the whales that frequent them?"

"That's what I mean, Ned."

"All the more reason to get to know them," Conseil concluded.

"But look! Look!" the Canadian cried with new excitement. "It's coming closer! It's coming toward us! It's teasing me—it knows I can't do a thing to it!"

Ned stamped his foot. Brandishing an imaginary harpoon, his hands actually trembled.

"These local whales," he asked, "are they as big as those in the northern seas?"

"Almost, Ned."

"Because I've seen huge baleen whales, professor, whales up to 100 feet in length. And I've heard that those rorqual whales off the Aleutian Islands get up to 150 feet long."[2]

---

2. This is a tad exaggerated, as Verne probably suspected. Today's largest whale is the blue whale, whose maximum length seems to be less than 120 feet.

Further, Verne's language in describing these super-whales seems to have troubled not only his English translators but his French compositors. The novel mentions the beasts twice, in almost identical terms. In I 1, Verne says the largest whales are "celles qui fréquentent les parages des îles Aléoutiennes, le Kulammak et l'Umgullick" (literally, "those that frequent the vicinity of the Aleutian Islands—the Kulammak and the Umgullick whales"). Then, in the present chapter, he refers to the critters as "le Hullamock et L'Umgallick des îles Aléoutiennes" (literally, "the Hullamock and the Umgallick whales from the Aleutian Islands"). Clearly, the compositors (or the editors, or maybe even Verne himself) were baffled by the animals' Eskimo names, since the spellings don't jibe. What's more, the book's first English translator, Louis Mercier, mistook the Eskimo terms as referring not to whales but to two heretofore unknown *island groups*: his I 1 reference reads "those that frequent those parts of the sea round the Aleutian, Kulammak, and Umgullick islands." Later English versions blandly recycle this mistake.

We can't swear to the accurate Eskimo spellings. The terms seem to be synonyms for the same gigantic animal—a blue whale, or just possibly a finback. So we go easy on modern readers and simply use the term "rorqual whales."

"That sounds exaggerated," I replied. "Those animals are only members of the genus *Balaenoptera* with dorsal fins, and like the sperm whales, they're usually smaller than the bowhead whale."

"Oh!" the Canadian cried again. His eyes had not left the ocean. "It's coming closer still, coming right up to us!"

Then he took up the thread of the conversation again.

"You talk of the sperm whale," he said, "as if it was a small beast! Yet I've heard people tell of gigantic sperm whales. They're supposed to be very clever cetaceans. It's said that some of them cover themselves with algae and fucus plants. People take them for little islands. They pitch camp on top, make themselves at home, light a fire . . ."

"And build houses," Conseil said.

"Yes, you comedian," Ned Land responded. "Then one fine day the animal dives and drags all its tenants down to the bottom of the ocean."

"Just like in the voyages of Sinbad the sailor," I laughed. "Oh Mr. Land, you're really fond of tall tales! Those are stupendous sperm whales! But—I just hope you don't believe in them!"

"Mr. Naturalist," the Canadian said in all seriousness, "when it comes to whales you can believe anything! Look at *that* one travel! Look how it slips away! Some people say those animals can circumnavigate the globe in fifteen days."

"That I don't deny."

"But what you doubtless don't know, Professor Aronnax, is that at the beginning of the world whales traveled even faster than they do now."

"Oh really, Ned! How come?"

"Because in those days their tails were like fishtails, completely vertical, thrashing the water from left to right, and right to left. But noticing that they swam too fast, our Creator twisted their tails, and since then they thrash the waves up and down, and they haven't been able to travel so fast."

"Fine, Ned," I said, and then I mimicked his own expression. "You expect us to fall for that?"

"Believe that," Ned said, "and I'll tell you there are whales 300 feet long that weigh 1,000,000 pounds."[3]

"That would be plenty big," I said. "But we must admit that certain cetaceans do grow to great size, since we hear that they furnish as much as 120 metric tons of oil."

"That I've seen," the Canadian said.

"And I believe you. I can believe too that certain baleen whales equal 100 elephants all rolled into one. Imagine the impact of such a mass launched at full speed ahead!"

"Does that mean," Conseil asked, "that they can really sink ships?"

3. The French gives 100,000 pounds, an evident typo since the very next paragraph states that these animals possess more than twice that weight (120 metric tons) in whale oil alone.

Ned's reference to these behemoths may be a sly dig at Aronnax's original hypothesis that *the enormous thing* was a gigantic cetacean.

"Ships? No. *But wait now!* It's a fact that in 1820—as a *matter* of fact, in exactly these southern seas!—a baleen whale rushed at the *Essex* and pushed it backward at a speed of four meters per second. The stern was flooded and the *Essex* went down fast."[4]

Ned gazed at me, mockingly askance.

"Well," he said, "for my part, I was once slapped by a whale's tail. I was in my longboat, of course. My companions and I were launched to an altitude of six meters. But of course, compared to the professor's whale, mine was a mere baby whale."

"Do they live very long? The whales, I mean," Conseil asked.

"A thousand years," the Canadian said authoritatively.

"Ned, how do you know *that!*" I exclaimed.

"Because people say so."

"And why do people say so?"

"Because people know so."

"No, Ned! People don't *know* so, they *suppose* so. And this is what they base their supposition on: When fishermen first chased whales, 400 years ago, those animals grew much larger than they do now. It was a logical inference, then, that in those days whales were allowed to live out a full life, and that today whales are smaller because they're *not* allowed to reach a ripe old age. That's why the Count de Buffon's encyclopedia says that whales can live— even *must* live—for a thousand years. You understand?"

Ned Land did not understand. He was not even listening. That baleen whale was coming still closer. Ned couldn't take his eyes off it.

"Oh!" he cried out."It's not just one whale, it's ten, no twenty, it's a whole gam! And I'm helpless, I'm tied hand and foot!"

"Friend Ned," Conseil suggested, "why don't you go ask Captain Nemo for permission to hunt—"

Before Conseil had finished his sentence, Ned had scooted down the hatch and raced in search of the captain. A few moments later the two of them appeared on the platform.

Captain Nemo studied that herd of cetaceans frolicking on the surface about a mile from the *Nautilus.*

"They're southern right whales," he said. "And there floats the fortune of a whole fleet of whalers."

"Well, sir," the Canadian asked, "can't I get out there and hunt them, just so I don't forget how to use a harpoon?"

"Hunt them—why?" Captain Nemo answered. "Just to destroy them? We don't use whale oil on board."

4. Indeed it did. This historical tragedy was recounted in T. F. Heffernan's eyewitness article *Stove by a Whale.* The *Essex* raised and pursued an adult whale that retaliated by ramming and sinking its tormentor. Hermann Melville is known to have studied Heffernan's narrative: it inspired the climax of *Moby Dick.*

One mild discrepancy. Verne blames the *Essex* catastrophe on a baleen whale (*baleine*); he should have specified a sperm whale (*cachalot*).

"But captain," the Canadian persisted, "in the Red Sea you let us hunt a dugong!"

"Then it was a question of getting fresh meat for the crew. Now it would be killing for the sake of killing. I know very well that's a privilege reserved for humanity, but I don't allow such murderous pastimes. In killing decent, inoffensive creatures like the southern right whale or the bowhead whale, people like you, Mr. Land, commit a reprehensible crime. Thus, your colleagues have already depopulated all of Baffin Bay, and they'll wipe out a whole class of useful animals. So just leave those poor cetaceans alone. They have enough natural enemies—like sperm whales, swordfish, sawfish—without your adding to their problems."

I leave to the reader's imagination what faces the Canadian made during this lecture on ethics. It was a waste of words to say these things to a born hunter. Ned Land gaped at Captain Nemo and clearly did not get the point. But the captain was right. The mindless, barbaric greed of some fishermen will someday make the baleen whale extinct.[5]

Ned Land whistled "Yankee Doodle" through his teeth, stuffed his hands in his pockets, and turned his back on all of us.

Meanwhile, Captain Nemo studied that herd of whales for a while and then said to me:

"I was right to say that baleen whales have enough natural enemies without counting human beings. These specimens are soon to face mighty opponents. Professor, eight miles to leeward, do you see those black specks moving about?"

"Yes, captain."

"Those are sperm whales—terrible beasts. I've sometimes met them in herds of 200 or 300! As for them, they're cruel, destructive animals, and people are right to kill *them*."

The Canadian whirled around at those words.

"Well then, captain," I suggested, "there's still time to act on behalf of the baleen whales—"

"No use running such risks, professor. The *Nautilus* needs no help in dispersing those sperm whales. It's armed with a steel ram just as effective as Mr. Land's harpoon, I imagine."

This time the Canadian didn't even shrug his shoulders. Attacking cetacean's with a ship's ram! Whoever heard of such a thing.

"Watch now, Professor Aronnax," Captain Nemo explained. "We'll show you a mode of hunting that you've never seen before. We'll take no pity on those ferocious cetaceans. They're nothing but mouth and teeth!"

---

5. As members of Greenpeace remind us, this eventuality is dangerously near. Some whale populations are now so thin that certain species may not endure even if their hunting ceases completely. And the extermination of whales could signal man's own suicide, according to David O. Hill. The more than 500,000 whales who once roamed the seas helped regulate the plankton economy. A major portion of the oxygen in our atmosphere is produced by this complex ecosystem. Wiping out the whale could jeopardize the supply of oxygen that both marine and human life depend on.

Mouth and teeth! There's no better way to describe the long-skulled sperm whale, which is sometimes more than twenty-five meters long. Its huge head makes up about a third of its body. It's better armed than the baleen whale, whose upper jaw is furnished with just whalebone—the sperm whale has twenty-five huge teeth twenty centimeters high, each of them cylindrical, conical on top, and weighing two pounds! Inside the upper part of that huge head, in big cavities separated by cartilage, there are stored 300 to 400 kilograms of that precious whale oil called "spermaceti." The sperm whale is awkward, more tadpole than fish, as Professor Fredol has said. It's poorly built, being "defective," so to speak, over the whole left side of its frame, hence able to see well only with its right eye.

Meanwhile, that monstrous herd of sperm whales was swimming closer. They had discovered the baleen whales and were racing on the offensive. I knew the sperm whales would win, not only because they were better built for fighting than their harmless adversaries, but also because they could stay longer underwater before needing to come up to breathe.

So there was no time to lose in running to the rescue of those baleen whales. The *Nautilus* dropped beneath the waves. Ned Land, Conseil, and I posted ourselves at the salon windows. Captain Nemo had made his way to the helmsman's side to operate his *Nautilus* as a weapon. Now I could hear the propeller speeding up and we moved faster.

Combat between the sperm whales and the baleen whales had already begun when we arrived on the scene. The *Nautilus* maneuvered to cut into that herd of long-skulled beasts. At first they paid little attention to this new monster joining the battle. But soon they had to guard against its blows.

What a fight! Even Ned Land got excited and began clapping his hands. Wielded in the captain's hands the *Nautilus* simply became a super-harpoon. Hurled against those fleshy masses, it ran them through and through, leaving behind wriggling halves of animals. When the sperm whales struck our sides with their tails, we hardly felt it; nor did we feel the full impact of the collisions we were causing. One sperm whale torn to bits, the *Nautilus* raced at another, tacked on the spot so as not to miss its prey, went ahead or astern, answered to its helm, dived when a sperm whale sank to deeper strata, came back up when it surfaced, struck it head-on or on the bias, chopped at it or ripped it up, and from any direction or at any speed, skewered it with that terrible ram.

What carnage! What a noise over the waves! What sharp hisses and snorts, peculiar to their species, issued from these terrified sperm whales. And lower in the water, in the usually calm strata, their tails churned up deep billows.

This Homeric massacre[6] lasted for an hour, and there was little chance the sperm whales could get away. Several times, ten or twelve of them would team

---

6. The overall scene of slaughter does resemble those Homer describes in the *Iliad*. In addition, Verne uses the Homeric trick of coldly describing the actual dissection that one warrior performs on another. Thus, when the *Nautilus* attacked "those fleshy masses, it ran them through and through, leaving behind wriggling halves of animals."

Mouth and teeth

up and try to crush the *Nautilus* with their sheer mass. Through the windows we could see their huge maws paved with teeth, their formidable right eyes. Losing all self-control, Ned Land hurled threats and insults at them. We could feel them clinging to our submarine like hounds atop a wild boar in the under-brush. But the *Nautilus,* gunning the propeller to its limit, carried them off, dragged them under, or forced them to the surface, with no concern for either their weight or the grip of their powerful jaws.

Finally that mass of sperm whales began to thin out. The waves grew quiet again. I felt us rising to the surface. The hatch was opened and we rushed out on the platform.

The sea was covered with mutilated corpses. A powerful explosion could not have cut up, torn, or shredded those masses of flesh with greater violence. We were floating in the midst of gigantic warty bodies, bluish on the back, whitish on the belly. A few terrified sperm whales were racing for the horizon. The waves were tinted red over an area of several miles—we were floating in a sea of blood.

Captain Nemo rejoined us.

"Well, Mr. Land?" he prompted.

"Well, sir," replied the Canadian, whose enthusiasm had subsided, "it is a terrible sight. But I'm a hunter not a butcher, and this is pure butchery, a massacre."

"A massacre of destructive creatures," the captain added. "And my *Nautilus* is not a butcher knife."

"I like my harpoon better," the Canadian said.

"To each his own," the captain said with an intense stare at Ned Land.

I was afraid Ned would yield to his violent instincts, with dreadful consequences for us all. But his anger was diverted by the sight of a baleen whale floating nearby.

This animal had been unable to escape the teeth of the sperm whales.[7] I recognized it as a southern right whale by its squat head and all-dark body. Anatomically, it can be distinguished from the white whale and the black right whale by the fact that its seven cervical vertebrae are joined, and it has two more ribs than its cousins. This poor specimen, now lying on its side, its belly bitten open, had died. Still hanging from its mutilated fin was a little baby whale that the mother had been unable to save from the slaughter. Her mouth was open, letting water flow in and out through its whalebone like a murmuring surf.

7. Reading modern zoological texts, we encounter no references to sperm whales preying on whalebone whales. The killer whale is a known pack hunter and, according to some eyewitness accounts, will overpower and feed on the gray whale. But the sperm whale seems to be a solitary hunter whose most ambitious prey is the giant squid.

Where did Verne get this notion? From Michelet's book *The Sea,* as we observed in a note for II 7. We do not know Michelet's basis for envisioning a combat between sperm whales and right whales. It does not seem to be factual.

Captain Nemo edged the *Nautilus* alongside the corpse. Two of his crewmen stepped out onto the whale and, to my astonishment, they started to milk the udders for all the liquid they contained, enough to fill two or three casks.

The captain offered me a cup of it and it was still warm. I could not help showing my distaste for such a beverage. He reassured me that it was an excellent drink, no different from cow's milk.

I tried it and he was right. And so that milk provided us with a useful reserve stock, because as salted butter or cheese, it would be a pleasant change from our usual ship's fare.

And from that day on, I noticed with great uneasiness that Ned Land's hostility toward Captain Nemo grew worse and worse. I realized I would have to keep a close watch on the Canadian.

THIRTEEN

The Ice Bank

THE *NAUTILUS* RESUMED its steady southerly course, following the 50th meridian with considerable speed. Did the captain hope to reach the pole? I didn't think so, because every effort to reach it so far had failed. Besides, the season was already well advanced, since March 13 in the Antarctic—when the equinoctial period begins there—corresponds with September 13 in the northern regions.

On March 14 at latitude 55° I saw floating ice, pale bits of debris twenty to twenty-five feet long, which formed reefs over which the sea burst into foam. The *Nautilus* kept to the surface. Having fished in Arctic waters, Ned was quite familiar with icebergs. But Conseil and I were admiring them for the first time.

In the sky toward the southern horizon we could see a dazzling white pillar of light. English whalers have dubbed it "ice blink."[1] No matter how dense the clouds are, they cannot obscure this phenomenon. It announces the presence of pack ice.

And in fact, we soon did see more massive blocks of ice shining with a brilliance that varied with the mist. Some of them contained green veins, as if they had been marked with wavy lines of copper sulfate. Others resembled enormous amethysts, reflecting the daylight from the myriad facets of their crystals. Others, tinted with a bright limestone sheen, would have provided enough marble to build a town.

The farther south we sailed, the more these floating islands gained in numbers and importance. Polar birds—petrels, cape pigeons, puffins—nested on them by the thousands. Their cries were deafening. Some of them apparently thought the *Nautilus* was a dead whale, and we could hear them pecking at the steel hull.

While we were navigating among these masses of ice, Captain Nemo spent a great deal of time on the platform. He studied these forsaken waters intently. Sometimes his calm gaze would become more animated. Did he feel more at

1. This optical phenomenon appears as a pillar in the sky over Antarctic sea ice. In some photographs it appears as a cross.

home here in the polar seas where humanity rarely visited, feel like the lord of these inaccessible areas? Perhaps. But he didn't speak. He would stand motionless, emerging from his meditations only when his helmsman's instincts took over. Then he would steer his *Nautilus* with consummate dexterity, dodging masses of ice sometimes several miles in length and seventy to eighty meters high. Often the horizon seemed completely blocked. And when we reached latitude 60° south, every passageway disappeared. Searching with care, he found a narrow opening. He glided into it audaciously, well aware that it would probably close behind him.

Steered by those expert hands the *Nautilus* passed by all those different masses of ice that are classified, according to size and shape, with a precision that charmed Conseil: *icebergs,* shaped like mountains; *ice fields,* which stretch out in smooth, limitless tracts; *drift ice,* or floating floes; and *ice packs,* or broken tracts, dubbed *patches* when they are circular and *streams* when they consist of long strips.

The temperature was quite low. In the outside air one of our thermometers registered −2° to −3° centigrade.[2] But we were warmly clad in furs, for which seals and polar bears had made the final sacrifice. Evenly heated by its electric apparatus, the interior of the *Nautilus* defied the most intense cold. Moreover, to find warmer temperatures we had only to drop just a few meters below the surface.

Two months earlier we would have enjoyed perpetual daylight in that latitude. But now we had nights three or four hours long, and later, six months of continuous darkness would descend on the circumpolar regions.

On March 15 we passed beyond the latitude of the South Shetland and South Orkney Islands. The captain told me that numerous tribes of seals had once lived on those islands but that English and American whalers, in a rage of destructiveness, had massacred all the adults, including pregnant females; where animation and life had once flourished, now there were only silence and death.

Following the 55th meridian, the *Nautilus* cut the Antarctic Circle before eight a.m. on March 16. Ice surrounded us on every side and closed off the horizon. Still, Captain Nemo progressed from one passageway to another, always heading south.

"But where is he going?" I asked.

---

2. This would be 28.4° to 26.6° Fahrenheit. The centigrade scale registers the freezing point of fresh water as 0° and the boiling point as 100°. This sensible scale was proposed by the Swedish astronomer Anders Celsius (1701–1744). In his honor the centigrade scale is today often called the Celsius.

By contrast, the scale named after German physicist Gabriel Fahrenheit (1686–1736) is awkwardly arbitrary: the freezing point is 32° and the boiling 212°. Conversion from one scale to another is accomplished with this equation: F = 1.8 C + 32.

One further point: on the centigrade scale, salt water freezes at −2°, a colder temperature than the freezing point of fresh water. So, in this passage, Aronnax is telling us that the *Nautilus* is lying in waters ready to freeze at any instant.

"Straight ahead," Conseil answered. "Ultimately, when he can't go any farther, he'll stop."

"I'm not so sure of that," I said.

But to be candid, I did admit to myself that I liked this new adventure. I am unable to describe the sublimity of those regions. The ice struck superb poses. Here, it took the form of an oriental town with many minarets and mosques; there, the shape of a city in ruins, flung to the ground by some earthquake. Our view was varied incessantly by the oblique rays of the sun, or swallowed up by gray fogs in the midst of blizzards. We would hear ice cracking and sliding and collapsing. We could see great icebergs somersaulting, altering the landscape like the changing scenery of a diorama.[3]

If the *Nautilus* was submerged when these disturbances occurred, we could hear great crashing noises echoing through the water, and the masses of toppling ice would create a fearsome backwash that could be felt in the deepest strata. The *Nautilus* then rolled and pitched like a boat abandoned to the fury of the elements.

Often, when there seemed to be no passageway in sight, I thought we were finally locked into the ice, but Captain Nemo, picking up the slightest clues, would once again find a way out. He was never wrong when he spotted slender threads of bluish water streaking through the ice fields. I felt sure now that he had considerable experience taking his *Nautilus* into Antarctic waters.

Nevertheless, on March 16 those tracts of ice did completely bar our way. It was not yet the Ice Bank but rather vast ice fields cemented together by the cold. But this barrier could not stop Captain Nemo—he hurled his ship against it with frightful violence. The *Nautilus* entered that brittle mass like a wedge, splitting it with terrible cracklings. It was an old-fashioned battering ram hurled with infinite power. Tossed aloft, the ice broke into pieces and fell back around us like hail. Through brute force alone our submarine hacked out a channel for itself. Occasionally our momentum would be so great that we would mount on top of the ice and crush it with our weight, or if we had slid under the ice, we would split it open by pitching back and forth, creating large gashes in the field.

Violent squalls assailed us in the daytime. Thick fogs made it impossible to see from one end of the platform to the other. The wind shifted abruptly to every point on the compass. Snow accumulated on the platform in such solid layers we had to chip it loose with pickaxes. When the temperature dropped merely to $-5°$ centigrade, the entire outer shell of the *Nautilus* was covered with ice. A ship's rigging would have been useless here because its tackle would have jammed in the grooves of the pulleys. Only a ship without sails, driven by electricity, could venture safely into such high latitudes.

---

3. To Verne's nineteenth-century readers, this was a dramatic comparison. Dioramas presented the onlooker with optical illusions and changing effects. The vista was a three-dimensional scene over which lights were played to vary the features; they were viewed through peepholes or out in the open.

Under these conditions the barometer readings were low, falling as far as 73.5 centimeters.[4] And we could no longer rely on the compass. Its needle would move wildly in opposite directions as we approached the south magnetic pole, which must not be confused with the South Pole proper. As a matter of fact, according to the astronomer Hansteen, this magnetic pole is located at approximately latitude 70°, longitude 130°, while Louis-Isidore Duperrey locates it at latitude 70°, 30′, longitude 135°. And so we had to transport compasses to different parts of the ship, take numerous readings, and strike a mean. Sometimes we could chart our route only by guesswork, not a satisfactory method considering our zigzagging through those passageways among constantly shifting landmarks.

Finally, on March 18, after twenty futile assaults, the *Nautilus* found itself absolutely blocked. We no longer faced an ice stream, patch, or field, but an endless, motionless barrier made up of icy mountains welded together.

"The Ice Bank!" said the Canadian.[5]

I realized that for Ned Land, and for every explorer who had gone before us, this was the great impassable obstacle. When the sun appeared briefly toward noon, Captain Nemo obtained a fairly exact reading for our position. We were at longitude 51° 30′ and latitude 67° 39′ south. So we were already deep into the Antarctic regions.

As for the liquid surface of the sea, there was no semblance of it in sight. Beyond the *Nautilus*'s ram there stretched a vast uneven plain, a tangle of confused ice masses, with all the pell-mell whimsicality of a river's surface just before the ice jam breaks up, but here on a gigantic scale. Here and there stood sharp peaks, slender spires rising 200 feet in the air; farther off, a series of steep, roughly hewn cliffs, tinted gray, tall mirrors reflecting the scant rays of a sun half lost in mist. And over this desolate realm of Nature a cruel silence reigned, silence scarcely broken by the flapping wings of petrels and puffins. Everything was frozen, even sound.

So here the *Nautilus* had to halt in its dangerous tour of the ice fields.

"Professor," Ned Land said to me, "if your captain gets any farther than this . . ."

"Yes?"

"He'll be a superman."

"Why do you say that, Ned?"

"Because no one can clear the Ice Bank. Your captain is a powerful man, but damnation, he's not more powerful than Nature, and where Nature draws a boundary line there you stop, like it or not."

4. In the English system this would be a barometer reading of 28.5—standardly the lowest reading and an automatic tempest situation. But Maury's *Physical Geography* asserts that "a low barometer" is common in Antarctic seas.

5. In Verne's time this was the phrase (*la banquise*) that his countrymen apparently used to identify a gigantic, still-undefined barrier of ice in the Antarctic. Based on the bearings Nemo will take in the next paragraph, his submarine is probably facing what will later be known as the Filchner Ice Shelf.

"Indeed, Ned Land, and still I'd like to know what lies beyond that Ice Bank! What irritates me most is a wall!"

"Master is right," Conseil put in. "Walls were invented to frustrate scientists. Walls should be outlawed everywhere."

"That's fine," the Canadian said, "but anybody can tell what's behind that Ice Bank."

"Exactly what?" I asked.

"Ice! And nothing but!"

"You seem to be sure of your facts, Ned, but I'm not. I've got to go *see* what is there."

"Professor, you'll have to give up that ambition. You've made it to the Ice Bank, and that's already an accomplishment. But you won't get any farther, even with your Captain Nemo and his *Nautilus*. Willy-nilly, he's got to go back north, to the land of normal people."

I had to agree with Ned Land that, until ships are built to navigate over the ice fields, they will have to stop at the Ice Bank.

And indeed, in spite of its efforts, in spite of the powerful means it had to split that ice, the *Nautilus* was now really locked in. Usually, when someone can't go any farther, he can at least turn back. But here, it was just as impossible to go back as it was to go forward, because all the passageways had frozen solid behind us. And if the *Nautilus* remained stationary for very long, it would soon become imbedded in the ice. And that is exactly what began to happen toward two p.m. Fresh ice formed along and then over the ship's sides with astonishing speed. I had to admit that Captain Nemo had acted recklessly.

I was on the platform. The captain was studying the situation for a while. Then he said:

"Well now, professor, what do you make of all this?"

"I think we're trapped, captain."

"Trapped! Whatever can you mean by that?"

"I mean we cannot move ahead, we cannot move back, we cannot move sideways. That's a standard definition of 'trapped,' at least in the populated areas of the world."

"So, professor, you really think the *Nautilus* won't be able to float clear?"

"Only with great difficulty, captain, since the season is too advanced for you to count on the ice breaking up naturally."

"Oh, professor," he replied in an ironic tone of voice, "you'll never change! You see only barriers and great difficulty. Now let me tell you—not only will the *Nautilus* break free, she will take us even farther!"

"Farther—south?" I asked, staring him in the face.

"Yes sir, she will take us to the pole."

"To the South Pole!" I exclaimed, unable to suppress a gesture of disbelief.

"Yes," he said coldly, "to the Antarctic pole, that unknown point where all the meridians cross. For as you know, the *Nautilus* does as I please."

Yes, I did know that. I knew this man was audacious to the point of rashness. But to overcome all the obstacles surrounding the South Pole, so much

An ice trap

more inaccessible than the North Pole, and even *that* hadn't yet been reached by the boldest navigators!—wasn't this an insane enterprise, which could occur only in the mind of a madman?

But then I got the idea of asking the captain if he had already discovered the South Pole, which, so far as the world knew, had never been trodden by a human being.

"No, professor," he replied, "but we shall discover it together. Where others have failed, I will succeed. I have never taken my *Nautilus* so far into these southernmost waters but, I repeat, it will go farther yet."

"I want to believe you, captain," I resumed in an ironic tone. "All right, I do believe you! Let's forge ahead! There are no barriers for us! Let's shatter that Ice Bank! Let's blow it up, and if it still resists, let's put wings on the *Nautilus* so we can fly over it!"

"Over it, professor?" Captain Nemo asked serenely. "No, not over it, but under it!"[6]

"Under it!" I cried out.

A sudden insight into the captain's plans had just flashed through my mind. I understood. The unique talents of the *Nautilus* were about to serve him once more in this superhuman enterprise!

"I see we're beginning to understand each other, professor," he said with a half smile. "You already see the potential—myself, I'd say the success—of this attempt. Projects that are impossible for an ordinary ship become easy for the *Nautilus*. If there's a continent at the pole, then of course we'll stop at the continent. But if the pole is washed by open sea, then we will sail right to the pole itself."

"Of course," I said, now swept along by the captain's line of reasoning, "while the surface of the sea has solidified into ice, its lower strata are free and open—thanks to that providential law that puts the maximum density of salt water one degree above the freezing point. And if I'm not mistaken, the portion of this Ice Bank that stands above the water is in a one-to-four ratio to the part below the water."

"Very nearly, professor. For each foot of iceberg above the sea, there are three more below it.[7] Now, since these ice mountains are never higher than 100 meters, it follows that they are submerged only to a depth of 300 meters. And what are 300 meters to the *Nautilus*?"

"Nothing, sir!"

---

6. Nemo is here anticipating the precise way in which the U.S. nuclear submarines *Nautilus* and *Skate* will negotiate the Northwest Passage in 1958.

7. Salt water freezes at $-2°$ centigrade, and it reaches its greatest specific gravity just before it hits that temperature. The heaviest water is that which is just about to freeze—and of course it has sunk to the lower strata, which remain fluid. Ice floats up to the surface because, having expanded, it is now lighter than the fluid water underneath.

Since Nemo and Aronnax know the "three to one ratio," they can estimate from the height of the above-surface ice just how deep the underwater ice goes, and where the "free" water begins.

"We could even go deeper to find that layer of temperature common to all the ocean waters, and there we would brave with impunity the −30° or −40° cold on the surface."

"Right, well put, captain!" I was growing more excited.

"Our main difficulty," Captain Nemo continued, "is that we'll be submerged several days with no chance to renew our air supply."

"Is that all? The *Nautilus* has big air tanks. We'll fill them and they can furnish all the oxygen we need."

"Well thought out, professor," the captain replied with an approving smile. "But just so you can't accuse me later of being rash, I'm going to mention all my objections now."

"Can there be any others?"

"Just one. If the South Pole is located in a sea, that sea could be frozen over, and we wouldn't be able to come to the surface."

"Goodness, captain, have you forgotten that the *Nautilus* is armed with a powerful ram? Can't we come up from below, strike the ice diagonally with the ram, and so break out into the open?"

"Well, professor, you are bursting with ideas today!"

"Besides, captain," I added enthusiastically, "why shouldn't we expect to find open sea at the South Pole as at the North Pole? The cold-temperature poles and the geographic poles do not coincide in either the Southern or Northern Hemispheres. Until we have proof to the contrary, we can suppose that at these two points there will be either land or an ice-free ocean."

"That's how I see it, professor. Let me just add that after overwhelming me with objections to my plan, you are now overwhelming me with arguments in its favor."

The captain was telling the truth. I was now the bolder one. I was now the one sweeping him along to the pole. I was leading the way, I was ahead of him . . . oh no, you poor fool! Captain Nemo knew all the time what the pros and cons were. He had been amusing himself, watching me being carried away by my daydreams of the impossible!

Nonetheless, he was losing no time. He gave a signal and the first mate appeared. The two men spoke rapidly in their incomprehensible language. Either the first mate had been briefed beforehand or he found the project perfectly feasible, because he showed no surprise at all.

But as impassive as the mate was, he was positively animated compared to Conseil when I told the lad of our plan to push on to the pole. He just uttered his usual:

"Whatever pleases master."

But Ned Land shrugged his shoulders higher than any had ever been shrugged before.

"Honestly, professor, you and your Captain Nemo, I pity you two!"

"But we *will* make it to the pole, Ned."

"Maybe, but you won't come back." And to prevent himself from "doing something desperate," as he phrased it, he went at once to his cabin.

Preparations for this bold enterprise were already under way. The *Nautilus*'s powerful pumps were forcing air into the tanks and storing it under high pressure. Near four p.m. Captain Nemo said that the hatches on the platform were soon to be shut. I took one last look at that massive Ice Bank we were about to clear. The weather was fair, the atmosphere reasonably clear, the cold quite brisk, specifically, −12° centigrade, but since the wind had died down, this temperature was not unbearable.

Some ten men, armed with picks, mounted the *Nautilus*'s sides and cracked loose the ice around the hull. It didn't take long—the fresh ice was still thin—and we were free. We all reentered the interior. The main ballast tanks were filling with the newly liberated water that had not yet frozen at our line of flotation, and the *Nautilus* started to sink.

I took a seat in the salon with Conseil. Through the open window we gazed into the lower strata of this southernmost sea. The thermometer was rising, and the needle on the pressure gauge moved across its dial.

Just as Captain Nemo had foreseen, at about 300 meters down we drifted beneath the undulating surface of the Ice Bank. But the *Nautilus* plunged deeper still, leveling off at 800 meters. The temperature of the water had risen two degrees, from −12° centigrade at the surface to −10° centigrade underneath.[8] Needless to say, the temperature inside the *Nautilus,* controlled by our electric apparatus, was much higher. Every maneuver was accomplished with perfect precision.

"With all due respect to master, I think we'll get past the Ice Bank," Conseil said.

"I'm sure we will," I answered with strong conviction.

Now that it was in open water, the *Nautilus* headed straight for the pole without leaving the 52nd meridian. From 67° 30′ to 90° we had twenty-two-and-a-half degrees of latitude still to cross, in other words, slightly more than 500 leagues. The *Nautilus* adopted a mean speed of twenty-six miles an hour, the speed of an express train. If it kept up that pace, we would reach the pole in 40 hours.

For part of the night the novelty of our situation kept Conseil and me at the salon window. The sea was illuminated by our beacon, showing that the depths were deserted. Fish apparently did not live in these imprisoned waters—for them it was only a passageway from the Antarctic Ocean to whatever open sea there was near the pole. We were traveling fast, as we could tell from the quivering of the long steel hull.

Toward two a.m. I went to snatch a few hours' sleep. Conseil did likewise. I did not meet Captain Nemo in the corridors. I assumed he was keeping to the pilothouse.

But at five a.m., March 19, I was back at my post in the salon. The electric

8. The French has an odd, obvious bobble: it gives −11° for the subsurface temperature, which conflicts with the cited two-degree rise. One or the other has to be a typo. We chose (and corrected) the former.

log indicated that we had reduced our speed. The *Nautilus* was rising cautiously to the surface, emptying its tanks very slowly.

My heart was pounding fast. Would we emerge in open water and breathe the polar air?

No. A sudden thud informed me that the ship had bumped the underside of the Ice Bank, still quite thick if we could gauge it from the dull sound of the collision. Indeed, we had "struck bottom," to use a nautical expression, but upside down and at a depth of 3,000 feet. That meant there was 4,000 feet of ice above us, 1,000 feet of it above the surface. So the Ice Bank was higher here than at the outskirts—not a very reassuring thought.

The *Nautilus* tried that experiment several times that day, every time bumping against that thick ceiling. Sometime we struck ice at a depth of 900 meters, denoting a thickness of 1,200 meters, of which 300 meters rose above the surface.[9] That thickness had tripled since the moment the *Nautilus* had dived beneath the ice.

I took careful notes on these varying depths and so obtained a submarine profile of that upside-down mountain chain stretching under the sea.

By evening there was no major change in our situation. The ice kept between 400 and 500 meters deep, obviously diminishing, but what a barrier still lay between us and the surface, and the open air!

By now it was eight p.m. The air inside the ship should have been renewed four hours earlier in accord with daily practice on board. I wasn't suffering very much, even though Captain Nemo had not yet begun to use his reserve supply.

My sleep was fitful that night, hope and fear alternating in my thoughts. I got up several times. The *Nautilus* continued groping. Toward three a.m. I noticed that we hit the underside of the Ice Bank at a depth of only fifty meters. So only 150 feet separated us from the surface! The Ice Bank was changing, little by little, into an ice field. The mountain was becoming a plain.

My eyes never left the pressure gauge. We kept mounting on a diagonal, lighting the ice above us. Topside and underside, the Ice Bank was subsiding, mile after mile growing flatter and thinner.

Finally, at six a.m. on that memorable day of March 19, the salon door opened. Captain Nemo came in and announced:

"The sea is open."

9. Despite earnest efforts by Nemo and Aronnax to clarify the three-to-one ratio adhered to by icebergs (see note 7 earlier), the French compositors—or someone in the halls of Hetzel—produced a notable mess in this paragraph and the one before it.

In the preceding paragraph, the French texts all give 1,000 feet above plus 1,000 below equals 2,000, which is far from the official ratio. For the general reader's sake, we've substituted 1,000 feet above plus 3,000 below equals 4,000. Then, in the present paragraph, the French gives 900 meters below plus 200 above equals 1,200 meters. We've corrected the obviously erroneous 200 to 300.

We've often harbored suspicions that Hetzel's staff altered Verne's text without consulting him. We also suspect that Verne did not always proof the typeset results. Given the blatant discrepancies in this instance, both of our suspicions seem plausible.

FOURTEEN

❧

The South Pole [1]

I RUSHED OUT onto the platform. Yes, open sea! Just a few sparse floes and some moving icebergs in a sea stretching far into the distance; hosts of birds in the air, myriads of fish in the water, water varying from intense blue to olive green, depending on its depths. Our thermometer registered 3° centigrade. It was as though a relative springtime had been hidden away behind the Ice Bank, whose masses were outlined far away on the northern horizon.

"Are we at the pole?" I asked the captain, my heart beating fast.

"I have no idea," he said. "I'll shoot the sun at noon."

"But can the sun get through these mists?" I gazed at the grayish sky.

"I need only a faint glimpse of it to establish my position," he said.

About ten miles to the south of the *Nautilus* a solitary isle rose to a height of maybe 200 meters. We headed toward it, but carefully, for these uncharted waters could be strewn with reefs.

An hour later we reached it, two hours later we had circled around it. It measured four to five miles in circumference. A narrow channel separated it from a considerable shore, perhaps a continent, whose limits we couldn't see. The very existence of that shore seemed to bear out one of Commander Maury's hypotheses. This ingenious American has noted that between the South Pole and the 60th parallel the sea is covered with floating ice of dimensions much greater than any encountered in the North Atlantic. From this fact he concluded that the Antarctic Circle contains a large land mass, because icebergs cannot form on the high seas but only along coastlines. According to his calculations, that frozen land mass surrounding the South Pole forms a vast ice cap whose width must reach 4,000 kilometers. [2]

1. When this novel appeared in 1871, both the North and South poles were still undiscovered—in real life. But Verne's titular hero in *The Adventures of Captain Hatteras* (1864) had attained the North Pole in fancy. That fictitious triumph, along with Nemo's at the South Pole in the present chapter, will strengthen public interest in polar exploration—until Robert Peary actually reaches the North Pole in 1909 and Roald Amundsen the South Pole in 1911.

2. Most of Maury's ideas cited here will prove to be true. Antarctica is a continent of more than 5,000,000 square miles. Its ice shelves—ranging up to 10,000 feet thick—"calve" the giant icebergs Nemo has been busy dodging.

Apprehensive of running his *Nautilus* aground, Captain Nemo halted three cable lengths from a beach dominated by superb stacks of rocks. The dinghy was placed in the water, and two men carrying instruments, the captain, Conseil, and I got in. It was 10 a.m. I had not seen Ned Land. In the presence of the South Pole, the Canadian probably disliked having to eat his words.

A few strokes of the oars brought our dinghy to the beach where we ran aground on the sand. Conseil was about to jump ashore but I held him back.

"Sir," I told Captain Nemo, "the honor of first setting foot on this land belongs to you."

"Yes, professor," he agreed, "and if I don't hesitate to touch land here, it's because no human being till now has left a footprint near the South Pole."

With this he leapt lightly onto the sand. His heart must have beat rapidly with keen excitement. He scaled an overhanging rock that led to a small promontory and there, standing quiet and motionless with his arms crossed and his eyes afire, he seemed to take possession of these southernmost regions. After five minutes of this ecstatic trance, he turned to us.

"Whenever you're ready, sir," he cried to me.

I got out, followed by Conseil, leaving the dinghy in the care of the two crewmen.

Over an extensive area, the soil was composed of that igneous gravel called "tuff," reddish in color as if made from crushed bricks. The soil was covered with slag, lava flows, and pumice stones. There was no mistaking its volcanic origin. Here and there little smoke holes gave out a sulfurous smell, indicating that the fires inside the earth still maintained their wide-ranging power. Nonetheless, when I climbed a high escarpment, I could see no volcanoes for miles around. Still, I remembered that in the Antarctic regions, on the 167th meridian at latitude 77°32′, Sir James Clark Ross had found the craters of Mt. Erebus and Mt. Terror in a fully active state.[3]

I found the vegetation on that desolate continent to be quite limited. A few lichens of the species *Usnea melanoxanthra* sprawled over the black rocks. The rest of the meager flora consisted of microscopic buds, some rudimentary diatoms with their single cell placed between two quartz-rich shells; plus some long purple and crimson fucus plants, supported by small air bladders and cast up on the beach by the surf.

The fauna fared better: the beach was sprinkled with mollusks—small mussels; limpets; smooth heart-shaped cockles; and especially some sea butterflies with oblong, membranous bodies whose heads consist of two rounded lobes. I also saw myriads of those northern sea butterflies three centimeters long, which a baleen whale can swallow by the thousands in one mouthful.[4]

---

3. Ross named these two volcanoes after his own ship the *Erebus,* and the *Terror* commanded by his subordinate, F. R. M. Crozier. They discovered the two volcanoes on January 28, 1841. Erebus is believed to be the only volcano still active in Antarctica today.

4. Today this whale food is called krill.

The water at the shoreline was alive with these charming pteropods, true butterflies of the sea.

Among other zoophytes, I saw in the shallows a few tree-shaped corals of a type that, according to Sir James Clark Ross, live in Antarctic seas as far down as 1,000 meters; then, some small alcyon coral, of the species *Procellaria pelagica*, called "little kingfishers";[5] and a great number of starfish peculiar to those climes, with some feather stars spangling the sand.

But where life most abounded was in the air. There, various species of birds fluttered and flew by the thousands, deafening us with their cries. Other fowl were crowding the rocks, gazing without fear as we passed, even pressing against our feet in a familiar way. These were auks, so agile and supple in the water that they are sometimes mistaken for bonitos, and yet so awkward and heavy on the land. They uttered outlandish cries, forming many public assemblies that were sober in gesture but extravagant in clamor.

Among other fowl I noted some sheathbills from the wading bird family: as large as pigeons, white in color, the beak short and conical, and the eyes framed in red circles. Conseil captured several, because when properly cooked, those winged creatures make an agreeable dish. Passing overhead were some sooty albatross, with four-meter wingspans, birds aptly dubbed "the vultures of the sea"; and some giant petrels, among others several with arching wings, called *quebrantahuesos*,[6] great killers and eaters of seals; some cape pigeons, a kind of small duck, the top of their bodies black and white: in short, a whole series of petrels, some whitish with brown borders on their wings, others blue and unique to the Antarctic waters, the former "so oily," I told Conseil, "that inhabitants of the Faroe Islands simply stick a wick in them before lighting them."

"Too bad," he responded, "that Nature doesn't fit them with wicks to start with. That way they would make perfect lamps."

About half a mile farther on, we found the ground completely riddled with penguins' nests, like burrows arranged for laying eggs, from which numerous birds emerged. Later Captain Nemo would have hundreds of them hunted because their black flesh is highly edible. They bray like donkeys. The size of a goose with slate-colored bodies, white undersides, lemon-yellow bands around their necks, those animals would allow themselves to be stoned to death without even trying to get away.

Meanwhile, the mists prevailed, and at eleven a.m. there was still no sun. Its absence worried me. Without it, we couldn't fix our position. How then could we know whether we had reached the pole?

When I rejoined Captain Nemo, he was leaning quietly against a boulder, gazing at the sky. He seemed impatient and baffled. But what could we do? This bold, powerful man could not command the sun as he did the sea.

5. This nickname has been given to such soft corals because they resemble the nests made by those birds.
6. Spanish: meaning "ospreys"; also called "sea eagles" or "fish hawks."

Antarctic aviary

Noon came without the sun having shown itself for a single moment. We couldn't even figure out where it was behind its curtain of mist. And then that mist began to condense into snow.

"Till tomorrow, then," the captain said quietly, and we went back to the *Nautilus* amidst whirling flurries.

There we found that the crew had cast out their nets, and I was eager to see what fish they were hauling in. Large numbers of migratory fish, fleeing from tempests in the subpolar zones, take refuge in the Antarctic seas, only, it must be said, to glide down the gullets of porpoises and seals. I noted some southern bullhead about one decimeter long, a species of white cartilaginous fish overrun with livid bands and armed with stings; then, some Antarctic rabbitfish three feet long, with very slim bodies, the skin a glossy silver white, the head rounded, the back equipped with three fins, the muzzle ending in a trunk that curves back toward the mouth. I found its flesh rather bland, despite Conseil's opinion that it was tolerable.

The snowstorm persisted until the next day, and it was impossible to stay on the platform. In the salon I wrote up the events of this polar excursion while listening to the cries of petrel and albatross frolicking in the midst of the blizzard. The *Nautilus* wasn't idle, cruising along the coast, advancing some ten miles farther south amid the half light left by the sun as it skimmed the edge of the horizon.

The next day, March 20, the snow stopped. The cold was much brisker, our thermometer registering $-2°$ centigrade. The fog vanished and I could hope that we would shoot the sun at noon.

Since Captain Nemo did not appear, the dinghy took only Conseil and myself to shore. Here the nature of the soil was the same: volcanic. Traces of lava, slag, and basalt were everywhere, but I could not find the crater that had ejected them. There as yonder, a myriad birds enlivened that part of the polar continent. But they were obliged to share their dominion with vast herds of marine mammals that gazed at us with their gentle eyes. These were seals of various species, some stretched out on the ground, others abed on drifting ice floes, many entering or leaving the sea. Never having dealt with humanity, they did not flee at our approach, and I counted enough of them to provision a few hundred ships.

"Ye gods," Conseil said, "it's good that Ned Land didn't come along."

"Why, Conseil?"

"Because that deranged hunter would kill every animal here."

"*Every* animal is an exaggeration, but I doubt we could have stopped him from harpooning several of these magnificent cetaceans. That would be an insult to Captain Nemo. He doesn't like to slaughter harmless animals except when they're needed as food."

"And he is right."

"He certainly is, Conseil. But tell me, have you finished classifying these superb specimens of marine fauna?"

"Master knows very well," he replied, "that I'm not yet adept at practical classification. But if master would just tell me the names of these animals. . . ."

"They're seals and walruses."

"Both of these genera," my learned Conseil hastened to say, "belong to the family Pinnipedia, order Carnivora, group Unguiculata, subclass Monodelphia, class Mammalia, branch Vertebrata."

"Nice work, Conseil, but these two genera of seals and walruses are divided into species, and, if I'm not mistaken, we have a chance here to actually look at them. So let's do just that."

It was eight a.m. We had four hours before the sun might show itself for our noon observations. I led the way toward a vast bay that made a crescent-shaped cut in the granite cliffs along the beach.

There, all about us as far as the eye could see, marine animals crowded the shore and the ice floes, and I swear, I looked about me involuntarily for old Proteus, that mythic shepherd who watched over King Neptune's huge flocks. Most of them were seals. They formed distinct male-and-female groups, the father watching over his family, the mother suckling her little ones, with some already strong enough to walk asserting their independence a few steps away. When these mammals wanted to move someplace else, they accomplished it in a series of little leaps, made by contracting their bodies; they're helped along by their imperfectly developed flippers which, as with their cousin the manatee, form genuine forearms. But in the water, their natural element, I must say they swim wonderfully thanks to their flexible backbones, narrow pelvises, close-cropped hair, and webbed feet. When they rest on shore, they recline in graceful positions. And so, seeing their gentle features, their expressive glances unsurpassed by those of the loveliest women, their clear, soft eyes, their charming attitudes, the ancients glorified them by metamorphosing the males into sea gods and the females into mermaids.

I pointed out to Conseil the highly developed cerebral lobes housed in those intelligent cetaceans. No mammals except human beings have such a quantity of cerebral matter.[7] And so they are quite teachable; they are easily domesticated, and I agree with certain naturalists who say these seals could well be trained as "hunting dogs" for fishermen.

The majority of them were sleeping on the rocks or the sand. Among those properly classified as seals—that is, those whose ears do not protrude from their heads, as they do with sea lions—I studied several varieties of the species *stenorhynchus*. They were three meters long, with white hair and bulldog heads with ten teeth in each jaw: four incisors in both the upper and the lower, plus two great canines shaped like the fleur-de-lis. Among them slithered some sea elephants, a kind of seal with a short, flexible trunk. They are the giants of the species, with bodies twenty feet in circumference and ten meters long! They did not move as we approached them.

7. In the nineteenth century, evidently, little was known about the cerebral matter of whales and porpoises—which modern scientists would rate as considerably brainier than seals.

"They aren't dangerous, are they?" Conseil asked.

"Not unless you attack them. When these giant seals are defending their young, their fury is terrible. It's not at all unusual for them to smash a fisherman's longboat to smithereens."

"They're within their rights," Conseil replied.

"I can't deny that."

Two miles farther on we were stopped by a headland that protected the bay from southerly winds. It dropped straight down to the sea, and surf foamed against it. From beyond that barrier we heard loud bellowings such as a herd of cattle might produce.

"Goodness," Conseil inquired, "a chorus of bulls?"

"No," I corrected him, "a chorus of walruses."

"Are they fighting?"

"Either fighting or playing."

"With all due respect to master, I'd like to see them."

"Then see them we must, Conseil."

And there we were, climbing over blackish rocks through sudden landslides and over stones slippery with ice. More than once I fell and hurt my backside. More prudent or more stable, Conseil scarcely ever stumbled, helping me up as he intoned:

"If master would just keep his feet farther apart, then master could more easily keep his balance."

When we reached the ridge at the top of the headland, I could see a vast white plain covered with walruses. They were romping with each other, bellowing not with anger but with joy.

Walruses resemble seals in the shape of their bodies and in the arrangement of their limbs. But walruses have no canines or incisors in their lower jaws, and the canines in their upper jaws consist of two tusks 80 centimeters long and 33 centimeters around at the socket. These teeth are made of solid ivory, without striations, they're harder than elephant tusks and don't yellow so quickly. Needless to say, walrus ivory is in high demand. As a result, walruses are the target of mindless hunting that will soon make them extinct, since their hunters indiscriminately massacre even pregnant females and youngsters at the rate of 4,000 walruses a year.

As I walked around these curious animals, I could observe them at my leisure since they did not move away from me. Their hides were thick, rough, and a reddish tan, their hair sparse and short. Some of them were four meters long. Calmer and less fearful than their Arctic cousins, they had not posted sentinels around their camp as northern walruses do.

After studying this community of tusked mammals, I thought of getting back to the *Nautilus*. It was eleven a.m., and if Captain Nemo found conditions favorable for shooting the sun, I wanted to be there. But I didn't see much hope that the sun would appear at noon. It was hidden from our view by clouds crushed massively together along the horizon. The sun seemed jealous, unwilling to light that part of the world for any human being.

Still I headed back toward the *Nautilus*. We walked along the edge of the cliffs. By eleven thirty we reached the place where we had landed. The dinghy had returned with the captain. I could see him standing on a block of basalt, his instruments nearby. His eyes were fixed on the northern horizon, along which the sun must have been describing its long arc.[8]

Without saying a word, I stood near him and waited. Noon arrived. As on the previous day, the sun made no appearance.

This was a quirk of fate. We did not know where we were, and if we couldn't fix our position by noon of the next day, we might never know whether we had actually been at the pole!

This was the problem: it was March 20. The next day, March 21, was the day of the equinox, when the sun would disappear beneath the horizon for six months, not counting refraction, and the long polar night would begin. After the September equinox, the sun had emerged above the northern horizon, rising in long spirals until December 21. On that day—the summer solstice of the southernmost regions—the sun had started back down, and on March 21 it would cast its last rays over the South Pole.

I told Captain Nemo what I was thinking and what I was afraid of.

"You're right, Professor Aronnax," he said. "If I can't shoot the sun tomorrow, I won't be able to try it again for another six months. But since fate has planted us here in time for March 21, it will be comparatively easy to take our bearings if the sun does appear at noon."

"Why so, captain?"

"Because when the sun is traveling through the sky in such long spirals, it's difficult to measure its exact altitude above the horizon, and our instruments can make serious errors."[9]

"What can you do, then?"

"Use only my chronometer. At noon tomorrow, March 21, if—after accounting for refraction—the sun's disk is cut exactly in half by the northern horizon, then I know I'm at the South Pole."

"True," I said, "but mathematically speaking, that wouldn't be exact proof because the equinox needn't fall precisely at noon."

"No doubt, professor, but the error couldn't be more than 100 meters, and for us that's close enough. So, till tomorrow. . . ."

Captain Nemo went back on board. Conseil and I explored the beach until 5 p.m. I found nothing unusual except a large auk's egg for which a collector would gladly have paid 1,000 francs. It was cream-colored, and the streaks and lines that embellished it, like so many hieroglyphics, made it a rare trinket. I

8. Aronnax only *knows in his mind* that the sun is moving along the horizon as described; because of the clouds, he can't *see* it.

9. Because the sun is sweeping in an arc close to the horizon and settling at the same time. By tomorrow, March 21, it will have settled so much more it will lie below the horizon. Dr. David Woodruff of New York University verified Verne's calculations in this passage back in the 1970s. He added that of course Nemo was working from standard astronomical tables.

entrusted it to Conseil and, holding it like precious porcelain from China, that careful, sure-footed lad delivered it to the *Nautilus* all in one piece.

There I placed it in one of the glass cases in our museum. I dined with gusto on an excellent piece of seal's liver, which reminded me of pork. And then, in Hindu fashion, I invoked the favors of the radiant orb of day and went to sleep.

When I mounted to the platform at 5 a.m. on the fateful day of March 21, I found Captain Nemo already there.

"The weather is letting up a bit," he told me. "I have high hopes now. After breakfast let's go ashore and pick out an observation post."

That settled, I went to find Ned Land. I wanted him to go with us. The obstinate Canadian refused, and I could see that his taciturnity and bad mood were growing day by day. But under the circumstances I finally felt better about his refusal. There were too many seals ashore, and I thought it best not to expose an unthinking fisherman to such temptations.

Breakfast under my belt, I went ashore. The *Nautilus* had moved a few miles farther on during the night. It now lay well out, a good league from the coast, which was dominated by a sharp peak 400 to 500 meters high. In addition to me, the dinghy carried Captain Nemo, two crewmen, and the instruments: a chronometer, a telescope, and a barometer.

During our crossing I saw numerous baleen whales of the three species peculiar to the southernmost seas: the bowhead whale, or the "right whale" as the English call it, which has no dorsal fin; the humpback whale of the genus *Balaenoptera* (meaning "winged whale"), beasts with wrinkled belly and vast whitish fins which, genus name regardless, do not really form wings; and the finback whale, yellow brown, the swiftest of all cetaceans. We could hear even those finbacks who were a long way off when they sent aloft great spouts of air and vapor, which looked like swirls of smoke. Herds of these different sea mammals played about in the calm water, and I could see that the Antarctic polar basin was now the refuge for these cetaceans so fiercely hunted down by whalers.

I also noted long, whitish strings of salps, a type of shellfish that lives in colonies, and some huge jellyfish swaying back and forth in the backwash of the billows.

We pulled up to shore at nine a.m. The sky was brightening, clouds were fleeing south. Mists were rising from the cold surface of the waters. Captain Nemo headed for the peak, which he no doubt wanted to use as his observatory. It was a painful climb up over sharp lava and pumice stones in an atmosphere reeking with sulfurous fumes from the smoke holes. For a man out of practice at walking on land, the captain scaled the steepest slopes with a litheness and agility that I could not equal and which hunters of Pyrenees mountain goats would have envied.

It took us two hours to reach the summit of the peak, which was half porphyry, half basalt. From there, we could look out over a vast sea that, toward the north, traced its boundary line clearly against the sky. At our feet we could see dazzling white fields, and over our heads, a pale azure sky clear of mists. To the north, the sun's disk looked like a ball of fire—it was already cut into by the horizon. From the bosom of the sea, whales were sending up jets of water like hundreds of magnificent bouquets. Far off, the *Nautilus* lay like another sleeping cetacean. Behind us, to the south and east there was an immense expanse of land, chaotically heaped with rocks and ice, whose limits we could not see.

Arriving at his post on the summit, Captain Nemo carefully determined its altitude by means of his barometer, because this factor had to be taken into account in his noon observations.

At 11:45 a.m., the sun—a golden disk we could see now only by refraction—was casting its last rays over this unknown continent and down to these seas still unplowed by humanity's ships.

Captain Nemo was using a special telescope that corrected the sun's refraction by means of a mirror—its eyepiece contained reticles.[10] He observed the sun sinking little by little along a very extended diagonal that reached below the horizon. I was holding the chronometer. My heart was pounding mightily. If the disappearance of the lower half of the sun's disk coincided with noon on the chronometer, then we were at the pole itself.

"Noon!" I cried.

"The South Pole!" Captain Nemo responded in a grave voice as he handed me the spyglass. Through it I could see the sun's disk cut into two exactly equal portions by the horizon.

I watched the shadows slowly climbing the slopes and the last rays of sunlight growing weaker at the peak. Then Captain Nemo put his hand on my shoulder and said:

"Professor, in 1600 the Dutchman Gheritk, driven by currents and storms, reached latitude 64° south and discovered the South Shetland Islands. On January 17, 1773, the illustrious Captain Cook, following the 38th meridian, reached latitude 67° 30′ south; and on January 30, 1774, via the 109th meridian, he got so far as 71° 15′.[11] In 1819 the Russian Bellingshausen reached the 69th parallel and two years later, the 66th at longitude 111° west.[12] In 1820 the Englishman Bransfield could not get past 65°. That same year the American Morrel, whose reports are dubious, went along the 42nd meridian and claims he discovered open sea at latitude 70° 14′. In 1825 the Englishman Powell was unable to pass beyond 62°. That same year an Englishman named Weddell, who was a simple seal fisherman, reached latitude 72° 14′ on the 35th meridian,

10. Grids for determining the scale or position of the object viewed.

11. Cook was ordered to search for a southern continent conjectured to exist by the geographer Alexander Dalrymple. He found no evidence to support the latter's theories and reported grumpily that if ever land were discovered in those terrible regions, "the world will derive no benefit from it."

12. Fabian von Bellingshausen sighted the first land ever seen inside the Antarctic Circle, a little island he named after Czar Peter I.

and 74° 15′ on the 36th.[13] In 1829 the Englishman Forster, captain of the *Chanticleer,* took possession of the Antarctic continent at latitude 63° 26′ and longitude 66° 26′. On February 1, 1831, the Englishman Biscoe discovered Enderby Land at latitude 68° 50′, on February 5, 1832, Adelaide Land at latitude 67°, and on that February 21, Graham Land at latitude 64° 45′. In 1838 the Frenchman Captain Dumont d'Urville was stopped by the Ice Bank at latitude 62° 57′, but he managed to discover the Louis-Philippe Peninsula; on January 21, two years later, at 66° 30′, he named the Adelie Coast and eight days later, the Clarie Coast at 64° 40′. And also in 1838 the American Wilkes advanced to the 69th parallel on the 100th meridian.[14] In 1839 the Englishman Balleny discovered the Sabrina Coast at the edge of the Antarctic Circle. Lastly, on January 12, 1842, the Englishman Sir James Clark Ross, with his ships *Erebus* and *Terror,* found Victoria Land in latitude 70° 56′ and longitude 171° 7′ east; then on January 23 he raised the 74th parallel, the farthest point reached up to that time; on January 27, he reached 76° 8′; the next day, 77° 32′; on February 2, he got as far as 78° 4′;[15] then late in 1842 he returned to 71° but could not get beyond it. And now, professor, on March 21, 1868, I myself, Captain Nemo, have reached the South Pole at 90°, and I take possession of this region of the globe that is equal in area to one-sixth of the known continents."

"In whose name, captain?"[16]

"In my own name, sir!"

So saying, Captain Nemo unfurled a black flag bearing a gold "*N*" on its quartered bunting. Then he turned toward the sun, whose last rays were flickering on the sea's horizon, and cried:

"Farewell, O sun! Leave us, O radiant orb! Go to thy rest beneath the open sea, and let six months of night spread their shadows over my new domains."[17]

---

13. James Weddell sailed into the sea that now bears his name. The English navigator also has a large brown seal named after him.

14. The French gives Wilkes as *English,* an error we've corrected. Charles Wilkes led the first-ever exploring expedition launched by the U.S. Navy.

15. This stood as the Farthest South in 1868, the record Nemo had to beat. In real life, it remained the record until 1900.

Incidentally, the French features an apparent compositor's error for Ross's discovery of Victoria Land: it cites the latitude as 76°56′. We've corrected this to read 70°56′.

16. A little more psychological fencing between Nemo and Aronnax, continuing the match begun in I 14. The professor was hoping that this occasion would reveal Nemo's nationality. The classic formula for such a moment runs: "I take possession of this territory in the name of His Majesty _____, the King of _____ ." Instead, Nemo claims to act as agent for no one but himself.

17. Here Verne presents Nemo as the ultimate rebel (the first and possibly the greatest of a series of rebels to be featured in his fiction). The black flag, of course, is the flag of piracy, of defiance of international law.

FIFTEEN

Accident or Incident?

W E BEGAN PREPARATIONS for departure at six a.m. the following day, March 22. The last gleams of twilight were melting into night. The cold was brisk and the constellations were glittering with surprising intensity. Straight overhead I saw the wondrous Southern Cross, the polar star of the Antarctic regions.[1]

Our thermometer registered −12° centigrade, and when the wind came up it caused the very air to bite. Ice floes were multiplying on the open sea. The water was congealing everywhere. Numerous blackish patches spread over its surface, announcing that new ice was forming. Clearly, that southernmost basin would freeze over during its six-month night and become absolutely inaccessible. What would the whales do? No doubt they went out under the Ice Bank to find open water As for seals and walruses, they were used to living in extreme cold and could stay on in this frozen desert. They know by instinct how to open holes in the ice fields and keep them open, and that's where they come to breathe. And when the birds have all migrated north to escape the cold, these seals and walruses remain as sole lords of the polar continent.

Now the ballast tanks were filling up with water and the *Nautilus* was slowly sinking. At a depth of 1,000 feet it leveled off, its propeller churning the waves as it headed due north at a speed of fifteen miles an hour. Toward afternoon we were already cruising under the vast frozen carapace of the Ice Bank.

Since the *Nautilus* could run afoul of some submerged block of ice, the salon panels were kept closed as a safety measure. So I spent the day rewriting my notes. My mind was immersed entirely in memories of the South Pole. We had actually reached that inaccessible spot without fatigue or danger, as easily as if we had gone there in a railroad train! And now we were actually escaping that area on a return trip! Would it provide as many surprises? I felt sure it would, for there seemed to be no end to this series of underwater marvels. During the five-and-a-half months that fate had kept us aboard the *Nautilus,* we had traveled

---

1. In the Southern Hemisphere, the traveler can use the constellation Crux, or the Southern Cross, to find his direction. He locates four of its stars that form the tips of an upright crucifix. The two center stars point to the south celestial pole.

14,000 leagues. And on this voyage longer than the earth's circumference, there were so many strange or terrifying events that kept us spellbound: that hunting trip in the Crespo Island forests; our running aground in the Torres Strait; the burial in the coral cemetery; the pearl fisheries of Ceylon; the dash through the Arabian tunnel; the volcanic fires of Santorin; the millions taken from the Bay of Vigo; the walk into Atlantis; discovering the South Pole! During the night those memories dissolved from one dream to another, giving my brain no rest at all.

At three a.m. I was awakened by a violent collision. I sat up in bed, trying to hear in the dark what was going on, when I was suddenly hurled into the middle of the cabin. Apparently the *Nautilus* had run aground and then heeled over sharply.

Feeling my way along the walls, I dragged myself down the gangways to the salon, where the ceiling lights were ablaze. The furniture had been knocked around. Fortunately, the glass cases were solidly attached to the floor and still stood in place. Because we were no longer vertical, the pictures on the starboard side were glued to the tapestries, while those on the port side hung a foot away from the wall. So the *Nautilus* was lying on its starboard side and, moreover, was immobilized.

I could hear footsteps and muffled voices. But Captain Nemo did not appear. Just when I was about to leave the salon, Ned Land and Conseil showed up.

"What happened?" I asked.

"We came to ask master that," Conseil replied.

"Damnation!" the Canadian cried. "I know what happened! The *Nautilus* has run aground, and judging from the way it's heeled over, I'd say we won't get free so easily as we did in the Torres Strait."

"You mean," I asked, "at least we're on the surface?"

"We have no idea where we are," Conseil said.

"But it's easy to find out," I realized.

I consulted the pressure gauge. To my great surprise it registered a depth of 360 meters.

"What's going on?" I exclaimed.

"We've got to ask Captain Nemo," Conseil said.

"But where is he?" Ned Land asked.

"Come with me," I told my two companions.

We left the salon. No one in the library. No one by the central companionway or near the crew's quarters. I figured that Captain Nemo was posted in the pilothouse. It seemed best to wait, so the three of us went back to the salon.

I won't repeat the Canadian's recriminations. He had a good case. I let him vent his foul mood without restraint or reply from me.

We remained for twenty minutes like this, trying to hear the slightest noise, when Captain Nemo appeared. He seemed not to see us. His face, usually so impassive, showed signs of uneasiness. In silence he consulted the compass and the pressure gauge, and then placed his finger on the map at a spot in the Antarctic.

Captain Nemo enters the salon

I hesitated to interrupt him, but a few minutes later, when he turned toward me, I repeated a phrase he had used in the Torres Strait:

"An incident, captain?"

"No, professor, this time it's an accident."

"Serious?"

"Maybe."

"Is there any immediate danger?"

"No."

"The *Nautilus* has run aground?"

"Yes."

"How did this happen?"

"Not through human error but through a caprice of Nature. We made no mistake in our maneuvers. Nevertheless, we can't prevent the laws of equilibrium from operating. We may brave the laws of humanity but we can't withstand the laws of Nature."

Captain Nemo had picked a strange time to philosophize. On the whole, his reflections had told me nothing.

"Do you mind telling me," I finally asked, "what has caused this accident!"

"A huge block of ice, a whole mountain, has turned over," he answered. "When icebergs are eroded at their base by warmer water or by repeated collisions, their center of gravity rises. At the crucial point, they must turn upside down. And that's just what happened here. One of these icebergs somersaulted and struck the *Nautilus,* which was cruising underwater. Then it slid under our hull and lifted us, with irresistible power, up into less congested strata, where we now lie on our side."

"But can't we float the *Nautilus* clear by emptying the ballast tanks, and so return to an upright position?"

"That's what we're doing, professor, you can hear the pumps working. And look at the pressure gauge: it shows that we're ascending. But that block of ice is rising with us, unfortunately, and until some other object stops its upward movement, our position won't change."

Indeed, the *Nautilus* still lay on its side. No doubt it would straighten up when the ice block stopped moving. But we couldn't know whether, at that moment, we would hit the underside of the Ice Bank and be horribly crushed between two frozen surfaces.

I was trying to figure out the possibilities. Captain Nemo never took his eyes off the pressure gauge. Since the iceberg had collapsed, the *Nautilus* had ascended about 150 feet, but it was still listing to starboard.

Suddenly I could feel the hull making a slight movement. Obviously the *Nautilus* was straightening a little. Objects hanging on the walls were going back to their normal positions as the walls approached the vertical. Nobody could speak. With hearts beating fiercely, we watched and felt the ship righting itself. The floor was becoming horizontal under our feet. Ten minutes passed.

"At last," I cried, "we are *upright!*"

"Yes," the captain agreed, heading toward the door of the salon.

"But do you think we can float free?"

"Surely. The ballast tanks aren't empty yet. And when they are, the *Nautilus* will rise to the surface."

The captain left, and I soon understood that he had given orders to halt the ascent of the *Nautilus*. Otherwise we would have hit the underbelly of the Ice Bank. It was better to stay free in midwater.

"That," Conseil said, "is what is known as a narrow escape."

"Yes, we could have been crushed between these two masses of ice, or at the very least, trapped between them. And then, with no way to renew our air supply. . . . Yes, we *have* had a narrow escape."

"If we really did escape," Ned muttered.

I didn't say anything to him—why renew a useless argument? Besides, at that moment the panels opened and light burst through the windows.

True, we were fully afloat. But on each side of the *Nautilus,* about ten meters away, there rose a dazzling wall of ice. And I saw walls above and below us. Above, because the underbelly of the Ice Bank stretched over us like an immense ceiling. Below, because that somersaulting iceberg, sliding bit by bit, had become jammed between the two side walls. The *Nautilus* was therefore enclosed in a genuine tunnel of ice about twenty meters wide and filled with tranquil water. But it should be easy to exit the tunnel by going either ahead or astern, and then sinking a few hundred meters deeper and proceeding in free water under the Ice Bank.

The overhead lights in the salon had been turned off, and still the room was brilliantly illuminated. The walls of ice were acting as powerful reflectors, sending the light of our beacon right back at us. I can't adequately describe the effects our electric rays produced on those huge, whimsically sculpted ice blocks. Their every angle, ridge, and facet gave off a different hue, depending on the nature of the veins running inside the ice. It was a dazzling mine of gems, in particular sapphires and emeralds whose jets of blue and green crisscrossed. Here and there, I could see opaline shades of great subtlety running among blazing points of light that were like so many fiery diamonds, shining so brilliantly my eyes could hardly stand it. The power of our beacon was increased a hundredfold, like a lamp shining through the biconvex lenses of a major lighthouse.

"Beautiful! How beautiful!" Conseil exclaimed.

"Yes," I agreed, "a wonderful spectacle. Isn't it, Ned?"

"Damnation yes! It's superb! I'm furious that I have to admit it. Nobody has ever seen its equal. But this sight could cost us our lives! And to be perfectly honest, I think we're looking at things that God never intended us to see!"

Ned was right, it was too beautiful. But suddenly a cry from Conseil made me turn around.

"What is it?" I asked.

"Master must close his eyes! Master must not look!"

He clapped his hands over his eyes.

"But what happened to you, my boy?"

"I've been stricken blind!"

Involuntarily, I glanced out the window, but my eyes couldn't stand the fiery light that seemed to consume the glass.

I realized what had happened. The *Nautilus* had just started off at great speed. All the glow and luster from the walls of ice had changed into flashes of lightning. The fires from those myriads of diamonds were combined, intensified. Propelled by its powerful engines, the *Nautilus* was moving through a sheath of blinding luminosity.

The panels moved shut. We kept our hands over our eyes, seeing nothing but those concentric gleams that assail the retina when we've stared too long at the sun. It took some time to calm our troubled vision.

Finally, we risked lowering our hands.

"My God, I would never have believed it," sighed Conseil.

"And I can't believe it yet," the Canadian grunted.

"When we get back on land," Conseil continued, "we'll feel so sophisticated, after seeing all these marvels of Nature, we won't ever get excited by those miserable continents and those pitiful creations of humanity! No, the inhabited world will be boring to us."

Such words from that impassive Fleming showed just how excited we had become. But the Canadian did not fail to throw cold water on our enthusiasm:

"The inhabited world! Don't let that worry you, Conseil. You'll never see that world again!"

By then it was five a.m. At that moment the *Nautilus* struck something ahead—I realized that the ram had just hit a block of ice. And this time it could be human error because this submarine tunnel, obstructed by such blocks, was not easy to navigate. I expected that Captain Nemo would change his course slightly, go around these obstacles, stay close to the walls. I felt certain that the way ahead could not be blocked entirely. Nevertheless, the *Nautilus* went into reverse.

"We're going astern?" Conseil asked.

"Yes," I replied. "The tunnel probably has no way out at this end."

"What then?"

"A simple maneuver. We'll back up and use the opening at the southern end. That's all."

I hoped in talking this way to appear more confident than I actually was. Meanwhile the *Nautilus* was moving backward at great speed.

"This way'll take longer," Ned said.

"What does it matter, a few hours more or less, so long as we get out."

"Yes," he repeated, "so long as we get out."

I took a leisurely stroll from the salon to the library. My companions remained seated and kept quite still. Soon I threw myself down on a divan and picked up a book and let my eyes roam mechanically over the print.

Fifteen minutes later Conseil came over and said:

"Does master find that book very interesting?"

"Very," I answered.

"I can believe it. Master is reading his own book."

"My own book?"

Indeed, I was holding my own work on the great submarine depths. I hadn't even realized it. I closed it and resumed my walking up and down. Ned and Conseil got up to go.

"No, stay, friends," I said, blocking their way. "Let's stay together until we get out of this cul-de-sac."

"Whatever pleases master," Conseil said.

For several hours I kept checking the instruments on the wall. The pressure gauge showed that the *Nautilus* kept at a constant depth of 300 meters, the compass that we were still heading south, the log that we were moving at a speed of twenty miles an hour, a speed that seemed excessive in such an enclosed space. But Captain Nemo must have been aware that he couldn't really go too fast, since by then minutes were worth ages.

At 8:25 there was a second collision, this time astern. I could feel the blood draining from my face. My companions came over. I took Conseil's hand and our eyes questioned each other, more directly than if our thoughts had been expressed in words.

Then the captain entered the salon. I went over to him and asked:

"Is our route barred to the south, too?"

"Yes, professor. When the iceberg turned over, it closed off every exit."

"Then we're—hemmed in on all sides?"

"Yes."

SIXTEEN

Lack of Air

S O THEN, THERE were impenetrable frozen walls above, below, and
around the *Nautilus*. We were prisoners of the Ice Bank! The Canadian
banged a table with his powerful fist. Conseil was quiet. I looked at the
captain. His face had resumed its habitual impassivity. His arms were
folded on his chest. He was meditating. And the *Nautilus* had stopped moving.

The captain finally broke into speech:

"Gentlemen," he said calmly, "there are two ways to die in these
circumstances."

This strange personage acted like a mathematics professor going over a
problem with his students.

"The first way," he went on, "is to be crushed to death. The second is to die
from lack of air. I'm not going to mention starving to death because the *Nautilus*'s food supplies would outlast us in any event. So let's concentrate on our
chances of being crushed or asphyxiated."

"As for asphyxiation, captain," I responded, "we have nothing to worry
about. Our air tanks are full."

"Right," Captain Nemo said, "but they hold only enough air for two days.
We've been buried underwater for thirty-six hours and our atmosphere is oppressive, we must renew it soon. And then in another forty-eight hours our
reserve air will be all used up."

"Well then, captain, let's break out of here in less than forty-eight hours!"

"We'll try it, at least. We'll cut through one of these walls."

"Which one?" I asked.

"Borings will tell us which one. I'm going to ground the *Nautilus* on the
lower surface. My men will get into their diving suits and attack the ice wherever it's thinnest.

"May we have the panels open in the salon?" I asked.

"No problem. We're not moving yet."

And he went out. Hissing sounds soon told me that the ballast tanks were
filling up with water. The *Nautilus* slowly settled and rested on the bottom at
a depth of 350 meters, the depth at which the lower shelf of ice lay submerged.

"My friends," I said, "we're in real trouble, but I'm counting on your courage and your strength."

"Professor," Ned answered, "this is not the time to bore you with my protests. I'll do my part for the common good."

"Great, Ned!" I held out my hand to the Canadian.

"And you know," he added, "I can handle a pickaxe as well as I handle a harpoon. Whatever the captain wants done, all he has to do is tell me."

"And he won't refuse your help. So come with me, Ned."

I led the Canadian to the room where some of the *Nautilus*'s crew were getting into their diving suits. I told the captain of Ned's offer, which was promptly accepted. The Canadian put on his sea costume and was ready as soon as the others. Each of them carried a Rouquayrol apparatus on his back, with a generous allowance of pure oxygen. This was a considerable but necessary drain on the ship's reserves. As for the Ruhmkorff lamps, they were unnecessary in this enclosed space brilliantly lighted by our beacon.

Once Ned was dressed I returned to the salon, where the panels were now open. I posted myself next to Conseil and studied the strata surrounding and supporting the *Nautilus*.

In a few minutes, we saw a dozen crewmen set foot on the ice shelf. Ned Land was easily recognized by his great height. Captain Nemo was out there too.

Before digging into the ice, he had to ascertain the best direction in which to work. Long bores were driven into the side walls, but after fifteen meters they were still impeded by the thickness of the ice. There was no point in attacking the ceiling for that was the Ice Bank itself, more than 400 meters high. Captain Nemo then bored into the lower surface and found that ten meters of ice separated us from the water below. Such was the thickness of that iceberg. From that point on, it was a question of chopping out a piece equal in surface area to the *Nautilus*'s waterline. That meant detaching about 6,500 cubic meters to create a hole big enough for the *Nautilus* to sink through

The men set to work at once with indefatigable energy. Instead of digging all around the ship, which would entail still greater problems, Captain Nemo outlined an immense trench on the ice, eight meters from our port quarter. Then his men simultaneously set to work with drills at several points on its circumference. Now they could start chipping with their pickaxes. Soon huge blocks of that compact matter were loosened from its mass. These blocks weighed less than water, and by a curious effect of specific gravity, each block took wing, so to speak, and floated up to the ceiling of the tunnel, which thus thickened above as much as it diminished below. But that didn't matter so long as the lower part was growing thinner.

After two hours of hard work, Ned came back inside, exhausted. He and his companions were replaced by a fresh crew, including Conseil and me. The first mate served as foreman of this second gang.

The water seemed especially cold at first, but wielding my pick soon warmed me up. I found I could work freely, even though I was undergoing a pressure of thirty atmospheres.

After two hours of work, I went inside to snatch some food and rest. I could tell at once the difference between the pure air supplied by my Rouquayrol tank and the *Nautilus*'s atmosphere, which was already charged with carbon dioxide. The *Nautilus*'s air had not been renewed in forty-eight hours, and its ability to sustain life had diminished considerably. Then, after twelve hours had elapsed, we had removed from the outlined area a slice of ice only one meter thick, about 600 cubic meters. Assuming we could equal that every twelve hours, it would still take five nights and four days to finish the job.

"Five nights and four days!" I told my companions. "And we have only two days' supply in the air tanks!"

"Without taking into account," Ned added, "that once we get out of this damned prison, we'll still be confined under the Ice Bank with no sure way of renewing our air supply."

An apt remark. Who could calculate the time needed to get out into the open air? Couldn't we all asphyxiate before we could surface? Were we and our ship destined to perish in this ice tomb? Our situation seemed terrible, but we faced it head-on, with everyone resolved to do his duty to the end.

As I had expected, during the night another one-meter slice was removed from that immense pit. But in the morning, when I was dressed in my diving suit and walking through water that was −6° to −7° centigrade, I noticed that little by little the side walls were getting closer together. The water farthest from the trench, since it was not warmed by the action of men and tools, was tending to freeze. Faced with this new, imminent danger, what now were our chances of salvation? How could we prevent that liquid medium from solidifying and shattering the hull of the *Nautilus* like glass?

I didn't tell my companions about this new danger. What good would it do to dampen the energy they were putting into our painful efforts to escape? But when I got back on board I notified Captain Nemo of this grave complication.[1]

"I know," he said in that calm tone that he could maintain through the worst emergencies. "It's one more danger, but I don't know what we can do about it. Our one chance of success lies in our working faster than the water freezes. We've got to get there first, that's all."

Get there first! I should have known that he would say that!

---

1. In this passage Verne lays out the standard approach for generations of later sci-fi writers. He puts his characters into a novel danger that only their advanced technology could have exposed them to in the first place. The world's first open-sea submarine gets caught between shifting slabs of ice. Verne must now anticipate each development growing naturally out of this crisis and counter it with all his ingenuity. He, his characters, and his readers are in unknown territory.

And his readers can begin to anticipate problems! For instance, some may wonder at what point Nemo's crew will be hacking away at ice too thin to support them? Verne has the option of raising such a question at about the point it will occur to the reader, or of ignoring it so that the reader can collaborate in building the suspense! Then Verne himself can climax the chapter by returning to the very idea that he seems to have overlooked.

For several hours that day I wielded my pickaxe with fierce determination. This work kept up my spirits. Moreover, working meant leaving the *Nautilus,* with its foul, weak air, and putting on the Rouquayrol apparatus and breathing its pure, invigorating oxygen.

Toward evening we had detached another one-meter layer from the trench. When I got back on board I was almost asphyxiated by the carbon dioxide that saturated the air. Oh, if only we had the chemical means to drive out that harmful gas! There was no *real* shortage of oxygen: all that water around us contained considerable quantities of it, and if we could have extracted it with our powerful batteries, we would have had all of it we needed. I had thought it all out, but it was no use because the carbon dioxide produced by our breathing had already pervaded very part of the ship. To absorb it we would have to fill containers with potassium hydroxide and shake them continually. But we had none of that chemical on board and nothing else could do the job.

That evening Captain Nemo was obliged to open the spigots on his air tanks and release a few whiffs of pure oxygen into the interior. If he hadn't done that, we might not have awakened from our sleep.

On that morning of March 26, I once again became a miner, working now on that fifth one-meter layer. The side walls and the ceiling were visibly thicker. It surely looked as if they would join up with each other before the *Nautilus* managed to break out. For a moment despair gripped me and I nearly let the pick slip out of my hands. What was the point of toiling like this if I was to die smothered and crushed by solidified water, a torture the most barbaric mind had not yet invented? I felt as if I was caught between the jaws of a monster, jaws irresistibly closing.

Directing our work and working himself, Captain Nemo passed me by. I tapped him on the arm and pointed to the walls of our prison. The starboard wall alone had advanced to a point less than four meters from the *Nautilus*'s hull.

The captain understood and motioned to me to follow him. We went on board, removing our diving suits, and went into the salon.

"Professor Aronnax, we have to do something on a heroic scale, or we'll be sealed up in this ice as if it were cement."

"Yes," I said, "but what!"

"Oh," he cried, "if only my *Nautilus* were strong enough to withstand that pressure without being crushed!"

"And then . . .?" I couldn't see what he was driving at.

"Don't you see that then the freezing of this water could help us? That this solidification could burst the ice around us as it bursts the hardest stones? Don't you see that it could liberate us instead of destroying us?"

"Oh yes, captain, maybe. But whatever resistance the *Nautilus* may possess, it couldn't withstand that much pressure; it would be flattened out like a sheet of iron."

"I know, professor, we can't rely on Nature to rescue us this time but only on our own ingenuity. We have to fight that freezing and stop it. Not only are the side walls closing in, but we don't have ten feet of water ahead of us or behind us. On every side the ice is gaining on us."

"How much longer," I asked, "will we be getting oxygen from the air tanks?"

The captain looked me straight in the eye.

"After tomorrow, our air tanks will be empty!"

I broke out in a cold sweat. But why should I have been shocked by his answer? We had plunged beneath the open waters at the pole on March 22. It was now March 26. We had lived off the ship's stores for five days. And what was left of the breathable air had to be saved for the crews working outside. Even today, my memories of that situation are so vivid that an involuntary terror comes over me: I feel short of breath as I write these lines!

Meanwhile, motionless and silent, Captain Nemo seemed lost in thought. An idea seemed to surface in his mind and he seemed to cast it aside. He shook his head. But suddenly these words escaped his lips:

"Boiling water!" he murmured.

"Boiling water?" I gasped.

"Yes; professor. We're confined in a relatively small space. If we pumped jets of boiling water into this area, wouldn't that raise the temperature and retard the freezing?"

"It's worth trying!" I said resolutely.

"So let's try it, professor."

First checking the thermometer, we saw it was $-7°$ centigrade outside. Then Captain Nemo led me to the galley where a large distilling machine was providing drinking water by means of evaporation. All the heat our batteries could produce was launched into the coils passing through the liquid. In a few minutes the water reached $100°$ centigrade. Captain Nemo directed the boiling liquid toward the pumps while new water was piped into the machine, in turn to arrive boiling hot at the pumps.

The captain now injected the hot water into the cold water outside. Three hours later our thermometer read $-6°$ out there. One degree gained! Two hours later the thermometer had risen to $-4°$.

After watching the captain as he checked every phase of the operation, I told him:

"It's doing the trick."

"I think so," he answered. "We won't be crushed—now we only have to worry about being asphyxiated."

During the night the temperature of the surrounding water rose to $-1°$ centigrade. The injections couldn't get it any higher. But I was reassured because seawater will not freeze until it drops to $-2°$ centigrade.

By the next day, March 27, we had wrenched six one-meter layers of ice from their socket. We only had four more meters to dig out. That meant forty-eight hours of work still left. And now the air could no longer be renewed inside. And that day it got worse and worse.

I felt I was carrying an oppressive weight. By three p.m. this sensation was overwhelming, agonizing. I yawned so wide I expected to dislocate my jaws. My lungs gasped in their effort to inhale that fuel necessary for life, a fuel that grew scarcer and scarcer. Mental torpor took hold of me. I lay outstretched, weak, almost unconscious. My gallant Conseil, showing the same symptoms and suffering the same as I was, never left my side. He would take my hand and encourage me, and I even heard him murmur:

"Oh, if only I could stop breathing and leave more air for master!"

To hear him talk that way brought tears to my eyes.

The more intolerable our situation became inside, the more eagerly we got into our diving suits to take our turns outside. Our picks resounded on that bed of ice. Our arms grew weary, hands were rubbed raw, but who cared about fatigue, what difference were aches and pains, if we had lifegiving air in our lungs! We were breathing, we were breathing!

Yet no one tried to prolong his work beyond the time allotted him. His shift completed, each man surrendered to a gasping companion that air tank that would revive him. Captain Nemo set the example and was the first to submit to this severe discipline. When his time was up, he yielded his apparatus to another and reentered the foul air on board, calm as always, unflinching, uncomplaining.

That day the quota was accomplished with special vigor because we could see that only two meters remained to be dug out. Only two meters between us and the open sea! But the ship's air tanks were nearly empty. The little air left had to be reserved for the workmen outside. Not one atom for inside the *Nautilus!*

When I went back on board, I felt half suffocated. What a night! I can't depict it, for such suffering defies description. Next day I was short-winded. Headaches and dizziness made me reel like a drunk. All my companions felt the same way. Some crewmen were at their last gasp.

That day, the sixth of our imprisonment, Captain Nemo decided that picks and pickaxes were too slow and he should try to crush the ice layer still separating us from the water below. The man had retained his composure and his energy. He had subdued physical pain with moral strength. He could still think, plan, and act.

At his command the craft was lightened, that is, raised from its ice bed by a change in its specific gravity. When it was afloat, the crew towed it, hauling it directly over the trench outlined to conform to the ship's waterline.[2] Then the ballast tanks took in water; the boat sank into its socket.

Now the entire crew returned on board and the double door leading to the outside world was shut. The *Nautilus* was resting on a layer of ice only one meter thick and pierced by bores in a thousand places.

2. Now Verne resolves the dilemma, as the previous note hints, by returning to a seemingly overlooked idea. This "ace in the hole" will prove not only practical but dramatic. As befits the climax of this grim adventure.

Death by suffocation

The crew opened the stopcocks on the ballast tanks and 100 cubic meters of water rushed in, increasing the *Nautilus*'s weight by 100,000 kilograms.

We waited, we listened, we ignored our pain, we hoped once more. We had staked our lives on this one last gamble.

Despite the buzzing in my head I could hear vibrations under our hull. We tilted. The ice cracked with a noise like paper tearing and the *Nautilus* was sinking.

"We're getting through!" Conseil murmured in my ear.

I couldn't answer him. I could only grasp his hand, squeezing it involuntarily.

All at once, dragged down by its terrific excess load, the *Nautilus* sank into the waters like a cannonball, dropping as if in a vacuum!

Our full electric power was applied to the pumps, which began to expel water from the ballast tanks. In a few minutes the pumps had checked our descent. The pressure gauge soon showed we were ascending. Going full speed, sweeping us northward, the propeller made our iron hull tremble down to its bolts.

But how long would it take to navigate under the Ice Bank and out into the open sea? Another day? I knew I could die before then.

Stretched out on a divan in the library, I was suffocating. My face was violet, my lips blue,[3] my mind not functioning. I no longer saw, no longer heard. I had lost all sense of time. I could not even contract my muscles.

I can't estimate how many hours I spent in that condition. But I was aware that my death agonies had begun. I realized I was about to die . . .

Suddenly I revived. Whiffs of air were reaching my lungs. Had we surfaced? Had we reached the end of the Ice Bank?

Not so! My two gallant friends, Ned and Conseil, were sacrificing themselves to save me. They had discovered that some few molecules of air remained in one of the Rouquayrol tanks. Instead of breathing it themselves they had saved it for me, and while they were suffocating they poured life into me drop by drop. I tried to push the tank away, but they held my hands, and for several moments I breathed voluptuously.

My eyes flew to the clock. Eleven a.m. It had to be March 28. The *Nautilus* was traveling at the frightful speed of forty miles per hour. It actually *writhed* in the water.

Where was Captain Nemo? Had he succumbed? Had his companions perished with him?

At that moment the pressure gauge showed we were no more than twenty feet from the surface. We were separated from fresh air by a thin ice field! Could we crash through it?

3. How can Aronnax tell that his face is purple, his lips blue, when he's lying on a divan without a mirror anywhere in sight? Verne wrote in those benighted times before Henry James made both author and reader jumpy about "point of view."

Perhaps! In any event, the *Nautilus* was going to try. I could feel it assuming an oblique position, lowering the stern, raising the ram. The captain had accomplished this maneuver by taking in more water in the tanks astern. Next, impelled forward and upward by its powerful engines, it attacked the ice field from underneath like a formidable battering ram. It split the ice a bit at a time, pulling back, then putting on full speed again into the ice, until at last, carried away by its own momentum, it shot through and out onto that frozen surface, crushing the ice beneath its weight.

The hatches were opened—one might say *wrenched* open—and waves of pure air came flooding into every part of the *Nautilus*.

Lack of Air

ॐ

SEVENTEEN

From Cape Horn to the Amazon

I CAN'T IMAGINE how I got out onto the platform. Maybe the Canadian had carried me there. But I was breathing. I was inhaling the bracing sea air. Next to me my two companions were getting drunk on those fresh molecules. We were the opposite of people who have suffered from long starvation: they must be very careful not to gulp down great quantities of food in a hurry. We did not have to practice such caution; we could take in fresh air by the lungful, and it was the sea breeze, the very sea breeze, that poured into us this voluptuous intoxication.

"Ah!" Conseil sighed. "Such wonderful oxygen. Master need not feel selfish about breathing it! There's enough for everybody."

Ned didn't say anything, but he opened his jaws wide enough to scare off a shark. And what powerful inhalations! He sucked in air like a furnace going full blast.

We soon regained our strength and when I was finally able to look around, I realized that we were alone on the platform. Not one crewman. Not even Captain Nemo. Those strange seamen on the *Nautilus* were satisfied with the air now circulating inside the ship. Not one of them had come up to enjoy the sea breeze.[1]

My first words were words of thanks and gratitude to my companions. Ned and Conseil had actually prolonged my life during the final hours of our ordeal. But no expression of gratitude could repay them fully for their devotion.

"Ah, professor," Ned Land replied, "don't even mention it! How could you give us any credit for something like that? It was simple, a matter of elementary arithmetic. Your life is worth more than ours! So we had to save you."

---

1. Here we have the most grotesque behavior yet from these strange seamen. It's enough for them that fresh air will now circulate through the vessel: they feel no need to dash on deck. Outlaws all, they are presumably toughened by resistance and rebellion. They toil in submarine mines, in ice traps, in combats with sperm whales and other aggressors. Their only rewards seem to be quiet satisfaction in helping the victims of oppression and plentiful opportunity to meditate on the past.

"No, no, Ned, it isn't worth more. No person is superior to a man as good and generous as you are."

"All right, if you say so." He was very embarrassed.

"And Conseil," I went on, "how you must have suffered!"

"Not too much, if master doesn't mind my saying so. I was a bit out of breath, but I was expecting to get used to it. When I saw master about to faint, I lost all desire to breathe. It took the wind out of me, so to—"

Now he seemed embarrassed, too, confused perhaps by the unexpected pun and his cliche.

"My friends," I tried to sum it up, "we are bound to each other forever, and I am under infinite obligation to you."

"And I'll take advantage of that," the Canadian exclaimed.

"Meaning what?" Conseil wanted to know.

"Meaning I'll have the right to drag you with me when I leave this infernal *Nautilus*."

"Incidentally," Conseil put in, "are we heading in a favorable direction?"

"Yes," I reassured them, "we're heading toward the sun, and here the sun means north."

"No doubt," Ned agreed, "but are we heading north into the Pacific or north into the Atlantic? Into inhabited or uninhabited areas?"

I didn't have an answer to those questions, but I was afraid Captain Nemo would take us not homeward but rather into that vast ocean that bathes both the Asian and the American shores. In that way he could both complete his tour of the submarine world and return to those seas where the *Nautilus* had its greatest freedom. But if we did go back to the Pacific, far from every populated area, what would happen to Ned's plans?

We would soon find out. The *Nautilus* was traveling fast. We cleared the Antarctic Circle and then headed for the promontory of Cape Horn. We were abreast of the tip of South America by seven p.m., March 31.

By then all our past sufferings were forgotten. All memory of that imprisonment under the Ice Bank faded from our minds. We dreamed only of the future. Captain Nemo no longer came into the salon or out onto the platform. Each day it was the first mate who marked our position on the chart and so I could figure out where we were heading. And that night it became obvious to me that we were returning north by the Atlantic route.

I passed on the good news to Ned and Conseil.

"Good news," Ned agreed, "but just where in the north are we going?"

"That I don't know yet."

"Maybe your captain, having discovered the South Pole, wants now to find the North Pole and then get to the Pacific through the famous Northwest Passage?"

"Now don't *dare* him to do that," murmured Conseil.

"Don't worry," the Canadian replied. "We will have left him before then."

"Nevertheless," Conseil added, "this Captain Nemo is a superman, and we shall never regret having known him."

"Especially after we've left him!" Ned replied.

Next day, April 1, when the *Nautilus* mounted to the surface shortly before noon, we sighted land to the west. It was Tierra del Fuego; early navigators gave it that name—Land of Fire—when they first saw the many columns of smoke that rose from the natives' huts.[2] Tierra del Fuego is a large island group, thirty leagues long and eighty leagues wide, extending between latitudes 53° and 56° south, and between longitudes 67° 50′ and 77° 15′ west. Its coast seemed flat but in the distance I could see high mountains. I even thought I could make out Mt. Sarmiento, which rises 2,070 meters above sea level; it's a block of shale shaped like a pyramid with a very pointy summit. Depending on whether it's veiled in mist or clear, it "announces bad or good weather," as Ned Land told me.

"Then it's a first-class barometer, my friend."

"Yes, professor, it's a natural barometer. And it served me well when I used to sail the narrows of the Strait of Magellan."

By now the peak was standing out distinctly against the sky. That "announced" good weather. And so it proved.

The *Nautilus* submerged and drew near the coast, cruising along it for just a few miles. Standing at the salon windows I saw some long creepers and gigantic fucus plants, bulb-bearing seaweed, specimens of which I had seen earlier in the open sea at the pole; with their glossy, sticky filaments, they measured as much as 300 meters long; genuine cables more than an inch thick and very tough, they are often used as mooring lines for ships. Another weed, known as velp, with leaves four feet long, was growing among the coral and carpeting the floor of the sea. It provided both nests and nourishment for myriads of crustaceans and mollusks, for crabs and cuttlefish. Seals and otters were dining sumptuously, combining meat from fish with ocean vegetables, somewhat like the English with their Irish stews.

The *Nautilus* sped rapidly over those lush, luxuriant depths. Toward evening we drew near the Falkland Islands, whose rugged summits I identified the next day. The sea was relatively shallow there. So not without good reason, I assumed that those two islands, together with the many islets surrounding them, were once part of the Magellan shores. The Falkland Islands were proba-

2. The Ona, Yahgan, and Alacaluf Indians who inhabited del Fuego were soon all but wiped out by Europeans who coveted the good pasture land, oil, and gold of these shores. The outcome of such colonial aggression is dramatized by Verne in his posthumously published novel (possibly reworked and completed by his son Michel) *The Survivors of the "Jonathan"* (1909). Early in the book the Magellan Strait is described as "belonging to no one. . . . It was not one of those well-ordered states where the police are interested in people's past lives and where it is impossible to remain unknown for long. Here, nobody was authorized to exercise authority, and a man could live in complete liberty, free of all constraint of law and custom." But when gold is found in del Fuego, the islands are overwhelmed by invaders from five continents, and foreign control is firmly established.

bly discovered by the famous navigator John Davys, who named them the Davys Southern Islands. Later Richard Hawkins named them the Maidenland, after the Virgin. At the beginning of the eighteenth century, Breton fishermen from Saint-Malo renamed them the Malouines, and finally, the British, to whom they now belong, called them the Falklands.

In those waterways our nets brought up some fine samples of algae, in particular certain fucus plants whose roots were laden with the world's best mussels. Geese and duck landed on the platform by the dozens and soon took their place on the ship's bill of fare. As for fish, I especially observed some bony fish of the goby genus, above all some gudgeon two decimeters long, sprinkled with white and yellow spots.

I also admired the many medusas, including the most beautiful of their breed, the compass jellyfish, found only in the Falkland seas. Some of them were shaped like a smooth semispheric umbrella, with red and brown stripes and a fringe of twelve symmetrical tentacles. Others looked like overturned baskets from which there trailed wide leaves and long red twigs. They swam with quiverings of their four leaflike arms, letting the rich tresses of their tentacles float in the water.[3] I would like to have preserved a few specimens of these delicate zoophytes, but they are clouds, shadows, illusions that dissolve, melt, or evaporate after they are removed from their native element.

When the last heights of the Falklands sank beneath the horizon, the *Nautilus* submerged to a depth between twenty and twenty-five meters and followed the South American coast. Captain Nemo did not show himself.

We did not leave those Patagonian waterways until April 3, cruising now under the ocean, then on the surface. The *Nautilus* passed the wide estuary at the mouth of the Rio de la Plata and on April 4 we lay abreast of Uruguay but fifty miles out. Still heading north, we followed the long windings of the shores of South America. By then we had navigated 16,000 leagues since our embarkation in the seas of Japan.

Toward eleven a.m. we cut the Tropic of Capricorn at the 37th meridian and passed well out from Cape Frio. It was clear, to Ned Land's great discomfort, that Captain Nemo had no love for Brazil's inhabited coasts because he traveled past at dizzying speed. Not even the swiftest fish or birds could keep up with us, and so the natural curiosities of those seas eluded our study.

We maintained this pace for several days, until on the evening of April 9, we sighted South America's easternmost tip, Cape São Roque. But then the *Nautilus* veered away again, searching for the lowest depths of a submarine valley hollowed out between that cape and Sierra Leone on the African coast. That valley forks into two arms parallel with the West Indies and ends to the north in an enormous depression 9,000 meters deep. Between there and the Lesser Antilles, the ocean's geologic profile features a steeply carved cliff six

---

3. Medusas are named after the Gorgon Medusa, a maiden who figures in Greek mythology. Her hair was a nest of snakes, and she could *petrify* anyone who looked her in the face. The medusas Aronnax is viewing can *paralyze* their prey with stingers on their tentacles.

kilometers high, and parallel with the Cape Verde Islands there is another wall no less imposing; between these two barriers lies the submerged continent of Atlantis. The floor of that immense valley is dotted with underwater mountains that give these submarine regions a very picturesque appearance. This information is based on certain hand-drawn charts I found in the *Nautilus*'s library, charts evidently prepared by Captain Nemo himself according to his own personal observations.[4]

For two days we visited those deep, deserted waters by using our slanting fins. The *Nautilus* would do long diagonal dives that would take us to every level. But on April 11 we rose abruptly, and we saw the shore at the mouth of the Amazon River, a vast estuary whose outpouring is so considerable that it freshens—desalts—the ocean over an area of several leagues.

We crossed the equator. Twenty miles to the west lay Guiana, a French territory where we might easily have found refuge. But the wind was blowing in strong gusts, and the furious waves were too much for our simple dinghy. Apparently Ned also understood that because he didn't even mention escaping to me. I made no allusion to his plans because I did not want to spur him into a rash venture doomed to failure.

I compensated myself for that delay by doing some interesting research. For those two days—April 11 and 12—the *Nautilus* stayed on the surface, and our dragnet brought up a simply miraculous catch of zoophytes, fish, and reptiles.

Some zoophytes were dredged up by the chain of our trawl. Most of them were beautiful sea anemones of the family Actinidia, including among other species the *Phyctalis protexta,* unique to that part of the ocean. Their small cylindrical trunk is adorned with vertical lines, mottled with red spots, and crowned with a marvelous blossoming of tentacles. As for the mollusks, they consisted of species I had already observed: some turret snails; some olive shells of the "tent olive" species with neatly intersecting lines and ruddy spots standing out vividly against a flesh-colored background; some strange spider conches that looked like petrified scorpions; some translucent glass snails; argonauts; exceedingly edible cuttlefish; and certain species of squid that naturalists of antiquity classified with the flying fish and which are now used as bait for catching codfish.

And there were several fish in those waterways that I had not yet had a chance to observe. Among cartilaginous fish: some brook lamprey, a kind of eel fifteen inches long, head greenish, fins violet, back bluish gray, belly a silvery brown with bright spots, iris of the eye encircled in gold, curious creatures that the Amazon must have swept out to sea because their natural habitat is fresh water; some sting rays, the muzzle pointed, the tail slender, long and armed with an extended, serrated sting; small sharks one meter long with gray and whitish flanks, their teeth arranged in several rows and bent backward, crea-

4. Nemo's charting of the *cliff* and *wall* cited by Aronnax suggests a portion of the Mid-Atlantic Ridge, one of the globe's most important geologic features. It is now known to be part of the Mid-Ocean Ridge that runs continuously for 40,000 miles along the bottoms of the world's oceans.

tures commonly known as carpet sharks; some batfish, a sort of reddish isosceles triangle half a meter long whose pectoral fins are attached by fleshy extensions that make them look like bats, although a horn-covered appendage near the nostrils earns them the nickname of sea unicorns; finally, some species of triggerfish, the cucuyo whose stippled flanks glitter with sparkling gold, and the leatherjacket, bright violet with an iridescent luster like a pigeon's throat.

I will conclude this catalog, somewhat dry perhaps but very exact,[5] with the series of bony fish that I observed: eels of the genus *Apteronotus* whose snow-white muzzle is very blunt, the body a lovely black and equipped with a very long, slender, fleshy whip; long sardines from the genus *Odontognathus,* like three-decimeter pike, resplendent with a bright silver glow; Guaranian mackerel with two anal fins; black-tinted rudderfish that fishermen catch by using torches—fish measuring two meters and boasting white, firm, plump meat that when fresh tastes like eel, but when dried, like smoked salmon; semired wrasse with scales only at the bases of their dorsal and anal fins; grunts on which gold and silver mingle their luster with that of ruby and topaz; yellow-tailed gilthead whose flesh is very dainty and whose phosphorescence betrays their presence in the water; porgies tinted orange, with slender tongues; croakers with golden caudal fins; black surgeonfish; four-eyed fish from Surinam, etc. And that "et cetera" will not prevent my citing one more fish that Conseil, with good reason, will remember long and well.

One of our nets brought up a very flat ray that weighed some twenty kilograms; if its tail had been chopped off, it would have formed a perfectly round disk. It was white underneath and reddish above, with large round spots of deep blue encircled in black, its hide quite glossy and ending in a double-lobed fin. Laid out on the platform, it struggled convulsively, trying to turn back over onto its stomach, and it was about to flip itself over the side and back into the water. But Conseil, unwilling to let the fish go, rushed at it and before I could stop him, he seized it with both hands.

He was immediately thrown down, legs in the air, half paralyzed, crying out: "Oh master! Master! Will you please help me!"

Now that was the first time the poor lad had not addressed me in the third person![6]

From Cape Horn to the Amazon

⧎

339

5. Another of Aronnax's "detour signs," hinting that the fish details are skippable. (WJM detects a pun in Aronnax's use of the word *dry,* to describe such a "wet" subject.)

6. This carefully set-up reversal can be viewed as simply a gag, or, more gravely, as Conseil's attempt to establish a more human relationship with his boss.

Beyond this, Conseil's lapse hints at a growing, pervasive strain in the *Nautilus*'s underwater existence—things are starting to erode and crumble. Aronnax notes that Nemo has gone into permanent hiding, that he "no longer came into the salon or out onto the platform." Next, Conseil will not only breach his own verbal etiquette, but in the following chapter a crewman will also drop his guard in a similar fashion. In still later chapters we'll see both Nemo and Ned sinking into deep depressions. We have a mounting sense of insanity and self-destruction spreading through the ship.

Verne still has several exciting episodes in store. But underneath them, his novel is now gathering impetus for its final catastrophe.

Ned Land and I sat him up and massaged his tightly cramped arms. By the time he had regained his five senses that eternal classifier was murmuring:

"Class of cartilaginous fish, order Chondropterygia with fixed gills, suborder Selacia, family Rajiiforma, genus electric ray!"

"Yes, my friend," I responded, "that was an electric ray that did this to you."

"Oh, master can trust me in this matter," he said. "I'll get my revenge on that animal!"

"How?"

"I'll eat it!"

And that is exactly what he did that very night, but purely for spite, because frankly, that animal was tough as leather.[7]

Poor Conseil had attacked an electric ray of the most dangerous species, the cumana. Living in a medium like water that conducts electricity, this bizarre animal can hurl lightning bolts at fish several meters away, so great is the power of its electric organ—an organ whose two main surfaces measure no less than twenty-seven square feet!

The *Nautilus* drew near the mouth of the Maroni River, on the coast of Dutch Guiana, on the next day, April 12. There we saw several groups of sea cows living in family units. These were manatees, who belong to the order Sirenia, like the dugong and Steller's sea cow.[8] Peaceful and inoffensive, these fine animals were six to seven meters long and must have weighed at least 4,000 kilograms each. I told Ned Land and Conseil how prescient Nature had assigned an important role to these mammals. Like the seals, manatees are destined to graze the submarine prairies, and so they destroy those masses of weeds that obstruct the mouths of tropical rivers.

"And do you know," I added, "what has happened since humanity has almost wiped out these useful races? Those weeds are rotting, they are fouling the air, and that poisoned air causes the yellow fever that devastates these remarkable countries. That toxic vegetation has increased beneath these warm seas of the Torrid Zone, and so the disease spreads unchecked from the mouth of the Rio de la Plata to Florida!"

And if Professor Toussenel is correct, this plague is nothing compared to the scourge that will strike our descendants once we have exterminated all whales and seals. Then, overpopulated with cuttlefish, jellyfish, and squid, the oceans will become vast centers of infection, since their waters will no longer contain "those vast stomachs that God has assigned to scouring the surface of the seas."[9]

7. Although inedible, the poor electric ray isn't good for much else at this point. Once he uses his electric charge, it takes him days to recharge his batteries.

8. The last member of the order Sirenia to be discovered, the first to be extinguished by the greed of man. The docile beasts were found in the Bering Strait by Dr. George Steller, a German naturalist, in 1741. The word spread. Within thirty years arctic fishermen killed off most of these sea cows. No more have been reported after Aronnax's time.

9. Yellow fever, it turns out, is not produced by putrefaction of uneaten marine vegetation. In 1900 it will be proven that the disease is caused by a virus transmitted by mosquitoes.

Conseil and the ray

Meanwhile, without holding these theories in disdain, the *Nautilus*'s crew captured half a dozen of these manatees. Essentially, it was a question of stocking the ship's pantry with their meat, which is superior to beef and veal. But the hunting of manatees was not an exciting sport. They offered no resistance to being struck down. And so several thousand kilos of meat were stored on board to be dried and preserved.

And that day the *Nautilus*'s food supply was further increased by a very strange way of fishing in seas that proved full of game. Our dragnet brought up in its meshes a certain number of fish whose heads are crowned with an oval plaque with fleshy edges. These were suckerfish, from the third family of sub-brachian Malacopterygia. Those flat disks atop their heads consist of transverse plates of movable cartilage between which these animals can create a vacuum, enabling them to fasten themselves to objects, like suction cups.

The remoras I had seen in the Mediterranean are akin to this species. But the creature in question here was the *Echeneis osteochara,* found only in these waters. Our crewmen took them out of the nets and put them in buckets of water.

This stage of the hunt completed, the *Nautilus* went nearer to the coast. There a number of sea turtles were sleeping on the surface. It would have been difficult to capture these precious reptiles, because they wake up at the slightest sound and their solid shell resists harpoons. But our suckerfish would help us capture the turtles with precision and certainty. Indeed, this animal is a living fishhook, promising wealth and happiness to the most inexperienced fisherman.

The *Nautilus*'s crew attached to the tails of the suckerfish a ring large enough not to cramp their movements, and to the ring they tied a long line, the other end of which was moored on board.

The crewmen threw the suckerfish into the sea and there they got to work immediately, attaching themselves to the shells of the turtles. Their tenacity was such that they would allow themselves to be pulled apart rather than relax their grip. When they were hauled back on board, the turtles came too!

That's how we captured several loggerheads, reptiles a meter wide, weighing 200 kilos each. Their shells are covered with large horny plates, thin, brown, and transparent with white and yellow markings; they fetch a good price in the market. Besides, their flesh was excellent to eat, tasting like the green turtles.

This fishing ended our sojourn in the waters near the Amazon, and that night the *Nautilus* was again headed for the high seas.

EIGHTEEN

Giant Squid

FOR SEVERAL DAYS the *Nautilus* sailed far from the American coast. Clearly it did not want to enter the Caribbean Sea or the Gulf of Mexico. It was not a question of trouble in shallow waters, since the mean depth of those seas is 1,800 meters; but strewn with islands and plowed by steamers, those waters probably would have made Captain Nemo feel extremely uncomfortable.

On April 16, we did sight Martinique and Guadeloupe from a distance of about thirty miles. For just an instant I got a glimpse of their lofty peaks.

The Canadian was quite disheartened. He had counted on being able to escape in the gulf, either by reaching shore or by pulling alongside one of the numerous boats plying a coastal trade from one island to another. Flight would have been quite easy there, if Ned had been able to seize the dinghy without the captain's knowledge. But in midocean it was unthinkable.

The Canadian, Conseil, and I had a pretty long talk on this subject. We had been prisoners aboard the *Nautilus* for six months. We had traveled 17,000 leagues and, as Ned Land put it, there was no reason to believe that it would ever end. Therefore he made a proposal I had not at all anticipated. We should pose this question to Captain Nemo, categorically: Do you plan to keep us prisoners on this ship indefinitely?

Such a step was distasteful to me. To my mind it could lead nowhere. We should hope for nothing from the commander of the *Nautilus* but rely only on ourselves. Besides, for some time now the man had grown more somber, more withdrawn, less sociable. He seemed to be avoiding me. I met him only at rare intervals. Formerly, he used to take pleasure in explaining the underwater world to me; now he left me to my own research and no longer came into the salon.

What changes had come over him? For what reason? I had done nothing to deserve this, and I could not blame myself. Was our presence on board beginning to be a burden or a nuisance to him? Even so, I had no illusions about his being ready to set us free.

So I begged Ned to let me think it over before taking action. If such a step provoked a refusal from the captain, it might certainly renew his suspicions, make our situation even more difficult, and jeopardize the Canadian's plans. Of course, I could not use our health as an argument. Except for that grueling ordeal under the Ice Bank at the South Pole, we had never enjoyed *better* health, neither Ned, Conseil, nor I. The nutritious diet, the invigorating sea air, the regular routine, the uniform temperature in which we lived—all these circumstances kept illness at bay. Moreover, for a man like Captain Nemo, who did not miss life on land, who was completely at home at sea, who could go wherever he wished, who could pursue that life of secrecy to which he seemed committed, I could understand such an existence. But not for us: we had not broken with humanity. For my part, I did not want my pioneering research to be buried with my bones. I had the right and the ability now to produce the definitive book on the sea, and I wanted that work to see the light of day.

And here once more, through the panels opening into those Caribbean waters ten meters below the surface, how many fascinating things I was able to study and enter in my daily notes! Among other zoophytes there were some Portuguese men-of-war known as *Physalia pelagica,* resembling huge oblong bladders with a pearly sheen, spreading their membranes to the wind, letting their blue tentacles drift like silken threads; to the casual eye, charming jellyfish, but to the touch, nettles oozing poisonous fluid. Among the articulates, there were some annelid worms a meter-and-a-half long, armed with a pink horn, furnished with 1,700 organs of locomotion, snaking through the water and throwing off every gleam in the solar spectrum. Among various fish, I saw some manta rays,[1] enormous cartilaginous fish ten feet long and weighing 600 pounds, their pectoral fin triangular, their midback slightly arched, their eyes at the edge of the face, at the front of the head; they floated like wreckage, sometimes fastening onto our windows like opaque shutters. There were some American triggerfish, dressed only in black and white; some feather-shaped gobies, long and plump, with yellow fins and a jutting lower jaw; some sixteen-decimeter mackerel with short, sharp teeth, fish covered with small scales and related to the albacore species. Next came clouds of red mullet corseted in golden stripes from head to tail, their resplendent fins quivering. These masterpieces of jewelry were once considered sacred to the goddess Diana and were much in demand by wealthy Romans. There was a saying about them: "He who catches them doesn't eat them!" Lastly, I saw golden angelfish, garbed in velvet and silk with emerald ribbons, passing by like lords and ladies of Verona; some spurred gilthead rushed by on the strength of their powerful thoracic fins; some thread herring fifteen inches long were wrapped in a phosphorescent gleam; some gray mullet thrashed the sea with their large fleshy tails; some red salmon seemed to mow the waves with their slicing pectorals; and silvery

---

1. The French gives *raies-molubars,* which Mercier's 1873 translation renders as "Malabar rays." This is unconvincing: II 1 and II 3 demonstrate that Verne spelled "Malabar" exactly as we do. A manta is indicated for two reasons: (1) Verne's description fits; (2) The manta (today classed in the family Mobulidae) used to sport the scientific name of *Mobula mobula.* So we're evidently staring at another compositor's error: the French needs to read *raies-mobulars.*

moonfish, worthy of their name, rose on the horizon of the waters like so many pale moons.

How many more marvelous specimens, many new to me, I might have observed if the *Nautilus* had not little by little settled to the lower strata! Our slanting fins directed us down to 2,000 meters, then to 3,500 meters. There animal life was represented only by some sea lilies; some starfish; some charming crinoids with bell-shaped heads, their straight stalks supporting little chalices; some top shell snails; some blood-red tooth shells; and some fissurella snails, a large species of coastal mollusk.

On April 20 we came back up to an average depth of 1,500 meters. The land nearest us was the Bahamas, spread out like a batch of cobblestones. There, tall submarine cliffs reared up, straight walls formed by stones arranged like bricks, between which there were black caves so deep our electric rays could not penetrate them.

Those stones were covered with huge weeds, immense sea tangle, gigantic fucus: a genuine trellis of water plants fit for a world of Titans.

Talking about these colossal plants, Conseil, Ned, and I were naturally led into a discussion of the colossal animals of the sea. The one was seemingly intended as food for the other. Nevertheless, as I peered through the windows of the *Nautilus*—which was almost motionless at the moment—I could see nothing among those long filaments but the principal articulates of the division Brachyura: spider crabs with long legs; violet crabs; and those sponge crabs found only in Caribbean waters.

It was about eleven o'clock when Ned Land drew my attention to a formidable swarming, wriggling movement out in those huge weeds.

"Well, those are the kinds of caves that squid live in," I said, "and I wouldn't be surprised to see some of those monsters in there."

"What!" Conseil put in. "Squid, simple squid from the class Cephalopoda?"

"No," I said, "giant squid. But Ned might have been seeing things. There's nothing like that out there."[2]

"Too bad," Conseil said. "I'd like to come face-to-face with one of those giant squid I've heard so much about—the ones that can drag a ship to the bottom of the abyss. They're called krak—"

"*Crock* is right," Ned cut in sarcastically.

"Krakens!" Conseil finished his word without wincing at Ned's witticism.[3]

"Nobody can convince me that such animals exist," Ned snorted.

"Why not?" Conseil asked. "We believed in master's narwhale!"

2. To Verne's original readers, this was an instant reminder of numerous appearances in the 1860s by giant oceangoing cephalopods.

3. As Ned's attitude indicates, these krakens were once thought to be products of the imagination. Today they are generally defined as "fabulous Scandinavian sea monsters." But with the wisdom of hindsight we can see that the Scandinavian mariners had actually spotted the kind of *giant squid* that would make scores of documented appearances in the Atlantic and Mediterranean during Aronnax's lifetime.

"And we were wrong, Conseil!"

"Yes, but there are probably lots of people who still do believe in it!"

"Probably, Conseil," I agreed. "But as for me, I'm determined now not to believe in such monsters until I've dissected one with my own hands."

"But doesn't master believe in giant squid?" Conseil asked me.

"Yikes!" the Canadian cried. "Who in Hades ever did believe in giant squid?"

"Lots of people, Ned, my friend."

"Maybe scientists but not fishermen."

"Pardon me, Ned. Fishermen *and* scientists."

"Why I—to whom you are speaking," Conseil said with the world's most serious tone of voice, "I recall perfectly seeing a big longboat dragged under the waves by the arms of a squid."

"You saw that?" the Canadian asked.

"Yes, Ned."

"With your own eyes?"

"With my own eyes."

"Where, may I ask?"

"At Saint-Malo," Conseil replied imperturbably.

"In the harbor?" Ned asked sarcastically.

"No, in a church."

"In a church!" the Canadian exclaimed.

"Yes, friend Ned. They had a painting that portrayed the squid in question."

"Oh great!" Ned burst into laughter. "Mr. Conseil has put me in my place."

"Actually, he's right," I said. "I've heard about that painting. But the story it portrays is taken from a legend, and you know how skeptical a naturalist has to be about legends. Besides, when it's a question of monsters, the human imagination always tends to run amuck. People not only claimed that squid could drag ships under, but a certain Olaus Magnus tells of a cephalopod a mile long that looked more like an island than an animal. There's also the story of the Bishop of Trondheim who set up an altar on a big rock. When he finished saying mass, the rock moved back into the sea. That rock was a giant squid."

"And that's all we know?" asked the Canadian.

"No," I went on, "another bishop, Bishop Pontoppidan of Bergen, tells of a giant squid so big a cavalry regiment could maneuver on it."

"They did go on, didn't they, those bishops of yore!" Ned Land said.

"Finally, the naturalists of antiquity describe some monsters with mouths as big as a gulf. They were so large they couldn't get through the Strait of Gibraltar."

"That story gets the prize," Ned said.

"But is there any truth in all these stories?" Conseil asked.

"None, my friends, none at least in those tales that pass the limits of probability and mount toward fable or legend. Still, there had to be something real to excite the imagination of those storytellers. We know for sure that there are species of squid that are very large, though still smaller than whales. Aristotle measured one squid as five cubits long—that's 3.1 meters. Our own fishermen often see squid that are over 1.8 meters long. And the museums of Trieste and Montpellier do have squid carcasses that are two meters in length. Besides—and here's the point!—naturalists figure that one of these animals only six feet long would have tentacles twenty-seven feet long! Now that would make a formidable monster."

"Does anybody fish for them nowadays?" the Canadian asked.

"Well, if they don't fish for them, sailors at least see them. A friend of mine—Captain Paul Bos of Le Havre—has often told me of the time he encountered one of these colossal monsters in the Indian seas. But the most astonishing event—which proves that these gigantic animals are really out there—took place just recently, in 1861."

"What happened?" Ned Land asked.

"Well, in 1861, to the northeast of Tenerife, and very nearly in the latitude we're in now, the crew of the gunboat *Alecton* spied a monstrous squid swimming nearby. Commander Bouguer brought his ship closer and his men attacked it with blows from harpoons and blasts from firearms, but without success, because bullets and blades passed through its soft flesh as if it were loose jelly. Then they tried many times to get a noose around the mollusk's body. When they finally succeeded in that, the noose slid as far as the caudal fins and stopped. Then they tried to haul the monster up on board, but it weighed so much that when they tugged on the rope, it simply pulled off the animal's tail, and, deprived of that embellishment, the squid disappeared beneath the waters."

"Finally, we have some real facts," Ned said.

"Indisputable facts, my gallant Ned. There have been many suggestions to call that animal 'Bouguer's Squid'."[4]

"How long was it?" the Canadian asked.

"About six meters long, wasn't it?" Conseil was at the window staring out at the crevices in the cliff.

"Exactly," I said.

---

4. Bouguer's ship the *Alecton* was probably named after Alecto, one of the Furies of Greek mythology. The French Academy scrutinized the *Alecton*'s report on the monster, refused to believe it, and concluded that the crew had really grappled with some oversize seaweed and had succumbed to mass hysteria.

The Academy was soon proved guilty of carrying scientific skepticism too far. Just five years after Aronnax's narrative, another squid attacked some cod fishermen off Newfoundland. They chopped off one of its tentacles, which proved to be 19 feet long. Many fishermen reported similar sightings in those waters until about 1880. Then giant squid also began making appearances in the Pacific: a specimen found off New Zealand had a total length of 57 feet.

Today, there are indications that the creatures may attain even greater lengths. Peter Benchley's blockbuster *Beast* (1991) features a giant squid (*Architeuthis dux*) some 100 feet long; and, according to *Reader's Digest,* Benchley believes that some specimens may even reach twice that size. (Incidentally, both Benchley and Verne picked similar West Indies stomping grounds for their respective monsters: Verne chose the Bahamas, Benchley Bermuda.)

"Wasn't its head crowned with eight tentacles that quivered in the water like a nest of serpents?"

"Precisely."

"And it had large bulging eyes—popeyes?"

"That's what they said, my boy."

"And wasn't its mouth like a parrot's beak but enormous?"

"Indeed, Conseil, you remember it all."

"Well now, with all due respect to master," Conseil responded serenely, "if that isn't Bouguer's Squid out there, it's one of his close relatives."

I stared at Conseil, while Ned Land rushed to the window and exclaimed:

"What a horrible beast!"

When I got to the window I could not repress a gesture of revulsion. Right before my eyes was a horrifying, quivering monster worthy of a place in the annals of teratology.[5]

It was a giant squid all right, eight meters long. It was traveling backward with great speed, right alongside us. It gaped with enormous eyes tinted sea green. Its eight arms—or more accurately, legs—were rooted in its head, which has earned these animals the name of *cephalopod*. Its arms stretched a distance twice the length of its body and they writhed like the serpentine hair of the Furies. We could plainly see its 250 suckers that lined the inner sides of the tentacles: they were shaped like semispheric capsules. Sometimes it fastened some of its suckers on the salon window by creating vacuums against it. The monster's mouth, a horn-covered beak shaped like a parrot's, opened and closed vertically. Its tongue, also made of a hornlike substance and armed with several rows of sharp teeth, would flicker out from between those genuine shears. What a freak of Nature! A bird's beak on a mollusk! Its body was spindle-shaped, swollen in the middle, a mass of flesh that must have weighed 20,000 to 25,000 kilograms. As it grew more irritated, its color changed rapidly, passing from livid gray to ruddy brown.

And just what was irritating that huge mollusk? No doubt the *Nautilus,* which was more formidable than itself, and on which its arms and suckers could find no real grip.[6] And yet what monsters they are, what vitality our Creator has given them, what vigor in their motions, thanks to their having three hearts!

It was mere chance that we had encountered this rare specimen and I didn't want to lose a moment in studying it. I repressed my horror at the mere sight of it and seizing pencil and paper, began to sketch it swiftly.

"Maybe this is the same beast the *Alecton* tried to capture," Conseil said.

5. An occult science devoted to the study of monstrosities and freaks.

6. This is an astute observation, given the little that was known about giant squid in Verne's day. Since then, sperm whales have often been found with numerous scars from these tooth-rimmed suckers. Likewise, the present description of squid experiencing extreme emotions like fury or irritation has been corroborated by Aronnax's successors.

A colossal squid

"Can't be," said the Canadian, "this one is all there, and that other one lost its tail."

"That's not necessarily so," I put in. "The arms and tails of these animals can grow again—a process called regeneration—and in seven years the tail on Bouguer's Squid has had plenty of time to regenerate."

"Besides," Ned was getting excited, "if this one isn't Bouguer's Squid, then maybe it's one of those!"

Indeed, other giant squid had appeared at the starboard window. I counted seven of them. They formed an escort for the *Nautilus,* and I could hear their beaks grinding on our iron hull. We were being escorted beyond our wildest fantasies.

I kept sketching. Those monsters kept pace with us with such precision that they seemed motionless. I could have traced them in outline on the window. Of course, we were only going at a moderate speed.[7]

All at once the *Nautilus* stopped. It was such a jolt that the ship trembled in every plate.

"Have we struck bottom?" I asked.

"Whatever, we're already clear," the Canadian responded. "See, we're floating."

Floating but not moving. We couldn't hear the blades of the propeller churning the waves. After a minute passed, Captain Nemo entered the salon with his first mate.

I hadn't seen him for quite a while. He seemed melancholy. Without saying anything to us—maybe not even seeing us—he went to the window, stared at those giant mollusks, and addressed a few words to his first mate, who left at once.

Soon the panels closed and the ceiling lights went on.

I approached the captain.

"A curious collection of squid," I said, with the carefree manner of an enthusiast in front of an aquarium.

"Yes, indeed, Mr. Naturalist, and we're going to fight them hand-to-hand."

Believing I had not heard him clearly, I stared at him and said:

"Hand-to-hand?"

"Yes, professor, our propeller is jammed. I think the horn-covered mandibles of a squid are entangled in the blades. That's why we can't move."

"And how are you going to handle this?"

"Mount back to the surface and massacre the vermin."[8]

"Not an easy job."

7. Again Verne is working with remarkably good information. Giant squid have been "logged" at 12 knots, and Nemo does seem to have been lazing all day so far.

8. Nemo's bitterness toward the giant squid seems odd for a man who is usually objective about natural phenomena. Perhaps these creatures, with their far-reaching tentacles, symbolize for him the power that the state has to interfere in the lives of its subjects.

"Indeed no. Our electric bullets aren't effective against such soft flesh — they don't meet enough resistance to explode. So we'll attack the beasts with axes."

"And with a harpoon, captain, if you'll accept my help," the Canadian said.

"I do accept it, Mr. Land."

"We'll go too," I said, and we followed Captain Nemo to the central companionway.

There were some ten crewmen, armed with boarding axes, ready for the assault. Conseil and I also took up axes and Ned Land a harpoon.

By then the *Nautilus* had reached the surface. A crewman at the top of the steps unscrewed the bolts holding the hatch in place. But the nuts were scarcely removed when the hatch was lifted with great violence, obviously pulled up by suckers on a squid's tentacle.

Immediately one of those long arms glided like a serpent into the opening, and twenty others were quivering above it. With a blow of his axe Captain Nemo chopped off that first arm and it slid writhing down the steps.

The moment we started crowding each other to get out on the platform, two more tentacles lashed the air, seized the seaman in front of Captain Nemo, and carried the man off with irresistible violence.

Captain Nemo gave a shout and sprang outside, the rest of us rushing after him.

What a scene! Seized by that tentacle and glued to its suckers, the wretched man was swinging in the air at the mercy of that elephantine trunk. He gasped, he choked, he cried out "Help! Help!" These words were *spoken in French!*[9] I was stupefied! So I had a compatriot on board, maybe several. I will hear his harrowing cry as long as I live.

The unfortunate man was doomed. Who could possibly wrench him from that powerful grip? Even so, Captain Nemo rushed at the giant mollusk and with a sweep of his ax hacked off another of its tentacles.[10] His first mate was struggling furiously with other squid crawling up the side of the ship. The entire crew now were flailing away with their axes, and Ned and Conseil and I sank our weapons into those masses of flesh. A violent, musky odor filled the air. It was horrible.

---

9. Fast on the heels of Conseil's verbal breakdown, another man on board the *Nautilus* finds himself in such straits that he drops his guard and begs for help in language truer to his own nature. Also, a page or two earlier, note that Captain Nemo is described as "melancholy." Something has been happening on board since that South Pole episode—a malaise that will increase by the chapter to the novel's end.

10. According to modern scientists, such tentacles can exceed the thickness of a man's thigh. By the by, Verne does make one bobble. He identifies the creature very decisively as a squid (*calmar*), an animal that sports ten tentacles. Verne, however, gives it only eight. In our opinion, this is one of the author's rare genuine blunders, and we're convinced that he should have known better: in I 18 he describes a smaller breed of squid . . . and there he does give it the regulation ten arms.

For an instant I thought the poor man entwined by the squid could be pulled free from its powerful suckers. Seven arms out of eight had been cut off. Only one arm was left writhing in the air, brandishing its victim like a feather. But when Captain Nemo and the first mate rushed at it, the animal shot out a jet of black liquid secreted by a pouch under its abdomen. It blinded us. When that cloud of black spray had dissipated, the squid was gone—and so was my wretched compatriot!

What rage now drove us against those monsters! We were beside ourselves. Ten or twelve squid had overrun the platform and sides. We were rolling pell-mell amid pieces of tentacles, writhing snakelike amid waves of blood and India ink.[11] It seemed as if these slimy tentacles grew back like the many heads of the Hydra. Every thrust of Ned Land's harpoon plunged into a sea-green eye and burst it. But suddenly my brave companion was overthrown by the tentacles of a monster he could not avoid.

Oh now I felt as if my heart would explode from excitement and horror! The squid's formidable beak was opening right over the fallen Canadian. The poor man was about to be chopped in two. I rushed to his rescue. But Captain Nemo was faster. His axe disappeared between those enormous mandibles. Miraculously saved, the Canadian stood up and plunged his harpoon deep into the squid's triple heart![12]

"One good turn deserves another," Captain Nemo told the Canadian. "I owed it to myself to pay you back!"

Ned bowed without answering.

That combat lasted for fifteen minutes. Defeated, mutilated, battered to death, those monsters gave up at last and sank beneath the waves.[13]

Captain Nemo, drenched in blood, stood still near the beacon. He gazed at that sea that had engulfed one of his companions. Huge tears streamed down his face.

11. Understandably, Aronnax describes this ink as *black*. According to modern observers, it's really a dark brown.

12. What Aronnax calls the triple heart is really three modified blood vessels; the squid doesn't have a heart in the standard, vertebrate sense.

13. In discussing these animals Verne uses three terms: (1) *calmar* (literally, squid); (2) *kraken* (literally, kraken, a many-armed Scandinavian sea monster); (3) *poulpe* (defined by *Grzimek's Animal Life Encyclopedia* as the French equivalent of kraken; in the 1860s it was simply a *generic* term for an animal having numerous feet or tentacles).

Shifts in meaning have caused some confusion since then. In the 20th century *poulpe* is sometimes used as a popular synonym for "octopus," but Verne clearly was not thinking of that animal. The exact French terms for octopus and cuttlefish are, respectively, *pieuvre* and *seiche*. Both were available and well known to Verne (see our note on Victor Hugo in II 19), but he carefully avoids both terms in this context. So, to reduce reader confusion, we use *squid* to stand in for both *calmar* and *poulpe*.

NINETEEN

❧

The Gulf Stream ¹

NONE OF US will ever be able to forget that terrible episode of April 20. I recorded it when I was still under the influence of my violent reactions to what had happened. Later I read it to Conseil and to the Canadian. They found it accurate but lacking in emotional impact. To recreate that horrendous ordeal would require the talents of our most illustrious poet, the author of *The Toilers of the Sea.*²

I said that Captain Nemo had wept while he was gazing into the waves. His grief was immense. It was the second companion he had lost since we had come aboard. And what an awful way to die! Crushed, strangled, battered by the formidable arms of a giant squid, ground up in its iron jaws, that companion was never to rest with his comrades in the tranquil waters of their coral cemetery.

As for me, it was the cry of despair he had uttered in the thick of battle that still tears at my heart. Forgetting the strange language they used on board, that poor Frenchman had resorted to his mother tongue to fling out his last appeal for help. And so, among the crew of the *Nautilus,* bound body and soul to

---

1. Verne's first readers had a reverential reaction to the very words "Gulf Stream." To them these words signified a miracle of Nature that guided a wide river of warm water to heat northern Europe. Their awe was increased by Maury's lyric prose, which emphasizes divine purpose. Europeans could thus bask in the belief that the entire globe was arranged for their benefit. But, as we shall see, today's scientists do not unanimously agree about the stream's impact on Europe's climates.

2. Written by Victor Hugo (1802–1885), this novel was published just three years before the present one. The most talked-about episode in *The Toilers* was a mortal combat between its hero Gilliatt and a rogue octopus (*pieuvre*) that lurked in an island cave in the English Channel. Verne was intimately familiar with this episode and expected the same of his readers.

So, Verne's comment that an evocative description of any such battle "would require the talents" of a Hugo is his sly perception of the stylistic chasm between himself and his famous forerunner. Hugo's description is much lengthier than Verne's, is packed with repetitive detail, and is dense in imagery, symbolism, and word music. By contrast, Verne is crisp and clinical: he swiftly establishes a scientific basis, borne out by his casting of the giant squid as villain (modern zoologists consider the octopus essentially harmless). Thereafter, Verne presents his facts and his action in a tight, clean, Dashiell Hammett-like prose that is miles from Hugo's lush prose-poetry.

Captain Nemo and like the captain a refugee from civilization, there had been a compatriot of mine, unknown to me. Had he been the only Frenchman in this mysterious brotherhood, apparently made up of persons from several nationalities? This became just one more of those unanswerable questions that gave me no peace.

Captain Nemo had retired to his cabin and I was not to see him again for a good while. But he was sad, despairing and irresolute—I could be sure of that just from the way the *Nautilus* behaved, the ship whose soul he was, the ship that reflected his every mood. The *Nautilus* no longer stayed on a fixed course. It came and went, drifting like a corpse abandoned to the waves. The propeller had been disentangled from the giant squid but it was rarely put to use. The captain let us cruise at random. He could not tear himself away from the scene of that last struggle, from the waters that had devoured one of his own!

Ten days went by like this. It was not until May 1, after we had sighted the Bahamas from the mouth of the Old Bahama Channel, that the *Nautilus* resumed a definite course: to the north. We were following the current of the sea's greatest river, which has its own banks, fish, and temperature. I mean the Gulf Stream.

It is indeed a river that flows freely through the middle of the Atlantic without mingling its own waters with the ocean's waters. It is a salty river, saltier than the sea surrounding it. Its mean depth is 3,000 feet, its mean width 60 miles. In some places its current moves at a speed of four kilometers an hour. The unvarying volume of its waters is greater than that of all the world's rivers combined.

The true source of the Gulf Stream, as recognized by Commander Maury, its point of departure so to speak, is located in the Bay of Biscay. There its waters, still lacking heat and color, begin to take form. It descends south along equatorial Africa, is warmed by the sun in the Torrid Zone, crosses the Atlantic, reaches Cape São Roque on the coast of Brazil, and divides into two branches, one of which is heated still further by the Caribbean. Then the Gulf Stream—whose function it is to restore the balance between the extremes of temperature and to mix tropical and northern waters—takes on its stabilizing role. Attaining a "white heat" in the Gulf of Mexico, it flows north along the American coast up to Newfoundland, is deflected by the cold current from the Davis Strait, and resumes its ocean course by following one of the globe's great-circle routes on a loxodromic curve.[3] It divides into two arms in the area of the 43rd parallel. One, helped by the northeast trade winds, returns to the Bay of Biscay and the Azores. The other bathes the beaches of Ireland and Norway in lukewarm water, meanders past Spitzbergen, where its temperature drops to 4° centigrade, and fashions the open sea at the pole.

It was on this oceanic river that the *Nautilus* was now navigating. Leaving the Old Bahama Channel, which is fourteen leagues wide and 350 meters deep,

3. On flat maps a curved line charting the shortest distance between two points; also called a rhumb line.

the Gulf Stream flows at about eight kilometers, or five miles, per hour. This speed tends to decrease as it heads north, a tendency we fervently hope continues, because, as the experts agree, if its speed and direction are modified, the European climates would undergo changes of incalculable consequences.

Toward noon I was on the platform with Conseil. I was trying to make him familiar with all the pertinent facts about the Gulf Stream. When I reached the end of my explanation, I suggested that he dip his hands into its current.

He did so, and he was astonished that he experienced no sensation of either hot or cold.

"That," I explained, "is due to the fact that the temperature of the Gulf Stream, as it leaves the Gulf of Mexico, is just about the temperature of your blood. The Gulf Stream is a vast dispenser of warmth, making it possible for the coasts of Europe to be decked in eternal greenery. Commander Maury puts it this way: If the heat of this current were fully utilized, it could keep a river of molten metal as big as the Amazon or the Missouri constantly in its molten state."

Where we were, the Gulf Stream was running 2.25 meters per second. So distinct is its current from the surrounding sea that its waters stand out against the ocean and operate on a different level from the colder waters. Gulf Stream water is darker and saltier, its pure indigo contrasting with the green waves of the sea. The line of demarcation is so clear that when the *Nautilus* was parallel with the Carolinas, her ram was in the Gulf Stream while her propeller was still beating the waves of the Atlantic.[4]

That current carried along with itself a whole world of moving creatures. Argonauts, so common in the Mediterranean, voyaged there in schools of great numbers. Among cartilaginous fish, the most remarkable were some rays whose long thin tails formed nearly a third of their body, which was a vast diamond shape twenty-five feet long. Next came some small one-meter sharks, the head wide with a short, rounded muzzle flaunting sharp teeth arranged in rows, and the body seemingly covered with scales.

Among bony fish I noted some grizzled wrasse found only in those seas; some deepwater gilthead whose iris gleamed like fire; some one-meter croakers whose large maws bristle with small teeth and who actually let out a thin cry; some black rudderfish like the ones I've already described; some blue dorados speckled with silver and gold; some parrot fish, true oceanic rainbows that can

4. Maury tried to explain the Atlantic currents as one regular system of circulation. But some recent researchers hold different views, claiming the system is really a network of thin, overlapping currents. Other students have disputed that the Gulf Stream's water is significantly warmer than the Atlantic proper, and still others credit Europe's moderate climates to currents of *air* rather than water.

Yet, for the general reader, Verne/Maury still holds up well. We checked a contemporary work of standard reference, the 1992 *World Book Encyclopedia,* and found it largely supportive of the information in Verne: (1) the Gulf Stream may diversify up north but is coherent throughout its mid-Atlantic oval; (2) its water ranges from 11° to 18° Fahrenheit warmer than the surrounding water; (3) its current is responsible for raising the air temperatures that in turn warm European shores.

rival the loveliest tropical birds in coloring; some banded blennies with triangular heads; some bluish flounder with no scales; toadfish decorated with a transverse yellow band in the shape of a Greek T; swarms of small freckled gobies stippled with brown spots; some lungfish with silver heads and yellow tails; various specimens of salmon; some slender mullet gleaming with a gentle glow that Lacépède dedicated to the memory of his wife; and finally, a handsome fish, the American cavalier, decorated by every honorary order, bedizened with their every ribbon, frequenting the shores of that great nation where ribbons and orders are held in such low esteem.[5]

I must add that during the night the Gulf Stream's waters were often so phosphorescent they almost rivaled our electric beacon, especially in the stormy weather that sometimes threatened us.[6]

On May 8, while parallel with North Carolina, we were off Cape Hatteras once more. There the Gulf Stream is 75 miles wide and 210 meters deep. The *Nautilus* seemed to be wandering aimlessly in these waters. There seemed to be no supervision, no surveillance on board. I must admit that it might have been easy to escape. The shores were inhabited and harbors were numerous. The sea was plowed endlessly by many steamers providing service between the Gulf of Mexico and New York or Boston, and it was overrun night and day by small schooners engaged in coastal trade. We could hope to be picked up. So it might well have been a favorable opportunity, even considering the fact that the *Nautilus* did keep itself at least thirty miles off the coasts of the Union.

But one unfortunate circumstance always put the Canadian's plans in doubt. The weather was extremely foul. We were approaching an area where storms are frequent, the very homeland of tornadoes and cyclones actually engendered by the current of the Gulf Stream. To confront an often angry sea in a frail dinghy could have been a race to a certain doom. Ned Land conceded this himself. So he champed at the bit, helpless victim of a violent homesickness that could be cured only by our escape.

"Professor," he told me that day, "this has got to stop. I've got to get to the bottom of this problem. Your Captain Nemo is heading out to the open sea—and heading north! But believe you me, I had enough of this at the South Pole and I won't go through it again at the North Pole!"

5. The French name for this mystery fish, as Verne gives it, is *le chevalier-américain*. But exactly what kind of fish *is* this so-called "American cavalier?" We don't claim to know for certain. In his 1976 annotated edition of the Mercier text, WJM referred to it as "the American knight" and speculated that "Aronnax must mean the *sea horse,* which looks like the knight on a chessboard. . . . it could well suggest a bluff, horse-faced soldier bedecked with ribbons and medals." Conversely, FPW's nominee is the American cavalla, also known as the king mackerel. It's a sleek, varicolored fish whose iridescent scales are likewise suggestive of rows of medals.

6. Throughout these pages Aronnax has been fascinated with *phosphorescence,* and he does not exaggerate its brightness. Today's marine scientists claim that this *bioluminescence* can rival sunlight. It's produced by a variety of underwater life, from microscopic organisms to luminescent fishes.

"What can we do, Ned, since it isn't safe to escape now?"

"I've already told you what we can do—talk to the captain! You didn't say a thing when we were close to your country. Now that we're close to mine, *I've* got to speak out! When I think that in a few days the *Nautilus* will be off Nova Scotia, and from Nova Scotia to Newfoundland there's a large gulf, and the St. Lawrence River empties into that gulf, and the St. Lawrence is *my* river, my river running by Quebec, *my* hometown—when I'm thinking about all this, my gorge rises and my hair stands on end! Honestly, professor, I get so furious I'd rather jump into the sea than stay here! I won't stay! I'm smothering!"

Clearly, the Canadian had exhausted his patience. His vigorous nature could not endure this prolonged imprisonment. Even his facial features were changing day by day as his moods grew darker. I was beginning to sense what he was suffering because now I also was gripped by homesickness. Nearly seven months had passed without our getting any news from land. Moreover, Captain Nemo's separating himself from me, his altered moods, his silence, especially since our fight with the giant squid, all this made me see things differently. I no longer felt the enthusiasm that I had when we first came on board. One had to be a Fleming like Conseil to accept these circumstances, living in a world made for whales and other denizens of the deep. Truly, if that young man had gills in place of lungs, he would have made the perfect cold fish![7]

"Well, professor?" Ned wanted a response.

"Ned, I understand that you want me to ask Captain Nemo what he intends to do about us?"

"Right."

"Even though he's already made that quite clear?"

"Yes, I want the question raised again, once and for all. Speak for just me, on my behalf, if that's the only way you can do it."

"But you know I see him rarely—he practically avoids me now."

"All the more reason for you to go talk to him."

"Well, I *will*, Ned."

"When?"

"When I see him."

"Professor, should I go and look for him myself?"

"No, let me do it. Tomorrow I—"

"Today," Ned insisted.

---

7. Beneath all the action, adventure, and marine biology, Verne has quietly been developing characterizations of considerable subtlety and complexity. Here, Aronnax's human weakness and human challenge spill out almost unconsciously in his narrative. The professor has been an ace avoider and procrastinator throughout the Second Part, and his comment in this chapter that "I don't like to have things hanging over my head" is almost comical in its self-deception. He is terrified of Ned's justifiable demands, fearful of confronting Nemo, and so in this passage he shifts the blame to poor, absent Conseil. The scapegoat method. In this chapter Verne will continue to portray Aronnax as a wavering coward . . . but ultimately his principles will inspire him to act with courage. He will emerge reborn in this sense: the courage he gains is the courage to beat down his own cowardice.

"Well, today then." I didn't want him to take action himself and mess things up completely.

Once he had left me, I composed myself. Since it had been settled that I'd ask the captain, I resolved to do it at once. I don't like to have things hanging over my head.

I went back to my cabin, where I could hear movements inside Captain Nemo's quarters. I could not pass up this chance. I knocked on his door. No response. I knocked again, then I tried the knob. The door opened.

I went in. Yes, the captain was there. Bent over his worktable, he apparently had not heard me. Intent on not leaving without having questioned him, I went over to his table. He looked up sharply, frowned, and said in a barely tolerable tone of voice:

"You here! What do you want!"

"To talk to you, captain."

"But I'm busy, professor, I'm working. I let you enjoy your privacy. Can't I have some for myself?"

This was no auspicious beginning. But I was determined to hold my ground, to carry out my mission.

"Captain," I said coolly, "I have to talk to you about something that cannot wait."

"And whatever could that be?" he answered sarcastically. "Have you discovered something that I missed? Have the secrets of the depths been revealed to you at last?"

We seemed to have reached a stalemate, but before I could try again he pointed to a manuscript lying on the table and said, now in a graver voice:

"This manuscript, professor, is written in several languages. It contains a summary of all my submarine research. God willing, it will not perish with me. It is signed with my name, it tells my complete life story, and it will be packed in a small, unsinkable box; the last man alive aboard the *Nautilus* will toss it into the sea, and it will go wherever fate, the winds, and the waves will take it."

The man's real name! His life story written by himself! So the secrets of his existence *might* someday be unveiled! And what he had just said gave me the perfect introduction to what I wanted to say:

"Captain, I'm all praise for this project of yours. I agree, the fruits of your research must not be lost! But I can't agree with the way you're going about it. Who knows where the wind will take that box, into whose hands it will fall? Isn't there a safer, surer way? Can't you or one of your people—"

"Never, professor," he cut that short.

"But my companions and I would be willing to safeguard this manuscript, if you would only give us our freedom—"

"Your freedom!" Captain Nemo exclaimed, standing up tall.

"Yes, captain, that is precisely what I have come to talk to you about. For seven months now we have been kept on your vessel, and in the name of my companions and myself, I must ask, do you plan to keep us forever?"

"Professor Aronnax, I'll give you the same answer now that I gave you seven months ago: Whoever boards the *Nautilus* must never leave it!"[8]

"Then you consign us to slavery!"

"Give it whatever name you please."

"But everywhere slaves have the right to regain their freedom! By any means necessary!"

"Who has denied you that right? Have I ever tried to chain you with your word of honor?"

He crossed his arms and stared at me.

"Captain, it isn't pleasant for either of us to go over this question a second time. But since we've started it, let's finish it. I repeat: it isn't just for my sake that I raise this question. For me, research is a relief, a great diversion, a lure, a passion that can make me forget everything else. Like you, I am a man ignored and unknown, living in the fragile hope that someday I can pass on to future generations the fruits of my labors, leaving them—figuratively speaking—in some box entrusted to waves and wind. In short, I can admire you and go along comfortably with you in a life I can only partly comprehend. But I still catch glimpses of other parts of your life that are surrounded by complications and mysteries that my companions and I cannot share. And even when our hearts could beat with yours, moved by your griefs or inspired by your courage or genius, we have had to repress in ourselves the slightest token of that sympathy that arises at the sight of something beautiful and good—whether it comes from friend or enemy. I guess it's that feeling of being excluded from your deepest concerns that makes our position unacceptable, impossible—even for me now but especially for Ned Land. Every man, by the very fact that he is human, deserves some consideration. Have you thought about how a love of freedom and hatred of slavery can drive a man like Ned Land to—vengeance? What he might be thinking, attempting, planning—?"

I had said it. Captain Nemo replied:

"Let Ned Land think, attempt, plan anything he wants, what does that matter to me? I didn't invite him on board! I don't keep him on board for my pleasure. As for you, Professor Aronnax, you are an intelligent person, you can understand even silence. And I am silent now. Let this be the last time you come to me to discuss this question, because the next time I won't even listen."

I left him. From that moment on our situation had become critical. I reported this conversation to my companions.

"At least now we know that we can't expect anything from that man," Ned said. "The *Nautilus* is approaching Long Island. That's where we'll go, no matter what the weather."[9]

But the skies became really threatening. There were conspicuous signs of a hurricane on the way. The atmosphere was turning white and misty. Slender

8. Is this another reason for the melancholy of the myrmidons? Do they become galley slaves?

9. The Nazis also picked Long Island as the best U.S. beach to land men from a submarine.

sheaves of cirrus clouds were followed on the horizon by layers of nimbocumulus. Other low clouds were speeding by. The sea, inflated by long swells, grew towering. Every bird had vanished, except for the petrels, those friends of the storms. Our barometer fell considerably, indicating a tremendous tension in the ambient haze. The mixture in our stormglass decomposed under the influence of the electricity that charged the air. A war of the elements was imminent.

Exactly when the *Nautilus* was drifting toward Long Island, some miles out from the New York harbor, in the daylight of May 13, the tempest burst.[10] Captain Nemo, from some inexplicable whim, instead of seeking safety beneath the waves, decided to brave it out on the surface. And so I am able to describe this contest of the elements from its very midst.

The wind blew from the southwest, at first a stiff breeze, in other words, with a speed of 15 meters per second, stepping up to 25 meters toward three p.m. That's where it qualified as a tempest.

Unshaken by these squalls, Captain Nemo had posted himself on the platform. He was lashed around the waist so he could withstand the monstrous breakers rushing over the ship. I also lashed myself in place, dividing my admiration between the tempest and that incomparable person who could face it head-on.

The raging sea was swept by huge tattered clouds that soaked themselves in the waves. There were no more of those smaller waves that can form in the hollows of the bigger ones. Just long, soot-colored undulations with crests so compact they did not foam. They were coming taller and taller, spurring each other on. Sometimes heeling over on its side, other times standing on end like a mast, the *Nautilus* rolled and pitched dreadfully.

Toward five p.m. a torrential rain fell, but it calmed neither sea nor wind. The hurricane was launched at a speed of 45 meters per second, that is, nearly 40 leagues an hour! It's under such conditions that houses flip over, roof tiles actually pierce wooden doors, iron railings snap, and twenty-four-pound cannonballs are shoved around. And yet in the midst of that turmoil the *Nautilus* confirmed the words of a learned engineer: "There is no well-constructed hull that cannot defy the sea!" That submarine boat was no resisting rock that waves could destroy—it was a steel spindle, obediently in motion, with no rigging or masting, able to brave the sea's fury with impunity.

I was studying these unleashed breakers in every detail. They measured up to 15 meters in height over a length of 150 to 175 meters. The speed of their propagation—about half the speed of the wind—was 15 meters per second. Their volume and power increased with the depth of the waters. Now I could see firsthand the role played by these waves—they imprison air in their flanks and force it down into the depths where its oxygen nurtures life. It is estimated

10. The French gives May 18, probably a compositor's error, because, as the next chapter reveals, the *Nautilus* will be off Newfoundland on that date. Our correction to May 13 assumes the common misreading of "3" for "8."

The king of tempests

that they can exert a pressure of up to 3,000 kilograms on every square foot of surface that they strike. It was such waves in the Hebrides that actually moved a stone block weighing 84,000 pounds. It was such waves in the storm of December 23, 1854, that destroyed part of Tokyo, Japan, and then went that same day at 700 kilometers an hour to crash on the beaches of America.[11]

As night came on, the storm increased in its violence. As in the 1860 cyclone on Réunion Island, our barometer fell to 710 millimeters, or 28 inches. At the close of day I saw a huge ship passing on the horizon, struggling painfully. It lay to at half steam in an effort to hold steady on the waves. It must have been one of those steamers on the lines out of New York to Liverpool or Le Havre. It soon vanished in the shadows.

At 10 p.m. the skies caught fire. The atmosphere was crisscrossed with violent flashes of lightning. I couldn't stand this brightness but Captain Nemo stared straight at it, seeming to suck in the soul of the storm. A terrible clamor filled the air, partly the howl of crashing breakers, partly the roar of the wind, partly the thunderclaps. The wind shifted to every point on the compass, leaving the east to pass through the north, the west, the south, returning to the east, counterclockwise, as opposed to storms in the Southern Hemisphere, which revolve clockwise.

Oh that Gulf Stream! It well merits its nickname of King of Tempests! All by itself it creates these formidable hurricanes by means of the difference in temperature between its currents and the surrounding air.

The rain was followed by a shower of fire. Droplets of water changed into exploding tufts. Was Captain Nemo courting a death worthy of himself, trying to be struck by lightning? With a terrifying pitching motion the *Nautilus* lifted its steel ram into the air, like a lightning rod, and I saw long sparks shooting down its length.

My strength shattered, I slid flat on my belly toward the hatch, opened it, and took refuge in the salon. The storm was at its peak of violence. I couldn't stand upright inside the ship.

Captain Nemo came back down toward midnight. I could hear the ballast tanks filling by degrees, and the *Nautilus* sank gently beneath the surface.

Through the salon windows I watched large fish, bewildered, passing like phantoms in those fiery waters. A few were struck by lightning right before my eyes.

The *Nautilus* was still descending. I thought it would reach complete calm at about 15 meters down. But no, the upper layers of the sea were still thrashing about too violently. We had to go down to 50 meters, looking for peace in the bowels of the ocean.

11. This "storm" was really a tidal wave produced by an earthquake. The French misdates the catastrophe as 1864. Since Verne began work on this novel in 1865, we assume that this time perspective would have prevented him from making such a slip. Once again the likeliest culprit is the compositor.

But once there, what tranquillity we found, what quiet, what peace all around us! Who could tell that a horrible hurricane was then raging on the surface of the sea?[12]

12. This passage anticipates Simon Lake's 1898 submarine voyage off Florida. Operating the first successful open-sea submersible, Lake imitated Nemo by taking refuge in the depths during a horrendous storm. Later, in his autobiography, Lake wrote: "Jules Verne . . . was the director-general of my life."

Meanwhile, Nemo's very presence on the surface during a hurricane is yet another indication of crumbling conditions on board. Insanity and self-destruction, as we suggested in an earlier note, are becoming more pervasive. First, Ned yells that he'd "rather jump into the sea" than continue on board. Second, we see Nemo preparing his figurative last will and testament by readying his autobiography and scientific secrets for jettisoning overboard. Third, we observe the captain, in a fit of madness reminiscent of Shakespeare's King Lear, braving a dangerous storm on the surface, "courting a death worthy of himself." The voyage is clearly winding down, and Verne's long-range control of his plot is indeed worthy of admiration.

In Latitude 47° 24′ and Longitude 17° 28′

A S A RESULT of the hurricane, we were flung back to the east. Any hope we had of escaping near New York or the St. Lawrence faded away. In despair, Ned Land shut himself up, like Captain Nemo. But Conseil and I never left each other.

I have said that the *Nautilus* was driven to the east. To be more accurate, I should have said to the northeast. Sometimes on the surface, sometimes below the surface, the ship wandered for days amid those fogs so dreaded by seafaring men. Those mists are caused mainly by melting ice, which keeps the atmosphere very damp. How many ships have been lost in those waterways as they were trying to identify the indistinct lights on the coast! How many wrecks have been caused by those opaque fogs! How many ships have gone aground on those reefs because the clear warning sound of the breaking surf was smothered by the howling of the winds! How many ships have rammed into each other, in spite of their running lights and the warnings sounded by their bosun's pipes and alarm bells!

And so, the floor of those seas looked like a battlefield where every ship defeated by Nature lay still, some already old and encrusted, others more recent and reflecting the light of our beacon on their iron work and their copper undersides. How many of these ships had gone down with all hands—their crews and crowds of immigrants—at those places marked as dangerous on the charts: Cape Race, St. Paul Island, the Strait of Belle Isle, the St. Lawrence estuary! And in only a few years, how many names have been supplied for the obituary columns by the Royal Mail, the Inman,[1] and the Montreal lines: by vessels named the *Solway,* the *Isis,* the *Paramatta,* the *Hungarian,* the *Canadian,* the *Anglo-Saxon,* the *Humboldt,* and the *United States,* all run aground; the *Arctic* and the *Lyonnais,* sunk in collisions; the *President,* the *Pacific,* and the *City of Glasgow,* lost for reasons unknown. And amid these somber wrecks the *Nautilus* navigated as if passing the dead in review.

---

1. These were magic names in the nineteenth century. The great Royal Mail Steam Packet Co. was started in 1838 and was unusual in that all its officers were Royal Navy. The Inman line was launched in 1850 by William Inman, whose target market was the immigrant trade.

Inman is misspelled "Inmann" in the French, We have corrected it to the usual spelling.

By May 15 we were off the southern tip of the Grand Banks of Newfoundland. This area is the product of marine deposits, a huge mass of organic particles brought either from the equator by the Gulf Stream, or from the North Pole by the countercurrent of cold water that skirts the American coast. There are also heaps of rocks dropped by the breaking up of the drifting ice. A vast charnel house forms there from the fish, mollusks, and zoophytes that die there by the billions.

The sea is not very deep at the Grand Banks, a few hundred fathoms at best. But toward the south there is a steep, abrupt depression, a hole 3,000 meters deep. There the Gulf Stream widens, losing its speed and some of its heat as it blossoms into an ocean.

Among the fish startled by the *Nautilus*'s passing through, I will cite the lumpfish, one meter long, blackish on top, orange on the belly, which practices monogamy, a custom rarely imitated by other fish; a large eelpout; a kind of emerald moray, good to the palate; wolffish, with big eyes in a head that resembles a dog's; some viviparous blennies whose eggs are hatched inside their bodies, like those of snakes; some bloated gobio, or black gudgeon, two decimeters long; and some grenadiers, silvery with long tails, speedy fish venturing far from their Arctic habitat.

Our nets also brought in a bold, tough, powerful fish, with strong muscles and prickles on its head and stings on its fins, a true scorpion two to three meters long. Mortal enemy of cod, blennies, and salmon, this was the bullhead of the northern seas, a fish with a gnarled body, entirely brown except for its red fins. The *Nautilus*'s crewmen had some trouble getting a grip on this spiny creature. Thanks to the shape of its gill covers, it can keep its lungs from drying out in the air, and so it can live out of water for a good while.

And just for the record, I will cite some small banded blennies that often follow ships into northern waters; some sharp-snouted carp unique to the north Atlantic; some scorpionfish; and the gadoid family, represented by their main species, the cod, which I was able to surprise in its favorite waters over those inexhaustible Grand Banks.

We could call these cod "mountain fish" because Newfoundland is in reality a submarine mountain. While the *Nautilus* was parting their thick ranks, Conseil could not repress his amazement:

"What—those are cod? But I always thought cod were flat, like flounder or sole!"

"Oh how naive you are! Cod are flat only in the fish market, where they're cut open and spread out flat, on display. But in the sea they're like mullet, spindle shaped, perfectly built for speed."

"If master says so, I believe it. But what crowds of them, what swarms!"

"Yes, my friend, and there'd be even greater swarms if they didn't have two great enemies: scorpionfish and human beings. Do you know how many eggs have been counted in just one female cod?"

"I'll exaggerate," Conseil said. "Five hundred thousand."

"Eleven million, my friend!"[2]

"Eleven million! I can't believe that unless I count them myself."

"So count them, Conseil. But it would be much easier to take my word for it. Besides, the French, English, Americans, Danes, and Norwegians catch them by the thousands. Human beings eat them in prodigious quantities, so if they weren't amazingly fecund, the seas would soon be depopulated of cod. In England and America alone, 5,000 ships, manned by 75,000 seamen, go after cod. On the average, each ship brings in a catch of 4,400 cod, or 22,000,000 in all. Off the coast of Norway the statistics are similar."

"All right, I'll take master's word for it. I won't count them."

"Count what?"

"Those 11,000,000 eggs. But may I say just one thing?"

"Yes?"

"If all their eggs hatched, just four cod could feed England, America, and Norway."[3]

As we skimmed over the bottoms of the Grand Banks, I could see clearly those long fishing lines, each armed with 200 hooks, that each boat dropped over the side by the dozens. Each line was fastened at the surface to a cork buoy, and on the bottom, to a small grappling iron. The *Nautilus* had to maneuver carefully to get through that underwater network!

But the ship did not tarry long in those frequented waters. We headed toward the 42nd parallel, the latitude of St. John's in Newfoundland and Heart's Content, where the Atlantic Cable terminates.

Instead of continuing north, the *Nautilus* swerved east, as if to follow that "telegraphic plateau" on which the cable rests, where numerous soundings had made it possible to map the floor with the utmost exactitude.

It was on May 17, about 500 miles from Heart's Content and 2,800 meters below the surface, that I first spotted the cable lying on the ocean floor. Since I had not prepared Conseil for this sight, he took it for a gigantic sea snake and was winding up to classify it. But I stopped him in time and to console him for his embarrassment, I gave him some background on the laying of the cable.

The first cable was put down during 1857–1858, but after it had transmitted about 400 telegrams, it went dead. In 1863 engineers constructed a

---

2. Actually it's Aronnax who is exaggerating. Today's naturalists claim that a typical female bears about one million eggs. Even from a very *large* female, eleven million would be an astonishing performance.

3. But only one or two individuals out of every million eggs will grow to adult fish. Further, as the original French compositors present it, the arithmetic in this sequence fails to jibe. For the benefit of the general reader, we've rectified two figures in this passage: we give 4,400 instead of the French's 40,000, and 22,000,000 instead of the French's 25,000,000. This way, Conseil's punch line adds up.

new cable that measured 3,400 kilometers long, weighed 4,500 metric tons, and was mounted on the *Great Eastern*.⁴ This project also miscarried.

Now on May 25 the *Nautilus,* 3,836 meters below the surface, found the exact place where the second cable had suffered the rupture that ruined the enterprise. It had happened 638 miles off the coast of Ireland. At two p.m. one day someone on the *Great Eastern* noticed that communications with Europe had just been interrupted. The electrical engineers on board decided to cut the cable before fishing it up, and by eleven p.m. they had reclaimed the damaged section. They repaired it, spliced it, and submerged it again. But a few days later it snapped again and this time it could not be recovered from the depths of the ocean.

But those Americans would not give up. The audacious Cyrus Field— who had risked his entire fortune promoting this project—called for a new bond issue. It sold out immediately. Another, much stronger cable was manufactured. Its sheaves of electric wire were insulated in a casing of gutta-percha, which in turn was wrapped in hemp, which then was covered with a metal sheath. The *Great Eastern* sailed again on July 13, 1866.

Everything went well, with just one exception. When they were unrolling this third cable, the electricians discovered that, in several places, someone had driven nails into it, apparently to cause its core to corrode. Captain Anderson, his officers, and the engineers put their heads together. Then they posted a warning that if the guilty person were caught in the act, he would be denied a trial and tossed overboard. There was no more sabotage of the Atlantic Cable.

When the *Great Eastern* was lying no farther than 800 kilometers from Newfoundland, on July 23, 1866, the cable brought them the telegraphed news that Prussia and Austria had agreed to an armistice after the Battle of Sadova. In heavy fog, the *Great Eastern* reached the port of Heart's Content on July 27. The enterprise had ended happily, and as its first cabled dispatch, young America sent to aging Europe these wise words so rarely understood: "Glory to God in the highest, and peace on earth to men of good will."

I knew I wouldn't see that electric cable in the mint condition in which it had left the factory. In fact that long snake was covered with bits of shell and bristling with foraminifera;⁵ a crust of caked gravel protected it from those mollusks that might bore into it. It was lying there, serene, sheltered from the sea's motions, under a pressure that actually favors transmission of that electric spark that goes from Europe to America in .32 of a second! The cable will probably last indefinitely because, as experts have observed, its casing of gutta-percha is actually improved by being bathed in salt water.

---

4. The only ship afloat big enough to lay all the cable in one trip. As a passenger vessel it was dogged by bad luck: too big for most ports, it was actually denied entrance to many stopping points. But the ship was a bonanza to Field.

5. Single-celled microorganisms with hard carapaces.

Besides, on this well-chosen submarine plateau the cable never lies at depths that could cause a break. The *Nautilus* followed it to its lowest point, 4,431 meters down, and there it rested with no stress or strain. Then we returned to the place where the 1863 accident had occurred.

There the ocean floor formed a deep valley, 120 kilometers wide, into which one could place Mt. Blanc without exposing its summit above the surface. This valley is closed off to the east by a sheer wall 2,000 meters tall. We arrived at that wall on May 28, and we were then not more than 150 kilometers from Ireland.

Was Captain Nemo about to continue north and beach us on the British Isles? No. To my great surprise he turned south toward European waters. As we swung around the Emerald Isle, I could see for an instant Cape Clear and the lighthouse on Fastnet Rock that guides thousands of ships setting out from Glasgow or Liverpool.

An important question then popped into my head. Would the *Nautilus* dare take on the challenge of the English Channel? Ned Land—who came out of isolation as soon as we approached land—never stopped questioning me. What could I say? Captain Nemo did *not* come out of isolation. After letting the Canadian glimpse the shores of America, would he now tease me with the coasts of France?

However, the *Nautilus* kept to its southerly course. On May 30 we sighted Land's End, cruising between the lowermost tip of England and the Scilly Islands, which we left behind to starboard.

If the captain intended to risk the English Channel, he would now have to turn sharply to the east. And he didn't.

All day long, on May 31, the *Nautilus* went round and round in a series of circles. I was intrigued as the ship seemed to be looking for a spot difficult to locate. At noon Captain Nemo himself came up to take our bearings. He didn't have a word for me. He looked more somber than ever. What was making him so sad? Was it our proximity to Europe? Did he still suffer from homesickness for the country he had abandoned? If not, what did possess him—remorse? regrets? For a long time such ideas occupied my mind, and I had a strong feeling that soon fate would betray the captain's secrets.

The next day, June 1, the *Nautilus* continued these same circular maneuvers. The ship was clearly trying to find a very specific point in the ocean. Again it was Captain Nemo who came up to shoot the sun. The seas were smooth, the skies immaculate. Eight miles to the east a large steamship was visible on the horizon. No flag was flapping from the gaff of its fore-and-aft sail, so I could not tell its nationality.

A few minutes before the sun passed its zenith, Captain Nemo raised his sextant and took his observations with the utmost precision. The absolute calm of the waves facilitated his work. The *Nautilus* lay motionless, neither rolling nor pitching.

I was on the platform watching. Our position determined, the captain pronounced these words:

"It's right here!"

He went below again. Had he noticed that that big vessel had changed its course and seemed to be heading for us? I couldn't tell.

I returned to the salon, the hatch was closed, and I heard the hissing sound of water entering the ballast tanks. The *Nautilus* began to submerge straight down because its propeller had been disengaged.

Some minutes later, 833 meters down, the ship rested on the seafloor.

The ceiling lights in the salon went out, the panels opened, and through the windows I could see, for half a mile around, the ocean brilliantly lit by our beacon light.

To port I saw nothing but an immensity of tranquil water.

But to starboard a large object, bulging on the ocean floor, captured my attention. At first glance it looked like some ruin covered with a snowlike mantle of whitened seashells. Studying it more carefully, I thought I could identify the swollen outlines of a ship shorn of its masts and sunk bow first. This wreck certainly dated from some remote decade. To be so encrusted with calcareous matter, this ship must have spent many a year on the ocean floor.

But what ship was it? Why had the *Nautilus* come to visit its grave? Was it something more than a maritime accident that had dragged this craft beneath the waves?

I couldn't figure it out, but next to me I heard Captain Nemo saying, very slowly:

"Originally this ship was named the *Marseillaise*. It was launched in 1762 and carried seventy-four guns. On August 13, 1778, commanded by La Poype-Vertrieux, it fought bravely against the *Preston*. On July 4, 1779, as part of the squadron under Admiral d'Estaing, it assisted in the capture of the island of Grenada. On September 5, 1781, under the Count de Grasse, it fought in the Battle of Chesapeake Bay. In 1794 the new Republic of France changed the name of this ship. On April 16 that year it joined the squadron at Brest under Rear Admiral Villaret de Joyeuse—he was entrusted with escorting a convoy of wheat coming from America under the command of Admiral Van Stabel. In that second year of the French Revolutionary Calendar, on the 11th and 12th days in the Month of Pasture, this squadron did battle with some English ships. Professor, today is June 1, 1868, or the 13th day in the Month of Pasture. Seventy-four years ago to the day, at this very spot in latitude 47°24′ and longitude 17°28′, this ship sank after a heroic fight. Its three masts gone, water in its hold, a third of its crew out of action, it preferred to be sunk with all its 356 sailors rather than surrender. With its flag nailed up on the afterdeck, it slipped beneath the waves with all its men shouting:

"Long live the Republic!"

"Then that's the *Vengeur!*" I cried.

"Yes, professor! The *Vengeur!*"

Captain Nemo crossed his arms and murmured, "What a beautiful name!"[6]

6. The *Vengeur* was an actual warship, its full name being *Le Vengeur du Peuple* (*The People's Avenger*). Its war record, as quoted by Nemo, consists entirely of encounters with the Royal Navy. The 1778 contest occurred near the English Channel. In 1779 the ship helped France recover a former Caribbean colony from the British. In 1781, as a U.S. ally, it fought against England during the American Revolution. Finally, in June 1794, it again fought the English— in an encounter known as the Second Battle of the Ushant, during which it was sunk by HMS *Brunswick*.

By showing Aronnax the *Vengeur*'s grave, Nemo the romantic hero is setting the stage for a scene of vast symbolic significance. And, of course, Nemo *has* seen that "the big vessel had changed its course and seemed to be heading for us . . ."

In Latitude

47°24′ and

Longitude

17°28′

☙

370

TWENTY-ONE

A Hecatomb [1]

H IS WAY OF commenting on this unexpected scene, first his giving
the history of the patriot ship, then his pronouncing those last words
with such strong emotion—the very name *Vengeur* whose significance could not escape me—all this combined to strike at the very
depths of my being. I could not take my eyes off the captain. Hands outstretched toward the sea, he contemplated that glorious wreck with blazing
eyes. Perhaps I might never learn his real identity, where he came from or
where he was headed, but more and more I could see the man as distinct from
the scientist. It was no ordinary distrust of humanity that kept Captain Nemo
and his crew shut up inside the *Nautilus*. It was rather a hatred so monstrous
or so sublime that the course of time could never weaken it.

Did that hatred also hunger for revenge? The future would soon tell me.

Meanwhile the *Nautilus* was rising slowly toward the surface and I
watched the *Vengeur*'s vague shape disappearing little by little. Soon a slight
rolling told me we were afloat in the open air.

At that moment I heard a dull *boom*. I looked at the captain. He didn't
move a muscle.

"Captain?" I said.

He did not respond.

I left him and mounted to the platform. Conseil and the Canadian were
already there.

"What caused that detonation?" I asked.

"A cannon," Ned Land replied.

---

1. A mass slaughter, a sacrifice of many victims. In ancient Greece, a hecatomb was a public
offering of 100 oxen to the gods, and Verne's chapter title is calculated to create suspense. We're
dealing, then, with a great, solemn sacrifice: after some *great offense* against the nature of things,
a community could make peace with the gods by *sacrificing the criminals*.

We sense that Nemo is already involved in dramatic ritual because of the tableau he has just
arranged on the ocean floor. *Just what was the great offense? Who are the criminals to be sacrificed?*
Such are the questions that would spring to the minds of Verne's original readers, well versed in
classical lore.

I looked toward the large ship I had noticed earlier. It was coming closer to us and we could see it was putting on steam. It was six miles away.

"What kind of ship is it?" I asked Ned.

"From its rigging, and the shortness of its masts, I bet it's a warship," the Canadian replied. "I hope it reaches us and, if need be, sinks this damned *Nautilus*."

"Friend Ned," Conseil protested, "what harm can it do the *Nautilus*? Can it attack us under the waves? Can it cannonade us at the bottom of the sea?"

"Ned," I asked, "can you tell its nationality?"

Creasing his brow, lowering his lids, and puckering the corners of his eyes for a few moments, the Canadian focused his marvelous gaze on the oncoming ship.

"No, professor," he decided, "I can't tell what country it's from—it's not flying its flag. But I still bet it's a man-of-war because a long pennant is fluttering from the peak of its mainmast."

For a quarter of an hour we watched the ship bearing down on us. It seemed inconceivable to me that it had discovered the *Nautilus* at that distance, much less known that it was a submarine.

Soon the Canadian announced that the oncoming craft was a huge battleship, a double-decker ironclad complete with a ram.[2] Dark, thick smoke poured from its twin funnels. Its furled sails merged with the lines of its yardarms. The gaff of its fore-and-aft sail held no flag. It was still too far away for us to tell the colors of its pennant, which floated on the breeze like a thin ribbon.

It was coming on fast. If Captain Nemo would just let it approach, this might be our chance to escape.

"Professor," Ned Land said, "if that ship comes within a mile of us, I'll jump into the water, and I suggest you follow me."

I didn't respond to the Canadian's advice but stared at the warship, which was looming larger on the horizon. Whether it was English, French, American, or Russian, it would surely welcome us aboard if we could just get to it.

"Master might well recall," Conseil said, "that we have some experience with swimming. Master can rely on me to tow him toward that ship. That is, if it pleases master to follow Ned."

Before I could answer, there was a puff of white smoke from the bow of the battleship. A few seconds later, there was a big splash near our stern as some heavy object landed in the water, and then I heard an explosion.

"What! They're firing at us!" I cried.

"Good lads!" the Canadian murmured.

2. During the American Civil War, the Union Navy demonstrated the value of rams as weapons, and many warships were so equipped at the time Aronnax is writing. Likewise, we already know that a ram is the only large offensive weapon that Nemo packs. But most navies will abandon the instrument by 1900. A major reason will be that in fleet maneuvers in 1875 and 1893, the Royal Navy will sink its own ships through accidental ramming!

"That means they don't see us as shipwrecked men, clinging to some wreckage, waiting to be rescued . . ."

"With all due respect to master . . . oh goodness gracious," Conseil put in, shaking off the water another cannonball had splashed all over him. "With all due respect, they have spotted the narwhale and they're cannonading the same."

"But it must be clear to them," I cried, "that there are human beings on it!"

"Maybe that is *why* they're firing." Ned gazed at me.

The truth dawned on me. No doubt the world now knew the facts about this so-called monster. No doubt the monster's encounter with the *Abraham Lincoln*—when the Canadian hurled his harpoon at it—had led Commander Farragut to recognize the narwhale as actually a submarine, much more dangerous than any supernatural cetacean!

Yes, that had to be it! And now on every sea they were hunting down this terrible engine of destruction!

Terrible indeed if, as we could well suppose, Captain Nemo had been using the *Nautilus* as an instrument of vengeance. That night in the middle of the Indian Ocean, when he had us locked up in that cell, he must have attacked some ship! That man now buried in the coral cemetery—was he a casualty of some collision engineered by the *Nautilus?* Yes, I told myself, this had to be the truth! One part of Captain Nemo's secret activities had been unveiled. And now, if his real identity was still unknown, at least the nations allied against him knew they were no longer chasing a chimerical creature but a person who had vowed eternal hatred of them!

So I realized, as that formidable series of events passed through my mind, that instead of finding friends on that warship, we would meet only pitiless enemies.

Shells were falling all around us. Some of them would hit the surface of the sea and ricochet into the distance. None of them reached the *Nautilus.*

The ironclad was now no more than three miles off. In spite of its violent cannonading, Captain Nemo had still not appeared on the platform. Yet, if one of those conical shells had scored a direct hit on the *Nautilus,* it could have been fatal to him.

The Canadian told me:

"We've got to do everything we can to get out of this mess. Let's signal them! Maybe they'll understand that we're innocent bystanders!"

Ned Land pulled his handkerchief out of his pocket, set to wave it in the air. But he had scarcely unfolded it when he was struck by an iron fist, and, despite his great brawn, he tumbled to the platform.

"Wretch!" the captain shouted. "Do you want to be riveted to the *Nautilus*'s ram before it charges that ship?"

Terrible to hear, the captain was still more terrible to see. His face was pale, perhaps because his heart had stopped beating for a moment. The pupils of his eyes were fiercely contracted. He was not speaking, he was *roaring.* Bending down, he shook Ned by his shoulders.

The captain and the Canadian

Then, leaving the Canadian he turned on the battleship, whose shells were raining about him, and shouted powerfully:

"O ship of an accursed country, you know who I am! And I don't need to see your colors to identify you! But see, I'll show you mine!"

And at the front of the platform Captain Nemo unfurled a black flag similar to the one he had left planted at the South Pole.

Just then a shell hit obliquely against the hull, ricocheted near the captain, and vanished into the sea.

Captain Nemo shrugged his shoulders. Then he turned on me:

"Go below!" he said curtly. "You and your companions—go below!"

"Sir!" I cried. "Are you going to attack that ship?"

"Professor, I'm going to sink that ship!"

"You wouldn't do that!"

"I will do that," he replied coldly. "You are ill-advised to pass judgment on me, professor. Fate has allowed you to see what you were never supposed to see. They have attacked me. The counterattack will be terrible. Go below!"

"From what country is that ship?"

"You don't know? So much the better! At least its nationality will remain a secret to you. Below!"

The Canadian, Conseil, and I could only obey. Now some fifteen of the *Nautilus*'s crewmen were surrounding their captain, looking with implacable hatred at the man-of-war bearing down on them. The same breath of vengeance seemed to animate their every soul.

As I was going below, another projectile scraped the *Nautilus*'s hull and I could hear its commander shout:

"Fire away, you demented ship! Waste your useless ammunition! You won't escape the ram of the *Nautilus*! But you shan't perish here! I won't let your wreckage mingle with that of the *Vengeur*."[3]

I got to my cabin. The captain and his first mate were still on the platform. The propeller started turning and the *Nautilus* speedily moved out of range of the battleship's guns. The warship pursued us, apparently, and I recalled how the captain, under such circumstances, would simply keep his distance.

But, unable to contain my impatience and anxiety, about four p.m. I walked out to the central companionway. The hatch was still open, and I ventured out onto the platform. The captain was still there, walking up and down in a state of agitation. He stared at the warship, which was now five or six miles to his leeward. He had his *Nautilus* circling around it like a wild beast, and allowing it to follow him, he was drawing it eastward. But he did not attack. Was he still trying to make up his mind?

I wanted to reason with him. But I had scarcely opened my mouth when he shut me up:

A Hecatomb

❦

375

3. The romantic hero will fling speeches at far-off people, or even at things or abstractions. Why doesn't Nemo use his regulation shipboard language in this speechifying? Apparently because his real audience isn't his crew but Aronnax.

"I am the law, I am the tribunal. I am the oppressed and there are my oppressors. Thanks to them, everything I loved was destroyed—everything I cherished and venerated—homeland, wife, children, my father and mother. There is everything I hate! So you be quiet!"[4]

I took one final look at the warship, which was putting on steam, and then I rejoined Ned and Conseil.

"We'll get away!" I exclaimed.

"Good!" Ned agreed. "But what country is that ship from?"

"I still don't know. But wherever it's from, it will be sunk before dark. In any case, it's better to perish with it than become accomplices in a reprisal the justice of which we can't gauge."

"That's how I feel," the Canadian replied coolly. "But let's wait until dark."

When night came, a deep silence prevailed on board. The compass showed me that the *Nautilus* had not changed its course. I could hear the propeller churning the waves with steady speed. The ship stayed on the surface, rolling sometimes to one side, sometimes to the other.

My companions and I had decided to jump overboard as soon as the warship drew close enough to hear us or to see us—for the moon, just three days short of waxing full, was shining bright. Once we were on board the warship, even if we could not ward off the blow that threatened it, we could at least do everything that circumstances permitted. Several times I thought the *Nautilus* was getting ready to attack. But it was content for now to let the warship approach and then suddenly to resume its apparent retreat.

As the night wore on without incident, we kept looking for our chance. We talked very little—we were too keyed up. Ned Land wanted to jump into the sea but I forced him to wait. The way I figured it, the *Nautilus* would attack the double-decker on the surface, at her waterline,[5] and it would be not only possible but easy to escape.

At three a.m., full of anxiety, I mounted to the platform. Captain Nemo had not left it. He stood in the bow, and a mild breeze was unfurling his flag about his head. He kept his eyes on the man-of-war. The intensity of his gaze seemed magically to attract it, pulling it along more surely than if he had it in tow!

The moon was passing its zenith. Jupiter was rising in the east. In the midst of this peaceful scene, the sky and the sea rivaled each other in tran-

---

4. Nemo has already said enough here. If he and his men have lost their homeland, then they are the victims of one of the conquering colonial powers, one of the great nineteenth-century imperialist nations. Their continued assaults on that nation, terrible though they may be, at least make some sense now. They are engaged in a unique kind of guerrilla warfare.

What homeland has Nemo lost? What imperialist nation is his great enemy? Verne will answer these questions only in a later novel. But in the present one there are, for the observant reader, several hints or clues as to that future answer, most recently in the immediately preceding chapter.

5. In other words, Aronnax assumes that the battleship is armored only *above its waterline,* that naked planking begins right below it.

quillity, and the sea offered the moon the loveliest mirror ever to reflect its image.

And when I compared that deep calm of the elements with the ferocious passions brewing inside this barely perceptible submarine, I felt a chill pass over my entire being.

The warship stood two miles off, always moving toward that phosphorescence that signaled the location of the *Nautilus*. I could see its running lights, green and red, plus its white lantern hanging from the large stay of its foremast. Its rigging was lit with a dim, flickering glow, showing that its furnaces were fired to the limit. Showers of sparks and flaming cinders escaped from the funnels, spangling the air with shooting stars.

Although I stayed there until six a.m., Captain Nemo seemed never to notice me. The vessel lay now a mile and a half off, and with the first gleam of dawn, it resumed its barrage. The moment could not be far away when the *Nautilus* would retaliate, and my companions and I would leave forever this man I dared not judge.

I was about to go below to alert them when the first mate came out on the platform, accompanied by several seamen. Captain Nemo didn't see them or didn't want to. They carried out certain very simple procedures that could be called the *Nautilus*'s version of "clearing the decks for action." First they lowered the manropes that formed a handrail around the platform. Then they pushed the pilothouse and the beacon housing down into the hull until they were flush with the deck. Now nothing protruded from the long steel surface of this cigar-shaped ship; there was nothing to hamper its maneuvers.

When I went back to the salon, I could see that we were still on the surface. Light filtered through the waves and the windows were enlivened by streaks of red from the rising sun. That terrible day of June 2 had dawned.

At seven a.m. the log showed me that the *Nautilus* was cutting down its speed.[6] That meant Captain Nemo was letting the warship get closer. The explosions were louder now. Shells furrowed the water around us and labored into the depths with strange whistles.

"Friends," I said, "this is it! Let's shake hands and then—God preserve us!"

Ned Land seemed resolute and Conseil calm, but I felt so nervous I could not contain myself. We walked swiftly into the library, but the moment I opened the door leading to the central companionway, I heard the hatch closed sharply overhead.

The Canadian rushed up the steps but I stopped him. A familiar hissing told me that the ballast tanks were filling, and in a few minutes the *Nautilus* had dropped several meters below the surface.

I understood that maneuver. It was too late for us to escape. The *Nautilus* did not intend to strike the double-decker *at* its waterline, where it was clad

6. The French gives five a.m., not only too early for the cited sunrise, but out of synch with Aronnax's earlier claim that he stayed topside till six a.m.

in impenetrable iron armor, but below its waterline, *below* the metal carapace.[7]

We were prisoners again, unwilling witnesses to a gruesome drama. But we hardly had time for reflection. Taking refuge in my cabin, we stared at each other without saying a word. I fell into a deep stupor; my thinking came to a dead stop. I hovered in that painful state in which we expect an explosion we can't escape. I waited, I listened, existing only through my sense of hearing.

Meanwhile the *Nautilus* had increased its speed. It was gathering momentum. Its entire hull was vibrating.

Suddenly I let out a cry. I could feel the collision but the impact was surprisingly light. I could feel the steel ram penetrating, I heard a rattling and scraping. Carried by its great momentum, the *Nautilus* had passed right through the warship like a sailmaker's needle through canvas!

I couldn't stay still. Frantic, going out of my mind, I sprang from my cabin and rushed into the salon.

Captain Nemo was standing there, mute, somber, implacable, looking through the port window.

An enormous mass was descending into the sea. To make certain he would not miss one detail of his victim's death agonies, he had the *Nautilus* descend side by side with the warship. Ten meters away, I could see its half-opened hull into which the sea was rushing with a sound of thunder, then its double rows of cannons and railings. The deck was covered with dark, agitated shadows.

The water was rising and those wretched men sprang up into the shrouds, clung to the masts, struggling in the sea. It was a human anthill, trapped by a surprise invasion from the ocean.

Paralyzed, stiff with horror, my hair standing on end, my eyes popping out of my head, I was short of breath, suffocating, speechless—for *I* was watching too, just like the captain, glued to the glass by an irresistible allure!

That enormous craft settled slowly. Following it down, the *Nautilus* kept watch on its every movement. All at once there was an explosion. The air compressed inside the ship sent its decks flying, as though the powder magazine had caught fire. The *Nautilus* swerved from the shock.

Now that unfortunate ship was sinking faster. I could see the crow's nests laden with victims, then the crosstrees bending from the weight of men hanging from them, and at last, the peak of the mainmast. Then the somber mass dropped from view, its crew of dead men sucked down by the swirling eddies.

I turned to Captain Nemo. That terrible dispenser of justice, that genu-

7. Nemo's diving *several meters* suggests that he has detected armor plate *below* the battleship's waterline as well. It was not unheard of. In 1859, for example, the British Admiralty had ordered two ironclads with armor extending *six feet below the waterline*. That would serve as excellent protection against both the guns and rams of other warships—but not, of course, against a futuristic *submarine* ram.

ine archangel of hate, was still staring downward. When it was all over, I followed him with my eyes as he walked toward his room and went in.

On the far wall, beneath the portraits of his heroes, I saw the portrait of a still young woman with two little children. Captain Nemo stared at them for a few moments, reached out his arms toward them, sank to his knees, and melted into sobs.[8]

8. Nemo apparently includes his own family among those martyrs to oppression that Aronnax listed in II 8. Why didn't the professor notice the portrait of the woman and children earlier? Aside from possible male chauvinism, Aronnax was busy identifying pictures of *famous* people, and in inferring an important conclusion about their overall significance.

A Hecatomb

⬿

379

TWENTY-TWO

The Last Words of Captain Nemo

THE PANELS CLOSED on this frightful scene, but the lights did not go on again in the salon. All was dark and still inside the *Nautilus*. With prodigious speed, traveling a hundred feet below the waves, we were putting that place of devastation well behind us. Where were we going? To the north? To the south? Where would this man flee after that horrifying reprisal?

I returned to my room, where Ned and Conseil were waiting quietly. Captain Nemo filled me with insurmountable horror. Whatever he had suffered at the hands of humanity, he had no right to mete out such punishment. And he had made me, if not an accomplice, at least an eyewitness to his fierce vengeance. All this surpassed belief.

When the lights went on again, about eleven a.m., I returned to the salon. No one else was there. I checked the various instruments. The *Nautilus* was fleeing north at twenty-five miles an hour, sometimes on the surface, sometimes thirty feet below it.

Once our position was marked on the chart, I could see that we were passing into the mouth of the English Channel and hurtling toward the northernmost seas at a frightful pace.

And so I could barely glimpse the rapid passing of some longnose sharks; some hammerhead sharks; spotted dogfish common to those waters; huge eagle rays; clouds of seahorse that resemble the knights in a chess game; eels quivering like fireworks serpents; armies of crab that fled sideways, crossing their pincers over their shells; and finally schools of porpoise that tried to outrace the *Nautilus*. But of course, at our speed it was impossible to observe, study, and classify them.

By that evening we had cleared 200 leagues up the Atlantic. Shadows gathered and darkness overran the sea until the moon came up.

Back in my room, I could not sleep. I was tormented with nightmares. That horrible scene of destruction was played over and over again in my mind's eye.

From that day on, I could not be sure where the *Nautilus* was taking us in the North Atlantic basin. Always at incalculable speed! Always in the midst of the high Arctic fogs! Did we call at the capes of Spitzbergen or the shores of

Novaya Zemlya? Did we cross such uncharted waters as the White Sea, the Kara Sea, the Gulf of Ob? Did we visit the Lyakhov Islands and the unexplored northern coast of Siberia? I just can't say. I couldn't even guess at the time any more. Were the clocks running down? As happens in the polar regions, it seemed that night and day no longer followed their regular patterns. I found myself being drawn into that strange domain where the overwrought imagination of Edgar Allan Poe moved with ease. Like his fabled Arthur Gordon Pym, I expected any moment to encounter that "shrouded human figure, very far larger in its proportions than any dweller among men," cast athwart that cataract that protects the outskirts of the pole![1]

I could be wrong when I estimate that the *Nautilus* went on sailing haphazardly for fifteen or twenty days. And I can't be sure how long it would have gone on that way if it had not been for the sudden catastrophe that ended our tour. Captain Nemo was no longer around. His first mate I never saw. Not one member of the crew was visible for an instant. The *Nautilus* drifted beneath the waves almost continuously. When it did surface to renew our air supply, the hatches opened and closed automatically. Our position was no longer marked on the chart. I had no idea where we were.

I should add that the Canadian had reached the end of his endurance and his patience. He stayed in his cabin and Conseil could not coax a single word out of him. Conseil was afraid that Ned would commit suicide in a fit of rage or in the deep melancholy of homesickness. And so Conseil stayed with Ned always.

Obviously we had all reached the end of our tether.

One morning—how would I know the exact date?—I fell into a heavy sleep in the hours before dawn, a painful, sickly sleep. I woke up to see Ned Land leaning over me, speaking in a low voice:

"We're going to make a break for it!"

I sat up.

"When?" I asked.

"Tonight. There's no more supervision or control on board. Everyone seems stupefied. Will you be ready, professor?"

"Of course. But where are we?"

"In sight of land. I saw it through the mist this morning. Twenty miles to the east of us."

"What country?"

"I have no idea. It doesn't matter. We're going to take refuge there."

"Yes, Ned! Let's make a break for it even if the sea swallows us up."

1. Verne will be obsessed by both Poe and Pym for decades to come. Poe ended his *Narrative of Arthur Gordon Pym* with a baffling cliffhanger, the phrases Verne has just quoted. Dissatisfied with this inconclusiveness, the Frenchman wrote a sequel entitled *The Sphinx of the Icefields* (1897), in which he provides natural explanations for Pym's seemingly supernatural happenings—including that gigantic "shrouded human figure" just mentioned.

Yet another Poe yarn will likewise be evoked in this penultimate chapter.

"The sea is rough, the wind is blowing hard. But a twenty-mile run in our dinghy doesn't worry me. It's a nimble boat. And inside it I've stowed away some food and flasks of water. The crew never caught on."

"I'm with you, Ned."

"What's more, if they do catch us, I'll fight them to the death."

"Then we'll fight and die together, Ned."

My mind was made up. After the Canadian left me, I went out on the platform. I could hardly stand up, the waves were beating against the ship with such force. The sky looked menacing, but since there was land in those thick mists, we had to risk it. We couldn't afford to lose a day or even an hour.

I went back down to the salon, fearing and yet hoping to meet Captain Nemo, wanting yet not wanting to see him. What would I say? How could I conceal the horror he now inspired in me? No, it was best not to meet him face to face. Best to try to forget him. And yet . . .!

How long that day seemed, my last on this submarine marvel. I stayed by myself. We avoided speaking to each other, for fear we'd betray ourselves in some way.

At six p.m., when dinner was served, I ate but I had no appetite. Despite my revulsion, I forced it down, not wanting to weaken myself.

At 6:30 Ned came into my room and told me:

"We shouldn't see each other again before we leave. At 10 p.m. the moon won't have risen yet, so we should take advantage of the darkness. At that time come up to the dinghy. Conseil and I'll be waiting there for you."

The Canadian left without giving me time to reply.

I wanted to check the *Nautilus*'s course, so I made my way to the salon. We were racing north-northeast at a frightful speed, fifty meters down.

I took one last look at the marvels of Nature, the masterpieces of art exhibited in this museum, this unrivaled collection doomed to perish someday in the depths of the sea, along with its collector. I wanted to stamp an indelible impression of all this in my memory. I stayed there an hour, basking in the light that fell from the luminous ceiling, reviewing those resplendent treasures in their glass cases. Then I returned to my cabin.

Dressing in heavy sea clothes, I assembled my notes and arranged them carefully in different pockets. My heart was beating mightily. I couldn't slow it down, no matter how I tried. I knew that my anxiety and agitation would be obvious to Captain Nemo, if he had a chance to observe me.

What was he doing at that moment? I put my ear to the door of his room. I could hear footsteps. Captain Nemo was surely there. He had not gone to bed. With his every step I imagined he was coming out to ask me why I wanted to escape! I felt unremitting alarm. My imagination magnified everything. The feeling became so acute I wondered whether it wouldn't be better to go into his cabin, dare him face to face, brave it out with word and deed!

Now that was the brainstorm of a madman. Fortunately I checked that crazy impulse and stretched myself out on my bed to quiet my nerves. I did calm down a little, but my overexcited mind kept recalling all my experiences on the *Nautilus,* all those lucky and unlucky happenings since I went overboard from the *Abraham Lincoln:* the hunt on the seafloor, the Torres Strait, our running aground, the Papuan savages, the coral cemetery, the tunnel of Suez, Santorin Island, the Cretan diver, the Bay of Vigo, Atlantis, the Ice Bank, the South Pole, our imprisonment inside the ice, the battle with the giant squid, the hurricane in the Gulf Stream, the *Vengeur,* and that ghastly sight of the warship sinking with all hands . . .! All those events passed before my eyes like backdrops unrolling upstage in a theatre. In that strange setting Captain Nemo grew fantastically, his features were accentuated and took on superhuman proportions. He was no longer one of my species, he was the Man of the Waters, the Genie of the Seas.

By then it was 9:30. I clasped my head in both hands to keep it from bursting. I closed my eyes. I didn't want to think anymore. One half hour still to wait! One half hour of nightmares that could drive me insane!

Just then I heard vague chords from the organ, melancholy harmonies to some indefinable melody[2], the wail of a soul longing to break its ties with the earth. I listened with all five senses at once, scarcely breathing, plunged like Captain Nemo into that musical trance that was drawing him to the edge of this world.

A sudden thought terrified me. Captain Nemo had left his room! He was out there in the salon, which I could have to walk through in order to escape. I would encounter him there for one final meeting. He would see me, maybe speak to me! One gesture from him could obliterate me, one word could chain me to his ship!

Even so, ten p.m. was about to strike—time to leave my cabin and join my companions.

I dared not hesitate, even if Captain Nemo stood in my way. I opened my door cautiously, but as it turned on its hinges it seemed to make a dreadful noise. But maybe I imagined that.

I moved slowly through the *Nautilus*'s dark corridors, stopping only in vain efforts to slow down my heart.

I reached the corner door of the salon and opened it gently. The room was completely dark, filled with soft chords from the organ. Captain Nemo was there but he didn't see me. Even in broad daylight I'm sure he wouldn't have noticed me, so completely was he immersed in his music.

I stepped inch by inch across the carpet, avoiding anything that would make a noise and betray my presence. It took me all of five minutes to get to the door at the far end that led into the library.

I was just about to open it when a gasp from Captain Nemo nailed me to the spot. I realized he was standing up, I could even glimpse him now in the faint light that came from the library. He was coming toward me, arms crossed, silent, not really walking but gliding like some spectral being. His chest was

2. Nemo seems to be playing some sort of plainsong—a simple, hymnlike, repetitive, deliberately monotonous melody of the kind used in liturgical chanting.

heaving with sobs. And he murmured these words, the last I would ever hear him speak:

"O Almighty God! Enough! Enough!"

Was this a vow of repentance escaping from his conscience . . .?

Desperate, I rushed through the library, up the central companionway, through the upper gangway, and arrived beneath the dinghy. I climbed through the hatch and there were Conseil and Ned Land!

"Let's get going," I exclaimed. "Let's go!"

"Right away!" the Canadian agreed.

Using the monkey wrench he had stowed away, Ned first closed and bolted the hatch in the *Nautilus*'s hull, then he closed and bolted the corresponding hatch in the dinghy, and finally started to loosen the bolts that held the dinghy to its socket in the hull of the submarine.

But then we heard a noise from the interior of the ship. Voices were shouting back and forth. What was it? Had somebody realized what we were doing? Ned Land was slipping a dagger into my hand.

"Good," I whispered, "we know how to die!"

The Canadian had paused in his work. But one word shouted twenty times, one terrible word, made it clear to me what was causing all the ruckus below in the *Nautilus*. We were not what the crew was so upset about.

"Maelstrom!" they were shouting. "Maelstrom!"[3]

The Maelstrom! Could a more frightful word have reached our ears in a more frightful situation? So we were in those dangerous waters off the Norwegian coast! Was the *Nautilus* being sucked into that huge whirlpool just when our dinghy was about to cast off from its hull?

As we well knew, at the turn of the tide the waters confined between the Faroe and Lofoten Islands rush out with irresistible violence, creating a whirlpool that no nearby vessel can escape. Monstrous waves race together from every point of the horizon. They form a pattern of eddies justly called "The Navel of the Ocean." It can pull in things that are 15 kilometers away, sucking down not only ships but whales, sometimes polar bears.

And that was where the captain had run his *Nautilus* unintentionally—or maybe intentionally! It was being swept around in a circle that was getting smaller and smaller. Still partly bolted to the ship's hull, our dinghy was also carried around at dizzying speed. I could feel us whirling, whirling, and I was

---

3. This "terrible word" is the first uttered by the crew to be understood by Aronnax. Has the crew been forced in time of stress to abandon its artificial language once again? More likely, they use the term "Maelstrom" because the word had attained international usage.

The word *maelstrom* derives from words meaning to *grind into meal*—an apt description, as Verne goes on to mention the "sharp rocks on the seafloor, where the hardest objects are smashed." Although it has become fashionable to debunk the Maelstrom in our century, the *Sailing Directions* for Norway notes that "much loss of life has resulted" from this whirlpool. It's one additional reason why Verne recalls Poe earlier in this chapter: we're now reminded of the American's story "A Descent into the Maelstrom," a tale that dramatizes not only this whirlpool's terror, but the possibility of escaping from it.

The whirlpool

experiencing that dizziness and nausea that such continuous motions can cause. We were in a state of terror, in the last stages of horror, our blood at a standstill in our veins, our nerves numb, drenched in cold sweat like the sweat from the throes of dying. And what a noise engulfed our frail dinghy! What roars echoing from miles around! What crashing sounds from the waters breaking against sharp rocks on the seafloor, where the hardest objects are smashed, where tree trunks are worn down into "a shaggy fur," as the Norwegians put it.

What a predicament to be in! We were endlessly tossed about. The *Nautilus* defended itself like a human being. I could hear its steel muscles cracking. Sometimes it stood up on end, throwing us up and down inside our steel envelope.

"We've got to hold on tight," Ned was saying, "and screw the nuts back onto the bolts. If we can stay attached to the *Nautilus,* we have a chance to—"

He was interrupted by a loud cracking sound. The bolts had given way, and yanked out of its socket, the dinghy was flung into the middle of the vortex like a stone shot from a sling.

My head hit an iron timber, and with this violent shock I lost consciousness.

TWENTY-THREE

Conclusion

AND SO CONCLUDES our voyage under the seas. What happened later that night, how the dinghy escaped the Maelstrom's powerful eddies, how Ned Land, Conseil, and I got out of that whirlpool alive, I am unable to say.[1] But when I regained my five senses, I was in a bed in a fisherman's hut on one of the Lofoten Islands. Safe and sound, my companions were at my bedside holding my hands. We embraced each other heartily.

For the moment we cannot even dream of getting back to France. There are no frequent, regular means of travel between the far-northern parts of Norway and the south. I have to wait for a steamboat that runs twice a month from North Cape.

So it is here, among these good people who have taken us into their house, that I am reviewing this account of our adventures. It is accurate. Nothing important has been omitted, nothing has been exaggerated. It is my faithful narrative of our incredible expedition into an element now inaccessible to human beings—but progress will surely show them the way.

Will anybody believe my story? I can't say. But it doesn't really matter. For I now have the power to speak with authority of those seas under which, in less than ten months, I have traveled 20,000 leagues in this tour of the submarine world—the power to describe the many marvels I have discovered in the Pacific, the Indian Ocean, the Red Sea, the Mediterranean, the Atlantic, the southernmost and northernmost waters!

But what happened to the *Nautilus*? Did it survive the clutches of the Maelstrom? Is Captain Nemo alive? Does he still seek opportunities for revenge, or was his need for reprisal sated by that last hecatomb? Will the waves someday carry to civilization that manuscript that gives his full life story? Will I ever know the real name of that man? Will we be able to infer, from the nationality of the stricken man-of-war, the nationality of Captain Nemo himself?[2]

---

1. The simplest explanation would be that the tide changed and the whirlpool smoothed out right after the dinghy broke loose.

2. Aronnax's wondering whether we shall ever know Nemo's history is Verne's implicit promise to deal with this issue in a later book. In *The Mysterious Island* (1875) Verne provides a

I hope so. I hope too that his powerful submarine has vanquished the sea inside its most terrible whirlpool and that the *Nautilus* has survived where so many ships have suffered defeat and death! If that is so, and Captain Nemo still inhabits the ocean—his adopted country—I hope the hatred has been appeased in that wild heart! I hope his contemplation of so many oceanic marvels will extinguish forever his passion for vengeance. I hope that the dispenser of justice will die, and that the man of science will prosper to continue his peaceful studies of the seas.[3] If his destiny is strange, it is also sublime. Haven't I known that strange sublimity myself? Haven't I spent ten months in that extranatural life? And to that question posed 6,000 years ago[4] in the Book of Ecclesiastes— "Who can fathom the depths of the abyss?"—only two men out of all humanity now have the right to respond.

Captain Nemo and I.

Conclusion

⌘

388

summary of Nemo's career, identifying the respective nationalities of both the captain and his oppressor. We've provided a new translation of this "summary" in the appendix that immediately follows.

3. Verne's symbolic end for Nemo is superb. Driven by madness and self-destructive despair, Nemo is sucked into a moral maelstrom of his own choosing. But as we learn in *The Mysterious Island,* he escapes from the whirlpool, sails the seas for another thirteen years, and atones by performing benevolent deeds. Thus Verne makes his own use of the classical significance of the whirlpool as a metaphor for death and rebirth.

4. Aronnax is reflecting the traditional belief about the date of the Bible. More recent studies in biblical history would cut the age of Ecclesiastes nearly in half.

APPENDIX

Captain Nemo's Life Story

(Excerpt from The Mysterious Island, *Third Part, Chapter 16)*

In The Mysterious Island *(1875) Verne finally revealed the name, nationality, and personal history of Captain Nemo, plus the identity of his great political enemy. The standard English translation of this sequel was prepared by the nineteenth-century British boys' author, W. H. G. Kingston, and it's his century-old text that we invariably encounter in U.S. libraries and bookshops. Unfortunately, Kingston's rendering of Nemo's biography is not at all faithful to Verne: the Englishman rewrites, cuts, and just plain fabricates, all in an effort to bring this crucial passage into line with the official British propaganda of his day. This political falsifying will become instantly apparent if you compare Kingston's text with our new close rendering.*

In preparing an authoritative translation of this significant excerpt, we worked from the Hetzel "grand in-8" edition at Rice University.

CAPTAIN NEMO WAS AN INDIAN — PRINCE DAKKAR, the son of a rajah in the formerly independent territory of Bundelkhand, and the nephew of Tippu, Sultan of Mysore, India's great national hero. When the prince was ten years old, his father sent him to Europe to receive a comprehensive education, with the ulterior motive of preparing the boy so that someday he could contend on equal terms with those he regarded as the oppressors of his country.

From age ten to age thirty, Prince Dakkar was trained in every discipline. He proved exceptionally gifted, possessed nobility of both mind and heart, and he pursued his studies far and wide, concentrating on science, literature, and the arts.

Prince Dakkar traveled throughout Europe. His wealth and station made him immensely popular, but worldly enticements held no attraction for him. Although he was both young and handsome, he remained grave, gloomy, and ravenous for knowledge—and in his heart he nursed an undying grudge.

The prince was full of hate. He hated the one country he had never wanted to visit, the one nation whose overtures he continually rejected. He hated England—and hated it all the more because he admired certain of its achievements.

Inside this Indian youth there seethed all the savage hatred that the victim feels for his vanquisher. There could be no love between the invaded and the invader. Prince Dakkar was the son of a sovereign who had pledged only token allegiance to the United Kingdom. He was born of the family of Tippu, Sultan of Mysore. He had been reared on a philosophy of revolution and revenge. He was a patriot with an overwhelming love for his poetic country, a country groaning under English shackles. This Indian had no desire to visit that cursed land which had enslaved his India.[1]

Prince Dakkar became an artist on whom artistic masterworks had a sublime effect, a scientist on speaking terms with all the higher sciences, a statesman trained in the foremost courts of Europe. To casual observers he probably came off as one of those international sophisticates, a do-nothing busybody, a wealthy wanderer, a haughty idealist, a citizen of the world with no permanent roots.

He was anything but. This artist, this scientist, this human being, was Indian through and through—Indian in his lust for revenge, in his hope of someday building enough power to reclaim his country's rights, drive out the foreigners, and restore national independence.

To that end, Prince Dakkar went home to Bundelkhand in 1849. He married a woman in the nobility who shared his concern for India's miseries. She bore him two children whom he dearly cherished. But all this domestic bliss did not distract him from the plight of his enslaved country. He kept watch for the right moment to take action. It finally arrived.

England's oppression may simply have become too much for the Hindu populace to bear. Prince Dakkar appealed to all these discontented people, won their support and filled their minds with an utter hatred for the foreigners. He campaigned across the entire Indian peninsula, not only in the free zones but in regions directly governed by the English. He gave a call to arms, a call for a return to the great days of Tippu, Sultan of Mysore, who died a hero's death at Seringapatam while defending his homeland.

The great Sepoy Rebellion broke out in 1857, and Prince Dakkar was its guiding spirit. He had organized that whole immense uprising. He had placed both his fortune and his talents at the service of this cause. He paid out both in person—he fought in the front lines, he risked his life side by side with the humblest-born of those warriors who rose up to liberate their country. He was wounded ten times in twenty skirmishes, yet when the rebellion had been quashed and every last freedom fighter lay dead, the prince still lived on.

Never before had the United Kingdom been in such danger of losing its power over India. The Sepoys had hoped to persuade other nations to side with the liberation movement, and if they had succeeded in this, it might have spelled the end of British control and influence on the Asiatic continent.

1. In the final, published versions of *20,000 Leagues,* Verne sows several clues that hint at these later revelations of Nemo's nationality and that of his hated enemy. As early as I 8, Aronnax speculates that the captain and his first mate "were born in the low latitudes," that they may have been "Spaniards, Turks, Arabs, *or Indians.*" Then, at the close of II 3, Nemo's ambivalent tag line can easily be read as an admission of his Indian birth.

As for identifying England as Nemo's antagonist, this is also hinted at in Aronnax's narrative. For instance, the mysterious "encounter" described in I 23 and 24 occurs in East Indies waters, a sector patrolled by the British. Likewise, the parallel, openly observed encounter in II 21 takes place near another British zone, the English Channel. But the clincher is found at the close of II 20: Nemo pays homage to the French warship *Vengeur.* That vessel's war record consists entirely of *battles against the British.*

However, the present biography does leave undiscussed two remaining issues concerning Nemo and his crew: (1) We learn nothing abut their mysterious shipboard language; (2) The international distribution of the crew is not explained—in I 18, Aronnax claims to identify certain sailors of Irish, Greek, Slavic, and even French extraction.

By that point Prince Dakkar was famous. Rather than working behind the scenes, he had fought in plain view. A reward was offered for his assassination, and when no traitors claimed it, his father, mother, wife, and children were seized without warning and put to death in his place. . . .

As usual, might makes right. Civilization marches on, and simply grabs whatever rights it needs. The Sepoys were defeated, and the land of the old rajahs sank back beneath the iron rule of England.

His life somehow spared, Prince Dakkar retreated into the mountains of Bundelkhand. Now all alone in this world, he loathed mankind, felt only hatred and horror for civilization, and resolved to leave it for good. He liquidated what remained of his fortune, gathered together some twenty faithful friends, and one day vanished utterly.

So where did Prince Dakkar go to find that freedom that eluded him throughout the inhabited world? Under the seas, in the ocean depths, beyond human reach.

The man of war became the man of science. On a desert island in the Pacific, he set up a shipyard where he designed and built a submarine boat. Using methods that may someday be revealed, he had learned how to harness the incomparable motive power of electricity. He knew how to generate it indefinitely and used it for his vessel's every need: locomotion, lighting, and heating. The ocean depths offered priceless treasures, innumerable fish, gigantic mammals, fields of seaweed and sargasso—not only everything preserved there by Nature, but everything lost there by mankind. Whatever the prince and his crew needed, the sea had it in abundance—it was the answer to a prayer, because he wanted no further contact with the shore. So he christened his submarine boat the *Nautilus*, named himself Captain Nemo, and vanished beneath the waves.

For many years the captain traveled the oceans from one pole to the other. Now an outcast from the inhabited world, he collected marvelous treasures from those undiscovered regions. Those millions in the Bay of Vigo, lost by Spanish galleons in 1702, furnished him with an inexhaustible source of wealth that he distributed to others as an anonymous benefactor, always favoring people who fought for the freedom of their countries.[2]

For a long while he had no contact with his fellow man when, on the night of November 6, 1867, three castaways came aboard his vessel. They were a professor from France, his manservant, and a Canadian fisherman. These three had been thrown into the sea during a collision between the *Nautilus* and a pursuing U.S. frigate, the *Abraham Lincoln.*

Captain Nemo learned from this professor that the world at large wavered between regarding the *Nautilus* as a giant mammal from the family Cetacea, or as a submarine boat housing a crew of pirates. In any case, the ship was now being hunted across the seven seas.

These three men had accidentally intruded on Captain Nemo's secretive existence, and he could easily have thrown them back into the ocean. He refrained, kept them on board as prisoners, and for the next seven months they participated in a marvelous underwater voyage that covered a distance of 20,000 leagues.

2. A case in point would be Crete's revolt against the Ottoman Empire, which Captain Nemo did indeed aid in this way. *Jules Verne*

One day, on June 22, 1868, these three men—who knew nothing of Captain Nemo's past—seized the *Nautilus*'s dinghy and managed to escape.[3] But at that exact moment the *Nautilus* was sucked into the vortex of the Maelstrom off the coast of Norway. Afterward, the captain thought that the three fugitives must have drowned in the depths of the whirlpool. So he was unaware that the Frenchman and his two companions had been miraculously washed ashore on one of the Lofoten Islands, that local fishermen had cared for them, and that the professor had returned to France and there published a book in which their strange, seven-month adventure aboard the *Nautilus* was written out and served up to an inquisitive public.

For a long while Captain Nemo continued to roam the seas. But gradually his friends died and were laid to rest in a coral cemetery on the floor of the Pacific. The *Nautilus* grew emptier and emptier, and finally, out of all those men who had found a haven in the ocean depths, only Captain Nemo remained.

By that point the captain was sixty years old. Now the only one left, he managed to return the *Nautilus* to one of those underwater harbors that he sometimes used as ports of call.

One of those ports was a cavern beneath Lincoln Island, and there the *Nautilus* took refuge.

The captain stayed there for six years, his seafaring days over, looking forward only to his death—to that moment when he would be reunited with his friends. . . .

Captain Nemo died of unnamed natural causes after aiding settlers on Lincoln Island. In the wake of his passing, volcanic upheavals destroyed the island, and the sea entombed Captain Nemo and his Nautilus *for eternity.*

3. The French features a discrepancy in the years given for Aronnax's arrival and departure from the *Nautilus*. The former is cited as 1866, the latter 1867, exactly *one year earlier* than the chronology in *20,000 Leagues*. Whether the blame lies with Verne or with Hetzel & Co. we can't say, but we've advanced the years here to match Aronnax's narrative.

Incidentally, Nemo's biography fixes a precise departure date (June 22), a date that the troubled Aronnax "couldn't even guess at" in his account.

ABOUT THE EDITORS

Walter James Miller, television and radio writer, critic, poet, and translator, is generally regarded as one of the leading Verne scholars. His more than sixty books include *The Annotated Jules Verne* (a Book-of-the-Month Club selection), *Engineers as Writers, Making an Angel: Poems*; critical commentaries on Vonnegut, Heller, Doctorow, Beckett; critical editions of Homer, Shakespeare, Conrad, Dickens, and Dumas. His articles, poems, and reviews have appeared in *The New York Times, New York Quarterly, Western Humanities Review, Literary Review, Explicator, College English, Authors Guild Bulletin, Science Fiction & Fantasy Book Review, Engineer, Transactions on Engineering Writing and Speech, Civil Engineering,* and many other periodicals and anthologies.

From the *Literary Review* he has won its Charles Angoff Award for Excellence in Poetry; from the Armed Forces Service League, a prize for military fiction; and from the Engineers' Council for Professional Development, a special award for his NBC-TV series, *Master Builders of America*.

A veteran of World War II, he has taught at Hofstra University, the Polytechnic University, Colorado State University, and is now Professor of English at New York University.

Writer, actor, and broadcaster, Frederick Paul Walter is based at the University of Houston where he's a staff announcer on KUHF, one of the nation's leading public radio stations. A longtime Jules Verne enthusiast, Walter graduated from Bradley University, worked initially as a college theater director, today balances his performing career with work as scriptwriter, lyricist, and copywriter, and has published crime fiction and numerous nonfiction pieces on opera and classical music. By a handy coincidence, he worked on this new translation of *Twenty Thousand Leagues under the Sea* while simultaneously moonlighting for a major marine exploration firm! He is a fervent amateur paleontologist.

The Naval Institute Press is the book-publishing arm of the U.S. Naval Institute, a private, nonprofit, membership society for sea service professionals and others who share an interest in naval and maritime affairs. Established in 1873 at the U.S. Naval Academy in Annapolis, Maryland, where its offices remain today, the Naval Institute has members worldwide.

Members of the Naval Institute support the education programs of the society and receive the influential monthly magazine *Proceedings* and discounts on fine nautical prints and on ship and aircraft photos. They also have access to the transcripts of the Institute's Oral History Program and get discounted admission to any of the Institute-sponsored seminars offered around the country. Discounts are also available to the colorful bimonthly magazine *Naval History*.

The Naval Institute's book-publishing program, begun in 1898 with basic guides to naval practices, has broadened its scope in recent years to include books of more general interest. Now the Naval Institute Press publishes about one hundred titles each year, ranging from how-to books on boating and navigation to battle histories, biographies, ship and aircraft guides, and novels. Institute members receive discounts of 20 to 50 percent on the Press's more than eight hundred books in print.

Full-time students are eligible for special half-price membership rates. Life memberships are also available.

For a free catalog describing Naval Institute Press books currently available, and for further information about joining the U.S. Naval Institute, please write to:

Membership Department
U.S. Naval Institute
291 Wood Road
Annapolis, MD 21402-5034
Telephone: (800) 233-8764
Fax: (410) 269-7940
Web address: www.usni.org